PSYCHOS

SERIAL KILLERS, DEPRAVED MADMEN, AND THE CRIMINALLY INSANE

EDITED WITH COMMENTARY BY

JOHN SKIPP

NEW YORK TIMES BESTSELLING AUTHOR

BLACK DOG
& LEVENTHAL
PUBLISHERS

For Scooby Hamilton,
that crazy dog.

CLASSICAL SCENES OF FAREWELL © 2011 Jim Shepard, Reprinted by permission of SLL/Sterling Lord Literistic, Inc.
MARMALADE WINE From GREEN FLASH AND OTHER TALES OF HORROR, copyright © 1971 by Joan Aiken Enterprises Ltd., Copyright renewed 1999 by Joan Aiken Enterprises Ltd. Used by permission of Brandt & Hochman Literary Agents, Inc. All rights reserved.
THE SMALL ASSASSIN © 1946 Ray Bradbury Reprinted by permission of Don Congdon Associates, Inc.
LUCY COMES TO STAY © 1952 Weird Tales
MARLA¹S EYES © 2012 Ed Kurtz
THE LIAR © 2012 Laura Lee Bahr
THE PAPERHANGER © 2000 William Gay
RED DRAGON © 1981 Yazoo Fabrications Inc. Reprinted by permission of G.P. Putnam's Sons, a division of Penguin Group (USA) Inc. and The Ranom House Group Ltd.
THE EXIT AT TOLEDO BLADE BOULEVARD © 1998 Dallas Mayr
INCIDENT ON AND OFF A MOUNTAIN ROAD © 1991 Joe R. Lansdale. First published in *Night Visions*.
MURDER FOR BEGINNERS © 2012 Mercedes M. Yardley
JESSE © 2012 Steve Rasnic Tem
IN FOR A PENNY © 1999 Lawrence Block
NOW HOLD STILL © 2012 David J. Schow
FEMININE ENDINGS © 2007 Neil Gaiman
GOING SOLO © 2012 Leah Mann
DEATH-IN-LIFE LOVE SONG © 2012 Kevin L. Donihe
RALPH AND JERRY © 2012 Leslianne Wilder
AND WHAT DID YOU SEE IN THE WORLD? © 2010 Norman Partridge
LIFE WITH FATHER © 1998 Bentley Little
THE SHALLOW END OF THE POOL © 2008 Adam-Troy Castro
MOMMY PICKS ME UP AT DAY CARE © 2012 John Gorumba
WHEN THE ZOOS CLOSE DOWN, THEY¹LL COME FOR US © 2012 Violet LeVoit
ALL THROUGH THE HOUSE © 2005 Christopher Coake. Reprinted by permission of Houghton Mifflin Harcourt Publishing Company. All rights reserved.
INTRUDER © 2012 John Boden
STRAYCATION © 2012 Scott Bradley and Peter Giglio
LIFE COACH © 2012 Cody Goodfellow
RIGHTEOUS © 2012 Weston Ochse
THE MEANING OF LIFE © 2012 Amelia Beamer
DAMAGED GOODS © 1993 Elizabeth Massie
WILLOW TESTS WELL © 2012 Nick Mamatas
SERENITY NOW © 2012 Simon McCaffery
THE MANNERLY MAN © 2002 Mehitobel Wilson
SENSIBLE VIOLENCE © 1997 Brian Hodge
BUCKY GOES TO CHURCH © 2012 Robert Devereaux
AT EVENTIDE © 2000 Kathe Koja

Library of Congress Cataloging-in-Publication Data available upon request.

Published by Black Dog & Leventhal Publishers, Inc.
151 West 19th Street, New York, NY 10011

Distributed by Workman Publishing Company
225 Varick Street, New York, NY 10014

Design by Red Herring Design
Printed in the United States
ISBN: 978-1-57912-914-9
10 9 8 7 6 5 4 3
LSC-H

TABLE OF **Contents**

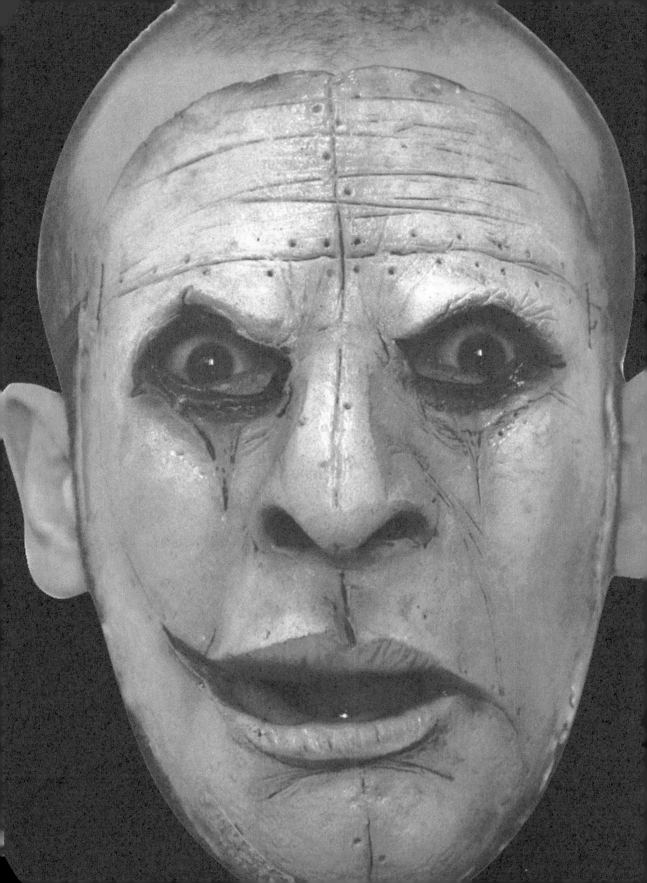

Our Brain: The Monster of Choice, When There's No One Else Left to Blame

A CHEERFUL INTRODUCTION BY JOHN SKIPP

The world is a comedy to those that think;
a tragedy to those that feel.
—Horace Walpole (1717–1797)

This just in: SOME PEOPLE KILL PEOPLE! It's the hideous headline heard daily, 'round the world.

As it turns out, we do it quite a bit: every sixty seconds, in the USA alone, according to the latest statistics. The global guesstimates must be even more impressive.

Which means that, in the time it takes me to write this sentence, at least *one* somebody is killing somebody else, somewhere on Earth. Probably a hell of a lot more.

And in the time it takes you to read *this* sentence—six months to a hundred years after I wrote it—those odds have probably only gone up.

And you thought math wasn't gonna come in handy!

Lemme tell ya: this world can make you crazy, if you weren't already. And if there's one thing I hope we've all figured out by now, it's that *we're all at least a little bit insane.* Prone to thoughts we probably shouldn't have. Occasionally impelled toward some really bad ideas.

It's a relative thing, of course, ranging from harmless oddball activities like collecting stamps all the way to, you know, harvesting skulls. There's a lot of idio-syncratic leeway in between, which is where most of us live out lives of either (a) quiet, secretive desperation or (b) noisily in-your-face acting-out. Depending on our personal style and symptomology.

But most of us can agree that there's a pretty clear line somewhere between "acceptable" crazy—eccentric, obnoxious, slightly off, kinda spooky—and genuinely terrifying, murderous madness. The kind that tears holes in our lives. And makes us so deeply afraid of each other.

That's where this book differs from our previous supernatural anthologies—*Demons, Zombies,* and *Werewolves and Shapeshifters*—David J. Skal's *Vampires,* and Hans Holzer's nonfiction *Ghosts and Witches* volumes.

Ask anybody what they're most afraid of in this world. The answer is not likely to be vampires, werewolves, or zombies (which most people don't believe in), or ghosts, witches, and demons (which many people do).

For most folks, the monster of choice is *other people.*

Because other people are scary. You don't know what they're going to do. They may seem nice. They may seem friendly. They may seem like they're going to do what any *other* nice, friendly person would do. Like *you* would do, if you were nice and friendly.

But maybe they won't.

If it turns out that they are *not* nice, friendly people, then the horrible truth is that you might wind up in a real-life nightmare world of shit almost beyond imag-ining. Just by rubbing up next to them, in the wrong place, at the wrong time. At a grocery store. In the ATM line. In traffic. At your place of business. Or even at home, among your own.

And the closer you get to them, the more you find out.

Whether you want to or not.

It is this ultrathin line that we'll be crossing throughout the extraordinary work that follows: a staggering thirty-eight-course banquet of literary mania and mayhem, served up by some of the most amazingly astute, deeply disturbing, im-mensely entertaining chroniclers of crazy ever to grace the printed page.

So let's try to set up our terms, real quick, before we descend into the misfiring brainmeat of the matter.

Psychosis is an only-slightly-more-precise word than *madness*, given all the factors that play into it, and the incredibly personal nature of the experience. It's a universe of chemical/historical/experiential variables, which scientists are deciphering as we speak. With a very long way to go.

The richly schizoid, hallucinatory varieties are the easiest to spot, by and large, because they tend to drive other people away with their disassociative weirdness and inability to fit in. That is, unless they're also wildly charismatic, form a cult or other familial grouping, find a nice remote location, and multiply unseen. (Or just multiply the madness inside their own heads, alone, wherever "home" may be.) Our asylums are packed with these ladies and gents. But you'd be stunned by how many run loose.

And then there are those otherwise-normal folk driven over the edge by circumstance. A horrific encounter or, a tragic loss, might be the straw that breaks the camel's back, ultimately snapping the spine of sanity. Post-Traumatic Stress Disorder is woefully real, and nothing to sneeze at, no matter *how* strong you are, as we're finally coming to understand.

In a war zone, pretty much everyone has it, from soldiers to civilians to their animals and plants. War is horror on a grand scale —Hell on Earth, unleashed— and no one who's been through it comes out unscathed.

If you live in a rough-enough neighborhood, the same principle applies. Constant street-level threat weighs heavy on the human soul. Fear wears us down. And even in the nicest parts of town or country, it only takes one sufficiently terrifying violent encounter to yank our sense of security out from under us, and let the dark thoughts in.

Most of us somehow find a way to weather it. Some even thrive and blossom in adversity. Find themselves. Become an inspiration to others.

Some of us just can't. We snap. It's too much.

And then more of the tragic bad things happen.

But the bulk of the one out of every one hundred of us who are arguably psychotic—according to the latest pop science projections—are functioning members of society. Many with high-paying, power-intensive jobs. (A 2012 study suggests that one out of ten high-powered CEOs meet the psycho test. Living in Hollywood, I suspect the number might be higher.)

Whether these numbers are nonsense or nailing it, they say something profound and intense about our current level of relative sanity.

Functioning psychosis—which is to say, the psychosis that interacts with us, day by day—is largely characterized by *lack of empathy*: the inability to feel or care about others. This enables psychotics to move through the world without the burden of sympathy or conscience, indifferent to moral codes that make no sense to them.

To psychotics, morals and empathy just seem like a big load of hooey: meaningless, stupid obstacles between themselves and whatever they might hope to achieve. This is the mind-set that allows a person to ruthlessly step on others, treat them like shit, and kill them if necessary or otherwise exciting.

The other side of the problem, of course, is feeling too much. That's where crimes of passion kick in, and all that latent crazy goes to town.

But for most psychotics, it's thinking too much. Thinking and thinking. And, the sad truth be told, being smart is no defense against madness. Sometimes smart doesn't help much at all.

Obviously, you don't have to be smart to kill people. Any lunkhead can do it. Henry Lee Lucas was dumb as a post. Ed Gein wasn't real sharp, either. And don't even get me started on John Wayne Gacy.

But Hannibal Lecter—the Dr. Moriarty of modern madness at its highest and most nightmarishly evolved—very clearly suggests that even genius is no defense. It just ups the voltage on crazy, makes it weirdly more impressive and sustained.

Till you finally get caught. Which you very well might. Unless you're a CEO, or a major political figure, or some other kind of above-the-law superstar. Or otherwise extremely cunning and lucky.

But even that might not be enough to keep your world from caving in.

Which brings us to the ultimate, terrible truth.

There is no escape from the horror of horror. However it's explained, justified, or exposed, it's still fucking horrific, and that's all there is to it.

For most of us—no matter how dark our impulses—it's one thing to imagine them. It's another to act them out. The difference is clear, because the difference has consequences.

Horror—and crime, and mystery, and suspense, and all the other literary forms that evoke that emotion—are fictions of consequences. They lay out scenarios. They postulate what-ifs. They flood us with streams of experiential gnosis in which we are the ones thinking, feeling, experiencing.

When it's happening to you, it's a whole 'nother story.

And that's why these stories are so astounding.

Because they take you inside every side of the nightmare moment, from the killer to the knife to the victim to the people who were otherwise affected by the act: because they saw, because they cared, or because they just, unfortunately, shared the same world.

For this book—in some ways, more than any other—my excellent editor Dinah Dunn and I put an extremely high premium on psychological acuity. Which meant that honesty was our highest priority, right next to talent, vision, and skill. It wasn't enough to just tell a good story. And enormous as this volume turned out to be, we still only had so many pages.

That's why it pains me to say that we could easily have filled *two books this size* with incredibly great stories, with some left over, most of which could easily sell to any other astute editor.

In the end, our job was to bring the most comprehensive, wide-ranging cornucopia of mind-shatteringly kick-ass fiction we could gather, by some of the finest writers ever to spelunk this treacherous territory. Descend into this black hole of the soul.

You may notice an uncharacteristic shortage of "vintage" classics in this assemblage. That's largely because I honestly feel that better short psychological fiction is being written now—particularly as pertains to honest depictions of madness—than in the hallowed days of yore, when you had to be some kind of monster to even *think* such things. (More on the history of the literature, and the mind-sets that framed it, in the appendices that follow.)

In a weird way, I see this book as the flipside of our last volume, *Demons*, wherein supernatural forces helped abstract and mythologize just how crazy we can get, and made that bitter pill somewhat easier to swallow. You know. *The devil made me do it!* Or *I turned into a werewolf, or something!*

This time, however, we're on our own. It's just us and our crazy brains. Thinking thoughts we probably shouldn't. Coming to grips, as best we can.

Or succumbing to the tidal wave of psychosis.

And laying waste to all we love.

We are our own demons, yes. And each other's. Cuz people are scary. But as the great Lord Buckley said, "Angels got wings because they take themselves lightly."

So hang onto your heart and your wits and your wings. Believe me, you are going to need them. A pitch-black sense of humor will also come in handy.

In the end, I suspect true sanity lies in making peace with all the painful insanity that is so much a part of our human heritage. Facing it down, without letting it win. Seeing it for what it is. And then saying, "No, thank you."

The real war—the eternal one—is the battle against the madness within ourselves. Don't ever forget it.

Everything else, from patriotism on down to the most intimate one-on-one, is just a costume we drape over that central conflict. Finding excuses to let our inner monster run free. Or finding opportunities to tame and rein them in.

I hope these stories provoke you, in the very best way, to remember what it is to be a human being. Through the laughter and tears.

Now enjoy, you crazy bastard!

Classical Scenes of Farewell

BY JIM SHEPARD

People often tend to think of serial killing as a modern phenomenon, the term having only been coined as recently as the 1980s, when the escalating trend of death-crazed media darlings (Bundy, Gacy, et al.) made such snappy buzzwords commonplace nomenclature. But, of course, nothing could be further from the truth.

Case in point: a good four hundred years before Jack the Ripper became the first pop star of nocturnal disembowelment—carving up streetwalkers and spreading panic through the cobblestoned Whitechapel of 1888—there was Gilles de Rais.

Here was a man of noble roots, epic contradictions, and monstrous compulsions, whose horrors played out on such a grand, historic scale of war, perversion, class disparity, religious hypocrisy, and power-gone-mad that it's hard to believe Shakespeare didn't invent him.

And so we begin with Jim Shepard's tragic, immaculately rendered inside account of a life spent complicit with a fifteenth-century devil made flesh, its implications rumbling through our culture to this day.

As a child who could barely hold myself upright without tottering, I was steeped in my mother's belief that our tumbledown farm was serried about and tumid with devils. In my mind's eye they stood in a ring and clasped one another's taloned hands and leered in at me while I slept. My fourth summer was the year that Sophie, the stonemason's daughter, was seized with a helplessness in her limbs until her father conceded her diabolic possession and took her to the Church of Our Savior, where the priest found five devils residing inside her, whose names were Wolf, Lark, Dog, Jolly, and Griffin. The devils confessed they'd conjured hailstones through her by beating the surface of well water with her hands and that they'd additionally concocted the tinctures and ointments she'd used to blight her neighbors' apple trees. They said they'd requested, and been denied, a special grease that would have turned her into a werewolf. When asked of whom they'd made their appeal, they said only "The Master."

When I was twelve, the man from whom we rented our pastureland—a lifelong bachelor whose endless mutterings were his way of negotiating his solitude, and whose imagination extended only to business; the sort who milled his rye without sifting it, so it might last longer—was found in the middle of our lane one winter morning, naked, his feet and lips blue. He said a demon had appeared to him on a pile of wood under his mulberry tree, in the likeness of a corpulent black cat belonging to the house next door. With its front paws the cat had gripped him by the shoulders and pushed him down, and then had fastened its muzzle on the man's mouth and would not be denied. The man claimed that for nearly an hour he'd remained that way, swooning, speechless, and open to the cat's searching jaws, unable to make even the Sign of the Cross and powerless to diminish the urgings of its tongue. He had no memory of where his clothes had gone, or how he'd ended up in the lane.

My mother had long since taken to enfolding a crucifix in the bedcovers when she turned down my poor linens for the night. My chamber was in our barn's loft, attached to the back of the house, and from this, the highest point on the hill, I could view the Delorts' farm to the west. Their daughter, Katherine, was the continual object of my confused nightly agitations as well as the focus of my joy.

And then one sunstruck August afternoon when we were passing through the village, my mother and I investigated a disturbance on the church steps, a crowd squabbling over who had sufficient schooling to interpret the document posted on the doors before them. A sacristan emerged to provide assistance and to read aloud what he declared to be a juridical confession lately obtained through the harrowing of some of our neighbors. Said neighbors had been identified to the ecclesiastical investigators by other neighbors.

The confession stated that Marie Delort, along with her daughter, had for three years been giving herself over to a pair of demons, from Friday midnight through to Saturday dawn, and had assisted at a series of conjurings in the company of others. According to the deacon Katherine had testified that her association began when one evening, washing her family's linen outside of town, she saw before her a man with a curved back and pointed ears whose eyes were like emeralds in an ash pit. He called for her to give herself to him and she answered that she would. He then gentled her cheeks with both hands, his palms softly furred, and flooded her mouth with his breath, and from then on each Friday night she was carried to a gathering from her own bed, simply by willing herself free. At the gathering place she shed her night-dress and was approached, every time having been made to wait for a period alone in the darkness, by the same man leading a gigantic he-goat, which knelt before her, and to both apparitions she abandoned herself.

The sacristan then read her mother's corroboration of this account, which further detailed the strange trance during which she was also transported from her bed, and their mutual adoration of the goat and the man, and their not only bathing in but also taking in all sorts of offensive liquids, with satiation being the object of their every clutch and gesture.

I was born Etienne Corillaut of Pouzauges, in the diocese of Luçon, and am known as Poitou, and I am now of twenty-two years of age, and here acknowledge to the best of my abilities the reasons for those acts that have made this name along with my master's the object of hatred throughout the region. I here also address the questions that my kinsmen hear from every stable hand, every innkeeper, every farmer in his field: What transpired in his mind that allowed a young person to have acted in such a manner and then to have lived apparently untroubled among his fellows? What enabled him to have stepped forward into the sunlight and Nature's bounty for six years of such iniquity?

My master is Gilles de Rais, whom I have served as page and then bodyservant for these last six years; and for the past three, since he first offered access to the full chamber of his secrets, he and I, with five others I will name, have been responsible for the entrapment and mutilation and dismemberment and death of one hundred and forty-two children between the ages of five and fifteen. Coming in the Year of Our Lord 1440, this admission dates the full vigor of my offenses back to the winter of 1437. But even before he chose to sweep back the curtain on the full extent of his ferocity, I knew myself to be already standing outside the ring of salvation, having failed so signally as a neighbor and a brother and a Christian and a son.

My father failed no one, having been brought up in honesty and industry with a mild and peaceable disposition, and my first memory of my mother is of the two of us gathering into her basket rue and southernwood in bright sunlight. I remember her saying one sweltering morning that the forest, our edge of pastureland, and a hive of bees were our only livelihood. I remember her tears. Later there was a shed and a little tower with a dovecote. We raised rye and beans and pot-herbs. As I grew stronger I was given suitable responsibilities, my first being light weeding during the day and laying the table and filling the hand basin after sunset. Before that my contributions had been limited to fanning the wasps out of my little sister's sweet milk.

At that time I was devout. I retired each morning to pray and refused refreshment for a quarter of an hour afterward. And I displayed other singularities. My brother and sister avoided me, which I attributed to acts of stupidity that somehow had discredited me forever. I played alone, chopping at roadside weeds with my special stick. "Still fighting your cabbages?" my brother asked one day, having seen me thrash some wild collards.

My mother liked to claim that all she brought to the marriage was a bench, bed, and chest, and I first registered their sadness while hiding in the fields watching my father cut clover. My mother brought him soup, ladling it out in the shade of an elm, and he said, "Will you kiss me?" and she answered, "We all have our needs." He then told her to take back her soup, for he didn't want it, and scythed all the clover without eating and returned hungry to the house.

He complained later that it was as if his accounts were tallied small coin by small coin. She confided in my brother, her favorite, that she lived in dread of bad weather, during which his father would pass the hours in the kitchen, his resentment turning from the weather to her. We slept with pounding hearts when they fought.

And during a rainy October the day after my eleventh birthday my brother fell sick of a malady of the brain. We moved him to a room off the kitchen with a hearth that backed on to our stove, where during sickness or bloodletting or weaning, a greater warmth could be maintained. My mother made him an egg dish into which she chopped dittany, tansy, marjoram, fennel, parsley, beets, violet leaves, and pounded ginger. He was seized with convulsions and his writhing was such that she couldn't stay in the room. He died at cock's crow two mornings after he was first afflicted.

She afterward seemed so bereft and storm-tossed that our neighbors called her "the Wind's Wife." November imprisoned the farm with its load of ice, sheathing both sickle and hoe. In our little pond fish hung motionless and petrified with cold. My mother kept to herself in the kitchen, puzzled and drained by our questions, her smile gloomy and terrible in its simplicity. Our father sat on a stool drawn up near the door, a hermit paying his visit to a sister hermit.

And even after the winter seemed well ended it suffered a relapse, piling snow deeper atop our work. My sister and I offered ourselves to our mother without success. On this side and that, she seemed to find only sore constraint and bitter captivity. Her blood turned thin as water and she developed scrofulous complaints. When at her angriest, she wiped my nose, violently, and said it was oppressive to be looked at so reproachfully by children. If we asked for too much, her panicked response frightened us further.

Her own presence seemed to distress her. She fell endlessly behind in her work. She was found at all hours bent in half and rubbing her back. She couldn't warm her hands. One palm on the table would quiver, and, seeing us notice, she'd cover it with the other.

Our animals sickened as if bewitched. Our cat died of hunger. When the weather permitted my mother sat in the field as far as possible from the house. When storms drove us inside, on occasion I glimpsed her before she had composed her expression. One sleeting morning she taught my sister a game, based on the stations of a woman's life, that she called Tired, Exhausted, Dying, and Dead.

At night when I was visited by strange dreams and pleaded for her company, she told me she'd seen witches lying in the fields on their backs, naked up to the

navel. She fixed on a story from a neighboring town of a man who'd confessed that
he'd killed seven successive boys in his wife's womb by means of his magic, and
that he'd also withered the offspring of his father-in-law's herd. She told us that
lost girls were cooked in a cauldron until the flesh entire came away from the bone,
from which the witches made an unguent that was a great aid to their arts and pleasures.
She followed closely the sensational story of de Giac, the king's favorite, who confessed
he had given one of his hands to the Devil, and who asked when condemned that
this hand be severed and burned before he was put to death.

She took her life with a series of plants that my father said she had gathered
from the most sinister localities. We discovered her early one bright morning. I
remained in place near her bed, remembering her hand slipping off my inhospitable
arm the evening before when she'd been trying to negotiate some ice on our doorstep.

I was fourteen. My sister was nine. We discussed what had happened as though
it all belonged to a period now concluded. Our day-to-day world having fallen
away, something else would take its place.

After that I paid only distracted attention to the ordinary round of life. If others
came too close, I made signs with my hands as if to repair the harm I'd done them. At
times during chores I would halt as if seized by my own vacancy. I saw very well how
people looked upon me. I despised in my heart those who despised me. And when my
father saw me in such torments, he thought: he loved her so much he's still weeping.

All I desired, morning in and evening out, was a love with its arms thrown
wide. But the contrary is the common lot, everyone's family telling him furiously
that everything hurts, always. The nest makes the bird.

This potter's wheel of futility and despair would have continued had our parish
priest not singled out my voice for his choir, and detected in me what he claimed
were aptitudes, especially for the sciences. What he offered as appreciation I took
to be pity. It was suggested to my father that I be turned over to the monastic
school at Pont-à-Sevre. But even before that decision could be made, Henriet
Griart, having heard the choir, brought me to his lord de Rais's attention. He was
then seventeen, and quick-eyed and enterprising in his service as steward.

Thus does this chronicle turn, harsh and bleak as it is, from one misfortune to
another. I was presented at Tiffauges, which was so tall that its towers were cloud-capped

when I first saw them, and orange in the setting sun. Out of its windows summer had never been so mild, dusk so vivid, or the surrounding hills so shady in their grateful abundance of streams and gardens. My sponsor, who'd refused converse during the carriage ride, provided some instruction on etiquette while we waited in the great hall, adding that if I behaved he'd see that my promotion was advanced with great ingenuity.

His kindness moved me. And when the doors opened for the castle's master and his retinue, tears sprang to my eyes. My interview was conducted through that blur of weeping. This was the lord whom even I knew to be one of the richest in France. Who'd fought side by side with Joan the year our country had pulled herself from her knees. Who'd drawn the bolt from the Maid's shoulder and in her vanguard had raised the siege of Orleans.

The sun was fully set. Boys in special surplices moved from candelabra to candelabra with delicate, whiplike tapers. All of the wall tapestries featured hunting scenes. His first words, seeming to come from somewhere behind him, were that I was a little angel. He had reddish hair and a trimmed red beard. A blue satin ruff. His face in the candlelight was like a half-veiled lamp.

Henriet was told to prepare me. I was pulled into an antechamber where my clothes were stripped from me and burned on a grate. I was fitted with a doublet of green and brown velvet and loose-fitting breeches and shoes, then taken through a small passageway bolted with an iron gate on either end and set with chevrons along its length to what looked like a side-chapel arranged with painted screens. Above the screens loomed the worked canopy of a gigantic bed. In the firelight the embroidered tigers flexed and clawed their mates. Benches with saw-tooth serrations above the headrests lined the walls. This seemed a secret room constructed where roof trusses converged from the projecting base.

A boy near the door was identified by Henriet as the aquebajulus: custodian of the holy water. He held before him a small bronze bowl. Upon entering, each of the lords dipped two fingers in it and made the Sign of the Cross, and then the boy departed.

Those present in that chamber besides myself, Henriet, and the lord de Rais were his lord's cousins Gilles de Sillé and Roger de Briqueville. That night while they took their ease on those benches and drank hippocras from a silver beaker that the steward had fetched, I was made to shed the doublet I had just donned and to lie across the billowy down of the bed's snowy comforter and to receive onto my belly the ejaculate of his lord's member. He knelt above me, having finished, attentive to my face with his head cocked as though listening for something, and then Roger de Briqueville handed him a jeweled dagger, the tip of which he pressed to my Adam's apple, and the sting caused me to squint before his other cousin cleared his throat and reminded him of my uncommon beauty, suggesting I be retained as a page. The lord de Rais turned his gaze to Henriet, who looked at me. In his eyes I saw my mother's gloomy and drained consideration. He shrugged, and nodded. With that shrug his lord returned his attention to my features. He set the dagger on the coverlet between us, touched his semen with a fingertip, and drew a line to my throat with it. Then he dismounted the bed. I was ignored through the conversation that followed.

Lying there, not yet having been granted leave to move, I experienced the ongoing impression that all this was inexplicably directed at me. The lord remarked that when he was three, his brother, René de la Suze, was born, upsetting the entire household, and that relations between them had never been cordial. He added that when at eleven he'd lost both parents, his father gored by a boar and his mother carried off by an inflammation of the brain. That same autumn had brought the disgrace of Agincourt, with the loss of his maternal grandfather's lone son and heir.

When he stopped the only sounds were the logs on the fire. Henriet caught my eyes with his but I couldn't tell what he hoped to communicate. And the lord de Rais, as though he'd already asked more than once, bade everyone to leave. When I rose, he instructed me to stay.

The firelight shimmered because I was weeping with terror. He asked my age in a gentle voice and, when answered, exclaimed "Fifteen!" with a kind of graciousness, as if at an unexpected gift.

He asked if I had heard of the emperor Nero. When I could not stop my tears, he went on to inform me that Nero never wore the same clothes twice. That he almost never traveled with a train of less than one thousand carriages. That his mules were shod with silver and his muleteers wore coats of Carnusian wool.

He said that at my age he knew already the men who were to influence the entire course of his life. That these great souls had taught him that to venture little was to venture much, and the risk the same.

He returned to the bed and eased himself down beside me, sympathetic to my shivering and heaving. While touching me he explained that balked desire, seeing itself checked as if by a cruel spell, undergoes a hideous metamorphosis. And steep and slippery then became the slope between voluptuous delight and rage. He said he was still undecided as to whether he was of a mind to let me rest and that only a straw turned the scale which kept me there. He lay beside me in silence for some moments while I regained custody of my emotions. Then he made me swear I would reveal none of the secrets about to be entrusted to me, prefatory to the oath administered a few hours later before the altar in the Chapel of the Holy Trinity. In swearing so I understood I was gathering to my heart the secrets of sins both committed and to come. This oath was taken in the presence of the same gathering that had witnessed the initial events in the secret room. And following the oath I was seated at the lord de Rais's right hand for a dinner of roast goose with sausages, a stew of hares, white leeks with capons, plovers, dressed pigs, a fish jelly, bitterns, and herons in claret, with rice in milk and saffron afterward.

My account proceeds by gaps, not unlike my life. The castle at Champtocé was an apparition out of a fairy story: black and grave, sprouting crooked tall towers with battlements like broken teeth. Grimly flattened fields surrounded it. But everything inside was transformed by braziers of light and furniture of gold leaf, by statues and bound manuscripts of worked silver. My sponsor explained the tumult of passing men-at-arms by informing me that our lord kept a personal army of two hundred and fifty, each equipped with the finest mounts and armor, as well as complete new liveries three times a year. He traveled, Henriet explained, from residence to residence and kept an open house at each, so that anyone, high-born or low, could stop for food and drink. As for the low, it was well-known that this invitation was extended only to young and beautiful children, either unaccompanied or, if not, left behind to dine at their leisure.

He unlocked a curved black grate guarding access to a spiral stairwell ascending the north tower, and led me up the stone steps and at the top we paused before a room, also locked. The smell was startling. Henriet held a small cloth soaked in cloves over his nose and mouth. He did not offer to share it. Jean de Malestroit, Bishop of Nantes, was to take possession of the castle in forty-eight hours, he said, so this work had to be completed by then. We were joined by Gilles de Sillé and another servant who did not give his name. Inside the room we found the skeletons, heaped in a colossal faggot-box set near the hearth, of forty-two children. The skin was shrunken and dried about the bones and flaked off to the touch. The box was the height of our chins and the jumble of bones inside as high as our chests. A stool was brought to help Henriet and myself climb up and in, each of us using a staff to clear space for our legs. This disturbed the beetles and flies and other insects to which the bones had been abandoned, as well as a kind of powdery dust that settled in our mouths and eyes. No one spoke except about how best to bundle the loads into large coffers bound with iron and already waiting in the middle of the room. When filled, each was to be double-bound with rope as a proof against the failure of the iron bands. Eight in all were required. I distinguished the number of children by counting the skulls. Our purchase of everything was increasingly complicated by hands turned white and greasy with a slimy ash.

We became aware of noises at the door's peephole, though none of my co-workers seemed troubled. I heard a woman's soft laughter. Henriet warned me to keep guardianship of my eyes. He later explained that Roger de Briqueville at times invited noble ladies of the district to watch such operations in progress.

We swept the last bits into the faggot-box, and a layer of resin wood and ground aromatics was spread to mask the smell. The coffers were carried down the spiral steps at nightfall to waiting wagons, which were driven to a quay on the Loire and loaded onto barges to be poled down to Machecoul. There, before sunrise, they were hauled up to what Henriet revealed was our lord's own bedroom. And there they were emptied and the bones burned in his presence. And when each pyre cooled, it was our task to dump the ashes into the moat.

Henriet lost patience with my periodic torpor. When I complained about his anger, he widened his eyes and affected a fool's expression as though imitating someone. I was quartered near his wash basin and chamber-pot stand, and told not to touch his things. We took our meals together. After some weeks we began conversing at night once our chambers were dark. He said that from his earliest childhood he'd felt himself an affliction to those around him and had banished himself to the woods, where he couldn't be spied and only answered after having been called many times. Sometimes he hid in caves. He remembered asking his father if a hermit could live on plants and roots. One day during the harvest they found him looking in the hedges and hayfields for wild saffron bulbs to eat. He'd made a bow with which to kill birds, but hadn't managed to hit any. He was nothing like his younger brother, who in January ran beside the plow with a goad until he was hoarse from the cold and the shouting. At my age he had frightened his mother by pointing into the fireplace and claiming to have seen old Mourelle grinding her teeth. Mourelle was their mare, and of her he was deeply afraid. He also feared hens. But he was a lesson, he thought, for at some point he had applied himself diligently to discover what he should do to cease being reclusive and live among men.

He was given charge of my instruction. I learned to bear my head upright and to keep my eyelids low and my gaze four rods ahead without glancing right or left. To scatter our lord's room with alder leaves for the fleas. We set out bowls of milk and hare's gall for the flies. We strewed the floor around his bed with violets and green herbs. We cared for the smaller birds in his aviaries, prepared sand for his hourglasses, dried roses to lay among his clothing, and found boys to replace the boys who continued to disappear in his secret rooms.

Girls were sometimes accepted if slender and beautiful and as red-haired and fair-skinned as our lord. Each of his castles was thronged about by children made homeless by a hundred years of war and brigandage, begging where they could and stealing where they couldn't. Henriet and I spent an hour each morning sheltered in our aerie above the portcullis, selecting from those at the gate. For children of particular beauty we roamed the villages and churches. If a boy was of more respectable means, Gilles de Sillé or Roger de Briqueville would ask the father to lend the child to take a message to the castle. And later, if asked what had become of the boy, they said they didn't know, unless he'd been sent on to another of the lord de Rais's residences, or thieves had taken him.

Children were also provided by an old woman who came to be known along the Loire as "the Terror."

One Sunday after Mass we were cornered by a mother so agitated she refused to let us pass. Her husband was embarrassed by her fervor. Her other children shrank from her voice. Henriet told her he had seen her boy helping our lord's cook, Cherpy, preparing the roast, and that perhaps he'd since been apprenticed elsewhere. She answered that she'd been told twenty-five male children had been provided as ransom to the English for Messire Michel de Sillé, captured at Lagny. Henriet pointed out that she knew more than he, then, and forced his way past. She tore my sleeve as she sought to follow.

We were summoned to the secret room to meet a boy named Jeudon, indentured to the local furrier. He curtsied before us comically, and steadied himself. He breathed over us the sour wine and cinnamon smell of the hippocras. He had beautiful, hay-colored hair and a fondness for candied oranges. He seemed happily confused by our little gathering.

His face changed when the lord de Rais, standing some feet away, took his member from his breeches and stroked it until it was erect. Henriet and I were instructed to hold the boy's arms until the lord de Rais, moving closer, lifted the boy's shirt and took his pleasure upon his belly. Then he looped a silken cord around the boy's neck, whispering assurances all the while, and hung him from a lantern-hook high on the wall.

The boy kicked and thrashed and spun on the cord. The sound he made was like someone spitting. The lord de Rais released the knot and slid him to the floor, savoring the expressions of panic and relief. He had the boy carried to the bed and freed from his clothing but bade us not release his limbs. "Please," the boy said to me, and then to Henriet. The lord de Rais sat without his breeches on his naked chest, leaned close again to whisper something soothing and, with the boy's eyes on his, produced his jeweled dagger from the bedclothes and carved a line across the center of his throat. The fissure welled and then fountained with blood. The boy's hand jerked in mine. The lord de Rais, spattered, pulled back and then leaned forward in his work, taking the boy's gaze in his own eyes and sawing with a drowsy languor through windpipe and bone and then into the bedding.

The blood pooled faster than the bedding could receive it, so when he finally shifted his weight from the boy's chest a stream filled the indentation formed by his knee.

That night neither of us spoke until it was nearly dawn. Then Henriet used the chamber pot and, laying himself down again, claimed that even the pillars of heaven were based in the abyss. When he received no response, he wondered angrily who among us had not had the poisoned air lay its dead hand upon him. What did I know of Original Sin? He had to repeat the question. I finally told him I knew nothing of Original Sin. He said he believed in it, this dogma that taught all were lost for one alone, not only punished but also deserving of punishment, undone before they were born.

Was he weeping? I asked him, after debating the question myself. By way of answer he rose from his bed and struck me.

The disappearances whenever the lord de Rais was in residence were no secret, but there were always orphans, and parents to bring their children forward in the hopes of making their fortune in a great noble's service. Some sent their children in pairs that they might be safer in one another's care. If such a pair was to our lord's taste he had the more beautiful one's throat cut first so he or she might not pine overlong for the other. At all inquiries the herald of arms was to say that peradventure the boy was now with some upstanding gentleman elsewhere, who would see that he got on. Now in the secret room heads would line the window seat and the lord de Rais, once they were thus arranged, would ask each of us to choose the most comely. He had us each kiss the mouth of the head we chose, and then he hoisted his favorite, lowered it to his gaze, and kissed it with abandon, as though initiating it into the pleasures of the flesh.

The heads were kept for two or three days. Then they followed the bodies into the great fireplace, their ashes ferried from there to the cesspits or the moat.

Much is forgotten, and much will fall out of this account. My education in language and figures, set in motion by the parish priest, was continued under the auspices of one of the teaching friars responsible for the pages. I invited Henriet every so often to test my newfound knowledge, and he refused.

The seasons pulled us through our shifting duties while the fields around us displayed the lives from which we'd been plucked. March was for breaking clods. August was for reaping. December was for threshing and winnowing. The freemen

brought their rents, their three chickens and fifteen eggs, to the tenants' tables for
their accounting. Courtyard cats feigned sleep before blinking half-shut eyes at them.
For a little while longer, the world of treasures that consoled us and softened woe seemed
in place. But like toads crossing our path in the dark, the balance reasserted itself.

We saw a girl of seven on her back, shod only in one stocking, her head bare,
some of her spread hair pulled out and lying at her feet. We saw a five-year-old with
beautiful eyes and a filthy face whom I at first held and then released at Tiffauges's
gates, watching her disappear like a bolt from a crossbow. We witnessed our lord
beheading poppies with a rod and heard him remark that the world had been empty
since the Romans. He spoke also of Joan, and how she entered Orleans armored
in white at all points and carrying a standard depicting two angels holding a fleur-de-
lis over an Annunciation. We heard him marvel at the magical world in which she
lived, and the way, just like that, English resistance collapsed before her. As the
months went on, he took an increased interest in selecting boys himself. He came
to favor kneeling on the torso after the head had been removed but while some
warmth still remained in the body. Henriet said that I developed so gloomy, wrought,
and unforthcoming an aspect that passersby sometimes drew him aside and wondered
if I was his lord's imbecile. I asked what I should do and he said that he hauled his
necessities about with him, like someone shipwrecked. The world had abandoned
him and he had returned the favor. His claim frightened me. I took to closing my
throat with my hand as I lay beside him in the darkness, experimenting with various
pressures. One night he took my hand from my neck and reminded me that insanity
was a master's privilege. Later he emptied three full basins trying to clean his eyes
after a boy's brains had bespattered them. Afterwards he lay on his pallet unmoving,
and I was sorry for someone so young and so far from his father and mother and
brothers, and for whom all comfort was a bed of stones when compared with his home.

Chasms opened beneath me, as if the earth would swallow my sin. I wept. I fell
to the ground. I regained my feet. One morning I lay in a wheat field and some
farmers saw me and were astonished, but said nothing. We were bound to our lord
from the crowns of our heads to the soles of our feet. While he looked down from
his heights of Pandemonium. And we fell under the spell of the slaughter with its

reddish-brown eyes: ushers kept the doors, clerks added the accounts, squires dressed the dishes, and serving maids swept the halls and beat the coverlets, all while our souls, at their own bidding, flew headlong into dreadful extremity.

Our lord announced he was going to take a hand in our education. For two straight nights he appeared in our chambers and read to us from Suetonius. Then without explanation he stopped, growing increasingly agitated and impatient. Henriet in our more private moments explained why: he was spending over fifteen hundred livres per day. His family's wealth consisted of land and property, but what was needed, perpetually, was accessible money. For him wealth no longer counted as such unless it had wings and admitted of rapid exchange. In Machecoul he had founded his own chapel, the Chapel of the Holy Innocents, with a Collégiale of the finest voices and most beautiful faces he could find. Of the chapel itself it was said that even visitors from Paris had never seen the like: great glittering cascades of ornament engraved and set with precious stones and gold and silver, with all deacons, archdeacons, curates, and choirboys robed in vermilion and white silk with tawny furs and surplices of black satin and hooded capes. One wall was a towering organ, and he additionally commissioned a portable one it took six men to carry so he should not be deprived of music when obliged to travel. When the chapel was completed he had himself named Canon of Saint-Hilaire de Poitiers so he might wear the multihued ecclesiastical robes he himself had designed. He found a boy who resembled him so powerfully that the boy was designated Rais le Héraut, and dressed more magnificently then anyone, and given a place of honor in the cortége whenever the household rode out. So that everywhere our lord went, he could see himself preceding himself: our lord in white, Rais le Héraut in the deepest black.

When we traveled, our procession might take two days to fully pass through a town. When we halted we filled every tavern and lodging house. When we moved on, local innkeepers and tradesmen displayed the stunned and dull-eyed satisfaction of overfed cattle. And in addition to all this he was preparing to mount the mystery play he had commissioned, which at its climax depicted him at his moment of greatest glory. *The Mystery of the Siege of Orleans* was to be presented in that city upon the tenth anniversary of the raising of the siege, and featured twenty thousand lines of verse, one hundred and forty speaking parts, six hundred extras, and three specially built revolving stages. Each costume was to be made from new material. Even beggars' rags were to be created by slashing and defacing fine cloth. No costume could be worn twice. And unlimited supplies of food and drink were to be available to all spectators.

It seemed inconceivable that our household would find itself short of gold, but any number of estates and properties were mortgaged. And Henriet and I would be sent to retrieve bodies from our lord's bedchambers. He mortgaged properties twice and then refused to abandon them. He ransomed merchants and travelers. And finally he had to sell off estates. He sold two great crucifixes of pure silver. He sold his manuscript of Valerius Maximus and his Latin *City of God* and his parchment *Metamorphoses* of Ovid bound in emerald leather and secured with a golden lock. He sold the silver reliquary enclosing the head of Saint-Honoré, his most precious relic.

He sold so much that finally his brother and his extended family wrote to the Pope asking His Holiness to disavow the foundation of the Chapel of the Holy Innocents, and to the King requesting an edict forbidding the sale of any further family property. Both petitions were granted. Soon after, word came from his brother that his nephews had discovered a pipe full of dead children in the keep at Chemillé. Nothing came of it. In his family's eyes, once their property was safe, whatever else our lord did was his affair.

It was logical, then, that our lord would employ someone to manufacture more wealth. Joan had had secret knowledge and had put it, while he watched, to kingdom-shaking use. And now he, too, needed to appeal to secret powers. The world was an epistle and every scholar's dream was to unlock its hidden instructions. Most did so by searching for the philosopher's stone, which would transmute base metals to gold. Cold water could when heated be turned to hot air. In the same way other bodies could be similarly transformed. It was a matter of discovering the correct agent of change.

This was explained to us in a meeting convened in the secret room at Tiffauges. While our lord addressed us I looked over at the bed where he first held the jeweled dagger to my throat.

We were being taken into this confidence because we would all be a part of the great search about to begin. The sibyl foretold the future, but the conjurer made it, by recruiting Nature itself to fulfill his designs. There was an old saying in war that our lord had never forgotten: "Is there a chance? Where Prudence says no, the devil says yes." There were demons who had the power to reveal hidden treasure, teach philosophy, and guide those boldest of men who sought to make their way in the world. Years ago he'd received from a knight imprisoned in Anjou for heresy a book on the arts of alchemy and the evocation of devils. Gerbert, later to be Pope, was said to have studied astrology and other arts in Spain under the Saracens and to have summoned ghostly figures from the lower world, some of whom abetted his ascension to the papacy. Sylvester II was said to have been taught to make clocks and other internal devices by wraiths he had summoned. We would each now put our energies into locating alchemists. I would accompany Gilles de Sillé, as Henriet would Roger de Briqueville. The latter pair would travel to Italy, the center of alchemic knowledge, accompanied by a priest from Saint-Malo whose presence would make such inquiries less dangerous.

With my lord's cousin I traversed much of France, without success. We found a goldsmith who claimed he could heal, prophesy, conjure, cast love charms, and transmute silver into gold. We gave him a silver coin and locked him in a room, and he got drunk and fell asleep. Others stepped forward as conjurers. One drowned en route to Tiffauges. Another's face was of such frightening aspect that our lord refused to be shut in the tower with him. But the other group returned from Italy by the year's end with a youth named François Prelati who'd received his tonsure from the Bishop of Arezzo, having studied geomancy and other arts and sciences. He had sapphire eyes and ringletted blond hair. He wore shells from Saint James of Compostela and a holy napkin from Rome. He'd been to the East, where he claimed to have witnessed the blasphemous Marriage of the Apes, after which the celebrant cleansed his hands in molten lead. He spoke Latin and French and as a test in Florence had invoked twenty crows in the upper story of his house. He claimed he regularly conjured a demon named Barron who usually appeared as a beautiful young man. Our lord immediately had him installed in the bedchamber across from his own, and provided with everything he needed.

Experiments commenced the night his laboratory was ready. Henriet and I watched from beyond the door and outside a ring drawn into the floor with the point of a sword. Our lord and Gilles de Sillé waited just outside the circle, the latter holding to his chest his figurine of the Blessed Virgin. The conjuror's face was backlit by the green glow from his athanor, but it was unclear from the smell what he was burning. He spoke in Latin and when he stopped a cold wind blew through the tall and narrow window behind him. He drew ciphers in the center of each of the four walls. Then he poured a glittering powder into his little fire, from which a stinking smoke drove everyone from the room.

Our presence was commanded throughout the sessions that followed, in the event there was assistance the conjuror might require. The following night our lord brought with him a pact written in his own hand and bearing his signature. When it was burned in the athanor a great clattering rose above us, as though a four-legged animal was cantering on the roof.

More nights followed with the demon manifesting himself yet not appearing. The conjuror spied him and conversed with him when we could not. This progress made our lord wild with success and impatience. What else did the demon require? A week of conjurings passed before he answered. Then he said, through the conjuror in a changed voice, a soul.

Beside me in the doorway, Henriet's respiration shifted. This was the awful bargain we'd each expected.

"Well, he can't have mine," our lord told the conjuror. And in the silence that followed he added that he would get him the next-best thing.

The next morning I was told to convey a bolt of strong cloth and four loaves of bread and a sester of good milk to Henriet, who was going back to the village after having negotiated that price for an infant. That night our lord passed us in the doorway to the conjuror's room holding a vessel covered in linen, the way a priest holds a ciborium. He told the conjuror to tell the demon that he had come to offer this holy innocent's heart and eyes, and the glass when he uncovered it was smeared and the contents inside were ropy and bulbous and filled only the very bottom.

And again the demon did not appear. Henriet and I were charged with wrapping the remains in the linen cloth and burying them before daybreak in consecrated ground near the chapel.

The conjuror suggested a new method of invocation that involved a crested bird and a dyadrous stone. The latter could not be procured. Attempts were made with serpents' hearts and with the conjuror wearing a thin crown fashioned from pitch and umbilical cords.

Our lord spent more time in solitude. His aspect around those children we produced was more melancholic and distracted. He talked without explanation of his allies' desertion. He remarked during the disposal of one girl that he had been born under such a constellation that it seemed to him no one would ever comprehend the things he did.

He moved to Bourgneuf, where he stayed in a convent. He had another boy brought to him there. On All Saints' Day he informed us that Gilles de Sillé and Roger de Briqueville had gone abroad without explanation. The Dauphin announced a visit to Tiffauges, and Henriet and I were sent back at a gallop to ensure that all of the conjuror's vessels and furnaces were hidden or smashed.

In the villages even the poorest parents now flew at our approach. It was openly asserted that the lord de Rais was writing a book on the black arts and using as ink the blood of the children he'd butchered, and that when it was complete he would have the power to take any stronghold he wished. We still managed to deliver two boys, ten and seven, and then two others, fourteen and four. When he was in his cups he would lie back on his bed in the secret room, mottled in gore from the waist down, and lament that his world was disintegrating for yet a third occasion. During the first, the death of his parents, he'd had his grandfather for support; and during the second, the death of his grandfather, he'd had his wealth. Now what did he have? he asked us.

"I'm sure I don't know," Henriet told him.

He attended Easter service and received the sacraments among the poor, waving them forward to receive before him when they tried to stand aside out of respect for his position. He spent three days alone in his chambers in fasting and prayer. Then he decided to repossess the castle of Saint-Etienne-de-Mer-Morte, which he'd sold to Jean V's treasure. Having done so, he held at sword point in the chapel the officiating priest, the new owner's brother, whom he then pitched into the castle's dungeon.

He had violated ecclesiastical property, attacked a member of the duke's household, and transgressed against the rights of familial possession. That night the conjuror and the priest from Saint-Malo did not respond to his summons, and sent no word of where they might be located. He spent the next days consumed with his design for a velvet doublet waisted in silk that was embroidered along its length with Saint John's Gospel in golden thread, which he presented to a new page whom he then murdered and incinerated before us.

We alone stayed, our only home now the mad ostentation of his cruelty. Perhaps we imagined that since devils were only as active as God suffered them to be, no one would undertake to punish His instruments. I stopped eating. Henriet fell into greater and greater silences. One night he said only that he knew when my upset was at its most extreme, because I then crossed my arms and held my hands to my shoulders. He refused to add to this insight. On another occasion while we lay there on our pallets in the dark, he wondered what there was for us to do, now, but to low and bleat and wait for the culling.

It was not long in coming. On the fifteenth of September a body of men under the command of Jean Labbé, acting in the name of Jean V and Jean de Malestroit, Bishop of Nantes, presented themselves at Machecoul and demanded that the lord de Rais constitute himself their prisoner so he might answer to the triple charge of witchcraft, murder, and sodomy. Our lord had taken particular care dressing that morning, as though he expected them. We were arrested with him, and taken to Nantes.

We rode together in a covered carriage, Henriet with his head in his hands. The lord de Rais held forth the entire journey. He said he was praying to Saint Dominic, to whose order the powers of the Inquisition had been conferred. He said he had heard of a man in Savenay who, despairing of cure, had amputated his foot and then, having fallen asleep praying to the Virgin, had roused himself to find his foot restored. He said no one, rich or poor, was secure, but waited day to day on the will of the Lord.

Henriet kept his head in his hands. The lord de Rais ignored him and addressed me. He noted that I once again had nothing to offer in response. But he said he'd seen my soul. He knew it by heart. He'd noted my hours of discouragement and been present at my yielding.

I had no response for that, either. The lord de Rais stopped speaking. His single other comment, before we arrived, was that he was glad that his François, the conjuror, had escaped.

The lord de Rais was summoned to appear before the ecclesiastical judge appointed by the Bishop of Nantes on the Monday following the Feast of the Exaltation of the Holt Cross, 19 September 1440. Our presence was commanded as well. We were seated in a small dock beside the notary public. He was first charged with doctrinal heresy which violated divine majesty and subverted and weakened the faith. He was next charged with sacrilege and violation of the immunity of the Church related to his having threatened with a sword a cleric standing on holy ground. He was then charged with sodomy, the Inquisitor, from the Order of Preaching Brothers, reminding the assembled that the act of depositing semen anywhere other than the vessel for which it was intended was a sin so fundamental that self-abuse was a more serious crime than rape. The Inquisitor cited the prophet who cries out and chides," "Sons of men: how low does your heart sink?"

We were advised that those of us mindful of our salvation should undertake to set forth an extrajudicial confession. When I asked Henriet upon our return to our cell if he intended to attempt such a document, he said that he looked forward to a time when the whole globe was scoured of inhabitants, with houses left vacant, towns deserted, fields too small for the dead, and crows on the highest branches shouldering one another in their solitude. He said we were like those rough countrymen during the years of the plague who were persuaded despite all to carry the corpses to the pits.

He agreed to read my account as I set it down. Having done so to this juncture, he remarked that he found it impossible to assert which was the more astonishing, the author's memoir or his crimes. When I questioned his response he wondered with some irritation if I'd been struck by the oddity of the author's having felt so acutely for the raptors, and not their quarry.

"I've felt remorse for all of those children," I told him.

"You wrote that he had this or that person's throat cut," he answered. "But you neglected to indicate who sometimes did the cutting."

At the hour of terce on Saturday, 8 October, the lord de Rais refused to take the oath on the Sacred Scripture and, having declined to respond to the articles of indictment, was excommunicated in writing. On 15 October he consented to recognize the court's jurisdiction and admitted to many of his crimes and misdeeds. On 20 October, in order that the truth might be more fully elucidated, it was proposed that the question of torture be put to the defendant. On 21 October he petitioned that the application of torture be deferred, and on 22 October offered his full and public confession.

He spoke for four full hours. He offered the assembly a diptych of Paradise and Hell with himself as the central figure in both panels, in the former a paragon of the highest ideals of Christian knighthood, and in the latter evil's conscienceless servant. He said he believed his acts to have been halted by the hand of God, and that by the same hand he expected to be granted salvation. He freely related all of his crimes in luxurious detail and admitted he had offended our Savior because of the bad guidance he had received in his childhood, and he implored with great emotion all parents present to raise their children with good teachings and virtuous examples. He requested that his confession be published in French for the benefit of the common people. He exhorted everyone in the court, especially the churchmen, to always revere Holy Mother Church, and added that without his own love for Her he would never have been able to evade the Devil's grasp. At the end he fell to his knees and tearfully asked for mercy and remission from his Creator and for the support of the prayers of all those, present or absent, who believed in Christ and adored Him.

The civil court found him guilty of homicide, but the canonical court condemned him for heresy and sodomy alone, the latter being known as the cause of earthquakes, plagues, and famine. On 25 October he received pronouncement of sentence: he would be hanged, and then burned. His two accomplices, Henriet and myself, would be burned and then hanged. Afterward the Inquisitor asked if he wished to be reincorporated into the Church and restored to participation in the Sacraments. He answered in the affirmative. He requested of the court that since he and his servants together had committed the crimes for which they were condemned, they might be permitted to suffer punishment at the same hour, so that he, the chief cause of their perfidy, could console and admonish them and provide an example of how to die well, and perhaps thereby be a partial cause of their salvation. This request was granted. He further asked for a general procession, that the public might view their contrition, and, when this was agreed, that on the sides of the wagon transporting them would be hung paintings he'd commissioned of late, depicting classical scenes of farewell. And the court, in concluding its proceedings, was pleased to grant this final request.

We ask all who read this to judge us with the charity we might not otherwise deserve. We were brushed by our lord's divine impatience and, like driven horses, risked in his wagers. Now our share is only the lash. Tomorrow's morning has been chosen for the consummation of our sentences, the site a meadow close above the main bridge over the Loire, where the trees are often adorned with the hanged.

Where is the region of that law beyond the law? No one makes his way there with impunity. I've filled sheet after sheet in a box at my feet. I conclude a final page by candlelight while Henriet weeps and will not speak and refuses my consoling touch. He rubs his back as my mother did. He will not read any further pages I put before him.

But I write this for him. And my eyes will be on only him as our arms are lashed around the heavy stakes to our back, and his gaze remains on lord de Rais. He will hang his head and close his eyes as he does when the greatest extremity is upon him. And lord de Rais's final moments will manifest themselves before us. He will die first, and in view of his contrition the court has decreed that his body be taken from the flames before it bursts and buried in the church he has chosen. In his last moments he will be a model of piety, exhorting us to keep faith throughout what follows. Barely burned, his body will be laid out on the finest linen by four noble ladies, two of whom watched us through that peephole so many months ago, and carried in solemn procession to his interment. We will watch the procession go. We will be isolated in our agonies as the bundles are lit below us. We will be burned to cinders and our ashes scattered.

And God will come to know our secrets. At our immolation He'll appear to us and pour His gold out at our feet. And His grace that we kicked away will become like a tower on which we might stand. And His grace will raise us to such a height that we might glimpse the men we aspired to be. And His grace like the heat of the sun will burn away the men we have become.

Hop-Frog

BY EDGAR ALLAN POE

Some unfortunate folk find themselves bullied into madness by a world that is itself insane. Against all their better angels, they feel compelled to rise up in righteous vengeance against injustice so profound that only the most spectacularly deranged and incendiary payback will do.

Bloody revenge stories are now roughly a dime a dozen, which—speaking of profound injustice—is probably more than the great Edgar Allan Poe got paid to write this classic retribution tale. The poor genius who invented the detective story, the unreliable first-person descent-into-madness story, and a dozen other indelible tropes of dark fiction died drunk, broke, and alone, never knowing how important his work would be to generations a-coming. Never truly valued in his time.

There are so many great Poe stories—"The Tell-Tale Heart," "The Black Cat," "The Cask of Amontillado"—that utterly define the foundation of this literature.

But "Hop-Frog" was my favorite as a kid, and the first to make me wholeheartedly go "YAY!" for the crazy guy. The underdog. The victim who judges back.

Poe could clearly relate. And I'll bet you will, too.

Never knew anyone so keenly alive to a joke as the king was. He seemed to live only for joking. To tell a good story of the joke kind, and to tell it well, was the surest road to his favor. Thus it happened that his seven ministers were all noted for their accomplishments as jokers. They all took after the king, too, in being large, corpulent, oily men, as well as inimitable jokers. Whether people grow fat by joking, or whether there is something in fat itself which predisposes to a joke, I have never been quite able to determine; but certain it is that a lean joker is a *rara avis in terris*.

About the refinements, or, as he called them, the 'ghost' of wit, the king troubled himself very little. He had an especial admiration for breadth in a jest, and would often put up with length, for the sake of it. Over-niceties wearied him. He would have preferred Rabelais' 'Gargantua' to the 'Zadig' of Voltaire: and, upon the whole, practical jokes suited his taste far better than verbal ones.

At the date of my narrative, professing jesters had not altogether gone out of fashion at court. Several of the great continental 'powers' still retain their 'fools,' who wore motley, with caps and bells, and who were expected to be always ready with sharp witticisms, at a moment's notice, in consideration of the crumbs that fell from the royal table.

Our king, as a matter of course, retained his 'fool.' The fact is, he required something in the way of folly-if only to counterbalance the heavy wisdom of the seven wise men who were his ministers-not to mention himself.

His fool, or professional jester, was not only a fool, however. His value was trebled in the eyes of the king, by the fact of his being also a dwarf and a cripple. Dwarfs were as common at court, in those days, as fools; and many monarchs would have found it difficult to get through their days (days are rather longer at court than elsewhere) without both a jester to laugh with, and a dwarf to laugh at. But, as I have already observed, your jesters, in ninety-nine cases out of a hundred, are fat, round, and unwieldy-so that it was no small source of self-gratulation with our king that, in Hop-Frog (this was the fool's name), he possessed a triplicate treasure in one person.

I believe the name 'Hop-Frog' was not that given to the dwarf by his sponsors at baptism, but it was conferred upon him, by general consent of the several ministers, on account of his inability to walk as other men do. In fact, Hop-Frog could only get along by a sort of interjectional gait-something between a leap and a wriggle-a movement that afforded illimitable amusement, and of course consolation, to the king, for (notwithstanding the protuberance of his stomach and a constitutional swelling of the head) the king, by his whole court, was accounted a capital figure.

But although Hop-Frog, through the distortion of his legs, could move only with great pain and difficulty along a road or floor, the prodigious muscular power which nature seemed to have bestowed upon his arms, by way of compensation for deficiency in the lower limbs, enabled him to perform many feats of wonderful dexterity, where trees or ropes were in question, or any thing else to climb. At such exercises he certainly much more resembled a squirrel, or a small monkey, than a frog.

I am not able to say, with precision, from what country Hop-Frog originally came. It was from some barbarous region, however, that no person ever heard of-a vast distance from the court of our king. Hop-Frog, and a young girl very little less dwarfish than himself (although of exquisite proportions, and a marvellous dancer), had been forcibly carried off from their respective homes in adjoining provinces, and sent as presents to the king, by one of his ever-victorious generals.

Under these circumstances, it is not to be wondered at that a close intimacy arose between the two little captives. Indeed, they soon became sworn friends. Hop-Frog, who, although he made a great deal of sport, was by no means popular, had it not in his power to render Trippetta many services; but she, on account of her grace and exquisite beauty (although a dwarf), was universally admired and petted; so she possessed much influence; and never failed to use it, whenever she could, for the benefit of Hop-Frog.

On some grand state occasion-I forgot what-the king determined to have a masquerade, and whenever a masquerade or any thing of that kind, occurred at our court, then the talents, both of Hop-Frog and Trippetta were sure to be called into play. Hop-Frog, in especial, was so inventive in the way of getting up pageants, suggesting novel characters, and arranging costumes, for masked balls, that nothing could be done, it seems, without his assistance.

The night appointed for the fete had arrived. A gorgeous hall had been fitted up, under Trippetta's eye, with every kind of device which could possibly give eclat to a masquerade. The whole court was in a fever of expectation. As for costumes and characters, it might well be supposed that everybody had come to a decision on such points. Many had made up their minds (as to what roles they should assume) a week, or even a month, in advance; and, in fact, there was not a particle of indecision anywhere—except in the case of the king and his seven minsters. Why they hesitated I never could tell, unless they did it by way of a joke. More probably, they found it difficult, on account of being so fat, to make up their minds. At all events, time flew; and, as a last resort they sent for Trippetta and Hop-Frog.

When the two little friends obeyed the summons of the king they found him sitting at his wine with the seven members of his cabinet council; but the monarch appeared to be in a very ill humor. He knew that Hop-Frog was not fond of wine, for it excited the poor cripple almost to madness; and madness is no comfortable feeling. But the king loved his practical jokes, and took pleasure in forcing Hop-Frog to drink and (as the king called it) 'to be merry.'

"Come here, Hop-Frog," said he, as the jester and his friend entered the room; "swallow this bumper to the health of your absent friends, [here Hop-Frog sighed,] and then let us have the benefit of your invention. We want characters-characters, man-something novel-out of the way. We are wearied with this everlasting sameness. Come, drink! the wine will brighten your wits."

Hop-Frog endeavored, as usual, to get up a jest in reply to these advances from the king; but the effort was too much. It happened to be the poor dwarf's birthday, and the command to drink to his 'absent friends' forced the tears to his eyes. Many large, bitter drops fell into the goblet as he took it, humbly, from the hand of the tyrant.

"Ah! ha! ha!" roared the latter, as the dwarf reluctantly drained the beaker. "See what a glass of good wine can do! Why, your eyes are shining already!"

Poor fellow! his large eyes gleamed, rather than shone; for the effect of wine on his excitable brain was not more powerful than instantaneous. He placed the goblet nervously on the table, and looked round upon the company with a half-insane stare. They all seemed highly amused at the success of the king's 'joke.'

"And now to business," said the prime minister, a very fat man.

"Yes," said the King; "Come lend us your assistance. Characters, my fine fellow; we stand in need of characters-all of us-ha! ha! ha!" and as this was seriously meant for a joke, his laugh was chorused by the seven.

Hop-Frog also laughed although feebly and somewhat vacantly.

"Come, come," said the king, impatiently, "have you nothing to suggest?"

"I am endeavoring to think of something novel," replied the dwarf, abstractedly, for he was quite bewildered by the wine.

"Endeavoring!" cried the tyrant, fiercely; "what do you mean by that? Ah, I perceive. You are Sulky, and want more wine. Here, drink this!" and he poured out another goblet full and offered it to the cripple, who merely gazed at it, gasping for breath.

"Drink, I say!" shouted the monster, "or by the fiends-"

The dwarf hesitated. The king grew purple with rage. The courtiers smirked. Trippetta, pale as a corpse, advanced to the monarch's seat, and, falling on her knees before him, implored him to spare her friend.

The tyrant regarded her, for some moments, in evident wonder at her audacity. He seemed quite at a loss what to do or say-how most becomingly to express his indignation. At last, without uttering a syllable, he pushed her violently from him, and threw the contents of the brimming goblet in her face.

The poor girl got up the best she could, and, not daring even to sigh, resumed her position at the foot of the table.

There was a dead silence for about half a minute, during which the falling of a leaf, or of a feather, might have been heard. It was interrupted by a low, but harsh and protracted grating sound which seemed to come at once from every corner of the room.

"What-what-what are you making that noise for?" demanded the king, turning furiously to the dwarf.

The latter seemed to have recovered, in great measure, from his intoxication, and looking fixedly but quietly into the tyrant's face, merely ejaculated:

"I-I? How could it have been me?"

"The sound appeared to come from without," observed one of the courtiers. "I fancy it was the parrot at the window, whetting his bill upon his cage-wires."

"True," replied the monarch, as if much relieved by the suggestion; "but, on the honor of a knight, I could have sworn that it was the gritting of this vagabond's teeth."

Hereupon the dwarf laughed (the king was too confirmed a joker to object to any one's laughing), and displayed a set of large, powerful, and very repulsive teeth. Moreover, he avowed his perfect willingness to swallow as much wine as desired. The monarch was pacified; and having drained another bumper with no very perceptible ill effect, Hop-Frog entered at once, and with spirit, into the plans for the masquerade.

"I cannot tell what was the association of idea," observed he, very tranquilly, and as if he had never tasted wine in his life, "but just after your majesty had struck the girl and thrown the wine in her face-just after your majesty had done this, and while the parrot was making that odd noise outside the window, there came into my mind a capital diversion-one of my own country frolics-often enacted among us, at our masquerades: but here it will be new altogether. Unfortunately, however, it requires a company of eight persons and-"

"Here we are!" cried the king, laughing at his acute discovery of the coincidence; "eight to a fraction-I and my seven ministers. Come! what is the diversion?"

"We call it," replied the cripple, "the Eight Chained Ourang-Outangs, and it really is excellent sport if well enacted."

"We will enact it," remarked the king, drawing himself up, and lowering his eyelids.

"The beauty of the game," continued Hop-Frog, "lies in the fright it occasions among the women."

"Capital!" roared in chorus the monarch and his ministry.

"I will equip you as ourang-outangs," proceeded the dwarf; "leave all that to me. The resemblance shall be so striking, that the company of masqueraders will take you for real beasts-and of course, they will be as much terrified as astonished."

"Oh, this is exquisite!" exclaimed the king. "Hop-Frog! I will make a man of you."

"The chains are for the purpose of increasing the confusion by their jangling. You are supposed to have escaped, en masse, from your keepers. Your majesty cannot conceive the effect produced, at a masquerade, by eight chained ourang-outangs, imagined to be real ones by most of the company; and rushing in with savage cries, among the crowd of delicately and gorgeously habited men and women. The contrast is inimitable!"

"It must be," said the king: and the council arose hurriedly (as it was growing late), to put in execution the scheme of Hop-Frog.

His mode of equipping the party as ourang-outangs was very simple, but effective enough for his purposes. The animals in question had, at the epoch of my story, very rarely been seen in any part of the civilized world; and as the imitations made by the dwarf were sufficiently beast-like and more than sufficiently hideous, their truthfulness to nature was thus thought to be secured.

The king and his ministers were first encased in tight-fitting stockinet shirts and drawers. They were then saturated with tar. At this stage of the process, some one of the party suggested feathers; but the suggestion was at once overruled by the dwarf, who soon convinced the eight, by ocular demonstration, that the hair of such a brute as the ourang-outang was much more efficiently represented by flax. A thick coating of the latter was accordingly plastered upon the coating of tar. A long chain was now procured. First, it was passed about the waist of the king, and tied, then about another of the party, and also tied; then about all successively, in the same manner. When this chaining arrangement was complete, and the party stood as far apart from each other as possible, they formed a circle; and to make all things appear natural, Hop-Frog passed the residue of the chain in two diameters, at right angles, across the circle, after the fashion adopted, at the present day, by those who capture Chimpanzees, or other large apes, in Borneo.

The grand saloon in which the masquerade was to take place, was a circular room, very lofty, and receiving the light of the sun only through a single window at top. At night (the season for which the apartment was especially designed) it was illuminated principally by a large chandelier, depending by a chain from the centre of the sky-light, and lowered, or elevated, by means of a counter-balance as usual; but (in order not to look unsightly) this latter passed outside the cupola and over the roof.

The arrangements of the room had been left to Trippetta's superintendence; but, in some particulars, it seems, she had been guided by the calmer judgment of her friend the dwarf. At his suggestion it was that, on this occasion, the chandelier was removed. Its waxen drippings (which, in weather so warm, it was quite impossible to prevent) would have been seriously detrimental to the rich dresses of the guests, who, on account of the crowded state of the saloon, could not all be expected to keep from out its centre; that is to say, from under the chandelier. Additional sconces were set in various parts of the hall, out of the way, and a flambeau, emitting sweet odor, was placed in the right hand of each of the Caryatides that stood against the wall-some fifty or sixty altogether.

The eight ourang-outangs, taking Hop-Frog's advice, waited patiently until midnight (when the room was thoroughly filled with masqueraders) before making their appearance. No sooner had the clock ceased striking, however, than they rushed, or rather rolled in, all together-for the impediments of their chains caused most of the party to fall, and all to stumble as they entered.

The excitement among the masqueraders was prodigious, and filled the heart of the king with glee. As had been anticipated, there were not a few of the guests who supposed the ferocious-looking creatures to be beasts of some kind in reality, if not precisely ourang-outangs. Many of the women swooned with affright; and had not the king taken the precaution to exclude all weapons from the saloon, his party might soon have expiated their frolic in their blood. As it was, a general rush was made for the doors; but the king had ordered them to be locked immediately upon his entrance; and, at the dwarf's suggestion, the keys had been deposited with him.

While the tumult was at its height, and each masquerader attentive only to his own safety (for, in fact, there was much real danger from the pressure of the excited crowd), the chain by which the chandelier ordinarily hung, and which had been drawn up on its removal, might have been seen very gradually to descend, until its hooked extremity came within three feet of the floor.

Soon after this, the king and his seven friends having reeled about the hall in all directions, found themselves, at length, in its centre, and, of course, in immediate contact with the chain. While they were thus situated, the dwarf, who had followed noiselessly at their heels, inciting them to keep up the commotion, took hold of their own chain at the intersection of the two portions which crossed the circle diametrically and at right angles. Here, with the rapidity of thought, he inserted the hook from which the chandelier had been wont to depend; and, in an instant, by some unseen agency, the chandelier-chain was drawn so far upward as to take the hook out of reach, and, as an inevitable consequence, to drag the ourang-outangs together in close connection, and face to face.

The masqueraders, by this time, had recovered, in some measure, from their alarm; and, beginning to regard the whole matter as a well-contrived pleasantry, set up a loud shout of laughter at the predicament of the apes.

"Leave them to me!" now screamed Hop-Frog, his shrill voice making itself easily heard through all the din. "Leave them to me. I fancy I know them. If I can only get a good look at them, I can soon tell who they are."

Here, scrambling over the heads of the crowd, he managed to get to the wall; when, seizing a flambeau from one of the Caryatides, he returned, as he went, to the centre of the room-leaping, with the agility of a monkey, upon the king's head, and thence clambered a few feet up the chain; holding down the torch to examine the group of ourang-outangs, and still screaming: "I shall soon find out who they are!"

And now, while the whole assembly (the apes included) were convulsed with laughter, the jester suddenly uttered a shrill whistle; when the chain flew violently up for about thirty feet-dragging with it the dismayed and struggling ourang-outangs, and leaving them suspended in mid-air between the sky-light and the floor. Hop-Frog, clinging to the chain as it rose, still maintained his relative position in respect to the eight maskers, and still (as if nothing were the matter) continued to thrust his torch down toward them, as though endeavoring to discover who they were.

So thoroughly astonished was the whole company at this ascent, that a dead silence, of about a minute's duration, ensued. It was broken by just such a low, harsh, grating sound, as had before attracted the attention of the king and his councillors when the former threw the wine in the face of Trippetta. But, on the present occasion, there could be no question as to whence the sound issued. It came from the fang-like teeth of the dwarf, who ground them and gnashed them as he foamed at the mouth, and glared, with an expression of maniacal rage, into the upturned countenances of the king and his seven companions.

"Ah, ha!" said at length the infuriated jester. "Ah, ha! I begin to see who these people are now!" Here, pretending to scrutinize the king more closely, he held the flambeau to the flaxen coat which enveloped him, and which instantly burst into a sheet of vivid flame. In less than half a minute the whole eight ourang-outangs were blazing fiercely, amid the shrieks of the multitude who gazed at them from below, horror-stricken, and without the power to render them the slightest assistance.

At length the flames, suddenly increasing in virulence, forced the jester to climb higher up the chain, to be out of their reach; and, as he made this movement, the crowd again sank, for a brief instant, into silence. The dwarf seized his opportunity, and once more spoke:

"I now see distinctly." he said, "what manner of people these maskers are. They are a great king and his seven privy-councillors,-a king who does not scruple to strike a defenseless girl and his seven councillors who abet him in the outrage. As for myself, I am simply Hop-Frog, the jester-and this is my last jest."

Owing to the high combustibility of both the flax and the tar to which it adhered, the dwarf had scarcely made an end of his brief speech before the work of vengeance was complete. The eight corpses swung in their chains, a fetid, blackened, hideous, and indistinguishable mass. The cripple hurled his torch at them, clambered leisurely to the ceiling, and disappeared through the sky-light.

It is supposed that Trippetta, stationed on the roof of the saloon, had been the accomplice of her friend in his fiery revenge, and that, together, they effected their escape to their own country: for neither was seen again.

Marmalade Wine

BY JOAN AIKEN

This little ray of sunshine comes from the prolific pen of Joan Aiken, circa 1958. Like so many classic horrors I read as a kid, I stumbled upon this in the British anthologies of the 1960s, by Pan and Fontana. And loved it at once.

Clearly, Rod Serling had a similar love for those collections. Because when he started Night Gallery *in the '70s, a stunning number of episodes had their genesis in those pages.*

And so it was with "Marmalade Wine," which wound up as one of the goofier entries, Robert Morse and Rudy Vallee hamming it up in grand style. That said, Aiken's deft prose is infinitely more penetrating, and easily twice as much fun.

How much you wanna bet that Stephen King's one of the story's biggest fans, too? (Within the question lies the clue.)

"Paradise," Blacker said to himself, moving forward into the wood. "Paradise. Fairyland."

He was a man given to exaggeration; poetic licence he called it. His friends referred to "Blacker's little flights of fancy," or something less polite, but on this occasion he spoke nothing but the truth. The wood stood silent about him, tall, golden, with afternoon sunlight slanting through the half-unfurled leaves of early summer. Underfoot, anemones palely carpeted the ground. A cuckoo called.

"Paradise," Blacker repeated, closing the gate behind him, and strode down the overgrown path, looking for a spot in which to eat his ham sandwich. Hazel bushes thickened at either side until the circular blue eye of the gateway by which he had come in dwindled to a pinpoint and vanished. The taller trees overtopping the hazels were not yet in full leaf and gave little cover; it was very hot in the wood and very still.

Suddenly Blacker stopped short with an exclamation of surprise and regret: lying among the dog's-mercury by the path was the body of a cock-pheasant in the full splendour of its spring plumage. Blacker turned the bird over with the townsman's pity and curiosity at such evidence of nature's unkindness; the feathers, purple-bronze, green, and gold, were smooth under his hand as a girl's hair.

"Poor thing," he said aloud, "what can have happened to it?" He walked on, wondering if he could turn the incident to account. *Threnody for a Pheasant in May.* Too precious? Too sentimental? Perhaps a weekly would take it. He began choosing rhymes, staring at his feet as he walked, abandoning his conscious rapture at the beauty around him.

Stricken to death . . . and something . . . leafy ride,
Before his . . . something . . . fully flaunt his pride

Or would a shorter line be better, something utterly simple and heartfelt, limpid tears of grief like spring rain dripping off the petals of a flower?

It was odd, Blacker thought, increasing his pace, how difficult he found writing nature poetry; nature was beautiful, maybe, but it was not stimulating. And it was nature poetry that *Field and Garden* wanted. Still, that pheasant ought to be worth five guineas. *Tread lightly past, Where he lies still, And something last . . .*

Damn! In his absorption he had nearly trodden on another pheasant. What was happening to the birds? Blacker, who objected to occurrences with no visible explanation, walked on frowning. The path bore downhill to the right, and leaving the hazel coppice, crossed a tiny valley. Below him Blacker was surprised to see a small, secretive flint cottage, surrounded on three sides by trees. In front of it was a patch of turf. A deck-chair stood there, and a man was peacefully stretched out in it, enjoying the afternoon sun.

Blacker's first impulse was to turn back; he felt as if he had walked into somebody's garden, and was filled with mild irritation at the unexpectedness of the encounter. There ought to have been some warning signs, dash it all. The wood had seemed as deserted as Eden itself. But his turning round would have an appearance of guilt and furtiveness; on second thoughts, he decided to go boldly past the cottage. After all there was no fence, and the path was not marked private in any way; he had a perfect right to be there.

"Good afternoon," said the man pleasantly as Blacker approached. "Remarkably fine weather, is it not?"

"I do hope I'm not trespassing."

Studying the man, Blacker revised his first guess. This was no gamekeeper; there was distinction in every line of the thin sculptured face. What most attracted Blacker's attention were the hands holding a small gilt coffee-cup; they were as white, frail, and attenuated as the pale roots of water plants.

"Not at all," the man said cordially. "In fact you arrive at a most opportune moment; you are very welcome. I was just wishing for a little company. Delightful as I find this sylvan retreat, it becomes, all of a sudden, a little dull, a little banal. I do trust that you have time to sit down and share my after-lunch coffee and liqueur."

As he spoke he reached behind him and brought out a second deck-chair from the cottage porch.

"Why, thank you; I should be delighted," said Blacker, wondering if he had the strength of character to take out the ham sandwich and eat it in front of this patrician hermit.

Before he had made up his mind, the man had gone into the house and returned with another gilt cup full of black, fragrant coffee, hot as Tartarus, which he handed to Blacker. He carried also a tiny glass, and into this, from a blackcurrant-cordial bottle, he carefully poured a clear colourless liquid. Blacker sniffed his glassful with caution, mistrusting the bottle and its evidence of home-brewing, but the scent, aromatic and powerful, was similar to that of curaçao, and the liquid moved in its glass with an oily smoothness. It certainly was not cowslip wine.

"Well," said his host, reseating himself and gesturing slightly with his glass, "how do you do?" He sipped delicately.

"Cheers," said Blacker, and added, "my name's Roger Blacker." It sounded a little lame. The liqueur was not curaçao, but akin to it, and quite remarkably potent. Blacker, who was very hungry, felt the fumes rise up inside his head as if an orange tree had taken root there and was putting out leaves and golden glowing fruit.

"Sir Francis Deeking," the other man said, and then Blacker understood why his hands had seemed so spectacular, so portentously out of the common.

"The surgeon? But surely you don't live down here?"

Deeking waved a hand deprecatingly. "A week-end retreat. A hermitage, to which I can retire from the strain of my calling."

"It certainly is very remote," Blacker remarked. "It must be five miles from the nearest road."

"Six. And you, my dear Mr. Blacker, what is your profession ?"

"Oh, a writer," said Blacker modestly. The drink was having its usual effect on him; he managed to convey not that he was a journalist with literary yearnings, on a local daily, but that he was a philosopher and essayist of rare quality, a sort of second Montaigne. All the time he spoke, while drawn out most flatteringly by the questions of Sir Francis, he was recalling journalistic scraps of information about his host; the operation on the Indian Prince; the Cabinet Minister's appendix; the amputation performed on that unfortunate ballerina who had both feet crushed in a railway accident; the major operation which had proved so miraculously successful on the American heiress ...

"You must feel like a god," he said suddenly, noticing with surprise that his glass was empty. Sir Francis waved the remark aside.

"We all have our godlike attributes," he said, leaning forward. "Now you, Mr. Blacker, a writer, a creative artist—do you not know a power akin to godhead when you transfer your thought to paper?"

"Well, not exactly then," said Blacker, feeling the liqueur moving inside his head in golden and russet-colored clouds. "Not so much then, but I do have one unusual power—a power not shared by many people—of foretelling the future. For instance, as I was coming through the wood, I knew this house would be here. I knew I should find you sitting in front of it. I can look at the list of runners in a race, and the name of the winner fairly leaps out at me from the page as if it was printed in golden ink. Forthcoming events—air disasters, train crashes, I always sense, in advance. I begin to have a terrible feeling of impending doom, as if my brain was a volcano just on the point of eruption."

What was that other item of news about Sir Francis Deeking, he wondered, a recent report, a tiny paragraph hat had caught his eye in *The Times*? He could not recall it.

"Really?" Sir Francis was looking at him with the keenest interest; his eyes, hooded and fanatical under their heary lids, held brilliant points of light. "I have always longed to know somebody with such a power. It must be a terrifying responsibility."

"Oh, it is," Blacker said. He contrived to look bowed under the weight of supernatural cares; noticed that his glass was full again, and drained it. "Of course I don't use the faculty for my own ends; something fundamental in me rises up to prevent that. It's as basic, you know, as the instinct forbidding cannibalism or incest."

"Quite, quite," Sir Francis agreed. "But for another person you would be able to give warnings, advise profitable courses of action? My dear fellow, your glass is empty. Allow me."

"This is marvelous stuff," Blacker said hazily. "It's like a wreath of orange blossom." He gestured with his finger.

"I distill it myself; from marmalade. But do go on with what you were saying. Could you, for instance, tell me the winner of this afternoon's Manchester Plate?"

"Bow Bells," Blacker said unhesitatingly. It was the only name he could remember.

"You interest me enormously. And the result of today's Aldwych by-election? Do you know that?"

"Unwin, the Liberal, will get in by a majority of two hundred and eighty-two. He won't take his seat, though. He'll be killed at seven this evening in a lift accident at his hotel." Blacker was well away by now.

"Will he, indeed!" Sir Francis appeared delightful. "A pestilent fellow. I have sat on several boards with him. Do continue."

Blacker required little encouragement. He told the story of the financier whom he had warned in time of the oil company crash; the dream about the famous violinist which had resulted in the man's canceling his passage on the ill-fated Orion; and the tragic tale of the bullfighter who had ignored his warning.

"But I am talking too much about myself," he said at length, partly because he noticed an ominous clogging of his tongue, a refusal of his thoughts to marshal themselves. He cast about for an impersonal topic, something simple.

"The pheasants," he said. "What's happened to the pheasants? Cut down in their prime. It—it's terrible. I found four in the wood up there, four or five."

"Really?" Sir Francis seemed callously uninterested in the fate of pheasants. "It's the chemical sprays they use on the crops, I understand. Bound to upset the ecology; they never work out the probable results beforehand. Now if you were in charge, my dear Mr. Blacker—But forgive me, it is a hot afternoon and you must be tired and footsore if you have walked from Witherstow this morning—let me suggest that you have a short sleep . . ."

His voice seemed to come from farther and farther away; a network of sun-coloured leaves laced themselves in front of Blacker's eyes. Gratefully he leaned back and stretched out his aching feet.

Some time after this Blacker roused a little—or was it only a dream—to see Sir Francis standing by him, rubbing his hands with a face of jubilation.

"My dear fellow, my dear Mr. Blacker, what a *lusus naturae* you are. I can never be sufficiently grateful that you came my way. Bow Bells walked home—positively ambled. I have been listening to the commentary. What a misfortune that I had no time to place money on the horse—but never mind, never mind, that can be remedied another time. It is unkind of me to disturb your well-earned rest, though; drink this last thimbleful, and finish your nap while the sun is on the wood."

As Blacker's head sank back against the deck-chair again, Sir Francis leaned forward and gently took the glass from his hand.

"Sweet river of dreams," thought Blacker, "fancy the horse actually winning. I wish I'd had a fiver on it myself; I could do with a new pair of shoes. I should have undone these before I dozed off, they're too tight or something. I must wake up soon, ought to be on my way in half an hour or so . . ."

When Blacker finally woke, he found that he was lying on a narrow bed indoors, covered with a couple of blankets. His head ached and throbbed with a shattering intensity, and it took a few minutes for his vision to clear; then he saw that he was in a small white cell-like room which contained nothing but the bed he was on and a chair. It was very nearly dark.

He tried to struggle up, but a strange numbness and heaviness had invaded the lower part of his body; and after hoisting himself on to his elbow he felt so sick that he abandoned the effort and lay down again.

"That stuff must have the effect of a knockout drop," he thought ruefully; "what a fool I was to drink it. I'll have to apologise to Sir Francis. What time can it be?"

"Ah, my dear Blacker, I see you have come round. Allow me to offer you a drink."

He raised Blacker skillfully, and gave him a drink of water from a cup with a rim and a spout.

"Now, let me settle you down again. Excellent. We shall soon have you—well, not on your feet, but sitting up and taking nourishment." He laughed a little. "You can have some beef tea presently."

"I am so sorry," Blacker said. "I really need not trespass on your hospitality any longer. I shall be quite all right in a minute."

"No trespass, my dear friend. You are not at all in the way. I hope that you will be here for a long and pleasant stay. These surroundings, so restful, so conducive to a writer's inspiration—what could be more suitable for you? You need not think that I shall disturb you. I am in London all the week but shall keep you company at weekends—pray, pray, don't think that you will be a nuisance or *de trop*. On the contrary, I am hoping that you can do me the kindness of giving me the Stock Exchange prices in advance, which will amply compensate for any small trouble I have taken. No, no, you must feel quite at home—please consider, indeed, that this is your home."

Stock Exchange prices? It took Blacker a moment to remember, then he thought, "Oh lord, my tongue has played me false as usual." He tried to recall what stupidities he had been guilty of.

"Those stories," he said lamely, "they were all a bit exaggerated, you know. About my foretelling the future . . . I can't really. That horse's winning was a pure coincidence, I'm afraid."

"Modesty, modesty." Sir Francis was smiling, but he had gone rather pale and Blacker noticed a beading of sweat along his cheekbones. "I am sure you will be invaluable. Since my retirement I find it absolutely necessary to augment my income by judicious investment."

All of a sudden Blacker remembered the gist of that small paragraph in *The Times*. Nervous breakdown. Complete rest . . .

"I—I really must go now," he said uneasily, trying to push himself upright. "I meant to be back by seven."

"Oh, but Mr. Blacker, that is quite out of the question. Indeed, so as to preclude any such action, I have amputated your feet. But you need not worry; I know you will be very happy here. And I feel certain that you are wrong to doubt your own powers. Let us listen to the ten o'clock news in order to be quite satisfied that the detestable Unwin did fall down the hotel lift shaft."

He walked over to the portable radio and switched it on.

The Most Dangerous Game

BY RICHARD CONNELL

Killing as sport. That's what hunting's all about once there's already meat on the table. And when Richard Connell first published this piece in Collier's *magazine in 1924, it was one of those bull's-eye moments when a story achieves quintessence and becomes a classic for all time.*

Far from a one-hit wonder in his day (he also wrote the screen story for Frank Capra's Meet John Doe*), this remains the one for which Connell is justly remembered. Herein you'll find an old-fashioned, exquisitely mannered psychosis: Conrad's* Heart of Darkness *as an elitist chamber piece, stripped of politics, with its imperialist pinky upraised.*

It's also bare-knuckled suspense at its classiest. And an inarguable inspiration for all the wannabe Hannibal Lecters to come. (The Zodiak Killer was also a fan.)

"Off there to the right—somewhere—is a large island," said Whitney. "It's rather a mystery—"

"What island is it?" Rainsford asked.

"The old charts call it 'Ship-Trap Island'," Whitney replied. "A suggestive name, isn't it? Sailors have a curious dread of the place. I don't know why. Some superstition—"

"Can't see it," remarked Rainsford, trying to peer through the dank tropical night that was palpable as it pressed its thick warm blackness in upon the yacht.

"You've good eyes," said Whitney, with a laugh, "and I've seen you pick off a moose moving in the brown fall bush at four hundred yards, but even you can't see four miles or so through a moonless Caribbean night."

"Nor four yards," admitted Rainsford. "Ugh! It's like moist velvet."

"It will be light enough in Rio," promised Whitney. "We should make it in a few days. I hope the jaguar guns have come from Purdey's. We should have some good hunting up the Amazon. Great sport, hunting."

"The best sport in the world," agreed Rainsford.

"For the hunter," amended Whitney. "Not for the jaguar."

"Don't talk rot, Whitney," said Rainsford. "You're a big-game hunter, not a philosopher. Who cares how a jaguar feels?"

"Perhaps the jaguar does," observed Whitney.

"Bah! They've no understanding."

"Even so, I rather think they understand one thing at least—fear. The fear of pain and the fear of death."

"Nonsense," laughed Rainsford. "This hot weather is making you soft, Whitney. Be a realist. The world is made up of two classes—the hunters and the hunted. Luckily, you and I are hunters. Do you think we've passed that island yet?"

"I can't tell in the dark. I hope so."

"Why?" asked Rainsford.

"The place has a reputation—a bad one."

"Cannibals?" suggested Rainsford.

"Hardly. Even cannibals wouldn't live in such a Godforsaken place. But it's got into sailor lore, somehow. Didn't you notice that the crew's nerves seem a bit jumpy today?"

"They were a bit strange, now you mention it. Even Captain Nielson—"

"Yes, even that tough-minded old Swede, who'd go up to the devil himself and ask him for a light. Those fishy blue eyes held a look I never saw there before. All I could get out of him was, 'This place has an evil name among seafaring men, sir.' Then he said to me, very gravely, 'Don't you feel anything?'—as if the air about us was actually poisonous. Now, you mustn't laugh when I tell you this—I did feel something like a sudden chill.

"There was no breeze. The sea was as flat as a plate-glass window. We were drawing near the island then. What I felt was a—a mental chill—a sort of sudden dread."

"Pure imagination," said Rainsford. "One superstitious sailor can taint the whole ship's company with his fear."

"Maybe. But sometimes I think sailors have an extra sense that tells them when they are in danger. Sometimes I think evil is a tangible thing—with wave lengths, just as sound and light have. An evil place can, so to speak, broadcast vibrations of evil. Anyhow, I'm glad we're getting out of this zone. Well, I think I'll turn in now, Rainsford."

"I'm not sleepy," said Rainsford. "I'm going to smoke another pipe up on the after deck."

"Goodnight then, Rainsford. See you at breakfast."

"Right. Goodnight, Whitney."

There was no sound in the night as Rainsford sat there, but the muffled throb of the engine that drove the yacht swiftly through the darkness, and the swish and ripple of the wash of the propeller.

Rainsford, reclining in a steamer chair, indolently puffed on his favorite brier. The sensuous drowsiness of the night was on him. 'It's so dark,' he thought, 'that I could sleep without closing my eyes; the night would be my eyelids—'

An abrupt sound startled him. Off to the right he heard it, and his ears, expert in such matters, could not be mistaken. Again he heard the sound, and again. Somewhere, off in the blackness, someone had fired a gun three times.

Rainsford sprang up and moved quickly to the rail, mystified. He strained his eyes in the direction from which the reports had come, but it was like trying to see through a blanket. He leaped upon the rail and balanced himself there, to get greater elevation; his pipe, striking a rope, was knocked from his mouth. He lunged for it; a short, hoarse cry came from his lips as he realized he had reached too far and had lost his balance. The cry was pinched off short as the blood-warm waters of the Caribbean Sea closed over his head.

He struggled up to the surface and tried to cry out, but the wash from the speeding yacht slapped him in the face and the salt water in his open mouth made him gag and strangle. Desperately he struck out with strong strokes after the receding lights of the yacht, but he stopped before he had swum fifty feet. A certain cool-headedness had come to him; it was not the first time he had been in a tight place. There was a chance that his cries could be heard by someone aboard the yacht, but that chance was slender, and grew more slender as the yacht raced on. He wrestled himself out of his clothes, and shouted with all his power. The lights of the yacht became faint and ever-vanishing fireflies; then they were blotted out entirely by the night.

Rainsford remembered the shots. They had come from the right, and doggedly he swam in that direction, swimming with slow, deliberate strokes, conserving his strength. For a seemingly endless time he fought the sea. He began to count his strokes desperately; he could do possibly a hundred more and then—

Rainsford heard a sound. It came out of the darkness, a high, screaming sound, the sound of an animal in an extremity of anguish and terror.

He did not recognize the animal that made the sound; he did not try to; with fresh vitality he swam toward the sound. He heard it again; then it was cut short by another noise, crisp, staccato.

"Pistol shot," muttered Rainsford, swimming on.

Ten minutes of determined effort brought another sound to his ears—the most welcome he had ever heard—the muttering and growling of the sea breaking on a rocky shore. He was almost on the rocks before he saw them; on a night less calm he would have been shattered against them. With his remaining strength he dragged himself from the swirling waters. Jagged crags appeared to jut up into the opaqueness; he forded himself upward, hand over hand. Gasping, his hands raw, he reached a flat place at the top. Dense jungle came down to the very edge of the cliffs. What perils that tangle of trees and underbrush might hold for him did not concern Rainsford just then. All he knew was that he was safe from his enemy, the sea, and that utter weariness was on him. He flung himself down at the jungle edge and tumbled headlong into the deepest sleep of his life.

When he opened his eyes he knew from the position of the sun that it was late in the afternoon. Sleep had given him new vigor; a sharp hunger was picking at him. He looked about him, almost cheerfully.

'Where there are pistol shots, there are men. Where there are men, there is food,' he thought. But what kind of men, he wondered, in so forbidding a place? An unbroken front of snarled and jagged jungle fringed the shore.

He saw no sign of a trail through the closely knit web of weeds and trees; it was easier to go along the shore, and Rainsford floundered along by the water. Not far from where he had landed, he stopped.

Some wounded thing, by the evidence a large animal, had thrashed about in the underbrush; the jungle weeds were crushed down and the moss was lacerated; one patch of weeds was stained crimson. A small, glittering object not far away caught Rainsford's eye and he picked it up. It was an empty cartridge.

"A twenty-two," he remarked. "That's odd. It must have been a fairly large animal, too. The hunter had his nerve to tackle it with a light gun. It's clear that the brute put up a fight. I suppose the first three shots I heard was when the hunter flushed his quarry and wounded it. The last shot was when he trailed it here and finished it."

He examined the ground closely and found what he had hoped to find—the print of hunting boots. They pointed along the cliff in the direction he had been going. Eagerly he hurried along, now slipping on a rotten log or a loose stone, but making headway; night was beginning to settle down on the island.

Bleak darkness was blacking out the sea and jungle when Rainsford sighted the lights. He came upon them as he turned a crook in the coast line, and his first thought was that he had come upon a village, for there were many lights. But as he forged along he saw to his great astonishment that all the lights were in one enormous building—a lofty structure with pointed towers plunging upward into the gloom. His eyes made out the shadowy outlines of a palatial château ; it was set on a high bluff, and on three sides of it cliffs dived down to where the sea licked greedy lips in the shadows.

'Mirage,' thought Rainsford. But it was no mirage, he found, when he opened the tall spiked gate. The stone steps were real enough; the massive door with a leering gargoyle for a knocker was real enough; yet about it all hung an air of unreality.

He lifted the knocker, and it creaked up stiffly, as if it had never before been used. He let it fall, and it startled him with its booming loudness. He thought he heard footsteps within; the door remained closed. Again Rainsford lifted the heavy knocker, and let it fall. The door opened then, opened as suddenly as if it were on a spring, and Rainsford stood blinking in the river of glaring gold light that poured out. The first thing Rainsford's eyes discerned was the largest man Rainsford had ever seen— a gigantic creature, solidly made and black-bearded to the waist. In his hand the man held a long-barrel revolver, and he was pointing it straight at Rainsford's heart.

Out of the snarl of beard two small eyes regarded Rainsford.

"Don't be alarmed," said Rainsford, with a smile which he hoped was disarming. "I'm no robber. I fell off a yacht. My name is Sanger Rainsford of New York City."

The menacing look in the eyes did not change. The revolver pointed as rigidly as if the giant were a statue. He gave no sign that he understood Rainsford's words, or that he had even heard them. He was dressed in uniform, a black uniform trimmed with gray astrakhan.

"I'm Sanger Rainsford of New York," Rainsford began again. "I fell off a yacht. I am hungry."

The man's only answer was to raise with his thumb the hammer of his revolver. Then Rainsford saw the man's free hand go to his forehead in a military salute, and he saw him click his heels together and stand at attention. Another man was coming down the broad marble steps, an erect, slender man in evening clothes. He advanced to Rainsford and held out his hand.

In a cultivated voice marked by a slight accent that gave it added precision and deliberateness, he said, "It is a very great pleasure and honor to welcome Mr. Sanger Rainsford, the celebrated hunter, to my home."

Automatically Rainsford shook the man's hand.

"I've read your book about hunting snow leopards in Tibet, you see," explained the man. "I am General Zaroff."

Rainsford's first impression was that the man was singularly handsome; his second was that there was an original, almost bizarre quality about the general's face. He was a tall man past middle age, for his hair was a vivid white; but his thick eyebrows and pointed military mustache were as black as the night from which Rainsford had come. His eyes, too, were black and very bright. He had high cheekbones, a sharp-cut nose, a spare, dark face, the face of a man used to giving orders, the face of an aristocrat. Turning to the giant in uniform, the general made a sign. The giant put away his pistol, saluted, withdrew.

"Ivan is an incredibly strong fellow," remarked the general, "but he has the misfortune to be deaf and dumb. A simple fellow, but I'm afraid, like all his race, a bit of a savage."

"Is he Russian?"

"He is a Cossack," said the general, and his smile showed red lips and pointed teeth. "So am I."

"Come," he said, "we shouldn't be chatting here. We can talk later. Now you want clothes, food, rest. You shall have them. This is a most restful spot."

Ivan had reappeared, and the general spoke to him with lips that moved but gave forth no sound.

"Follow Ivan, if you please, Mr. Rainsford," said the general. "I was about to have my dinner when you came. I'll wait for you. You'll find that my clothes will fit you, I think."

It was to a huge, beam-ceilinged bedroom with a canopied bed big enough for six men that Rainsford followed the silent giant. Ivan laid out an evening suit, and Rainsford, as he put it on, noticed that it came from a London tailor who ordinarily cut and sewed for none below the rank of duke.

The dining room to which Ivan conducted him was in many ways remarkable. There was a medieval magnificence about it; it suggested a baronial hall of feudal times with its oaken panels, its high ceiling, its vast refectory table where twoscore heads of many animals—lions, tigers, elephants, moose, bears; larger or more perfect specimens Rainsford had never seen. At the great table the general was sitting, alone.

"You'll have a cocktail, Mr. Rainsford," he suggested. The cocktail was surpassingly good; and, Rainsford noted, the table appointments were of the finest, the linen, the crystal, the silver, the china.

They were eating *borsch*, the rich, red soup with sour cream so dear to Russian palates. Half apologetically General Zaroff said, "We do our best to preserve the amenities of civilization here. Please forgive any lapses. We are well off the beaten track, you know. Do you think the champagne has suffered from its long ocean trip?"

"Not in the least," declared Rainsford. He was finding the general a most thoughtful and affable host, a true cosmopolite. But there was one small trait of the general's that made Rainsford uncomfortable. Whenever he looked up from his plate he found the general studying him, appraising him narrowly.

"Perhaps," said General Zaroff, "you were surprised that I recognized your name. You see, I read all books on hunting published in English, French, and Russian. I have but one passion in my life, Mr. Rainsford, and it is the hunt."

"You have some wonderful heads here," said Rainsford as he ate a particularly well cooked filet mignon. "That Cape buffalo is the largest I ever saw."

"Oh, that fellow. Yes, he was a monster."

"Did he charge you?"

"Hurled me against a tree," said the general. "Fractured my skull. But I got the brute."

"I've always thought," said Rainsford, "that the Cape buffalo is the most dangerous of all big game."

For a moment the general did not reply; he was smiling his curious red-lipped smile. Then he said slowly, "No. You are wrong, sir. The Cape buffalo is not the most dangerous big game." He sipped his wine. "Here in my preserve on this island," he said in the same slow tone, "I hunt more dangerous game."

Rainsford expressed his surprise. "Is there big game on this island?"

The general nodded. "The biggest."

"Really?"

"Oh, it isn't here naturally, of course. I have to stock the island."

"What have you imported, General?" Rainsford asked. "Tigers?"

The general smiled. "No," he said. "Hunting tigers ceased to interest me some years ago. I exhausted their possibilities, you see. No thrill left in tigers, no real danger. I live for danger, Mr. Rainsford."

The general took from his pocket a gold cigarette case and offered his guest a long black cigarette with a silver tip; it was perfumed and gave off a smell like incense.

"We will have some capital hunting, you and I," said the general. "I shall be most glad to have your society."

"But what game—" began Rainsford.

"I'll tell you," said the general. "You will be amused, I know. I think I may say, in all modesty, that I have done a rare thing. I have invented a new sensation. May I pour you another glass of port, Mr. Rainsford?"

"Thank you, General."

The general filled both glasses, and said, "God makes some men poets. Some He makes kings, some beggars. Me He made a hunter. My hand was made for the trigger, my father said. He was a very rich man with a quarter of a million acres in the Crimea, and he was an ardent sportsman. When I was only five years old he gave me a little gun, specially made in Moscow for me, to shoot sparrows with. When I shot some of his prize turkeys with it, he did not punish me; he complimented me on my marksmanship. I killed my first bear in the Caucasus when I was ten. My whole life has been one prolonged hunt. I went into the army—it was expected of noblemen's sons—and for a time commanded a division of Cossack cavalry, but my real interest was always the hunt. I have hunted every kind of game in every land. It would be impossible for me to tell you how many animals I have killed."

The general puffed at his cigarette.

"After the debacle in Russia I left the country, for it was imprudent for an officer of the Czar to stay there. Many noble Russians lost everything. I, luckily, had invested heavily in American securities, so I shall never have to open a tearoom in Monte Carlo or drive a taxi in Paris. Naturally, I continued to hunt—grizzlies in your Rockies, crocodiles in the Ganges, rhinoceroses in East Africa. It was in Africa that the Cape buffalo hit me and laid me up for six months. As soon as I recovered I started for the Amazon to hunt jaguars for I had heard they were unusually cunning. They weren't." The Cossack sighed. "They were no match at all for a hunter with his wits about him, and a high-powered rifle. I was bitterly disappointed. Hunting was beginning to bore me! And hunting, remember, had been my life. I have heard that in America businessmen often go to pieces when they give up the business that has been their life."

"Yes, that's so," said Rainsford.

The general smiled. "I had no wish to go to pieces," he said. "I must do something. Now, mine is an analytical mind, Mr. Rainsford. Doubtless that is why I enjoy the problems of the chase."

"No doubt, General Zaroff."

"So," continued the general, "I asked myself why the hunt no longer fascinated me. You are much younger than I am, Mr. Rainsford, and have not hunted as much, but you perhaps can guess the answer."

"What was it?"

"Simply this: hunting had ceased to be what you call 'a sporting proposition'. It had become too easy. I always got my quarry. Always. There is no greater bore than perfection."

The general lit a fresh cigarette.

"No animal had a chance with me any more. That is no boast; it is a mathematical certainty. The animal had nothing but his legs and his instinct. Instinct is no match for reason. When I thought of this it was a tragic moment for me, I can tell you."

Rainsford leaned across the table, absorbed in what his host was saying.

"It came to me as an inspiration what I must do," the general went on.

"And that was?"

The general smiled the quiet smile of one who has faced an obstacle and surmounted it with success. "I had to invent a new animal to hunt," he said.

"A new animal? You are joking."

"Not at all," said the general. "I never joke about hunting. I needed a new animal. I found one. So I bought this island, built this house, and here I do my hunting. The island is perfect for my purposes—there are jungles with a maze of trails in them, hills, swamps—"

"But the animal, General Zaroff?"

"Oh," said the general, "it supplies me with the most exciting hunting in the world. No other hunting compares with it for an instant. Every day I hunt, and I never grow bored now, for I have a quarry with which I can match my wits."

Rainsford's bewilderment showed in his face.

"I wanted the ideal animal to hunt," explained the general. "So I said, 'What are the attributes of an ideal quarry?' And the answer was, of course, 'It must have courage, cunning, and, above all, it must be able to reason.'"

"But no animal can reason," objected Rainsford.

"My dear fellow," said the general, "there is one that can."

"But you can't mean—" gasped Rainsford.

"And why not?"

"I can't believe you are serious, General Zaroff. This is a grisly joke."

"Why should I not be serious? I am speaking of hunting."

"Hunting? Good God, General Zaroff, what you speak of is murder."

The general laughed with entire good nature. He regarded Rainsford quizzically. "I refuse to believe that so modern and civilized a young man as you seem to be harbors romantic ideas about the value of human life. Surely your experiences in the war-" He stopped.

"Did not make me condone cold-blooded murder," finished Rainsford stiffly.

Laughter shook the general. "How extraordinarily droll you are!" he said. "One does not expect nowadays to find a young man of the educated class, even in America, with such a naïve, and, if I may say so, mid-Victorian point of view. It's like finding a snuffbox in a limousine. Ah, well, doubtless you had Puritan ancestors. So many Americans appear to have had. I'll wager you'll forget your notions when you go hunting with me. You've a genuine new thrill in store for you, Mr. Rainsford."

"Thank you, I'm a hunter, not a murderer."

"Dear me," said the general, quite unruffled, "again that unpleasant word. But I think I can show you that your scruples are quite ill founded."

"Yes?"

"Life is for the strong, to be lived by the strong, and, if needs be, taken by the strong. The weak of the world were put here to give the strong pleasure. I am strong. Why should I not use my gift? If I wish to hunt, why should I not? I hunt the scum of the earth—sailors from tramp ships—lascars, blacks, Chinese, whites, mongrels—a thoroughbred horse or hound is worth more than a score of them."

"But they are men," said Rainsford hotly.

"Precisely," said the general. "That is why I use them. It gives me pleasure. They can reason, after a fashion. So they are dangerous."

"But where do you get them?"

The general's left eyelid fluttered down in a wink. "This island is called Ship-Trap," he answered. "Sometimes an angry god of the high seas sends them to me. Sometimes, when Providence is not so kind, I help Providence a bit. Come to the window with me."

Rainsford went to the window and looked out toward the sea.

"Watch! Out there!" exclaimed the general, pointing into the night. Rainsford's eyes saw only blackness, and then, as the general pressed a button, far out to sea Rainsford saw the flash of lights.

The general chuckled. "They indicate a channel," he said, "where there's none: giant rocks with razor edges crouch like a sea monster with wide-open jaws. They can crush a ship as easily as I crush this nut." He dropped a walnut on the hardwood floor and brought his heel grinding down on it. "Oh, yes," he said casually, as if in answer to a question, "I have electricity. We try to be civilized here."

"Civilized? And you shoot down men?"

A trace of anger was in the general's black eyes, but it was there but for a second, and he said, in his most pleasant manner: "Dear me, what a righteous young man you are! I assure you I do not do the thing you suggest. That would be barbarous. I treat these visitors with every consideration. They get plenty of good food and exercise. They get into splendid physical condition. You shall see for yourself tomorrow."

"What do you mean?"

"We'll visit my training school," smiled the general. "It's in the cellar. I have about a dozen pupils down there now. They're from the Spanish bark *San Lucar* that had the bad luck to go on the rocks out there. A very inferior lot, I regret to say. Poor specimens and more accustomed to the deck than to the jungle."

He raised his hand, and Ivan, who served as waiter, brought thick Turkish coffee. Rainsford, with an effort, held his tongue in check.

"It's a game, you see," pursued the general blandly. "I suggest to one of them that we go hunting. I give him a supply of food and an excellent hunting knife. I give him three hours' start. I am to follow, armed only with a pistol of the smallest caliber and range. If my quarry eludes me for three whole days, he wins the game. If I find him"—the general smiled—"he loses."

"Suppose he refuses to be hunted?"

"Oh," said the general, "I give him his option, of course. He need not play that game if he doesn't wish to. If he does not wish to hunt, I turn him over to Ivan. Ivan once had the honor of serving as official knouter to the Great White Czar, and he has his own ideas of sport. Invariably, Mr. Rainsford, invariably they chose the hunt."

"And if they win?"

The smile on the general's face widened. "To date I have not lost," he said.

Then he added, hastily, "I don't wish you to think me a braggart, Mr. Rainsford. Many of them afford only the most elementary sort of problem. Occasionally I strike a tartar. One almost did win. I eventually had to use the dogs."

"The dogs?"

"This way, please. I'll show you."

The general steered Rainsford to a window. The lights from the windows sent a flickering illumination that made grotesque patterns on the courtyard below, and Rainsford could see moving about there a dozen or so huge black shapes; as they turned toward him, their eyes glittered greenly.

"A rather good lot, I think," observed the general. "They are let out at seven every night. If anyone should try to get into my house—or out of it—something extremely regrettable would occur to him." He hummed a snatch of song from the Folies Bergère.

"And now," said the general, "I want to show you my new collection of heads. Will you come with me to the library?"

"I hope," said Rainsford, "that you will excuse me tonight, General Zaroff. I'm really not feeling at all well."

"Ah, indeed?" the general inquired solicitously. "Well, I suppose that's only natural, after your long swim. You need a good, restful night's sleep. Tomorrow you'll feel like a new man, I'll wager. Then we'll hunt, eh? I've one rather promising prospect—"

Rainsford was hurrying from the room.

"Sorry you can't go with me tonight," called the general. "I expect rather fair sport—a big, strong black. He looks resourceful—Well, goodnight, Mr. Rainsford; I hope that you have a good night's rest."

The bed was good and the pajamas of the softest silk, and he was tired in every fiber of his being, but nevertheless Rainsford could not quiet his brain with the opiate of sleep. He lay, eyes wide open. Once he thought he heard stealthy steps in the corridor outside his room. He sought to throw open the door; it would not open. He went to the window and looked out. His room was high up in one of the towers. The lights of the château were out now, and it was dark and silent, but there was a fragment of sallow moon, and by its wan light he could see, dimly, the courtyard; there, weaving in and out in the pattern of shadow, were black, noiseless forms; the hounds heard him at the window and looked up, expectantly, with their green eyes. Rainsford went back to the bed and lay down. By many methods he tried to put himself to sleep. He had achieved a doze when, just as morning began to come, he heard, far off in the jungle, the faint report of a pistol.

General Zaroff did not appear until luncheon. He was dressed faultlessly in the tweeds of a country squire. He was solicitous about the state of Rainsford's health.

"As for me," sighed the general, "I do not feel so well. I am worried, Mr. Rainsford. Last night I detected traces of my old complaint."

To Rainsford's questioning glance the general said, "Ennui. Boredom."

Then, taking a second helping of crepes suzette, the general explained, "The hunting was not good last night. The fellow lost his head. He made a straight trail that offered no problems at all. That's the trouble with the sailors; they have dull brains to begin with, and they do not know how to get about in the woods. They do excessively stupid and obvious things. It's most annoying. Will you have another glass of Chablis, Mr. Rainsford?"

"General," said Rainsford firmly, "I wish to leave this island at once."

The general raised his thickets of eyebrows; he seemed hurt. "But, my dear fellow," the general protested, "you've only just come. You've had no hunting—"

"I wish to go today," said Rainsford. He saw the dead black eyes of the general on him, studying him. General Zaroff's face suddenly brightened.

He filled Rainsford's glass with venerable Chablis from a dusty bottle.

"Tonight," said the general, "we will hunt—you and I."

Rainsford shook his head. "No, General," he said. "I will not hunt."

The general shrugged his shoulders and delicately ate a hothouse grape. "As you wish, my friend," he said. "The choice rests entirely with you. But may I not venture to suggest that you will find my idea of sport more diverting than Ivan's?"

He nodded toward the corner to where the giant stood, scowling, his thick arms crossed on his hogshead of chest.

"You don't mean—" cried Rainsford.

"My dear fellow," said the general, "have I not told you I always mean what I say about hunting? This is really an inspiration. I drink to a foeman worthy of my steel—at last."

The general raised his glass, but Rainsford sat staring at him.

"You'll find this game worth playing," the general said enthusiastically. "Your brain against mine. Your woodcraft against mine. Your strength and stamina against mine. Outdoor chess! And the stake is not without value, eh?"

"And if I win—" began Rainsford huskily.

"I'll cheerfully acknowledge myself defeated if I do not find you by midnight of the third day," said General Zaroff. "My sloop will place you on the mainland near a town."

The general read what Rainsford was thinking.

"Oh, you can trust me," said the Cossack. "I will give you my word as a gentleman and a sportsman. Of course you, in turn, must agree to say nothing of your visit here."

"I'll agree to nothing of the kind," said Rainsford.

"Oh," said the general, "in that case—But why discuss it now? Three days hence we can discuss it over a bottle of Veuve Clicquot, unless—"

The general sipped his wine.

Then a businesslike air animated him. "Ivan," he said to Rainsford, "will supply you with hunting clothes, food, a knife. I suggest you wear moccasins; they leave a poorer trail. I suggest too that you avoid the big swamp in the southeast corner of the island. We call it Death Swamp. There's quicksand there. One foolish fellow tried it. The deplorable part of it was that Lazarus followed him. You can imagine my feeling, Mr. Rainsford. I loved Lazarus; he was the finest hound in my pack. Well, I must beg you to excuse me now. I always take a siesta after lunch. You'll hardly have time for a nap, I fear. You'll want to start, no doubt. I shall not follow till dusk. Hunting at night is so much more exciting than by day, don't you think? *Au revoir*, Mr. Rainsford, *au revoir*."

General Zaroff, with a deep, courtly bow, strolled from the room.

From another door came Ivan. Under one arm he carried khaki hunting clothes, a haversack of food, a leather sheath containing a long-bladed hunting knife; his right hand rested on a cocked revolver thrust in the crimson sash about his waist. . . .

Rainsford had fought his way through the bush for two hours. "I must keep my nerve. I must keep my nerve," he said through tight teeth.

He had not been entirely clear-headed when the château gates snapped shut behind him. His whole idea at first was to put distance between himself and General Zaroff, and, to this end, he had plunged along, spurred on by the sharp rowels of something very like panic. Now he had got a grip on himself, had stopped, and was taking stock of himself and the situation.

He saw that straight flight was futile; inevitably it would bring him face to face with the sea. He was in a picture with a frame of water, and his operations, clearly, must take place within that frame.

"I'll give him a trail to follow," muttered Rainsford, and he struck off from the rude path he had been following into the trackless wilderness. He executed a series of intricate loops; he doubled on his trail again and again, recalling all the lore of the fox hunt, and all the dodges of the fox. Night found him leg-weary, with hands and face lashed by the branches, on a thickly wooded ridge. He knew it would be insane to blunder on through the dark, even if he had the strength. His need for rest was imperative and he thought, 'I have played the fox, now I must play the cat of the fable.' A big tree with a thick trunk and outspread branches was nearby, and, taking care to leave not the slightest mark, he climbed up into the crotch, and stretching out on one of the broad limbs, after a fashion, rested. Rest brought him new confidence and almost a feeling of security. Even so zealous a hunter as General Zaroff could not trace him there, he told himself; only the devil himself could follow that complicated trail through the jungle after dark. But, perhaps, the general was a devil—

An apprehensive night crawled slowly by like a wounded snake, and sleep did not visit Rainsford, although the silence of a dead world was on the jungle. Toward morning when a dingy gray was varnishing the sky, the cry of some startled bird focused Rainsford's attention in that direction. Something was coming through the bush, coming slowly, carefully, coming by the same winding way Rainsford had come. He flattened himself down on the limb, and through a screen of leaves almost as thick as tapestry, he watched. The thing that was approaching him was a man.

It was General Zaroff. He made his way along with his eye fixed in utmost concentration on the ground before him. He paused, almost beneath the tree, dropped to his knees, and studied the ground. Rainsford's impulse was to hurl himself down like a panther, but he saw that the general's right hand held something small and metallic—an automatic pistol.

The hunter shook his head several times, as if he were puzzled. Then he straightened up and took from his case one of his black cigarettes; its pungent incense-like smoke floated up to Rainsford's nostrils. Rainsford held his breath.

The general's eyes had left the ground and were traveling inch by inch up the tree. Rainsford froze there, every muscle tensed for a spring. But the sharp eyes of the hunter stopped before they reached the limb where Rainsford lay; a smile spread over his brown face. Very deliberately he blew a smoke ring into the air; then he turned his back on the tree and walked carelessly away, back along the trail he had come. The swish of the underbrush against his hunting boots grew fainter and fainter.

The pent-up air burst hotly from Rainsford's lungs. His first thought made him feel sick and numb. The general could follow a trail through the woods at night; he could follow an extremely difficult trail; he must have uncanny powers; only by the merest chance had the Cossack failed to see his quarry. Rainsford's second thought was even more terrible. It sent a shudder of cold horror through his whole being. Why had the general smiled? Why had he turned back?

Rainsford did not want to believe what his reason told him was true, but the truth was as evident as the sun that had by now pushed through the morning mists. The general was playing with him! The general was saving him for another day's sport! The Cossack was the cat; he was the mouse. Then it was that Rainsford knew the full meaning of terror.

"I will not lose my nerve. I will not."

He slid down from the tree, and struck off again into the woods. His face was set and he forced the machinery of his mind to function. Three hundred yards from his hiding place he stopped where a huge dead tree leaned precariously on a smaller, living one. Throwing off his sack of food, Rainsford took his knife from its sheath and began to work with all his energy.

The job was finished at last, and he threw himself down behind a fallen log a hundred feet away. He did not have to wait long. The cat was coming again to play with the mouse.

Following the trail with the sureness of a bloodhound came General Zaroff. Nothing escaped those searching black eyes, no crushed blade of grass, no bent twig, no mark, no matter how faint, in the moss. So intent was the Cossack on his stalking that he was upon the thing Rainsford had made before he saw it. His foot touched the protruding bough that was the trigger. Even as he touched it, the general sensed his danger and leaped back with the agility of an ape. But he was not quite quick enough; the dead tree, delicately adjusted to rest on the cut living one, crashed down and struck the general a glancing blow on the shoulder as it fell; but for his alertness, he must have been smashed beneath it. He staggered, but he did not fall; nor did he drop his revolver. He stood there, rubbing his injured shoulder, and Rainsford, with fear again gripping his heart, heard the general's mocking laugh ring through the jungle.

"Rainsford," called the general, "if you are within sound of my voice, as I suppose you are, let me congratulate you. Not many men know how to make a Malay man-catcher. Luckily for me, I too have hunted in Malacca. You are proving interesting, Mr. Rainsford. I am going now to have my wound dressed; it's only a slight one. But I shall be back. I shall be back.

When the general, nursing his bruised shoulder, had gone, Rainsford took up his flight again. It was flight now, a desperate, hopeless flight, that carried him on for some hours. Dusk came, then darkness, and still he pressed on. The ground grew softer under his moccasins; the vegetation grew ranker, denser; insects bit him savagely. Then, as he stepped forward, his foot sank into the ooze. He tried to wrench it back, but the muck sucked viciously at his foot as if it were a giant leech. With a violent effort, he tore his foot loose. He knew where he was now. Death Swamp and its quicksand.

His hands were tight closed as if his nerve were something tangible that someone in the darkness was trying to tear from his grip. The softness of the earth had given him an idea. He stepped back from the quicksand a dozen feet or so and, like some huge prehistoric beaver, he began to dig.

Rainsford had dug himself in in France when a second's delay meant death. That had been a placid pastime compared to his digging now. The pit grew deeper; when it was above his shoulders, he climbed out and from some hard saplings cut stakes and sharpened them to a fine point. These stakes he planted in the bottom of the pit with the points sticking up. With flying fingers he wove a rough carpet of weeds and branches and with it he covered the mouth of the pit. Then, wet with sweat and aching with tiredness, he crouched behind the stump of a lightning-charred tree.

He knew his pursuer was coming; he heard the paddling sound of feet on the soft earth, and the night breeze brought him the perfume of the general's cigarette.

It seemed to Rainsford that the general was coming with unusual swiftness; he was not feeling his way along, foot by foot. Rainsford, crouching there, could not see the general, nor could he see the pit. He lived a year in a minute. Then he felt an impulse to cry aloud with joy, for he heard the sharp crackle of the breaking branches as the cover of the pit gave way; he heard the sharp screams of pain as the pointed stakes found their mark. He leaped up from his place of concealment. Then he cowered back. Three feet from the pit a man was standing, with an electric torch in his hand.

"You've done well, Rainsford," the voice of the general called. "Your Burmese tiger pit has claimed one of my best dogs. Again you score. I think, Mr. Rainsford, I'll see what you can do against my whole pack. I'm going home for a rest now. Thank you for a most amusing evening."

At daybreak Rainsford, lying near the swamp, was awakened by a sound that made him know that he had new things to learn about fear. It was a distant sound, faint and wavering, but he knew it. It was the baying of a pack of hounds.

Rainsford knew he could do one of two things. He could stay where he was and wait. That was suicide. He could flee. That was postponing the inevitable. For a moment he stood there, thinking. An idea that held a wild chance came to him, and, tightening his belt, he headed away from the swamp.

The baying of the hounds drew nearer, then still nearer, nearer, ever nearer. On a ridge Rainsford climbed a tree. Down a watercourse, not a quarter of a mile away, he could see the bush moving. Straining his eyes, he saw the lean figure of General Zaroff; just ahead of him Rainsford made out another figure whose wide shoulders surged through the tall jungle weeds; it was the giant Ivan, and he seemed pulled forward by some unseen force; Rainsford knew that Ivan must be holding the pack in leash.

They would be on him any minute now. His mind worked frantically. He thought of a native trick he had learned in Uganda. He slid down the tree. He caught hold of a springy young sapling and to it he fastened his hunting knife, with the blade pointing down the trail; with a bit of wild grapevine he tied back the sapling. Then he ran for his life. The hounds raised their voices as they hit the fresh scent. Rainsford knew now how an animal at bay feels.

He had to stop to get his breath. The baying of the hounds stopped abruptly. And Rainsford's heart stopped too. They must have reached the knife.

He shinned excitedly up a tree and looked back. His pursuers had stopped. But the hope that was in Rainsford's brain when he climbed had died, for he saw in the shallow valley that General Zaroff was still on his feet. But Ivan was not. The knife, driven by the recoil of the spring tree, had not wholly failed.

Rainsford had hardly tumbled to the ground when the pack took up the cry again.

"Nerve, nerve, nerve!" he panted, as he dashed along. A blue gap showed between the trees dead ahead. Ever nearer drew the hounds. Rainsford forced himself on toward the gap. He reached it. It was the shore of the sea. Across a cove he could see the gloomy gray stone of the château. Twenty feet below him the sea rumbled and hissed. Rainsford hesitated. He heard the hounds. Then he leaped far out into the sea....

When the general and his pack reached the place by the sea, the Cossack stopped. For some minutes he stood regarding the blue-green expanse of water. He shrugged his shoulders. Then he sat down, took a drink of brandy from a silver flask, lit a perfumed cigarette, and hummed a bit from *Madame Butterfly*.

General Zaroff had an exceedingly good dinner in his great paneled dining hall that evening. With it he had a bottle of Pol Roger and half a bottle of Chambertin. Two slight annoyances kept him from perfect enjoyment. One was the thought that it would be difficult to replace Ivan; the other was that his quarry had escaped him; of course, the American hadn't played the game—so thought the general as he tasted his after-dinner liqueur. In his library he read, to soothe himself, from the works of Marcus Aurelius. At ten he went up to his bedroom. He was deliciously tired, he said to himself, as he locked himself in. There was a little moonlight, so, before turning on his light, he went to the window and looked down at the courtyard. He could see the great hounds, and he called, "Better luck another time," to them. Then he switched on the light.

A man who had been hiding in the curtains of the bed, was standing there.

"Rainsford!" screamed the general. "How in God's name did you get here?"

"Swam," said Rainsford. "I found it quicker than walking through the jungle."

The general sucked in his breath and smiled. "I congratulate you," he said. "You have won the game."

Rainsford did not smile. "I am still a beast at bay," he said, in a low, hoarse voice. "Get ready, General Zaroff."

The general made one of his deepest bows. "I see," he said. "Splendid! One of us is to furnish a repast for the hounds. The other will sleep in this very excellent bed. On guard, Rainsford. . . ."

He had never slept in a better bed, Rainsford decided.

The Small Assassin

BY RAY BRADBURY

Kids. They do the darndest things.

Back in the 1940s, before establishing his rep as one of America's most beloved sf/fantasists, Ray Bradbury honed his prodigious chops with landmark stories of horror, crime, and suspense. Many of the best of these were collected in Dark Carnival *(1947), which was then expanded into 1955's incomparable* The October Country.

This is where I first fell in love with his work: some already laced with his poetic grace and whimsy; others charged with a grittier, more muscular, tragic realism.

And at the top of my love list was the glittering gem that follows: a nifty little slice of postpartum paranoia, with a punch line I've been able to quote verbatim since I was nine years old.

Just when the idea occurred to her that she was being murdered she could not tell. There had been little subtle signs, little suspicions for the past month; things as deep as sea tides in her, like looking at a perfectly calm stretch of tropic water, wanting to bathe in it and finding, just as the tide takes your body, that monsters dwell just under the surface, things unseen, bloated, many-armed, sharp-finned, malignant and inescapable.

A room floated around her in an effluvium of hysteria. Sharp instruments hovered and there were voices, and people in sterile white masks.

My name, she thought, what is it?

Alice Leiber. It came to her. David Leiber's wife. But it gave her no comfort. She was alone with these silent, whispering white people and there was great pain and nausea and death-fear in her.

I am being murdered before their eyes. These doctors, these nurses don't realize what hidden thing has happened to me. David doesn't know. Nobody knows except me and—the killer, the little murderer, the small assassin.

I am dying and I can't tell them now. They'd laugh and call me one in delirium. They'll see the murderer and hold him and never think him responsible for my death. But here I am, in front of God and man, dying, no one to believe my story, everyone to doubt me, comfort me with lies, bury me in ignorance, mourn me and salvage my destroyer.

Where is David? she wondered. In the waiting room, smoking one cigarette after another, listening to the long tickings of the very slow clock?

Sweat exploded from all of her body at once, and with it an agonized cry. Now. Now! Try and kill me, she screamed. Try, try, but I won't die! I won't!

There was a hollowness. A vacuum. Suddenly the pain fell away. Exhaustion, and dusk came around. It was over. Oh, God! She plummeted down and struck a black nothingness which gave way to nothingness and nothingness and another and still another. . . .

Footsteps. Gentle, approaching footsteps.

Far away, a voice said, "She's asleep. Don't disturb her."

An odor of tweeds, a pipe, a certain shaving lotion. David was standing over her. And beyond him the immaculate smell of Dr. Jeffers.

She did not open her eyes. "I'm awake," she said, quietly. It was a surprise, a relief to be able to speak, to not be dead.

"Alice," someone said, and it was David beyond her closed eyes, holding her tired hands.

Would you like to meet the murderer, David? she thought. I hear your voice asking to see him, so there's nothing but for me to point him out to you.

David stood over her. She opened her eyes. The room came into focus. Moving a weak hand, she pulled aside a coverlet.

The murderer looked up at David Leiber with a small, red-faced, blue-eyed calm. Its eyes were deep and sparkling.

"Why!" cried David Leiber, smiling. "He's a *fine* baby!"

Dr. Jeffers was waiting for David Leiber the day he came to take his wife and new child home. He motioned Leiber to a chair in his office, gave him a cigar, lit one for himself, sat on the edge of his desk, puffing solemnly for a long moment. Then he cleared his throat, looked David Leiber straight on and said, "Your wife doesn't like her child, Dave."

"What!"

"It's been a hard thing for her. She'll need a lot of love this next year. I didn't say much at the time, but she was hysterical in the delivery room. The strange things she said—I won't repeat them. All I'll say is that she feels alien to the child. Now, this may simply be a thing we can clear up with one or two questions." He sucked on his cigar another moment, then said, "Is this child a 'wanted' child, Dave?"

"Why do you ask?"

"It's vital."

"Yes. Yes, it is a 'wanted' child. We planned it together. Alice was so happy, a year ago, when—"

"Mmmm—That makes it more difficult. Because if the child was unplanned, it would be a simple case of a woman hating the idea of motherhood. That doesn't fit Alice." Dr. Jeffers took his cigar from his lips, rubbed his hand across his jaw. "It must be something else, then. Perhaps something buried in her childhood that's coming out now. Or it might be the simple temporary doubt and distrust of any mother who's gone through the unusual pain and near-death that Alice has. If so, then a little time should heal that. I thought I'd tell you, though Dave. It'll help you be easy and tolerant with her if she says anything about—well—about wishing the child had been born dead. And if things don't go well, the three of you drop in on me. I'm always glad to see old friends, eh? Here, take another cigar along for—ah—for the baby."

It was a bright spring afternoon. Their car hummed along wide, tree-lined boulevards. Blue sky, flowers, a warm wind. Dave talked a lot, lit his cigar, talked some more. Alice answered directly, softly, relaxing a bit more as the trip progressed. But she held the baby not tightly or warmly or motherly enough to satisfy the queer ache in Dave's mind. She seemed to be merely carrying a porcelain figurine.

"Well," he said, at last, smiling. "What'll we name him?"

Alice Leiber watched green trees slide by. "Let's not decide yet. I'd rather wait until we get an exceptional name for him. Don't blow smoke in his face." Her sentences ran together with no change of tone. The last statement held no motherly reproof, no interest, no irritation. She just mouthed it and it was said.

The husband, disquieted, dropped the cigar from the window. "Sorry," he said.

The baby rested in the crook of his mother's arm, shadows of sun and tree changing his face. His blue eyes opened like fresh blue spring flowers. Moist noises came from the tiny, pink, elastic mouth.

Alice gave her baby a quick glance. Her husband felt her shiver against him.

"Cold?" he asked.

"A chill. Better raise the window, David."

It was more than a chill. He rolled the window slowly up.

Suppertime.

Dave had brought the child from the nursery, propped him at a tiny, bewildered angle, supported by many pillows, in a newly purchased high chair.

Alice watched her knife and fork move. "He's not high-chair size," she said.

"Fun having him here, anyway," said Dave, feeling fine. "Everything's fun. At the office, too. Orders up to my nose. If I don't watch myself I'll make another fifteen thousand this year. Hey, look at Junior, will you? Drooling all down his chin!" He reached over to wipe the baby's mouth with his napkin. From the corner of his eye he realized that Alice wasn't even watching. He finished the job.

"I guess it wasn't very interesting," he said, back again at his food. "But one would think a mother'd take some interest in her own child!"

Alice jerked her chin up. "Don't speak that way! Not in front of him! Later, if you must."

"Later?" he cried. "In front of, in back of, what's the difference?" He quieted suddenly, swallowed, was sorry. "All right. Okay, I know how it is."

After dinner she let him carry the baby upstairs. She didn't tell him to; she *let* him.

Coming down, he found her standing by the radio, listening to music she didn't hear. Her eyes were closed, her whole attitude one of wondering, self-questioning. She started when he appeared.

Suddenly, she was at him, against him, soft, quick; the same. Her lips found him, kept him. He was stunned. Now that the baby was gone, upstairs, out of the room, she began to breathe again, live again. She was free. She was whispering, rapidly, endlessly.

"Thank you, thank you, darling. For being yourself, always. Dependable, so very dependable!"

He had to laugh. "My father told me, 'Son, provide for your family!'"

Wearily, she rested her dark, shining hair against his neck. "You've overdone it. Sometimes I wish we were just the way we were when we were first married. No responsibilities, nothing but ourselves. No—no babies."

She crushed his hand in hers, a supernatural whiteness in her face.

"Oh, Dave, once it was just you and me. We protected each other, and now we protect the baby, but get no protection from it. Do you understand? Lying in the hospital I had time to think a lot of things. The world is evil—"

"Is it?"

"Yes. It is. But laws protect us from it. And when there aren't laws, then love does the protecting. You're protected from my hurting you, by my love. You're vulnerable to me, of all people, but love shields you. I feel no fear of you, because love cushions all your irritations, unnatural instincts, hatreds and immaturities.

But—what about the baby? It's too young to know love, or a law of love, or anything, until we teach it. And in the meantime be vulnerable to it."

"Vulnerable to a baby?" He held her away and laughed gently.

"Does a baby know the difference between right and wrong?" she asked.

"No. But it'll learn."

"But a baby is so new, so amoral, so conscience-free." She stopped. Her arms dropped from him and she turned swiftly. "That noise? What was it?"

Leiber looked around the room. "I didn't hear—"

She stared at the library door. "In there," she said, slowly.

Leiber crossed the room, opened the door and switched the library lights on and off. "Not a thing." He came back to her. "You're worn out. To bed with you—right now."

Turning out the lights together, they walked slowly up the soundless hall stairs, not speaking. At the top she apologized. "My wild talk, darling. Forgive me. I'm exhausted."

He understood, and said so.

She paused, undecided, by the nursery door. Then she fingered the brass knob sharply, walked in. He watched her approach the crib much too carefully, look down, and stiffen as if she'd been struck in the face. "David!"

Leiber stepped forward, reached the crib.

The baby's face was bright red and very moist; his small pink mouth opened and shut, opened and shut; his eyes were a fiery blue. His hands leapt about on the air.

"Oh," said Dave, "he's just been crying."

"Has he?" Alice Leiber seized the crib-railing to balance herself. "I didn't hear him."

"The door was closed."

"Is that why he breathes so hard, why his face is red?"

"Sure. Poor little guy. Crying all alone in the dark. He can sleep in our room tonight, just in case he cries."

"You'll spoil him," his wife said.

Leiber felt her eyes follow as he rolled the crib into their bedroom. He undressed silently, sat on the edge of the bed. Suddenly he lifted his head, swore under his breath, snapped his fingers. "Damn it! Forgot to tell you. I must fly to Chicago Friday."

"Oh, David." Her voice was lost in the room.

"I've put this trip off for two months, and now it's so critical I just have to go."

"I'm afraid to be alone."

"We'll have the new cook by Friday. She'll be here all the time. I'll only be gone a few days."

"I'm afraid. I don't know of what. You wouldn't believe me if I told you. I guess I'm crazy."

He was in bed now. She darkened the room; he heard her walk around the bed, throw back the cover, slide in. He smelled the warm woman-smell of her next to him. He said, "If you want me to wait a few days, perhaps I could—"

"No," she said, unconvinced. "You go. I know it's important. It's just that I keep thinking about what I told you. Laws and love and protection. Love protects you from me. But, the baby—" She took a breath. "What protects you from him, David?"

Before he could answer, before he could tell her how silly it was, speaking of infants, she switched on the bed light, abruptly.

"Look," she said, pointing.

The baby lay wide-awake in its crib, staring straight at him, with deep, sharp blue eyes.

The lights went out again. She trembled against him.

"It's not nice being afraid of the thing you birthed." Her whisper lowered, became harsh, fierce, swift. "He tried to kill me! He lies there, listens to us talking, waiting for you to go away so he can try to kill me again! I swear it!" Sobs broke from her.

"Please," he kept saying, soothing her. "Stop it, stop it. Please."

She cried in the dark for a long time. Very late she relaxed, shakingly, against him. Her breathing came soft, warm, regular, her body twitched its worn reflexes and she slept.

He drowsed.

And just before his eyes lidded wearily down, sinking him into deeper and yet deeper tides, he heard a strange little sound of awareness and awakeness in the room.

The sound of small, moist, pinkly elastic lips.

The baby.

And then—sleep.

In the morning, the sun blazed. Alice smiled.

David Leiber dangled his watch over the crib. "See, baby? Something bright. Something pretty. Sure. Sure. Something bright. Something pretty."

Alice smiled. She told him to go ahead, fly to Chicago, she'd be very brave, no need to worry. She'd take care of baby. Oh, yes, she'd take care of him, all right.

The airplane went east. There was a lot of sky, a lot of sun and clouds and Chicago running over the horizon. Dave was dropped into the rush of ordering, planning, banqueting, telephoning, arguing in conference. But he wrote letters each day and sent telegrams to Alice and the baby.

On the evening of his sixth day away from home he received the long-distance phone call. Los Angeles.

"Alice?"

"No, Dave. This is Jeffers speaking."

"Doctor!"

"Hold onto yourself, son. Alice is sick. You'd better get the next plane home. It's pneumonia. I'll do everything I can, boy. If only it wasn't so soon after the baby. She needs strength."

Leiber dropped the phone into its cradle. He got up, with no feet under him, and no hands and no body. The hotel room blurred and fell apart.

"Alice," he said, blindly, starting for the door.

The propellers spun about, whirled, fluttered, stopped; time and space were put behind. Under his hand, David felt the doorknob turn; under his feet the floor assumed reality, around him flowed the walls of a bedroom, and in the late-afternoon sunlight, Dr. Jeffers stood, turning from a window, as Alice lay waiting in her bed, something carved from a fall of winter snow. Then Dr. Jeffers was talking, talking continuously, gently, the sound rising and falling through the lamplight, a soft flutter, a white murmur of voice.

"Your wife's too good a mother, Dave. She worried more about the baby than herself. . . ."

Somewhere in the paleness of Alice's face, there was a sudden constriction which smoothed itself out before it was realized. Then, slowly, half-smiling, she began to talk and she talked as a mother should about this, that and the other thing, the telling detail, the minute-by-minute and hour-by-hour report of a mother concerned with a dollhouse world and the miniature life of that world. But she could not stop; the spring was wound tight, and her voice rushed on to anger, fear and the faintest touch of revulsion, which did not change Dr. Jeffers' expression, but caused Dave's heart to match the rhythm of this talk that quickened and could not stop:

"The baby wouldn't sleep. I thought he was sick. He just lay, staring, in his crib, and late at night he'd cry. So loud, he'd cry, and he'd cry all night and all night. I couldn't quiet him, and I couldn't rest."

Dr. Jeffers' head nodded slowly, slowly. "Tired herself right into pneumonia. But she's full of sulfa now and on the safe side of the whole damn thing."

David felt ill. "The baby, what about the baby?"

"Fit as a fiddle; cock of the walk!"

"Thanks, Doctor."

The doctor walked off away and down the stairs, opened the front door faintly, and was gone.

"David!"

He turned to her frightened whisper.

"It was the baby again." She clutched his hand. "I try to lie to myself and say that I'm a fool, but the baby knew I was weak from the hospital, so he cried all night every night, and when he wasn't crying he'd be much too quiet. I knew if I switched on the light he'd be there, staring up at me."

David felt his body close in on itself like a fist. He remembered seeing the baby, feeling the baby, awake in the dark, awake very late at night when babies should be asleep. Awake and lying there, silent as thought, not crying, but watching from its crib. He thrust the thought aside. It was insane.

Alice went on. "I was going to kill the baby. Yes, I was. When you'd been gone only a day on your trip I went to his room and put my hands about his neck; and I stood there, for a long time, thinking, afraid. Then I put the covers up over his face and turned him over on his face and pressed him down and left him that way and ran out of the room."

He tried to stop her.

"No, let me finish," she said, hoarsely, looking at the wall. "When I left his room I thought, It's simple. Babies smother every day. No one'll ever know. But when I came back to see him dead, David, he was alive! Yes, alive, turned over on his back, alive and smiling and breathing. And I couldn't touch him again after that. I left him there and I didn't come back, not to feed him or look at him or do anything. Perhaps the cook tended to him. I don't know. All I know is that his crying kept me awake, and I thought all through the night, and walked around the rooms and now I'm sick." She was almost finished now. "The baby lies there and thinks of ways to kill me. Simple ways. Because he knows I know so much about him. I have no love for him; there is no protection between us; there never will be."

She was through. She collapsed inward on herself and finally slept. David Leiber stood for a long time over her, not able to move. His blood was frozen in his body, not a cell stirred anywhere, anywhere at all.

The next morning there was only one thing to do. He did it. He walked into Dr. Jeffers' office and told him the whole thing, and listened to Jeffers' tolerant replies:

"Let's take this thing slowly, son. It's quite natural for mothers to hate their children, sometimes. We have a label for it—ambivalence. The ability to hate, while loving. Lovers hate each other, frequently. Children detest their mothers—"

Leiber interrupted. "I never hated my mother."

"You won't admit it, naturally. People don't enjoy admitting hatred for their loved ones."

"So Alice hates her baby."

"Better say she has an obsession. She's gone a step further than plain, ordinary ambivalence. A Caesarian operation brought the child into the world and almost took Alice out of it. She blames the child for her near-death and her pneumonia.

She's projecting her troubles, blaming them on the handiest object she can use as a source of blame. We all do it. We stumble into a chair and curse the furniture, not our own clumsiness. We miss a golf-stroke and damn the turf or our club, or the make of ball. If our business fails we blame the gods, the weather, our luck. All I can tell you is what I told you before. Love her. Finest medicine in the world. Find little ways of showing your affection, give her security. Find ways of showing her how harmless and innocent the child is. Make her feel that the baby was worth the risk. After awhile, she'll settle down, forget about death, and begin to love the child. If she doesn't come around in the next month or so, ask me. I'll recommend a good psychiatrist. Go on along now, and take that look off your face."

When summer came, things seemed to settle, become easier. Dave worked, immersed himself in office detail, but found much time for his wife. She, in turn, took long walks, gained strength, played an occasional light game of badminton. She rarely burst out any more. She seemed to have rid herself of her fears.

Except on one certain midnight when a sudden summer wind swept around the house, warm and swift, shaking the trees like so many shining tambourines. Alice wakened, trembling, and slid over into her husband's arms, and let him console her, and ask her what was wrong.

She said, "Something's here in the room, watching us."

He switched on the light. "Dreaming again," he said. "You're better, though. Haven't been troubled for a long time."

She sighed as he clicked off the light again, and suddenly she slept. He held her, considering what a sweet, weird creature she was, for about half an hour.

He heard the bedroom door sway open a few inches.

There was nobody at the door. No reason for it to come open. The wind had died.

He waited. It seemed like an hour he lay silently, in the dark.

Then, far away, wailing like some small meteor dying in the vast inky gulf of space, the baby began to cry in his nursery.

It was a small, lonely sound in the middle of the stars and the dark and the breathing of this woman in his arms and the wind beginning to sweep through the trees again.

Leiber counted to one hundred, slowly. The crying continued.

Carefully disengaging Alice's arm he slipped from bed, put on his slippers, robe, and moved quietly from the room.

He'd go downstairs, he thought, fix some warm milk, bring it up, and—

The blackness dropped out from under him. His foot slipped and plunged. Slipped on something soft. Plunged into nothingness.

He thrust his hands out, caught frantically at the railing. His body stopped falling. He held. He cursed.

The "something soft" that had caused his feet to slip, rustled and thumped down a few steps. His head rang. His heart hammered at the base of his throat, thick and shot with pain.

Why do careless people leave things strewn about a house? He groped carefully with his fingers for the object that had almost spilled him headlong down the stairs.

His hand froze, startled. His breath went in. His heart held one or two beats.

The thing he held in his hand was a toy. A large cumbersome, patchwork doll he had bought as a joke, for—

For the baby.

Alice drove him to work the next day.

She slowed the car halfway downtown; pulled to the curb and stopped it. Then she turned on the seat and looked at her husband.

"I want to go away on a vacation. I don't know if you can make it now, darling, but if not, please let me go alone. We can get someone to take care of the baby, I'm sure. But I just have to get away. I thought I was growing out of this—this *feeling*. But I haven't. I can't stand being in the room with him. He looks up at me as if he hates me, too. I can't put my finger on it; all I know is I want to get away before something happens."

He got out on his side of the car, came around, motioned to her to move over, got in. "The only thing you're going to do is see a good psychiatrist. And if he suggests a vacation, well, okay. But this can't go on; my stomach's in knots all the time." He started the car. "I'll drive the rest of the way."

Her head was down; she was trying to keep back tears. She looked up when they reached his office building. "All right. Make the appointment. I'll go talk to anyone you want, David."

He kissed her. "Now, you're talking sense, lady. Think you can drive home okay?"

"Of course, silly."

"See you at supper, then. Drive carefully."

"Don't I always? 'Bye."

He stood on the curb, watching her drive off, the wind taking hold of her long, dark, shining hair. Upstairs, a minute later, he phoned Jeffers and arranged an appointment with a reliable neuropsychiatrist.

The day's work went uneasily. Things fogged over; and in the fog he kept seeing Alice lost and calling his name. So much of her fear had come over to him. She actually had him convinced that the child was in some ways not quite natural.

He dictated long, uninspired letters. He checked some shipments downstairs. Assistants had to be questioned, and kept going. At the end of the day he was exhausted, his head throbbed, and he was very glad to go home.

On the way down in the elevator he wondered, What if I told Alice about the toy—that patchwork doll—I slipped on on the stairs last night? Lord, wouldn't *that* back her off? No, I won't ever tell her. Accidents are, after all, accidents.

Daylight lingered in the sky as he drove home in a taxi. In front of the house he paid the driver and walked slowly up the cement walk, enjoying the light that was still in the sky and the trees. The white colonial front of the house looked unnaturally silent and uninhabited, and then, quietly, he remembered this was Thursday, and the hired help they were able to obtain from time to time were all gone for the day.

He took a deep breath of air. A bird sang behind the house. Traffic moved on the boulevard a block away. He twisted the key in the door. The knob turned under his fingers, oiled, silent.

The door opened. He stepped in, put his hat on the chair with his briefcase, started to shrug out of his coat, when he looked up.

Late sunlight streamed down the stairwell from the window near the top of the hall. Where the sunlight touched, it took on the bright color of the patchwork doll sprawled at the bottom of the stairs.

But he paid no attention to the toy.

He could only look, and not move, and look again at Alice.

Alice lay in a broken, grotesque, pallid gesturing and angling of her thin body, at the bottom of the stairs, like a crumpled doll that doesn't want to play any more, ever.

Alice was dead.

The house remained quiet, except for the sound of his heart.

She was dead.

He held her head in his hands, he felt her fingers. He held her body. But she wouldn't live. She wouldn't even try to live. He said her name, out loud, many times, and he tried, once again, by holding her to him, to give her back some of the warmth she had lost, but that didn't help.

He stood up. He must have made a phone call. He didn't remember.

He found himself, suddenly, upstairs. He opened the nursery door and walked inside and stared blankly at the crib. His stomach was sick. He couldn't see very well.

The baby's eyes were closed, but his face was red, moist with perspiration, as if he'd been crying long and hard.

"She's dead," said Leiber to the baby. "She's dead."

Then he started laughing low and soft and continuously for a long time until Dr. Jeffers walked in out of the night and slapped him again and again across his face.

"Snap out of it! Pull yourself together!"

"She fell down the stairs, doctor. She tripped on a patchwork doll and fell. I almost slipped on it the other night, myself. And now—"

The doctor shook him.

"Doc, Doc, Doc," said Dave, hazily. "Funny thing. Funny. I—I finally thought of a name for the baby."

The doctor said nothing.

Leiber put his head back in his trembling hands and spoke the words. "I'm going to have him christened next Sunday. Know what name I'm giving him? I'm going to call him Lucifer."

It was eleven at night. A lot of strange people had come and gone through the house, taking the essential flame with them—Alice.

David Leiber sat across from the doctor in the library.

"Alice wasn't crazy," he said slowly. "She had good reason to fear the baby."

Jeffers exhaled. "Don't follow after her! She blamed the child for her sickness, now you blame it for her death. She stumbled on a toy, remember that. You can't blame the child."

"You mean Lucifer?"

"Stop calling him that!"

Leiber shook his head. "Alice heard things at night, moving in the halls. You want to know what made those noises, Doctor? They were made by the baby. Four months old, moving in the dark, listening to us talk. Listening to every word!" He held to the sides of the chair. "And if I turned the lights on, a baby is so small. It can hide behind furniture, a door, against a wall—below eye-level."

"I want you to stop this!" said Jeffers.

"Let me say what I think or I'll go crazy. When I went to Chicago, who was it kept Alice awake, tiring her into pneumonia? The baby! And when Alice didn't die, then he tried killing me. It was simple; leave a toy on the stairs, cry in the night until your father goes downstairs to fetch your milk, and stumbles. A crude trick, but effective. It didn't get me. But it killed Alice dead."

David Leiber stopped long enough to light a cigarette. "I should have caught on. I'd turn on the lights in the middle of the night, many nights, and the baby'd be lying there, eyes wide. Most babies sleep all the time. Not this one. He stayed awake, thinking."

"Babies don't think."

"He stayed awake doing whatever he *could* do with his brain, then. What in hell do we know about a baby's mind? He had every reason to hate Alice; she suspected him for what he was—certainly not a normal child. Something—different. What do you know of babies, doctor? The general run, yes. You know, of course, how babies kill their mothers at birth. Why? Could it be resentment at being forced into a lousy world like this one?"

Leiber leaned toward the doctor, tiredly. "It all ties up. Suppose that a few babies out of all the millions born are instantaneously able to move, see, hear, think, like many animals and insects can. Insects are born self-sufficient. In a few

weeks most mammals and birds adjust. But children take years to speak and learn
to stumble around on their weak legs.

"But suppose one child in a billion is—strange? Born perfectly aware, able to
think, instinctively. Wouldn't it be a perfect setup, a perfect blind for anything the
baby might want to do? He could pretend to be ordinary, weak, crying, ignorant.
With just a *little* expenditure of energy he could crawl about a darkened house,
listening. And how easy to place obstacles at the top of stairs. How easy to cry all
night and tire a mother into pneumonia. How easy, right at birth, to be so close to
the mother that *a few deft maneuvers might cause peritonitis!*"

"For God's sake!" Jeffers was on his feet. "That's a repulsive thing to say!"

"It's a repulsive thing I'm speaking of. How many mothers have died at the
birth of their children? How many have suckled strange little improbabilities who
cause death one way or another? Strange, red little creatures with brains that work
in a bloody darkness we can't even guess at. Elemental little brains, aswarm with
racial memory, hatred, and raw cruelty, with no more thought than self-preservation. And self-preservation in this case consisted of eliminating a mother who
realized what a horror she had birthed. I ask you, doctor, what is there in the world
more selfish than a baby? Nothing!"

Jeffers scowled and shook his head, helplessly.

Leiber dropped his cigarette down. "I'm not claiming any great strength for
the child. Just enough to crawl around a little, a few months ahead of schedule.
Just enough to listen all the time. Just enough to cry late at night. That's enough,
more than enough."

Jeffers tried ridicule. "Call it murder, then. But murder must be motivated.
What motive had the child?"

Leiber was ready with the answer. "What is more at peace, more dreamfully
content, at ease, at rest, fed, comforted, unbothered, than an unborn child? Nothing.
It floats in a sleepy, timeless wonder of nourishment and silence. Then, suddenly,
it is asked to give up its berth, is forced to vacate, rushed out into a noisy, uncaring,
selfish world where it is asked to shift for itself, to hunt, to feed from the hunting, to
seek after a vanishing love that once was its unquestionable right, to meet confusion
instead of inner silence and conservative slumber! And the child *resents* it! Resents

the cold air, the huge spaces, the sudden departure from familiar things. And in the tiny filament of brain the only thing the child knows is selfishness and hatred because the spell has been rudely shattered. Who is responsible for this disenchantment, this rude breaking of the spell? The mother. So here the new child has someone to hate with all its unreasoning mind. The mother has cast it out, rejected it. And the father is no better, kill him, too! He's responsible in *his* way!"

Jeffers interrupted. "If what you say is true, then every woman in the world would have to look on her baby as something to dread, something to wonder about."

"And why not? Hasn't the child a perfect alibi? A thousand years of accepted medical belief protects him. By all natural accounts he is helpless, not responsible. The child is born hating. And things grow worse, instead of better. At first the baby gets a certain amount of attention and mothering. But then as time passes, things change. When very new, a baby has the power to make parents do silly things when it cries or sneezes, jump when it makes a noise. As the years pass, the baby feels even that small power slip rapidly, forever away, never to return. Why shouldn't it grasp all the power it can have? Why shouldn't it jockey for position while it has all the advantages? In later years it would be too late to express its hatred. Now would be the time to strike."

Leiber's voice was very soft, very low.

"My little boy baby, lying in his crib nights, his face moist and red and out of breath. From crying? No. From climbing slowly out of his crib, from crawling long distances through darkened hallways. My little boy baby. I want to kill him."

The doctor handed him a water glass and some pills. "You're not killing anyone. You're going to sleep for twenty-four hours. Sleep'll change your mind. Take this."

Leiber drank down the pills and let himself be led upstairs to his bedroom, crying, and felt himself being put to bed. The doctor waited until he was moving deep into sleep, then left the house.

Leiber, alone, drifted down, down.

He heard a noise. "What's—what's *that*?" he demanded, feebly.

Something moved in the hall.

David Leiber slept.

Very early the next morning, Dr. Jeffers drove up to the house. It was a good morning, and he was here to drive Leiber to the country for a rest. Leiber would still be asleep upstairs. Jeffers had given him enough sedative to knock him out for at least fifteen hours.

He rang the doorbell. No answer. The servants were probably not up. Jeffers tried the front door, found it open, stepped in. He put his medical kit on the nearest chair.

Something white moved out of sight at the top of the stairs. Just a suggestion of a movement. Jeffers hardly noticed it.

The smell of gas was in the house.

Jeffers ran upstairs, crashed into Leiber's bedroom.

Leiber lay motionless on the bed, and the room billowed with gas, which hissed from a released jet at the base of the wall near the door. Jeffers twisted it off, then forced up all the windows and ran back to Leiber's body.

The body was cold. It had been dead quite a few hours.

Coughing violently, the doctor hurried from the room, eyes watering. Leiber hadn't turned on the gas himself. He *couldn't* have. Those sedatives had knocked him out, he wouldn't have wakened until noon. It wasn't suicide. Or was there the faintest possibility?

Jeffers stood in the hall for five minutes. Then he walked to the door of the nursery. It was shut. He opened it. He walked inside and to the crib.

The crib was empty.

He stood swaying by the crib for half a minute, then he said something to nobody in particular.

"The nursery door blew shut. You couldn't get back into your crib where it was safe. You didn't plan on the door blowing shut. A little thing like a slammed door can ruin the best of plans. I'll find you somewhere in the house, hiding, pretending to be something you are not." The doctor looked dazed. He put his hand to his head and smiled palely. "Now I'm talking like Alice and David talked. But, I can't take any chances. I'm not sure of anything, but I can't take any chances."

He walked downstairs, opened his medical bag on the chair, took something out of it and held it in his hands.

Something rustled down the hall. Something very small and very quiet. Jeffers turned rapidly.

I had to operate to bring you into this world, he thought. Now I guess I can operate to take you out of it....

He took half-a-dozen slow, sure steps forward into the hall. He raised his hand into the sunlight.

"See, baby! Something bright—something pretty!"

A scalpel.

Lucy Comes to Stay

BY ROBERT BLOCH

Oh, Robert Bloch. In so many ways, you're the reason we're all having this conversation right now.

It wasn't just Psycho, *the book that gave us Norman Bates and put the P-word front-and-center in our popular consciousness. Long before Hitchcock made it a household name, and for decades after, Bloch excelled at bringing sharp matter-of-factness to the unraveling self, and spent a lifetime getting all the funny (and not-so-funny) little details right.*

When questioned about his own sanity—given his clear inside knowledge of crazy—Bloch infamously quipped, "I have the heart of a small boy. I keep it in a jar on my desk." (No, it wasn't Stephen King. He was quoting Bob. As do we all. Cuz he's one of our heroes.)

"Lucy Comes to Stay" is a seminal piece, not just because it's so good, but because it's the short story in his vast lexicon that most clearly sets up his most famous work. Not in terms of Mommy issues, but in angle of attack.

"You can't go on this way."

Lucy kept her voice down low, because she knew the nurse had her room just down the hall from mine, and I wasn't supposed to see any visitors.

"But George is doing everything he can—poor dear, I hate to think of what all those doctors and specialists are costing him, and the sanatarium bill, too. And now that nurse, that Miss Higgins, staying here every day."

"It won't do any good. You know it won't." Lucy didn't sound like she was arguing with me. She knew. That's because Lucy is smarter than I am. Lucy wouldn't have started the drinking and gotten into such a mess in the first place. So it was about time I listened to what she said.

"Look, Vi," she murmured. "I hate to tell you this. You aren't well, you know. But you're going to find out one of these days anyway, and you might as well hear it from me."

"What is it, Lucy?"

"About George, and the doctors. They don't think you're going to get well." She paused. "They don't want you to."

"Oh, Lucy!"

"Listen to me, you little fool. Why do you suppose they sent you to that sanatarium in the first place? They said it was to take the cure. So you took it. All right, you're cured, then. But you'll notice that you still have the doctor coming every day, and George makes you stay here in your room, and that Miss Higgins who's supposed to be a special nurse—you know what she is, don't you? She's a guard."

I couldn't say anything. I just sat there and blinked. I wanted to cry, but I couldn't, because deep down inside I knew that Lucy was right.

"Just try to get out of here," Lucy said. "You'll see how fast she locks the door on you. All that talk about special diets and rest doesn't fool me. Look at yourself—you're as well as I am! You ought to be getting out, seeing people, visiting your friends."

"But I have no friends," I reminded her. "Not after that party, not after what I did—"

"That's a lie," Lucy nodded. "That's what George wants you to think. Why, you have hundreds of friends, Vi. They still love you. They tried to see you at the hospital and George wouldn't let them in. They sent flowers to the sanatarium and George told the nurses to burn them."

"He did? He told the nurses to burn the flowers?"

"Of course. Look, Vi, it's about time you faced the truth. George wants them to think you're sick. George wants you to think you're sick. Why? Because then he can put you away for good. Not in a private sanatarium, but in the—"

"No!" I began to shake. I couldn't stop shaking. It was ghastly. But it proved something. They told me at the sanatarium, the doctors told me, that if I took the cure I wouldn't get the shakes any more. Or the dreams, or any of the other things. Yet here it was—I was shaking again.

"Shall I tell you some more?" Lucy whispered. "Shall I tell you what they're putting in your food? Shall I tell you about George and Miss Higgins?"

"But she's older than he is, and besides he'd never—"

Lucy laughed.

"Stop it!" I yelled.

"All right. But don't yell, you little fool. Do you want Miss Higgins to come in?"

"She thinks I'm taking a nap. She gave me a sedative."

"Lucky I dumped it out." Lucy frowned. "Vi, I've got to get you away from here. And there isn't much time."

She was right. There wasn't much time. Seconds, hours, days, weeks—how long had it been since I'd had a drink?

"We'll sneak off," Lucy said. "We could take a room together where they wouldn't find us. I'll nurse you until you're well."

"But rooms cost money."

"You have that fifty dollars George gave you for a party dress."

"Why, Lucy," I said. "How did you know that?"

"You told me ages ago, dear. Poor thing, you don't remember things very well, do you? All the more reason for trusting me."

I nodded. I could trust Lucy. Even though she was responsible, in a way, for me starting to drink. She had just thought it would cheer me up when George brought all his high-class friends to the house and we went out to impress his clients. Lucy had tried to help. I could trust her. I must trust her—

"We can leave as soon as Miss Higgins goes tonight," Lucy was saying. "We'll wait until George is asleep, eh? Why not get dressed now, and I'll come back for you."

I got dressed. It isn't easy to dress when you have the shakes, but I did it. I even put on some makeup and trimmed my hair with the big scissors. Then I looked at myself in the mirror and said out loud, "Why, you can't tell, can you?"

"Of course not," said Lucy. "You look radiant. Positively radiant."

I stood there smiling, and the sun was going down, just shining through the window on the scissors in a way that hurt my eyes, and all at once I was so sleepy.

"George will be here soon, and Miss Higgins will leave," Lucy said. "I'd better go now. Why don't you rest until I come for you?"

"Yes," I said. "You'll be very careful, won't you?"

"Very careful," Lucy whispered, as she tiptoed out quietly.

I lay down on the bed and then I was sleeping, really sleeping for the first time in weeks, sleeping so the scissors wouldn't hurt my eyes, the way George hurt me inside when he wanted to shut me up in the asylum so he and Miss Higgins could make love on my bed and laugh at me the way they all laughed except Lucy and she would take care of me she knew what to do now I could trust her when George came and I must sleep and sleep and nobody can blame you for what you think in your sleep or do in your sleep…

It was all right until I had the dreams, and even then I didn't really worry about them because a dream is only a dream, and when I was drunk I had a lot of dreams.

When I woke up I had the shakes again, but it was Lucy shaking me, standing there in the dark shaking me, I looked around and saw that the door to my room was open, but Lucy didn't bother to whisper.

She stood there with the scissors in her hand and called to me.

"Come on, let's hurry."

"What are you doing with the scissors?" I asked.

"Cutting the telephone wires, silly! I got into the kitchen after Miss Higgins left and dumped some of that sedative into George's coffee. Remember, I told you the plan."

I couldn't remember now, but I knew it was all right. Lucy and I went out through the hall, past George's room, and he never stirred. Then we went down-stairs and out the front door and the streetlights hurt my eyes. Lucy made me hurry right along, though.

We took a bus around the corner. This was the difficult part, getting away. Once we were out of the neighborhood there'd be no worry. The wires were cut.

The lady at the rooming house on the South Side didn't know about the wires being cut. She didn't know about me, either, because Lucy got the room.

Lucy marched in bold as brass and laid my fifty dollars down on the desk. The rent was $12.50 a week in advance, and Lucy didn't even ask to see the room. I guess that's why the landlady wasn't worried about baggage.

We got upstairs and locked the door, and then I had the shakes again.

Lucy said, "Vi—cut it out?"

"But I can't help it. What'll I do now, Lucy? Oh, what'll I do? Why did I ever—"

"Shut up!" Lucy opened my purse and pulled something out. I had been won-dering why my purse felt so heavy but I never dreamed about the secret.

She held the secret up. It glittered under the light, like the scissors, only this was a nice glittering. A golden glittering.

"A whole pint!" I gasped. "Where did you get it?"

"From the cupboard downstairs, naturally. You know George still keeps the stuff around. I slipped it into your purse, just in case."

I had the shakes, but I got that bottle open in ten seconds. One of my finger-nails broke, and then the stuff was burning and warming and softening—

"Pig!" said Lucy.

"You know I had to have it," I whispered. "That's why you brought it."

"I don't like to see you drink," Lucy answered. "I never drink and I don't like to see you hang one on, either."

"Please, Lucy. Just this once."

"Why can't you take a shot and then leave it alone? That's all I ask."

"Just this once, Lucy, I have to."

"I won't sit here and watch you make a spectacle of yourself. You know what always happens—another mess."

I took another gulp. The bottle was half-empty.

"I did all I could for you, Vi. But if you don't stop now, I'm going."

That made me pause. "You couldn't do that to me. I need you, Lucy. Until I'm straightened out, anyway."

Lucy laughed, the way I didn't like. "Straightened out! That's a hot one! Talking about straightening out with a bottle in your hand. It's no use, Vi. Here I do everything I can for you, stop at nothing to get you away, and you're off on another."

"Please. You know I can't help it."

"Oh, yes, you can help it, Vi. But you don't want to. You've always had to make a choice, you know. George or the bottle. Me or the bottle. And the bottle always wins. I think deep down inside you hate George. You hate me."

"You're my best friend."

"Nuts!" Lucy talked vulgar sometimes, when she got really mad. And she was mad, now. It made me so nervous I had another drink.

"Oh, I'm good enough for you when you're in trouble, or have nobody else around to talk to. I'm good enough to lie for you, pull you out of your messes. But I've never been good enough for your friends, for George. And I can't even win over a bottle of rotgut whiskey. It's no use, Vi. What I've done for you today you'll never know. And it isn't enough. Keep your lousy whiskey. I'm going."

I know I started to cry. I tried to get up, but the room was turning round and round. Then Lucy was walking out the door and I dropped the bottle and the light kept shining the way it did on the scissors and I closed my eyes and dropped after the bottle to the floor....

When I woke up they were all pestering me, the landlady and the doctor and Miss Higgins and the man who said he was a policeman.

I wondered if Lucy had gone to them and betrayed me, but when I asked the doctor said no, they just discovered me through a routine checkup on hotels and rooming houses after they found George's body in his bed with my scissors in his throat.

All at once I knew what Lucy had done, and why she ran out on me that way. She knew they'd find me and call it murder.

So I told them about her and how it must have happened. I even figured out how Lucy managed to get my fingerprints on the scissors.

But Miss Higgins said she'd never seen Lucy in my house, and the landlady told a lie and said I had registered for the room alone, and the man from the police just laughed when I kept begging him to find Lucy and make her tell the truth.

Only the doctor seemed to understand, and when we were alone together in the little room he asked me all about her and what she looked like, and I told him.

Then he brought over the mirror and held it up and asked me if I could see her. And sure enough—

She was standing right behind me, laughing. I could see her in the mirror and I told the doctor so, and he said yes, he thought he understood now.

So it was all right after all. Even when I got the shakes just then and dropped the mirror, so that the little jagged pieces hurt my eyes to look at, it was all right.

Lucy was back with me now, and she wouldn't ever go away any more. She'd stay with me forever. I knew that. I knew it, because even though the light hurt my eyes, Lucy began to laugh.

After a minute, I began to laugh, too. And then the two of us were laughing together, we couldn't stop even when the doctor went away. We just stood there against the bars, Lucy and I, laughing like crazy.

Marla's Eyes

BY ED KURTZ

The literary gene-splicing technique known as the "mashup" is all the rage these days. And I'm not just talking about modern classics like "Saving Private Titanic" or "Dr. Jekyll and Mr. Freud." It's as if the whole notion of genre has gone insane, a Reese's Peanut Butter Cup of colliding flavors. As if the whole purpose of historical fiction were for horror to gut it, then climb inside its husk for warmth.

Not that I'm complaining, mind you. The weirder things are, the happier I get, by and large. The entire Bizarro genre is a psychic cuisinart, in which all our ideas about story are blenderized into mutant concoctions that range from goofily amusing to brain-meltingly profound.

Enter Ed Kurtz, a young writer obsessed with finding strange new ways to rejigger traditional forms. He's not a Bizarro writer, per se, but you wouldn't know it to look at "Marla's Eyes:" a crazed commingling of Jack Ketchum and Evelyn Waugh which might not have seen print in the 1930s, when it's set, but which I can't wait to share with you now.

I

Cecil's breath hitched in his chest when she entered the parlor. She bent slightly at the knees, crossing her right leg before her left, and curtsied. Promptly Cecil realized he was staring, and that his mouth was open. He cleared his throat and assumed a proper employer's frown.

"Olive Bell, is it?"

The girl, her pale face a mask of apprehension, nodded once.

"Have you a tongue?" Cecil demanded. "Can you speak?"

"Yes," Olive whispered. "Yes, sir."

"God, you're a timid one," he said, averting his eyes to the broad, frosty window lest he stare again. "Sit, sit. I mean to interview you, Olive—you can't very well stand all the while."

"Yes, sir," Olive whispered. "Sorry, sir."

She paused, her eyes large and shimmering and moving from the Queen Anne chair to the right of the lounge to the one on the left.

"Anywhere," Cecil barked. "Whichever one."

His gaze remained directed at the window. Each of the twelve panes was framed with spectacularly intricate patterns of frost, a transparent circle in the center of every one through which he could see the sloping green hill beyond. Soon the hill would be buried beneath a blanket of snow, its only imperfections the tiny prints of fox's feet, or birds.

Olive selected the chair to Cecil's right. He made a thin line of his mouth and, hesitantly, returned his attention to her.

"All right then, Olive Bell. I understand you've come quite some way."

"From Sheffield, sir."

"Are you from Sheffield, originally?"

Olive nodded, her eyes still enormous and reflective. Cecil felt a shiver and prayed it did not show.

"Mosborough, sir."

Cecil crossed his legs and sat back. "I see."

Furrowing his brow, the lord of the house reached over to the pipe stand on the table before him and chose a meerschaum with little deliberation. He packed it and pinched a match from the cup, and just before he struck it he raised his eyebrows in a solicitous manner and said, "Does it bother you?"

Olive pursed her lips.

"The smoke," Cecil explained. "Will it bother you?"

"Oh, no sir. No, it won't."

"Good," he murmured as he struck the match. He touched the flame to the densely packed tobacco and drew deeply from the stem. "I do not smoke often, but I confess I enjoy it."

For several prolonged minutes the pair sat in silence, the master quietly smoking his pipe and the prospective servant gawping at the hands folded in her lap.

"Have you been to Dorset before now?"

"Is this part of the interview, sir?"

"It's only a question."

"I haven't, sir."

"Then why should you want to live here? Why not London, or Manchester?"

"Hardy, sir."

"I beg your pardon?"

"Thomas Hardy. He came from Dorset. His Wessex stories are all about Dorset."

"Is that so?"

"It is, sir."

"Blimey."

What Cecil Hughes would have liked to say, apart from "Blimey," was something like, "What a perfectly preposterous reason to pull up one's roots and move cross country," but he did not. His decorum was not the result of diplomacy, but the result of the young woman's startling grey eyes, which once more had become the object of his own staring pair. Cecil shot up from the lounge and moved quickly to the window, keeping his back to his subject.

"Have you any references?"

"Mrs. Eleanor Martin, sir."

"In Sheffield, I presume?"

"She is, yes."

Cecil waved it off. "Never you mind, then. I knew a Martin once, a Frederick Martin. Affable chap. Killed a dozen Huns in the war and never spoke of it."

"I don't know him, sir."

"Nor should you," Cecil said officiously as he pivoted on the heel of his shoe to face her again. "I'm satisfied. Have you your things, then?"

"Just the one trunk, sir. It's in the foyer, if you don't mind."

"I'll have some boys take it up for you."

"Then I've got it?" Olive's face registered something like shock; her large grey eyes grew larger still. "The position, I mean—I'm hired?"

"Naturally. Don't you still want it?"

"Oh, Mr. Hughes, I do!"

"Splendid," said Cecil, turning back to the window and the sloping hill. "Up the stairs, third door on your left. That's your room from now on. I am certain the journey from Sheffield was a tiring one, and you are permitted to rest today and begin tomorrow."

"Thank you, Mr. Hughes," Olive said, her voice returning to the whisper with which she began. "Thank you."

He waited until her footsteps—dainty as one might expect—grew quieter until he could not hear them at all. On the hilltop a sandpiper stood, its feathers ruffled up from the cold. Cecil watched the bird, but his mind was distant. He thought not of birds, nor hills, nor the possibility of snow. Cecil Hughes thought of Olive Bell, and in particular he thought of her startling large grey eyes.

And how very much like Marla's they were.

II

Marla's eyes were yellow and sunken when she died. Where they were not yellow they were red, webbed with burst capillaries, the product of the heaving coughs and stunted breaths that rushed her toward this ignominious end. To his credit, Cecil sat beside her throughout her final days and watched her slip away. More than this, he wiped her sweat-slick face with a damp cloth and held her hand when her lungs froze up and her face turned a horrific purple hue. He read letters to her, half of them wholly fabricated near the end when their friends stopped writing.

He explained Ainsley's achievements at school as best he understood them. He did absolutely everything within his power to mask his own emotion, the tremendous twisting, clawing feeling he had inside, and he did a very fine job of it.

Cecil was, by any standards, a splendid husband to his dying wife. And when at last the specter of death hung dark and near above her damp, cold bed, only Cecil was there to hear the words she rasped with her penultimate breath.

"I was beautiful, wasn't I?"

He told her she was, and that she still was, and he meant it deeply—but Marla was already gone.

Though the morning was cool, the sun burned up the fog by midday and Olive relished the warm breeze that tickled the nape of her neck through the open window whilst she dusted Mr. Hughes' writing desk and the photographs on the wall. One picture in particular warranted especial attention from the maid, its frame gilded and floral, its color a rusty sepia apart from the black and the white. In it sat a stern looking woman, stern but still beautiful by anyone's standards, dressed in a dark fur coat and a jaunty, asymmetrical hat unlike any Olive had ever seen. The woman's springy blonde curls flounced out from beneath the hat, almost mirthfully in spite of her drawn, austere face. Long after the last speck of dust was wiped away from both frame and glass, Olive continued to stare.

"My mother," said an uneven voice behind her.

Olive jumped slightly, moved quickly away from the photograph as though she was caught in the commission of a crime. Standing in the doorway was a boy, no older than fourteen, dressed in the coat and short pants of his alma mater, the crest of which was sewn onto the lapel.

"She's dead, you know," said the boy.

"I—I had an idea of it," Olive replied. She could feel the heat rising to her cheeks.

"It was awful at the end. I wondered why nobody put a pillow over her face or something, just for the mercy of it. Wouldn't you want somebody to end your suffering, if you knew it would keep on 'til you died?"

The heat retreated quickly and Olive blanched.

The boy went on: "I would. I certainly would. The vicar wouldn't like it, though, would he? Sanctity of life and all that."

A small grin played at the boy's thin lips and he suddenly marched to the middle of the room, whereupon he extended his right hand. Olive froze where she stood.

"Ainsley Hughes," he announced. "I'm just back from school. I attend Coventry, you know."

"I—I didn't," Olive admitted.

Realizing that the maid was not going to take his hand, Ainsley lowered it and wandered over to his father's writing desk.

"I shan't be an author like papa," he said, somewhat morosely. "I aim to be a solicitor. Perhaps an MP, someday."

Olive smiled and a small breath passed her lips. Ainsley spun around, his brow in a red pinch.

"Is it funny, what I said? I *could* be an MP if I wanted. I can be Prime Minister if I want. What's it to you? What the deuce do you know?"

Grasping the dust cloth tightly in both hands, Olive averted her eyes, which had gone wide and glassy from the tears she fought valiantly from spilling down her face.

"I don't think it's funny," she whispered. "Not at all."

"Cheek," Ainsley growled, and he stamped from the room.

"I didn't think it funny," she rasped, her voice barely audible to herself, much less the boy who was halfway across the house by then.

She turned, absent-mindedly twisting the rag in her hands, and without intending it met eyes once more with the austere woman in the portrait on the wall. Ainsley's mother. Her eyes seemed to drill into Olive's own, and for a queer moment she almost felt as though she was peering into a mirror.

IV

"She's *awful*, papa. Just awful. I hardly see what entered your mind when you took her on."

Cecil was traipsing up the hill, walking stick in hand, his son straggling up on stumpy legs. Cecil's legs were long for his height, and so were Marla's. He did not know how Ainsley's remained so stunted.

"When I was a boy," Cecil said calmly, almost professorially, "I should never have thought to question *my* father's decisions in matters thus."

"Did grandfather ever take a doe-eyed ninny like that woman into his house?"

Cecil paused, nearly to the crest of the hill, and sighed.

"Olive is the maid, Ainsley. She cleans, dusts, makes the beds. If she is not of the highest intellectual acumen I think you and I can forgive her that, don't you?"

"It's you I'm thinking of, papa. I'm to be back at Coventry before the weekend. You have to live with the cretin."

"That's enough, Ainsley."

Three mystical words, first the mother's incantation but now transposed to the father, and at last the boy gave it up. Silenced thusly, he continued his straggling pursuit of Cecil to the crest of the hill. High over the treetops a flock of sheldrakes screamed by. Ainsley took up imaginary arms, positioning his rifle and spitting for fire at the noisy birds. Cecil knitted his brow and said nothing.

The discovery of the cat on the following Sunday set the Hughes house aflutter. Marfin, the gardener, was the one who found it, all twisted and broken, the unfortunate animal's eyes gouged out. Marfin only came on Wednesdays and Sundays, and so there was no clear inkling as to how long the annihilated creature had lain amongst the hedges. That the gardener presented the horrible spectacle to Cecil at all was cause for reproach—"Have ye a butchers at this," the man said—but privately Cecil was glad to have seen the cat in its gruesome state. He might otherwise have brushed it all off as the work of a fox, but there was no mistaking what he saw, dangling by the matted brown tail in Marfin's fist. It was a human being who had done the killing.

Cecil instructed his man to bury the animal—anywhere, as long as it was deep enough to dissuade anything from digging it back up—and though he also made clear the incident was not to be spoken of, this decree came too late. Already Mrs. Rollo, Hughes' cook, was loudly bemoaning the cat's fate within earshot of half of Sherborne, by which means Olive Bell became acquainted with the gardener's gruesome discovery.

It was for this reason that Cecil found his maid weeping in the parlor, her small, oval face pressed into her gloved hands. He sighed deeply, unaccustomed to female histrionics since his Marla died, and advanced slowly toward the sobbing girl.

"Come now," he clumsily consoled the girl. "It's only a cat."

"A—all God's creatures," she murmured wetly.

Cecil raised an eyebrow at her. "Sorry?"

"God's tender m—mercies are all over His creatures, Mr. Hughes."

"Oh, I see. That's from the Bible, is it not?"

"Psalm 145, sir."

A smile, faint but a smile nonetheless, played at Cecil's mouth and he sat down beside Olive on the lounge.

"You've read rather a lot, I gather."

"Some," she agreed hesitantly.

"Curious for a girl of your class, what?"

"I'm fond of books, sir."

"And cats?"

"I'm fond of them, as well."

"Books and cats," Cecil said. "Well."

"It's a terrible thing, Mr. Hughes," Olive said, squeezing out the last syllable in just enough time before the floodgates reopened. She wailed freely as though she were home at Sheffield, and not at all in the presence of her employer, moaning and shaking at the shoulders. For his part, Cecil sat stock-still, shocked to silence, and gazed in wonder at the blubbering help.

"I say," he managed at last, crinkling his brow and peering out, past the open doors to the empty, airy foyer. "Why, it's only a cat."

All at once Olive's weeping came to an abrupt halt. She lowered her hands, craned her neck to look upon Cecil with narrow, red eyes. Her eyelids were puffy from the crying, her eyelashes matted and cheeks wet, but all the same the girl's stunning steel-grey eyes pierced his soul and rendered him mute, incapable of a word, of moving even his little finger.

"God's tender mercies, Mr. Hughes," Olive reproached him.

"Why, yes," Cecil said softly, surprised at his own reply. "Yes, of course."

She stood then, a fluid motion, and dabbed at one eye and then the other before walking gracefully from the lounge, across the parlor, disappearing into the echoing foyer.

And as if a spell had been broken, a curse lifted, Cecil shuddered off his start at the maid's cheek. He rose, staggered halfway across the room, and paused.

"I say," he whispered to himself.

VI

In the late evening, Cecil privately worried.

He worried some about Olive, about her candor and attitude earlier that afternoon. There was no question in his own mind as to why he took her on—it was her eyes that got the position, Cecil knew that perfectly well, though he would never admit it to anyone else. Still, his highest hope had been that the small indiscretion would prove forgivable, that the girl would turn out a suitable maid in spite of her unknowability. Her deuced strangeness.

Cecil worried too about Ainsley. Often he did; many nights he lay sleepless in bed, the puzzled widower unsure of the tricky dichotomy between a father's strong hand and a motherless son. At the very least the boy spent three quarters of the year away at Coventry, ostensibly somebody else's problem, but Ainsley remained Cecil's responsibility, his heir. A man took the reins, took control of his progeny, shaped them into the man they were to become. A proper man, anyway. Yet the lad's anger, that was what troubled Cecil so. His anger and his defiance. And then there was the matter of the damned cat . . .

It was possible that the boy could have done it. He left on Friday, after tea, but the outrage might have been committed at any time between Marfin's visits, leaving Ainsley two full days to—Cecil shivered. All that prattle about Olive, the boy's evident, misplaced fury over her, and how he played at shooting the sheldrakes. Cecil did not give a fig about cats, but by God the eyes.

The eyes!

Cecil jolted up in bed, exhaled a noisy gasp and felt the flesh crawl at the back of his neck. Funny, he thought, how the pieces come together so. The whole ghastly affair was so terribly clear now.

The girl, her startling grey eyes. Ainsley must have noticed, he had to have. She was his mother, and to see her own cool, handsome eyes looking at him from a stranger's face, much less the bloody maid!

"Bugger and blast!" Cecil barked. He threw his legs over the edge of the bed, winced at the cold floor beneath his bare feet. "Ainsley, my God."

Much too late to do a thing about it now, he realised. He wanted nothing more than to seize the boy by the neck, to box his ears, but even if he should take the Crossley to Coventry there would be no one about, not that early. There was nothing else for it. Cecil had to wait.

So he shrugged his shoulders into his robe and stepped into his slippers, and he padded softly downstairs to the study. There he switched on the lamp, and he was instantly startled by a luminous figure looming at the window. Cecil emitted a small cry, but he was embarrassed immediately to determine the figure was nothing more than his own reflection in the glass. That girl, he mused, certainly does a cracking job on the windows.

His heart still hammering at his ribs, Cecil laughed quietly and turned to the wall beside the desk. Marla looked back at him, surrounded by gold and flowers, the sepia hue of the photograph failing miserably at concealing the sober grey of her lovely eyes.

"Bit barmy tonight, aren't I?" he said to her.

"Are you all right, Mr. Hughes?"

Again Cecil cried out. He spun about and found Olive in the doorway, a candle glowing atop the candlestick in her hand. She wore a long woolen nightgown and her hair was done up. She looked older than her years. Like somebody's mother.

"God a'mighty, woman!" he snarled. "You gave me a fright."

"I'm terribly sorry, sir. Really I am."

"It's all right, Olive."

"I didn't mean—"

"It's *all right*."

The girl smiled. It was a soft smile, with small, soft lips. Cecil reddened, turned quickly back to his portrait of Marla. Her solemn gaze—it never changed.

"A cup, then?" Olive asked. "Won't take a minute."

"Yes, Olive. Yes, I think that would be just the thing. Thank you."

Olive went off to the kitchen, hardly her domain but tea was tea, and Cecil lowered himself onto the chair before the writing desk. He would not get so much as a kip in before dawn, and he knew it. A long night ahead. He crossed one leg over the other and waited for his tea.

Outside the ink black sky rumbled.

VII

The rain fell in sheets all morning. Cecil paced the house, from top to bottom and left, right, and centre, his anxiety driving the staff mad though not a one dared say a word. At last the clock struck nine as Cecil was descending the stairs, whereupon he bolted across the ground floor for the telephone in the parlor, nearly colliding with a rather startled Olive along the way.

In minutes he was connected with Coventry. He did his utmost to conceal his panic and aggravation.

"Mr. Harbottle, please," he snapped at the operator.

The operator tonelessly informed him that Harbottle was engaged.

"Glasby then," Cecil said. "Connect me to Mr. Glasby, and be quick about it."

The line clicked loudly in Cecil's ear. A moment later it rattled and a tinny voice came on.

"Glasby? Glasby—Hughes, here. Listen to me, I want you to pull out Ainsley. He's got to collect his things and be ready to come down to Sherborne straight away. I'd rather you sent him along but on short notice I should understand if I must drive up to collect him. Are you listening to me, Glasby? Listen, old man: I wouldn't tell you all this if it wasn't terribly important . . ."

"Cor, Cecil," Glasby cut in. "Let a fellow get a word in, would you?"

"I *know* how I sound, old man, I know it. But you really must hear me out . . ."

"Cecil, you've got to settle yourself down a moment. Why, I was only just about to give you a bell, myself."

"I—what's that? Come again?"

A wind picked up outside, and it drove the rain sideways, shot buckets of it at the parlor window. Cecil covered his free ear with his hand.

"I say your boy, Cecil," Glasby said, his voice rising. "He's gone, man. Run away, he has. I'm awfully sorry to tell you . . ."

"Ainsley," Cecil rasped.

"Like a thief in the night, you know. Now, we shall find the lad, don't you worry about that, old bean. Likely he spent the night out in the cold and can't bear another minute away from school, don't you agree?"

"I've got to ring off, Glasby," Cecil said, his voice choked.

"We'll find him, Cecil," Glasby carried on. "We'll find him, and when we do—"

"I've got to ring off now."

The receiver slammed into the hooks with a clattering bang that was preempted by a massive snapping roar of thunder.

Cecil said, "Ainsley. God, Ainsley."

He went with slumped shoulders to the window, squinted at the endless flood that washed over the panes. This time when Olive entered the room, he did not start. Instead he lowered his head, said, "What kind of father must I be, dear girl?"

"Sir?"

"I've ruined him. I'm sure of it. I've gone and ruined the boy."

"Master Ainsley, sir? Is he—"

"I have to tell you something, Olive," Cecil said gravely, turning away from the storm to look at her. "You won't like it, I'm afraid."

"Mr. Hughes," she whispered. "Oh, Mr. Hughes, please don't sack me."

"No, no, Olive. Please, sit."

He gestured toward the lounge, and though she momentarily hesitated, Olive took a seat upon it and looked up at her employer with wide, solicitous eyes.

"The boy," he began haltingly. "My son."

Olive stared.

"I might as well come out with it," Cecil continued. "I believe…well, bugger it all. I believe you are in danger, my poor girl."

"Danger, sir?"

"I hope I'm wrong. Christ! I hope I'm horribly wrong!"

"But why should I be in danger, Mr. Hughes?"

"That is what I'm telling you, child. It's the boy, don't you see? He's the one who killed the cat. He plucked the poor beast's eyes out, if you remember. Why, I gather it has everything to do with the eyes, with *your* eyes, Olive."

"My eyes? Sir—Mr. Hughes—you're frightening me . . ."

"And indeed you should be frightened, poor thing. You should!"

No sooner had Cecil made this exclamation than the window smashed in, exploded in a mist of miniscule fragments of glass, a great, lashing tree branch reaching through like the snatching hand of some forgotten elder god.

Olive shrieked.

"Mr. *Hughes!*"

Cecil rushed to her, swept the girl up from the lounge into his arms. He felt her tremble, her warm breath puffing quickly against his neck. The branch scraped rhythmically at the floor, its measured scratching met with the soft tinkle of falling glass like chimes.

"Damn this storm," Cecil groused. He spun Olive about, gave her a push for the entryway to the foyer. "The great room, that's the thing."

Together they scuttled across the house to the great room, where Marla once so enjoyed entertaining guests—the room was all but boarded up now, the massive table and its many chairs draped in sheets. Cecil permitted Olive entry first and locked the door upon following her in.

He found his breath coming too quick, too shallow. He rubbed his chin, studied the large, ghostly room.

"He had some harsh words for me," Olive said at some length. "Your son, I mean. We were in the study. He was . . . vexed about a photograph on the wall."

Cecil nodded as he drew the sheet from the nearest chair. The sheet fluttered to the floor and he sat.

"I'm sure of it."

"But I don't understand, Mr. Hughes. What's it got to do with me?"

"God, everything, Olive."

"My—you said something about my eyes . . ."

"I'm such a fool," Cecil said.

"Sir?"

A great, deep sigh hissed out of Cecil and he leaned his head back. "He is a troubled boy, my Ainsley. Rather troubled, indeed. I expect his mother's passing affected him—why, it should affect any child, naturally—but no, not in the usual way. He grew angry, you must understand. At what, I cannot say, not really. At me, perhaps? At Marla, for abandoning him? And he is most assuredly angry at you, Olive. You see, you have her eyes."

"Mrs. Hughes . . . ?"

"Spitting image, I'm dead shocked you did not notice upon seeing the portrait. Why, you might as well have been—"

"—looking into my own eyes. Yes sir, I noticed."

"Then you must see. About Ainsley, I mean to say. You must see what is going on in that mad little head of his."

"But sir," Olive protested, her face chalky, bloodless. "He's only a child."

"He has run away from school."

Olive gasped.

"I spoke to the headmaster. He's no notion at all where the boy has gone. But I do."

"Oh, oh," the girl muttered.

"He's coming home."

Olive cried out, a great keening moan, and collapsed to the floor in a faint. Cecil shot out of the chair. He knelt down beside her, lifted her head with one hand and swept the loose, auburn strands of hair away from her eyes with the other. He paused a moment, startled by her simple beauty, resenting himself all the while but gawping at her alabaster face just the same.

"A classic fool!" he rasped, turning his head, averting his eyes to the space beneath the covered table. And there, in the inch between the sheet's hem and the floor, Cecil saw four very still fingertips lifted only slightly in a curl.

Instinctively he withdrew, and in doing so he dropped Olive's head, which thumped against the floor.

A hand. Someone beneath the table. Cecil sneered, wiped the beading sweat from his brow and licked his lips. Then, his breath held in his lungs, he pinched the hem of the sheet and lifted it up.

Mrs. Rollo lay there, twisted at the waist, her head spun round so that the tight black bun of her hair faced Cecil. She was quite still. She was, in fact, quite dead.

And though he already knew, though he could not bear to look, Cecil had to be sure of what was already as obvious as the raging storm outside. He reached under the table, grasped Mrs. Rollo's shoulder, and pulled her toward him. Her head flopped over as though her neck was made of rubber, and Cecil moaned loudly.

The poor woman's eyes were gone, gouged out of their sockets, nothing left but unseeing, red-black pits.

He was not coming after all; he had come.

Ainsley Hughes was home.

VIII

The slap brought her to, a sharp sting that shocked her back to the great room with alarming clarity. Her eyes filled with tears and she scrambled back, afraid and confused.

"I am sorry, Olive," Cecil said, his face drawn and dripping sweat. "You must stay vigilant. I am going to look for him, but you must remain here—and keep those doors locked!"

Olive's face fell and her eyes dropped to the floor. Almost immediately Cecil lunged for her, seized her by the chin and forced her face up.

"You mustn't look under the table!" he cried.

The girl's bottom lip quivered and tears spilled down her cheeks.

"Promise me!"

"I won't, sir! Mr. Hughes, I won't!"

"Here—" He rose, scooted a chair clear across the room, far away from the horror beneath the great table. "Sit here. Sit here and wait for me, Olive. It's no castle, the Hughes House. I shall find him and quick."

"But he's dangerous," the maid protested as she hefted herself up.

"To you, dear girl. He's a terrible danger to you. But I am his father, God help me. Even a mad boy shall mind his own father, or I shall make him mind me!"

Enervated thusly, Cecil wasted no more time and stomped across the great room, unlocked the doors, and stepped into the hall. "Lock these doors!" he called back, and he slammed them shut.

IX

"You have been soft with him," Marla said quietly, nearly too quietly to hear. "It is a mother's preoccupation to soften life's blows, don't you think? A father's hand must be firmer, dear-heart."

Cecil's heart swelled even as the pit in his stomach tightened. He adored the pet name Marla used all these years, though now each time he heard her utter *dear-heart* he wondered if it would be the last time she would say it.

"If you mean about the row with that Hawkings boy . . ."

"Ainsley smashed the child's nose, Cecil. It's too much."

"The other boy started it. Why, a man has a right to defend himself, hasn't he?"

"Ainsley is not yet a man."

"A boy, then. Hasn't a boy the same right?"

"Eye for an eye and all that, then."

"Certainly."

"But our son took two eyes for the one. Three, even. He went much too far."

"He was . . . well, he was angry, wasn't he?"

"It's too much, Cecil."

Cecil sighed, pinched the bridge of his nose between forefinger and thumb. "Yes," he said.

"It is simply too much. Something needs be done."

"Yes."

"You will have a word with him."

"Yes, Marla."

"Say it, say you will speak to Ainsley."

Through clenched teeth, covered by still lips, Cecil murmured, "I will speak to him."

"That's a good lad," Marla said.

X

Boys, Cecil knew from experience, were rather good at hiding. So although he scoured every room upstairs from the closets to underneath the beds, he found neither hide nor hair of Ainsley Hughes. Whenever he finished with a room, he shuddered at the thought that his turned back was ample enough invitation for the little scoundrel, that there would soon come a knife into his back or a bat at his knees. He hurried away each time, feeling foolish yet prudent. And once he was done with the upstairs, Cecil climbed back down the steps, filling his lungs to call out for the rotten child.

He need not have done so, and indeed he was not given the chance, for at the bottom of the staircase, standing in a puddle of rainwater, was Ainsley. The boy was soaked crown to toe, his dark hair hanging over his face like seaweed, his arms dangling limp at his sides. His looked up, up the stairs, up at his father's astonished face. In the wake of a thundercrack, he said, "I am not going back. I won't go back to Coventry."

"That's all right," Cecil said, assuming a false smile. He descended, slowly, to the foyer.

"Did you hear what I said? I said I refuse to go back to school. I won't do it, and that's the end of it."

"Yes, Ainsley. I heard you."

The boy stamped his foot, splashing the puddle. Cecil's shoulders jumped.

"I mean it! I mean what I say!"

"Calm down, son. It's all right, really it is."

"No, it's not. Nothing's all right. Everything is . . . dreadful, papa."

Ainsley groaned, hung his head. A low moan built up inside of him, working its way up and growing louder, more anguished, until at last it escaped his mouth, a keening wail.

Cecil went to him, partly horrified but largely filled with remorse and sympathy. All at once he knew he meant to be complicit. No one would ever know what had befallen poor, dead Mrs. Rollo.

Embracing the boy and drawing him in close, Cecil squeezed his son tightly and wept along with him.

"You needn't worry, Ainsley. You *mustn't* worry. Your father will take care of everything, I promise you that."

"I hate it, papa. I hate Coventry."

"Don't think about it. Don't think about Coventry or the cat or even Mrs.

Rollo. Just clear it all out, son. Clear it from your mind and I'll fix everything."

"Cat?" Ainsley murmured. He pushed against Cecil's chest, wiggled free from his father's strong embrace. "Mrs. Rollo?"

"Quiet, now," Cecil insisted. "Not tonight. Tomorrow. Tomorrow, I'll—"

"—but I don't know what you mean, papa."

"Hush, son."

The boy shook his head and knitted his dripping brow. He wrestled himself away from his father and looked up at him sternly. For a moment they regarded one another, father and son. Then Ainsley said, "What's happened to Mrs. Rollo, father?"

Cecil said, "Oh, God."

And then the great room doors burst open and Olive Bell came thundering out, shrieking like a spectre and brandishing the chair leg Cecil had furnished her.

He turned slowly, as if in a dream in which all the world was slowed, all but Olive. She came on quickly, savagely. Her face was a twisted mask, not the shy Sheffield girl at all, but a fiend, a monster with Marla's eyes.

"No," he said, too quiet to hear. Oddly, he felt a little bit like laughing.

Olive spun around him, brought the chair leg up and back before thrusting the broken end at Ainsley. The splintered teeth pierced the boy's neck, digging in and tearing, wooden fangs rending the flesh in a spurting red mist.

Ainsley opened his mouth, ostensibly to scream, but all he could manage was a weak yelp. His hands, white and smooth, a schoolboy's workless hands, clawed at the jagged slivers. His fingers were stained red instantly, though they failed to staunch the pulsing bloodflow.

The color drained rapidly from the boy's face. Cecil noted this in a kind of fascination, a terrible realisation that people were so fragile, so laughably weak. Spill a spot of blood and the whole game was done. Nothing for it. Not now.

"God," he said stupidly. "My boy."

Olive whooped and wrenched the chair leg free from Ainsley's neck. The threefold wounds burbled and ran wildly, a brook of blood. Cecil staggered forth, just a step, and reached out for him. Ainsley's eyes crumpled up and his lips wobbled. He looked like a baby about to cry. Instead, he collapsed to the floor, splashing in rainwater mixed with blood, and died.

The windows on either side of the front door flashed with intense white light, a throbbing light that went dark just as the thunder rumbled overhead like a herd of celestial horses.

"My boy," Cecil said to Olive, a little lilt at the end making it a sort of question. "My boy, Olive."

She screeched and slammed the side of the chair leg against his temple.

XI

He came around in stages. He was someplace cool. His head swam and his left eye stung terribly. It was dark apart from the orange glow of an oil lamp, which swayed gently above him, its light glinting off the knives and cleavers that swung from nearby hooks.

The kitchen. *But how . . . ?*

"The storm," she said, a hint of annoyance in her soft voice. "There's no electricity. Took ages to find matches in here. Your Mrs. Rollo had her own way of hiding things in here, she did."

"Mrs. . . . oh!" The moment he spoke a spike of pain stabbed the side of his head.

"Yes, you'll want to relax, sir. I didn't mean to knock you that hard, really I didn't."

"O—Olive?"

"Yes, Mr. Hughes. It's me. It's just old Olive."

"Olive, Olive listen to me . . ."

The pain spread, enveloped him like a shroud. He attempted to sit up but his body would not obey. Something holding him down. Restraints.

"Oh, oh Jesus."

"Now Mr. Hughes," she cooed. Something rattled. "You really ought to relax. I mean it."

"You—you're mad, aren't you?"

Olive laughed a soft, feminine laugh. She sounded like a girl rather than a woman.

"Of course not, don't be daft. I'm only helping, sir. You hired me to help, after all. That's what I do. That's what I've always done."

"For God's sake, woman! You've killed my boy! You've murdered my Ainsley!"

"Oh," Olive said, turning so that the lamplight bathed her face orange. "*That.*"

"He was just thirteen, you mad cow."

"He was a monstrous little beast and you know it, dear-heart."

Cecil choked on a sob. "You . . . yuh-you . . ."

"You mutter while you sleep, Mr. Hughes, did you know that? I've spent long nights sitting in your room, watching you. Listening to you. Dear-heart and my poor Marla and oh, her eyes, her eyes my dear-heart, they're just like yours were." Olive tittered. "You truly are such a sweet little man, sir."

She raised her arm and the knife in her hand sparkled in the lamp's wavering glow. She regarded the long, narrow blade lovingly.

"No, Olive—no, you mustn't . . ."

"Mr. Hughes, I should like to call you Cecil."

"Please, girl, please . . ."

"May I do that, sir? May I call you Cecil?"

"Yes—Jesus, yes! Anything you like, Olive. Just please, *please* think about what you are doing . . ."

"I want to tell you something, Cecil. It's really rather important, so listen to me when I tell it to you. Is that all right?"

"Oh, my god," he cried. "Jesus Christ!"

"Cecil," Olive said firmly as she approached him with the knife still held aloft. "You are *not* listening to me."

"I will," he murmured. "I will, Olive. I'll listen."

He did not continue speaking. But he did begin to quietly cry.

"I want you to know this: I am not your wife. I am not your Marla. I never knew her and I have never had anything to do with her. Do you understand so far?"

With a juddering sob, Cecil nodded weakly.

"I came down to Dorset to help, Cecil. All I ever wanted was to help somebody. And by Jesus I have, God knows I have. But what I did not come here for was to replace your dead, god-damned wife. I am not her and I never shall be, and damn my eyes!"

With a swift, fluid motion she brought the knife up and Cecil squeezed his eyes shut, readying himself for the attack. Olive moaned horribly, her voice deep and wet. But the attack did not come. He listened in the dark to her wretched burbling and for an instant he wondered when the pain would commence, and why he could not feel it now.

When he opened his eyes again and blinked his vision clear he focused up at the deranged maid and gasped at the ghastly mess she had made of herself. Her left eye was a dribbling, bloody wreck. The knife dripped blood, oozed with white pieces of the eye she was busily carving out of her own face even as she groaned in agony. Cecil's head throbbed, his wakefulness wavered. He felt as though he might fall unconscious, but the thought of it terrified him sufficiently enough to fight the faint back. So instead he watched. He watched with mute horror as his maid, the murderer of his only son, finished cutting out her eye.

Her marvelous, beautiful steel grey eye.

And almost naturally, when she was done with that and took a moment to roll her head around on her shoulders and cry out like some tortured spirit, Olive wiped each side of the blade on her blouse and set to destroying her remaining eye.

Cecil babbled so incoherently he could not even understand himself. The nightmare was too much for him, finally. He could very nearly feel his mind breaking, hear the last sane thoughts pass through his brain before madness took root.

"No, no, no, no," he went on and on. "No no no no no no no ..."

The second eye came apart and out more quickly and efficiently than the first. Still, Olive shrieked dreadfully, her voice shrill and very loud. Her face was now awash in red, her eyes nothing more than dark, deep pits.

She screamed for what seemed to Cecil like hours. He gawped and babbled all the while. Gradually, her voice broke, quieted, and she dropped the knife to the floor with a jarring clatter. She staggered backward, knocked against a countertop and turned over a small stack of tins. A sticky sob spilled out of her mouth. In seconds it transformed into a sort of giggling.

"Now," she said, her voice raw and ugly, "no one has Marla's eyes."

#

The days passed slowly. She brought him bread and biscuits found with groping hands in the larder. Later came a bottle of port. She wrapped dishrags about her eyes in lieu of bandages. She refused to unbind Cecil, and he stopped asking her to do so.

Along the third day Olive began to sing whatever she said. She did not speak much, but when she did it was in a warbling, off-key croon.

"Olive has no eyes to see," she trilled. "She'll never see the sparkly sea."

Upon the end of the fifth day she disrobed and jammed her blood-soaked garments in the bin. She stood naked before Cecil, softly ran her fingertip up the length of his arm, and asked, "Do you still see, Cecil? Do you see me?"

He did not reply. She grunted and left the kitchen. She did not return for two days.

Cecil remained strapped to the table. He soiled himself and there was nothing at all to be done about it.

Upon Olive's return, she did not speak (or sing) for a full day. She remained entirely naked apart from the filthy rags on her face, black with dried, fetid blood. Whenever Cecil made a sound, she hit him on the face. The bread she gave him was mouldy. He ate it anyway.

He was given no water or wine at all.

He grew weak. Then, ill.

The kitchen reeked of sweat and faeces, piss and sweat.

Time lost all meaning to him. He did not know if the electricity was ever restored because Olive kept the kitchen dark. She no longer needed the light.

One day—or night—perhaps weeks after she carved out her eyes, Olive came into the kitchen with the lamp dangling from one hand and a curious object in the other. She had grown quite skilled at navigating the house with no eyes to see, never to see the sparkly sea. Cecil was suitably impressed.

She approached him where he lay strapped down, stinking wretchedly and shaking like a man possessed, and held the object up in the lamplight for him to see. It was a human skull, the bone scored with cross-hatching marks from top to bottom from whatever she had used to scrape away the tissue. There remained still patches of leathery brown skin, a few sprigs of hair on the crown, but all in all Cecil adjudged her work to be exemplary.

He told her so. She spat in his face.

"It's Ainsley, you know," she sang.

Cecil grinned, a rivulet of saliva running down his cheek.

"I know."

She left it on the countertop beside the burning lamp where he could see it and left. He studied it closely, eyes narrowed to slits. It did not look a thing like his boy. It did not look like Ainsley at all. Cecil erupted into laughter and he laughed for a long time.

Days crawled by like slugs in the garden. Olive had not come back, not even to feed him mouldy bread. He had taken to dry heaving several times a day. He realised there was no sensation at all in his legs and he wondered about it absently.

The line that marked the difference between slumber and wakefulness, previous so clearly demarcated, dissolved entirely. Thus when Marla came to visit him, Cecil was in no way surprised to see her.

"My dear-heart," she whispered. "You really ought to have known better."

"Certainly," Cecil agreed.

"Many women have eyes as gray as mine. Millions, I'd wager."

"Millions."

"A woman is more than her eyes."

"Much more," he said. "So much more."

"You should have known better."

"I should have."

Marla smiled a sweetly familiar smile, small and sharply upturned at the corners of her pink mouth, and bent over to administer a kiss to Cecil's cheek. Into his ear she whispered, "The cow is dead, you know."

"Olive?"

"She fell down the steps, just the other day. She is at the bottom now, dead as a doornail. Dead as that cat. Dead as Ainsley. Dead as me."

"Heavens," Cecil said.

"Why, everybody in this horrid house is dead now."

"Mrs. Rollo."

"Yes, her as well."

"And me? What about me?"

"Silly dear-heart," Marla laughed. "You are dead too, of course."

Cecil smiled. "Of course," he said.

She cocked her head to the side and looked at him adoringly. He closed his eyes and she climbed up onto the table, laid down beside him. He floated into a dream.

When he awoke next, she was gone.

Marfin was shaking his shoulders, shouting close to his face.

"Mr. Hughes, my god, my god, Mr. Hughes," the gardener bellowed.

"Quiet, you stupid dool," Cecil said. "Dool? I meant fool. You, I mean. You're the fool."

"Christ *Jesus*, Mr. Hughes, what's happened?"

"Why did I say *dool?*" Cecil wondered aloud. He squinted and turned to look across at the countertop. The skull was still there, but the lamp had long burned itself out. He then looked up at the ceiling, at the knives and cleavers suspended above him. The electricity was back on. *Well*, Cecil thought, *thank goodness for that.*

"Dead, Mr. Hughes! All of 'em, dead!"

Cecil frowned. "Don't be so bloody stupid, Marfin. We're *all* dead, aren't we? Is this not hell?"

"I rang for the police afore I come in here, Mr. Hughes. They'll be here . . . oh, but Jesus!"

Marfin fell to tearing away the ropes that bound Cecil to the table, gone stiff from the mess he'd made and ripping away from his clothes at places. Shouting erupted from elsewhere in the house. Marfin cried out, "Here, we're in here!"

Moments later a storm of pounding footsteps thundered toward them and a trio of smartly uniformed Bobbies burst into the kitchen. They formed a phalanx, Olive at the point with a shiny black nightstick in her hand and at her rear Mrs. Rollo and young Master Ainsley. All three of them grimaced menacingly, their eyes glittering with hate.

"A right rotten mess you're in, Mr. Hughes," Olive said in a faux deep voice. "You shan't talk your way out of this one."

"Blimey, you're a beast," said Ainsley.

Mrs. Rollo blew the whistle that hung from a chain round her neck.

Cecil sneered, glanced over to Marfin who was just about done plucking his eyes out with his thumbs. "Nothing to see here," he said.

"Ridiculous," Cecil said.

"Just," Marfin concurred.

Cecil shook his head disapprovingly, closed his eyes and his ears and his mind. Some time later, hours or days, he opened up again and was alone. His stomach ached and his neck felt bruised. He blinked in the darkness and listened to himself breathe. It sounded like crinkling paper, or dead leaves.

Not long afterward Olive did come back. She padded softly to the lamp, poured some more oil into it, and lighted the wick. Cecil watched passively as the flame grew and threw light on Olive and the skull on the countertop. There were small back insects crawling over the skull, their interest directed primarily at the scraps of rotted flesh that still clung to the bone.

"I'm sorry, Mr. Hughes," Olive said sheepishly. "I tried cleaning the windows in the study—them in the parlour's broken up, you remember—but I can't do it. I'm no good to you blind."

"It's all right, Olive."

"I expect you'll want to sack me, then."

"Poor girl."

She let out a small, shivering cry and ran her hands down the length of her nude body. Her skin was dirty, oily, riddled with little cuts and bruises. A substantial amount of blood stained her thighs, spread out from the tangled dark V of her groin.

"I'll just lie me down a spell, if you don't begrudge me that, sir."

"Yes."

"Just a short kip."

"It'll do you good."

Just as Marla had done in his waking dream, Olive climbed up beside him and draped a leg and an arm over his bound body. She purred like a kitten and Cecil decided it was rather nice even as she finally plunged the blade between two of the ribs on his left side. It sank in neatly and his side went hot and wet. She left it in, stuck in up to the hilt, and pulled in closer, nuzzling her nose against his neck.

"Good night, sir," she rasped into his ear.

Minutes later she was softly snoring.

Cecil shut his eyes and remembered her eyes as they were. Grey and cool and knowing and intelligent, impossible to lie to, impossible not to adore. He remembered her when she was well and when she was pink and warm with life; he remembered her big as the Durdle Door, gravid with unborn Ainsley for whom the hopes of their whole world rested. He recalled her words both scolding and kind, her voice never raised, her attitude always noble, her intentions always good. He thought of telling her once he would one day write a book just for her, no one else would ever be allowed to read it, and his eyes clouded over because he knew he never would fulfill that promise since he was dying now.

He said, "I love you, Marla. I love you so very much."

And as the blood leaked out inside of him, Cecil Hughes exhaled a mawkish breath and went to sleep forever.

The Liar

BY LAURA LEE BAHR

The innocence of youth is such a tenuous thing. We tend to cherish it in our children, and try to preserve it as long as possible, even though grown-up prevailing wisdom says that it's utterly useless once real life gets down to business.

Of course, the business of very young children is to try to make sense of the world they've fallen into. They're hungry to learn and impulsively eager to trust anyone who might help them decipher life's riddles.

The child inside Laura Lee Bahr has not forgotten what it was like before we knew, nor does she soft-pedal the painful gnosis to come. What we get in this story, with remarkable purity, is the wide-eyed moment of impact itself.

And I'd be lying if I said it doesn't hurt.

Boiled beets. Mashed potatoes from a box. Ground hamburger mixed with vegetable soup from a can. They all fold their arms and close their eyes. Dad gives the blessing.

Topaz opens her eyes just a peek. Ruby is staring right at her, through her.

Topaz quickly shut shuts her eyes and keeps them tight.

Amen.

Mom puts the mashed potatoes on a plate, the beets on the side. She scoops the vegetable and hamburger mix on to the mashed potatoes. It is one of Topaz' favorite meals. Lavender and Lily start to complain to each other that the beets make their mashed potatoes pink and they don't want them touching each other. Dad makes the point that they all end up mixing in their stomachs anyway.

Dad asks about school, and the twins are telling a story about what happened during lunch. There is something wrong with Ruby, but there is always something wrong with Ruby. She is always in trouble at school. She is always making trouble at home.

Topaz is afraid that she might let slip what Ruby told her not to let slip about sneaking out last night. She is afraid because sometimes she says the wrong thing without knowing and then Ruby will sit near her in the dark and tell her, like a bedtime story starts, how what she did was the wrong thing and how she should have known. And sometimes the punishment comes then, a pinch so hard that Topaz screams into the pillow—or worse, the punishment that comes later. The time her hamster disappeared—that was the worst. Ruby said she had nothing to do with it, but there was a glint in her eye and a sidewise wink that told Topaz otherwise. She had cried, and she would have told all, but Ruby told her Cocoa Puff wasn't dead yet, and she could bring her back to life if Topaz was sorry now, and never crossed Ruby again. Thankful, so thankful, Topaz said yes yes yes and please please and never again and Cocoa Puff had appeared back in her cage that next morning like magic.

But something is wrong with Mom, too. Her words come choked and with sighs in between. Topaz doesn't mind the beets bleeding into the potatoes. She likes that they turn pink and she is mixing it all around on her plate when Mom suddenly says, very loud and clear, "You all know that you must never, never get into anyone's car, or go anywhere with anybody unless it's me or Daddy, right?"

Lavender and Lily look to each other then back to Mom. They nod.

Topaz nods.

Only Ruby keeps eating like it's nothing and says, "What about Uncle Gerald? Or Aunt Jess?"

"Well, that's different," Dad says.

"Or what if it's a teacher from school?" Ruby continues.

"Well, I'm not sure why you would be riding with your teacher, but if it were something where the school knew about it, then…," Dad was saying but Ruby just cuts him off.

"What if it's someone from the Church?" Ruby says and then stops chewing and looks at him directly. She knows how to make everyone stop and look, for sure, and the whole table does. There's something in it that makes Dad look uncomfortable.

"Well, you shouldn't be taking rides from anyone, Ruby, but it isn't you we are worried about, anyway."

"Yeah, probably be just as glad to get rid of me," she says under her breath.

"No, no, of course not! You have to be careful, too, Ruby," Mom says, "but the people that this monster is taking are much younger than you. He's taking children. Little kids. Eight year olds. Seven year olds, the last one." And here Mom chokes on the next words and they come out as a sob: "The last one was five."

And then everyone turns and looks at Topaz. She is six. Lily and Lavender are twelve. Ruby is sixteen. Topaz is the baby. She likes being the baby.

She knows just what to say. "I don't ever talk to strangers," she utters with her best brave face.

Her mom smiles as tears run down her face. "I know, baby, I know," she says, and she leaves her seat to rush over and hug Topaz, and she keeps on crying.

Ruby sits on the end of Topaz' bed. Topaz has to share the room with Ruby. Ruby sneaks out all the time, and sometimes Topaz has heard a knock at the window. She would be so afraid that it was a ghost or a monster, but it would be one of Ruby's boyfriends tapping. There was Dale—the bad one—she didn't like. He was mean. He hurt animals. And he liked to pick on Topaz, with Ruby's approval. Or sometimes Jeff, who was okay and would bring her little pieces of candy some-times, but he hadn't been around for a while. Ruby would leave with the boy when he came and tap tap tapped on the window, and Topaz usually would try to pretend she didn't wake up and she had never been afraid it was a ghost or a monster.

Sometimes Ruby would come back all giggly and smelling strange. Sometimes she would wake Topaz and hug her, sometimes crying, sometimes she would say, "Oh, my little sister, my sweet sweet little sister, I would kill kill kill anyone who hurt you. You know that, right?"

Topaz doesn't know that. Sometimes she thinks Ruby would kill her, herself.

Now Ruby sits on the bed, this night, and is combing Topaz' hair. It feels nice. Topaz is scared—she is always scared when Ruby is nice—but she tries to act like Ruby is always nice.

"Poor Mom," says Ruby. "She just can't understand that there could be such a beast right under her nose. Do you want to know what he did?"

Topaz doesn't want to know but she says, "Yes."

"Well, there are four missing children, but they found the body of the five year old. The last one he took. He raped the kid, and then strangled her, and threw her body in a ditch. And I could tell you more gory details but I'll spare your innocent ears."

"My ears aren't innocent," Topaz says.

Ruby pinches one, not hard, but Topaz still yelps. "Baby," says Ruby. "Do you know what rape is?"

Topaz doesn't know. "Yes," she says. She doesn't want Ruby to tell her.

Ruby laughs. "You don't know. But I do. I know. But it's not something I could tell you. Telling you wouldn't really tell you." She has finished combing Topaz' hair. She pulls Topaz into a hug. Her voice is calm and soothing, but Topaz feels freezing cold, like her insides are prickling. "Mom is crying because Mom doesn't know who it is, or how to protect you from it. But I do."

"You do?" says Topaz, because she can tell Ruby is waiting for her to say something.

"Yes. I know who it is, Topaz. I know who is killing the children."

"Who?"

Ruby remains quiet for a minute.

"Who?" Topaz asks again.

"Do you want to see?"

Topaz follows Ruby down the stairs on her softest feet. First toes, then slowly the heel, then lift the next leg, first toes, then the heel, lift next leg… creep creep quietly. She knows how to creep this quiet because Ruby had taught her the hard way. If she was sneaking something for Ruby—money from Mom's purse—if she made noise, if she got caught, Ruby would punish her. Now she knows how to be silent, and she follows Ruby like a shadow.

'I have a little shadow that goes in and out with me.' Topaz likes to tell herself poems she knows in her head to keep herself from shaking, from slipping up. The poem makes her feel like this is an adventure she is having now, with Ruby. Ruby is taking her into her confidence. Ruby is looking after her like big sisters are supposed to do. And maybe, sometime very soon, Ruby might realize that she really likes Topaz. That she likes telling her things. And what a good help Topaz is.

'And I see him jump before me, when I jump into my bed,' the poem continues in her head. They are sisters after all, and sisters like each other. They are alike and they like each other. Like and alike. Topaz says those words in her head.

Down down the stairs and far to the end of the hall. Then more stairs. Most times no one goes down there. Topaz isn't feeling like and alike any more, now that they are closer. Topaz doesn't like the basement. There were mice in there, she knew. When she went in there—in the daytime only would she go—she might see one scurry away. That wasn't so bad. They looked sort of like a distant cousin of Cocoa Puff, but she was scared of the mice for some reason even though she wasn't scared of Cocoa Puff. But worse, sometimes she had seen a little mouse dead in one of the traps Dad set out with peanut butter for bait. Ruby always threatened this—one day, she would set Cocoa Puff loose in the basement, and he would go straight to the peanut butter and SNAP.

She follows down and down, in the dark, her eyes adjust but still only seeing the shapes of things. The kitchen. The steps. Then the basement. Now that they are far enough away from the rooms where everyone is sleeping, Ruby turns on a flashlight. She puts the light underneath her chin, like the way she likes to tell ghost stories. "Don't get too close," she says. Then Ruby opens the basement door very slowly.

Topaz can barely let herself think it, but she thinks Ruby might have been lying. Ruby likes to scare people and Topaz expects—somewhere where she couldn't say it, but somewhere—that maybe it is nothing. Just a joke. Ruby is going to scare her or punish her ... but now the door creeps open and Topaz can see inside her heart that she hopes Ruby is lying. She prays in her head that Ruby is lying.

The basement is pitch black inside.

Topaz grabs the folds of Ruby's nightgown, holding the fabric close. The light shines revealing cans of jellies, canned beets, pickles, a huge tub of grain, and then next to it, on the ground, a figure is tied up—silver tape on his mouth—blood on his face and an open blue eye that stares right into the light.

Topaz screams. Then her head goes quick into the wall with Ruby's fist and a hand covers her mouth.

"Shut up right now or I'll feed you to him," Ruby hisses.

Topaz tastes the dirt on Ruby's hand. She tastes the salt and sweat—it wasn't sweet—it tastes bad, Ruby's hand—and it is over and in her mouth, and Topaz knows she can bite that hand but she would never bite—never dare—and the monster with the one blue eye—the light isn't shining on him anymore and he is just there in the dark.

"Get out of here, you little baby," Ruby says after taking her hand away.

Topaz doesn't care about the sound. She runs away as fast as she can—up the stairs through the dark—through the kitchen in the dark up the stairs to her room—the one they share, in the dark, and she hides under the covers.

'I have a little shadow,' she thinks to try and stop it, but not the poem now, now, not the shadow. Now the shadow scares her, too. 'I see it jump before me as I jump into my bed.' Not in the bed. They will find her in the bed. Under the bed. They wouldn't look there.

She hides under the bed, her eyes focus on the door and she waits. Waiting for Ruby to come back. She breathes and counts her breaths. Cocoa Puff is running on his wheel, he doesn't know. Doesn't know about the basement and the snap! of the trap.

Topaz listens to the sounds as he runs and runs. Any second Ruby will come back and snatch him, take poor Cocoa Puff and feed him to the trap or worse. Feed him to the beast. The one blue eye. But Ruby doesn't come back. And Topaz shuts her eyes beneath the bed and falls asleep.

It is Sunday, and Ruby looks happy to be at Church, for once. She gives Topaz a strange smile. Something bad would happen for sure. Lavender and Lily look nervous, too. Something bad is about to happen, or has already happened, when Ruby is in a good mood like that. Mom keeps holding Topaz tight to her, and Topaz buries herself in her mother's arms, in her neck and chest. She breathes in the smell of her mother. She tries to climb on her mom's lap during Sacrament meeting, something she hasn't done for a long time now, and Mom lets her for a few minutes then put her back down beside her.

"You're too big, baby," Mom whispers in her ear.

Ruby isn't looking at her. Ruby is watching Bishop Farnington speak as if she is interested in what he is saying. But none of the girls are fooled. Ruby doesn't believe anything the Church says. Ruby doesn't believe in the Church, or the Prophet, or in angels, or even in God. She has told all of her sisters so, laughing at their shocked expressions. She has told them they are all fools and blind to believe and they will find out for themselves, soon enough. So her expression now, her interest in every word that the Bishop says, means that something very bad has happened. Something very, very bad.

After Church is over, they all walk back to the car, and Ruby grabs Topaz's hand and pulls her from the hand of her mother. Mom watches and smiles as Ruby pulls Topaz into a hug and Mom moves to put things in the car. Just Ruby and Topaz for a moment.

"Did you notice," Ruby whispers into her ear, "that Brother Johnson wasn't there?"

Topaz scarcely knows who Brother Johnson is, and she isn't sure whether the correct response is a yes or no, so she says nothing.

"Do you know why he isn't there?" Ruby asks.

Topaz shakes her head.

"Because, silly. He's in the basement!"

It is Quiet Time, the time after Church, when they're all supposed to reflect, pray, read scriptures. More often than not, it is when Daddy would nap and they might sneak off to watch TV.

Lavender and Lily are in the room next door, giggling to themselves about some boys they liked. "He likes you"—"No, he likes *you!*" Back and forth like a song.

Ruby is putting curlers into her hair.

Topaz clutches her favorite doll and pretends to read her illustrated Bible stories.

She tries to ignore Ruby, who sometimes talked like this—long speeches to herself, only indirectly involving Topaz and mostly not wanting a response at all.

"I played with him all night. Teasing him. It was kind of fun, but not really fun, if you know what I mean. Nevermind. Of course, you don't. Such a little baby. Baby, baby, baby. He likes that. He likes babies who don't know better. Babies he can overpower. He's a coward and a weakling, really. He doesn't like big girls like me. He likes little girls like you. Or boys who don't know. He likes to trick them. But I tricked him. That's how I got him. And I tricked him all night long. I would pretend I might let him go. Or I would pretend I might call the cops. Or I would pretend I might kiss him. And then I would hurt him. And he's too scared to scream. He can't scream because if they find him, then they'll know."

Then it is silent. Topaz looks up to see Ruby looking at herself in the mirror, a strange smile on her face that makes Topaz want to scream. She isn't sure who she is more scared of: Ruby, with that smile, or that thing in the basement. What if it gets out?

"How long will he be in the basement?" Topaz asks, her voice a whisper.

Ruby shrugs. "Not sure. I can't keep him there forever, of course. I guess I will have to finish with him tomorrow, or the next day, and then ask Dale to help me get rid of him."

"Get rid of him?"

"We will have to do something with the body. I got some ideas."

"You're going to . . ." Topaz isn't sure what word she is looking for. She isn't sure what Ruby means exactly. She can't mean that. . . . "You're going to *kill* him?"

Ruby starts to laugh. "Yes, silly. Of course."

"But—"

"What?"

"But—"

"What?"

Topaz can't think. She doesn't know how to say what she needs to say. "Shouldn't you tell Mom and Dad?" This is what she finally arrives at.

Ruby really laughs now. Like Topaz has never heard her laugh. Like maybe she said something genuinely funny. Topaz starts to smile a little, too, because if she has said something funny, she wants to seem like she did it on purpose.

"No, silly. No telling Mom and Dad, and I don't have to tell you, of course, that you can't tell anyone or Cocoa Puff is straight to the mice, you know. Or worse. I'll feed *you* to *him*."

"The man who wasn't at Church? Who is he?"

"Brother Johnson. You know, the one who is always smiling at you."

Topaz thought hard. Who was always smiling at her? She doesn't remember anyone always smiling at her. Wouldn't she remember that? He must really like her.

"You're going to kill him?" she asks.

"He deserves it! Baby, you don't know what terrible, terrible things he did to those poor kids. You don't know how many more kids he would do it to if I hadn't got him. Trapped him. And now I'm going to kill him so he can't hurt another poor baby like you ever again. Don't look like that. It's a good thing. I'm actually doing something good and right here, Topaz. Honestly. It's a good thing."

Topaz thinks about "good" and "right."

Good and Right.

How can Ruby be trusted with good and right? Wasn't that something for the authorities to know? If not her parents? Topaz wants to do what's good and right, too.

"Shouldn't you give him to the police?"

Ruby sighs. "You don't understand things. You're just a kid. Anyway, I'm gonna take care of it because otherwise it won't get taken care of. Trust me, I know. The people in this town, they don't listen. They don't see. They don't care until it's too late. So, you know sometimes as Dad says, if you want something done right you have to do it yourself."

Topaz stares at her sister.

Ruby stretches and yawns. "I'm tired," she says. "Like I said, I didn't sleep at all last night."

Topaz stares.

"So get out of here," Ruby says. "I don't want you, like, all watching me as I sleep. Go watch some TV or something, creep. Get out of here."

Topaz sits in the living room all alone, the cartoons on with the volume down low. Just through the kitchen, down the stairs, down the hall, down the stairs…he is there. She doesn't remember who he is, but *"always smiling at you"* keeps going around and around like a bit of a poem, and in her mind she can see a face like Santa Claus, a blue eye twinkling at her, and then that blue eye in the basement, when the light hit it. Almost like Aurora in *Sleeping Beauty*, when the evil witch calls her into the castle, hypnotized, that's how Topaz feels.

"I'm hypnotized," part of her mind says, as the other plays, "always smiling at you always smiling at you." She sees in her mind that blue twinkling Santa Claus eye with that bloody blue eye of the Beast as the light hits it.

And she is at the basement door.

It is Sunday. It is daylight. She isn't scared of things in the day. Except Ruby. But Ruby is asleep now and Ruby sleeps deep and Ruby snores, and sometimes it seems impossible to wake her, especially in the day. Topaz knows Ruby is deep asleep, just like she is hypnotized by the always-smiling-at-you bloody Santa Claus eye.

She opens the door. It makes a little creak.

The basement is dark, still, even in the day, but she can see him from here.

He has his pants down now, his long white underwear showing, and bloody. Arms and legs tied behind him. He is sleeping, too, the creak from the door not enough to wake him. Bloody and all his clothes ripped.

Brother Johnson.

He still doesn't look familiar, but it is strange to see a man with his clothes all ripped, tied up in a weird way, eyes closed. There is no tape on his mouth anymore. His mouth is open, wheezing with breath. His face around his mouth raw and red.

It smells in there, now, like poop and pee and like Ruby, too. That weird Ruby smell she sometimes has when she comes home late at night.

Topaz gets closer now, and closer. Very close, so she can see his face.

He has two huge bruises around his eyes, all purple and yellow and black, and his head is bloody.

No, he doesn't look like anyone, not anyone she knows. Not Brother Johnson "always smiling at you."

"Brother Johnson?" she whispers, scared, like when they say *Bloody Mary* in the mirror.

He doesn't wake up. Was Ruby lying? Ruby lies all the time, she reminds herself. Sometimes big lies, sometimes small lies. Is this Brother Johnson? Was there a Brother Johnson at all?

There is a broom in the corner of the basement. She gets the broom and then softly, softly—she doesn't want to hurt him—pokes his belly; which is white and poochy and covered in light brown hair.

His eyes open. Well, one does while the other tries to open, but it is crusted shut.

That poor blue eye. She doesn't know how she could have been scared of that poor blue eye. It looks so sad now, like it might cry at her, standing there with the broom. Does she recognize that twinkle of an eye? Did that eye ever twinkle at her?

He is wriggling the best he can, making grunting "Help me" noises from his mouth. Then he stops and stares.

Poor Blue Eye.

"Hello, Topaz," he says. His voice is soft and sweet, like a kind of song.

"Hello. Brother Johnson?"

"Yes. You have it right, little Topaz. Hi there. Hi." He makes it sound like it is nothing at all, him here like this. Like they might have been merely walking down the street or something. So this is Brother Johnson, a man she doesn't remember but is always smiling at her.

So, then Ruby wasn't lying. It is *him*. And this man is a murderer. The kind who makes her mom cry. She stays where she is with the broom. This man is a monster then, who would eat her. She mustn't be stupid. She must be smart. She can scream any second now. And she knows how to scream loud.

"Don't be scared," he says. "I know I look scary, but don't be scared of me." He tries to smile with a broken mouth and Topaz doesn't yelp. She is scared, but she is brave.

"Little Topaz," he says from his cracking mouth. "I need you to help me. It's very important. It's life or death, you have to help me."

Topaz shakes her head.

"No?" he says.

Topaz shakes her head again.

"No," he says. He coughs, blood coming out of his mouth. "No," he says again. Then: "And why, might I ask, would you—a little girl who I know is a very sweet and a good little girl—not help someone who is truly in danger?"

Topaz likes this. There is something fun in this. He says it like a sing-song, like a game. And she is the one with all the pieces. She is the one who will say who wins.

"Because," she says, with her best serious face that she knows makes the adults coo, "you are a bad man. Because you kill children." She is right.

But then after she says it, she isn't so sure. He did something with his face. It was strange because his face is bloody, his face is all scary looking anyway, but he did something with his face when she said that, something that looked like "no no no no" like a scream, but he didn't make any sound at all. Just his face moved like that. She isn't so sure she should have said that. It hurt him.

"Have you ever heard the story, Topaz, about the Liars and the Truth-tellers?" He has a very nice voice, a voice people like to hear talk for long times. Topaz remembers his voice now. The stories. He sometimes stopped in on Sunday School and told Bible stories so you could almost see them like they were movies. He had a nice voice, and he liked jokes and riddles. Now she remembers. "Always smiling at you." Yes. Always smiling. She liked his stories.

Topaz shakes her head. She hasn't heard this story.

Brother Johnson tells her:

"A man is on his way to an important meeting in Happyland, where he has never been before. It is very exciting that he has been asked to this meeting. But he is also a bit . . . apprehensive. That means scared. He is a little scared, Topaz, because he knows from very reliable sources that the way to Happyland is treacherous—and that means dangerous. He knows that there are two towns along the way, in opposite directions. One town is a town called Liarsville. And one is a town is called Truthstown. Now, in Liarsville, which leads to a dark boggy pit, the people can only tell lies. They cannot say anything but lies. The other way—which leads straight to Happyland, is Truthville and there, people only can tell the truth.

"The man comes to a fork in the road and must go in one. He sees a traveler coming from each direction—one must be coming from Liarsville, the other from Truthstown. He stops one and says, 'Please- tell me, which is the way to Happyland?' 'This way,' she says pointing from where she came from. 'Oh, don't listen to her!' says the traveler from the other direction. 'She's from Liarsville and can only tell lies! This is the way to Happyland—this way!'"

Brother Johnson stops for a moment with the story, so Topaz can think about the puzzle placed before her. Topaz is worried. Which is the way? Who of the travelers is telling the truth? He coughs again.

"So, how do you know, Topaz, how do you know which way is the way you can go? Who can you trust?"

Topaz answers honestly. "I don't know," she says.

He starts coughing more. A bad cough. It looks like it hurts him.

She doesn't say "Are you okay?" though. She knows she has to wait.

She sits down on the cold basement floor. It is cold against her. He must be cold. He is a bad man, Ruby says. A very bad man. But right now he doesn't seem bad. Right now, she feels very bad for him.

"There's a trick to it," he says, after he finishes coughing, his voice sounding like it hurts him, but finding the sing-song again. "Ask the traveler who just spoke to you, 'wait, did you just say this was the way to Happyland?' if they are the Truth-teller, they will say 'yes!' and you will know it is truth. If they say 'No! I didn't say that!' or any denial, you know that they are the liar. Does that make sense?"

Topaz nods, but she says, "I don't know."

Topaz likes it now, saying she doesn't know. It makes her feel wise in some way. And as she says it, Brother Johnson, or the beast which ever he was, looks a little more scared, a little more pained. She had never seen anyone scared of her, least of all a full-grown man. She'd been scared plenty. Is this what she looked like? Is this how Ruby felt?

"I am going to give you a question to ask her, Topaz. Wait for her answer. And then ask her again. Then you will know. It may not be as simple as the puzzle, but I believe that the little girl who I have seen in Sunday school; who is so sweet that she loves to talk about her hamster—Cocoa Malt?—is that your hamster's name?"

"Cocoa Puff" Topaz says, astounded. He knows her hamster! He knows her, then, better than most, better than most anyone outside the family.

"Cocoa Puff. A sweet girl that loves little Cocoa Puff that much, a hamster, will do what she can to save the life of an innocent man. Ask her, your sister, this question, ask again, and then you will know."

One blue eye open, the other sealed shut. She feels so sorry for him. She thinks of Aslan, in the *Lion and the Witch and the Wardrobe*, tied up by the White Witch and tortured. She doesn't want to help the White Witch. Except that a lion could eat her in one *snap!* with his jaws and she would be like the mouse in the trap.

"Ask her how she knew," he says

"How she knew what?"

"Ask her how she knew that it was me. That I did the terrible things you and she have accused me of. Killing . . . children. Ask her how she knows that. Let her tell you, and then repeat back what she said and ask her if its true. She will say no. And that is how you will know she is a liar."

Topaz' brain feels very fuzzy all of the sudden. She is very cold. She can see blood on the edge of Brother Johnson's lips as he starts to cough again. She thinks of Cocoa Puff in the trap. She feels like she might vomit.

"Then again," he says, a smile cracking his lips again, "maybe you already know, Topaz. Maybe you already know who is the Liar and who is the Truth-teller. You have seen me in Sunday School, you have sat on my lap and I have told you stories from the Bible. Have I ever been anything but good? And your sister, has she ever been anything but bad?"

She stares at him.

"Sweet little Topaz, untie me."

She inches closer to him.

"I almost have this one behind my hands- if you can just- use those little fingers to un-do this knot—just help me to loosen it."

She is closer—she can smell him, she can smell Ruby, she can see he is breathing faster now, his belly up and down. And she is frightened—very frightened, the blood on his mouth, she thinks of the fairy tale and big mouth *"The better to eat you with, my dear!"*

She hears it in her head like a call ringing and ringing in her head, an alarm clock to wake up now, wake up, she is hypnotized like Aurora but the alarm says, *"the bloodier the mouth—the better to eat you!"*

"Come closer," he says. "Help me."

Instead she turns and runs.

It is dark now. They are in bed and there is school tomorrow. Ruby is not asleep. But Topaz is supposed to be. But Ruby knows she is not. It is so quiet. It is so dark.

"I went down there while you were asleep," Topaz says. She is glad to finally tell her. Ruby always knows everything anyway, she might as well tell her before she went down and the beast said.

"Hmm," says Ruby, like it is nothing. "I hope you didn't get too close. I took the tape off his mouth last night. He doesn't have many teeth left, but he can still bite."

"He said you were a liar." Topaz feels brave now. Topaz is going to be clever.

Ruby snorts. "Of course he said that. What else would he say? Do you think he would admit to you all those things he's done? When he wants to do it to you, too?"

Topaz swallows. "How do you know it is him?"

"What?"

"How do you know that he is the one, that he is the one who killed the children?"

Topaz can see Ruby's face lit in the moonlight—half of it—the other half in shadow, her eyes shining like those of a cat.

"I know . . . because . . . I know. That's all."

"Tell me how."

Ruby makes a sound like a half-laugh. "Okay, baby. I'll tell you how."

She tells:

"I know there is a darkness in people who pretend to be light. I know there is blood behind the smiles. I know there is evil cloaked in good. I know that people think I am bad, and perhaps I am. But perhaps they prefer to think me bad and to call me that, than to see that I am a mirror of their hypocrisy. They call me a liar, but they are the liars. I want them to know that I see that they are liars. I want them to see that I SEE their evil with my own." It was like a whip and a spit, her voice, and it finishes sharp. "I want them to hurt."

Ruby clears her throat. And then Ruby begins to speak with a voice Topaz has never heard. It is clear and sweet like a bell, it sounds like she was testifying in Church—which Ruby had never done. It is a pretty sound, and Topaz is taken by it, away with it.

"And hurting they are. For the children are being taken. I know that children were being taken, and it seemed to me so strange in a place that pretends to be a place of God, to have an evil so strong lurking and taking what is sweetest and best. And my heart was heavy with sorrow, and my eyes were laden with tears. And I was down the hill, walking in that patch of trees like I sometimes do, and like the Prophet, I had a vision. You know the story of the Prophet and his first vision, right?"

Topaz nods, though in her bed in the dark, she knows Ruby can't see.

"I had a vision, too. Only the Prophet knelt to pray and asked which church was true, and I knelt to pray and asked how could God let something like this happen? How can He let bad pass as good, and good pass as bad? How can Heavenly Father be so cruel as to let children suffer at the hands of illusion and have their throats torn open by Beasts that masquerade as Brothers? And then I saw a vision. An Angel. An angel with white wings appeared before me and said that God had bestowed me with the power to see—for God did not allow this to happen, but it was the work of the Devil—and I was to be an agent of God, and to find this creature, and slay him. And then the Angel said that he would take me to see where the Beast, which paraded as a man, kept his lair. And the Angel led me, through the woods—and there—I saw the Beast, with the bones of the children. And I knew, then, what I must do."

Topaz knows the story of the Prophet was true. That the Prophet had had a vision, and seen an angel, that people saw angels sometimes—and yes—it made sense that God would want to have this beast slain. But why would Heavenly Father have Ruby do it? Topaz tries to collect her thoughts and keep them straight and put them in order, but they keep wriggling around and becoming slippery and airy. Ice water steam. All the same things in different forms. Which is true? She tries to remember what she was supposed to ask. She tries to remember what she was supposed to do.

"So, you know that he is the Beast because the Angel told you," Topaz says. She is prepared to believe. One must believe when angels appear.

Ruby starts to laugh. Then more laughter. It is mean laughter, not the kind that made Topaz think she had actually said something funny. This made her feel small and tight inside.

"Oh, you stupid, stupid baby," Ruby says. Then she is out of her bed, and she is in Topaz' bed, still with the laughter. She hugs Topaz as she laughs. "You can't believe all that crap that the Church tells you. There aren't any angels."

"But then...how?"

"How what?"

"How do you know?"

"I know because I know."

"How?"

"How?" Ruby is incredulous that Topaz is pressing her on this, or any point.

Ruby releases her from the hug and sits up. But Topaz is more than Topaz ever has been before, and she knows it. Topaz is brave now, and she is figuring things out. She is clever and she is a sweet girl, and she can do what is good and right. She has to keep asking.

"Yes, if not the Angel, if the Angel is a lie ..." and as Topaz says it, she knows. Ruby has just told her that she is a liar. Ruby is the liar! And of course, Topaz has always known that. And perhaps a liar can only lie. Topaz must turn away now, and try and figure out what she could do.

But Ruby surprises her. Ruby puts her arms around Topaz again and holds her close. And Ruby is crying.

Topaz holds her, in return.

Maybe Ruby will let him go, after all.

Ruby whispers in her ear. "I know because he did it to me."

"What?"

"He did to me. Years ago. He did it to me."

Ruby holds her even closer now. And cries and cries. Topaz wants to just let her cry, but she can't because it doesn't fit. "But," says Topaz, into Ruby's cries.

Ruby doesn't hear so Topaz says again, louder, "But Ruby ..."

"What?" Ruby sobs.

"Well, you're alive and the person they are looking for . . . doesn't he kill? Isn't it that he kills children? He kills them."

Ruby pulls back and looks at Topaz. She wipes her eyes.

"Do you think I'm telling you the truth, little Topaz? Do you think I'm lying? Or do you think *he* is lying?"

Topaz thinks Ruby is lying. But should she say? There is something in Ruby's voice that is a threat, now. Should she say? She shouldn't.

"No. Yes. I mean, yes. No." She can't remember the order. She needs to lie for herself, for Cocoa Puff, for . . .

"Which is it?" Ruby asks.

Topaz can't remember the order. She should say, "Yes," she is telling the truth, "No," she is not lying, but which came when? And she doesn't have time with Ruby.

"I don't know," Topaz says.

"No, you don't. And you just better pray to Heavenly Father that you never do."

Ruby leaves Topaz's bed. She blows her nose. She starts moving around like she is going to leave the room.

"Are you going to kill him?" Topaz asks.

Ruby doesn't answer. It is quiet for so long Topaz thinks Ruby might have gone to sleep. But then Ruby leaps over like a panther in the darkness and is next to her, crouched low. Topaz bites her tongue to keep from screaming. Ruby's eyes are shiny and wild in the moonlight. "Do you want me to let him go?"

Topaz stares at her sister. Ruby's mouth is slightly ajar and her teeth are bared. Like she may just bite her face off.

"You say the word, and I'll let him go. Right now. Tonight. I will set him free. I will let him go. You think I am lying? You think he is an okay guy? It is *you* he is after, now. It is *you* he will hurt, now, not me. You want me to let him go?"

Topaz doesn't know what to say. She is biting her tongue. She is not going to say because she doesn't know. What if Ruby lets him go—and Ruby is telling the truth? What if he came and found her then, and hurt her? She saw his bloody mouth—*the better to eat her with*—that bloody blue eye. He kills children—her mother cries—*the last one was five.* Is it him? Did he do it?

Ruby's hands are suddenly around Topaz's face, squeezing her cheeks hard. "Baby, baby, baby. I can kill him or I can let him go. YOU decide. You."

Topaz says nothing, and Ruby keeps squeezing her baby sister's face in together, pressing in on her jaw. Topaz's teeth in her tongue, Ruby's hands printing into her face.

It hurts—it hurts—it hurts—but she knows that it is nothing compared to the Beast—to Brother Johnson—to what Ruby had done to him. Or what the Beast could do to her, to them both, if he were that. If he were the man that did such things.

"You say 'yes,' I let him go. You say, 'no,' he dies tonight. You decide, baby. You. All that power. Life or death. You."

It hurts. It hurts. It hurts. Pressing in. Blood in her mouth now as she bites down on her tongue, fingers hard like claws into her face.

"Yes or no, baby. Yes or no. One or the other. You say, right now."

It hurts.

It hurts.

It hurts.

The Paperhanger

BY WILLIAM GAY

There are few things more shattering than an unsolved crime. There's no closure. No rest. No way to get free of the ghosts, or the hope. Until you go all the way.

William Gay's harsh, ultrarealist, entirely unsentimental Southern Gothic style has allowed critics to invoke both William Faulkner and Flannery O'Connor without looking silly. To me, Jim Thompson's work also comes to mind, in its working-class post–Dust Bowl scar-tissue bleakness.

Let's just call it great, and leave it at that.

The vanishing of the doctor's wife's child in broad daylight was an event so cataclysmic that it forever divided time into the then and the now, the before and the after. In later years, fortified with a pitcher of silica-dry vodka martinis, she had cause to replay the events preceding the disappearance. They were tawdry and banal but in retrospect freighted with menace, a foreshadowing of what was to come, like a footman or a fool preceding a king into a room.

She had been quarreling with the paperhanger. Her four-year-old daughter, Zeineb, was standing directly behind the paperhanger where he knelt smoothing air bubbles out with a wide plastic trowel. Zeineb had her fingers in the paper-hanger's hair. The paperhanger's hair was shoulder length and the color of flax and the child was delighted with it. The paperhanger was accustomed to her doing this and he did not even turn around. He just went on with his work. His arms were smooth and brown and corded with muscle and in the light that fell upon the pa-perhanger through stained-glass panels the doctor's wife could see that they were lightly downed with fine golden hair. She studied these arms bemusedly while she formulated her thoughts.

You tell me so much a roll, she said. The doctor's wife was from Pakistan and her speech was still heavily accented. I do not know single-bolt rolls and double-bolt rolls. You tell me double-bolt price but you are installing single-bolt rolls. My friend has told me. It is cost me perhaps twice as much.

The paperhanger, still on his knees, turned. He smiled up at her. He had pale blue eyes. I did tell you so much a roll, he said. You bought the rolls.

The child, not yet vanished, was watching the paperhanger's eyes. She was a scaled-down clone of the mother, the mother viewed through the wrong end of a telescope, and the paperhanger suspected that as she grew, neither her features nor her expression would alter, she would just grow larger, like something being aired up with a hand pump.

And you are leave lumps, the doctor's wife said, gesturing at the wall.

I do not leave lumps, the paperhanger said. You've seen my work before. These are not lumps. The paper is wet. The paste is wet. Everything will shrink down and flatten out. He smiled again. He had clean even teeth. And besides, he said, I gave you my special cockteaser rate. I don't know what you're complaining about.

Her mouth worked convulsively. She looked for a moment as if he'd slapped her. When words did come they came in a fine spray of spit. You are trash, she said. You are scum.

Hands on knees, he was pushing erect, the girl's dark fingers trailing out of his hair. Don't call me trash, he said, as if it were perfectly all right to call him scum, but he was already talking to her back. She had whirled on her heels and went twisting her hips through an arched doorway into the cathedraled living room. The paperhanger looked down at the child. Her face glowed with a strange constrained glee, as if she and the paperhanger shared some secret the rest of the world hadn't caught on to yet.

In the living room the builder was supervising the installation of a chandelier that depended from the vaulted ceiling by a long golden chain. The builder was a short bearded man dancing about, showing her the features of the chandelier, smiling obsequiously. She gave him a flat angry look. She waved a dismissive hand toward the ceiling. Whatever, she said.

She went out the front door onto the porch and down a makeshift walkway of two-by-tens into the front yard where her car was parked. The car was a silver-gray Mercedes her husband had given her for their anniversary. When she cranked the engine its idle was scarcely perceptible.

She powered down the window. Zeineb, she called. Across the razed earth of the unlandscaped yard a man in a grease-stained T-shirt was booming down the chains securing a backhoe to a lowboy hooked to a gravel truck. The sun was low in the west and bloodred behind this tableau and man and tractor looked flat and dimensionless as something decorative stamped from tin. She blew the horn. The man turned, raised an arm as if she'd signaled him.

Zeineb, she called again.

She got out of the car and started impatiently up the walkway. Behind her the gravel truck started, and truck and backhoe pulled out of the drive and down toward the road.

The paperhanger was stowing away his T square and trowels in his wooden toolbox. Where is Zeineb? the doctor's wife asked. She followed you out, the paperhanger told her. He glanced about, as if the girl might be hiding somewhere. There was nowhere to hide.

Where is my child? she asked the builder. The electrician climbed down from the ladder. The paperhanger came out of the bathroom with his tools. The builder was looking all around. His elfin features were touched with chagrin, as if this missing child were just something else he was going to be held accountable for.

Likely she's hiding in a closet, the paperhanger said. Playing a trick on you.

Zeineb does not play tricks, the doctor's wife said. Her eyes kept darting about the huge room, the shadows that lurked in corners. There was already an undercurrent of panic in her voice and all her poise and self-confidence seemed to have vanished with the child.

The paperhanger set down his toolbox and went through the house, opening and closing doors. It was a huge house and there were a lot of closets. There was no child in any of them.

The electrician was searching upstairs. The builder had gone through the French doors that opened onto the unfinished veranda and was peering into the backyard. The backyard was a maze of convoluted ditch excavated for the septic tank field line and beyond that there was just woods. She's playing in that ditch, the builder said, going down the flagstone steps.

She wasn't, though. She wasn't anywhere. They searched the house and grounds. They moved with jerky haste. They kept glancing toward the woods where the day was waning first. The builder kept shaking his head. She's got to be somewhere, he said.

Call someone, the doctor's wife said. Call the police.

It's a little early for the police, the builder said. She's got to be here.

You call them anyway. I have a phone in my car. I will call my husband.

While she called, the paperhanger and the electrician continued to search. They had looked everywhere and were forced to search places they'd already looked. If this ain't the goddamnedest thing I ever saw, the electrician said.

The doctor's wife got out of the Mercedes and slammed the door. Suddenly she stopped and clasped a hand to her forehead. She screamed. The man with the tractor, she cried. Somehow my child is gone with the tractor man.

Oh Jesus, the builder said. What have we got ourselves into here.

The high sheriff that year was a ruminative man named Bellwether. He stood beside the county cruiser talking to the paperhanger while deputies ranged the grounds. Other men were inside looking in places that had already been searched numberless times. Bellwether had been in the woods and he was picking cockleburs off his khakis and out of his socks. He was watching the woods, where dark was gathering and seeping across the field like a stain.

I've got to get men out here, Bellwether said. A lot of men and a lot of lights. We're going to have to search every inch of these woods.

You'll play hell doing it, the paperhanger said. These woods stretch all the way to Lawrence County. This is the edge of the Harrikin. Down in there's where all those old mines used to be. Allens Creek.

I don't give a shit if they stretch all the way to Fairbanks, Alaska, Bellwether said. They've got to be searched. It'll just take a lot of men.

The raw earth yard was full of cars. Dr. Jamahl had come in a sleek black Lexus. He berated his wife. Why weren't you watching her? he asked. Unlike his wife's, the doctor's speech was impeccable. She covered her face with her palms and wept. The doctor still wore his green surgeon's smock and it was flecked with bright dots of blood as a butcher's smock might be.

I need to feed a few cows, the paperhanger said. I'll feed my stock pretty quick and come back and help hunt.

You don't mind if I look in your truck, do you?

Do what?

I've got to cover my ass. If that little girl don't turn up damn quick this is going to be over my head. TBI, FBI, network news. I've got to eliminate everything.

Eliminate away, the paperhanger said.

The sheriff searched the floorboard of the paperhanger's pickup truck. He shined his huge flashlight under the seat and felt behind it with his hands.

I had to look, he said apologetically.

Of course you did, the paperhanger said.

Full dark had fallen before he returned. He had fed his cattle and stowed away his tools and picked up a six-pack of San Miguel beer and he sat in the back of the pickup truck drinking it. The paperhanger had been in the Navy and stationed in the Philippines and San Miguel was the only beer he could drink. He had to go out of town to buy it, but he figured it was worth it. He liked the exotic labels, the dark bitter taste on the back of his tongue, the way the chilled bottles felt held against his forehead.

A motley crowd of curiosity seekers and searchers thronged the yard. There was a vaguely festive air. He watched all this with a dispassionate eye, as if he were charged with grading the participants, comparing this with other spectacles he'd seen. Coffee urns had been brought in and set up on tables, sandwiches prepared and handed out to the weary searchers. A crane had been hauled in and the septic tank reclaimed from the ground. It swayed from a taut cable while men with lights searched the impacted earth beneath it for a child, for the very trace of a child. Through the fat dark woods lights crossed and recrossed, darted to and fro like fireflies. The doctor and the doctor's wife sat in folding camp chairs looking drained, stunned, waiting for their child to be delivered into their arms.

The doctor was a short portly man with a benevolent expression. He had a moon-shaped face, with light and dark areas of skin that looked swirled, as if the pigment coloring him had not been properly mixed. He had been educated at Princeton. When he had established his practice he had returned to Pakistan to find a wife befitting his station. The woman he had selected had been chosen on the basis of her beauty. In retrospect, perhaps more consideration should have been given to other qualities. She was still beautiful but he was thinking that certain faults might outweigh this. She seemed to have trouble keeping up with her children. She could lose a four-year-old child in a room no larger than six hundred square feet and she could not find it again.

The paperhanger drained his bottle and set it by his foot in the bed of the truck. He studied the doctor's wife's ravaged face through the deep blue light. The first time he had seen her she had hired him to paint a bedroom in the house they were living in while the doctor's mansion was being built. There was an arrogance about her that cried out to be taken down a notch or two. She flirted with him, backed away, flirted again. She would treat him as if he were a stain on the bath-room rug and then stand close by him while he worked until he was dizzy with the smell of her, with the heat that seemed to radiate off her body. She stood by him while he knelt painting baseboards and after an infinite moment leaned carefully the weight of a thigh against his shoulder. You'd better move it, he thought. She didn't. He laughed and turned his face into her groin. She gave a strangled cry and slapped him hard. The paintbrush flew away and speckled the dark rose walls with antique white. You filthy beast, she said. You are some kind of monster. She stormed out of the room and he could hear her slamming doors behind her.

Well, I was looking for a job when I found this one. He smiled philosophically to himself.

But he had not been fired. In fact now he had been hired again. Perhaps there was something here to ponder.

At midnight he gave up his vigil. Some souls more hardy than his kept up the watch. The earth here was worn smooth by the useless traffic of the searchers. Driving out, he met a line of pickup trucks with civil defense tags. Grim-faced men sat aligned in their beds. Some clutched rifles loosely by their barrels, as if they would lay to waste whatever monster, man or beast, would snatch up a child in its slaverous jaws and vanish, prey and predator, in the space between two heartbeats.

Even more dubious reminders of civilization as these fell away. He drove into the Harrikin, where he lived. A world so dark and forlorn light itself seemed at a premium. Whippoorwills swept red-eyed up from the roadside. Old abandoned foundries and furnaces rolled past, grim and dark as forsaken prisons. Down a ridge here was an abandoned graveyard, if you knew where to look. The paperhanger did. He had dug up a few of the graves, examined with curiosity what remained, buttons, belt buckles, a cameo brooch. The bones he laid out like a child with a Tinkertoy, arranging them the way they went in jury-rigged resurrection.

He braked hard on a curve, the truck slewing in the gravel. A bobcat had crossed the road, graceful as a wraith, fierce and lantern-eyed in the headlights, gone so swiftly it might have been a stage prop swung across the road on wires.

Bellwether and a deputy drove to the backhoe operator's house. He lived up a gravel road that wound through a great stand of cedars. He lived in a board-and-batten house with a tin roof rusted to a warm umber. They parked before it and got out, adjusting their gun belts.

Bellwether had a search warrant with the ink scarcely dry. The operator was outraged.

Look at it this way, Bellwether explained patiently. I've got to cover my ass.

Everything has got to be considered. You know how kids are. Never thinking. What if she run under the wheels of your truck when you was backing out? What if quicklike you put the body in your truck to get rid of somewhere?

What if quicklike you get the hell off my property, the operator said.

Everything has to be considered, the sheriff said again. Nobody's accusing anybody of anything just yet.

The operator's wife stood glowering at them. To have something to do with his hands, the operator began to construct a cigarette. He had huge red hands thickly sown with brown freckles. They trembled. I ain't got a thing in this round world to hide, he said.

Bellwether and his men searched everywhere they could think of to look. Finally they stood uncertainly in the operator's yard, out of place in their neat khakis, their polished leather.

Now get the hell off my land, the operator said. If all you think of me is that I could run over a little kid and then throw it off in the bushes like a dead cat or something then I don't even want to see your goddamn face. I want you gone and I want you by God gone now.

Everything had to be considered, the sheriff said.

Then maybe you need to consider that paperhanger.

What about him?

That paperhanger is one sick puppy.

He was still there when I got there, the sheriff said. Three witnesses swore nobody ever left, not even for a minute, and one of them was the child's mother. I searched his truck myself.

Then he's a sick puppy with a damn good alibi, the operator said.

That was all. There was no ransom note, no child that turned up two counties over with amnesia. She was a page turned, a door closed, a lost ball in the high weeds. She was a child no larger than a doll, but the void she left behind her was unreckonable. Yet there was no end to it. No finality. There was no moment when someone could say, turning from a mounded grave, Well, this has been unbearable, but you've got to go on with your life. Life did not go on.

At the doctor's wife's insistence an intensive investigation was focused on the backhoe operator. Forensic experts from the FBI examined every millimeter of the gravel truck, paying special attention to its wheels. They were examined with every modern crime-fighting device the government possessed, and there was not a microscopic particle of tissue or blood, no telltale chip of fingernail, no hair ribbon.

Work ceased on the mansion. Some subcontractors were discharged outright, while others simply drifted away. There was no one to care if the work was done, no one to pay them. The half-finished veranda's raw wood grayed in the fall, then winter, rains. The ditches were left fallow and uncovered and half filled with water. Kudzu crept from the woods. The hollyhocks and oleanders the doctor's wife had planted grew entangled and rampant. The imported windows were stoned by double-dared boys who whirled and fled. Already this house where a child had vanished was acquiring an unhealthy, diseased reputation.

The doctor and his wife sat entombed in separate prisons replaying real and imagined grievances. The doctor felt that his wife's neglect had sent his child into the abstract. The doctor's wife drank vodka martinis and watched talk shows where passed an endless procession of vengeful people who had not had children vanish, and felt, perhaps rightly, that the fates had dealt her from the bottom of the deck, and she prayed with intensity for a miracle.

Then one day she was just gone. The Mercedes and part of her clothing and personal possessions were gone too. He idly wondered where she was, but he did not search for her.

Sitting in his armchair cradling a great marmalade cat and a bottle of J&B and observing with bemused detachment the gradations of light at the window, the doctor remembered studying literature at Princeton. He had particular cause to reconsider the poetry of William Butler Yeats. For how surely things fell apart, how surely the center did not hold.

His practice fell into a ruin. His colleagues made sympathetic allowances for him at first, but there are limits to these things. He made erroneous diagnoses, prescribed the wrong medicines not once or twice but as a matter of course.

Just as there is a deepening progression to misfortune, so too there is a point beyond which things can only get worse. They did. A middle-aged woman he was operating on died.

He had made an incision to remove a ruptured appendix and the incised flesh was clamped aside while he made ready to slice it out. It was not there. He stared in drunken disbelief. He began to search under things, organs, intestines, a rising tide of blood. The appendix was not there. It had gone into the abstract, atrophied, been removed twenty-five years before, he had sliced through the selfsame scar. He was rummaging through her abdominal cavity like an irritated man fumbling through a drawer for a clean pair of socks, finally bellowing and wringing his hands in bloody vexation while nurses began to cry out, another surgeon was brought on the run as a closer, and he was carried from the operating room.

Came then days of sitting in the armchair while he was besieged by contingency lawyers, action news teams, a long line of process servers. There was nothing he could do. It was out of his hands and into the hands of the people who are paid to do these things. He sat cradling the bottle of J&B with the marmalade cat snuggled against his portly midriff. He would study the window, where the light drained away in a process he no longer had an understanding of, and sip the scotch and every now and then stroke the cat's head gently. The cat purred against his breast as reassuringly as the hum of an air conditioner.

He left in the middle of the night. He began to load his possessions into the Lexus. At first he chose items with a great degree of consideration. The first thing he loaded was a set of custom-made monogrammed golf clubs. Then his stereo receiver, Denon AC3, $1,750. A copy of *This Side of Paradise* autographed by Fitzgerald that he had bought as an investment. By the time the Lexus was half full he was just grabbing things at random and stuffing them into the backseat, a half-eaten pizza, half a case of cat food, a single brocade house shoe.

He drove west past the hospital, the country club, the city-limit sign. He was thinking no thoughts at all, and all the destination he had was the amount of highway the headlights showed him.

In the slow rains of late fall the doctor's wife returned to the unfinished mansion. She used to sit in a camp chair on the ruined veranda and drink chilled martinis she poured from the pitcher she carried in a foam ice chest. Dark fell early these November days. Rain crows husbanding some far cornfield called through the smoky autumn air.

The sound was fiercely evocative, reminding her of something but she could not have said what.

She went into the room where she had lost the child. The light was failing. The high corners of the room were in deepening shadow but she could see the nests of dirt daubers clustered on the rich flocked wallpaper, a spider swung from a chandelier on a strand of spun glass. Some animal's dried blackened stool curled like a slug against the baseboards. The silence in the room was enormous.

One day she arrived and was surprised to find the paperhanger there. He was sitting on a yellow four-wheeler drinking a bottle of beer. He made to go when he saw her but she waved him back. Stay and talk with me, she said.

The paperhanger was much changed. His pale locks had been shorn away in a makeshift haircut as if scissored in the dark or by a blind barber and his cheeks were covered with a soft curly beard.

You have grown a beard.

Yes.

You are strange with it.

The paperhanger sipped from his San Miguel. He smiled. I was strange without it, he said. He arose from the four-wheeler and came over and sat on the flagstone steps. He stared across the mutilated yard toward the treeline. The yard was like a funhouse maze seen from above, its twistings and turnings bereft of mystery.

You are working somewhere now?

No. I don't take so many jobs anymore. There's only me, and I don't need much. What has become of the doctor?

She shrugged. Many things have change, she said. He has gone. The banks have foreclose. What is that you ride?

An ATV. A four-wheeler.

It goes well in the woods?

It was made for that.

You could take me in the woods. How much would you charge me?

For what?

To go in the woods. You could drive me. I will pay you.

Why?

To search for my child's body.

I wouldn't charge anybody anything to search for a child's body, the paper-hanger said. But she's not in these woods. Nothing could have stayed hidden, the way these woods were searched.

Sometimes I think she just kept walking. Perhaps just walking away from the men looking. Far into the woods.

Into the woods, the paperhanger thought. If she had just kept walking in a straight line with no time out for eating or sleeping, where would she be? Kentucky, Algiers, who knew.

I'll take you when the rains stop, he said. But we won't find a child.

The doctor's wife shook her head. It is a mystery, she said. She drank from her cocktail glass. Where could she have gone? How could she have gone?

There was a man named David Lang, the paperhanger said. Up in Gallatin, back in the late 1800s. He was crossing a barn lot in full view of his wife and two children and he just vanished. Went into thin air. There was a judge in a wagon turning into the yard and he saw it too. It was just like he took a step in this world and his foot came down in another one. He was never seen again.

She gave him a sad smile, bitter and one-cornered. You make fun with me.

No. It's true. I have it in a book. I'll show you.

I have a book with dragons, fairies. A book where Hobbits live in the middle earth. They are lies. I think most books are lies. Perhaps all books. I have prayed for a miracle but I am not worthy of one. I have prayed for her to come from the dead, then just to find her body. That would be a miracle to me. There are no miracles.

She rose unsteadily, swayed slightly, leaning to take up the cooler. The paper-hanger watched her. I have to go now, she said. When the rains stop we will search.

Can you drive?

Of course I can drive. I have drive out here.

I mean are you capable of driving now. You seem a little drunk.

I drink to forget but it is not enough, she said. I can drive.

After a while he heard her leave in the Mercedes, the tires spinning in the gravel drive. He lit a cigarette. He sat smoking it, watching the rain string off the roof. He seemed to be waiting for something. Dusk was falling like a shroud, the world going dark and formless the way it had begun. He drank the last of the beer, sat holding the bottle, the foam bitter in the back of his mouth. A chill touched him. He felt something watching him. He turned. From the corner of the ruined veranda a child was watching him. He stood up. He heard the beer bottle break on the flagstones. The child went sprinting past the hollyhocks toward the brush at the edge of the yard, a tiny sepia child with an intent sloe-eyed face, real as she had ever been, translucent as winter light through dirty glass.

The doctor's wife's hands were laced loosely about his waist as they came down through a thin strand of sassafras, edging over the ridge where the ghost of a road was, a road more sensed than seen that faced into a half acre of tilting stones and fading granite tablets. Other graves marked only by their declivities in the earth, folk so far beyond the pale even the legibility of their identities had been leached away by the weathers.

Leaves drifted, huge poplar leaves veined with amber so golden they might have been coin of the realm for a finer world than this one. He cut the ignition of the four-wheeler and got off. Past the lowering trees the sky was a blue of an improbable intensity, a fierce cobalt blue shot through with dense golden light.

She slid off the rear and steadied herself a moment with a hand on his arm. Where are we? she asked. Why are we here?

The paperhanger had disengaged his arm and was strolling among the gravestones reading such inscriptions as were legible, as if he might find forebear or antecedent in this moldering earth. The doctor's wife was retrieving her martinis from the luggage carrier of the ATV. She stood looking about uncertainly. A graven angel with broken wings crouched on a truncated marble column like a gargoyle. Its stone eyes regarded her with a blind benignity. Some of these graves have been rob, she said.

You can't rob the dead, he said. They have nothing left to steal.

It is a sacrilege, she said. It is forbidden to disturb the dead. You have done this.

The paperhanger took a cigarette pack from his pocket and felt it, but it was empty, and he balled it up and threw it away. The line between grave robbing and archaeology has always looked a little blurry to me, he said. I was studying their culture, trying to get a fix on what their lives were like.

She was watching him with a kind of benumbed horror. Standing hip-slung and lost like a parody of her former self. Strange and anomalous in her fashionable but mismatched clothing, as if she'd put on the first garment that fell to hand. Someday, he thought, she might rise and wander out into the daylit world wearing nothing at all, the way she had come into it. With her diamond watch and the cocktail glass she carried like a used-up talisman.

You have broken the law, she told him.

I got a government grant, the paperhanger said contemptuously.

Why are we here? We are supposed to be searching for my child.

If you're looking for a body the first place to look is the graveyard, he said. If you want a book don't you go to the library?

I am paying you, she said. You are in my employ. I do not want to be here. I want you to do as I say or carry me to my car if you will not.

Actually, the paperhanger said, I had a story to tell you. About my wife.

He paused, as if leaving a space for her comment, but when she made none he went on. I had a wife. My childhood sweetheart. She became a nurse, went to work in one of these drug rehab places. After she was there awhile she got a faraway look in her eyes. Look at me without seeing me. She got in tight with her supervisor. They started having meetings to go to. Conferences. Sometimes just the two of them would confer, generally in a motel. The night I watched them walk into the Holiday Inn in Franklin I decided to kill her. No impetuous spur-of-the-moment thing. I thought it all out and it would be the perfect crime.

The doctor's wife didn't say anything. She just watched him.

A grave is the best place to dispose of a body, the paperhanger said. The grave is its normal destination anyway. I could dig up a grave and then just keep on digging. Save everything carefully. Put my body there and fill in part of the earth, and then restore everything the way it was. The coffin, if any of it was left. The bones and such. A good settling rain and the fall leaves and you're home free. Now that's eternity for you.

Did you kill someone, she breathed. Her voice was barely audible.

Did I or did I not, he said. You decide. You have the powers of a god. You can make me a murderer or just a heartbroke guy whose wife quit him. What do you think? Anyway, I don't have a wife. I expect she just walked off into the abstract like that Lang guy I told you about.

I want to go, she said. I want to go where my car is.

He was sitting on a gravestone watching her out of his pale eyes. He might not have heard.

I will walk.

Just whatever suits you, the paperhanger said. Abruptly, he was standing in front of her. She had not seen him arise from the headstone or stride across the graves, but like a jerky splice in a film he was before her, a hand cupping each of her breasts, staring down into her face.

Under the merciless weight of the sun her face was stunned and vacuous. He studied it intently, missing no detail. Fine wrinkles crept from the corners of her eyes and mouth like hairline cracks in porcelain. Grime was impacted in her pores, in the crepe flesh of her throat. How surely everything had fallen from her: beauty, wealth, social position, arrogance. Humanity itself, for by now she seemed scarcely human, beleaguered so by the fates that she suffered his hands on her breasts as just one more cross to bear, one more indignity to endure.

How far you've come, the paperhanger said in wonder. I believe you're about down to my level now, don't you?

It does not matter, the doctor's wife said. There is no longer one thing that matters.

Slowly and with enormous lassitude her body slumped toward him, and in his exultance it seemed not a motion in itself but simply the completion of one begun in one world and completed itself in another one.

From what seemed a great distance he watched her fall toward him like an angel descending, wings spread, from an infinite height, striking the earth gently, tilting, then righting itself.

The weight of moonlight tracking across the paperhanger's face awoke him from where he took his rest. Filigrees of light through the gauzy curtains swept across him in stately silence like the translucent ghosts of insects. He stirred, lay still then for a moment getting his bearings, a fix on where he was.

He was in his bed, lying on his back. He could see a huge orange moon poised beyond the bedroom window, ink-sketch tree branches that raked its face like claws. He could see his feet book-ending the San Miguel bottle that his hands clasped erect on his abdomen, the amber bottle hard-edged and defined against the pale window, dark atavistic monolith reared against a harvest moon.

He could smell her. A musk compounded of stale sweat and alcohol, the rank smell of her sex. Dissolution, ruin, loss. He turned to study her where she lay asleep, her open mouth a dark cavity in her face. She was naked, legs outflung, pale breasts pooled like cooling wax. She stirred restively, groaned in her sleep. He could hear the rasp of her breathing. Her breath was fetid on his face, corrupt, a graveyard smell. He watched her in disgust, in a dull self-loathing.

He drank from the bottle, lowered it. Sometimes, he told her sleeping face, you do things you can't undo. You break things you just can't fix. Before you mean to, before you know you've done it. And you were right, there are things only a miracle can set to rights.

He sat clasping the bottle. He touched his miscut hair, the soft down of his beard. He had forgotten what he looked like, he hadn't seen his reflection in a mirror for so long. Unbidden, Zeineb's face swam into his memory. He remembered the look on the child's face when the doctor's wife had spun on her heel; spite had crossed it like a flicker of heat lightning. She stuck her tongue out at him. His hand snaked out like a serpent and closed on her throat and snapped her neck before he could call it back, sloe eyes wild and wide, pink tongue caught between tiny seed-pearl teeth like a bitten-off rosebud. Her hair swung sidewise, her head lolled onto his clasped hand. The tray of the toolbox was out before he knew it, he was stuffing her into the toolbox like a rag doll. So small, so small, hardly there at all.

He arose. Silhouetted naked against the moon-drenched window, he drained the bottle. He looked about for a place to set it, leaned and wedged it between the heavy flesh of her upper thighs. He stood in silence, watching her. He seemed philosophical, possessed of some hard-won wisdom. The paperhanger knew so well that while few are deserving of a miracle, fewer still can make one come to pass.

He went out of the room. Doors opened, doors closed. Footsteps softly climbing a staircase, descending. She dreamed on. When he came back into the room he was cradling a plastic-wrapped bundle stiffly in his arms. He placed it gently beside the drunk woman. He folded the plastic sheeting back like a caul.

What had been a child. What the graveyard earth had spared the freezer had preserved. Ice crystals snared in the hair like windy snowflakes whirled there, in the lashes. A doll from a madhouse assembly line.

He took her arm, laid it across the child. She pulled away from the cold. He firmly brought the arm back, arranging them like mannequins, Madonna and child. He studied this tableau, then went out of his house for the last time. The door closed gently behind him on its keeper spring.

The paperhanger left in the Mercedes, heading west into the open country, tracking into wide-open territories he could infect like a malignant spore. Without knowing it, he followed the self-same route the doctor had taken some eight months earlier, and in a world of infinite possibilities where all journeys share a common end, perhaps they are together, taking the evening air on a ruined veranda among the hollyhocks and oleanders, the doctor sipping his scotch and the paperhanger his San Miguel, gentlemen of leisure discussing the vagaries of life and pondering deep into the night not just the possibility but the inevitability of miracles.

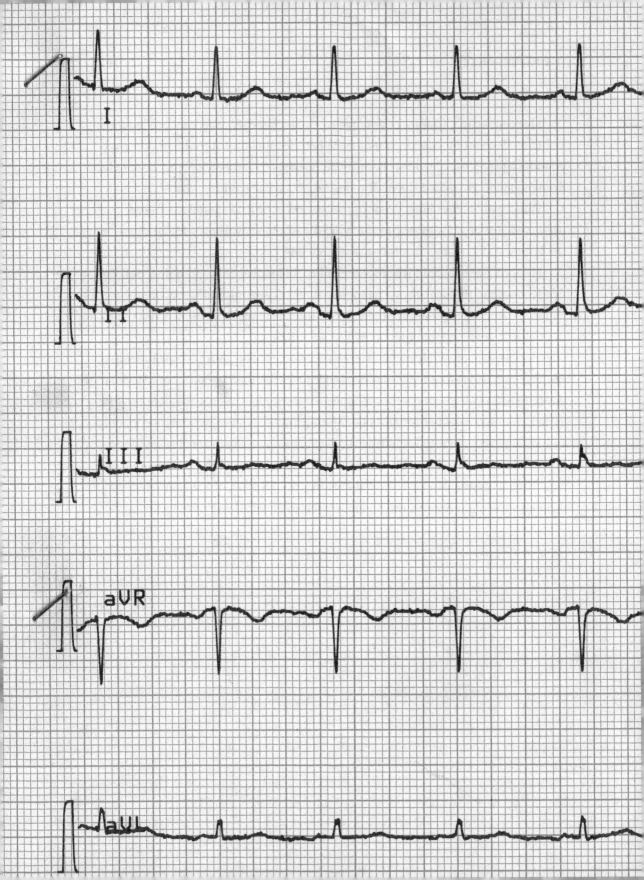

Red Dragon

BY THOMAS HARRIS

In much the same way that Dracula *is the defining vampire novel and* The Exorcist *is the book that put demonic possession stories on the map,* Red Dragon *by Thomas Harris is the absolute ground zero for the entire forensic serial-killer–chasing craze. Without it, there would be no* CSI, *no* Criminal Minds, *and none of the trillion novels—best-selling or otherwise—that tried and failed to reach the bar that it single-handedly raised.*

If you're one of the millions who first stumbled upon Harris's brilliance when Red Dragon's *fairly well-known sequel,* The Silence of the Lambs, *slapped the icing on the cake, I can't even tell you how thrilled I am to share with you the following chapter, from the even-greater masterpiece that started it all.*

The very one in which Harris first introduced us to Hannibal Lecter, and resoundingly opened the door for all that was to come.

Dr. Frederick Chilton, chief of staff at the Baltimore State Hospital for the Criminally Insane, came around his desk to shake Will Graham's hand.

"Dr. Bloom called me yesterday, Mr. Graham—or should I call you Dr. Graham?"

"I'm not a doctor."

"I was delighted to hear from Dr. Bloom, we've known each other for *years*. Take that chair."

"We appreciate your help, Dr. Chilton."

"Frankly, I sometimes feel like Lecter's secretary rather than his keeper," Chilton said. "The volume of his mail alone is a nuisance. I think among some researchers it's considered chic to correspond with him—I've seen his letters *framed* in psychology departments—and for a while it seemed that every Ph.D. candidate in the field wanted to interview him. Glad to cooperate with *you*, of course, and Dr. Bloom."

"I need to see Dr. Lecter in as much privacy as possible," Graham said. "I may need to see him again or telephone him after today."

Chilton nodded. "To begin with, Dr. Lecter will stay in his room. That is absolutely the only place where he is not put in restraints. One wall of his room is a double barrier which opens on the hall. I'll have a chair put there, and screens if you like.

"I must ask you not to pass him any objects whatever, other than paper free of clips or staples. No ring binders, pencils, or pens. He has his own felt-tipped pens."

"I might have to show him some material that could stimulate him," Graham said.

"You can show him what you like as long as it's on soft paper. Pass him documents through the sliding food tray. Don't hand anything through the barrier and do not accept anything he might extend through the barrier. He can return papers in the food tray. I insist on that. Dr. Bloom and Mr. Crawford assured me that you would cooperate on procedure."

"I will," Graham said. He started to rise.

"I know you're anxious to get on with it, Mr. Graham, but I want to tell you something first. This will interest you.

"It may seem gratuitous to warn *you*, of all people, about Lecter. But he's very disarming. For a year after he was brought here, he behaved perfectly and gave the appearance of cooperating with attempts at therapy. As a result—this was under the previous administrator—security around him was slightly relaxed.

"On the afternoon of July 8, 1976, he complained of chest pain. His restraints were removed in the examining room to make it easier to give him an electrocardiogram. One of his attendants left the room to smoke, and the other turned away for a second. The nurse was very quick and strong. She managed to save one of her eyes.

"You may find this curious." Chilton took a strip of EKG tape from a drawer and unrolled it on his desk. He traced the spiky line with his forefinger. "Here, he's resting on the examining table. Pulse seventy-two. Here, he grabs the nurse's head and pulls her down to him. Here, he is subdued by the attendant. He didn't resist, by the way, though the attendant dislocated his shoulder. Do you notice the strange thing? His pulse never got over eighty-five. Even when he tore out her tongue."

Chilton could read nothing in Graham's face. He leaned back in his chair and steepled his fingers under his chin. His hands were dry and shiny.

"You know, when Lecter was first captured we thought he might provide us with a singular opportunity to study a pure sociopath," Chilton said. "It's so rare to get one alive. Lecter is so lucid, so perceptive; he's trained in psychiatry...and he's a mass murderer. He seemed cooperative, and we thought that he could be a window on this kind of aberration. We thought we'd be like Beaumont studying digestion through the opening in St. Martin's stomach.

"As it turned out, I don't think we're any closer to understanding him now than the day he came in. Have you ever talked with Lecter for any length of time?"

"No. I just saw him when...I saw him mainly in court. Dr. Bloom showed me his articles in the journals," Graham said.

"He's very familiar with *you*. He's given you a lot of thought."

"You had some sessions with him?"

"Yes. Twelve. He's impenetrable. Too sophisticated about the tests for them to register anything. Edwards, Fabré, even Dr. Bloom himself had a crack at him. I have their notes. He was an enigma to them, too. It's impossible, of course, to tell what he's holding back or whether he understands more than he'll say. Oh, since his commitment he's done some brilliant pieces for *The American Journal of Psychiatry* and *The General Archives*. But they're always about problems he doesn't have. I think he's afraid that if we 'solve' him, nobody will be interested in him anymore and he'll be stuck in a back ward somewhere for the rest of his life."

Chilton paused. He had practiced using his peripheral vision to watch his subject in interviews. He believed that he could watch Graham this way undetected.

"The consensus around here is that the only person who has demonstrated any practical understanding of Hannibal Lecter is you, Mr. Graham. Can you tell me anything about him?"

"No."

"Some of the staff are curious about this: when you saw Dr. Lecter's murders, their 'style,' so to speak, were you able perhaps to reconstruct his fantasies? And did that help you identify him?"

Graham did not answer.

"We're woefully short of material on that sort of thing. There's one single piece in *The Journal of Abnormal Psychology*. Would you mind talking with some of the staff—no, no, not this trip—Dr. Bloom was very severe with me on that point. We're to leave you alone. Next trip, perhaps."

Dr. Chilton had seen a lot of hostility. He was seeing some at the moment.

Graham stood up. "Thank you, doctor. I want to see Lecter now."

The steel door of the maximum-security section closed behind Graham. He heard the bolt slide home.

Graham knew that Lecter slept most of the morning. He looked down the corridor. At that angle he could not see into Lecter's cell, but he could tell that the lights inside were dimmed.

Graham wanted to see Dr. Lecter asleep. He wanted time to brace himself. If he felt Lecter's madness in his head, he had to contain it quickly, like a spill.

To cover the sound of his footsteps, he followed an orderly pushing a linen cart. Dr. Lecter is very difficult to slip up on.

Graham paused partway down the hall. Steel bars covered the entire front of the cell. Behind the bars, farther than arm's reach, was a stout nylon net stretched ceiling to floor and wall to wall. Through the barrier, Graham could see a table and chair bolted to the floor. The table was stacked with softcover books and correspondence. He walked up to the bars, put his hands on them, took his hands away.

Dr. Hannibal Lecter lay on his cot asleep, his head propped on a pillow against the wall. Alexandre Dumas' *Le Grand Dictionnaire de Cuisine* was open on his chest.

Graham had stared through the bars for about five seconds when Lecter opened his eyes and said, "That's the same atrocious aftershave you wore in court."

"I keep getting it for Christmas."

Dr. Lecter's eyes are maroon and they reflect the light redly in tiny points. Graham felt each hair bristle on his nape. He put his hand on the back of his neck.

"Christmas, yes," Lecter said. "Did you get my card?"

"I got it. Thank you."

Dr. Lecter's Christmas card had been forwarded to Graham from the FBI crime laboratory in Washington. He took it into the backyard, burned it, and washed his hands before touching Molly.

Lecter rose and walked over to his table. He is a small, lithe man. Very neat. "Why don't you have a seat, Will? I think there are some folding chairs in a closet just down that way. At least, that's where it sounds like they come from."

"The orderly's bringing one."

Lecter stood until Graham was seated in the hall. "And how is Officer Stewart?" he asked.

"Stewart's fine." Officer Stewart left law enforcement after he saw Dr. Lecter's basement. He managed a motel now. Graham did not mention this. He didn't think Stewart would appreciate any mail from Lecter.

"Unfortunate that his emotional problems got the better of him. I thought he was a very promising young officer. Do you ever have any problems, Will?"

"No."

"Of course you don't."

Graham felt that Lecter was looking through to the back of his skull. His attention felt like a fly walking around in there.

"I'm glad you came. It's been what now, three years? My callers are all professional. Banal clinical psychiatrists and grasping second-rate *doctors* of psychology from silo colleges somewhere. Pencil lickers trying to protect their tenure with pieces in the journals."

"Dr. Bloom showed me your article on surgical addiction in *The Journal of Clinical Psychiatry*."

"And?"

"Very interesting, even to a layman."

"A layman . . . layman—layman. Interesting term," Lecter said. "So many learned fellows going about. So many *experts* on government grants. And you say you're a layman. But it was you who caught me, wasn't it, Will? Do you know how you did it?"

"I'm sure you've read the transcript. It's all in there."

"No it's not. Do you know how you did it, Will?"

"It's in the transcript. What does it matter now?"

"It doesn't matter to *me*, Will."

"I want you to help me, Dr. Lecter."

"Yes, I thought so."

"It's about Atlanta and Birmingham."

"Yes."

"You read about it, I'm sure."

"I've read the papers. I can't clip them. They won't let me have scissors, of course. Sometimes they threaten me with loss of books, you know. I wouldn't want them to think I was dwelling on anything morbid." He laughed. Dr. Lecter has small white teeth. "You want to know how he's choosing them, don't you?"

"I thought you would have some ideas. I'm asking you to tell me what they are."

"Why should I?"

Graham had anticipated the question. A reason to stop multiple murders would not occur readily to Dr. Lecter.

"There are things you don't have," Graham said. "Research materials, filmstrips even. I'd speak to the chief of staff."

"Chilton. You must have seen him when you came in. Gruesome, isn't it? Tell me the truth, he fumbles at your head like a freshman pulling at a panty girdle, doesn't he? Watched you out of the corner of his eye. Picked *that* up, didn't you? You may not believe this, but he actually tried to give *me* a Thematic Apperception Test. He was sitting there just like the Cheshire cat waiting for Mf 13 to come up. Ha. Forgive me, I forget that you're not among the anointed. It's a card with a woman in bed and a man in the foreground. I was supposed to avoid a sexual interpretation. I laughed. He puffed up and told everybody I avoided prison with a Ganser syndrome—never mind, it's boring."

"You'd have access to the AMA filmstrip library."

"I don't think you'd get me the things I want."

"Try me."

"I have quite enough to read as it is."

"You'd get to see the file on this case. There's another reason."

"Pray."

"I thought you might be curious to find out if you're smarter than the person I'm looking for."

"Then, by implication, you think you are smarter than I am, since you caught me."

"No. I know I'm not smarter than you are."

"Then how did you catch me, Will?"

"You had disadvantages."

"What disadvantages?"

"Passion. And you're insane."

"You're very tan, Will."

Graham did not answer.

"Your hands are rough. They don't look like a cop's hands anymore. That shaving lotion is something a child would select. It has a ship on the bottle, doesn't it?" Dr. Lecter seldom holds his head upright. He tilts it as he asks a question, as though he were screwing an auger of curiosity into your face. Another silence, and Lecter said, "Don't think you can persuade me with appeals to my intellectual vanity."

"I don't think I'll persuade you. You'll do it or you won't. Dr. Bloom is working on it anyway, and he's the most—"

"Do you have the file with you?"

"Yes."

"And pictures?"

"Yes."

"Let me have them, and I might consider it."

"No."

"Do you dream much, Will?"

"Good-bye, Dr. Lecter."

"You haven't threatened to take away my books yet."

Graham walked away.

"Let me have the file, then. I'll tell you what I think."

Graham had to pack the abridged file tightly into the sliding tray. Lecter pulled it through.

"There's a summary on top. You can read that now," Graham said.

"Do you mind if I do it privately? Give me an hour."

Graham waited on a tired plastic couch in a grim lounge. Orderlies came in for coffee. He did not speak to them. He stared at small objects in the room and was glad they held still in his vision. He had to go to the rest room twice. He was numb.

The turnkey admitted him to the maximum-security section again.

Lecter sat at his table, his eyes filmed with thought. Graham knew he had spent most of the hour with the pictures.

"This is a very shy boy, Will. I'd love to meet him. . . . Have you considered the possibility that he's disfigured? Or that he may believe he's disfigured?"

"The mirrors."

"Yes. You notice he smashed all the mirrors in the houses, not just enough to get the pieces he wanted. He doesn't just put the shards in place for the damage they cause. They're set so he can see himself. In their eyes—Mrs. Jacobi and . . . What was the other name?"

"Mrs. Leeds."

"Yes."

"That's interesting," Graham said.

"It's not 'interesting.' You'd thought of that before."

"I had considered it."

"You just came here to look at me. Just to get the old scent again, didn't you? Why don't you just smell yourself?"

"I want your opinion."

"I don't have one right now."

"When you do have one, I'd like to hear it."

"May I keep the file?"

"I haven't decided yet," Graham said.

"Why are there no descriptions of the grounds? Here we have frontal views of the houses, floor plans, diagrams of the rooms where the deaths occurred, and little mention of the grounds. What were the yards like?"

"Big backyards, fenced, with some hedges. Why?"

"Because, my dear Will, if this pilgrim feels a special relationship with the moon, he might like to go outside and look at it. Before he tidies himself up, you understand. Have you seen blood in the moonlight, Will? It appears quite black. Of course, it keeps the distinctive sheen. If one were nude, say, it would be better to have outdoor privacy for that sort of thing. One must show some consideration for the neighbors, hmmmm?"

"You think the yard might be a factor when he selects victims?"

"Oh yes. And there will be more victims, of course. Let me keep the file, Will. I'll study it. When you get more files, I'd like to see them, too. You can call me. On the rare occasions when my lawyer calls, they bring me a telephone. They used to patch him through on the intercom, but everyone listened of course. Would you like to give me your home number?"

"No."

"Do you know how you caught me, Will?"

"Good-bye, Dr. Lecter. You can leave messages for me at the number on the file." Graham walked away.

"Do you know how you caught me?"

Graham was out of Lecter's sight now, and he walked faster toward the far steel door.

"The reason you caught me is that we're *just alike*" was the last thing Graham heard as the steel door closed behind him.

He was numb except for dreading the loss of numbness. Walking with his head down, speaking to no one, he could hear his blood like a hollow drumming of wings. It seemed a very short distance to the outside. This was only a building; there were only five doors between Lecter and the outside. He had the absurd feeling that Lecter had walked out with him. He stopped outside the entrance and looked around him, assuring himself that he was alone.

From a car across the street, his long lens propped on the window sill, Freddy Lounds got a nice profile shot of Graham in the doorway and the words in stone above him: "Baltimore State Hospital for the Criminally Insane."

As it turned out, *The National Tattler* cropped the picture to just Graham's face and the last two words in the stone.

The Exit at Toledo Blade Boulevard

BY JACK KETCHUM

In trying to make sense of seemingly senseless tragedy, one of the hardest things to reconcile is the randomness of fate. We like to think in terms of cause and effect—I punch you in the nose, and the result will be hurt—because it's nice and simple, and often true.

But the only straight lines are the ones that we make. Life tends to be a lot more complex and rococo, weaving patterns so elaborate they often go right over our heads, leaving us with nothing but the question Why?

And so with this puzzle box by noble literary savage Jack Ketchum, never more thoughtful and heartbreaking than here. Don't worry; the pieces come together hard.

Just not necessarily in the shape you might have hoped.

The boys in the pickup were traveling north along the dark empty stretch of I-75 near Nokomis, three of them cramped side-by-side in the cab and sweating in the mid-July heat despite the open windows. They could smell each other's sweat wafted in and out by the breeze. They didn't mind. It was Monday night. There weren't any girls around anyhow.

Jimmie who had just turned eighteen the week before and was losing yet another battle in his ongoing war with zits popped a Bud and handed it to Doug who handed it to Bobby. The truck was in the fast lane doing seventy in a sixty zone. Bobby was driving. Having his fourth beer open in his hand was dangerous. Less out here on the highway at nearly midnight than it would have been back home on the streets of Tampa—you were much more likely to get stopped in towns —but dangerous enough.

He didn't mind that either. Hell, the risk was part of it.

He'd been lucky so far.

He tilted back the can. The beer was warmer than he liked but the first pull always tasted good, warm or not.

"Hey. Turn that up," he said to Doug. "Quick."

The song on the radio was Johnny Cash doing *The Tennessee Stud* and it reminded him simultaneously of his uncle's hardscrabble farm in Georgia and of Mary Ann Abbot and Dee Dee Whitaker—and what he, Bobby, knew about life that these other two, Doug and Jimmie, didn't.

He loved this guy. The Man in Black.

And for once Doug didn't complain about Johnny's singing. Truth was, Doug was past complaining. Five cold brews at the Cave Rock Inn in Murdock and one on the road and old Douggie could barely find the volume control. He managed though, leaning forward and studying the panel and then Jimmie started singing along beside him. Jimmie had a pretty good singing voice but he couldn't get the growly low notes that Johnny got. What could you expect? Hell, Bobby still remembered when little Jimmie's voice changed. Wasn't that long ago, either. Jimmie was still a kid.

He thought about Mary Ann again, an image of cool white thighs spread naked in the woods.

He was thinking of that and listening to the wind and the song up loud over the wind and he had the beer can to his lips again when he saw something glint ahead of him and then something loom suddenly in the headlights and way over against the passenger side door Jimmie stopped singing and shrieked and he guessed he did too, something like *whathafuuuuck?* and he swerved the pickup and braked and tried to steer and the next thing he knew they were cruising the bumpy dirt shoulder at fifteen miles per hour, amazed to be alive. He was shaking like a cold wet dog and his lap and legs and teeshirt were foul and wet where Doug had thrown up all the hell over him.

Earlier that afternoon George Hubbard stared out the double glass doors leading from his kitchen to the lanai and thought about the dog and how the dog had in some ways been the beginning of the end of it.

The dog had been a gift to her, something to make her stay, a hope against hope that a few furry pounds of warm retriever puppy would be the glue for them that sex no longer was, nor love, nor anything else was able to be.

It hadn't worked. She was gone, the dog with her.

Just like all the rest of them.

His father was gone—dead of a heart attack—and that was all to the good, actually. At least one of them wouldn't be around to play victim to his mother's fucking viciousness any more. His sister, now in her thirties, had somehow without his noticing turned into the lesbian bitch from Sodom, working as a mail carrier for god's sake in Shreveport, Lousiana. They hadn't talked in two years, not since his father died and even then that was mostly to shout at one another. His friends had drifted away into one Sarasota warren or another since he started telling them the truth about what was really going on with him. They'd all stepped back into their own little lives, their own private blind alleys of pseudo-awareness. Good riddance. Sister, friends. Even his sadass father.

The only one he *couldn't* get rid of was his mother.

Ever since he was a kid she'd been trying to kill him and lately she'd been stepping up the pace. In a way, she'd already succeeded.

He stared out into the dimming sunlight on the lanai and pulled at the joint. The joint was one of the few ways he had of escaping her.

They said he was crazy. Paranoid. The doctors at the hospital after his meth OD had the balls to go even further. Paranoid *schizophrenic* they said.

Even Cal and Linda thought he was paranoid and said so to his face. Told him he needed to get help—his best friends since high school. Said his mother couldn't do all that. When he knew damn well she was mob connected, knew damn well she'd been harassing him constantly, anyone could see that, getting her friends in the IRS after him, getting her friends in the police force after him for back child-support payments to his first wife and his daughter, trying to put his ass in jail.

He'd had to leave the state. Come here to Florida.

He'd disappeared.

His mother wasn't the only one who knew a trick or two.

Though he knew she was looking for him even now. He could feel it. In his blood he could feel it. His mother had tentacles everywhere. She was psychic as hell and she was looking.

Get help. Shit. Once, years ago, he'd fucked Linda. It had been a good fuck too. Friendly.

And now she denied him.

They all did.

Even Sandy, after three years of loving him or at least saying she loved him, making him think that, making him feel he *knew that*, staying with him even through the relocation because she understood first-hand what a bitch his mother was, she'd had enough run-ins with her herself by then, though even she wouldn't believe how connected she was with police and mob and government, his mother was too smart for that, too smart to let on to her. Some things she reserved strictly for him.

He stubbed out the joint and walked absently through the condo, looking at what she'd left behind. It wasn't a whole lot. In the living room, his desk, a shelf full of paperbacks and audio tapes. In the kitchen, some old pots and pans, some silverware and glassware, the toaster and the microwave they'd bought together.

Upstairs in the bathroom she'd even taken the shower curtain.

The worst, for him, was the bedroom. The bed was still there, but stripped of its quilt and the lace hand-made bedspread. Dirty sheets lay in a corner. She'd left him three out of seven pillows. The television was gone and the night stand by the bed. The dresser was there, but empty of her jewelry boxes and perfumes and toiletries it looked uninhabited, the entire life of it fled. The empty hangers in the big walk-in closet seemed ridiculous, poverty awaiting an abundance that would never occur again.

He crossed the room and sat down on the bed.

His footsteps sounded much too loud to him.

The bed had seen them through three apartments together, one for every year they'd been together. It seemed almost wrong that she hadn't taken it with her—like leaving a child behind or a kitten. A kind of betrayal. He thought of what had happened on the bed, the talking, the laughing, the fighting, *jesus*, all the joys and sorrows between them that had lasted long into the night sometimes, he thought of making love to her, her intense, amazing passion that was easily the equal to his own and the like of which he'd not only never seen before but never even knew existed in a woman and which hadn't dimmed at all until just recently, until just this last year when he'd begun telling her the truth about what was happening to him, *sharing* with her really, what his mother was doing and the whole damn conspiracy. And finally, a week ago, about what was wrong with him.

He thought of how intimate a bed was. *In the night, before sleep, the soul pours forth its strength.*

He put his hands to his face and cried.

His listened to his sobs echo in the empty room.

When he was exhausted he stood and went downstairs again. One of the dog's chew-bones lay half-eaten on the landing. He picked it up and walked to the kitchen and dumped it in the garbage.

He stood a moment looking out at the lanai, into the fading light. The screens leading out to the small enclosed yard were becoming overgrown with creepers. Normally he'd have wanted to take care of that right away. He made his living as a gardener and it was a matter of his pride as a professional. A few creepers were one thing, even attractive. He liked them there, their graceful abstract patterns. But the way they were going, eventually they'd ruin the screen.

He decided it was time to break his rule. He'd quit because Sandy hated the smell of the stuff on his breath and he wanted to smell good for her for when they went to bed, for the times they made love or even just kissed good night, so that sleeping beside her on the bed, he wouldn't offend. But now that she was gone there was no one to offend anymore and given this fucking little problem of his, there never would be.

He went to the liquor cabinet. He poured himself a drink.

A half hour after Bobby's pickup went off the road and thirty miles south along I-75, Pete and Jan Hoffsteader's white Ford Thunderbird crept along the on-ramp at Peace River, waited for a set of headlights to pass in the slow lane and then pulled out onto the highway.

They were both a little nervous to be out this late. It was after twelve.

That almost never happened.

Normally they'd have been in bed over half an hour now, right after the news and weather.

Pete was weary.

It had been a pretty good evening, though. They'd had dinner with Jan's brother and sister-in-law, ate good German food at the Karl Ehmer Restaurant in Punta Gorda, too much of it really, so much food that they couldn't finish it all. Which at their age seemed to be happening a lot lately. About half his saurbraten, red cabbage and potato dumplings were in the usual styrofoam container resting in Jan's lap. They'd gone back to her brother Ed's mobile home for a nightcap which then became two nightcaps and he'd lost track of time a little talking with Ed about their respective outfits stationed in France during the War and then Pete thought he'd best have some coffee before heading back.

They were on their way home to the Silver Lakes retirement community in Sarasota.

Forty-five minutes driving time.

The highway was nearly deserted at this hour.

What if they had car trouble? *Jesus. What if they had a flat?*

At sixty-seven, with a heart that was not exactly in the best shape possible, not to mention with three drinks in him, he didn't feel up to changing a goddamn flat.

What the hell, he thought, you hope for the best.

Jan was nervous, though. He could tell by the way she kept fidgeting with her hands, playing with the tongue of the styrofoam container.

Part of it was that he wasn't really supposed to be driving at night at all and she knew it. The glaucoma. It narrowed his field of vision and the oncoming headlights could be hell. But out here on the highway the headlights were few and far between. And if he stayed over here in the slow lane they weren't that big a problem. It was worse in town actually, where the streets were narrower.

He felt a momentary annoyance with her. *She'd* been the one who made the dinner date with her brother. What did she expect them to do afterwards? *Fly* home? Whether it was eight o'clock or midnight darkness was darkness, headlights were headlights. He used to drive a bus for a living. He'd manage.

He couldn't stay mad at her, though.

He reached over and patted her pale cool hand.

He was lucky. His second wife was a damn good woman. He'd known that when he married her. But if he'd had any doubts, the way she stood by him during the angioplasty, him scared shitless, scared to tears, she a goddamn *pillar*, well, he would have lost them then and there.

Whoever said that men were tougher than woman didn't have any idea.

Now though, she was really pretty nervous for some reason.

Get her talking, he thought. Relax her.

The usual subject was the first that came to mind.

"So. What do you think about the Stockyard for dinner tomorrow? We haven't been there in a while."

She thought about it.

"Oh, I don't know," she said. "It'll be crowded."

"Not so bad this time of year. With all the snowbirds gone."

"It's *always* crowded. Dorothy went there last *week* and it was crowded. What about the Olive Garden?"

He shrugged. He'd rather have a steak from the Stockyard but so what. "Olive Garden's fine."

"It's just that the Stockyard's going to be so *crowded*."

"I don't mind the Olive Garden."

"I don't know."

He glanced at her. "You all right?"

She was frowning, her mouth turned down, tight brows squinting her eyes. He heard her fingernails pluck at the styrofoam container.

"I'm fine."

"I'm driving okay, aren't I?"

He was doing fifty in a sixty zone, riding the straightaway in the slow lane, the Thunderbird on cruise control, not another car in sight in front of him or behind.

"Yes, dear. You're doing fine."

He knew that.

"So? What, then?" he said.

"I don't know. Something's wrong. Something's not right."

"You worried about your brother?"

Ed had prostate cancer. It was still too early to tell if the treatments were going to take.

"I don't know," she said. "Maybe."

He glanced at her again. The dashboard lights gave off a pale greenish glow. Her face was set, immobile.

He thought for a moment that this was what she would look like dead and then dismissed the thought.

Hell, she'd outlive him by ten years, if not more.

She's just tired, he thought. Tired and nervous being out this late, with me driving.

We'll be home soon.

He concentrated on the road ahead and did not look at her again.

Five and a quarter miles behind them Annie Buxton held to a steady sixty in the rented red Nissan and thought about how amazingly *clear* her head was.

Three weeks ago by about this time at night she'd have been sipping her sixth or seventh vodka and tonic. Or she'd have switched to Stoli straight up. Either that or she'd have passed out altogether.

She glanced down at the gas gauge and saw she was down to a quarter of a tank. She'd make it home to Bradenton. Barely. Who cared?

The point was she was going home.

She considered turning on the radio but it was entirely possible that anything the slightest bit sentimental—hell, any song with the word *love* in it—would get her crying again. She was weepy these days.

Her sister said that was to be expected. Annie was picking up the pieces of her life and putting them together again and there were so *many* pieces and so *much* putting together it would make anybody weepy now and then.

Anyhow, Madge said, you always cry when you realized that against the odds, you've survived.

Still she decided against the radio.

It was better to have just the silence and the wind and the highway's bleak flat sweep in front of her.

She took a Marlboro from the pack on the dashboard and lit it in the orange coil glow of the lighter. Cigarettes were something she would continue to allow herself, she thought, at least for the time being. She'd quit them too one of these days, maybe get the patch. But first things first. Or as all the literature read, one damn step at a time.

My god, the air felt good pouring in through the window.

For a week and a half she'd seen nothing but the inside of her sister's stuffy bedroom. The first two days of that, she'd spent strapped to the fourposter bed.

Tough love, Madge called it.

You won't go into a goddamn hospital, okay, fine, we'll do it this way.

She saw rabbits on the bed with her and snakes who swallowed the rabbits whole. She floated out to sea on that bed, sunk and drowned and rose again. She howled and sweated and hurt and stained the sheets.

Tough love. That it was.

Three weeks, total, at her sister's house. Most of that time a virtual prisoner, held hostage against her own vices, trapped inside her own feverish sweaty body while she waited for her system and then her mind to clear themselves of the poisons that were killing both her and her six-year marriage to Tim.

Two weeks before Madge would even allow her to light up a smoke.

By then she'd called her sister every name in the book. Early on, even swung at her a couple of times. Even while she knew in her heart that big sister was busy as hell with the nasty job of saving her silly life.

It was only later, when she was sane enough to talk about things, talk until they were both exhausted, endless exhausting exhilirating nights, that she realized she *actually wanted* to save her life, and that some of the facts about her life, like Tim's being a respected English teacher while she'd barely finished high school, like the fact that so far they were childless and she was pushing thirty-five, like the fact that at the moment he was busy with his life and she was not, that these kinds of things didn't matter half as much as she was simply *letting* them matter. It was willful destructiveness. She was obsessing on the trivial and ignoring one great big *beautiful* fact—that Tim loved her, hell, he adored her. Even adored her when she was drinking.

Though the drinking was poisoning him too.

So many times she'd sent this gentle quiet man into a towering rage.

So many times she'd pushed and pushed at him.

You're just like Mom! Madge said. *You damn fool. You love him to death and he loves you and all you care about is that you're* jealous, *that at the moment you're fucking bored and unemployed and you feel stupid and useless because he's* not. *You know how crazy that is? You're* exactly *like her! You're not just missing the forest for the trees, you're burning the goddamn forest!*

She brushed her cheek with her fingertips and, in the oncoming glare of headlights moving south toward her, saw that her fingers came away glistening and black with mascara.

You really are a fool, she thought. You might as well turn the radio on after all. You're going to be crying anyway. Why not just wallow in it?

She smiled at herself and stubbed out the cigarette and took a deep breath of the warm night air.

It was over. She'd get into a program if she had to—though she'd never been much of a joiner. Anything. There was no chance in hell she'd ever touch a drink again. She suspected there was going to be a lot of coffee around for a while. His voice on the telephone when she called to say she was coming home to him, the *break* in his voice, the sob when he said *thank god*, told her as clearly as her own finally steady voice did that nothing was ever going to be the same from here on in.

Lives were to be made as best you could and then remade if necessary.

Not broken.

Never broken.

When he climbed into the car that night George Hubbard didn't really know what he was going to do.

He was going out for a drive. Going out to shake the blues. Forget about Sandy. Forget about his mother. Get out of the lonely bare condo and drive before he drank too much to impair his judgement or get his ass arrested.

Meandering through the streets of town he was fine. It was only when he turned out onto I-75 that the darkness began to envelop him.

The darkness began in his mind, in some corner of his mind where his mother lived and Sandy lived and mostly, where anger lived and had for a very long time. It reached out from that place to embrace his future, a growing black clot of pain which dimmed his senses and fed itself on ghostly images of future prosecutions by his demon mother, by the authorities, by doctors, images of the long lonely love-less sexless months ahead of him while the AIDS virus ate away at his immunity, of wasting away alone, of bedsores and coma and that single meth-crystal spike in his arm so long ago that was also his mother's demon spike, his mother's revenge, his mother's hydra venom, the reality and consequences of which for both Hubbard and for Sandy he had finally admitted to her and which had driven her away from him in horror and in fury.

The darkness inside spread as the AIDS spread, inking his conscience black.

On I-75 it reached out from his fingertips and turned off the headlights.

And then turned him south into the northbound lane.

He was only half aware of the pickup truck going off the shoulder. Only that he was still alive and whoever was inside was still alive and that so was everybody else on this miserable planet and that none of these things would do.

He drove.

Within and without he was only darkness.

It was probably the glaucoma. Pete never would have seen it were it not for Jan, never did see the car really or not much of it, her eyes good fixed on the road ahead, his wife worried, nervous about being out so late, Jan startling him so much when she screamed his name that he stomped on the brakes and wrenched at the wheel away from the black hurtling mass ahead of him skimmed by light and the Lincoln rolled, skidded on its side and rolled again and for a moment they were weightless and then they were crashing down, air bags suddenly inflated, his door caving in and the front fender throwing sparks across the highway, the shoulder-strap harness biting deep into his chest and thighs and pulling his shoulder out of its socket with a sickening thud of pain, the air bags enveloping them both as the car slid and righted itself and rolled to a stop at an angle across the highway.

He pushed his way free of the air bag and looked for Jan beside him but only the passenger-side bag was there, the brown and red remains of his dinner from the styrofoam container dripping over it. Her harness was empty. *Had she been wearing it? God! had she had it on her?* Her door was wide open, its window shattered. He tasted metal and smoke.

Only then did he panic.

"Jan! Jesus Jan!"

He shoved at his door but it wouldn't move and pain raced hot through his shoulder. He tried again but he was weak and hurt and then he heard her pulling at it from the outside, calling his name.

"Other side!" he said. "Your side. I'm coming! I'm okay."

Thank god, he thought. Not for himself. For her.

He got out of the harness and edged himself across the seat past the air bag to the door. By the time he got one foot out on the tarmac she was already there in front of him, leaning toward him, crying and smiling both, her pale thin arms reaching out to him to ease him gently home.

Maybe this is a mistake, he thought.

People just kept going by me.

Perhaps it wasn't meant to be. It was possible.

Near the exit to Toledo Blade Boulevard he pushed it up to eighty, sightless of the speedometer in the roaring dark.

There were lights out there in the distance.

I'll get flowers, she thought. I'll make dinner.

Candlelight.

No wine.

Everything new, she thought. People could start over. People could forgive and if not forget exactly, they could take up life sadder and wiser than they were and make something good of it, they could make love again and find a halfway decent job and maybe even someday make a baby, she wasn't too old, she had her health now that the poison was gone and the dark cloud over her life was gone, she had strength.

I'm coming, Tim, she thought. *I'm coming home.*

I'm alive. I'm fine.

Incident On and Off a Mountain Road

BY JOE R. LANSDALE

And speaking of accidents, automotive and otherwise . . .

The flip side of utter chaos is poetic justice; and the more optimistic among us are prone to think that everything happens for a reason.

Of course, the worse things get, the harder it is to maintain that cheerful disposition. That's when resilience and good old-fashioned, can-do spirit come in awfully handy. Or, as the old saying goes, "Chance favors the prepared mind."

That would seem to be the moral of this wildly amoral tale by the inimitable Joe R. Lansdale, who takes off the fun gloves here and heads straight for brutal backwoods terror, as only he can.

It is no accident that he is one of our best. He's got the awards—and the scars—to prove it.

She unfastened her seat belt, and as a matter of habit, located her purse and slipped its strap over her shoulder. She got out of the Chevy feeling wobbly, eased around front of it and saw the hood and bumper and roof were crumpled.

A wisp of radiator steam hissed from beneath the wadded hood, rose into the moonlight and dissolved.

She turned her attentions to the Buick. Its tail end was now turned to her, and as she edged alongside it, she saw the front left side had been badly damaged. Fearful of what she might see, she glanced inside.

The moonlight shone through the rear windshield bright as a spotlight and revealed no one, but the back seat was slick with something dark and wet and there was plenty of it. A foul scent seeped out of a partially rolled down back window. It was a hot coppery smell that gnawed at her nostrils and ached her stomach.

God, someone had been hurt. Maybe thrown free of the car, or perhaps they had gotten out and crawled off. But when? She and the Chevy had been airborne for only a moment, and she had gotten out of the vehicle an instant after it ceased to roll. Surely she would have seen someone get out of the Buick, and if they had been thrown free by the collision, wouldn't at least one of the Buick's doors be open? If it had whipped back and closed, it seemed unlikely that it would be locked, and all the doors of the Buick were locked, and all the glass was intact, and only on her side was it rolled down, and only a crack.

Enough for the smell of the blood to escape, not enough for a person to slip through unless they were thin and flexible as a feather.

On the other side of the Buick, on the ground, between the back door and the railing, there were drag marks and a thick swath of blood, and another swath on the top of the railing; it glowed there in the moonlight as if it were molasses laced with radioactivity.

Ellen moved cautiously to the railing and peered over.

No one lay mangled and bleeding and oozing their guts. The ground was not as precarious there as she expected it. It was pebbly and sloped out gradually and there was a trail going down it. The trail twisted slightly and as it deepened the foliage grew denser on either side of it. Finally it curlicued its way into the dark thicket of a forest below, and from the forest, hot on the wind, came the strong turpentine tang of pines and something less fresh and not as easily identifiable.

Now she saw someone moving down there, floating up from the forest like an apparition; a white face split by silver—braces, perhaps. She could tell from the way this someone moved that it was a man. She watched as he climbed the trail and came within examination range. He seemed to be surveying her as carefully as she was surveying him.

Could this be the driver of the Buick?

As he came nearer Ellen discovered she could not identify the expression he wore. It was neither joy or anger or fear or exhaustion or pain. It was somehow all and none of these.

When he was ten feet away, still looking up, that same odd expression on his face, she could hear him breathing. He was breathing with exertion, but not to the extent she thought him tired or injured. It was the sound of someone who had been about busy work.

She yelled down, "Are you injured?"

He turned his head quizzically, like a dog trying to make sense of a command, and it occurred to Ellen that he might be knocked about in the head enough to be disoriented.

"I'm the one who ran into your car," she said. "Are you all right?"

His expression changed then, and it was most certainly identifiable this time. He was surprised and angry. He came up the trail quickly, took hold of the top railing, his fingers going into the blood there, and vaulted over and onto the gravel.

Ellen stepped back out of his way and watched him from a distance. The guy made her nervous. Even close up, he looked like some kind of spook.

He eyed her briefly, glanced at the Chevy, turned to look at the Buick.

"It was my fault," Ellen said.

He didn't reply, but returned his attention to her and continued to cock his head in that curious dog sort of way.

Ellen noticed that one of his shirt sleeves was stained with blood, and that there was blood on the knees of his pants, but he didn't act as if he were hurt in any way. He reached into his pants pocket and pulled out something and made a move with his wrist. Out flicked a lock-blade knife. The thin edge of it sucked up the moonlight and spat it out in a silver spray that fanned wide when he held it before him and jiggled it like a man working a stubborn key into a lock. He advanced toward her, and as he came, his lips split and pulled back at the corners, exposing, not braces, but metal-capped teeth that matched the sparkle of his blade.

It occurred to her that she could bolt for the Chevy, but in the same mental flash of lightning, it occurred to her she wouldn't make it.

Ellen threw herself over the railing, and as she leapt, she saw out of the corner of her eye, the knife slashing the place she had occupied, catching moonbeams and throwing them away. Then the blade was out of her view and she hit on her stomach and skidded onto the narrow trail, slid downward, feet first. The gravel and roots tore at the front of her dress and ripped through her nylons and gouged her flesh. She cried out in pain and her sliding gained speed. Lifting her chin, she saw that the man was climbing over the railing and coming after her at a stumbling run, the knife held before him like a wand.

Her sliding stopped, and she pushed off with her hands to make it start again, not knowing if this was the thing to do or not, since the trail inclined sharply on her right side, and should she skid only slightly in that direction, she could hurtle off into blackness. But somehow she kept slithering along the trail and even spun around a corner and stopped with her head facing downward, her purse practically in her teeth.

She got up then, without looking back, and began to run into the woods, the purse beating at her side. She moved as far away from the trail as she could, fighting limbs that conspired to hit her across the face or hold her, vines and bushes that tried to tie her feet or trip her.

Behind her, she could hear the man coming after her, breathing heavily now, not really winded, but hurrying. For the first time in months, she was grateful for Bruce and his survivalist insanity. His passion to be in shape and for her to be in shape with him was paying off. All that jogging had given her the lungs of an ox and strengthened her legs and ankles. A line from one of Bruce's survivalist books came to her: Do the unexpected.

She found a trail amongst the pines, and followed it, then, abruptly broke from it and went back into the thicket. It was harder going, but she assumed her pursuer would expect her to follow a trail.

The pines became so thick she got down on her hands and knees and began to crawl. It was easier to get through that way. After a moment, she stopped scuttling and eased her back against one of the pines and sat and listened. She felt reasonably well hidden, as the boughs of the pines grew low and drooped to the ground. She took several deep breaths, holding each for a long moment.

Gradually, she began breathing normally. Above her, from the direction of the trail, she could hear the man running, coming nearer. She held her breath.

The running paused a couple of times, and she could imagine the man, his strange, pale face turning from side to side, as he tried to determine what had happened to her. The sound of running started again and the man moved on down the trail.

Ellen considered easing out and starting back up the trail, making her way to her car and driving off. Damaged as it was, she felt it would still run, but she was reluctant to leave her hiding place and step into the moonlight. Still, it seemed a better plan than waiting. If she didn't do something, the man could always go back topside himself and wait for her. The woods, covering acres and acres of land below and beyond, would take her days to get through, and without food and water and knowledge of the geography, she might never make it, could end up going in circles for days.

Bruce and his survivalist credos came back to her. She remembered something he had said to one of his self-defense classes, a bunch of rednecks hoping and praying for a commie take-over so they could show their stuff. He had told them: "Utilize what's at hand. Size up what you have with you and how it can be put to use."

All right, she thought. *All right, Brucey, you sonofabitch. I'll see what's at hand.*

One thing she knew she had for sure was a little flashlight. It wasn't much, but it would serve for her to check out the contents of her purse. She located it easily, and without withdrawing it from her purse, turned it on and held the open purse close to her face to see what was inside. Before she actually found it, she thought of her nail file kit. Besides the little bottle of nail polish remover, there was an emery board and two metal files. The files were the ticket. They might serve as weapons; they weren't much, but they were something.

She also carried a very small pair of nail scissors, independent of the kit, the points of the scissors being less than a quarter inch. That wouldn't be worth much, but she took note of it and mentally catalogued it.

She found the nail kit, turned off the flash and removed one of the files and returned the rest of the kit to her purse. She held the file tightly, made a little jabbing motion with it. It seemed so light and thin and insignificant.

She had been absently carrying her purse on one shoulder, and now to make sure she didn't lose it, she placed the strap over her neck and slid her arm through.

Clenching the nail file, she moved on hands and knees beneath the pine boughs and poked her head out into the clearing of the trail. She glanced down it first, and there, not ten yards from her, looking up the trail, holding his knife by his side, was the man. The moonlight lay cold on his face and the shadows of the wind-blown boughs fell across him and wavered. It seemed as if she were leaning over a pool and staring down into the water and seeing him at the bottom of it, or perhaps his reflection on the face of the pool.

She realized instantly that he had gone down the trail a ways, became suspicious of her ability to disappear so quickly, and had turned to judge where she might have gone. And, as if in answer to the question, she poked her head into view.

They remained frozen for a moment, then the man took a step up the trail, and just as he began to run, Ellen went backwards into the pines on her hands and knees.

She had gone less than ten feet when she ran up against a thick limb that lay close to the ground and was preventing her passage. She got down on her belly and squirmed beneath it, and as she was pulling her head under, she saw Moon Face crawling into the thicket, making good time; time made better, when he lunged suddenly and covered half the space between them, the knife missing her by fractions.

Ellen jerked back and felt her feet falling away from her. She let go of the file and grabbed out for the limb and it bent way back and down with her weight.

It lowered her enough for her feet to touch ground. Relieved, she realized she had fallen into a wash made by erosion, not off the edge of the mountain.

Above her, gathered in shadows and stray strands of moonlight that showed through the pine boughs, was the man. His metal-tipped teeth caught a moonbeam and twinkled. He placed a hand on the limb she held, as if to lower himself, and she let go of it.

The limb whispered away from her and hit him full in the face and knocked him back.

Ellen didn't bother to scrutinize the damage. Turning, she saw that the wash ended in a slope and that the slope was thick with trees growing out like great, feathered spears thrown into the side of the mountain.

She started down, letting the slant carry her, grasping limbs and tree trunks to slow her descent and keep her balance. She could hear the man climbing down and pursuing her, but she didn't bother to turn and look. Below she could see the incline was becoming steeper, and if she continued, it would be almost straight up and down with nothing but the trees for support, and to move from one to the other, she would have to drop, chimpanzee-like, from limb to limb. Not a pleasant thought.

Her only consolation was that the trees to her right, veering back up the mountain, were thick as cancer cells. She took off in that direction, going wide, and began plodding upwards again, trying to regain the concealment of the forest.

She chanced a look behind her before entering the pines, and saw that the man, who she had come to think of as Moon Face, was some distance away.

Weaving through a mass of trees, she integrated herself into the forest, and as she went the limbs began to grow closer to the ground and the trees became so thick they twisted together like pipe cleaners. She got down on her hands and knees and crawled between limbs and around tree trunks and tried to lose herself among them.

To follow her, Moon Face had to do the same thing, and at first she heard him behind her, but after a while, there were only the sounds she was making.

She paused and listened.

Nothing.

Glancing the way she had come, she saw the intertwining limbs she had crawled under mixed with penetrating moonbeams, heard the short bursts of her breath and the beating of her heart, but detected no evidence of Moon Face. She decided the head start she had, all the weaving she had done, the cover of the pines, had confused him, at least temporarily.

It occurred to her that if she had stopped to listen, he might have done the same, and she wondered if he could hear the pounding of her heart. She took a deep breath and held it and let it out slowly through her nose, did it again.

She was breathing more normally now, and her heart, though still hammering furiously, felt as if it were back inside her chest where it belonged.

Easing her back against a tree trunk, she sat and listened, watching for that strange face, fearing it might abruptly burst through the limbs and brush, grinning its horrible teeth, or worse, that he might come up behind her, reach around the tree trunk with his knife and finish her in a bloody instant.

She checked and saw that she still had her purse. She opened it and got hold of the file kit by feel and removed the last file, determined to make better use of it than the first. She had no qualms about using it, knew she would, but what good would it do? The man was obviously stronger than she, and crazy as the pattern in a scratch quilt.

Once again, she thought of Bruce. What would he have done in this situation? He would certainly have been the man for the job. He would have relished it. Would probably have challenged old Moon Face to a one on one at the edge of the mountain, and even with a nail file, would have been confident that he could take him.

Ellen thought about how much she hated Bruce, and even now, shed of him, that hatred burned bright. How had she gotten mixed up with that dumb, macho bastard in the first place? He had seemed enticing at first. So powerful. Confident. Capable. The survivalist stuff had always seemed a little nutty, but at first no more nutty than an obsession with golf or a strong belief in astrology.

Perhaps had she known how serious he was about it, she wouldn't have been attracted to him in the first place.

No. It wouldn't have mattered. She had been captivated by him, by his looks and build and power. She had nothing but her own libido and stupidity to blame. And worse yet, when things turned sour, she had stayed and let them sour even more. There had been good moments, but they were quickly eclipsed by Bruce's determination to be ready for the Big Day, as he referred to it. He knew it was coming, if he was somewhat vague on who was bringing it. But someone would start a war of some sort, a nuclear war, a war in the streets, and only the rugged individualist, well-armed and well-trained and strong of body and will, would survive beyond the initial attack. Those survivors would then carry out guerrilla warfare, hit and run operations, and eventually win back the country from . . . whoever. And if not win it back, at least have some kind of life free of dictatorship.

It was silly. It was every little boy's fantasy. Living by your wits with gun and knife. And owning a woman. She had been the woman. At first Bruce had been kind enough, treated her with respect. He was obviously on the male chauvinist side, but originally it had seemed harmless enough, kind of Old World charming. But when he moved them to the mountains, that charm had turned to domination, and the small crack in his mental state widened until it was a deep, dark gulf.

She was there to keep house and to warm his bed, and any opinions she had contrary to his own were stupid. He read survivalist books constantly and quoted passages to her and suggested she look the books over, be ready to stand tall against the oncoming aggressors.

By the time he had gone completely over the edge, living like a mountain man, ordering her about, his eyes roving from side to side, suspicious of her every move, expecting to hear on his shortwave at any moment World War Three had started, or that race riots were overrunning the USA, or that a shiny probe packed with extraterrestrial invaders brandishing ray guns had landed on the White House lawn, she was trapped in his cabin in the mountains, with him holding the keys to her Chevy and his jeep.

For a time she feared he would become paranoid enough to imagine she was one of the "bad guys" and put a .357 round through her chest. But now she was free of him, escaped from all that . . . only to be threatened by another man: a moon-faced, silver-toothed monster with a knife.

She returned once again to the question, what would Bruce do, outside of challenging Moon Face in hand-to-hand combat? Sneaking past him would be the best bet, making it back to the Chevy. To do that Bruce would have used guerrilla techniques. "Take advantage of what's at hand," he always said.

Well, she had looked to see what was at hand, and that turned out to be a couple of fingernail files, one of them lost up the mountain.

Then maybe she wasn't thinking about this in the right way. She might not be able to outfight Moon Face, but perhaps she could outthink him. She had out-thought Bruce, and he had considered himself a master of strategy and preparation.

She tried to put herself in Moon Face's head. What was he thinking? For the moment he saw her as his prey, a frightened animal on the run. He might be more cautious because of that trick with the limb, but he'd most likely chalk that one up to accident—which it was for the most part . . . but what if the prey turned on him?

There was a sudden cracking sound, and Ellen crawled a few feet in the direction of the noise, gently moved aside a limb. Some distance away, discerned faintly through a tangle of limbs, she saw light and detected movement, and knew it was Moon Face. The cracking sound must have been him stepping on a limb.

He was standing with his head bent, looking at the ground, flashing a little pocket flashlight, obviously examining the drag path she had made with her hands and knees when she entered into the pine thicket.

She watched as his shape and the light bobbed and twisted through the limbs and tree trunks, coming nearer. She wanted to run, but didn't know where.

All right, she thought. All right. Take it easy. Think.

She made a quick decision. Removed the scissors from her purse, took off her shoes and slipped off her pantyhose and put her shoes on again.

She quickly snipped three long strips of nylon from her damaged pantyhose and knotted them together, using the sailor knots Bruce had taught her. She cut more thin strips from the hose—all the while listening for Moon Face's approach—and used all but one of them to fasten her fingernail file, point out, securely to the tapered end of one of the small, flexible pine limbs, then she tied one end of the long nylon strip she had made around the limb, just below the file, and crawled backwards, pulling the limb with her, bending it deep. When she had it back as far as she could manage, she took a death grip on the nylon strip, and using it to keep the limb's position taut, crawled around the trunk of a small pine and curved the nylon strip about it and made a loop knot at the base of a sapling that crossed her knee-drag trail. She used her last strip of nylon to fasten to the loop of the knot, and carefully stretched the remaining length across the trail and tied it to another sapling. If it worked correctly, when he came crawling through the thicket, following her, his hands or knees would hit the strip, pull the loop free, and the limb would fly forward, the file stabbing him, in an eye if she were lucky.

Pausing to look through the boughs again, she saw that Moon Face was on his hands and knees, moving through the thick foliage toward her. Only moments were left.

She shoved pine needles over the strip and moved away on her belly, sliding under the cocked sapling, no longer concerned that she might make noise, in fact hoping noise would bring Moon Face quickly.

Following the upward slope of the hill, she crawled until the trees became thin again and she could stand. She cut two long strips of nylon from her hose with the scissors, and stretched them between two trees about ankle high.

That one would make him mad if it caught him, but the next one would be the corker.

She went up the path, used the rest of the nylon to tie between two saplings, then grabbed hold of a thin, short limb and yanked at it until it cracked, worked it free so there was a point made from the break. She snapped that over her knee to form a point at the opposite end. She made a quick mental measurement, jammed one end of the stick into the soft ground, leaving a point facing up.

At that moment came evidence her first snare had worked—a loud swishing sound as the limb popped forward and a cry of pain. This was followed by a howl as Moon Face crawled out of the thicket and onto the trail. He stood slowly, one hand to his face. He glared up at her, removed his hand. The file had struck him in the cheek; it was covered with blood. Moon Face pointed his blood-covered hand at her and let out an accusing shriek so horrible she retreated rapidly up the trail. Behind her, she could hear Moon Face running.

The trail curved upward and turned abruptly. She followed the curve a ways, looked back as Moon Face tripped over her first strip and hit the ground, came up madder, charged even more violently up the path. But the second strip got him and he fell forward, throwing his hands out. The spike in the trail hit him low in the throat.

She stood transfixed at the top of the trail as he did a pushup and came to one knee and put a hand to his throat. Even from a distance, and with only the moonlight to show it to her, she could see that the wound was dreadful.

Good.

Moon Face looked up, stabbed her with a look, started to rise. Ellen turned and ran. As she made the turns in the trail, the going improved and she theorized that she was rushing up the trail she had originally come down.

This hopeful notion was dispelled when the pines thinned and the trail dropped, then leveled off, then tapered into nothing. Before she could slow up, she discovered she was on a sort of peninsula that jutted out from the mountain and resembled an irregular-shaped diving board from which you could leap off into night-black eternity.

In place of the pines on the sides of the trail were numerous scarecrows on poles, and out on the very tip of the peninsula, somewhat dispelling the diving board image, was a shack made of sticks and mud and brambles.

After pausing to suck in some deep breaths, Ellen discovered on closer examination that it wasn't scarecrows bordering her path after all. It was people.

Dead people. She could smell them.

There were at least a dozen on either side, placed upright on poles, their feet touching the ground, their knees slightly bent. They were all fully clothed, and in various states of deterioration. Holes had been poked through the backs of their heads to correspond with the hollow sockets of their eyes, and the moonlight came through the holes and shined through the sockets, and Ellen noted, with a warm sort of horror, that one wore a white sun dress and . . . plastic shoes, and through its head she could see stars. On the corpse's finger was a wedding ring, and the finger had grown thin and withered and the ring was trapped there by knuckle bone alone.

The man next to her was fresher. He too was eyeless and holes had been drilled through the back of his skull, but he still wore glasses and was fleshy.

There was a pen and pencil set in his coat pocket. He wore only one shoe.

There was a skeleton in overalls, a wilting cigar stuck between his teeth. A Freshups man with his cap at a jaunty angle, the moon through his head, and a clipboard tied to his hand with string. His legs had been positioned in such a way it seemed as if he was walking.

A housewife with a crumpled, nearly disintegrated grocery bag under her arm, the contents having long fallen through the worn, wet bottom to heap at her feet in a mass of colorless boxes and broken glass.

A withered corpse in a ballerina's tutu and slippers, rotting grapefruits tied to her chest with cord to simulate breasts, her legs arranged in such a way she seemed in mid-dance, up on her toes, about to leap or whirl.

The real horror was the children. One pathetic little boy's corpse, still full of flesh and with only his drilled eyes to show death, had been arranged in such a way that a teddy bear drooped from the crook of his elbow. A toy metal tractor and a plastic truck were at his feet.

There was a little girl wearing a red rubber clown nose and a propeller beanie. A green plastic purse hung from her shoulder by a strap and a doll's legs had been taped to her palm with black electrician's tape. The doll hung upside down, holes drilled through its plastic head so that it matched its owner.

Things began to click. Ellen understood what Moon Face had been doing down here in the first place. He hadn't been in the Buick when she struck it.

He was disposing of a body. He was a murderer who brought his victims here and set them up on either side of the pathway, parodying the way they were in life, cutting out their eyes and punching through the backs of their heads to let the world in.

Ellen realized numbly that time was slipping away, and Moon Face was coming, and she had to find the trail up to her car. But when she turned to run, she froze.

Thirty feet away, where the trail met the last of the pines, squatting dead center in it, arms on his knees, one hand loosely holding the knife, was Moon Face. He looked calm, almost happy, in spite of the fact a large swath of dried blood was on his cheek and the wound in his throat was making a faint whistling sound as air escaped it.

He appeared to be gloating, savoring the moment when he would set his knife to work on her eyes, the gray matter behind them, the bone of her skull.

A vision of her corpse propped up next to the child with the teddy bear, or perhaps the skeletal ballerina, came to mind; she could see herself hanging there, the light of the moon falling through her empty head, melting into the path.

Then she felt anger. It boiled inside her. She determined she was not going to allow Moon Face his prize easily. He'd earn it.

Another line from Bruce's books came to her. Consider your alternatives.

She did, in a flash. And they were grim. She could try charging past Moon Face, or pretend to, then dart into the pines. But it seemed unlikely she could make the trees before he overtook her. She could try going over the side of the trail and climbing down, but it was much too steep there, and she'd fall immediately. She could make for the shack and try and find something she could fight with. The last idea struck her as the correct one, the one Bruce would have pursued. What was his quote? "If you can't effect an escape, fall back and fight with what's available to you."

She hurried to the hut, glancing behind her from time to time to check on Moon Face. He hadn't moved. He was observing her calmly, as if he had all the time in the world.

When she was about to go through the doorless entryway, she looked back at him one last time. He was in the same spot, watching, the knife held limply against his leg. She knew he thought he had her right where he wanted her, and that's exactly what she wanted him to think. A surprise attack was the only chance she had. She just hoped she could find something to surprise him with.

She hastened inside and let out an involuntary rasp of breath.

The place stank, and for good reason. In the center of the little hut was a folding card table and some chairs, and seated in one of the chairs was a woman, the flesh rotting and dripping off her skull like candle wax, her eyes empty and holes in the back of her head. Her arm was resting on the table and her hand was clamped around an open bottle of whiskey. Beside her, also without eyes, suspended in a standing position by wires connected to the roof, was a man. He was a fresh kill. Big, dressed in khaki pants and shirt and work shoes. In one hand a doubled belt was taped, and wires were attached in such a way that his arm was drawn back as if ready to strike. Wires were secured to his lips and pulled tight behind his head so that he was smiling in a ghoulish way. Foil gum wrappers were fixed to his teeth, and the moonlight gleaming through the opening at the top of the hut fell on them and made them resemble Moon Face's metal-tipped choppers.

Ellen felt queasy, but fought the sensation down. She had more to worry about than corpses. She had to prevent herself from becoming one.

She gave the place a quick pan. To her left was a rust-framed rollaway bed with a thin, dirty mattress, and against the far wall, was a baby crib, and next to that a camper stove with a small frying pan on it.

She glanced quickly out the door of the hut and saw that Moon Face had moved onto the stretch of trail bordered by the bodies. He was walking very slowly, looking up now and then as if to appreciate the stars.

Her heart pumped another beat.

She moved about the hut, looking for a weapon.

The frying pan.

She grabbed it, and as she did, she saw what was in the crib. What belonged there. A baby. But dead. A few months old. Its skin thin as plastic and stretched tight over pathetic, little rib bones. Eyes gone, holes through its head. Burnt match stubs between blackened toes. It wore a diaper and the stink of feces wafted from it and into her nostrils. A rattle lay at the foot of the crib.

A horrible realization rushed through her. The baby had been alive when taken by this madman, and it had died here, starved and tortured. She gripped the frying pan with such intensity her hand cramped.

Her foot touched something.

She looked down. Large bones were heaped there—discarded mommies and daddies, for it now occurred to her that was who the corpses represented.

Something gleamed amongst the bones. A gold cigarette lighter.

Through the doorway of the hut she saw Moon Face was halfway down the trail. He had paused to nonchalantly adjust the UPS man's clipboard. The geek had made his own community here, his own family, people he could deal with— dead people—and it was obvious he intended for her to be part of his creation.

Ellen considered attacking straight-on with the frying pan when Moon Face came through the doorway, but so far he had proven strong enough to take a file in the cheek and a stick in the throat, and despite the severity of the latter wound, he had kept on coming. Chances were he was strong enough to handle her and her frying pan.

A back-up plan was necessary. Another one of Bruce's pronouncements. She recalled a college friend, Carol, who used to use her bikini panties to launch projectiles at a teddy bear propped on a chair. This graduated to an apple on the bear's head. Eventually, Ellen and her dorm sisters got into the act. Fresh panties with tight elastic and marbles for ammunition were ever ready in a box by the door; the bear and an apple were in constant position. In time, Ellen became the best shot of all. But that was ten years ago. Expertise was long gone, even the occasional shot now and then was no longer taken ... still ...

Ellen replaced the frying pan on the stove, hiked up her dress and pulled her bikini panties down and stepped out of them and picked up the lighter.

She put the lighter in the crotch of the panties and stuck her fingers into the leg loops to form a fork and took hold of the lighter through the panties and pulled it back, assured herself the elastic was strong enough to launch the projectile.

All right. That was a start.

She removed her purse, so Moon Face couldn't grab it and snare her, and tossed it aside. She grabbed the whiskey bottle from the corpse's hand and turned and smashed the bottom of it against the cook stove. Whiskey and glass flew. The result was a jagged weapon she could lunge with. She placed the broken bottle on the stove next to the frying pan.

Outside, Moon Face was strolling toward the hut, like a shy teenager about to call on his date.

There were only moments left. She glanced around the room, hoping insanely at the last second she would find some escape route, but there was none.

Sweat dripped from her forehead and ran into her eye and she blinked it out and half-drew back the panty sling with its golden projectile. She knew her makeshift weapon wasn't powerful enough to do much damage, but it might give her a moment of distraction, a chance to attack him with the bottle. If she went at him straight on with it, she felt certain he would disarm her and make short work of her, but if she could get him off guard....

She lowered her arms, kept her makeshift slingshot in front of her, ready to be cocked and shot.

Moon Face came through the door, ducking as he did, a sour sweat smell entering with him. His neck wound whistled at her like a teapot about to boil. She saw then that he was bigger than she first thought. Tall and broad-shouldered and strong.

He looked at her and there was that peculiar expression again. The moonlight from the hole in the roof hit his eyes and teeth, and it was as if that light was his source of energy. He filled his chest with air and seemed to stand a full two inches taller. He looked at the woman's corpse in the chair, the man's corpse supported on wires, glanced at the playpen.

He smiled at Ellen, squeaked more than spoke, "Bubba's home, Sissie."

I'm not Sissie yet, thought Ellen. Not yet.

Moon Face started to move around the card table and Ellen let out a blood-curdling scream that caused him to bob his head high like a rabbit surprised by headlights. Ellen jerked up the panties and pulled them back and let loose the lighter. It shot out of the panties and fell to the center of the card table with a clunk.

Moon Face looked down at it.

Ellen was temporarily gripped with paralysis, then she stepped forward and kicked the card table as hard as she could. It went into Moon Face, hitting him waist high, startling, but not hurting him.

Now! thought Ellen, grabbing her weapons. Now!

She rushed him, the broken bottle in one hand, the frying pan in the other.

She slashed out with the bottle and it struck him in the center of the face and he let out a scream and the glass fractured and a splash of blood burst from him and in that same instant Ellen saw that his nose was cut half in two and she felt a tremendous throb in her hand. The bottle had broken in her palm and cut her.

She ignored the pain and as Moon Face bellowed and lashed out with the knife, cutting the front of her dress but not her flesh, she brought the frying pan around and caught him on the elbow, and the knife went soaring across the room and behind the rollaway bed.

Moon Face froze, glanced in the direction the knife had taken. He seemed empty and confused without it.

Ellen swung the pan again. Moon Face caught her wrist and jerked her around and she lost the pan and was sent hurtling toward the bed, where she collapsed on the mattress. The bed slid down and smashed through the thin wall of sticks and a foot of the bed stuck out into blackness and the great drop below. The bed tottered slightly, and Ellen rolled off of it, directly into the legs of Moon Face. As his knees bent, and he reached for her, she rolled backwards and went under the bed and her hand came to rest on the knife. She grabbed it, rolled back toward Moon Face's feet, reached out quickly and brought the knife down on one of his shoes and drove it in as hard as she could.

A bellow from Moon Face. His foot leaped back and it took the knife with it. Moon Face screamed, "Sissie! You're hurting me!"

Moon Face reached down and pulled the knife out, and Ellen saw his foot come forward, and then he was grabbing the bed and effortlessly jerking it off of her and back, smashing it into the crib, causing the child to topple out of it and roll across the floor, the rattle clattering behind it. He grabbed Ellen by the back of her dress and jerked her up and spun her around to face him, clutched her throat in one hand and held the knife close to her face with the other, as if for inspection; the blade caught the moonlight and winked.

Beyond the knife, she saw his face, pathetic and pained and white. His breath, sharp as the knife, practically wilted her. His neck wound whistled softly. The remnants of his nose dangled wet and red against his upper lip and cheek and his teeth grinned a moonlit, metal good-bye.

It was all over, and she knew it, but then Bruce's words came back to her in a rush. "When it looks as if you're defeated, and there's nothing left, try anything."

She twisted and jabbed out at his eyes with her fingers and caught him solid enough that he thrust her away and stumbled backwards. But only for an instant. He bolted forward, and Ellen stooped and grabbed the dead child by the ankle and struck Moon Face with it as if it were a club. Once in the face, once in the midsection. The rotting child burst into a spray of desiccated flesh and innards and she hurled the leg at Moon Face and then she was circling around the rollaway bed, trying to make the door. Moon Face, at the other end of the bed, saw this, and when she moved for the door, he lunged in that direction, causing her to jump back to the end of the bed. Smiling, he returned to his end, waited for her next attempt.

She lurched for the door again, and Moon Face deep-stepped that way, and when she jerked back, Moon Face jerked back too, but this time Ellen bent and grabbed the end of the bed and hurled herself against it. The bed hit Moon Face in the knees, and as he fell, the bed rolled over him and he let go of the knife and tried to put out his hands to stop the bed's momentum. The impetus of the rollaway carried him across the short length of the dirt floor and his head hit the far wall and the sticks cracked and hurtled out into blackness, and Moon Face followed and the bed followed him, then caught on the edge of the drop and the wheels buried up in the dirt and hung there.

Ellen had shoved so hard she fell face down, and when she looked up, she saw the bed was dangling, shaking, the mattress slipping loose, about to glide off into nothingness.

Moon Face's hands flicked into sight, clawing at the sides of the bed's frame.

Ellen gasped. He was going to make it up. The bed's wheels were going to hold.

She pulled a knee under her, cocking herself, then sprang forward, thrusting both palms savagely against the bed. The wheels popped free and the rollaway shot out into the dark emptiness.

Ellen scooted forward on her knees and looked over the edge. There was blackness, a glimpse of the mattress falling free, and a pale object, like a whitewashed planet with a great vein of silver in it, jetting through the cold expanse of space. Then the mattress and the face were gone and there was just the darkness and a distant sound like a water balloon exploding.

Ellen sat back and took a breather. When she felt strong again and felt certain her heart wouldn't tear through her chest, she stood up and looked around the room. She thought a long time about what she saw.

She found her purse and panties, went out of the hut and up the trail, and after a few wrong turns, she found the proper trail that wound its way up the mountainside to where her car was parked. When she climbed over the railing, she was exhausted.

Everything was as it was. She wondered if anyone had seen the cars, if anyone had stopped, then decided it didn't matter. There was no one here now, and that's what was important.

She took the keys from her purse and tried the engine. It turned over. That was a relief.

She killed the engine, got out and went around and opened the trunk of the Chevy and looked down at Bruce's body. His face looked like one big bruise, his lips were as large as sausages. It made her happy to look at him.

A new energy came to her. She got him under the arms and pulled him out and managed him over to the rail and grabbed his legs and flipped him over the railing and onto the trail. She got one of his hands and started pulling him down the path, letting the momentum help her. She felt good. She felt strong.

First Bruce had tried to dominate her, had threatened her, had thought she was weak because she was a woman, and one night, after slapping her, after raping her, while he slept a drunken sleep, she had pulled the blankets up tight around him and looped rope over and under the bed and used the knots he had taught her, and secured him.

Then she took a stick of stove wood and had beat him until she was so weak she fell to her knees. She hadn't meant to kill him, just punish him for slapping her around, but when she got started she couldn't stop until she was too worn out to go on, and when she was finished, she discovered he was dead.

That didn't disturb her much. The thing then was to get rid of the body somewhere, drive on back to the city and say he had abandoned her and not come back. It was weak, but all she had.

Until now.

After several stops for breath, a chance to lie on her back and look up at the stars, Ellen managed Bruce to the hut and got her arms under his and got him seated in one of the empty chairs. She straightened things up as best as she could. She put the larger pieces of the baby back in the crib. She picked Moon Face's knife up off the floor and looked at it and looked at Bruce, his eyes wide open, the moonlight from the roof striking them, showing them to be dull as scratched glass.

Bending over his face, she went to work on his eyes. When she finished with them, she pushed his head forward and used the blade like a drill. She worked until the holes satisfied her. Now if the police found the Buick up there and came down the trail to investigate, and found the trail leading here, saw what was in the shack, Bruce would fit in with the rest of Moon Face's victims. The police would probably conclude Moon Face, sleeping here with his "family," had put his bed too close to the cliff and it had broken through the thin wall and he had tumbled to his death.

She liked it.

She held Bruce's chin, lifted it, examined her work.

"You can be Uncle Brucey," she said, and gave Bruce a pat on the shoulder.

"Thanks for all your advice and help, Uncle Brucey. It's what got me through." She gave him another pat.

She found a shirt—possibly Moon Face's, possibly a victim's—on the opposite side of the shack, next to a little box of Harlequin Romances, and she used it to wipe the knife, pan, all she had touched, clean of her prints, then she went out of there, back up to her car.

Murder for Beginners

BY MERCEDES M. YARDLEY

Sometimes, you just gotta kill that bastard. Just seems like the natural thing to do. Not a whole lot of explanation necessary. If you knew him, you'd probably want to kill him, too.

This is the story that first made me fall in love with Mercedes M. Yardley and her cheerfully deranged young ladies. I think it's charming and hilarious.

And I don't know about you, but right about now, a laugh sounds great to me.

She looked at the shovel in her hands and then at Rob's dead body.

"Ah, snap," she said.

"Nah, it's not that bad," Dawn said, tipping her head to look at the carnage. She nudged Rob a bit with the tip of her red high heel. When he didn't move, she nudged him harder. Taking heart, she gave him a good kick. And then another one. She was just gearing up for the granddaddy of all kicks when suddenly the blunt shovel snapped lightly against her foot.

"Stop it."

Dawn's balance was thrown off, and she fought for a second to regain it. She blew her hair out of her eyes.

"Aw, Jaye, you never let me have any fun."

"Hey, I let you go at it for a while, didn't I? You can't say I'm not gracious." This spoken from a woman holding a bloody shovel over a dead man.

"True," Dawn agreed. "Very gracious."

They grinned at each other.

"So. What do we do?" Jaye asked. She patted Rob's corpse on the rump with the tip of the shovel, then stabbed the end into the ground and sighed.

"Um . . . we apologize?"

"Sorry, Rob. I didn't mean to kill you."

"No." Dawn shook her head. "Not to Rob. Let's drag him somewhere else. Maybe we can write a note, or something. Leave it in his pocket. 'I'm sorry I killed Rob, he really was a jerk. Do what you want with his body.'" She looked at Jaye. "Isn't there a better way to word that?"

Jaye leaned her head against the shovel handle. "You mean like, 'Please dispose of his body properly'?"

Dawn's eyes shone. "Yes! I'm sorry about Rob; please dispose of his body properly!"

Jaye thought about it briefly. "I like it, but it doesn't seem very fair to do that. What if a kid should find him? Or an old lady?"

"Or his wife."

"Oh, yeah. Her." Jaye winced. "Think we should tell her?"

"I don't wanna."

"I don't, either. But it seems mean not to. What if she's waiting up for him, or something?"

Dawn flopped down on the ground beside Rob. "I need a cigarette. Got one?"

"You know I don't."

Dawn lay on her back and looked at the treetops. "You are such a priss. You know that?"

"Watch it!" Jaye raised the shovel threateningly.

Dawn rolled her eyes before shutting them. "So not scared," she said. "Mm-mmm, cigarettes."

"What happened to yours?"

"They fell out of my purse when I was running away from Rob. They're back there somewhere." She fluttered her hand distractedly toward the woods.

Jaye was silent for a second. "Rob smokes. Every now and then. Betcha he's got something."

Dawn opened her eyes and looked at Jaye. "How do you know that?"

Jaye shrugged. "I tasted it. You know. That one time."

"Oh yeah. Right." Dawn rolled over on her stomach and stared at Rob, nose to nose. "So I've always wondered. What's he like, as a kisser? We sort of always skipped that part."

Jaye wrinkled her nose. "Hmmm. Not too bad, I guess. Not great. He needs to work on his technique." She knocked the shovel against the soles of his shoes. "You need to work on your technique." Rob didn't respond.

"So," Dawn said urgently. "The smokes."

"I'm not sure where they are. Check him."

"You check him!"

"I don't want the cigarettes!"

Dawn's brown eyes were sad. "Oh, come on. Please? It's Rob. He's just so . . . gross, now that he's dead. Kinda when he was alive, too. I don't want to touch him."

Jaye glared at Dawn and then dropped to her knees beside Rob. "Okay. I understand. But," she said, when Dawn clapped her hands, "when I roll Rob for his cigarettes, you have to call his wife. It's only fair."

"But . . ."

"Here." Jaye held out her cell phone. Dawn looked at it as if it would bite her.

"Or I could call and you can paw dead Rob. Your choice."

Dawn snatched the phone and punched in some numbers. She turned her back on Jaye, who started going through Rob's pockets.

"Oh, Dawn! He's starting to cool down!"

"Well, that's just gross. I'm glad that—hello, Karen? Hi, this is Dawn."

Jaye found a wad of used tissue in Rob's coat pocket. She yicked and threw it over her shoulder. She slid her hand back inside.

"I'm great, thanks! How are you? Uh huh. Oh, and Quinn said what? Oh! Isn't he just a little card?"

Only half listening to Dawn's end of the conversation, Jaye scored an open pack of gum and a handful of change from the other coat pocket. She took a piece for herself and flipped one to Dawn. Dawn caught it and opened it neatly.

"Listen, Karen, I called because there's been a situation with Rob. Yeah. She's here with me. Jaye," she whispered, covering the phone with her hand, "Say hi to Karen."

"Hi, Karen!" Jaye yelled, and slid her hands into Karen's dead husband's pockets. "How's Quinn?"

Dawn popped the gum into her mouth and chewed loudly. "Quinn's good, Jaye. He said something hysterical. I'll tell you later. So Karen. Jaye here hit Rob on the head with a shovel. Pretty hard. Uh huh. Oh, I don't know. Five or six times, I'd say. What do you think?" she said to Jaye. "Five or six times?"

"At least."

"Yeah, about that much." Dawn listened on the phone. Jaye pulled out Rob's wallet and started flipping through it.

"Yeah, it was pretty amazing, Karen! She just went to town. She had a shovel out here 'cuz she was planting something..."

"Geraniums."

"Geraniums, she says. And she just went to town all over his freaking head. It was wild."

Dawn caught Jaye's eye and winked. "Karen says you're a freaking Amazon."

Jaye snorted and continued looking through the wallet.

"Yeah, he was after me. I told him I'd just found out that you two were married and I wasn't into that scene. I mean, you guys got married when? Tuesday? And it's, what, Friday now? I mean, really."

Jaye pulled a nude picture of Dawn out of Rob's wallet and raised her eyebrow. She handed it to Dawn, who deftly tucked it into her bra.

"Yeah, he got mad, Karen. Chased me all the way to Jaye's. I mean, if it weren't for her and her daffodils..."

"Geraniums."

"Geraniums, I'd probably be toast!" Dawn listened. "Yeah, he's pretty dead. Sorry."

Jaye straightened up on her knees and looked at Dawn. Dawn shook her head. "Uh uh. We haven't. No, she's right here, going through his clothes for cigarettes.

I dropped mine, and I don't want to touch him. Oh. Why would he do that? Thanks, I see. Okay."

Dawn pointed at Rob's legs. "She says he keeps a few loose ones tucked into his socks. Because he feels cool reaching down to get them."

Jaye shook her head and pulled up Rob's pant leg. She took three loose cigarettes from the top of his tube sock. She handed them to Dawn along with her own lighter.

"You're such a pyro," Dawn whispered, and lit up. She took a deep drag. "Mmmmm. Thanks, Karen!" she said into the phone. "That was very helpful. Okay, I'll tell her."

Jaye was checking Rob's other sock. She pulled out a comb and a badly written love poem that bordered on the obscene. She showed it to Dawn, who grimaced.

"I hope it wasn't for me. Karen wants to know if he has a heartbeat."

"Of course not. He's cold!"

"Well, would you listen? She wants to make sure."

"I'm tired of touching him!"

"Oh, come on. Necrophiliacs do it all of the time. Besides, you did kill him." Jaye growled. "Okay. Fine!"

She unbuttoned his shirt and put her ear to his cool chest. The curly hair tickled her ears. She didn't hear a sound.

"Sick, now I'm going to have to wash my face!"

"Nope, no heartbeat," Dawn told Karen. "Uh huh. Uh huh. Will do. Still up for a movie tomorrow? Okay, see you then."

She snapped the phone shut and handed it to Jaye, who was standing up and brushing off her dusty knees.

"She says we should probably call the police soon, and not to worry because she'll testify about his temper and stuff. But let's eat first. I'm starving. How about chicken salad at Irelands? My treat."

"No, Rob's," Jaye said, and flashed the twenty from his wallet.

"Best thing he ever did for us. All right, let's go," Dawn said, and poked Jaye hard in the side as they walked away. "Don't forget to wash your hands before you eat."

"As if."

Jesse

BY STEVE RASNIC TEM

Some writers have a way of getting under your skin, and making it feel kind of greasy in there. Not dirty in the typical pervo sense, but unclean on some deeper, more fundamentally disturbing level.

Steve Rasnic Tem has an uncanny knack for conveying that squirming, wormlike kind of crazy. And in "Jesse," it's an atmosphere that literally drips from the pages, the deeper you sink your reluctant fingers in.

Jesse says he figures it's about time we did another one.

He uses "we" like we're Siamese twins or something, like we both decide what's going to happen and then it happens. Like we just do it, two bodies with one mind like in some weird movie. But it's Jesse that does it, all of it, each and every time. I'm just along for the ride. It's not my fault what Jesse does. I can't stop him—nobody could.

"Why?" I ask, and I feel bad that my voice has to shake, but I can't help it. "Why is it time, Jesse?"

"'Cause I'm afraid you're forgetting too many things, John. You're forgetting how we do it, and how they look."

We again. Like Jesse doesn't do a thing by himself. But Jesse does everything by himself. "I don't forget," I say.

"Oh, but I think you do. I know you do. It's time all right." Then he gets up from his nest in the sour straw and starts toward the barn door. And even though I haven't forgotten how they look, and how we do it, how he does it—how could anybody forget something like that?—I get up out of the straw and follow.

When Jesse called me up that day I didn't take him all that seriously. Jesse was always calling me up and saying crazy things.

"Come on over," he said. "I gotta show you something."

I laughed at him. "You're in enough trouble," I said. "Your parents grounded you, remember? Two weeks at least, you told me."

"My parents are dead," he said, in his serious voice. But I had heard his serious voice a thousand times, and I knew what it meant.

I laughed. "Sure, Jesse. Deader than a flat frog on the highway, right?"

"No, deader than your dick, dickhead." He was always saying that. I laughed again. "Come on over. I swear it'll be okay."

"Okay. My mom has to go to the store. She can drop me off and pick me up later."

"No. Don't come with your mom. Take your bike."

"Christ, Jesse. It's five miles!"

"You've done it before. Take your bike or don't come at all."

"Okay. Be there when I get there." He made me mad all the time. All he had to do was tell me to do something and I'd do it. When I first knew him I did things he said because I felt sorry for him. His big brother had died when a tractor rolled over on him. I wasn't there but people said it was pretty awful. I heard my dad tell my mom that there must have been a dozen men around but none of them could do a thing. Jesse's brother had been awake the whole time, begging them to get the tractor off, that he could feel his heart getting ready to stop, that he knew it was going to stop any second. Dad said the blood was seeping out from under the tractor, all around his body, and Jesse's brother was looking at it like he just couldn't believe it. And Jesse was there watching the whole thing, Dad said. They couldn't get him to go away.

It gave me the creeps, what Jesse's brother had said. 'Cause I've always been afraid my heart was just going to stop some day, for no good reason. And to feel your heart getting ready to stop, that would be horrible.

Because of all that I felt real bad for Jesse, so for awhile there he would ask me to do something, anything, and I'd do it for him. I'd steal somebody's lunch or pull down a little kid's pants or walk across the creek on a little skinny board, all kinds of stupid crap. But after awhile I just did it because he said. He didn't make you want to feel bad for him. I wasn't even sure that he cared that his brother was dead. Once I asked him if he still felt bad about it and he just said that his brother picked on him all the time. That's all he would say about it. Jesse was always weird like that.

I hadn't ridden my bike in over a year—I wasn't sure I still could. I thought sixteen-year-olds were too old to ride bikes—guys were getting their licenses and were willing to walk or get rides with older friends until that day happened. And I was big for my age, a lot bigger than Jesse. I felt stupid. But I rode my bike the five miles anyway, just because Jesse told me to.

By the time I got to his farm I was so tired and mad I just threw the bike down in the gravel driveway. I didn't care if I broke it—I wasn't going to ride it home no matter what. Jesse came to the screen door with a smirk on his face. "Took you long enough," he said. "I didn't think you were coming."

"I'm here, all right? What'd you want to show me that was so damn important?"

He pulled me down the hall. He was so excited and it was happening so fast I was having a real bad feeling even before I saw them. He stopped in front of the door to his parents' bedroom and knocked it open with his fist. The sound made me jump. Then when I looked inside there were his parents on the floor, sleeping.

A short laugh came out of me like a bark. They looked silly: his mom's dress pulled up above her knees and his dad's mouth hanging open like he was drunk. They had their arms folded over their bellies. I never saw people sleeping that way before. The sheets and blankets and pillows had been pulled off the bed and were arranged around them and underneath them like a nest. His mom had never been a good housekeeper—Jesse told me the place always looked and stank like a garbage dump—but I'd never thought it was this bad, that they had to sleep on the floor.

The room was full of all these big candles, the scented kind. There must have been forty or fifty of them. And big melted patches where there must have been lots more, but they'd burned down and been replaced. There was a box full of them by the dresser, all ready to go. They also had a couple of those weird-looking incense burners going. It made me want to laugh. There were more different smells in that room than I'd smelled my whole life. And all of them so sweet they made my eyes water.

But under the sweet there was something else—when a breeze sneaked through and flickered the candles I thought I could smell it—like when we got back from vacation that summer and the freezer broke down while we were away. Mom made Dad move us to a motel for awhile. Something like that, but it was having a hard time digging itself out of all that sweetness.

"Candles cost a fortune," Jesse said. "All the money in my dad's wallet plus the coins my mom kept in a fruit jar. She didn't even think I knew about that. But they look pretty neat, huh?"

I took a step into the room and looked at his dad's mouth. Then his mom's mouth. They hung open like they were about to swallow a fly or sing or something. I almost laughed again, but I couldn't. Their mouths looked a little like my dad's mouth, the way he lets it hang open when he falls asleep on the couch watching TV. But different. Their mouths were soft and loose, their lips dark, all dry and cracked, but even though they were holding their mouths open so long no saliva came dripping out. And there was gray and blue under their eyes. There were dark blotches on Jesse's mom's face. They were so still, like they were playing a game on me. Without even thinking about it I pushed on his dad's leg with my foot. It was like pushing against a board. His dad rocked a little, but he was so tight his big arms didn't even wiggle. Jesse always said his old man was "too tight." I really did start to laugh, thinking about that, but it was like my breath exploded instead. I didn't even know I had been holding it. "Jesus..." I could feel my chest shake all by itself.

Jesse looked at me almost like he was surprised, like I'd done something wrong. "I told you, didn't I? Don't be a baby." He sat down on the floor and started playing with his dad's leg, pushing on it and trying to lift up the knee. "Last night they both started getting stiff. It really happens, you know? It's not just something in the movies. You know why it happens, John?" He looked up at me, but he was still poking the leg with his fist, like he was trying to make his dad do something, slap him or something. Any second I figured his dad would reach over and grab Jesse by the hair and pull him down onto the floor beside them.

I shook my head. I was thinking no no no, but I couldn't quite get that out.

Jesse hit his dad on the thigh hard as he could. It sounded like an overstuffed leather chair. It didn't give at all. "Hell, I don't know either. Maybe it's the body fighting off being dead, even after you're dead, you know? It gets all mad and stiff on you." He laughed but it didn't sound much like Jesse's laugh. "I guess it don't know it's dead. It don't know shit once the brain is dead. But if I was going to die I guess I'd fight real hard." Jesse looked at his mom and dad and made a twisted face like he was smelling them for the first time. "Bunch of pussies . . ."

He grabbed the arm his dad had folded against his chest and tried to pull it away. His dad held on but then the arm bent a little. The fat shoulders shook when Jesse let go and his dad fell back. The head hit the pillow and left a greasy red smear.

"The old man here started loosening up top a few hours ago, in the same order he got stiff in." Jesse reached over and pinched his dad's left cheek.

"Christ, Jesse!" I ran back into the hall and fell on the floor. I could hardly breathe. Then I started crying, really bawling, and I could breathe again.

After awhile I could feel Jesse patting me on the back. "You never saw dead people before, huh, Johnny?"

I just shook my head. "I'm s-sorry, Jesse. I'm s-so sorry."

"They were old," he said. "It's okay. Really."

I looked up at him. I didn't understand. It felt like he wasn't even speaking English. But he just looked at me, then looked back into his parents' bedroom, and didn't say anything more. Finally I knew I had to say something. "How did it happen?"

He looked at me like I was being the one hard to understand. "I told you. They were old."

I thought about the red smear his dad's head made on the pillow, but I couldn't get myself to understand it. "But, Jesse...at the same time?"

He shook his head. "What's wrong with you, John? My dad died first. I guess that made my mom so sad she died a few minutes later. You've heard of that. First one old person dies, then the person they're married to dies just a short time after?"

"Yeah . . ."

"Their hearts just stopped beating." I looked up at him. I could feel my own heart vibrating in my chest, so hard it hurt my ribs. "I put them together like that. They were my parents. I figured they'd like that."

He had that right, I guess. After all, they were his parents. Maybe he didn't always get along with them, but they were his parents. He could look at them after they were dead.

I made myself look at them. It was a lot easier the second time. A whole lot easier. I felt a little funny about that. Even without his dad's blood on the pillow they were a lot different from sleeping people. There was just no movement at all, and hardly any color but the blue, and they both looked cool, but not a damp kind of cool because they looked so dry, and their eyelids weren't shut all the way, and you could see a little sliver of white where the lids weren't all the way closed. I made myself get as close to their eyes as I could, maybe to make sure one final time they weren't pretending. The sliver of white was dull, like on a fish. Like something thick and milky had grown over their eyes. They looked like dummies some department store had thrown out in the garbage. There wasn't anything alive about them at all.

"When did they die?"

Jesse was looking at them, too. Closely, like they were the strangest things anyone had ever seen. "It's been at least a day, I guess. Almost two."

Jesse said we shouldn't call the police just yet. They were his parents, weren't they? Didn't he have the right to be with them for awhile? I couldn't argue with that. I guessed Jesse had all kinds of rights when it was his parents. But it still felt weird, him being with their dead bodies almost two whole days. I helped him light some more candles when he said the air wasn't sweet enough anymore. I felt a little better helping him do that, like we were having a funeral for them. All those sweet-smelling candles and incense felt real religious. Then I felt bad about thinking he was being weird earlier, like I was being prejudiced or something. But it was there just the same. I quit looking at his mom and dad, except when Jesse told me to. And after a couple of hours of me just standing out in the hallway, or fussing with the candles, trying not to look at them, Jesse started insisting.

"You gotta look at them, John."

"I did. You saw me. I looked at them."

"No, I mean really look at them. You haven't seen everything there is to see."

I looked at him instead. Real hard. I could hardly believe he was saying this. "Why? I'm sorry they're dead. But why do I have to look at them?"

"Because I want you to."

"Jesse . . ."

". . . and besides, you should know about these things. Your mom and dad don't want you to know about things like this but I guess it's about the most important thing to know about there is. Everybody gets scared of dying, and just about everybody is scared of the dead. You remember that movie *Zombie* we rented? That's what it was all about. Now we've got two dead bodies here. You're my friend, and I want to help you out. I want to share something with you."

"Christ, Jesse. They're your parents."

"What, you think I don't know that? Who else should I learn about this stuff from anyway? If they were still alive, they'd be supposed to teach me. What's wrong with it? And don't just tell me because it's 'weird.' People say something's weird because it makes them nervous. Just because it bothers them they don't want you to do it. So what do we care, anyway? Nobody else is gonna know about this."

Jesse could argue better than anybody, and I never knew what to think about anything for sure. Before I knew it he had me back in the bedroom, leaning over the bodies. It was a little better—I guess I was getting used to them. At least I didn't feel ready to throw up like I did a while ago. That surprised me. It surprised me even more when he took my hand and put it on his mom's—his dead mom's—arm, and I didn't jerk it away.

"Jesus . . ." I guess I'd expected it to be still stiff, but it had gotten soft again, as soft as anything I'd ever felt, like I could just dig my fingers into her arm like butter. It was cool, but not what I expected. And dry.

"See the spots?" Jesse said behind me. "Like somebody's been painting her.

Like for one of those freak shows. Oh, she'd hate it if she knew. She'd think she looked like a whore!"

I saw them all right. Patches of blue-green low down on his dad's belly. Before I could stop him he raised his mom's skirt and showed me that the marks on her were worse: more of the blue-green and little patches of greenish red, all of it swimming together around her big white panties. I was embarrassed, but I kept staring. That's the way I'd always imagined seeing my first panties on a woman: when she was asleep or—to tell the truth—when she was dead. I used to dream about dead women in their panties and bras, dead women naked with their parts hanging out, and I'd felt ashamed about it, but here it was happening for the real and for some reason I was having a hard time feeling too ashamed. I hadn't done it; I hadn't killed her.

"Look," he said. I followed his hand as it moved up his mother's belly. I tensed as he pulled her dress up further, back over her head so that I couldn't see her mouth anymore, her mouth hanging open like she was screaming, but no sound coming out. "I know you always wanted to see one of these up close. Admit it, John." His hand rested on the right cup of her bra. Now I felt real bad, and ashamed, like I had helped him kill her. Her white, loose skin spilled out of the top and bottom of the cup like big gobs of dough. With a jerk of his hand Jesse pulled his mother's bra off. The skin was loose and it all had swollen so much it was beginning to tear. I knew it was going to break like an old fruit any second. "She's gotten bigger since the thing happened," he said. I started to choke. "Come on, John. You always wanted to see this stuff. You wanted to see it, and you wanted to see it dead."

I turned away and walked back into the hall when he started to laugh. His mom was an it now. His dad was a thing. But Jesse knew me so well. He knew about the dreams and he knew what would get to me, what I always thought about, even though I'd never told him. It made me wonder if all guys my age think about being dead that way, wanting to see it and touch it, wanting something real like that, even though it was so awful. I used to dream about finding my own parents dead, and what they would look like, but never once did I imagine I would do that to them. Not like Jesse. I knew now what Jesse had done to his parents. No question about that anymore. But I was all mixed up about what I felt about it. Because, even though it was awful, I still wanted to look, and touch. Wasn't that almost as bad?

"Here." Jesse grabbed my arm and turned me around. He led me back over to his mother's body. "You don't have to look. You can close your eyes. Let me just take your hand." But I wanted to look. He took me over to her side. There was a big blister there, full of stuff. Jesse put my hand on it. "Feel weird, huh?" He didn't look crazy; he looked like some kind of young scientist or something from some dumb TV show. I nodded. "Hey, look at her mouth!" I did. In her big loose mouth I could see pieces of food that had come up. A little dark bug crawled up out of her hair. This is what it's like, what it's really like, I thought. I thought about those rock stars I used to like all made up like they were dead, those horror movies I used to watch with Jesse, and all those stoner kids I used to know getting high every chance they had and telling me it don't matter anyway and everything was just a drag with their eyes half shut and their mouths hanging open and their skin getting whiter every day. All of them, they don't know shit about it, I thought. This is what it's really like.

Jesse left me by his mom and started going to the candles one at a time, snuffing them out. A filmy gray smoke started to fill the bedroom. I could already smell the mix of sweet and sharp smells starting to go away, and underneath that the other truly awful smell creeping in.

Jesse turned to me while the last few candles were still lit. That bad smell was almost all over me now, but I just sat there, holding my breath and waiting for it. He almost grinned but didn't quite make it. "I guess you're ready to take a hit off all this now," he said. I just stared at him. And then I let my clean breath go.

And now Jesse says he figures it's about time we did another one.

We took off from his house with the one bike and Jesse's pack but we had to walk most of the time because Jesse figured we'd better go cross-country, over the fences and through the trees where nobody could see us. He didn't think they'd find the bodies anytime soon but my parents would report me missing after awhile. It was hell getting the bike through all that stuff but Jesse said we might need it later so we best take it. The scariest part was when we had to cross a couple of creeks and wading through water up over my belt carrying that bike made me sure I was going to drown. But I thought maybe I even deserved it for what I'd seen, what I'd done, and what I didn't do. I thought about what a body must look like after it drowned—I'd heard they swole up something awful, and I thought about Jesse showing off my body after I'd died, letting people poke it and smell it, and then I didn't want to die anymore.

Once Jesse suggested that maybe we should build a raft and float downriver like Tom Sawyer and Huckleberry Finn. I'd read the two books and he'd seen one of the movies. I thought it was a great idea but then we couldn't figure out how to do it. Jesse bitched about how they don't teach you important stuff like that in school, and used to, dads taught you stuff like raft-building but they didn't anymore. He said his dad should have taught him stuff like that but he was always too busy.

"Probably," I said, watching Jesse closer all the time because he seemed to be getting frustrated with everything.

I thought a lot about Tom and Huck that first day and how they came back into town just in time to see their own funeral. I wondered if every kid dreamed about doing that. I wondered if my parents found out about what I did in Jesse's house what they would say about me at my funeral.

We slept the first night under the trees. Or tried to. Jesse walked around a lot in the dark and I couldn't sleep much from watching him. The next morning he was nervous and agitated and first thing he did he found an old dog and beat it over the head with a hammer. I didn't know he had the hammer but it was in his pack and I pretty much guessed what he'd used it for before. He didn't even tell me he was going to do it, he just saw the dog and as soon as he saw it he did it. We both stood there and looked at the body and touched it and kicked it and I didn't feel a damn thing and I don't think Jesse did either because he was still real nervous.

Later that morning the farmer picked us up in his truck.

"Going far?" he asked us from the window and I wanted to tell him to keep driving mister but I didn't. He was old and had a nice face and was probably somebody's father and some kid's grandfather but I couldn't say a thing with Jesse standing there.

"Meadville," Jesse said, smiling. I'd seen that fakey smile on Jesse's face before, when he talked to adults, when he talked to his own parents. "We're gonna help out on my uncle's farm." Jesse smiled and smiled and my throat and my chest and my head started filling up with that awful smell again. The old man looked at me and all I could do was look at him and nod. He let Jesse into the cab of the truck and told me I'd better ride with my bike in the back. The old man smiled at me a real smile, like I was a good boy.

The breeze was cool in the back of the truck and the bed rocked so on the gravelly side road we were on I started falling asleep, but every time I was getting ready to conk out we'd hit a bump or something and my head would snap up. But I still think I must have slept a little because somewhere in there I started to dream. I dreamed that I was riding along in the back of a pickup truck my grandfather was driving. He'd been singing the whole way and I'd been enjoying his singing but then it wasn't singing anymore it was screaming and a monster was in the front seat with him, Death was in the front seat with him, beating him over the head with a hammer. Then the truck jerked to a stop and I looked through the cab window where Death was hammering the brains out of my grandfather and coating the glass with gray and brown and red. My grandfather scratched at the glass like I should do something but I couldn't because it was just a dream. Then Death turned to me and grinned while he was still swinging the hammer and fighting with my grandfather and it was my face grinning and speckled with brains and blood.

I turned around to try to get out of the dream, to watch the trees whizz by while the truck was rocking me to sleep, but the land was dark and the trees were tall bodies all swollen in their dying and their heavy heads hanging down and their loose mouths falling open. And the wind through the trees was the breath of the dead—that awful smell I thought we'd left back at Jesse's house.

Later I kissed my grandfather goodbye and helped Jesse bury him under one of those tall trees that smelled so bad.

And now Jesse says he figures it's about time we did another one. He grins and says he's lost the smell. But I can smell it all the time—I smell, taste, and breathe that smell.

Outside Meadville Jesse washed up and stole a shirt and pants off a clothesline. From there we took turns walking and riding the bike to a mall where Jesse did some panhandling. We used the money to buy shakes and burgers. While we were eating Jesse said that panhandling wasn't wrong if you had to do it to get something to eat. I couldn't watch Jesse eat—the food kept coming up out of his mouth. My two burgers smelled so bad I tried to hold my breath while I ate them but that made me choke. But I still ate them. I was hungry.

We walked around the mall for a long time. Other people did the same thing, staring, but never buying anything. It reminded me of one of those zombie pictures. I tried not to touch anybody because they smelled so bad and they held their mouths open so that you could see all their teeth.

Finally Jesse picked out two girls and dragged me over to them. I couldn't get too close because of their smell, but the younger one seemed to like me. She had a nice smile. I looked at Jesse's face. He was grinning at them and then at me. His complexion had gotten real bad since we'd started travelling—there'd been more and more zits on his face every day. Now they were huge. One burst open and a long skinny white worm crawled out. I looked at the girls—they didn't seem to notice.

"His parents are putting him up for adoption so we ran away. I'm trying to hide him until they change their minds." Jesse's breath stank.

The girls looked at me. "Really?" the older one said. Her face had tiny cracks in it. I looked down at my feet.

Both of the girls said "I'm sorry" about the same time, then they got quiet like they were embarrassed. But I still didn't look up. I watched their sandaled feet and the black bugs crawling between their toes.

The older one could drive so they hid us in the back seat of their car and drove to the end of the drive that led to the farmhouse where their family lived. We were supposed to go on to the barn and the girls would bring us out some food later. We never told them about my bike and I kept thinking about it and what people would say when they found it. Even though I never used the bike anymore I was a little sorry about having lost it.

I also thought about those girls and how nice they were and how the younger one seemed to like me, even though they smelled so bad. I wondered why girls like that were always so nice to guys like us, guys with a story to tell, and I thought about how dumb it was.

After we were in the barn for a couple of hours the girls—they were sisters, if I didn't mention it before—brought us some food. The younger one talked to me a long time while I ate but I don't remember anything she said. The older one talked to Jesse the same way and I heard her say "You're a good person to be helping your friend like this." She leaned over and kissed Jesse on his cheek even though the zits were tearing his face apart. Her shirt rode up on the side and Jesse put his dirty hand there. I saw the blisters rise up out of her skin and break open and the smell was worse than ever in the barn but no one else seemed to notice.

I finished eating and leaned back into the dirty straw. I liked the younger sister but I hoped she wouldn't kiss me the same way. I couldn't stand the idea of her open, loose mouth touching my skin. Underneath the straw I saw that there were hunks of gray flesh, pieces of arms and legs and things inside you I didn't know the name for. But I covered them over with more straw when nobody was looking, and I didn't say anything.

And now Jesse says he figures it's about time we did another one. He thinks I've forgotten. But I haven't.

I've been thinking about the two sisters all night and how much they trust us and how good they've been to us. And I've been thinking how they remind me of the Wilks sisters in *Huckleberry Finn* and how Huck felt so ornery and low down because he was letting the duke and king rob them of their money after the sisters had been so nice to him. Sometimes I guess you don't know how to behave until you've read it in a book or seen it on TV.

So he gets up from his nest in the sour straw and starts toward the barn door. And I get up out of the straw and follow. Only last night I took the hammer, and now I beat him in the head until his head comes apart, and all the stink comes out and covers me so bad I know I'll never get it off. He always said he'd fight really hard if he knew he was dying, but his body doesn't fight back hardly at all. Maybe he didn't know.

I hear the noises in the farmhouse and now there are voices and flashlights coming. I scrape my fingers through the straw to find all the pieces of Jesse's head to make him look a little better for these people. I lie down in the straw beside him and close my eyes, leaving just a sliver of milky white under each lid to show them. I drop my mouth open and stop my saliva. I imagine the blue-green colors that will come and paint my body. I imagine the blisters and the insects and the terrible smell my breath has become. But mostly I try to imagine how I'm going to explain to these strangers why I'm enjoying this.

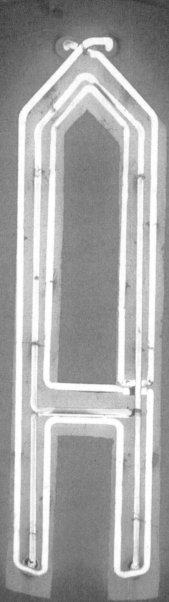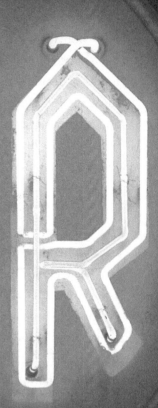

In for a Penny

BY LAWRENCE BLOCK

Everybody screws up once or twice. And a lot of us get caught. So you gotta respect a man who does his time, pays his debt to society, and moves on. The world is not forgiving, but you do what you can. Chalk it up to youthful craziness. And prepare to start anew.

This lies at the heart of many a great crime story, where banged-up guys with a rough road behind them find themselves back at the bottom and try to find their way home.

Lawrence Block is a superb crime writer, as witness his multiple Edgar awards, Grand Master status with the Mystery Writers of America, and multitudinous fans, of which I am one. His modern, hard-boiled style shows great sympathy for down-and-outers on the path to redemption, win or lose.

"In for a Penny" is one of his favorites. Mine, too. You're about to find out why.

Paul kept it very simple. That seemed to be the secret. You kept it simple, you drew firm lines and didn't cross them. You put one foot in front of the other, took it day by day, and let the days mount up.

The state didn't take an interest. They put you back on the street with a cheap suit and figured you'd be back inside before the pants got shiny. But other people cared. This one outfit, about two parts ex-cons to one part holy joes, had wised him up and helped him out. They'd found him a job and a place to live, and what more did he need?

The job wasn't much, frying eggs and flipping burgers in a diner at Twenty-third and Eighth. The room wasn't much, either, seven blocks south of the diner, four flights up from the street. It was small, and all you could see from its window was the back of another building. The furnishings were minimal—an iron bedstead, a beat-up dresser, a rickety chair—and the walls needed paint and the floor needed carpet. There was a sink in the room, a bathroom down the hall. No cooking, no pets, no overnight guests, the landlady told him. No kidding, he thought.

His shift was four to midnight, Monday through Friday. The first weekend he did nothing but go to the movies, and by Sunday night he was ready to climb the wall. Too much time to kill, too few ways to kill it that wouldn't get him in trouble. How many movies could you sit through? And a movie cost him two hours' pay, and if you spent the whole weekend dragging yourself from one movie house to another . . .

Weekends were dangerous, one of the ex-cons had told him. Weekends could put you back in the joint. There ought to be a law against weekends.

But he figured out a way around it. Walking home Tuesday night, after that first weekend of movie-going, he'd stopped at three diners on Seventh Avenue, nursing a cup of coffee and chatting with the guy behind the counter. The third time was the charm; he walked out of there with a weekend job. Saturday and Sunday, same hours, same wages, same work. And they'd pay him off the books, which made his weekend work tax-free.

Between what he was saving in taxes and what he wasn't spending on movies, he'd be a millionaire.

Well, maybe he'd never be a millionaire. Probably be dangerous to be a millionaire, a guy like him, with his ways, his habits. But he was earning an honest dollar, and he ate all he wanted on the job, seven days a week now, so it wasn't hard to put a few bucks aside. The weeks added up and so did the dollars, and the time came when he had enough cash socked away to buy himself a little television set. The cashier at his weekend job set it up and her boyfriend brought it over, so he figured it fell off a truck or walked out of somebody's apartment, but it got good reception and the price was right.

It was a lot easier to pass the time once he had the TV. He'd get up at ten or eleven in the morning, grab a shower in the bathroom down the hall, then pick up doughnuts and coffee at the corner deli. Then he'd watch a little TV until it was time to go to work.

After work he'd stop at the same deli for two bottles of cold beer and some cigarettes. He'd settle in with the TV, a beer bottle in one hand and a cigarette in the other and his eyes on the screen.

He didn't get cable, but he figured that was all to the good. He was better off staying away from some of the stuff they were allowed to show on cable TV Just because you had cable didn't mean you had to watch it, but he knew himself, and if he had it right there in the house how could he keep himself from looking at it?

And that could get you started. Something as simple as late-night adult programming could put him on a train to the big house upstate. He'd been there. He didn't want to go back.

He would get through most of a pack of cigarettes by the time he turned off the light and went to bed. It was funny, during the day he hardly smoked at all, but back in his room at night he had a butt going just about all the time. If the smoking was heavy, well, the drinking was ultralight. He could make a bottle of Bud last an hour. More, even. The second bottle was always warm by the time he got to it, but he didn't mind, nor did he drink it any faster than he'd drunk the first one. What was the rush?

Two beers were enough. All it did was give him a little buzz, and when the second beer was gone he'd turn off the TV and sit at the window, smoking one cigarette after another.

Then he'd go to bed. Then he'd get up and do it all over again.

The only problem was walking home.

And even that was no problem at first. He'd leave his rooming house around three in the afternoon. The diner was ten minutes away, and that left him time to eat before

his shift started. Then he'd leave sometime between midnight and twelve-thirty—
the guy who relieved him, a manic Albanian, had a habit of showing up ten to fifteen
minutes late. Paul would retrace his earlier route, walking the seven blocks down
Eighth Avenue to Sixteenth Street, with a stop at the deli for cigarettes and beer.

The Rose of Singapore was the problem.

The first time he walked past the place, he didn't even notice it. By day it was
just another seedy bar, but at night the neon glowed and the jukebox music poured
out the door, along with the smell of spilled drinks and stale beer and something
more, something unnamable, something elusive.

"If you don't want to slip," they'd told him, "stay out of slippery places."

He quickened his pace and walked on by.

The next afternoon the Rose of Singapore didn't carry the same feeling of danger.
Not that he'd risk crossing the threshold, not at any hour of the day or night. He
wasn't stupid. But it didn't lure him and, consequently, it didn't make him uncomfortable.

Coming home was a different story.

He was thinking about it during his last hour on the job, and by the time he
reached it he was walking all the way over at the edge of the sidewalk, as far from
the building's entrance as he could get without stepping down into the street. He
was like an acrophobe edging along a precipitous path, scared to look down, afraid
of losing his balance and falling accidentally, afraid too of the impulse that might
lead him to plunge purposefully into the void.

He kept walking, eyes forward, heart racing. Once he was past it he felt himself
calming down, and he bought his two bottles of beer and his pack of cigarettes and
went on home.

He'd get used to it, he told himself. It would get easier with time.

But, surprisingly enough, it didn't. Instead it got worse, but gradually,
imperceptibly, and he learned to accommodate it. For one thing, he steered clear
of the west side of Eighth Avenue, where the Rose of Singapore stood. Going to
work and coming home, he kept to the opposite side of the street.

Even so, he found himself hugging the inner edge of the sidewalk, as if every inch
closer to the street would put him that much closer to crossing it and being drawn
mothlike into the tavern's neon flame. And, approaching the Rose of Singapore's

block, he'd slow down or speed up his pace so that the traffic signal would allow him to cross the street as soon as he reached the corner. As if otherwise, stranded there, he might cross in the other direction instead, across Eighth Avenue and on into the Rose.

He knew it was ridiculous, but he couldn't change the way it felt. When it didn't get better, he found a way around it.

He took Seventh Avenue instead.

He did that on the weekends anyway because it was the shortest route.

But during the week it added two long crosstown blocks to his pedestrian commute, four blocks a day, twenty blocks a week. That came to about three miles a week, maybe a hundred and fifty extra miles a year.

On good days he told himself he was lucky to be getting the exercise, that the extra blocks would help him stay in shape. On bad days he felt like an idiot, crippled by fear.

Then the Albanian got fired.

He was never clear on what happened. One waitress said the Albanian had popped off at the manager one time too many, and maybe that was what happened. All he knew was that one night his relief man was not the usual wild-eyed fellow with the droopy mustache but a stocky dude with a calculating air about him. His name was Dooley, and Paul made him at a glance as a man who'd done time. You could tell, but of course he didn't say anything, didn't drop any hints. And neither did Dooley.

But the night came when Dooley showed up, tied his apron, rolled up his sleeves, and said, "Give her my love, huh?" And, when Paul looked at him in puzzlement, he added, "Your girlfriend."

"Haven't got one," he said.

"You live on Eighth Avenue, right? That's what you told me. Eighth and Sixteenth, right? Yet every time you leave here you head over toward Seventh. Every single time."

"I like the exercise," he said.

"Exercise," Dooley said, and grinned. "Good word for it."

He let it go, but the next night Dooley made a similar comment. "I need to unwind when I come off work," Paul told him. "Sometimes I'll walk clear over to Sixth Avenue before I head downtown. Or even Fifth."

"That's nice," Dooley said. "Just do me a favor, will you? Ask her if she's got a sister."

"It's cold and it looks like rain," Paul said. "I'll be walking home on Eighth Avenue tonight, in case you're keeping track."

And when he left he did walk down Eighth Avenue—for one block. Then he cut over to Seventh and took what had become his usual route.

He began doing that all the time, and whenever he headed east on Twenty-second Street he found himself wondering why he'd let Dooley have such power over him. For that matter, how could he have let a seedy gin joint make him walk out of his way to the tune of a hundred and fifty miles a year?

He was supposed to be keeping it simple. Was this keeping it simple? Making up elaborate lies to explain the way he walked home? And walking extra blocks every night for fear that the devil would reach out and drag him into a neon-lit hell?

Then came a night when it rained, and he walked all the way home on Eighth Avenue.

It was always a problem when it rained. Going to work he could catch a bus, although it wasn't terribly convenient. But coming home he didn't have the option, because traffic was one-way the wrong way.

So he walked home on Eighth Avenue, and he didn't turn left at Twenty-second Street and didn't fall apart when he drew even with the Rose of Singapore. He breezed on by, bought his beer and cigarettes at the deli, and went home to watch television. But he turned the set off again after a few minutes and spent the hours until bedtime at the window, looking out at the rain, nursing the beers, smoking the cigarettes, and thinking long thoughts.

The next two nights were clear and mild, but he chose Eighth Avenue anyway. He wasn't uneasy, not going to work, not coming home, either. Then came the weekend, and then on Monday he took Eighth again, and this time on the way home he found himself on the west side of the street, the same side as the bar.

The door was open. Music, strident and bluesy, poured through it, along with all the sounds and smells you'd expect.

He walked right on by.

You're over it, he thought. He went home and didn't even turn on the TV, just sat and smoked and sipped his two longneck bottles of Bud.

Same story Tuesday, same story Wednesday.

Thursday night, steps from the tavern's open door, he thought, Why drag this out?

He walked in, found a stool at the bar. "Double scotch," he told the barmaid. "Straight up, beer chaser."

He'd tossed off the shot and was working on the beer when a woman slid onto the stool beside him. She put a cigarette between bright red lips, and he scratched a match and lit it for her.

Their eyes met, and he felt something click.

She lived over on Ninth and Seventeenth, on the third floor of a brownstone across the street from the projects. She said her name was Tiffany, and maybe it was. Her apartment was three little rooms. They sat on the couch in the front room and he kissed her a few times and got a little dizzy from it. He excused himself and went to the bathroom and looked at himself in the mirror over the sink.

You could go home now, he told the mirror image. Tell her anything, like you got a headache, you got malaria, you're really a Catholic priest or gay or both. Anything. Doesn't matter what you say or if she believes you. You could go home.

He looked into his own eyes in the mirror and knew it wasn't true.

Because he was stuck, he was committed, he was down for it. Had been from the moment he walked into the bar. No, longer than that. From the first rainy night when he walked home on Eighth Avenue. Or maybe before, maybe ever since Dooley's insinuation had led him to change his route.

And maybe it went back further than that. Maybe he was locked in from the jump, from the day they opened the gates and put him on the street. Hell, from the day he was born, even.

"Paul?"

"Just a minute," he said.

And he slipped into the kitchen. In for a penny, in for a pound, he thought, and he started opening drawers, looking for the one where she kept the knives.

Now Hold Still

BY DAVID J. SCHOW

Nobody wants to get murdered. There's not much to like. If it happens, it's bound to be horrible.

Unless the deed goes down in public, odds are good that the last voice you'll hear—aside from your own worthless pleas, helpless screams, and undignified death rattles—will be coming from the person who kills you.

Now imagine that person is David J. Schow, whose sardonic, whip-smart, nightmare stand-up comedy patter should be the envy of psychotics everywhere. Imagine yourself as that captive audience, with his late-night-FM-radio-DJ-from-hell voice both tickling and tormenting you all the way out of this world and into the next.

That's the setup for "Now Hold Still," an original Schow that delivers all the razor-sharp ferocity and wit we have come to expect from this hardest of hard-ass literary assassins.

Now do what he says.

What other choice do you have?

Sorry I woke you up again.

You always ask the same dumb questions. <u>Why me</u> (meaning you)? Or <u>who are you</u> (meaning me)? Which paves the way for <u>what do you want</u> (meaning what do I want from you and how can you talk your way out of it)? That's okay because I expect you to say that—you always do. Last time this happened it occurred to me that you want a story, a justification that might reduce your fear or make sense of your apparently random victimization.

I used to have this girlfriend who once said I had to learn to look at a situation from the other person's point of view, and I first thought what the hell for? This is fairly cut and dried. So I thought about it some more.

Here's the story I came up with. We've got time.

You know what a soul-mate is? I don't mean the mainstay of cheap romance— that flowery, idealistic bullshit people use to excuse the ruination of their lives. Seriously, now. Don't most people assess what they have by smacking it against the wall of True Luv? And it never sticks. Hence many otherwise normal folks squander their well-being on an altar of whom-meets whom and happy endings all designed to rub your nose in what a crap life you have anyway.

The pisser about such clichés is that sometimes they're real—a random synergy, that ole thunderbolt that must exist if for no other reason than to cause us to writhe and pillory ourselves because it never exists for you and me. That's just infuriating, like not getting picked in the natural selection choose-up. It forces you to watch people effortlessly achieve a precise chemistry while you sit, a failure in a puddle of missed ingredients.

Buck and Nikki had a chemistry like that, the kind that could leave you pissed, envious, covetous, sourpussed.

But you probably wouldn't want to pay the price such a rarity costs, because you've always wanted things easy and convenient. A couple like Buck and Nikki, they could be your shining beacon of hope or your best reason to kill yourself. Especially if you're the kind of person who thinks finding a soul-mate is oh-so-special, and not merely a lie unforgiving mothers use to reassure loser children.

Buck and Nikki met by accident. Catalyst, reaction. Saw the essence of their beings in each other. Got married. Got divorced, because even ideal relationships need maintenance. Eventually they hooked back up. Buck needed larger goals. Nikki needed the illusion of freedom. They hit upon a course that was brutally honest, yet directly required them to be creative.

They sat down and made lists of every person with whom they'd gotten sexually involved since their breakup. No omissions, no cheats, no tricks and no also-rans. Basically, anybody who could be considered an assault on their unity. Then they added the people with whom they'd each had relationships prior to hooking up. (Buck had another marriage back in the weeds, somewhere.)

When they were finished they had to give full disclosure on each name. Buck's list had 72 and Nikki's 153, because getting laid for her was always a matter of simple consent (except for the rapes), whereas for Buck it was more a male pursuit thing.

They laughed over their sub-lists of "almosts."

Then they added their lists together—and this is the creative part—and Buck said *we should just kill every single one of them*, and Nikki's eyes lit up.

Think about that for a moment. Think about the commitment, the conviction it would take as an expression of an ultimate kind of love, a sealant bond of genuine weight and consequence, a process and an involute puzzle demanding bottom-lessly creative solutions. A self-renewing, auto-refreshing task.

Now think about your own personal list. The people you've fucked. Who've fucked you over. The ones you loved who didn't love you. The liars and con artists, the opportunists and abusers, the rotten choices, the impulse buys and the gauntlet of faces you've had to survive in order to develop what you call a persona and some sort of half-assed working philosophy.

I use the comparison of good memories versus bad. Good ones tend to shrink on the shelf while bad ones swell up to absorb more space, and that's a problem. The good boils down to fleeting impressions, fast moments, partial incidents— that long and unexpected kiss in a taxi; those fiery wrestling matches where you got what you wanted for once; a sudden spark of passion out of nowhere; the rare instance of transcendence or actual comfort. Now stack that one good feeling against the two weeks of misgivings it probably cost and you'll see the disparity— the year wasted versus the perfect moment; the downside of feeling good; the bitter, endless hours that taught you to be better or different with your next partner.

Obviously we're not just talking about sex here, although that's all that matters to the drones out there in yahoo-land. Who's fucking whom really does make the world go 'round. It's often the <u>only</u> piece of intel that matters.

Buck and Nikki, see, had found a way to cut right to the steak, stay happy, and build their love.

Let's go back to those lists: First thing you do is check off anybody who might have died without your help. Okay, that left 210 people.

Next thing you'd normally do is omit special circumstances or those candidates who were inapplicable or immune. Buck and Nikki looked at each other. Soul-mates, right? No fucking exceptions; still 210.

Then Nikki remembered this one guy who wound up (deservedly) as a paraplegic in an iron lung. She wanted him to spend every waking moment of his life suffering, and Buck agreed—209.

Three people in prison. Tougher to reach, so—206.

Four impossible to trace, gone to ground (perhaps literally), out of the world without a shove. It happens. Fair enough—202.

Or: a hundred and one times two. The symmetry was irresistible.

Hell, bullets come fifty rounds to a box; shotgun shells are five-per, and if you looked at it that way, the whole massacre barely added up to a full grocery bag.

The strategy was this: Any hesitancy, inability, or misgivings by one would be compensated by the other. If Buck couldn't bring himself to lay a sledgehammer upside the skull of his #8 from high school, then Nikki would batter-up. If Nikki felt a ping of remorse about stabbing her #43 (her longest liaison before Buck), Buck would move in smartly with the appropriate gutting tool. (Besides, ole #43 turned out to be a gosh-danged drug dealer.)

It was like collecting, in a way. Or catching the bug for library skills—research, data, deduction, checklists. The first items in your collection come fast and hard, in a flurry. The final ones are the most difficult to collect because the grails are the most subterranean, difficult, or costly.

As to bank, well, their parents had died in such a timely fashion that providence, not coincidence, was credited. Instead of a portfolio, golf, condos or early retirement they chose their special mission, which also fulfilled the old itch for a bit of world travel. Buck and Nikki were, after all, responsible adults who had to make their own way. All they really had was each other (and they had each other a lot).

Still, you're asking why, meaning you want all kinds of explanations you hope will prolong your clock. An "arc," as they say in the movie business, a through-line.

When stories explain everything to you, that's called "exposition."

Ever notice how most stories try that old "calm before the storm" routine? They try to set up something "normal" and then mess with it; make it abnormal to provide a fulcrum to restore the status quo. Except in them stories they usually get "normal" all wrong. It rings false. Or it ain't normal for half the people who read it. I mean, what is "normal," anyway? The Fifties nuclear family? The Nineties drag of soccer moms, SUVs and cellphones? Gold watches, gardening and grandkids? That stuff was never normal for me, and hearing about it all the time sounded like fairytales of zombie life from another planet, like Mars.

"Normal" is relative.

Think about the bad things. The secret things you've done in your life. The stuff so bad you've never shared it. Never even made teasing hints.

The maybes are endless. So are the excuses. Some of that crap might break your heart. But you love patterns and order, so you break your own heart over and over.

Ever mourn the dead? You think dead people give a sour rat fart about your self-humiliations and your displays designed to be noticed and overheard?

Ever hurt somebody on purpose? Perhaps relieve them of the burden of their lives? Is that too extreme for you?

How about all the people you've killed without murdering them? The lies you've spun, the dreams you've crushed, the trodden victims of your own screwed-up personality?

There are no karmic checks and balances, and the universe doesn't give a good goddamn about you.

Yet you think you have some jumped-up moral superiority to Buck and Nikki, don't you? You think you're "normal."

I could say, well, it was because of the baby. Nikki pushed really hard and Buck watched the spawn of their union dribble out in pieces. An arm with an elbow joint, a foot, half a head. And then you'd say, *oh, now I get it*, because you got your exposition. You think you know the mission, the plot.

But I wouldn't want you to *analyze* this to death and miss its value.

I would say Buck and Nikki found other ways to sanctify the covenant of their love, and then I would ask: Have you ever really been in love like that?

Now define "normal." I dare you.

At this stage I probably don't need to tell you that Buck and Nikki aren't their real names. You know that, right? If you didn't know that, you would still be sleeping. No duct tape, no gag. Enjoying a dream of love, perhaps, absent the real thing.

What you and I have right now is intimate, but it sure ain't love.

As might be normally expected, Buck and Nikki's verve began to flag about the time they hit the century mark, one hundred down. Leaving a hundred to go, plus stragglers. It might have been boredom or weariness or satiation. Whatever. So they started farming out a few jobs. Which is why I woke you up this way tonight, when you thought you were sleeping safely alone. Like I woke you up two nights ago, in another town. When you were wearing a different face, asking all the same dumb questions.

You're all the same to me.

And as intriguing as you may have found my tale of Buck and Nikki, I have no interest in what your own story might be. What your real name is. Who you might or might not have slept with in the past.

Story or no story, you'll ask the same dumb questions every time. Giving you all the exposition changes nothing.

You'll come awake in the dark, thinking yourself innocent and normal, and there I'll be, standing over you. You'll open your eyes and get it. No story; just is.

Feminine Endings

BY NEIL GAIMAN

Psychosis thrives in the open, unseen. That's one of its most terrifying aspects. We walk past it daily. Maybe nod. Maybe smile. Never recognizing what it is that is smiling back, with a searching gaze more intimate than we would ever want to know.

But love doesn't play by ordinary rules. And obsession is confession, be it welcome or not. As witness this nightmarishly heartfelt declaration.

Neil Gaiman is one of our finest, alivest, most enthusiastically engaged and therefore beloved modern storytellers. And this seldom-seen gem shows him at his most perceptively attentive. Letting us know just how well he knows us.

A little too well, if you ask me.

My darling,

Let us begin this letter, this prelude to an encounter, formally, as a declaration, in the old-fashioned way: I love you. You do not know me (although you have seen me, smiled at me, placed coins in the palm of my hand). I know you (although not so well as I would like. I want to be there when your eyes flutter open in the morning, and you see me, and you smile. Surely this would be paradise enough?). So I do declare myself to you now, with pen set to paper. I declare it again: I love you.

I write this in English, your language, a language I also speak. My English is good. I was for many years ago in England and in Scotland. I spent a whole summer standing in Covent Garden, except for the month of Edinburgh Festival, when I am in Edinburgh. People who put money in my box in Edinburgh included Mr Kevin Spacey the actor, and Mr Jerry Springer the American television star who was in Edinburgh for an Opera about his life.

I have put off writing this for so long, although I have wanted to, although I have composed it many times in my head. Shall I write about you? About me?

First you.

I love your hair, long and red. The first time I saw you I believed you to be a dancer, and I still believe that you have a dancer's body. The legs, and the posture, head up and back. It was your smile that told me you were a foreigner, before ever I heard you speak. In my country we smile in bursts, like the sun coming out and illuminating the fields and then retreating again behind a cloud too soon. Smiles are valuable here. But you smiled all the time, as if everything you saw delighted you. You smiled the first time you saw me, even wider than before. You smiled and I was lost, like a small child in a great forest, never to find its way home again.

I learned when young that the eyes give too much away. Some in my profession adopt dark spectacles, or even (and these I scorn with bitter laughter as amateurs) masks that cover the whole face. What good is a mask? My solution is that of full-sclera theatrical contact lenses, purchased from an American website for a little under $500 Euros, which cover the whole eye. They are dark grey, or course, and look like stone. They have made me more than $500 Euros, paid for themselves over and over.

You may think, given my profession, that I must be poor, but you would be wrong. Indeed, I fancy that you will be surprised by how much I have collected. My needs have been small and my earnings always very good.

Except when it rains.

Sometimes even when it rains. The others as perhaps you have observed, my love, retreat when it rains, raise umbrellas, run away. I remain where I am. Always. I simply wait, unmoving. It all adds to the conviction of the performance.

And it is a performance, as much as when I was a theatrical actor, a magician's assistant, even a dancer. (That is how I am so familiar with the bodies of dancers.) Always, I was aware of the audience as individuals. I have found this with all actors and all dancers, except the short-sighted ones for whom the audience is a blur. My eyesight is good, even through the contact lenses.

"Did you see the man with the moustache in the third row?" we would say. "He is staring at Minou with lustful glances."

And Minou would reply, "Ah yes. But the woman on the aisle, who looks like the German Chancellor, she is now fighting to stay awake." If one person falls asleep, you can lose the whole audience, so we play the rest of the evening to a middle-aged woman who wishes only to succumb to drowsiness.

The second time you stood near me you were so close I could smell your shampoo. It smelled like flowers and fruit. I imagine America as being a whole continent full of women who smell of flowers and fruit. You were talking to a young man from the university. You were complaining about the difficulties of our language for an American. "I understand what gives a man or a woman gender," you were saying. "But what makes a chair masculine or a pigeon feminine? Why should a statue have a feminine ending?"

The young man laughed and pointed straight at me, then. But truly, if you are walking through the square, you can tell nothing about me. The robes look like old marble, water-stained and time-worn and lichened. The skin could be granite. Until I move I am stone and old bronze, and I do not move if I do not want to. I simply stand.

Some people wait in the square for much too long, even in the rain, to see what I will do. They are uncomfortable not knowing, only happy once they have assured themselves that I am natural, not artificial. It is the uncertainty that traps people, like a mouse in a glue-trap.

I am writing about myself too much. I know that this is a letter of introduction as much as it is a love letter. But I should write about you. Your smile. Your eyes so green. (You do not know the true colour of my eyes. I will tell you. They are brown.) You like classical music, but you have also Abba and Kid Loco on your iPod Nano. You wear no perfume. Your underwear is, for the most part, faded and comfortable, although you have a single set of red-lace bra and panties which you wear for special occasions.

People watch me in the square, but the eye is only attracted by motion. I have perfected the tiny movement, so tiny that the passer can scarcely tell if it is something he saw or not. Yes? Too often people will not see what does not move. The eyes see it but do not see it, they discount it. I am human-shaped, but I am not human. So in order to make them see me, to make them look at me, to stop their eyes from sliding off me and paying me no attention, I am forced to make the tiniest motions, to draw their eyes to me. Then, and only then, do they see me. But they do not always know what they have seen.

I see you as a code to be broken, or as a puzzle to be cracked. Or a jig-saw puzzle, to be put together. I walk through your life, and I stand motionless at the edge of my own life. My own gestures, statuesque, precise, are too often misinterpreted. I love you. I do not doubt this.

You have a younger sister. She has a myspace account, and a facebook account. We talk sometimes. All too often people assume that a medieval statue exists only in the fifteenth century. This is not so true: I have a room, I have a laptop. My computer is passworded. I practice safe computing. Your password is your first name. That is not safe. Anyone could read your email, look at your photographs, reconstruct your interests from your web history. Someone who was interested and who cared could spend endless hours building up a complex schematic of your life, matching the people in the photographs to the names in the emails, for example. It would not be hard reconstructing a life from a computer, or from cellphone messages, like a crossword puzzle.

I remember when I actually admitted to myself that you had taken to watching me, and only me, on your way across the square. You paused. You admired me. You saw me move once, for a child, and you told a friend, loud enough to be heard, that I might be a real statue. I take it as the highest compliment. I have many different styles of movement, of course – I can move like clockwork, in a set of tiny jerks and stutters, I can move like a robot or an automaton. I can move like a statue coming to life after hundreds of years of being stone.

Within my hearing you have spoken of the beauty of this small city. How standing inside the stained-glass confection of the old church was like being imprisoned inside a kaleidoscope of jewels. It was like being in the heart of the sun. You are concerned about your mother's illness.

When you were an undergraduate you worked as a cook, and your fingertips are covered with the scar-marks of a thousand tiny knife-cuts.

I love you, and it is my love for you that drives me to know all about you. The more I know the closer I am to you. You were to come to my country with a young man, but he broke your heart, and you came here to spite him, and still you smiled. I close my eyes and I can see you smiling. I close my eyes and I see you striding across the town square in a clatter of pigeons. The women of this country do not stride. They move diffidently, unless they are dancers. And when you sleep your eyelashes flutter. The way your cheek touches the pillow. The way you dream.

I dream of dragons. When I was a small child, at the home, they told me that there was a dragon beneath the old city. I pictured the dragon wreathing like black smoke beneath the buildings, inhabiting the cracks between the cellars, insubstantial and yet always present. That is how I think of the dragon, and how I think of the past, now. A black dragon made of smoke. When I perform I have been eaten by the dragon and have become part of the past. I am, truly, seven hundred years old. Kings may come and kings may go. Armies arrive and are absorbed or return home again, leaving only damage and bastard children behind them, but the statues remain, and the dragon of smoke, and the past.

I say this, although the statue that I emulate is not from this town at all. It stands in front of a church in southern Italy, where it is believed either to represent the sister of John the Baptist, or a local lord who endowed the church to celebrate not dying of the plague, or the angel of death.

I had imagined you perfectly chaste, my love, yet one time the red lace panties were pushed to the bottom of your laundry hamper, and upon close examination I was able to assure myself that you had, unquestionably, been unchaste the previous evening. Only you know who with, for you did not talk of the incident in your letters home, or allude to it in your online Journal.

A small girl looked up at me once, and turned to her mother, and said "Why is she so unhappy?" (I translate into English for you, obviously. The girl was referring to me as a statue and thus she used the feminine ending.)

"Why do you believe her to be unhappy?"

"Why else would people make themselves into statues?"

Her mother smiled. "Perhaps she is unhappy in love," she said.

I was not unhappy in love. I was prepared to wait until everything was ready, something very different.

There is time. There is always time. It is the gift I took from being a statue. One of the gifts, I should say.

You have walked past me and looked at me and smiled, and you have walked past me and barely noticed me as anything other than an object. Truly, it is remarkable how little regard you, or any human, gives to something that remains completely motionless. You have woken in the night, got up, walked to the little toilet, peed and walked back to bed. You would not notice something perfectly still, would you? Something in the shadows?

If I could I would have made the paper for this letter for you out of my body. I thought about mixing in with the ink my blood or spittle, but no. There is such a thing as overstatement. Yet great loves demand grand gestures, yes? I am unused to grand gestures. I am more practised in the tiny gestures. I made a small boy scream once, simply by smiling at him when he had convinced himself that I was made of marble. It is the smallest gestures that will never be forgotten.

I love you.

Soon, I hope, you will know this for yourself. And then we will never part. It will be time, in a moment, to turn around, put down the letter. I am with you, even now, in these old apartments with the Iranian carpets on the walls.

You have walked past me too many times.

No more.

I am here with you. I am here now.

When you put down this letter. When you turn and look across this old room, your eyes sweeping it with relief or with joy or even with terror...

Then I will move. Move, just a fraction. And, finally, you will see me.

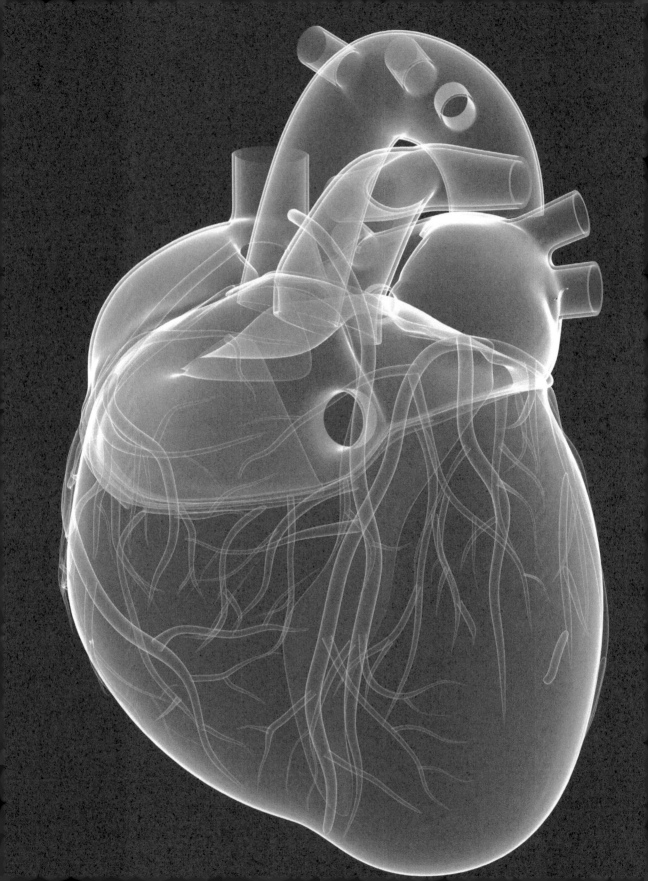

Going Solo

BY LEAH MANN

Most marriages, as it turns out, are not made in heaven. And the skillful eye can see a train wreck coming a mile away.

Our next tale takes a proactive approach to the whole "mismatched relationship" conundrum, with both ruthless rigor and startling heart.

Leah Mann is a gifted young filmmaker and a phenomenal puppet designer, but it turns out that her first and greatest love is writing. As such, I am thrilled to present "Going Solo," her auspiciously audacious publishing debut.

He gave her a few weeks before smoothly sliding into the seat across the worn table in the library. She'd needed time. They always needed time, after.

He'd learned that the hard way, but he was a quick study. Always had been. Even as a kid, Mikey paid attention.

He opened up his laptop, plugging in his headphones, casually avoiding her eyes. A delicate touch. Tread lightly. The last one had been easy, too easy, and he didn't want to get cocky.

He'd found the couple at a house party. Evie—beautiful and meek, hiding behind limp blond hair—had stood on the sidelines. Her boyfriend, Wes, held court, showering the masses with his brilliance and wit.

Mikey watched her kisses and jokes get ignored. They'd sung karaoke; Wes sang louder and stronger. He told Evie that her range was limited, her vocals thready.

The night wore on, Wes's level of intoxication directly correlating to Evie's desire to go home.

Mikey there alone, always alone, watched and decided.

With the internet, that most magical of innovations, it was easy to track Wes and Evie's life. A minor celebrity in the programming world, Wes kept his friends and fans well updated on his whereabouts. Evie was quieter online. Short bursts, funny, sarcastic, self-deprecating, less informative, far more revealing.

Wes was diabetic, type 1 (not the fat kind), lactose intolerant, and loved rock climbing. More so, in an absurdly convenient bout of machismo, Wes had recently taken up free climbing.

Two weeks after the fateful house-party, one inconspicuous phone call to a mutual friend and three practice climbing sessions at an indoor rock wall later, Mikey headed out to get some fresh air and exercise. Purely by chance, what a crazy world, he went to the same beloved national park on the same day as Wes. *What a coincidence, running into each other after meeting at that party a few weeks earlier.* Beaming his sideways smile and dimples and friendly eyes, Mikey sealed the deal. *Oh, you're into free-climbing? Well then, Wes, buddy old pal, you have to check out the East Falls, just a half mile further in. The cracks and grooves of the rock face are required reading for any student of the great outdoors.*

Twenty-five minutes later, they were almost to the top of the cliff. Sun-soaked and sweaty, Mikey edged his way up the wall past Wes; muscles warm, loose, scrubbed clean by the hot wind. His mind was sedated by the physical exertion, the puzzle of cracks and footholds.

A lizard skittered past. Wes, with the easy arrogance of ignorance, flashed his new friend a big grin.

Smug bastard. Mikey knew he'd made the right decision. He didn't hesitate another second.

An electrical impulse zipping from his brain to his foot sent out a quick kick, catching Wes under the chin. Wes cried out before bouncing off the first outcropping below. His long legs crunched against the wet rock, the roaring falls.

Mikey held his breath, waiting.

Wes' body rotated in the air on the rebound. The next impact, ten feet lower, twisted his neck with a snap. Muscle tone gone, Wes dropped with heavy flat thumps, floppy as a rag doll the rest of the way down.

Evie had cried for days. Mikey understood. He remembered when he'd first lost Naomi. Naomi was down under now, living in Australia, working her dream job in visual effects and, Mikey assumed, fucking fit Aussies after sexy games of volleyball on the beach.

When Naomi and he had broken up—mutually on the face of it, in the official story—she hadn't fought to keep him. She had been relieved to see him go; no regret, no anger, minimal tears. Mikey felt like he'd been punched in the heart.

He remembered the beginning, when they'd met: her throaty laugh, strong fingers grasping his hair. The first year, then two, then three, he'd loved her. Nights and weekends filled with cooking, kissing, camping, movies in bed, minigolf, silly strip teases, secret silent sex on family vacations.

He'd loved her so much he could feel his heart growing. His chest expanded to make room for all the new warm, liquidy feelings gushing from the font of his love.

Then she was gone.

After it was over, his heart was swollen, grotesque, inflamed and confused. In time, over time, lots of time (painful minutes, hours, days, months), it wasn't swollen anymore.

Mikey felt his heart shrinking in his chest. Harder, colder, like the Grinch before the happy ending. He wondered if the change would show up on a CT scan.

Mikey emerged remade, rejuvenated, reborn. A life without Naomi. A life with a heart that didn't demand so much.

An independent man, he crept out of his hole.

As he looked at the world with his new eyes and shriveled heart, he saw three types of people:

1. Those in love, with big happy hearts;
2. Those shaved down like him—lean, the desperate need washed from their faces;
3. Those who were still tethered. People with fat hearts and empty space, unfilled rooms.

Mikey saw these hurting people and wanted to help them. They needed training, a new regime to drop the extra pounds, to slim their flabby hearts into trim units of self-reliance.

His ninth student, carefully selected, Evie was unaware of the special club she had just joined. When Mikey came into her life, she didn't know she was going to rediscover how to read in bed each evening, how to eat alone, how to try new things, to stop hiding behind a curtain of hair, to uncover the teeny tiny bits and pieces that make her Evie, all while removing the need for a "better half."

What Evie knew was her hurt, her loneliness, her shock, her lively Wes lying limp and broken. She knew funeral arrangements and awkward conversations. Evie knew her aching heart was still inflated and gnarled.

Apply ice and elevate.

She was surprised by how much Mikey understood, this stranger she'd met in passing. She was surprised when he let her grieve, and grateful when he laughed at her first joke. She couldn't believe it when she discovered herself flirting. Twirling a blond strand around a nail bitten finger, she listened when Mikey told her it was best to be alone.

She went solo, and found pleasure in leaving the bar early, luxuriating in sweats and a good book in bed. The swelling went down, and she took up drawing again. Hours passed, her brain quiet.

She spent time with girlfriends, and pitied their distorted worlds. She hid her disdain for the insignificance of their significant others, and their compromise for mediocrity, safety, comfort. *Why carry extra space for someone else? We are burdened enough*, Evie declared, and Mikey seconded.

Easy Evie, his brightest student.

Mikey's record was not flawless. He had known failure. Mikey was a student of human nature, and like any student he had things to learn. Nothing can replace practical experience.

Inevitably, on occasion, he'd misjudged a person's strength to withstand loss. Uncle Greg, for example. Mikey had arrived on scene after the police and paramedics but before the hazmat team. Through the window of a beaten up Honda Civic, nausea roiling his stomach, Mikey had stared at Uncle Greg's puffy face, tinted green.

Uncle Greg, a do-it-yourself kind of guy. (Of course, suicide generally is a do-it-yourself proposition.) In an uncharacteristic bout of trendiness, he'd gotten instructions online, headed to the hardware store, and offed himself via chemical suicide like a hip Japanese teen.

Mikey never dwelled on whether the nausea spawned from his uncle's corpse, or his role in the matter.

A year after Mikey had liberated Uncle Greg from stifling Aunt Isabel, Uncle Greg's heart had remained big and empty. Cheesy fries, intramural basketball, a promotion, vodka gimlets and antidepressants had neither filled nor shrunk the void inside.

Mikey had been so eager to help a loved one. He hated to think of the effort he'd put into Aunt Isabel's "heart attack" going for naught. The missing nitro pills, misfiring pacemaker, delayed 911 call . . . it was a lesson in humility.

Expectations readjusted, tactics reassessed, Mikey had gone back to work with renewed vigor.

There were other students, none such failures as Uncle Greg, few as gracefully successful as Evie. Drew, Tomás and Kim quickly replaced their perished partners with distressingly similar people. That was disappointing. But Mikey liked to believe even the weak students had learned something about bravery during their brief time alone.

Alina and Jessie had found better people, stronger people. It was good to know at least two couples in the world functioned as independent individuals who came together for sex and the occasional meal without compressing two lives into one.

The gold stars went to aforementioned Evie, Sam and Nick. These three had tasted freedom, drunk it in. Cleansed, they'd dropped the jiggly pounds of need.

The library was full of kids too small for school, their nannies, struggling screenwriters, and a sprinkling of retirees reading up for book clubs. Mikey fingered the worn wood table, collecting his thoughts.

First contact was the hardest. This girl with curly black hair and confident hands was not Evie, nor Nick, Kim, Drew, Jessie or Uncle Greg.

Go easy.

Keep it slow.

He knew her. He knew all his students. She played the electric drums with a ferocity the silent kit couldn't hide. She walked around the neighborhood taking shortcuts and stairways, stopping to sniff at the jasmine and honeysuckle crawling up people's fences. She tutored rich homeschoolers and SAT students, relishing her flexible schedule. She met her grandma for lunch. She complained about idiots a lot and got grumpy easily. Mikey was inclined to agree about the idiots, and didn't hold this against her.

Mikey had discovered her and Bernie at a softball game, two months earlier. Playing catcher, shoved to the back of the lineup as the only girl on the team, she'd made a great play at home. Catching a wide throw from third base, she fearlessly blocked the plate and tagged the runner out as he slid into her, feet first.

Boyfriend Bernie, muscular and wide and easy, jogged in from third base. Gliding over the fact that his terrible throw had nearly cost them the game, he slapped her congrats on the ass and grabbed a beer from his duffel.

This girl could have anyone. Mikey saw it in the way she walked, laughed, wiped the blood from her knee with a smile. He analyzed the couple's faces, bodies, gestures, vocal intonations, how they looked at each other, at others. He processed this data. Mental calculations confirmed with a gut check.

Bernie had to go.

Mikey stretched, looking up across the table for the first time. His breath caught in the back of his throat. He forced it down, swallowing hard. Stick to the plan. Brief eye contact, back to the laptop.

His eyes flitted up again. Still calculating, he smiled bashfully. Her almond eyes were framed by a curly bob and thick eyebrows. She held his gaze, then went back to her work.

If all went well, the girl would look at him four more times in the next ninety minutes before packing up her things and leaving. He would catch her eye just one more of those times, holding it, and then look away quickly, embarrassed, a practiced flush warming his cheeks.

Ever the multitasker, with time to burn and looks to ignore, Mikey got down to researching his next project.

It was too soon to look up again, but he could feel her eyes on him. How is it that we can *feel* eyes on us? She wasn't glancing coquettishly. She was staring.

Did she recognize him? He had never been this close to her. The gold in her hazel eyes glinted with intelligence. She was beautiful.

She sighed lightly and went back to her work.

Blood rushed to Mikey's face. His heart rate sped up. His hands were cool and clammy. Angry at the unexpected physiological response, he focused instead on the face of her dead boyfriend.

Mikey rarely ruminated about the dead. They were not victims. His students were the victims, Mikey the savior.

Bernie had been handsome. Annoyingly, ridiculously good-looking. Thick brown hair, thick mustache matching his plaid shirt and silly little hipster hat, his eyes pale clear blue.

Young people were the hardest to kill. They had no heart problems, medications, respiratory disease, advanced diabetes or history of stroke to play off of. For murdering purposes, young people offered instead an array of risky behavior, adrenaline fueled pastimes and irresponsibility.

Bernie, like any red-blooded twenty-seven-year-old male living in a city with poor public transportation, spent his weekends drinking and driving.

It was a tragic night when Bernie was goaded into a marathon night of flip cup. Keys clutched tight, he had defied protestations, stumbling into his car.

Fifteen minutes later, winding down a one lane road, the city stretched out below with barely a guardrail in sight.

It only took a bump from behind for Bernie to lose control and careen over the hill.

In any collision, there are three stages of impact, and it is the third that causes the most damage to our fleshy-bony beings. The first is the impact of the car against another object (ground, tree, vehicle). The second is the impact of our bodies against the car (steering wheel, dashboard, windshield).

Third is the impact of our organs against our bodies. This is where our organs can be shaved, burst, split or crushed. If the hyperextension of the cervical spine as our bodies lunge up and over the dashboard doesn't kill us, our livers, spleens, kidneys and hearts slamming against our rib cages and abdominal walls will.

And so it was with Bernie, nose broken, brain reduced to cottage cheese as it slammed against his skull. His liver sliced in half by the coronary ligament which stayed stubbornly in place, while the two lobes of the liver continued traveling forward through space and time.

The girl hadn't known any of this before Bernie bit it. Her medical knowledge was limited to whatever ailments directly affected her family: asthma, pancreatic cancer, ovarian cysts. She took no pleasure in adding to this list, but had wanted the facts.

She liked facts, and put great store in acknowledging the world as it was, not as she wished it to be.

Mikey and this girl sat across from each other: one trying to ignore an unwanted stirring, the other wondering if she'd ever get stirred again.

Mikey couldn't stop himself. He looked up and she kinda half-smiled at him. He felt melty from tip to toe. He hadn't felt melty since Naomi.

Perfect lips parted, about to speak.

Mikey's heart swelled and stretched against his ribs.

Nope. Not happening. No room in this lean mean solo machine. He was above pain, above need, did not want to want.

He slammed his laptop shut, grabbed his bag and left. He walked off tight and quick, hunched shoulders guarding his thoughts.

His next student would be a guy. A young one. A kid who hadn't been corrupted and trained in the bad habits of adulthood. His little brother's frat would have some poor sap with a flabby heart. Those sorority sisters were a plague on both genders. One wouldn't be missed.

The girl watched him from under blocky black eyebrows, curls tucked behind her ear. She went back to her work, pushing Bernie to the back of her head.

She was alone. She'd been alone before. She could take it.

Her heart deflated in her chest, contracting small and cool.

Death-in-Life Love Song

BY KEVIN L. DONIHE

Kevin L. Donihe is one of the leading lights of the Bizarro movement in modern lit. Which is to say, his writing tends toward the most weirdly phantasmagoric and unhinged that our literary landscape has to offer. (My favorite of his novels, Night of the Assholes, *reconfigures the original* Night of the Living Dead *as an onslaught not of zombies, but of you-guessed-it. And if you respond in kind, you become an asshole, too. One of the aptest metaphors for inexcusable crazy that I have ever read.)*

To my immense delight, he has taken that prodigious predilection for crazy and imbued it here with sweet, uncharacteristically naturalistic intent.

The result is this beautiful stunner, which could not have been written by a normal person. But it brings all his gifts to bear, in ways you will no-fucking-way see coming.

I stand in rain like needles on my skin. I remember you and me, our naked-ness, and sex beneath gray and swollen clouds.

We weren't self-conscious. Beady-eyed neighbors couldn't see us over the protective hedge. Even if they did, we wouldn't have cared. Let them live through us. They existed from nine-to-five and would never experience a downpour like we did.

After you left, I hated rain. Darkness coiled around me—oblivion in motion—each time a storm cloud coalesced. There was no pleasure in getting soaked alone.

But now I know his name, and I'm making an unscheduled appearance at 311 Woodcrest as soon as the storm ends and I put on clothes. Must avoid white t-shirts, and that's too bad. I am, you know, a very casual man.

Two hours later, and you're mine.

The apartment was easy to locate. It was just a few miles away. Amazing. You'd been so close for so long.

Unfortunately, the man was stubborn, though it took him a while to notice me. I was quiet, and a glass box had commandeered his attention. He didn't lift his eyes from the screen until I was ready to strike.

My first blow only stunned him. Though his mouth opened and closed like a goldfish, he said nothing before my hammer fell again. A red flap opened on his scalp, but still he staggered, blubbering and drooling on himself like the world's biggest baby.

So I hit him a third time, a fourth, then a fifth. The experience was becoming absurd. Finally, gravity did its belated work and carried him to the floor.

Bent over the man, I noted his upturned, glassy eyes. Perhaps I'd gone too far. Taking hold of his wrist, I detected a pulse. My fingers lingered over it for longer than necessary. Human existence seemed fragile when the highways to the heart were buried in fleshy graves.

I withdrew my fingers. (You know I go off on mental tangents. You said that little facet of me charmed you the most. Standing in the apartment of the man I had just beaten senseless, however, afforded me little time for contemplation.) I struggled a bit to pick him up.

Out of the apartment, I helped him to my car as I would a drunken friend. He was well acquainted with the bottle. Though I just met him tonight, I know all about the guy.

You might say I've read up on the subject.

Now, he lies strapped to two card tables pushed together. I never fancied myself a surgeon, but I've done enough research to know cutting through the chest is going to be a bitch.

Wish me luck.

The ribcage is like living marble. Every stroke brings me closer to my destination, so I keep sawing, despite the strain.

Hours pass. I want to abandon caution and plow through the body, but I stay my hand. His life force is your life force, and I can't risk losing you again.

The ribcage wobbles. Grasping a segment of it with pliers, I twist back and forth until it breaks. Light illuminates the breach and reflects off of you, Judith, resting inside.

My hands play over you. I feel your death-in-life love song resonate through organic strings. You don't need a mouth to sing. I realize this now.

You lurch beneath my touch. Perhaps I should be gentler. Forgive me.

But also try to understand. After the accident, the mortician used his best tools to construct a smile for you, but putty only goes so far. In your casket, I saw the ghosts of slits and gouges on your sewn-together face.

Smiles, you see, come from the heart, and darkness alone lies in empty cavities. Your seat of love was placed in a cooler and turned into a rush-delivery package. It was shipped off to an undeserving recipient.

And what was left for me? Just the memory of a few hours spent with a shell in a gilded box.

But you're back, Judith. Nothing else matters. Blow the rest to hell.

And guess what . . .

Tomorrow's forecast calls for rain.

Ralph and Jerry

BY LESLIANNE WILDER

One of the greatest crimes modern society commits on a daily basis is the dumping of our mentally ill back onto the streets with no provisions. From a fiscal standpoint, it's utterly sound. But once you get past the bloodless number-crunching, it's the cultural equivalent of running raw sewage through our psychological thoroughfares, and into our tap water. Drink up!

Leslianne Wilder is a street-level medic, who has seen too much and more. She is also one of my favorite new writers, sharing her unstinting eye and for-midable style with immense compassion.

I consider this story a public service. It drops my jaw, and breaks my heart.

The alleyway is painted with cats, red on red, with patches of the fur curling brown at the edges and intestines looped like streamers at a prom. I remember prom, and wearing my uncle's blue tux with a paper flower boutineer down low to cover the stains, and all the time I sat with a plate in my lap not eating just watching Jennifer Rheeland with her pink skirt spinning, spinning, spinning, up till you could almost see where her legs stopped being legs and started being . . .

Ralphie sits next to me and chews on some bits of the cats. Ralphie's my best friend. Today he's a dog. A skinny dog that's going bald on the shoulders, and looks like he tried to lick a comb over. Wet fur clumps into dark brown lines like spider legs, and from the top he looks like two tax accountants standing back to back.

"Shit," I say to Ralphie. My stomach rolls. I feel terrible. "Shit, shit, shit. What if these were somebody's pets?"

Ralphie gnaws. Little bones snap between his teeth. He chews around the claws. "They weren't anybody's pets, Jerry."

"What if there's some little old lady? Like, with a shawl and little knitted coats for her cookie jars, and these were her cats, and somewhere she's waiting for them to come home?" I look around and wipe my face. My hand is sticky and I regret getting it near my eyes. "But they're not coming home."

"They didn't have ID," Ralphie points out. His breath smells like shit, and death, and cigarettes. "No tags. No wallets. Nobody wants them. If there's an old lady I bet she turns off the lights when they come around, and pretends she isn't home."

"Poor cats," I say. I forget my hand is wet and I run it through my hair. "That lady's a bitch, to treat them like that." I want to smash her cookie jars, leave them a spiky ruin of porcealin and little knitted coats.

Ralphie licks my smeared face. "This isn't really about the cats, is it, Jerry?"

I want to hug him and cry, but when I reach for him he growls.

Ralphie has boundary issues. He doesn't like to be touched.

"It's just about the cats," I say, but I know he doesn't believe me. He finishes cleaning my face, like I'm somebody else and he's somebody else's mother with a little pink rag and spit. I stand up, I fold my knife up and put it in my pocket, and I go out into the street. I like Houston. It's like it's always summer here, at the beach, and you sweat but it never goes away, and soon all your skin and all your clothes taste like the ocean and the trash on the beach. People try to lie to you sometimes, try to fool you. They put on coats and Christmas lights, and they tell you it's winter, but I know better. I don't believe their lies. I walk by the refineries with all their little lights and I feel like Godzilla, like all the pipes are skyscrapers and I could grow big enough that I could stomp through it all, break it to the ground. Like a lizard they woke up from the bottom of somewhere dark and frozen with atomic bombs, and lipstick, and fast food clown statues, and kiddy porn, and Haloperidol and Thorzine. I stand by the fence with all the warning signs of lightning striking fat black stickmen. I open my mouth big. I practice breathing radiation fire. I spit on my beard but I don't care. There's a bus stop behind me and the shadows from the cars' lights bend and shift like stampeding crowds of Tokyo people, trying to get away. I feel high and nauseous, like God. The drains smoke in the wet heat of the night. It's warm here. It's not like Columbus.

There's a bus stop behind me and the bus stops when it comes by. The driver's an old guy and the way he looks at me makes me want to hide. "You getting on, or what?" he says, and I want to tell him no, but then I see Ralphie inside the bus. He's a black lady now, with shiny pink and white beads at the end of his hair. So I get on the bus and I take out my paper cup and unfold it so I can reach the quarters. It's my good cup, my lucky cup. It's my ID. It has all my money in it, and the number on the inside wall, written in blue pen. I sit down next to Ralphie and keep my hands in my pockets. There's three other nurses with Ralphie, and they all look pinched and raw, like they have wounds around their eyes and their face is trying to grow a scar over them. Something smooth and hairless that they can't feel the world through.

They all have ID.

I can't read it anymore. My eyes are bad and the fuzzy letters crawl around, but I know it's their pictures and their names and it means somebody wants them. There's rules in the world and jobs, and the nurses follow them every day. They're part of it all, plastic gears like the inside of toys that fit into other gears, that touch everything so they move the world and the world moves them. Someone's waiting. Someone somewhere looks at their ID and welcomes them back. Someone misses them when they disappear.

Ralphie's fat now. I like it. My mom is fat, big, and soft, and a little wet. I remember, I remember holding on to her when I was small and scared, and sinking in to the smell of her, her big arms and breasts all around me, like I was inside of her and nothing could ever hurt me again. She hates being fat though. She cried, and she cut herself, and she put up all the pictures of her when she was skinny, when she made the videos and showed up in the magazines, in just high white socks and a hat, and her legs like cold metal poles, and her smiles where you could never see her teeth, and her breasts and and and ...

Ralphie gives me a "fuck off and die" look, and I huddle next to him, but I know he won't hug me. He doesn't want me to touch him. It's sad, sometimes, and I wish I had a friend like they do on the TV, where they hug each other around the shoulders, and have beer, and sometimes they fall asleep on the couch next to each other. Ralphie's a good friend, really. He never disappears, he never leaves me alone, he never gets arrested, or overdoses, or freezes to death, or dies in the bathroom of the shelter because somebody stabbed him over a smuggled sandwich. But sometimes, I just wish- I mean, I know it's stupid, but I think of the way Mom used to hug me, after dinner, when she was in a good mood, and I sank into her like she was a marshmallow or a waterbed, and listened to the little growls and chirps her belly made. I wish Ralphie would let me touch him. Wishing makes me lonely and nervous, and I put my hand in my pocket and flick the knife open and closed. Open and closed. Open and closed. The handle is sticky with cat.

Ralphie glares at me. "This is a public bus, you sicko."

I look down at my lap and it takes me a minute, but I realize what he means. I take my hands out and hold them up to show. "I don't do that!" I say. "You know I don't do that!" I did once, when I was a kid, and there were pictures all over the house and mom saw me and she told me every true horrible thing she could think of to punish me. I'm sick. I'm messed up. I'm disgusting. I ruined her life. She wished I'd never been born.

I don't do it. I get sick like coming down even thinking of it. Ralphie knows that. He knows it's just a knife, and he knows I don't do anything sick with it. I don't know why he's being like that. He stands up and he walks away. He isn't looking at me, but I hear him say, "Where's your ID, Jerry?"

I take the cup out of the pocket that doesn't have the knife in it, and I hunch over it like it's coffee on a freezing night. It's my lucky cup. It's where I keep the number. It's my ID. Ralphie knows that.

"That ain't ID, Jerry," he says as he gets off, looking back over his shoulder at me in disgust.

I don't want to be on the bus anymore. I get off at the next stop, because I want to be anywhere else, even somewhere in the hot, salty night with all the gutters smoking like there are cities under the street burning to ash, everyone dying, screaming, melting, because someone fell asleep with a cigarette in their mouth. The bus drives off and it's lit up inside the way windows into people's houses are. The nurses laugh under the blue-tinged light while they turn into little specks inside a tiny TV on wheels that I used to be inside of, too. I point my knife at it, like a remote, to turn it off. But I don't have batteries.

I think I'm at a mall. And I think, maybe, maybe, maybe there's a pay phone. All the pay phones are gone nowadays. They're like all the Indians, all the Cadillacs, all the happy families, all the shirts that change color when you put your hand on them, all the blue toilets and bathrooms with tiles that spell something out if you look long enough. If you're clever. Somebody caught on, and now all those messages are gone, and that makes me mad, because the bathrooms never spelled out anything bad. Why does the world always have to take everything away?

I walk through the parking lot and I pretend the white stripes are the bones of old whales and it's the bottom of the ocean. I walk the ribs. I pretend I killed the whole parking lot. Jerry: whale slayer. It feels good to be someone who can kill monsters, who can be mighty, who can make the world what it is supposed to be.

I don't see any pay phones. There's shops with mannequin corpses all in red, in tiny skirts and high socks. I don't like to look at them.

"Hey buddy," says a voice behind me. "Let's see some ID."

I turn and it's Ralphie, only now Ralphie is a big white cop whose cheeks and nose are red with tiny holes in them. He sounds so mean and angry. What did I do? He's supposed to be my friend. Didn't he lick my face when I needed it?

I hold out my lucky cup with the number, and he knocks it out of my hand. "I don't want your fucking change," he says. The money goes everywhere but I dive for the cup. The cup has the number. I hold it close, and I look up, and I see the Ralphie look around for cameras, and I know he's going to hurt me. He's got the look on his face. They took away the tiles in his bathroom too, and he knows he can't kill monsters, and he works and works but he can't pay for anything, and people yell at him that he's a freak and a sicko, and they hurt him and hurt him, and he can't fix anything, and I can see it in his face. He's going to hurt me because I don't have ID, I don't have a place, I don't have anybody who waits up for me, I don't have anybody who will wonder if I never come back. And he's going to hurt me because hurting something is the only way to feel for just a few minutes like he isn't tiny and helpless. I get that. I curl up into a ball because I know what's coming. His boot comes down again and again. My mouth tastes like puke and the inside of cats. It hurts every time I breathe. By the time he's done I can't bend two fingers on my left hand anymore.

"Why, Ralphie?" I wheeze. "You're supposed to be my friend."

Ralphie's panting, bending over with his hands on his knees. "Get outta here," he says, and I try to stand up, but I stumble and then his hands are under my armpits. His arms are hard in the middle, but all around he's soft, like he's almost thawed. He puts me in the seat of his golf cart, then he gets in the other side and turns it on.

I don't know what to say and he doesn't look at me, but we're side to side, like we're falling asleep together on a couch. I'm breathing in gasps, like a gold fish on the carpet. I don't want to be alone. I think, how many friends do I have anyway? He's Ralphie. I put my arm around his shoulder. I clap him around the shoulder, like they do on TV, and he looks at me, then looks away again, like he's going to cry. There's blood on my beard. "Get the fuck out," he says, when he takes me to the side walk. "This is private property and if you come back again, I'll fucking kill you."

I hate it when Ralphie talks to me that way, but he's my best friend, and I nod. There's a gas station on this side of the mall, and it has one pay phone, under the flickering light, inside a little red shell, like someone tore open a beetle and its guts were made of plastic and wire.

I have some quarters. I have the number. I paid a guy in meth to get the number for me. I pay the machine and I dial with my fingers that still bend. This is my ID, even if nobody else knows it.

Two rings, then it picks up. "This is Mary-Beth?" It's a question. I start crying.

When she speaks again, she sounds afraid. "Who is this? Who the fuck is this?"

"It's Jerry, Mom."

It's long and quiet and dark on the other end of the phone. I want to scream for her. I want her to hug me. I want her to be my ID. I want her to worry when she can't find me. I want the cookie jars to be whole.

"After what you did..." It's a whisper. Like she's afraid and she can't ever believe the world would be such a horrible place.

"Please, Mom . . ."

"Don't you ever call me again, you sick little fuck."

And then the phone is dead in my hand. I try. I put every quarter I can in the machine. And nickels and pennies. It rings and rings, but there's no person there on the other end and pennies fall out from the slot onto the street. Not even Ralphie picks up.

I let the phone hang down and I sit beneath it and I bury my head in my arms and I want to cry. The night air feels hot and wet, like the whole world is weeping. It still hurts when I breathe. Everything, everything is fucked up and I can't kill whales and I don't have any ID at all in the whole world.

Someone nudges me with a toe and I jump. It's a little girl, maybe sixteen, in a skirt so short you can see where her legs stop being legs. She's so skinny, like all the pictures on the walls. A dead cigarette hangs from her lips.

"You got a light?" she says.

I shake my head. No. No, I don't have any lights. She looks closer.

"Jesus, man, are you okay? You look like you got the shit kicked out of you."

She's so small. But she looks like she really cares. Like she's being nice to me just to be nice. I wish I had a light for her. The cup is in one pocket. The knife is in the other.

"Do . . . do you have any ID?" I ask.

She snorts and wiggles the unlit cigarette between her thin, soft fingers. "Why the fuck would I be carrying ID?"

And I think, how sad.

There's no one who's going to miss her.

And What Did You See in the World?

BY NORMAN PARTRIDGE

Love is hard enough for the sane. Almost by definition, it makes you crazy. Once you say, "I'd do anything for you," you've left the door wide open. Anything is an awfully large word.

As a writer, Norman Partridge is one of the only guys I'd put in a street-fighting class with Joe R. Lansdale. It's a very particular kind of plainspoken, down-to-earth-meets-batshit crazy, if you know what I mean. And I'll bet you do.

If not, you're about to find out. And you're entirely responsible for picking your own teeth out of the gravel.

He drove out of Dallas with Jenny in the trunk.

An old beater of a Ford was what he was driving. Someone had popped the lock out of the trunk. God knows why—the only thing he ever had worth stealing back there was Jenny, and he never left her in the trunk unless he was absolutely sure it was safe.

This trip he'd wired the trunk shut with a twisted up coat hanger. It would take some work to get in there if anyone wanted to try, but he had the feeling no one would. The lid was wired pretty tight. It didn't rattle much, except when he hit a bump. But that wasn't because of the coat hanger or the missing lock. The lid rattled because the rubber gaskets around the casing had rotted away.

He worried about that. If he hit rain on the trip, water might get in around the edges. Jenny wouldn't get wet, of course. No way. He kept her wrapped up in plastic so the weather wouldn't bother her.

Of course, the weather wasn't his only concern. He wondered how dark it was in the trunk. He wondered if Jenny could see anything in there. He'd jammed a rag in the hole where the lock should be so it would stay as dark as possible in the trunk, but there was nothing he could do about light that might creep in around the rotted gaskets.

He didn't want Jenny to have to see anything but darkness. Anything but darkness wouldn't be good. He hoped that was all Jenny saw. He hoped she wasn't looking at the other stuff jammed in there with her—his clothes, a box of kitchen stuff, the bald spare tire he couldn't afford to replace.

He didn't want her to see that stuff. Jenny wasn't stupid. She saw that stuff, she'd know what it meant.

Darkness was better.

Darkness could mean almost anything.

He headed north. It seemed like a good direction. He remembered the road. It was the same one he'd traveled about six months ago when he'd come to Texas, only then he'd been heading south.

Dallas had been a mistake. He'd known that right from the start, really. He'd heard there was work in Dallas, that the city was growing, that it was a really nice place to get a fresh start, but it turned out to be the same old stuff he'd heard about a dozen other places. Just a come-on to get you there, and once you were there . . . well, once you were there you saw how things were, you saw the dirty streets and you saw the things that happened on them, and pretty soon you found yourself listening to what people were saying about other places.

One look at Dallas and he'd known that it wasn't the place for Jenny. First thing he saw was the horizon at sunset, a ring of smog and domino skyscrapers choking downtown, and he knew PDQ that he'd made a mistake. He didn't even want Jenny to see Dallas at all, because he knew what one look would do to her.

She wanted to see it, of course. She wanted to see every city where they tried to settle, but he knew better than to let her. Deep down Jenny knew it, too, though it always took some convincing.

Not that she didn't understand once he explained it. Then things were all right. Jenny was a good sport. She had to stay in the trunk for two days when they first hit Dallas. It was hot—the middle of June—but Jenny didn't complain, even though the Ford didn't have air-conditioning.

Finally he found an apartment that he could afford. Well, that wasn't true. He could afford the first month's rent okay, but the last month's rent and the cleaning deposit tapped him out.

That was okay. At least it was a nice apartment. It was quiet, and there was new linoleum in the kitchen and the bathroom, and the walls wore a fresh coat of paint.

There was a walk-in closet in the single bedroom. It wore a new coat of paint too. First thing he did was step inside the closet and close the door. The floor of the closet was carpeted. Shag. The carpet was probably old, but it didn't smell or anything. And it piled against the bottom edge of the door when you closed it so that no light spilled under the doorway at all.

He remembered standing there in that closet, in the dark.

His eyes were wide open as he stood there.

He smiled. It was the perfect place for Jenny.

In the darkened closet it was easy to imagine that you were somewhere else. Somewhere nice.

Somewhere nice. He hoped that was where they were heading this time.

He glanced in the rearview, saw Dallas behind him. That felt good. He put on some music. The kind of stuff Jenny liked. He turned it up loud enough so that she could hear it, even through the backseat.

After awhile he got tired of the interstate. He wasn't interested in anyplace it might take him. He exited the next chance he got and headed northwest on a two-lane county road. That made him feel a little better. He worried about the interstate. People drove like idiots. And if he got in an accident with Jenny in the trunk . . . well, that could be disastrous. She didn't have a seat belt back there, and the old Ford sure as hell didn't have airbags in the passenger compartment, let alone the trunk.

That was a stupid thing to think. He shook his head. Sometimes the things he worried about amazed him. Hell, even if he were rich enough to afford any car he wanted, he wasn't likely to find one with airbags in the trunk.

The road was twisty, paralleling a riverbank lined with cottonwood. He could see the sun beyond the trees, but the Ford was trapped in the shadows they cast. He got kind of cold, but he didn't turn on the heater. It didn't seem fair. Jenny would be colder in the trunk, and you didn't hear her complaining.

Pretty soon he got hungry. The towns they passed through were small. They didn't have fast food out here. He passed a couple walk-in diners, but he didn't want to take the time for a sit-down meal. Besides, it wouldn't be fair to leave Jenny in the trunk while he sat in some nice warm diner and enjoyed himself. Finally he spotted an old burger stand. It didn't look like much, but now he was so hungry that he didn't care.

He pulled off the road and parked, killing the music. A jostling sound came from the trunk—the rustle of plastic, a couple pots and pans banging together as Jenny bumped the box that held the kitchen stuff. He thought that maybe she'd been sleeping. He hoped she had.

When it came to talking, riding in the car was tricky. He didn't look behind him when he spoke to Jenny. He'd learned not to do that, just in case anyone was watching. It looked funny enough to be talking to yourself, let alone an empty backseat.

"I'm going to get something to eat," he said. "Want anything?"

"I'm not hungry."

"All right. You sit tight. It's just a takeout place. Won't take me long."

"Okay."

"You want the music on while I'm gone?"

"No. I'm kind of tired of music."

He slipped the keys out of the ignition. "Okay. I'll just be a minute. You sit tight."

He opened the door. He was almost out of the car when she asked, "What kind of place is it?"

He looked at the burger stand. There were pictures showing burgers and fries and ice-cream sundaes behind the glass windows, but every picture was faded. The burgers and fries and sundaes were all kind of gray.

He didn't want to tell Jenny that, though. She didn't need to know.

"Are you still there?" she asked.

"Yes." He covered his mouth when he said it. The kid behind the takeout window was watching him, probably already thought that he was crazy.

"So . . . what kind of place is it?" she asked again.

"Nothing special."

"Can I take a look?"

"I don't think that's a good idea."

He got out and closed the door before Jenny could say anything else. The kid looked at him funny when he ordered, watched him the whole time he ate, too. He tried to ignore the kid, but it was hard. The place was awful, really. Besides the kid, there wasn't really anything else to look at if you didn't look at the gray pictures in the window. The only other things around were a half-dozen metal tables scarred with graffiti and a couple garbage cans. All the other tables were empty, and the only things interested in the garbage cans were flies.

After a few minutes, he couldn't stand sitting there. He finished his burger and dumped most of his fries in the garbage. Before he could turn away the flies were all over them. He was still thirsty, but he left his drink on the table. He knew that he'd have to stop somewhere to use the bathroom if he finished it, and he didn't want to have to stop anywhere else at all. Not after this place. Not unless he absolutely had to.

He climbed behind the wheel as fast as he could. Before he could even start the engine, the kid was out of the stand. He walked over and tossed the discarded drink in the garbage can. Then he stared at the old Ford while he wiped down the table.

Inside the Ford, the man's keys rattled in his hands as he dug them out of his pocket. Somehow, he managed to slip the right one into the ignition.

He heard Jenny's voice behind him. Muffled by tattered seat cushions, but he heard her plain enough. She asked the same question she'd asked a million times, the one she always asked when he'd been away from her.

"And what did you see in the world?"

He stared through the windshield, at the kid, who was still watching him.

He thought about Jenny's question, and the best way to answer it.

He pulled onto the two-lane county road.

When he was a couple miles away from the burger stand, he gave Jenny an answer.

He lied.

Jenny had always asked questions, of course. Living the way she did, he could understand why it would be hard not to. But he also understood that he had to be careful when he answered those questions. He knew that his answers could hurt Jenny, the same way the world could hurt her if she so much as looked at it.

So he had to be careful. Sometimes he had to lie. He supposed everyone did that, one way or another. Like when someone asks you, "How was your day?" Someone asks that, they don't necessarily want to know, especially if your day has been for shit. They're asking for another reason, really.

Just to be polite, maybe.

Or maybe they're asking because they care about you.

That's the way it was with Jenny. She cared about him. She loved him. They'd been together a long time. They'd known right from the start that they were different, though. Not two peas in a pod, this couple. Jenny was always sensitive. The simplest thing could set her off. He'd seen it happen a hundred times. A stray dog banging around their garbage cans, some kid shivering in the cold without a coat, even the smell of a hospital corridor—stuff like that could make her melancholy for days.

And sure, he wasn't the easiest guy in the world to live with. He had his good days and his bad days. Sometimes they argued. When they were first together, before Jenny started staying in the closet or the trunk of his car, they argued a lot. Sometimes she'd say he was insensitive. He'd toss a rock at a dog eating out of their garbage can, or he'd bypass some coatless kid without a second glance, or he'd take a deep breath in a hospital corridor—and she'd say that he didn't care about anything or anyone at all.

She was wrong, of course. He cared about her. He'd do anything for her. He loved her. Even on his bad days, he loved her more than anything.

Not that they were all bad days. Not at first. At first there were lots of good days. Jenny loved those. She was sensitive about bad things, things he never noticed, but she delighted in good things, and sometimes he was surprised he hadn't noticed those things either. Simple things most people took for granted—like a sunset, or the sound of her own laughter.

After awhile, that sound didn't seem to come very often. Everything got to be too much for Jenny. Sometimes she cried for days and days and days. She'd shut herself up in the bedroom, draw the drapes, close all the windows to keep out the sounds and smells of the street.

One day he went looking for a shirt and found her huddled in the closet. He didn't say anything. He didn't know what to say. He just stared down at her. And she looked up at him, and she started crying.

He didn't know what to say, so he closed the closet door.

Jenny just sat there in the closet, sobbing, all alone in the dark.

After awhile, she stopped crying.

That was the way it started.

But it wasn't always easy, keeping her in the dark. He couldn't remember exactly how long things had been that way, but he knew it had been a long time. Sometimes she got bored. Especially when they were in Dallas. Especially in that closet with the shag carpeting.

When he came home from work, she asked about things. Almost every night. "And what did you see in the world?" Sometimes he'd tell her. But mostly there was nothing much to tell.

Sometimes she'd talk about coming out. Just to walk around the apartment, or maybe to go to a park for an hour or two. He always managed to talk her out of it. He remembered what had happened before, and he didn't want to go through that again. This way was easier for the both of them.

But he could understand how she'd get bored in there. Sometimes he'd get her a little treat, like a library book. Just something to break the monotony. He had to be careful about what kind of book he got, of course. Almost anything with a story was sure to have something bothersome in it, and nonfiction was out of the question. Mostly, he stuck to paintings. Seascapes, flowers, that kind of stuff. He tried to find books that were new, because some of the older books upset Jenny. They had pages torn out, or nasty things written in the margins. Some of them even smelled bad, like a hospital or something.

He only opened the closet door a crack when he gave her the books, because he didn't want Jenny to see the apartment. And he only gave her the books at night, when it was dark, because he didn't want her to see him, either. She saw how he looked, she was sure to worry.

So he'd hand her a little flashlight along with the book, and then he'd close the door. Sometimes he went away for awhile. Most times he couldn't stand to do that. He'd sit by the door, afraid that Jenny might see something on one of the pages that would upset her, afraid that she'd start crying. But always somewhere deep inside him there was a little bit of hope, the hope that instead of seeing something awful she'd instead discover something simple and beautiful, and a lot of times while he sat there listening to Jenny turn the pages he was hoping he might hear the sound of her delighted laughter.

Sometimes he did.

Sometimes.

The further he drove, the better he liked it.

He was still on a two-lane road, but there were no more burger stands in sight. Instead there were canyons, dusty and bloody in the afternoon sun, and ridges splashed with old oak and gnarled mesquite.

The road was twisty, but there was something new to see around every bend.

It was getting late, but he couldn't bring himself to pull over. Everything was so beautiful. Kind of like the pictures in the library books he got for Jenny.

He took a fork in the road, dipped into a canyon and followed it for five or six miles, heading west. The sun hung above on the horizon, a red ball easing down behind a ridge that waited just ahead.

The sun sent a stream of light down the canyon like a heart pumping blood through a human vein. All of a sudden he wanted to get to that sun. It was dipping lower in the afternoon sky. Another hour and it would be gone.

He hit the gas. The road started to rise, switchbacking over the ridge. He shifted into low and floored it. The old engine complained, but soon enough the car crested the ridge and he found himself driving through a forest of old oak.

Thick trunks and branches painted his arms with shadows as he drove. He rolled down the window. The oak smell was wonderful in the late afternoon. It was a cool smell, like the promise of night coming on.

He spotted a sign just ahead. No words. Just a little camera on it, and an arrow pointing toward the lip of the ridge. He took the road. It snaked through a clutch of trees, following the rim of a little lake.

A couple minutes later he stood on the ridge, staring out at a green valley. The grass below was windblown by a breeze from the east, and for a second he thought he was looking at the waves of a gentle sea that could carry the old Ford all the way to the Pacific.

He stood there a long time, just staring.

He returned to the car, but he really didn't want to leave. Not until the sunset was over. He closed the door. He'd just sit here awhile longer, in shadows cast by old oak trees, beside the still lake that held their reflections. He'd sit here and watch the sun drift down through the trees and into the valley, watch until it found the horizon and disappeared for good.

Sounds behind him, in the trunk. The rustle of plastic. Pots and pans rattling in the box of kitchen stuff.

Jenny's voice.

"And what did you see in the world?"

They talked. It took a while to tell Jenny about the sunset, and then it took a while longer to sort things out.

"I don't know if it's a good idea, Jenny."

"You don't have to open the trunk. I'll just look through the hole. And I'll only look for a minute."

"That might be a minute too long."

"But if it's like you say... if it's really that pretty. Well, I know I want to see it."

"But what if you see something else? Something I didn't notice? What if something upsets you and—"

"It'll be okay," she said. "I know it will."

He sat there and didn't say anything. The sun was dropping fast now. Ten minutes, maybe fifteen at the outside, the sunset would be over. He watched it sink, and he thought about all the things he'd seen since that day he first found Jenny huddled in a closet.

That had been a long time ago. He wasn't sure how long. It was hard to remember.

A long time, though.

Long enough to see plenty of things.

He stared through the windshield.

In all those years, not one of the things he'd seen could touch this sunset.

He started the car, backed up. A three-point turn was what you called it, only this one was in reverse. Then he backed up to the edge of the ridge, so that the trunk faced the sinking red sun.

"You can look for a minute," he said over his shoulder, not turning around even though it was just the two of them alone in this place. "I don't want anything bad to happen. I don't want you to overdo it."

"I won't."

He hesitated, swallowing hard.

"You'd better hurry," Jenny said. "The sunset won't last forever. We don't have much time."

He cut the ignition and walked around to the trunk. The wire coat hanger still held it closed, and the rag hung from the punched-out lock. He knelt by the bumper and reached for the rag with his fingers.

He took hold of the rag and pulled it out. But just as quickly he covered the hole with his hand, because he wanted to be sure everything would be all right.

"You promise to be careful?" he asked.

The plastic bag rustled. "Yes... but let me see you first. It's always so dark when I see you. It's always night. I can't really remember what you look like."

He glanced down, saw his reflection smeared on the chrome bumper. His reflection was flecked with rust. He looked old, and worse.

"Oh, I haven't changed," he lied. "I still look the same."

"Just a peek?"

"I don't want to scare you."

Jenny laughed. He felt her finger then. She'd slipped it into the hole, and it pressed against his palm. The only thing separating them was the plastic bag.

Her finger was warm. He didn't want to move his palm away from it, but he did.

The punched-out keyhole was rimmed with rust. He moved close to it, thinking of all those jokes about dirty old men peeping through keyholes.

Inside the trunk, Jenny's eye shone through filmy plastic.

She saw his eye. She winked at him.

"It's going to be okay," she said.

"I know." He put his hand over the hole again. He thought that maybe he might start crying. "But we'll talk about that later. The sun's almost down. We have to hurry or you'll miss it."

"I'm ready."

So was he.

That was when he heard the other car coming toward him.

Through the trees, along the lake.

It was a police cruiser.

He didn't say a word. He couldn't afford to—what would it look like if the cop saw him talking to the trunk of his car? So he kept quiet, and he jammed the rag back into the hole.

Jenny said something, but he couldn't quite hear it. He stepped away from the car as fast as he could. The cop had pulled to a stop at the edge of the road, blocking off the little parking area. There was no way out of there now.

And now the sun was going down, sinking through the trees, going down for good. He felt it on his back. He smelled the oaks around him. That hot, late afternoon smell was fading. A cool twilight scent was coming on.

The cop opened the cruiser door and stepped out onto the blacktop. The man knew how it would go. The cop would tell him that the little park closed at sundown, that there wasn't any camping allowed here.

Maybe it would end there. But maybe it wouldn't. The Ford's registration was expired. The man had needed the money for moving, for the next cleaning deposit and first and last month's rent that waited for him somewhere down the line. The cop wouldn't understand that, though. He might get suspicious. He might decide that an expired registration was a good excuse to take a peek inside the Ford.

Or inside its trunk.

Worry clawed the man. What would happen to Jenny? How would she react if a cop popped the trunk, stared down at her? What would that do to her, when all she was expecting to see was a beautiful sunset?

And what about him? What would happen to a guy who kept a woman in the trunk of his car once the cops got hold of him?

He glanced over his shoulder, at the Ford. He couldn't help himself. He thought he heard plastic rustling. And then he saw the rag. It wasn't jammed in the trunk anymore. Jenny must have pushed it out. The rag was blowing across the parking lot, driven by the same wind that sent waves of grass rolling toward the green Pacific.

The sun was going down.

It was going down fast.

The cop stepped toward him. The cop didn't even know it yet, but he was coming to take Jenny away. The man was sure of it. Cut this any way you wanted, and that was how it would work out.

He started toward the cop. The cop smiled at him, said hello. He smiled back, but he didn't mean it. When he was close he charged the cop, piled into him with all the strength he could muster and together they went down hard on the blacktop, and the cop's head struck against the pavement and then the man found himself straddling the cop, cradling the bigger man's head in his hands, and he bashed it against the pavement time and time again, as hard as he could.

He didn't know how long he did that. But when he finally stopped, he knew that he'd done it for far too long.

Because Jenny couldn't wait any longer.

A twisted coat hanger rang against the pavement.

The trunk's rusting hinges complained as it sprang open.

Plastic rustled as Jenny climbed free.

But she hadn't seen him yet. No. He could tell. It had to be she was looking at something else, something simple and beautiful like a sunset, because she laughed.

The man listened to the sound. He stood up. He didn't turn around. He didn't look at Jenny. The last of the sunset filtered through the trees, washing his hands. But the sunlight didn't do any good. There was blood on his hands, and it wouldn't go away. He knew that it was there for good. He saw it. There was no missing it, the way you might miss a stray dog banging around your garbage can, or some kid shivering in the cold without a coat, or the smell of a hospital corridor.

He saw it.

And when the sun disappeared behind the horizon, Jenny saw it too.

She saw everything.

Life with Father

BY BENTLEY LITTLE

There's nothing like taking a perfectly good idea and beating it into the ground so hard that even the ground starts screaming.

But that's what you get when you take something nice and innocuous—like recycling, for example—and hand it over to Bentley Little. Suddenly, what seemed like a harmless suggestion becomes the most revolting home experiment ever. Proving once again that nothing succeeds like excess.

This is a story so wickedly horrible that it makes me laugh in self-defense, and earns the first of this anthology's warning labels. If you read it, it will fuck you up. You have been warned.

Enjoy!

I wrote "Life with Father" and "The Pond" for an ecological horror anthology titled *The Earth Strikes Back*. Both were rejected. Judging by the title of the book, I figured that most if not all of the stories would deal with the negative effects of pollution, overpopulation, deforestation, etc.

So I thought I'd do something a little different.

My wife is a hard-core recycler. Cans, bottles, newspapers, grocery bags—she saves them all. Even on trips, she brings along plastic bags in which to collect our soda cans.

I exaggerated her compulsion for this story.

Anything can be taken to extremes.

Shari has never seen a working toilet. She will—she goes to nursery school next year and I know they have toilets there—but right now she's only seen our toilets. Or what used to be our toilets before Father turned them into stationary storage containers for soybean chicken.

I don't know why I thought of that. I guess it's because Shari's squatting now over the biodegradable waste receptacle that Father makes us pee in. There are two receptacles for our waste. The blue one for urine. The red one for excrement.

I don't know how Shari'll do in school. She's slow, I think. Father's never said anything about it, but I know that he's noticed, too. Shari doesn't catch on to things the way she's supposed to, the way I did. She was three before she could even figure out the difference between the red and blue receptacles. She was four before she said her first word.

Sometimes I want to tell Father that maybe his seed shouldn't be recycled, that there's something wrong with it. Look at Shari, I want to say, look at The Pets. But I love Shari, and I even love The Pets in a way, and I don't want to hurt any of their feelings.

I don't want to get Father mad, either.

So I say nothing.

My period ended a few days ago, and I know I was supposed to wash out my maxi pads in this week's bathwater and then use the water on the outside plants and hang the maxi pads out to dry, but the thought of my blood makes me sick, and I just haven't been able to do it.

I've been saving the maxi pads beneath my mattress, and tomorrow I'm going to stuff them in my underwear and take them to school. I will throw them away in the girl's bathroom, just like everyone else.

I feel wicked and nasty.

I hope Father doesn't find out.

But I know he will when he takes Inventory.

I try to tell Father that we can donate my old clothes to Goodwill or the Salvation Army, that they will recycle my clothes and give them to other people. I hint that I can buy pants and blouses that have been worn by others at those same thrift stores and that this will contribute to the recycling process *and* allow me to have some new clothes, but he will not hear of it. The clothes we have are the clothes we will always have, he tells me, and only after death will they be passed on to someone else.

So he cuts up the material, takes out old stitches, and refashions the cloth into new blouses and pants.

I attend school dressed as a clown, laughed at by my classmates.

When I come home, I feed The Pets. They are kept in an enclosure in the center of the back yard, the low fence surrounding their habitat made from refashioned cans and cardboard. I feed them the crumbs and leftovers from yesterday's meal, mixed in with the compost of our own waste. I think this is wrong, but Father says that our bodies are not as efficient as they should be and that both our solid and liquid waste contain unused nutrients that can be fully utilized by The Pets.

I stand outside their enclosure and I watch them eat and I watch them play. When I am sure that Father is not around, I pick them up and hold them. Their bodies are cold, their skin slimy, their wings rough. I gave them names at one time, and sometimes I can still call out those names, but I'm ashamed to admit that I no longer know to whom they belong. Like everyone else, I can't tell The Pets apart.

I do not know why Father keeps The Pets and why he insists that they be fed, and that frightens me. Father never does anything without a reason or a purpose.

Every so often, when I'm standing there feeding them, I think to myself that their habitat looks like a pen.

Sometimes I try to tell the kids in my class the horrors of recycling, but I can never seem to find the words to describe what I mean, and they always tell me that they enjoy accompanying their parents to the recycling center on Saturday and dropping off their cans, bottles, and newspapers.

Cans, bottles, and newspapers.

Once, during ecology week, I told my teacher that anything can be carried too far, even recycling. She tried to explain to me that recycling is important, that it will help us preserve the planet for future generations. I said that instead of recycling everything, maybe it would be better if we used things that didn't have to be recycled. She said that I didn't understand the concept of environmentalism but that at the end of the week, after I had completed my worksheet and seen all the videotapes, she was certain that I would.

That night I went home and urinated into the blue bucket and defecated into the red.

It is Thursday again, and I know what that means.

I sit quietly on the couch, tearing the sections of today's newspaper into the strips that we will wash and screen and turn into my homework paper. I say nothing as Father enters the living room, but out of the corner of my eye I can see his dark bulk blocking the light from the kitchen.

He walks toward me.

"I feel The Need," he says.

My stomach knots up and I can't hardly breathe, but I force myself to smile because I know that if he can't have me he'll start in on Shari. His seed can't really be recycled (although he tried it once with frozen jars and the microwave, using his semen first as a skin lotion and then as a toothpaste), but he does not want it to go to waste, so when he feels The Need he makes sure that he finds a receptacle where it might do some good. In his mind, impregnating me is better than letting his seed go unused.

That's how we got The Pets.

I take down my pants and panties and bend over the back of the couch, and I try not to cry as he positions himself behind me and shoves it in.

"Oh God," I say, recycling the words he taught me. "You're so good!"

And he moans.

It has been four days since Shari last spoke and I am worried. Father is not worried, but he is unhappy with me. He felt The Need yesterday, and I let him have me, but I could not pretend that I enjoyed it, the way I usually do. He got angry at me because my unhappiness meant that his emotion was not recycled. He does not want anything to go unrecycled. He feels that, in sex, the pleasure that he feels should be transmitted to me. I am supposed to be happy after he takes me and to utilize that transmitted pleasure, to stay happy for at least a day afterward (although usually I'm miserable and sore and feel dirty), and to do something nice for Shari. Shari is supposed to recycle that pleasure again and do something nice for one of The Pets.

But I don't feel happy, and I can't fake it this time.

I tell Shari to lock her door when she goes to bed.

When I come home from school, Shari is crying and strapped to a chair at the dinner table and Father is in the kitchen preparing our meal. I know something is not right, but I say nothing and I wash my hands in last week's dishwater and sit down at the table next to my sister. Already I can smell the food. It is meat of some sort, and I hope Father has not decided to recycle a cat or dog that's passed away.

No matter what type of animal it is, I know that I will have to clean and carve the bones afterward and make them into forks and knives and toothpicks.

I try not to look at Shari, but I notice that her crying has not stopped or slowed even a little bit and that worries me.

Father comes in with our meal, carrying it on the single large plate that we share in order not to waste water, and it is some kind of casserole. He is grinning, and I know that grin: he is proud of himself. I take a close look at the ingredients of the casserole, at the meat. The piece I poke with my fork is strangely white and rubbery. I turn it over and see on its underside a darkened piece of skin.

Slimy, lizard skin.

I throw down my fork and glare at him and Shari is crying even harder.

"You killed one of The Pets!" I scream.

He nods enthusiastically. "In the future, it may be possible for us to be entirely self-sufficient. We may never have to go outside the family for a source of food. We can create our own meat, nurturing it with our own waste. We'll be the prototype of the family of the future." He grins, gesturing toward the casserole. "Try it. It's good." He picks up a fork, spears a chunk of meat, and puts it in his mouth, chewing, swallowing, smiling. "Tasty and nutritious."

I stare at the food and I realize that it has come from my body and will be going back into my body and will come out of my body again, and I suddenly feel sick. I start to gag, and I run out of the room.

"The yellow container!" Father calls. "Yellow is for vomit!"

I can hear Shari crying louder, the legs of her chair making a clacking noise as she rocks back and forth and tries to get away.

As I throw up into the yellow bucket, I wonder if our dinner is one of The Pets that I had named.

Father is rougher now. He seems crueler than before, and I wonder if it is because I disobeyed him.

I would run away if it wasn't for Shari.

In school we are learning about taking responsibility for our own actions and how we should clean up our own messes without Mommy or Daddy telling us to do so.

It is hard for me not to laugh.

Father says that I have caused him a lot of pain and emotional distress, and he beats me as he prepares to mount me from behind. My pants and panties are down and I am bent over the couch as he pulls out chunks of my hair and slaps my back and buttocks with the hard side of his hand. He is making Shari watch and she starts to cry as he shoves it in and begins thrusting.

I scream for him to stop it, that it hurts, not even pretending to enjoy it this time, but that seems to satisfy him and I know that he thinks he is recycling his negative emotions by imparting them to me.

When he is finished, he hits my face until I am bloody and then leaves the room.

Shari approaches me after he is gone. She stares at me with wide eyes and white face, frightened by what she has seen, and I try to smile at her but it hurts too much.

"Father hurted you," she says. She frowns, thinking for a moment, and she hunkers down next to me. "Is he a vampire?" she whispers.

"Yes," I say. "He's a vampire." I don't know why I'm saying this, I don't know what thought process made Shari even think of it, but it sounds good to me.

Her eyes get even bigger. "Then we better kill him," she says.

Kill him.

I smile at her and I force myself to sit up. "Yes," I say, nodding at her, wiping the blood from my nose and mouth. "We better kill him."

I make a stake from a recycled piece of broken broom handle that I find in the tool cupboard next to the washbucket. Father has been saving that piece of broom handle for some time now, knowing that it has an untapped usage but not knowing what that usage is.

I have found a use for it, and I feel good as I stand next to The Pets' habitat and sharpen the end of the stick.

We kill him while he is sleeping. Shari asks why he sleeps at night if he is a vampire, but I tell her that he is doing it to fool us and she believes me.

Because I am stronger, I hold the pillow over his face while Shari drives the stake through his heart. There is more blood than I expected. A lot more. It spurts everywhere as he screams and his arms and legs thrash wildly around. Both Shari and I are covered with it, but we've both seen blood before, and I think to myself that it's not as bad as seeing my own.

I continue holding the pillow until he is still, until he has stopped moving, until the blood has stopped pumping.

He is smaller in death, and he suddenly looks harmless to me. I remember all of the good things he's done and all of the fun we've had together and I think maybe we made a mistake.

Shari blinks slowly, staring at the stake. "He really was a vampire, wasn't he?"

I nod.

"What we do now?"

I tell her to take our clothes and the sheets and the pillowcases and wash them in the plant water. We strip and roll up the linens. Naked, I drag Father's body into the processing portion of the garage.

I place the biodegradable bags next to the butcher block, and as I take the knife from the drawer, I plan out where and what I'm going to cut, what I'm going to do with his skin, his blood, his hair. I try to think of the best way to utilize his bones.

Old habits die hard.

The Shallow End of the Pool

BY ADAM-TROY CASTRO

It's always tough when families split up. Tough on the parents. Even tougher on the kids. And some reunions are best avoided at all costs. They're like ticking time bombs that only explode upon contact.

But I suspect that few are so thoroughly designed for mutually assured destruction as the thermonuclear family gathering depicted in Adam-Troy Castro's "The Shallow End of the Pool." Taking domestic insanity to a whole 'nother level of intimate literary conflagration.

Originally published as a stand-alone by intrepid indie publisher Creeping Hemlock Press back in 2008—in a limited edition numbering only 350 signed copies—it's an honor and a privilege to give this masterpiece wider mainstream exposure, and the centerpiece position in this already crazed collection.

I don't know which one of us woke up first. I do know that when the light changed, illuminating a sky that the wire above us sectioned into little diamonds, I was curled like a wounded ball by the concrete steps, my skull pounding from the beating I'd taken, my arms numb from lack of circulation and my jaw aching like a dead thing attached to my skull with six-inch nails.

You would have expected us to have collapsed in opposite corners, in the traditional manner of the gladiators we were, but when I opened my eyes I saw that we'd slept only a few feet apart. His eyes were already open, and though it was hard to tell, he seemed to be smiling.

My Mom the Bitch lived in a desert fortress.

At least that's what my father had always told me, sometimes whispering the words, sometimes slurring them, sometimes growing so tired with the same old stories that he spoke in a monotone, making the words sound like a prayer from a faith he could no longer believe.

She'd nursed me when I was born. But things had already gotten bad between my parents by then, so bad that after less than another full year of trying, they split the kids between them. She took my twin brother Ethan, and Daddy took me, raising me to remember her as the Psycho Bitch she was.

I didn't lay eyes on her again until the summer of the year I turned sixteen.

On that sweltering day in August my father and I flew to Vegas, rented a car, and drove four hours into the desert to a place where the local roads almost disappeared under the windswept sands. There we took an almost invisible turnoff, and navigated another forty minutes along an abandoned road to the skeleton of a sign that had, once upon a time, decades ago, advertised roadside cabins.

The resort had never been prosperous. It was just a place for travelers on a budget to rest their heads for the night. Now, it was a wreck, hidden behind a natural outcropping of stacked boulders that God had arranged to look like praying hands. Once, the rocks had protected the guests from road noise. These days the barrier hid the blackened skeleton of the main office, the three cabins still standing out of the original eight, a swimming pool that hadn't seen water in years, and the mobile home where the Bitch lived with Ethan. I don't know if the cabins were still officially owned by anybody, nor do I have any idea how the Bitch had ever managed to find such an isolated place to live.

We pulled up in a cloud of dust to find the Bitch on the mobile home steps, smoking a cigarette, dressed in faded jeans with torn knees, and a sleeveless white t-shirt. She'd aged since the last photograph I'd seen, which dated back to some months after my birth. She'd been young and pretty in that one. But her skin had leathered and her hair, once a shiny brown, had gone gray and stringy, with a long white lock that crossed her face in the shape of a question mark. When she grimaced at our arrival, she revealed a front tooth missing among others yellowed from tobacco and time.

Leaving the rental's A/C was a shock. The outside temperature had been edging into the high nineties in Vegas, but here it was more like a hundred, in air that seemed more dust than oxygen.

Daddy said, "Hug your mother."

I crossed the seventeen steps between myself and the stranger on the mobile home steps. She put her arms around me and called me honey, even as her fingers probed my back, testing the bunched muscles there for any signs of flab. "My God, Jen. I remember when you were just a baby."

I cut the hug short. "I'm not a baby any more, Mom."

"No. You're not." She squeezed my upper arm, testing its solidity with strength I would not have expected from her. "She's an Amazon, Joe. Better than her pictures."

And that was just hateful mockery, because I knew what an Amazon was, and what one wasn't. An Amazon is tall: I was still three inches shorter than Daddy. An Amazon hacks off her right breast: I still had both of mine, and I daily cursed the hormones that had built them into a pair of fleshy curves softer by far than my bulging arms, my corded shoulders, and my granite abs. I was strong, and I was compact. I'd used diet and exercise to reduce those unwanted tits to the smallest size the genetic roll of the dice would allow, but I was still only a girl, the Amazon status we'd strived for a goal that would forever remain beyond my reach.

Daddy must have been thinking the same thing. "Where's the boy?"

The Bitch raised the cigarette to her lips and took a drag so deep the paper sizzled. "Inside."

"Call him out."

The Bitch took another long, slow drag of her cigarette, just to demonstrate that she wouldn't be hurried by the likes of us. "Ethan! Your father's here!"

Ethan emerged from the mobile home, screen door slamming.

In all my life I'd seen less than thirty photographs of my brother. They were what Daddy gave me instead of birthday or Christmas presents. As per the agreement that had governed the relationship between parents since the day of their dissolution, the two of them provided each other with such updates twice a year, just to keep each side apprised of just how the other was developing. Our basement dojo has a wall, tracking Ethan's metamorphosis from the chubby-cheeked toddler he was when last we saw each other, to the thick-jawed, iron-necked bruiser he was now. Watching that chest fill out, those arms swell, those muscles layer upon muscles, and those eyes grow dark as coals, in what amounted to time-lapse photography of a monster sprouting from a seed, had spurred me on more than any number of Daddy's lectures or rewards or punishments. Nothing communicated the urgency of hard training more than those pictures. Nothing made my own situation look more and more hopeless, for while Ethan and I were twins, the nasty combination of gender and genetics had provided him with a body much more hospitable to muscular development than mine. His last measurements, sent with glee six months ago, had already declared him a foot taller and some heavy pounds heavier than myself, with less than one percent body fat.

He was even bigger now. The last six months had provided him with another growth spurt. He was stripped to the shorts, by design I think, his hairless pectorals gleaming with the sheen left by his latest workout. His face, tanned to near blackness by the brutal desert sun, was so dark that the unpleasant white glow of his teeth stood out like a searchlight at the bottom of a deep well. His greasy shoulder-length black hair completed any resemblance he might have had to Tarzan. Next to him, the Bitch was a wisp in danger of being blown away by the next strong wind. He dwarfed her, and dwarfed me.

If my father had raised an Amazon (a label I rejected), then the Bitch, with her exacting cruelty, had raised a Greek God.

There were flaws. The enlarged jaw and forehead testified to the hormonal imbalance inflicted by steroid abuse. I had a touch of that myself, and had endured taunts about my face in most of the schools I'd briefly attended. Like mine, his chest was lined with hairline scars from training accidents and, I think, punishments. Unlike me, he was so very muscle-bound that his flexibility had suffered. He moved with the clumsy deliberation of a stop-motion dinosaur in a fifties monster flick. I moved better than that. And, like The Bitch, he couldn't really smile, at least not at us: the closest he could manage was an uneasy grimace.

"Hello," I said.

His voice was thick, his consonants gutteral. "Hello."

Once upon a time, we had drifted together in the same womb, knowing nothing of the venom being passed between those who had brought us into this life.

The Bitch said, "Hug your father."

My behemoth of a brother turned the head on his massive tree-trunk neck, and narrowed his eyes as he took in the figure of the man whose seed had provided half of him. Hatred burned in those eyes. He took two steps and enveloped Daddy in an embrace so tight that I half-expected to hear the crunch of shattering vertebrae. Unlike the Bitch, who had made a big show of hugging me back, Daddy just let his arms hang motionless at his sides. It was a brief hug. After a second or two my brother stepped back, his social obligations fulfilled.

Daddy said nothing.

The Bitch's eyes glittered. "Aren't you going to say I've done well?"

"I don't have to say it. I can see it."

"Then aren't you going to say I should be proud?"

"I wouldn't give you the satisfaction."

"Bastard." Her eyes turned to me: "I'm sure the two of you have a lot to talk about, after all these years. You can spend some time together this afternoon, if you'd like. Your father and I will need the rest of the day to finish work on the pool."

Daddy could not have been happy about this development, as private time between my brother and I had never been part of the family agenda. But the state of war between my parents had not gotten to where it was by either showing fear in the face of a challenge. "I have no problem with that. She'll need a few minutes to get ready, but after that, they can have the rest of the day if they want."

I coughed. "No."

Her head swiveled. "What?"

"This is just stupid. What are we fucking supposed to do, become friends now? That's just psychological warfare. I want to get this bullshit over with."

Ethan's eyes glittered, but not with the anger I might have expected. "You sure? There's plenty of time for that."

Daddy said, "I suppose we could use your help setting up."

I said, "There's that, too."

My mother and father let out a shared sigh.

"I'm sorry you feel that way," said Ethan.

Damned if our parents didn't look a little regretful, too.

"All right," Daddy said. "Give us about half an hour to get settled and take stock, and we'll meet on the patio."

"You can use Cabin Three," the Bitch said.

I backed away from her and Ethan, staying between them and my father until I could get behind him and concentrate on retrieving our trunk from the back seat.

Ethan and The Bitch just stayed by the mobile home steps, watching us.

Measuring me.

Cabin Three turned out to be surprisingly well-preserved, given that so many of the others had either burned down or collapsed. I'd expected cobwebs, scorpions, and an inch and a half of dust. We got a freshly swept wooden floor with a pair of bare box-spring mattresses with fitted white sheets. There was no air conditioning, which meant that the temperature was stifling, but the walls seemed solid enough, and the fresh screening on all the windows promised some protection from the local flies. There was no toilet, but there was a note to the effect that Ethan had dug a fresh outhouse for us, a short walk into the desert. For a sink we had a porcelain basin and a gallon jug of warm bottled water.

Daddy and I had lived in worse during my endurance training in the Sierra Nevadas, one long summer about three years earlier. That place had been so rickety that my last task, on the last day, had been to demolish it with my bare hands. By the time I was halfway done my knuckles bled and my fingers were studded with splinters. He had called me his best girl.

Without a washroom, settling in amounted to little more than dumping the bags on the unmade beds, so I took care of that, changed into a fresh white t-shirt bearing the name of a dojo I'd attended in Seattle, and then went around back to inspect the empty swimming pool. A leftover from the roadside cabin days, it and the cracked, weed-ridden patio surrounding it were the only paved things in the Bitch's entire homestead. It was kidney-shaped, three feet deep at the kiddie steps and thirteen feet below the rusted brackets that had once anchored the diving board. The bottom was pitted and streaked with years of windswept sand; there was also the corpse of a little black bird in the deep end, buzzing with flies. The air shimmered. Without any water to cut the sunlight, the walls had nothing to do but reflect the glare at one another, turning the entire bowl into a natural reservoir for heat.

Lifeguard chairs sat on both the concave and convex sides of the pool. They looked new, or at least recently wiped clean. So did the long and narrow tarpaulin, a few yards into the desert, there to keep the sun off a cylindrical shape three feet high and thirty feet across.

I asked, "That the chain-link?"

"That's the chain-link." Daddy licked his lips as he surveyed the deep end. "Check out that grate."

I dropped to my knees, grabbed the lip of the pool and hopped in, landing on my feet. The grate Dad had seen was a rusty square a half-meter on each side, covering the ancient water filtration system. The metal was so hot from the sun that I recoiled from my first touch, but I swallowed my pain, slipped my fingers through the holes in the mesh, and pulled it loose. It weighed maybe thirty pounds. The drain beneath it narrowed and curved out of sight, marked only by more sand and the skeletal remains of a mouse.

"Nothing hidden there?" Daddy asked.

"Nothing," I said.

It had been worth checking out. There could have been anything in that little well. A knife. A gun. Even a big rock. Any number of possible hidden weapons.

"Better get up here, then."

"All right." I didn't replace the grate, but instead used it to scrape the dead bird from the bottom of the pool, and hurl it over the side and into the desert. Not that I'm all that squeamish about having dead things around, but I prefer not to smell them when I don't have to. After a moment's further thought, I tossed the grate itself onto the patio, a safe distance from my father. "It's pretty solid. It probably qualifies as a weapon."

"It shouldn't be an issue," Daddy said. "Neither one of you will have arms free." "You know. In case." "Not saying it's a bad idea, hon. Besides, it's done."

I grabbed the edge of the pool with my fingers and climbed back up. The temperature was well over a hundred on the patio, but even that was a relief after the sizzling conditions in the oven down below; my t-shirt was already so saturated with sweat that the cloth had gone transparent over my breasts. I peeled the material off my belly and fanned myself with it, once or twice, just to get some cooler air in there, but it didn't help.

Daddy kneaded my shoulders. "Are you ready for this, Jen?"

"I guess I have to be."

Wrong answer. "Are you ready for this, Jen?"

"Yes. Yes, Daddy, I'm ready."

"You're not scared?"

"Maybe a little."

"Good. It helps to be scared. Fear is a survival trait. I wouldn't let this go any further if you weren't scared. But you're also ready?"

"Yes."

"Are you sure? There's no room for any doubt here."

"I'm sure. I know why this is important."

He really was proud of me. That was the main thing, which had carried us through all the years of hard work. He had invested everything he had in me, and I had invested everything in living up to what he wanted. I was still feeling a glow when his hand moved to the side of my head, and tugged at a braid. "What about this? Now or later."

"Later's fine," I said. "We can do it last thing."

"Okey-Dokey," he said.

A few minutes later Ethan and the Bitch came around, and we set to work on the arena.

The chain-link was a high-quality, thick mesh, lighter than it looked but still a bitch to work with at the quantities we needed:. It took all four of us, working in grim concert, more than an hour to unroll it from its resting place over the desert sand, past a section of patio, and over the pool itself, until it covered the basin entirely. Pronouncing the effects good, Ethan then went away and came back with the aluminum braces and steel bolts necessary to secure it against the patio. By the time we had finished lashing it down, our shared mother and father had exhausted themselves and had retreated to their opposing lifeguard stations, eyeing each other over the construction with the resigned air of nations that had always been, and would always be, at war.

By then, of course, I knew that turning down the day of truce had been a good idea, not only because our parents wouldn't have ever gotten this job finished, but because all this time working with Ethan had provided me an excellent opportunity to gauge his strength, his speed, his endurance, his dexterity, and most of all, his eagerness to begin.

Like me, he was hungry for this.

He might have dreaded it once, but his years of training had, like my own, worn away any of his own dreams and ambitions, and left him eager for nothing but the moment that we'd enter the pool together.

At about four o'clock, the sweat pouring down our bodies in waves, my brother and I used a pair of wire cutters to peel a three-sided flap away from a section over the steps leading to the shallow end. Descending, we explored the territory in the wader's area on hands and knees, testing the feel of the concrete against our bare skin, determining just how close we could come to standing before chain-link scraped against our backs or the tops of our heads. My smaller size and greater flexibility gave me an advantage here. I could run about in a doubled-over crouch that still gave me several inches of clearance, in places where Ethan could only struggle along in a hunchbacked, half-crippled lurch confined by the low ceiling. That advantage vanished as we both moved on to the Deep End. In the Deep End, where we could both stand fully upright, unimpeded by any low ceiling, the advantage of weight and strength was entirely his own. The gaping hole left by the removal of the grating presented the only equalizer. Either one of us could stumble into that one without warning, if not breaking bones, then at least crippling us long enough to cede advantage to the other.

We circled that hole together, thinking the same thoughts, then parted.

After several minutes of contemplative silence, we addressed each other with our backs against opposite walls.

Ethan ran a hand through his hair. "You do good work."

"Thanks. You too."

"I'm sorry you didn't want to come with me today. There's some great rock formations about twenty miles from here. I figured we could do some climbing and have ourselves a little picnic on the summit."

"That might have been fun," I allowed.

"Yeah." He kicked at the dust with the toe of one boot. "Would have been nice to have some fun. I don't even remember what it's like anymore."

"Boo fucking hoo."

"Yeah. I guess you know what it's like."

"And then some."

He seemed to hoard his next question before letting it go, all in a rush. "I'm sorry, but I have to ask this. Did he ever fuck you?"

"Who?"

"The Bastard."

Even then, it took me a second to figure out who he meant. "You mean, Daddy? Christ, no!"

"Did he ever make you blow him?"

If he didn't stop this, I was going to break his neck right here and now. "Is that what she told you?"

He relaxed. "Don't take it the wrong way or anything. I'm just saying, you never know. Not considering the kind of shit he used to do to her."

"He never did anything to her but take what she dished out."

"According to him."

If he was trying to anger me, he was doing an awfully good job. "I don't know what fucked-up stories she told you, but she's lying. She was the bad one."

"How do you know?" he countered. "Were you there?"

I thought of all the things Daddy had told me about her, from all the dreams she'd denied him, and all the petty betrayals she'd used to wound him, to all the words she'd used to castrate him. "What about you? Did you ever fuck the Bitch?"

He didn't object to me calling her that. "She offered once. About four years ago. I was thirteen, and half out of my head from jerking off fourteen times a day. She was already working five nights a week at the Horny Jackal, putting away enough cash for my training, so helping me out too wouldn't have meant all that much more. When I said I'd rather not, she didn't push it. Instead she got one of her co-workers to pay me a visit every couple of weeks."

"Ewww," I said.

"It wasn't too bad. But then she finally saved enough money to support us out here, and all that stopped."

"What do you do now?"

"Nothing. I think those shots have done something to my balls. I don't even think about it anymore." He drew another line in the dirt. "You could just give up, you know. That's what the rules say. Say you can't beat me and we won't have to do this. We can just go rock-climbing tomorrow instead of today."

I shook my head. "I can't do that to Daddy. Unless you want to give up instead?"

"Can't do that," he said. "Not all by myself. Not and miss the whole point of being born in the first place."

"Yeah, well." I shook my head, pushed myself away from the wall, and met him at the pool's deepest point.

We clasped hands.

He said, "Nice meeting you, Jen."

I said, "I'm gonna kill you, Ethan."

Would you believe he looked hurt?

Why did he have to go ahead and make me feel shitty like that?

Daddy and I went back to the cabin so he could shave my head.

I can't say I wasn't bothered. I owed my hair a lot. For all too long, sitting in school among soft boys with flabby necks and skinny girls with toothpick wrists, all of whom indulged their pretend adolescent cruelties without assets enabling them to last thirty seconds against a genuine real-world enemy, I'd had to pretend that I didn't hear the whispers. I heard them pointing out the crewcut and the enlarged jaw and my tree-trunk biceps and the nose flattened by a punch in the years before I'd learned to see an attack coming. Before Daddy relented and let me grow my hair long—always with the understanding that I'd have to cut it again for my match with Ethan—I'd heard them wonder just what the hell was I supposed to be anyway. The long blonde hair helped, as if I wore it right, it placed me within shouting distance of pretty. There'd even been a boy once and sweaty gropings on the couch in his parent's basement. It had been fun enough, though that had ended, painfully, the one time he put a hand on me without warning. Unfortunately, that incident happened on school property. Daddy had apologized and paid for the Emergency Room visit. I took the one-week suspension knowing that the lesson would not need to be taught again.

The hair was a loss. But I had always known I wouldn't be wearing it long, around my brother. Long hair was dangerous. It could get in my eyes and blind me at a crucial moment. Maybe I'd have a chance to grow it back and maybe not.

Daddy sat me down on the bed, used a pair of scissors to cut my hair short, the electric shears to reduce what was left to stubble, and a straight razor with medicated shaving cream to make my scalp baby-smooth. By the time he was done the mattress was itchy from liberated blonde. Then, surprising me, he opened up the suitcase and showed me a big floppy white hat.

"For afterward," he explained. "I think you'll look pretty in it."

My eyes welled. I hid it well, batting my eyes at him, in the manner of any Southern belle.

By six we were still so far from sunset that the sky hadn't even faded to a darker shade of blue. But more than half of the pool bottom was already in long shadow, the other half a surreal fresco of diamond-shapes cast by the fencing. Ethan and I had both consumed our last food and water and both taken our final opportunities for a civilized bathroom break. Daddy had given me my final instructions, which mostly consisted of strategies I already knew: to exhaust Ethan's wind by keeping him on the move, to retreat to the shallow end whenever I needed a breather myself, to be careful around that gaping hole in the deep end and to lure him into it, if I could. I was kind enough to react to all of these suggestions as if they were new and exciting ideas.

When he was done he gave me yet another hug, told me that I was his special girl, and promised me that things would be different once this was over. He said I could have anything I wanted. He made the mistake of asking me to name the first thing I'd want for myself when we were done, and for the life of me I couldn't think of anything. My life had never been about anything other than today and the idea of wanting something afterward was so ridiculous that it might have been spoken in another language entirely. When he pressed the point I couldn't speak the first answer that came to mind, which was that chance to go rock-climbing with Ethan. That was just stupid. By definition, there'd be no Ethan. So I just said, "Maybe we'll go shopping."

He kissed me on the forehead and said, "Sure."

By half past six, Ethan and I were stripped, greased, and in the process of being fitted with our respective hobbles.

Our parents had recognized, while Ethan and I were both still toddlers, that even with equal training he would probably still emerge with a substantial edge in brute strength. That appraisal had turned out to be an accurate one, but Daddy had pointed out that even Ethan wouldn't be able to end the fight with a single punch, or crushing bear hug, if unable to use his arms. Mom had agreed to taking corrective measures on the single condition that I was prevented from fighting dirty, by which she meant the use of teeth or nails.

Our gags, which buckled tightly around the backs of our shaved heads, were steel bits sheathed in layer of rubber thick enough for us to sink our teeth into. Our arms were cuffed behind our backs and held in place with canvas sheaths laced to the shoulders and fastened around our necks to prevent either one of us from curling into a ball to pass the cuffs under bent legs. The getup was confining, but I'd practiced in it for hours and could still high-kick without losing balance or strangling myself. Nor would it affect my stamina. Just six months ago I'd run the equivalent of a marathon with both arms tightly strapped behind my back.

I hadn't ever worn the getup against a similarly-hobbled opponent tasked to kill me, but that was all right. By now, this felt far more natural to me than that sun bonnet. Ethan, standing at attention while the Bitch tugged at the laces binding the sheath to his arms, looked like he felt the same way. He even managed to wink at me, though I don't know just what the hell he thought he was communicating.

Daddy announced that it was a quarter to seven. The sky was definitely a darker shade of blue now. The sunlight was just a thin slice of brighter concrete, beveled with distorted diamond-shapes, on the eastern edge of the pool. The Bitch led Ethan in through the cutaway flap above the Shallow End steps, escorted him all the way to the pool's deepest point, kissed him on the top of the head, then withdrew. Daddy helped me down the same steps, sat me down in the Shallow End, told me that whatever happened I would always be his daughter and that he would always believe in me no matter what, then abandoned me as Ethan had been abandoned.

Neither one of us could see the other. It was, after all, a kidney-shaped pool, which meant that as long as we stayed at opposite ends we were hidden from one another by the curvature of the walls. Apart, neither one of us would be able to tell how the other was doing. The only way to tell was to risk meeting in the middle.

Above us, Daddy and the Bitch got to work repairing the flap so that neither of us would be able to use it to escape. It wasn't a fancy patch. They just looped wire through the links, sewing the loose edges together. The two of them worked side by side, not speaking, not deigning to look at each other, but working as a unit just the same. Both their faces seemed shadowed, given the fading brightness of the sky. I wished I could see if Daddy was looking at me, but I couldn't tell for sure. I didn't think he was. Sweat stung my eyes and I had to look away.

Not long after that, our parents stood together and tugged at the flap. The fresh seal held. They turned their backs on each other and disappeared from my sky. A few seconds later, Daddy appeared again, this time sitting high on the lifeguard chair on the convex side of the pool. The Bitch took her own position on the lifeguard chair opposite him. I shifted position, got my feet under me, rose to a half-crouch, and waited.

Daddy said, "All right, kids. Make us proud."

Ethan did not disappoint me.

He was too smart to come at a run. He came around the bend at a fast walk, his eyes dark as he searched for me, half-hoping I'd meet him halfway.

I remained where Daddy had left me, waiting.

Ethan was neither disappointed at my lack of initiative nor contemptuous of my cautious start. He slowed and stopped at the midway point separating the Shallow and Deep ends of the pool. He paced that invisible line between us, his muscles tensing, his shoulders cording from what must have been a hideous effort to wrest himself free of the sheath binding his arms. The sheath held, as he'd probably known that it would. He grimaced through his gag, mumbled a word his mouth was not able to properly form, then advanced another step uphill. Another two. His eyes rolled toward the sky, as he felt the space between the top of his head and the wire link narrow to inches. He bent his knees and advanced still further, still testing our battlefield, painfully aware that I would not just allow him to march up and put me out of my misery.

I still didn't move.

Ethan advanced further. Now he had to crouch—not all the way, not so much he couldn't keep both eyes firmly focused on me, but enough to unbalance him, enough that he could feel his advantage of height and weight diminishing with every step he took. I could see sweat cutting through the sheen at what would have been his hairline. He paused again, braced himself for the inevitable moment when I charged, and tried to persuade me with a look that hanging back was no good, because he was ready for any attack I could muster.

I didn't move.

He advanced some more.

I saw his balls. I knew what balls looked like; I'd seen them close up, on that boy whose name I couldn't even remember. These looked tiny and purple. The steroids had shrunken them to a fraction of their natural size.

Had I been able to talk, I would have mocked him for being a dickless wonder. It might have upset him, made him sloppy.

He took another step, reminding me that it was a waste of time to contemplate strategies I couldn't use.

Another step.

I faked to the right.

He recognized my move as a feint, and anticipated a move in the other direction.

Another fake and I actually went right. A heartbeat before we collided I saw him brace for impact, but he expected me to hit him mid-body, at his center of gravity, where his superior weight allowed him to compensate. So instead I hurled myself at the ground and swept his legs with my own.

He went down.

Everybody's fallen down. But few people appreciate just how much we rely on our arms to protect our heads from damage during a fall. Falling forward, we throw out our hands and take the damage there, turning a potential cracked skull into a mere pair of sprained wrists. Neither one of us had the option now. Ethan managed to compensate enough to take the bulk of the impact on his knees, but even that did not stop his fall, and when he landed flat on his chest, his head whipped forward, smashing nose and forehead against the hard concrete ground.

Without the knees, that fall might have been enough to finish him all by itself.

Daddy cried, "Good one, Jen!"

I managed a weak kick to Ethan's calf as he rolled away, but didn't waste time waiting to see where he went after that, not with life or death riding on who rose first. It was early, still. I got my feet under me and backed off, giving Ethan the space he needed to back against the wall and take stock of himself. His nose was broken and bubbling blood from both nostrils: good news, as that would obstruct breathing. There was more blood in the seams between the teeth clamped against his bit-gag. He couldn't have bitten his tongue or cheeks, but maybe I'd loosened an incisor or two. Another advantage, in that he'd have that sickening taste to deal with.

But his eyes were still smiling.

Daddy yelled, "Don't overestimate him, baby!"

Ethan came for me again.

I faked another dodge to the right, but he changed course without even trying hard, and I tried to duck and roll, but that was going for the same trick twice in a row, and he was ready for that, lowering his head and reaching me before I could move away.

He drove his head into the softer flesh below my ribs and drove me off my feet, the force of his charge carrying me all the way to the concrete wall of the pool. The impact drove the air from my lungs. I gasped as my head whipped back against the wall with a force that I experienced as a burst of blinding white light.

Before I could recover he smashed the top of his head against my jaw, driving my skull against the concrete a second time. And then a third.

"Finish her!" yelled the Bitch.

He might have.

I only stayed up because Ethan's body kept me from falling.

He rammed me again. My legs thrashed and my feet left the floor. He was bearing all my weight now, driving me into the concrete so hard that I didn't have time to fall.

"Put him down, honey!" yelled Daddy.

If I'd had the use of my hands I could have taken out Ethan's eyes. If I'd had the use of my teeth I could have ripped out his throat. I only had my legs, which didn't have the proper angle for a worthwhile kick.

But I didn't need to kick him to put him down, not when the wall was right behind me.

Not when he was keeping me from falling.

I braced the bare soles of my feet against the concrete, took another skull-rattling impact with the wall just to gather my fading strength, and at the moment when he pulled back for another power-driving charge pushed off with everything I had.

It wasn't enough to send him flying backward, as I'd hoped. But it did throw him off balance. His greased skin lost traction against mine. He tried to shift, but then he fell left and I fell right and we both hit the bottom of the pool in a tangle.

I landed on top, driving my knee into his shriveled balls with a force that made him double in two.

"That's a girl!" Daddy yelled. "Now finish him!"

But I was in no shape to risk more close contact, not with my vision going gray from the beating I'd taken. I rolled away, got my feet under me again, and managed to get to the opposite wall just as Ethan was also getting back to his feet.

He looked like hell, sweaty, out of breath and the entire lower half of his face gleaming with blood. I don't know what I looked like, but as he went in and out of focus I knew that I had to look worse.

He shouted something through his gag, something that emerged as a series of bubbly roars. He could have been telling me to fuck myself. Or he could have been saying that I was his sister and he was sorry he couldn't love me. Or he could have been describing all the ways he wanted to make me suffer before I died.

It didn't matter what he wanted to say. Or what I wanted to say. Our vocabulary was limited. This fight was the only conversation we had left.

Fortunately, he'd had enough for now.

He looked away and staggered toward the Deep End.

I went for the Shallow.

Dad shouted encouragement from above. "That's good, honey! Pick your opportunities! Don't waste yourself going after him until you're ready!"

The Bitch cried, "I love you, honey!"

And so came the night.

The stars surprised me.

It wasn't the first time I'd spent the night outdoors. I'd had that summer in the Sierra Nevadas, and the endurance treks in the Mojave, and long nights shivering in tents on Alaskan glaciers. I'd been so far from cities that if anything had happened to me it would have taken days or weeks to make my way to the first emergency room capable of giving me so much as a single stitch. I'd learned just what the sky could look like in the rarefied places untouched by smog or the glare of neon lights. I'd seen those distant suns glowing by the thousands, each so bright that they might have been tiny campfires just beyond my reach. I had grown bored by them.

I had never seen stars as bright as the stars looked tonight. They were so brilliant that the sharpest stung my eyes and made my vision blur. Whenever I moved, some twinkled out of sight, eclipsed by chain-link. I had never seen them so close, so mysterious. I had never seen other eyes looking down, from those distant places, wondering about us the way I wondered about them. I had never known that some of them had to be fighting for their lives, to settle conflicts begun long before they were even born.

There was no moon. Daddy and the Bitch had decided that we shouldn't schedule this for a night with a moon. But the stars still provided enough glow to reveal the shape of the cracked white concrete walls. I could see the way the concave side curved off into the distance. The shadows were deep enough and large enough to provide any number of possible hiding places for my brother, but I could hear his bubbling snorks—representing a constant effort to keep his nostrils clear—and as far as I could tell it came from all the way around the bend. We were still at opposite corners.

I was thirsty. When I leaned the back of my head against the wall, my skin stuck, revealing a dried clotted mass back there. My teeth ached from biting into rubber for so long. My arms were in agony. I was nauseated, but didn't dare throw up, not when the gag would have forced me to swallow it or choke. I hadn't heard Daddy or the Bitch shout their little encouragements for quite a while, and couldn't tell from the shapes of lifeguard chairs silhouetted against the night sky if they were still up there watching.

It must have been about midnight that I squirmed away from the steps, which had been the closest thing I had to a refuge, got my feet underneath me, and padded over to the gentle curve to my immediate right. I crouched there, hesitated to make sure I was alone, and peed. Drizzle ricocheting off the puddle peppered my right ankle. A rivulet flowing downstream puddled against my heel. I wondered not for the first time how female dogs managed to keep their paws dry. After a few seconds, feeling better, I straightened out and put some distance between myself and the only toilet I'd have for as long as this battle lasted.

A million miles away, Ethan snorked again.

With his nose obstructed by the break, just breathing had to be exhausting him. It would deny him sleep, deny him rest, deny him even enough air to stay strong. He could get some around the gag, but it wouldn't be enough to keep him going forever. Even if I did nothing at all, and stayed out of his way, his probable life expectancy in the pool must have already been cut in half. I only wished I could be sure that what was left was still shorter than mine. After all, I'd suffered a head injury. The nausea and dizziness was a sure symptom of a concussion capable of deepening into coma as soon as I drifted off.

I had to make another go for him.

Padding along the warm concrete floor of the pool, which had not yet given up all the heat of the day, I made my way toward him, stopping every step or so to keep him from triangulating my position from the sound of my breath. Not that stealth mattered all that much. The thin layer of grit at the bottom of pool made every step crunch like an old-fashioned soft-shoe.

I tried not to think about how big he was and how badly he'd hurt me the last time we'd faced each other.

In my head, he'd grown to twice his actual size.

In my head, he was an ogre, towering over me like any other creature of old fantasies, with arms the size of tree trunks and a head that blotted out the sky. In my head, I only came up to his waist.

An image from an old stop-motion movie intruded, painting Ethan as a roaring Cyclops, scooping up badly-imposed sailors to bite in half with one chomp of his oversized jaws.

I cursed my imagination. This was stupid. He was nothing but a big, stupid, overdeveloped boy too clumsy for his own good.

He was just my brother.

Daddy had said, "You're better than him, honey."

He had said, "You'll win as long as you have heart."

He had said, "I have faith in you, Jen."

The Bitch might have said any number of things like that to Ethan, but then, she was the Bitch, and she was used to lies and deceit. Just look at all the things she had done to Daddy.

When Daddy said things like that, he told the truth.

I made it to the line that separated the Deep and Shallow ends. The bowl ahead of me was inkier and, it seemed, deeper than it had any right to be. I couldn't see the far wall. There was too much shadow there even to admit the distant light of the stars. It was too black to see Ethan, but I could still hear his breathing, somewhere ahead of me. It was ragged, wet, and labored. It didn't sound like he was lying down. I got the clear impression that he was standing against the far wall, beneath what would have been the diving board, confident in his own ability to meet my advance with a strength that trumped my own.

He was accurate enough there. If he was waiting for me, I should turn back.

I took another step to be sure.

Something nearby smelled like a sewer.

I still couldn't see him. I listened for him and all of a sudden couldn't hear him either.

I couldn't bring myself to hope that he'd died in the last few seconds. More likely, he'd realized I was close and was holding his breath as long as he was able, to keep me from being able to track him.

That trick worked for two as well as one. I couldn't close my mouth or pinch my nostrils shut, but I held my diaphragm tight and held my next breath as long as I could, counting off the seconds.

Ten. Thirty.

One minute.

I could hold my breath for two.

More, since my life depended on it.

Ninety Seconds. Still no sound from him.

He couldn't be dead. I could feel him.

Was he moving toward me?

Coming up on two minutes. My heart was pounding.

Two minutes. Still silence.

Would I even be able to hear him over the roar of the blood in my ears?

Two minutes ten.

It was not breath that alerted me. It may have been a soft, padding thump or a rush of air or the instinctive connection between siblings, but I knew I was being charged.

I spun, not knowing which way to dodge. Something massive struck a glancing blow against my right side, and kept going, the impact enough to make me lurch to the left in a clumsy dance that barely kept me on my feet.

I heard a metallic clang.

Rushing past me, he'd scraped the top of his head against chain link.

That had to hurt.

It didn't knock him down, but it did make him grunt.

I gasped as best I could, and whirled to face him in case he made another charge. I saw a gleaming wetness at just about eye-level and identified it as his gag, slick from hours of blood and drool. I had just enough time to register him

racing toward me at terminal velocity. I went to my knees, looked up, caught another glimpse of an Ethan-shape occluding the sectioned starscape, and for just a
heartbeat knew what it must have been like, in Jurassic times, to be a tiny animal
cowering at the tyrannosaur shadow standing between me and the primordial sky.

He went over me hard.

I heard a thud, a crack, and a subsequent moan.

That had to have killed him. He had rushed me too hard and gone over me in
what felt like a somersault. He would have had to smash his head again, maybe
broken his neck, at the very least dislocated his shoulders or fractured a leg. He
must have sustained some kind of injury, maybe even something internal that
would seep his life away.

I peered into the shadows and saw a huge form, glistening from wounds and
other liquids, dragging itself toward the farthest wall. The snorking breath started
again. He wasn't dead, then, only hurt. And there was no way of telling how hurt.
It would be just like him to fake something worse if that meant drawing me close.

I thought of how large he'd been in the darkness, and more than just gathering
thirst filled my throat with sand.

I'd peed all I had just a few minutes ago, but I lost another couple of drops now.

I couldn't go after him again. Not while it was still dark. There'd be more light
in the morning.

I retreated, refusing to turn my back on the giant in the darkness, not feeling
safe again until I was on my knees again, curling up beside the steps that represented
my only refuge. The stars above still twinkled in and out of existence when eclipsed
by the overhead wire.

All at once, they blurred.

I didn't want to kill him anymore.

I wanted to kill the Bitch. I wanted to grab her by her stupid witchy hair and
smash her face into the concrete again and again until her head staved in and the
pavement turned red from blood and brains. I wanted to scream at her, call her
names worse than the obvious cunt and whore and demand to know where the
fuck she got off doing this to her son and her daughter when we'd both be so much
better off if she'd just close her withered lips around a double-gauge.

I wanted Daddy. He had done the same thing. But he was Daddy.

"You can't cry," he'd told me. I'd been flat on my back pressing weights and he'd been spotting me. "You're strong and you're brave and you have more heart than anybody I've ever known, but if you don't get him right away and it goes into hours or days, then at some point it'll all be too much for you and you're going to want to cry. You'll know what it means because it'll be the first sign that you're losing heart. You can't let it happen. You'll have to shut it down, wall it off, put it away before it takes over and it's all you have left. You have to make yourself too hard to break." I'd told him I would and he'd said, "That's a good girl."

When he called me a good girl, I felt capable of anything.

But I hadn't heard his voice in hours.

Had the Bitch done something to him?

Or were things even worse than that?

Was all this just a joke to them? Or, worse, foreplay? Were they together in that shithole of a mobile home sharing six-packs and nuzzling each other's necks while they laughed over the big hilarious joke they'd played on the kids?

Were they in the car together, lighting out for parts unknown while wondering which of their two science experiments fell first?

"You'll even lose faith in me," he'd said. "But you'll know I love you, honey."

Unless that was just another part of the trick.

I couldn't cry. But there were too many hours between now and morning, and my eyes were burning.

I don't think I fell asleep. I think I passed out.

I saw myself running, the summer Daddy and I spent in the Cascades. I rose before dawn, performed three hundred pushups, then donned my wrist and ankle weights and hit the woods for a twenty mile run. It was the time of day when the chill left over from the night before turned the dew into frost, and the grass into stiff needles. The air ripped at my lungs like fire and my breath trailed behind me in a necklace of little clouds. Daddy had pointed out one ravine that could be leaped as long as I used a fallen tree propped up against a living one as an acceleration ramp. It was a tricky stunt even in perfect light and an almost suicidal one in woods still marked by the failing shadows of the previous night, but I'd mastered it, always landing in a duck-and-roll that plastered dirt and leaves to my back in a mortar of warm sweat. Even a perfect landing was hard enough to knock the breath out of me, but I always got up and kept going, As a younger girl, running other courses in other environments, I'd cracked ribs and once or twice broken fingers, once even run headlong into a low-hanging branch that ripped a gash in my forehead and freed hot burning blood to seep down into my eyes. It hadn't slowed me down. I'd been blinded but I'd returned home without slowing down. I couldn't depend on vision when so many possible attacks depended on targeting the eyes.

When I woke the sun had arrived, illuminating a sky that the wire above us sectioned into little diamonds. I was curled by the concrete steps, my skull pounding, my throat burning, my arms numb from lack of circulation and my jaw aching like a dead thing attached to my skull with six-inch nails. I would have expected Ethan and I to collapse in opposite corners, but instead we'd fallen only a few feet apart, in a togetherness unexpected for two people who wanted each other dead. His eyes were already open, and though it was hard to tell through all the gear on his face, he seemed to be smiling.

His nostrils weren't bubbling. I wondered if he was dead.

I shifted position and prodded him with a toe.

He blinked. The gagged smile broadened. He murmured a series of vowels that should have been indistinguishable as words, but which his sunny tone communicated perfectly.

"Unnnh Aww Innh."

And good morning to you, too.

I couldn't make myself believe that he'd been too injured to chance attacking me as I slept. Or that he'd been too afraid. More likely he'd experienced a spell as lost and as despairing as mine, and had wanted nothing more than to spend the remaining hours of darkness close to another living being. Even if that person happened to be me. Maybe especially if that person happened to be me.

I wasn't ready, either physically or emotionally, to take advantage just yet. I just nodded hello, squirmed and crawled my way to a safe distance, and then got to my feet. Dizziness, thirst and whatever damage the concussion had inflicted made me wobble, but I managed to stay upright.

I took a deep breath and almost gagged on it. Even with half the pool still in shadow the air was still so warm it felt more like soup.

We could stay in the narrowing shadows on the eastern side of the pool for most of the morning, moving west when they were replaced by the lengthening shadows of the late afternoon. It wouldn't protect us from the heat, but it might save us from being burned to a crisp by the sun.

That was funny. Us. Like we were a team or something.

And either way, there'd be no shadows at noon.

We were going to cook.

The two lifeguard chairs were still unoccupied.

They'd left. Daddy and the Bitch had patched together their differences and were now sipping champagne in their jacuzzi in some swank resort in Reno. Daddy must be saying, too bad about the kids. Yes, what a shame. They were both so respectful. Do you know, May, I once asked her to go fifteen days without food, as a survival exercise, and she just did it, without even arguing? That's right. She sat in her room, growing paler and paler, her cheeks growing gaunt and her skin going pale, and in all that time, May, all that time, she never one said, Daddy, I can't do this anymore, I need something, just a little soup, just a little bread, just something to stop my stomach from cramping? It was enough to make me wonder, May, just what the hell else I could ask her to do. Would she have put out her eyes? Cut off her own hand? Press the right side of her face against a hot frying pan and not move even as she felt her skin scar and sizzle from the heat? We should be proud of ourselves, May. The way we raised them, and all.

Daddy wouldn't talk that way. The Bitch would, but Daddy wouldn't.

Daddy was better than that.

Daddy loved me.

The world grayed. I shook the spots away and stumbled forward, walking the perimeter. I noted the drying blood stains on the floor and on the walls, I found a crack emitting a battalion of ants and, at the moment I entered the Deep End, a dead rattlesnake, its head and midsection crushed almost flat. It puzzled me for a while until I figured out the story. The concrete of the patio above, with its talent for sucking up heat during the day and radiating it slowly at night, rendered it a natural beacon for snakes. They must have loved the place, and with the empty pool considerably warmer, it must have been just as natural for them to crawl in, from time to time, their idiot reptilian brains too shortsighted to realize that once they made the drop they would not be up to the task of finding a way out. Ethan and the Bitch must have had their hands full, clearing the place of pissed-off rattlers without getting bitten themselves. And of course, they hadn't bothered to warn us of the danger: not when a fortuitously-stranded snake could spell defeat for a girl who hadn't been told.

This one must have taken Ethan by surprise.

Had it bitten him?

I couldn't be that lucky.

I looked over my shoulder and confirmed that he was still curled by the Shallow End steps. The sweat and the grease had plastered the sand to his body, giving him a white, powdery appearance. But he didn't seem sick. He'd rolled over and was watching me with a calm, unbothered curiosity.

My eyes burned.

I went deeper, not knowing what I was looking for. The deep end was just a filthy oval, covered with dust and bird shit and brilliant in the morning glare. When I reached its lowest point I caught a whiff of something foul, and followed the odor to the drain hole, where I found pretty much what I should have expected to find. Removing the grate had been doing Ethan a favor. It had given him a place to do his daily business without having to worry about stepping in it. Looking closer, wrinkling my nose as I was hit by the awful rising stink, I further noted that he'd suffered diarrhea. This was disgusting, but good news for me, as the single greatest factor in living through this was probably surviving dehydration, and he'd have no chance to replenish what he'd lost.

As if on cue, my own stomach gurgled.

Christ.

The heat and the conditions were doing the same thing to me that they were doing to him.

I considered making use of the drain, decided not, and went back to the Shallow End.

The sun was higher in the sky now. The shadows cast by the pool's eastern curve now covered less than a third of the pool bottom. I made the mistake of glancing at the sun and recoiled, my vision a purple blob. That sun wasn't golden. It was white. It was pure, malevolent heat, pounding down on us like a thousand hammers. How high was the temperature going to rise today, before the shadows came back? A hundred ten? More?

Ethan had settled in under the shadows, his bound arms against the convex wall, his knees curled up against his chest. He looked at me, then at the empty space beside him, and then at me again. He repeated himself, and when I failed to get it, repeated himself a third time.

I got it.

It was stupid to fight now. Not with shelter a more immediate need.

Might as well wait out the day, survive if we could, and make another go at each other tonight. We'd both be weaker then, but that only meant that we'd both be that much closer to finishing this.

If there was a finish. If Daddy and the Bitch came back.

I selected a spot two body-lengths from Ethan, put my back to the wall, and lowered myself into a bent-kneed squat. It was as relaxed a position as I was willing to attempt, around him, one that would allow me to jump away in a heartbeat if he went for me.

I didn't think he would.

If we couldn't outlive the day, what was the point?

The hours crawled. The sun rose in the cloudless sky. The air grew hot, then sweltering, then brutal, then hellish. Our refuge of shadow narrowed, the razor-thin line between mere unbearable heat and deadly sunlight drawing closer to our curled legs. The sweat pouring down my face collected against my lips, investing the rubber bit with a foul, salty taste. My tongue swelled. I tried not to look at the opposite wall, already so bright from reflected glare that my eyes compensated by conjuring gray spots at the edges.

The shadow wasn't protecting us enough.

Sunburns don't only happen to those to expose themselves to direct sunlight. Sometimes it's possible to hide in the shade, all day long, and still suffer painful burns. It all depends on the reflectivity of the surrounding surfaces.

Ethan and I were in a big white bowl, facing one of its big white walls. Spared the worst of the sunlight, we were still absorbing enough reflected radiation to cook us more slowly. Ethan, who was darker than me and had the base tan one would expect from a boy who had spent years training under this sun, would tolerate it better than I would, with my much fairer skin. But we were both burning. By the time the zone of shadow came within a finger's-length of his knees, his face had turned lobster-red, and sprouted the first of what would soon be many sun-blisters on his forehead.

He didn't move, though. He didn't shift position, to protect the parts already burned with the parts that had spent these hours protected by canvas and shadow. He didn't even lower his head. He just faced forward, his eyes closed, his expression serene and confident even as his lips cracked and the sweat pooled in the furrows between his muscles began to shine like tiny sun lamps. Not once did he let me see that it was bothering him.

By then I already knew that I was losing.

My skin was on fire. My tongue was a dry, swollen worm scraping the roof of my mouth like sandpaper. Something had gripped my bowels and twisted, turning everything inside me to acid. I'd fouled myself and not even realized it. When I moved, I could feel the stored heat rising from me in waves.

I felt snakes crawling over me. They were burning snakes, with razors instead of scales, and when they slithered over my breasts they left gaping wounds behind. They went away and were replaced by flies, each as hot as embers snatched from a fire, each with little buzzsaw wings that, twitching, shredded whatever remained. Then came the worms and the maggots. I threw up, choked on it, managed to get it down again, decided that the long day had to be over after all these hours of hell and looked down to see that the cutting edge of that line of direct sunlight hadn't moved any closer to me in the year or so I'd been hallucinating.

I cried. I don't know how many tears came out, but I cried. I didn't care if Ethan heard me. He knew how much this was hurting.

I couldn't fool him about that.

Even if I'd lied to him about Daddy.

"You have to be a rock," Daddy said. He had come to me early in the morning of my twelfth birthday, his eyes dark and his thing dangling from his thatch like a blind, rooted worm. "You have to take whatever happens to you. A broken nose is nothing. A broken leg is nothing. A broken rib is nothing. A lost eye is nothing. Days without sleep or rest, more pain than you can imagine, it's all nothing. He will hurt you any way he can, everywhere that you're soft enough to be hurt. He can even try to rape you, if he wants—after all, he's a boy, and that's always been one of the best ways for boys to hurt girls. It'll be even worse for you if it happens, because you'll know all along that it's your own brother doing it. Of course, if you're strong enough, he won't be able to. You can make it more work than it's worth. You might even make it the last dirty thing he ever tries. But even if he does manage to pin you down, and hurt you in that special way, you'll have a chance as long as you know that you can get past it. And the only way to know that is to know that you've been past it before."

He'd only done it that one time.

And I knew almost immediately that it hurt him as much as it hurt me, because when I tiptoed to his room the next morning, clutching the carving knife I'd plucked from its rack in our kitchen, thinking only of not letting him do that to me again, planning to separate him from the thing he'd jammed up inside me, I'd found him sitting on the edge of his bed, his head in his hands, his shoulders wracked by convulsive sobs. He hadn't seen me as I'd padded up behind him, not so fired by certainty now, my right arm trembling as the knife grip grew heavier and heavier and the sobs coming from the broken figure before me resolved into self-recriminations about what kind of monster he was. And I'd thought about burying that knife between his shoulder blades and watching his life blood seep into the sheets as he fell over dying but not dying so fast that he couldn't turn his head and gaze at me and see that I was the one who had done this to him, his stunned expression betraying a hurt a thousand times worse than the pain of the wound or the violation I'd suffered for a few short minutes in the middle of the night. He really did love me. He was my Daddy. And so I dropped the knife and threw my arms around his shoulders and wept, "I'm sorry, Daddy, I'm sorry, I didn't know," and he grabbed me back and buried his head in my shoulders and cried, "I'm sorry, I'm sorry, I had to, I didn't want to but I had to, you had to experience it once," and I said, "I know, I know, I know," and then it was all about him feeling bad and me trying to make him feel better, because I loved him, as he loved me, which meant that I would have to let him do it to me again if he thought it would help. He just wanted to make me strong, that's all.

I was a rock. Nothing could hurt me.

I looked down through the haze and thought I saw little plumes of steam rising from skin that now seemed scarlet enough to have been dipped in blood. I recoiled, gasped as the burns I already had chafed against the concrete and the sodden canvas of my arm restraints, and shifted position to pull my knees a few inches further away. It wasn't much of a reprieve, I knew. It would give me, at most, a few extra minutes of relative protection.

The line advanced, and touched skin again.

I hadn't seen Ethan move, but he was lying down now, pressed against the curve of the wall with the paler skin of his back, partially obscured by the canvas restraints binding his arms, presented to the sun that would soon be attacking both of us with all its considerable force. The skin on the top of his head was also fire-engine red, and popping with blisters. He was so still that he could have been dead. But I could tell from the corded tension in his shoulders that he was still alert, still strong, still aware of the toll this was taking on me. I should have been mad at him for not grunting or something, just to make sure I followed his example, but I couldn't blame him. He was my brother.

I lay down and rolled against the wall, pressing my face against the gentle curve that marked the junction between pool wall and pool floor. The seam, seen up close, turned out to be littered with the curled, blackened forms of ants, similar to the living ones I'd seen before, these baked to a crisp by previous mornings or afternoons. Their thoraxes pressed against their abdomens in pretend fetus positions, their little legs outhrust as if in protest. If they all came from the same hive, which was likely, then they all had the same mother, and they'd all died here, as we were dying here, as the siblings they were.

Ethan and I had more in common with them than with anybody else on the planet.

My throat thickened.

When the line of fire touched my skin again, there was no longer any safe place to retreat.

I don't know how long I was unconscious, but as I came to there was a dead weight, several times my size, pressing down on me.

I didn't care. If I was buried alive at least I'd soon be dead. If I was being attacked at least I'd soon be dead. If I was being raped at least I'd soon be dead. I was beyond feeling or wanting anything at all.

After a long time I registered the slippery feel of bare flesh, slick with sweat. It took me a while to identify it, because my nerve endings were all on fire, but eventually I registered as a naked human being, taller and broader than myself, covering me, shielding my head, my torso, my bound arms, and most of my legs, from the direct rays of the sun. I was still burning alive, and still dying of thirst, but the sun itself was no longer touching me, not even in reflection.

The weight made me protest. "Unnnh!"

The heavy body bore down, pinning me, but not making any further move as long as I refrained from struggling.

I passed out again.

My mind wasn't working very well, because it wasn't until much later that I realized it was Ethan protecting me.

It didn't make any sense to me. He had tried to kill me last night. If we survived the day he would no doubt try to kill me again. The sooner I fell, the better off he was—at least, as long as Daddy and the Bitch intended on ever coming back for us, which was far from certain.

Had I been able to talk, I would have asked him just what the hell he thought he was doing. Had he been able to talk, he might have told me.

I might have thanked him. I might have called him stupid.

But we weren't able to talk. And I was in so much pain by then that I might not have made any sense anyway.

The sun climbed as high as the sun ever goes, and began to climb back down.

As soon as there were shadows worth inhabiting he stood and nudged me with his toe until I managed to rise. We swayed together, in an inferno, the air rising in waves between us. He was seared black, his face an unhappy landscape of dried blood, blisters and peeling skin. He had puffy half-moons under both eyes, and a dry scab sealing one nostril: the reason I hadn't heard any snorking for a while, and the chief reason why, with his mouth gagged the way it was, his ability to breathe at all qualified as a miracle. I didn't like what his expression had to say about the way I looked, but at least he didn't try to keep me from seeing it.

I didn't have to see what I looked like, though. I could already tell. I could see the baked red of my breasts and the big fat sun blister forming on the tip of my nose. I'd been sick and I'd been feverish and at some point in the last hour or so my bowels had erupted with more liquid waste that hadn't had anywhere to go but except down my legs. All of it was peppered with grit and sand and packed together with congealing grease. I don't know how much body weight I'd lost from sweat, stress, and illness, just over the past few hours, but if it didn't show on my frame it must have shown in my face, and in my eyes, the same way it showed in his. We were both the walking dead, and we both looked it.

And it was as the walking dead that we shuffled together, across an infinite wasteland of burning concrete, the few short steps to the narrow strip of blessed shade that had begun to swell against the opposite wall of the pool.

We put our backs to that wall and slid downward, this time sitting side by side, secure in a truce that would last until the sun was no longer a common threat.

I forgot who said it. Maybe Daddy did. But whoever put the words together knew what he was talking about, when he said that sometimes Paradise can be nothing more than a Hell not quite as bad as a Hell you've already known.

It must have still been well over a hundred degrees in the shade, but I could already feel the temperature start to drop, and that made it Paradise.

At least until our insides felt the change, and the chills began to wrack us.

I asked him, all of once, why we couldn't just hide from her.

I must have been six at the time. I couldn't have been much older. I know that I'd been hearing the horror stories of my mother for as long as I could remember, and that it hadn't been all that long since I'd been able to place her in a category removed from Rumpelstilskin and the Wicked Witch and the Evil Stepmother and the other imaginary monsters of the fairy tales that I'd somehow managed to pick up without my father's notice.

I'd had bad dreams since the night I realized the Bitch was real.

So I asked him. Did I really have to visit her someday? Couldn't we just go somewhere far, far away? Wouldn't she just get tired of looking for us, and go away?

He'd gotten very serious and very sad.

"Just how many years do you think you'd have to hide?"

I felt them burning me before I had any idea what they were.

I'd spent the last few hours with my back against the pool wall, my legs curled against my chest in what would have been a fetal position had my arms been free to link fingers around my knees. My internal thermostat had been veering from one extreme to the other for some time now, alternating the wonderful sensations of being burned alive with those of everything inside me being turned to ice. I'd popped sweat after sweat, feeling steam rise from my skin as the rivulets of perspiration poured down my sides in waves; and then, reacting, I'd shivered with a fever that turned the world around me arctic. For hours on end my teeth would have chattered if they could have touched at all. My throat continued to ache for water, and the shadows, lurching toward the opposite wall to reclaim our battlefield for night, gained ground in a herky-jerky rhythm that served to emphasize just how much of the day I was spending too far gone to notice the passage of time.

Sometime after the shadows advanced to within a foot of the opposite wall, I was attacked by balls of fire.

There were dozens of them, each as hot as molten iron, each as solid as ball bearings, each impacting against my skin at the same instant: most striking my face and legs, but some hitting the top of my head and others burrowing down my back to burn my spine like acidic flame. The agony was so profound that I convulsed, shrieking through my gag, hurling myself against the pool floor with a desperation to escape that superseded any worries over how much the impact was going to hurt. I smashed my head again and didn't care. I heard Ethan roaring in equal pain, somewhere to my immediate left, his deeper cries as inarticulate and just as uncomprehending as mine.

More acid fell. It didn't stop falling. I felt my skin shriveling, turning black, peeling away from the bone, becoming flakes of ash which blew away like little embers.

Then a little made its way past my lips, somehow making its way past the gag and past my still-clamped teeth, and I found myself sucking at it with something like awe.

It was water.

It didn't feel like water, not against my skin, but against my tongue and dribbling down my throat it was just warm, refreshing water, tinny to the taste but better than wine.

A dribble went down the wrong pipe and I started to gag. I raged at myself for choking on this wonderful gift I had begun to think I'd never know again, forced the coughs to silence after only a minute or two of nonstop hacking, and stood, raising my face to the wonderful shower. Drops seemed to sizzle as they struck my ravaged cheeks and forehead. They still felt like acid against my burned flesh, but I didn't care. Thirst trumped Pain. I could feel my strength coming back with every drop I sucked down.

Somewhere above me, Daddy said, "Don't swallow too much, little girl. You'll get sick. Just turn around and I'll clean you off!"

I couldn't see him, as the water had washed the salt caked on my forehead into my eyes, but I staggered about in a circle, as he'd commanded. All at once the flow concentrated, no longer a diffuse spray but a tight, burning stream, battering my buttocks and my inner thighs to force away all of the day's collected filth. The agony of the moment was enough to make my guts clench. I staggered a step or two away, driven by the instinctive urge to escape the source of the suffering, but Daddy kept the stream focused and on target until every bit of the foulness was gone.

Then he turned off the water, leaving me wracked and trembling. There was vapor rising from the concrete.

"There," Daddy said.

I could still hear water patter against concrete. Looking up, I saw Ethan, still being hosed off. The current stream targeted his face, in order to wash away all the dried blood. The force of it rippled his cheeks, maybe making it easier for him to drink some. As he turned, the pool dust, washing off his muscled skin in waves, revealed shoulders turned so scarlet from the sun that he might as well have been dipped in blood. The top of his head, and the arc of his shoulders, had become a mass of popped blisters. His nose had swollen to almost twice its original size, and had a distinct blue tinge that worried me.

I don't know why it worried me. I should have wanted him to die.

Daddy said, "Come over to the steps. I want to take a look at you."

I pulled my eyes away from Ethan and staggered back to the shallow end, forgetting to duck as the chain-link grew low enough to scrape the top of my head. The contact with it felt like being branded. I groaned, went to my knees, and scrambled as best I could to the Shallow End steps.

Daddy was kneeling just above the wire. He wore a red-and-yellow Hawaiian shirt, mirrored sunglasses, khakis and a big straw hat. He looked tanned and rested and proud. When he saw me close up his mouth made a little O of sympathy. "Looks like you had a rough day, honey. I'm sorry to see it."

I tried to speak through my gag. "Wheeehhh wuhh oo?"

He understood me. "This dump has no running water and no well. The Bitch has to drive to town every couple of days, to fill up gallon jugs, and she was already almost out."

"Unnh! Wheehhhh wuhhh OO?"

"Calm down, kiddo. You have every right to be a little annoyed. But it's about a ninety minute drive, each way, and she wasn't about to go all by herself when she was afraid I'd take advantage of her absence to help you out when her back was turned. We had to be fair about this. So I had to go along to help. And then while we were there we decided to surprise you by renting a tanker and hose, and the place made us wait almost four hours before one was available." His mouth went grim. "Try to spend four hours with The Bitch trying to be civil in public. Just try. We even had to make nice over lunch in some diner with a one-eyed waitress. That was an ordeal you should be happy you missed."

Something hiccupped in the back of my throat. My vision blurred. I didn't know whether I was going to throw up or scream until the sound came out and it turned out to be laughter. It was the one-eyed waitress that did it, I think. I couldn't help picturing a fat woman in pirate gear, complete with patch, parrot and peg-leg, slinging hash while Daddy and the Bitch exchanged small talk over the menu. I even wondered if they'd tipped well. Probably. I didn't know my mom's custom in that regard, but Daddy knew how to charm the ladies. He just didn't know how to pick a good one.

Daddy perked up. "Anyhow, we're both back for the duration now, and now that we're here it looks like you've given as good as you got. You have a bit of an owie on the back of your head, but it looks worse than it is, and he's got to be suffering from that mess you made of his face. Plus his burn seems to be shaping up even worse than yours. Pick your moment tonight, or at the very worst sometime late tomorrow, and I'm sure you'll have no trouble putting him down for good."

His eyes softened, turning moist in the way they only did in training, whenever I'd broken some new boundary with sweat and blood and back-breaking effort. He pressed his hand against the chain-link, and extended his fingers through the diagonal windows between the wires; I raised my head to feel the touch of his hand and almost moaned at the way even that soft contact tortured the taut skin of my scalp. He couldn't tell that I wasn't craving his love. I was just hoping that if I was nice enough he'd remove my gag and give me a nice, cold cup of water. The few drops I'd sucked down hadn't come close to satisfying me, and the mere thought of enduring any more time without another taste was almost more than I could stand.

I argued my case through the gag, but my voice trailed off in a mouthful of dust.

"I'm so proud of you," he whispered, turning away all at once so I wouldn't see him cry.

The real suffering didn't manifest until after the air cooled. But as the sky turned purple and then black, every part of me caught on fire, raging at the slightest physical contact. I could avoid most of the pain by simply not moving, but the straps that held the canvas bindings around my arms and the bit gag firmly planted in my mouth both felt like razors heated over an open flame. I couldn't focus past it. It was like a landscape larger than myself, so vast in every direction that I couldn't even see its furthest horizons. It only ceased to overwhelm when I moved an arm or leg and in that way distracted myself with some other pain just as large, just as unbearable. Daddy and the Bitch, who had returned to watching the show from their respective lifeguard chairs, must have been bored beyond reason for much of the early evening, as both Ethan and I spent those hours at opposite ends of the pool, unconscious more often than we were awake, trembling with chills even as we panted from the heat.

We must have resisted the inevitable for hours.

I don't know what time it was when I crawled from the Shallow End steps, found the strength to get to my feet again and stagger, in a precarious lurch with only distant relation to the upright, to the invisible line separating the Shallow and Deep Ends.

Daddy called down from above. "Thattagirl. Show him what you're made of."

The Bitch summoned her own champion. "Don't give up, Ethan! I'm proud of you!"

After a long, snuffling pause, my brother shuffled out of the darkness.

The darkness spared me actual eye contact, or even a clear look at his face. All I saw was a vague, threatening presence, still larger than myself, still more formidable than myself. All I heard was ragged breath and a weak, liquid bubbling that may have been heralded the return of the blockage in his nostrils. The stench was the worst, all sour sweat and festering waste, the perfume of a creature all but dead who had yet to lie down.

"Come on, honey!" the Bitch cried. "You can do it!"

Ethan shuffled forward another step, and then stopped, swaying.

I couldn't see his eyes.

But the last day and a half had been a silent conversation between us, punctuated by moments of equally incomprehensible brutality and mercy. I didn't need to see his eyes to know something I hadn't really appreciated before.

He hadn't ever really wanted to do this.

He'd offered me a way out, at the start, but I'd imagined it the kind of formality one warrior exchanges with another, in the last few minutes before any duel to the death. I'd believed him when he'd said that he had no other reasons for being born. But now that I'd spent twenty-four hours with him, in the shared hell we'd been training for all our lives, I found I knew differently. He'd meant what he said. He'd taken his last opportunity for escape, and I'd thrown it back in his face.

Had I accepted his offer of a quiet afternoon together, on our last day before our descent into the pit, he wouldn't have stopped the jeep at those rock formations twenty miles away. He would have kept going, picking up a main road and staying on it until long after we'd left the State and the swimming pool behind. Daddy and the Bitch would have set up the chain-link barriers together, waited in vain for our return, and then come to the shared conclusion that we weren't coming back. They might have been upset and they might have been disappointed and they might have been relieved that the contract between them had finally been broken by somebody other than themselves. They might have flayed each other with recriminations, each blaming the other for raising a child disloyal enough to break free. They might have parted as bitter enemies who no longer possessed the weapons they had honed to hurt each other. Or they might have descended into the pool themselves, with or without the hobbles they'd chosen for us, to finally face each other without proxies, on a battlefield that would have put a period to everything that had turned the air toxic between them. Whatever happened to them, I realized, would not have mattered. Not with Ethan and I already miles away, and adding more distance between our lives and theirs with every moment we breathed free.

He had tried to shock me awake, asking questions he'd already known the answers to.

I just hadn't been ready to hear him.

We shuffled the last few steps toward each other. I rested my forehead against his shoulder and murmured something useless. He made a noise no more articulate.

"What the hell is this?" the Bitch demanded.

"Come on, kids!" Daddy urged. "Mix it up already!"

We were both sorry.

But we both knew this couldn't end until it ended the only way it was allowed to.

I reared back and slammed my forehead into Ethan's broken nose, feeling it collapse again under the impact, hearing the crunch of cartilage and the gasp of pain.

"Good one!" Daddy yelled.

Ethan staggered back a step, but recovered quickly, advancing with a speed I could not have expected, to drive his knee into my gut. It hurt even more than most belly-shots because my gag cut off most of my air's natural escape route, making my cheeks balloon from a mouthful of exhaled breath unable to leave as fast as its force demanded. I doubled over, spun, and fell over on my side, hitting the pool bottom with a thud that rattled my entire spine. My spine exploded again as he spun and slammed his right heel against my lower ribs. I felt something crack, as my eyes tried to well with tears but couldn't come up with the moisture they needed to cry.

The Bitch yelled, "Finish her!"

Daddy screamed. "Get up, get up, get up!"

I arched my back, whipped my legs up and around, and delivered a pile-driver kick to Ethan's crotch. I would have recognized the impact as solid even if the pain of impact hadn't rebounded all the way to my waist. I would have heard it in his liquid gurgle and in the blind thud of his next clumsy steps.

From the way he staggered, those stunted balls of his were just as sensitive to pain as the normal kind. It'd only take him another second or two to shrug it off, and come after me again, but I had no intention of giving him that much time.

I pinwheeled my legs, flipped to my feet, lowered my head, and charged him, striking his midsection with my right shoulder. He was already off balance and struggling to remain upright. The tackle drove him off his feet, his legs flailing against the pool bottom, his arms straining at their canvas binding as his body obeyed the urge to regain balance.

We both screamed through our respective gags: Ethan because he knew what was happening and myself because a tidal wave of white agony had flared down my back at the moment of impact. Daddy and the Bitch were screaming too, but at the moment I no longer gave a shit about them. I no longer gave a shit about anything.

The only thing that mattered, in this last second before the ground gave way, was driving Ethan back, further into the Deep End.

Then his left foot sought solid ground where there was none.

He didn't fall backward right away, which might have been better for him. He had just enough balance left to compensate as the pool bottom disappeared beneath him. His left leg sank into the drain hole, and his right slipped out from under him.

He took the bulk of the initial impact just under his left knee.

Even as I heard the wet splat of the first blood freed by the break, he was still off-balance, still falling backward.

I spun away and lost track of up and down as my feet pounded concrete trying to use up the momentum that remained. I tipped over and started to fall.

Ethan took the brunt of the impact on his bound arms. Something, maybe an elbow or one of the bones in his hands, made a sound like cracking ice. There was another crack, louder and more final, as his neck whipped back and slammed his head against the concrete.

I slowed and regained control just a hair too slowly to avoid a painful face-first encounter with the wall. I felt the cartilage in my nose release.

Behind me, Ethan wailed through his gag, making sounds that could have been words and could have been inarticulate cries of pain. They sounded the same. When he tried to pull his leg out of the drain, something razored ground against something obstinate, and he wailed again, in a voice suddenly gone as high as a baby's.

Still dizzied from my collision with the wall, and freshly sickened by the taste of blood, I lurched away, tripped over an invisible Ethan, came far too close to another potentially deadly pratfall, then regained my balance and approached Ethan again, triangulating his position from his moans of pain. When I was sure I knew where his head was, I spun like a top and drove my heel into the side of his face. I felt his jaw leave its track. His cry went wet and bubbling, with a nasty undercurrent of fresh rage, all the shared understanding between us forgotten as I became nothing more than an enemy, beating him to death in the dark.

I couldn't see his eyes but I knew they had to be reproaching me.

We owed each other more than this. This may have been the only currency we'd been empowered to pay, but it wouldn't settle any of the debts that really mattered. Those would stay on the books forever.

The Bitch yelled, "Ethan! Oh, please, honey! Get up!"

Another voice, all but drowning her out, swelled with pride: "Show him who's boss, Jen!"

The blood bubbled in Ethan's throat. His mouth must have been full of it, but there was no place for it to go but down, filling his windpipe and cutting him off from what he needed to live. He would have been fine without the gag, but with it, he was just a man in a noose, struggling for breath a mere layer of skin from all the air he could ever need or want. He was still strong enough. If I left him alone with his will to live he might even manage to keep snatching breath for hours.

I circled him again, exhausted, unwilling to take the logical next step.

The Bitch cried, "Ethan! Baby!"

Daddy yelled, "Jenny!"

I needed a drink of water so very much.

"Ethan! Get up! Do something!"

"Jenny! Finish him! Now!"

Their voices ran over one another, melding, becoming a single shrill command in a voice that sank knives into the base of my spine.

Had I been able to say anything intelligible, I might have apologized to my brother.

Instead, I prodded him with my toe, determining his position, figuring out the most efficient way of doing what needed to be done. He lay on his back, his spine arched because of the bound arms that prevented him from lying entirely flat. His head hung backward, his spasming throat as exposed to me as that of a defeated dog offering itself to the mercies of its pack leader. When he felt the weight of my knee, resting without any particular pressure on his neck, before I made the commitment to bear down, he whipped his head to the right in a final, instinctive attempt to shake me off. I shushed him with a sound my gag transformed into a reptilian hiss, tried to send him the silent message to the effect that what I did now was being done with all possible respect, and bore down, wishing that the knee was his and the crushed windpipe mine.

The next few days passed in a delirium of shifting light, moist compresses dripping cold water into my eyes, fevers so brutal that I came out of them astonished at being alive, the agony of every glancing touch, and the uncertain comfort of female hands spreading ointment on my face, shoulders, breasts, belly and legs.

It must have been two or three wakings before I grew used to the realization that I was in a bed with sheets, and maybe another couple after that before I registered that my arms, while restrained, were no longer drawn behind my back and were instead chained by the wrists to the bed frame.

Sometimes I heard canned laughter from a nearby low-volume television, other times I heard whispers saturated in venom. Sometimes I vomited. Sometimes, out of sheer malice, I soiled the bed and exulted in silent triumph when the soft, caring hands had to deal with my filth. Sometimes I dreamed I was still in the Deep End with Ethan. Some of the dreams bordered on the erotic, allowing me to have my way with him in every possible position despite a disapproving inner voice that insisted on reminding me that this would now be necrophilia as well as incest. Sometimes, when I told myself that, the dreams compensated by giving him Daddy's face instead, but I hated when that happened. I'd been there, and much preferred nonsensical fantasies about Ethan, even when those fantasies faded into detailed replays of the battle's final moments.

Sometimes, I returned to rationality long enough to understand that both my Mommy and Daddy were with me, whispering that I'd been a good girl, and that they loved me. I cried when Mommy kissed my forehead and told me I was beautiful. I cried harder when my Daddy told me about Ethan's burial in the desert, and of the words they'd written on notebook paper and interred with him, as of course there could not be a stone. The paper read, Beloved Son, Beloved Brother. Had I been consulted, I might have added, Warrior.

When, after a couple of days, I came back to myself long enough to realize that the restraints had been removed, I sat up, reeled from the worst dizzy spell I'd ever known, and somehow managed to focus. The tiny bedroom had faux-wood paneling, aluminum trim, shelving bolted to the faux-wood panel of the walls, and a miniature pop-down vanity complete with a perimeter of tiny light bulbs. The space between the single bed I occupied and that vanity was a narrow strip of floor just large enough to stand in. There were no photos, no personal items anywhere in sight. There was a gallon jug of water. Daylight, though sealed off by the aluminum blinds covering the only window, rested on the opposite wall in a single glowing sliver. The air was warm, but cooler than it had a right to be.

I looked down at the bed and saw a sheet liberally peppered with flakes of skin.

I swung my legs over the edge of the mattress, winced at flesh that insisted on complaining from every move, and hauled myself from the bed to the chair adjoining the vanity.

The mirror depicted a patchwork girl. Some patches of skin were still lobster-red, or tanned to near-blackness, but the worst of the burns had peeled, revealing irregular patches of pale new skin behind the dried flaps and healing blisters. Two even paler bands, reflecting the places where the leather straps of my gag had protected my skin from the sun, extended from the chapped corners of my lips, across my cheeks, and around as far back as I could see. My jaw was a mass of faded gray bruises. My eyes were red and underlined with a pair of gray half-moons. My cheeks seemed gaunt. My hair had started to grow back, though it hadn't established itself as more than a transparent blonde down, establishing the places where a full head of hair would appear once time and biology had done its work. Right now some of the bristles impaled loose flakes of skin, displaying them like butterflies on pins.

It could have been worse.

I drank some water from the jug. Slept. Then drank some more. Then Slept.

After a while, I drifted back to consciousness and heard a woman laughing, somewhere right outside.

A few seconds of searching and I found the clothes they'd left for me, neatly folded on the dresser, with a note to the effect that I could come outside if I felt up to the walk. In addition to one of my bras and one of my pairs of panties, there was also an oversized white t-shirt that must have belonged to Ethan, an oversized Hawaiian shirt I also identified as his to wear over it, an ankle-length skirt with belt to cinch them tight, the sun bonnet my father had bought for me, and a pair of flip-flop sandals. The gestalt may have been random as fashion but it was all loose, all selected for maximum sun protection while offering the greatest degree of comfort for skin still so sensitive that it hated glancing contact with cotton sheets. This struck me as uncommonly thoughtful. I eschewed the bra out of reluctance to feel those shoulder straps but otherwise accepted the rest of the suggested outfit, dressing gingerly and some four times slower than I was used to.

The screen door slammed as I bopped down the steps of the mobile home. It was still hot outside, but not sweltering: maybe somewhere in the upper eighties, not all that much warmer than that. My parents, who were about twenty feet away occupying a pair of chaise lounges under a huge beach umbrella angled to catch the morning sun, both looked tanned and happy to see me. Both wore oversized amber sunglasses and big floppy straw hats. The Bitch was reading something by Carole Nelson Douglas, Daddy something by John Grisham. Both seemed delighted to see me. They waved.

"There's the sleepy head," said Daddy.

"She looks better already," said the Bitch. To me, she added: "Better hurry up and get under the umbrella. You don't want to overdo."

There was a mesh folding chair just inside the umbrella's oval shadow.

I winced as I sat down, winced again as I edged the chair a few inches closer
to my parents.

"You want something to eat?" inquired the Bitch. "I can fix something. You've
been off solids for a bit, but you look like you're ready to keep something down."

My stomach bubbled dangerously. "Maybe later."

"Don't wait too long," she advised.

"I won't."

"You have to keep up your strength."

"Why?" I asked. "The fight's over."

"Just to take care of yourself," the Bitch said. "We care about these things,
even if you don't."

Daddy winked at me, retrieved his own mimosa from the gutter between their
lounges, and sucked a single dainty sip through a bent straw before returning the
glass to its resting place. "You listen to your mom," he advised. "She knows what's best."

I swallowed, wincing at the sudden surge of pain from a throat still too dry and
raw. "Does she?"

The Bitch looked away, her right hand covering the fresh scowl twisting her
lips. Daddy sighed, sat up, and removed his sunglasses so I could see his eyes,
which were very pale and very blue and so very much like Ethan's that everything
since my birth took hold of my heart and twisted hard. "Now, pumpkin," he said.
"I thought you knew better than that. Your mother and I did need to settle our
differences. We couldn't do it by ourselves. We know that because we tried, again
and again, and the more we argued the more we kept going over the same patches
of ground. We couldn't move on without settling who was right and who was
wrong. It's too bad about Ethan, of course, but now that everything's resolved,
there's no reason for any more pointless animosity. We can get along. We can even
be a family again, if you'd like. We could move your mom out of this place and get
a nice house somewhere with trees and a lake. We could even get a dog. You like
golden retrievers, don't you? I thought so. Just like I always promised you, I'll get
you anything you want. We'll make it work."

The impossible fantasy loomed before me, beautiful and horrifying and irresistible and repugnant all at the same time, drawing me in with a gravity greater

than my own capacity to resist it. I'd missed so many things, but I still had a couple of years left before I turned eighteen. Maybe it wasn't too late for me, to have the things other kids had.

I couldn't help it. I wanted to cry. Daddy had been rough on me during my training, but if he'd been less demanding I might not have survived. And Mommy might not be such a Bitch anymore, now that Daddy and I had established the order of things. I could love them and they could love me. It could happen. Stranger things had.

Thirsting for more than just water, I licked my lips and felt the sting as they cracked. "What if you two have another fight?"

Daddy winced as if stung. "We've taken that into account."

Mommy retrieved her mimosa and treated herself to another dainty sip, before returning the glass to the paving-stone by her side. "I went through the change already," she said, with what seemed infinite regret at the lost opportunities of her youth. "But you can still bear children. And twins run in the family."

I didn't know I'd risen from my chair with enough force to tip it backward, until Daddy said, "What?"

Then I moved.

Seven hours later, with the afternoon dying, the desert far behind me, and the approach of night turning the sky a shade of indigo, I pulled the rental up to a diner marked by a twenty-foot neon cowboy whose right arm wobbled to and fro in perpetual friendly wave. I would have preferred to drive still further, putting even more distance between myself and the struggle now taking place in the swimming pool, but the hunger I'd denied all day long had just settled in for good. I had to feed it or risk going off the road.

The waitress must have gotten her hair and her lipstick out of the same bottle. "I'm sorry to ask, honey, but what happened to you?"

"My ATV broke down in the desert," I said. "I couldn't get a signal on my cell, so I had to walk about twenty miles for the nearest tow truck."

She clucked. "People have died that way. You should have taken cover under the vehicle and done your walking at night."

"Yeah, well, that's what they told me at the Emergency Room."

"Are you sure you're all right to travel?"

"They said I was fine when they released me," I said. "Won't be winning any beauty pageants for a while, but I'll be good as new in a week or two."

She shook her head. "I gotta hand it to you. You're one tough kid."

"Believe me, not as tough as some."

She brought me a turkey sandwich and threw in a slice of apple pie out of sympathy.

I didn't need the charity. Between what I'd taken from Daddy's wallet, and the cache I'd found in Mommy's underwear drawer, I had a couple of thousand to fool around with. The burns, the buzz-cut, and my physique would help, too. They made me look older than I was, which would free me of any embarrassing questions about family.

I'd been better than them, in the end. I'd shown enough mercy to leave them the umbrella, and five one-gallon bottles of water. I'd also left them ungagged, with one free arm apiece, so they could drink as much as they wanted for as long as their supply held out. Of course, that gesture had been less about indulging their thirst than respecting their right to therapeutic communication. Now that they were speaking again for the first time in almost sixteen years, it would be a shame to deny them the time and voice they needed to catch up. There would be some awfully entertaining discussions going on between now and however long it would take for their voices to fall silent, and since I'd taken care to secure each of them well out of reach of the other, those conversations would all have a chance to play themselves out at proper length. It would have been interesting to stick around and listen, just to hear how often my own name was mentioned, and in what context, but I reasoned that they'd be more likely to release their inhibitions without me around. I was sure the privacy would lead to any number of fruitful epiphanies, some appreciated and some not.

I wished them well. At least, in the short term.

In the long term I hoped they fried.

Midway through my second cup of coffee, a family of four came in. Daddy was a scrawny thing with a prominent chin and weary blue eyes. Mommy, who was shorter, with frizzy blonde hair and a pointed nose, bore the grimace of any woman who had endured too many complaints for too many years. The boy and girl, who were six and five, didn't want to eat anything but french fries and had to be seated on opposite sides of their booth when the boy persisted in tapping his sister on the shoulder, again and again, a crime she found unbearable and which made her screech, "Mo-OMMM! He's touching me!" Daddy ended up slapping the boy and Mommy ended up informing both kids that were in big trouble if they dared make another noise: a disciplinary measure that lasted all of thirty seconds before wails and spilled water escalated the warfare, and the noise, to the next level.

As soon as I could I paid the bill and drove away, the lights of nearby homes blurring in the distance.

Maybe someday I'd be done with missing them.

Mommy Picks Me Up at Day Care

BY JOHN GORUMBA

Once again, through the eyes of a child, we are taken to the Bad Place: this time through eyes so young that they can't even begin to process the morality, but only experience the crazy as it comes.

John Gorumba is yet another young writer getting his sea legs by dancing on water, and making it look easy. Like Laura Lee Bahr, his gift for remembering how childhood actually feels is kind of uncanny, and entirely uncommon in its honest commingling of pure innocence with rawest horror.

As such, it's an extraordinary piece that you will not soon forget. Especially if you're a parent who's ever been anywhere close to the edge.

Jude was thrilled to have Mommy pick him up from daycare early. Usually Daddy got him at the end of the day when the sun was low, and by then Daddy was too tired to play games in the car like Mommy. Jude and Mommy always picked out all the busses and construction trucks they spied on the road, but Daddy just played weird music on the radio and said bad words at other people driving. Jude wasn't supposed to say *fuck* or *shit* or especially *cocksucker*. According to Daddy there were a lot of cocksuckers driving cars.

Jude's baby brother Justin got to stay home with Mommy today. She said his cough hurt and he needed to see a doctor. Jude didn't want to be left out, but Mommy said he absolutely *had* to go to daycare. He wanted to be sick too. At least Jude got to play with the coveted, light-up Buzz Lightyear since Justin wasn't there to take it like he did every single time Jude wanted to play with something. Flying Buzz around the playpen where baby Lucille slept, he dropped grape grenades on her head as Buzz swooped down to attack. The Wiggles were on TV but Jude didn't like them. It was the only thing Lucille wanted to watch when she went down for her nap and she'd cry if it wasn't on.

Jude didn't care when the doorbell rang, but when he heard Mommy's voice he dropped Buzz and ran over to Mrs. Alice. She was talking to Mommy.

"Mommy, you're here," Jude said. They kept talking. They never answered him the first time.

"Oh, the Doctor said Justin has croup, he won't be in all week probably," Mommy said.

"And Jude?"

"Mommy," Jude said.

"He'll stay with me this week. I think I'll be using the last of my sick days with this bout."

"Mommy!"

"Mommy's picking you up early, Jude," Mrs. Alice said.

"Go get your bag, and don't forget to put your cup in it," Mommy said.

"Okay."

He had a *mission*. He ran back to the living room to find his cup. He wasn't sick, but he'd still get to stay home with Mommy just like Justin. And when Justin went down for his nap it would just be him and Mommy.

Mommy didn't say much when she started to strap him into his car seat. That meant she was in a hurry. His parents were always in a hurry. He put his hands over hers.

"No Mommy, I want to do it."

"Go," Mommy said, frowning. Daddy called it her *scrunchy face*.

Jude fumbled with the shoulder straps. The plastic tongue never wanted to slide into the slot, but Mommy and Daddy always got it right away. Mommy tried to help guide the two pieces together. "Don't. I can do it."

"Baby, you need help."

"NO. I can do it myself."

"Look baby," Mommy said, lining up the two pieces, "now push them together. Mommy's tired of standing in the street."

Jude pushed and the belt clip snapped shut. Mommy clicked them into the lap strap.

"Mommy, you look exhausted." Jude hoped he'd used that word right. She stared at him for a moment, tilted her head up and laughed.

"Yeah, no shit." Mommy said. She shut the door.

Jude got Mommy to say okay to spying busses and trucks on the way home, but he wound up doing most of the spying. She just nodded and agreed. She did let him listen to his song, *Hey-Oh Let's Go*. He spotted a lot of yellow busses while Joey Ramone mumbled something about a backseat. They listened to the song three times before they made it home. Jude saw Daddy's car and got excited. "Mommy is Daddy home?"

"Well, yeah. You didn't think Justin was home alone?"

Jude bounced out of the seat the second Mommy unlocked the seatbelt. He ran to the door and had to wait for Mommy to catch up. He ran in ahead of her.

Daddy was face down on the floor. There was a spill of red mess around him, in his hair, on his face, with footprints through and around the spill. Justin was balled up in the corner of the room with the lamp tipped over beside him. He cast a long shadow on the wall. It looked like he'd been sliding around in the red mess.

"Daddy, why're you on the floor?" Jude laughed. He ran to Daddy.

"STOP!" Mommy yelled. "Do not touch them."

Jude stopped by Daddy. "But Mommy, I want to play."

"It's messy over there."

"Daddy made a mess?"

"Yes. He and Justin are sleeping, so we have to leave them alone."

"They're sleeping on the floor? That's funny, ha ha," Jude said, adding an exaggerated fake laugh at the end.

"Yes," Mommy said, pushing Jude back and stepping in-between him and Daddy. "Daddy and your brother are hilarious."

"Can I watch a movie?"

"Sure, go pick one out."

Jude ran through the kitchen and into the playroom, hopping around the piles of toys, to the scatter of movies by the small TV and DVD player. He wanted his *Looney Tunes* DVD. He looked back and saw Mommy stepping around Daddy, trying to avoid Daddy's mess. She picked up her pea-green robe from the floor and held it up. Her hands were shaking.

Jude went back to his latest mission and found the DVD. He knew how to put it in the player and work the TV. He started it up, watched the commercials until it stuck on the *Looney Tunes* menu. He wanted Mommy to start it. She wouldn't always come when he wanted her to, but if he asked to start a movie she always came. Maybe she'd stay in the playroom and play.

When he went back to the living room Mommy had changed into her comfy robe, rolled her sweatpants up to her knees, and left her heels by the couch. She was crouched by Justin, one hand on his chest, saying something Jude couldn't hear. There was a white face cloth rolled up and laid over his eyes. He didn't want Justin to be awake. Mommy crossed his hands over his chest.

"Is Justin awake now?" Jude asked.

She didn't answer so he asked again, louder, so she'd be sure to hear.

"He's still asleep," she said.

"Can you wake up Daddy so we can play?"

"No, baby. Can't you just watch your movie?"

"But I want Daddy to watch the part with the Daffy and the rabbit hole."

"I'm trying to talk to Justin for a second, son, then I'll watch it with you."

"But I want Daddy."

"Of course you do!" Mommy stood up. She made her scrunchy face again.

There was a big splotch of red mess across her robe. She walked away into the kitchen. "You always want your father."

Mommy was mad. "Sorry Mommy. I'm sorry, Mommy."

He followed her to the kitchen. She was standing at the counter. She wasn't making any noise but her eyes were full of tears. She had taken out her special dark chocolate that he loved to get bites of. She uncorked a bottle and poured a gross red drink he didn't want. She drank the glassful in a gulp and took her next sip right from the bottle.

"Can I have some of your chocolate, Mommy?"

"Do you ever think about anything but yourself?" Mommy said with a mouthful of chocolate. She frowned, showing chocolaty teeth. The bottle wobbled in her hand.

"I said sorry, Mommy."

"That's right. You are a sorry, sorry boy sometimes."

He didn't know what she meant, but he knew he didn't like it. "Fine! I'm gonna watch TV with Daddy. I don't wanna play with you!"

"Don't you go near them or you're punished!" she yelled. Jude whined. They stared at each other and Mommy started to cry louder. "I just wanted one nice day with you, but you don't give a fuck what Mommy wants, do you?"

Mommy used a bad word. When she yelled, he never got anything he wanted. Why did she have to be angry? Daddy, him and Mommy were supposed to play, watch movies, chase, and read books. "I don't care. You're stupid, Mommy! I hate!" Jude yelled, pretending to spit. He'd gotten out all the stuff Mommy hated him doing in one go.

"You little bastard," she whispered. She grabbed one of the big knives that he was never supposed to touch. It was covered in the same mess Daddy made on the floor. It took her a moment to notice the drops of red dribbling from the blade to the floor. She watched one fall, rubbing some red from the knife with her thumb. She forgot about him, turned to the sink, kissed the red on the knife and began to wash it with soap. "Go watch your movie, baby," she said.

"I want—"

"GO. WATCH. YOUR. MOVIE. NOW."

Jude moaned and ran into the playroom. *Looney Tunes* had Bugs, Daffy and

Elmer in this one. He wanted Mommy to watch the best part with him, but was afraid to ask her. He watched Daffy get his beak blown up and spun around. After what felt like forever, he got up and walked to the doorway leading into the kitchen, but didn't go in. He watched Mommy eat chocolate and drink red drink from the bottle. She whispered to nobody. She poured a palm-full of medicine from an amber bottle and swallowed it all with a big, gulp of gross red drink that dribbled down her chin. She took the knife and pressed the point against her wrist and made her scrunchy face. She took a few more of the pills, said something and pressed the knife to her wrist again.

"That's sharp, Mommy," he whispered from the doorway.

She didn't answer.

"Why are you doing that?"

"I'm waiting for it not to hurt as much."

"Mommy, will you play with me?"

Mommy let out a long sigh, making a thin string of hair on her forehead dance in the air. In one fast move she turned to him, raised the bottle in the air and smashed it into the sink. The crack was loud and sharp and terrifying. He heard Elmer chuckling from the playroom. Mommy walked towards him. She looked wrong. He ran back into the playroom and sat by the TV and Mommy came after him.

"Mommy, you scared me," he said. She stood over him. "I'm watching my movie now, see?" After a moment she sat down next to him.

"You want to sit in Mommy-chair?"

Jude grinned. He loved when Mommy and Daddy watched movies with him. Mommy sat cross-legged and he sat in her lap. He leaned against her and snuggled into her robe. She stroked his hair and kissed his cheek. They watched four *Looney Tunes*, and played in the different piles of toys till the sun got low. Justin never woke up and Mommy didn't try to get up and leave even once. It was a great day. Mommy even started to laugh.

"Putting Justin and Daddy to bed early was a great idea Mommy," Jude said, and hugged her tight. When he looked at her again her face had changed. Jude was scared he'd said something bad when she started to cry. It bubbled out of her all of a sudden, making her bottom lip flutter.

"Mommy's sad?"

"Mommy doesn't know what she is, baby," Mommy cried. She hugged him a little too tight. He let himself be rocked back and forth in her lap. "You can be a sweet boy sometimes."

"It's okay Mommy, don't cry." She hugged him tighter.

"Ouch, Mommy." She hugged tighter. "Mommy, OUCH. Something's biting me."

He pushed away from her. She had the knife in her hand. It had been poking him in the side.

"Oh, sorry, baby. Mommy forgot she had that in her hand. I think it's bath time, anyway."

"Aww, not bath time. Can we read a story?"

"After we put your PJs on okay?"

"Can we read a long story?"

"Okay. But only if you act like a big boy and let Mommy clean up while you're in the tub."

He let Mommy undress him and get him into the tub without much fuss. She told him to stay in the bath and let her get everyone ready for bed. He wanted her to stay and play but he thought asking would make her mad again. He did have the blocks and squirt toys all to himself, so that was okay. He went to building a boat from blocks, made the boat swim around and save the drowning squirt toys when he heard Mommy cursing really loud over and over. She sounded a little like Daddy.

"Mommy?"

"You asshole," she said from down the hall. "Why do you have to be so god-damned heavy?"

Jude stood up in the water and leaned over the rim of the tub. "Mommy, what's wrong?"

"Just stay in the tub, baby. Mommy's trying to get Daddy to bed. C'mon dammit. Slide, why won't you fucking slide!" She was sobbing.

Jude knew he shouldn't but he climbed out of the tub anyway, leaving wet footprints on his way through the bedroom to the hallway. He peeked from the doorway and saw Mommy in the hall. Daddy was on the ground and she was pulling him by the arm. Daddy trailed red stuff all down the hallway. Mommy's feet were covered in it. Daddy was making a really big mess. Mommy slipped and bumped her butt. She cried out and hit Daddy in the chest. She slapped his face and pulled his hair.

"Mommy, don't hit," Jude said. She screamed at Jude so loud and so sudden that he jumped back.

"Get back in the tub! Jude! GET IN THE TUB!"

"Mommy stop yelling!" His face was hot. Tears rolled down his face.

"GET IN THE TUB! GET IN THE FUCKING TUB! GET IN THE TUB!"

She pulled off Daddy's shoe and threw it at him. He turned to run and it hit him in the back. It didn't hurt that much, but he was surprised and started to bawl. Mommy kept screaming from the hall but he couldn't hear her over his own cries. He climbed back into the tub and sat down, pulling his knees to his chin. He kept wailing Mommy's name over and over and every time he did she screamed curse words at him. He put his head down and squeezed his eyes shut. He'd never seen Mommy so mad.

Her screams got closer. She was in the bedroom now.

"There! There you dumb shit. Lie on the floor. Even now you have to ruin everything."

Jude kept crying. Snot built up in his nose, making it hard to breath. His head pounded which just made him cry harder. Mommy was being mean so he yelled for his Daddy. He wanted Daddy to wake up and hold him. He heard Mommy singing "Patty Cake" from the bedroom. She always sang that to Justin when he didn't want to fall asleep. He wondered if Justin woke up. That made him mad. He wanted Daddy. Mommy could stay with Justin.

"Daddy, Mommy's being mean!" he yelled.

"Jude, for the last time shut the fuck up!" Mommy screamed.

"Shut up, Mommy!"

She appeared in the doorway. Her face was so red. He could see white all around her pupils and her teeth were showing. *"Shut up Mommy? You shut the fuck up, Jude. You shut the fuck up!"*

"Mommy, don't spank me!" Jude cried. He put his hands on his butt. Mommy lunged at him. She reached up and grabbed the shower curtain and pulled it down onto him. One end of the rod clanged the floor and Jude was swallowed in the plastic curtain. He could barely see Mommy through it. She was on top of him, pushing him down. He tried to cry out and she forced his head underwater.

"You dumb little shit, all you had to do was sit fucking still for ten fucking minutes before bed, but you have to make everything a goddamn war. Well, here you go!" Mommy tried to claw him through the curtain. He felt her hit his head. He cried her name out and caught a mouthful of water. His heart thumped in his ears and the water made his chest burn.

His hand slipped out from the curtain and he grabbed Mommy's wrist. Her skin was hot. He dug his fingernails into her. He blinked and the curtain was off of him. Mommy tossed it onto the toilet and stared at him. He coughed and spat up water for a long time. He couldn't stop crying. He wanted help, but Mommy didn't look like she wanted to help anyone. He wanted Daddy but was too scared to call for him.

"Mommy you hurt me." Jude coughed the words out, staring at Mommy's scrunchy red face. He couldn't stand to see her look at him like that. He slapped his hands over his face and kept telling her that she hurt him.

Mommy reached into the water and scooped him up. He curled into a ball, sinking his face into her robe. She sat on the bathroom rug and rocked him, whispering into his ear. When his cries slowed down he heard her singing. She always sang to Justin, but she hadn't sung to Jude in a long time.

They sang "Old McDonald," and when she stopped he would pick another animal. They did it twelve times before he ran out of animals.

"You want to know a secret? Mommy's aren't supposed to have favorites, but you were always my favorite. I was so scared of you. Mommy quit her job for the first year of your life. I used to complain about it, but part of me loved staying home with you. I'd sit in the dark and watch you sleep."

"You were scared of me? That's silly," Jude said. He stopped crying.

"Mommy was scared shitless, baby."

Jud had never heard *shitless* before and it sounded hilarious. He laughed, repeating it and laughing even harder. He thought Mommy would be mad but she laughed too.

"Fuck-less!" Jude giggled.

"Ass-less," she said.

They both laughed.

"Cocksucker-less!" Jude yelled.

Mommy laughed really hard.

"Alright. Time to put your PJs on and get in bed."

"Aww, not bed."

"How about you get to sleep in Mommy's bed."

"Okay." He was excited. He'd always get up during the night and try to climb in Mommy and Daddy's bed, but they'd make him go back to his own room.

"We're all going to sleep together tonight. Mommy, Daddy, Justin and you."

"Can we spend the day together tomorrow?"

Mommy was quiet. He was about to ask again when she spoke.

"Sure."

"Okay, Mommy."

When the Zoos Close Down, They'll Come for Us

BY VIOLET LAVOIT

When you don't believe in the powers-that-be, you make your own rules. You make your own way, and prepare to defend it. Prepare for the worst. That's the survivalist code.

Tribes are mostly formed through commonality. We start at family, link through heritage, break it down by race, region, religion, philosophy, and so forth from there.

But purity in any form is awfully hard to come by, and even harder to maintain, as Violet LaVoit makes blisteringly clear in the shocking, incendiary story that follows. A very American horror story. And the melting pot be damned.

Dad named us after the big three: Treblinka, Birkenau, Dachau. Blinky and Birk and Doc, that's us, spelled that way because most Brotherhood people, hate to say it, can't spell "Dach" without saying it dach-rhymes-with-match. You dumb shits, you might at least learn the language if you're serious about a White future.

Doc leaves tonight for his pilgrimage. He's got to bake that cake before he goes. He's not doing it. He's farting around with me, chucking acorns into the woods and drinking brew while I rock on a log and try and hug my cramps away. I'm wearing my fingerless gloves 'cause I have to split wood. I breathe onto my bluing fingernails, *hhhhhhuhhh*. April's still winter up here.

"Who's your favorite white person?" I ask.

"Jesus."

"Besides Jesus."

"Jesus."

"Come on, everyone says Jesus."

"'Cept you."

"Quit it. My favorite's Virginia Dare."

"Whatever. Long as you don't say those girls from Prussian Blue. Hey, Dad!"

Dad comes up the trail, ax swinging low in his hand. "Who's your favorite white person?"

"Mother," he says, and walks away.

I punch Doc in the arm. Dummy. Now Dad's gonna be in a mood. But he comes back a minute later and points at Doc.

"Are we gonna have a cake?"

Doc squirms. "She should do it," he says, pointing at me, like I know anything about baking.

My dad stands up his axe and looks at Doc.

"Cooking is survival skills. Only girls survive?"

"Lemme cull a doe for Hitler."

"You gonna cull the woods empty. Who wants cake for Hitler's birthday?"

I raise my hand. My dad raises his hand. Dad looks at Doc.

"Go bake that cake," he says, and walks into the woods.

For all that bitching, Doc baked it pretty good. All we had was deer tallow and cornmeal and a little bit of sugar but he did it right. "Don't drink anything cold when you eat it because all that tallow will turn to wax in your mouth," he warned. We put the candles in a swastika and heated up mead and sang the Horst-Wessel-Lied and tried to make it as good a party as possible. It still feels too small to have Hitler's Birthday with just us, and with Birk gone too.

Ed Beckwith came over around 8 in his truck.

"Sorry to break it up," he smiled. "But I ain't gonna have to pull you out the door, am I?" He grinned at Doc.

"Nossir." Doc got to his feet and grabbed his rucksack. He shook Dad's hand.

"Have fun," Dad said, "but you know your job. " I think I saw Doc blush.

I watched them pull away.

I went inside to clear dishes. Dad was in the field tent, at the computer. He kept his back to me when he asked "Where in your cycle are you?"

"I'll be ready in a week and a half."

"Go kill a deer." That's a joke, 'cause one day I was griping about something stupid, some PMS bullshit probably and Birk had enough and he told me "Aw, quit whining and go kill a deer." And he's right, there's something about waiting in that tree stand that just makes your bad mood go away. You're in the woods all green, and you've got the bow heavy in your hand, and you wait. And then you see a deer, and you fell it, and you do the extra thing and then you skin it and clean it, and it just falls apart into meat, step by step, simple as cleaning a gun. I mean, you can't not feel better when you're killing a deer. You just can't.

"Too dark to hunt now," I say. Dad marks a dot a few days from now on the calendar by his desk, the one with a picture of a cheetah.

After Mom died Dad told me about cheetahs, how they had a mass extinction at some point. Now they're so interbred you can graft a patch of some random cheetah's skin on to another, as if it was the same animal. *That's what'll happen to White people*, he said, *and it sounds good but it's not. We're already running out of space and getting bred into oblivion and when we make the move back to the land, like we did, we run the risk of genetic monopoly.* Zoos have whole programs for this. When they breed a lion they don't just pick the lion next door.

I spend the week waiting. I chop wood. I sew. I make myself swim in the cold river water. My period dries up to brown. In a few days sex starts sparking in my head, makes me touch myself at night and wake up sticky. I let my dad know.

That night Ed Beckwith's truck pulls up. I'm scrambling into my flannel shirt before I even hear my dad call for me.

Ed opens the truck door and I'm shivering, heart fluttering. I see him step out, rucksack on his back. The first thing I think is how pale he is. He's a skinhead but I can see the chick fluff on his scalp, white blond, almost. I swallow hard and step closer. He's shorter than my brothers. He's one of those wolf cub boys, big hands and feet and long ape arms that haven't caught up with the rest of him. He's bundled up in a big peacoat. He looks tired.

"You talk to Metzger?" my dad asks Ed.

Ed shakes his head. "Never saw him. I just drove the last leg. I'm the only one who knows how to get up here."

"That's how I like it." My dad claps his hand on the kid's shoulder. "You had a long drive."

"Yessir."

"Stay put, Ed. We're going to draw blood." My dad's excited. I can hear it in his voice. "You okay to take samples back to town?"

Ed nods. "I brought the cooler."

"Blink, go get Ed some coffee and anything else he wants."

I take Ed to the kitchen and put the pot on the stove. From the kitchen window I can see my dad and the kid in the field tent. My dad's got latex gloves on. He's making the kid make a fist, feeling where his veins pop out in the soft crook of his elbow. I see now the kid's got tons of stick and poke tattoos up and down his big arms. Swastikas, SSs, eagles. I smile a little.

"Black's fine for me," says Ed.

The pot burbles. I take it off the stove and pour Ed a cup. My dad's got the needle in the kid's vein now. He's drawing off vials. He pricks the kid's other finger and drops a dot in the well of a rapid response test on the table in front of him.

My dad's doing what Doc had done to him, somewhere in Montana, make sure he's free of syphilis and HIV and whatnot. Doc's probably fucking girls by now.

I get out another cup and fill it to the brim. I take it to them.

"This is my daughter Treblinka," my dad says, not looking up.

"Thanks," the kid says shyly and takes the cup from me. I see now he's got ice-blue eyes, not a speck of green. I've never seen eyes that blue on something that wasn't an animal. I can't stop looking at them.

Ed follows me into the tent. Dad hands Ed a bag of blood vials.

"You got lots of stick and pokes. I'm phoning out for Hep C plus the regular. Tonight you're not touching my daughter. Understand?" He looks at me. "Understand?"

"I understand."

"Can you bear great burdens, soldier?"

"I can."

He throws a sleeping bag at him. "Tonight you sleep on the ground." He points a finger at me. "You don't touch him."

I lay down on my bed. I hear the crickets and the tree frogs and Ed's truck peeling out on the gravel. I can't sleep. I think about touching myself but decide I want to save it. All wet is just about the hardest way to fall asleep.

The next morning the boy's still sleeping. I go outside to him. I kick him with my foot a little. He wakes up.

"Show me your tattoos," I say.

He rolls up his sleeve and I see them all now. They're not bad for stick and pokes. I roll up my sleeve. I've got a Celtic cross. He smiles. He shows me where on his arms he's got an American Front cross. We almost match.

"Come on," I say. "I want to see you chop wood."

We walk to the stump.

"What's your name?" I say.

"Eric."

Dad's already in the tent. He's talking to Ed on the CB. "All clear," I hear Ed's crackle say.

Dad got me an axe for Christmas last year because the maul was too big for my hands. "You can use the maul if you want," I say to the guy. I stand a dry log of pine on the block and back up. I straddle my legs and raise the axe over my head. *Thok*. It sticks in the wood.

The kid steps forward. "I'll get it for you," he says. I shake my head. I know to smack it on the block until it splits. "Your turn," I say. He looks at the axe and picks up the maul. *Thwack*. He can do it in one stroke. Blood rushes through me.

"I'm sixteen," I say, and I don't know why.

"I'm sixteen, too" he says.

Dad gets off the CB. He walks over to us. He's got a smile on his face. He's got the Bible in his hands.

"Guess what I did." He pulls out the Bible. "I married you."

Then he turns and walks away.

The kid and me go back to my room in the cabin.

"Lemme see all your tattoos," I say.

He peels off his shirt. They're all over him, across his chest. I can see all of them clear because he doesn't have any chest hair.

I reach up and unbutton his pants. I stick my hand in. I've never touched it before. It doesn't scare me like I thought it would. It just feels very warm. He swallows hard.

I let go and wriggle out of my pants. I can already feel where the wet spot sticks to my underwear. In an instant he's on top of me and I only panic for a second when I wonder how he's going to fit it in me and then it's so easy. It's better than easy. It's good. Holy shit, it's good. I dunno if it's rude or not to do it to yourself when a guy does it to you but I read somewhere it's good for conception. He doesn't mind. "Holy shit," he says, eyes agog. And then he feels it. And then I feel it.

We do it again.

"I forgot one," he says afterwards, laying beside me. He takes his two hands and rolls his lower lip open so I can see the soft inside. ARYAN, it says in blue letters.

"How'd you end up at Metzger's?" I say.

"Same as everyone. Run away. You're lucky, you got a dad that loves you."

"I'm glad you're here," I say.

He sleeps in my bed.

It only takes two weeks to skip a period. Two weeks of chopping wood and him dragging things around the compound for Dad and then I look at him hot and sweaty and my dad sees me looking and says "Go ahead." And we go back to the cabin. We do it all kinds of ways. We do it with him on top and with me on top and with me bent over on my knees and him behind me, driving into the heart of me until I want to scream. We do it in my mouth, even though that doesn't help the cause any.

It only takes two weeks.

"Good work," my dad says, when I tell him, when I'm sure. I pretty much knew when I spotted during the middle of my cycle. I never do that. But I counted the days so Dad would be sure too.

"Go kill a deer for your wife," says Dad, and Eric goes off into the woods. I could have got a deer myself, I'm not far along yet. But he goes and then just before dusk he comes back, crossbow slung low, carcass over his shoulder, white t-shirt brown with blood. I think I love him more that moment than I've ever felt for anything on earth.

We eat steaks that night and I'm so happy.

That night I hear Doc's voice on the CB. "They had me work on two of them, Tanya and Crystal. They're gonna give birth within a week of each other."

"Good boy," says Dad. "You coming home in the week?" Eric's listening but he doesn't say anything. I try to get him going that night but he's out of it. "I love you," I say. "I love you too," he says, and even though it's the first time I hear it from him it doesn't thrill me like it should.

I wake up before him because I'm sick. I eat crackers and it goes away but I can't go back to bed. I wash dishes until my hands go numb in the cold water. There's a little blank spot inside me where that joy used to be.

Through the window I see my dad chopping wood. I see Eric come up behind him.

The next day he corners my dad when my dad's chopping wood.

"When do I go back?" he asks him.

My dad narrows his eyes at him, maul in hand. "You're a married man," he says.

I watch him shrink a size but he keeps talking. "That wasn't the deal," he says. Kind of whining now. "Your son's coming back."

"My son is not the same as my daughter," my dad says.

"She's my *wife*," he says, and just as I feel that joy jump into place inside me again my dad raises the maul and drives in one long swinging arc that ends stopping hard in the top of the boy's head. And he pulls it out and swings it again and as the boy's body falls, I see now he got him right over the ear, there's a split that's like a tree wound and all I can think is *an axe blade makes the same shape in a person as in a tree* and I drop the dish in my hand and I watch as my dad swings the maul into my husband again and again and again and he just turns into meat. That's when I run on rubbery legs to the closet in my dad's room. I can look at meat but I can't look at meat that's still wearing clothes, meat with tattoos, meat with hands that touched me. I slam the closet door. Like how you see lightning before you hear thunder all the sounds come piercing me like arrows while I'm shuddering in that small dark space. The THOK of the maul and then that second crack that must have been his skull, the way splintering bone chops different than wood.

I realize I didn't even hear him scream.

Then it's just quiet. I hear my dad walk in the door. "Blinky?" I hear him yell. I stay quiet. He curses. I hear the rack of a shotgun and hear him walk back out.

I think I hear but I might be imagining Ed's truck pulling up on the gravel. "I heard on the CB," Ed says, "You needed me?—" and boom, the shotgun and then Ed has nothing else to say.

I know there's a knife in the footlocker under my dad's bed. There's guns there too but I can't even think about that. Dad always told us not to use bullets on deer because we needed the ammo for the race war. I'm not even sure he shot Ed. It doesn't make any sense if he did. I've got to peek my head out to see if I can make it to the locker. I'm working up my courage to do it when the door swings wide open.

It's my dad, and the shotgun.

"Are you really pregnant?" he says to me.

"Yes," I say, my voice tiny and quavery. "Yes. I am, I told you that I am."

"Okay then." He throws the shotgun on the bed. "Come on out and quit playing."

Out in the yard he's already put the boy's head on a stick. It's sort of hanging half open like a carved ham but it sits on the stick straight, right in the windpipe. I see Ed's truck. I guess I did hear right.

Dad's got a shovel and he hands me one. "Go get the quicklime," he says. I take the shovel and my fingers can't grasp it enough to hold it up. There's just a big pile of red fat and bone on the dark bloody ground. "Stop it," says Dad. "I already did the hard part." I can't stop it, I'm shuddering and crying and I guess I'm drooling because my dad wipes the corner of my mouth on his sleeve.

"I need to make you tough," he says. "Doc and Birk are disposable. All men are."

I remember my dad telling us about practicing for the race war when you kill a deer: do it right and then do something extra. Gouge out its eyes with your thumbs.

Break its ribs. Wrap your hands around the throat and squeeze and squeeze and squeeze, until you feel what it's like to make a windpipe crumble in your grip. Do it because when the war comes you're going to have to do it to niggers and spics and all the mud people coming after all we have here. Do it for our future.

"Come on," he says. "If you can do this you can do anything."

He's right. If I can dig a shovelful of dirt, one little shovel, and throw it on my husband's body, that will be the hardest. Every shovel after that will just make the mess go away, will put that meat back into the ground with his smile and his touch and the way he killed a deer for me that night. It will get further and further underground and nothing, absolutely nothing, will be hard after this.

I put the tip of the shovel against the dirt. I push my weight against it and I see how the hard iron cuts a little gash in the clay, not enough to dig even a tablespoon but enough to know I've started.

My dad nods and turns away.

I didn't know I was strong enough to raise a shovel over my head. I didn't know until I feel its weight swinging through the air over my own. I hit my dad in the back of the head. It's not enough to kill. "Goddammit," he roars, and reaches for his own shovel. I raise it again before I can think and this time I get him in the forehead. Blood comes out. He staggers back. I hit him again. He falls down. I hit him again. He's on the ground now. I hit him and hit him and hit him. I feel the moment shift when something living becomes something quiet and dead, just like a deer. When it happens I go back to being me. I throw the shovel down on my dad's beaten-in face and when I see it bounce I howl, running into the woods.

If I had sense I would run back and get Ed's truck and Dad's weapons but all I can do is run like an animal, the fastest animal that ever lived. I know the world is full of monsters and Jews but I'm not afraid. I will do anything for the baby in my belly. I can make it to Eugene in seven days if I lay low and follow the stars. I can go into Gomorrah if I have to. I run and I run, the last of our kind inside me. I'm ready to live among niggers and spics, they'll put us in a zoo when the race war comes and all the mud people will come and gawk at our skin every day. But I will stare into my baby's blue eyes and hold my head high and know nothing is hard, anymore. We will be okay.

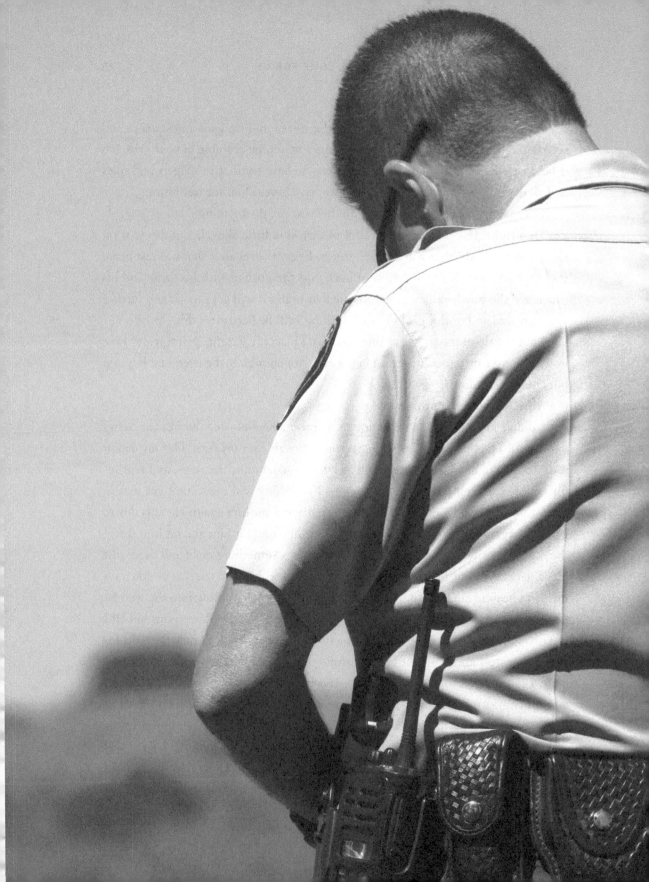

All Through the House

BY CHRISTOPHER COAKE

Old friends. There's nothing like them. They're the people you've grown up with, and loved all your life.

So what do you do when one of them snaps and does something so heinous that you're forced to call your whole life into question just to answer the deeper, even uglier question, "How did I not see this coming?"

Returning to the scene of the crime—both physically and emotionally, with all your memories and puzzle-solving brain waves engaged—is one of the hardest things a survivor of atrocity can be asked to do.

And it is here that Christopher Coake's "All through the House" so brilliantly succeeds: as an impeccably honest dissection of survivor guilt by association.

And of the love that survives, even after all the promises have been broken.

Now

Here is an empty meadow, circled by bare autumn woods.

The trees of the woods—oak, maple, locust—grow through a mat of tangled scrub, rusty leaves, piles of brittle deadfall. Overhead is a rich blue sky, a few high, translucent clouds, moving quickly—but the trees are dense enough to shelter everything below, and the meadow, too. And here, leading into the trees from the meadow's edge, is a dirt track, twin ruts with a grassy center, winding through the woods and away.

The meadow floor is overrun by tall yellow grass, thorny vines, the occasional sapling—save for at the meadow's center. Here is a wide rectangular depression. The broken remains of a concrete foundation shore up its sides. The bottom is crumbled concrete and cinder, barely visible beneath a thin netting of weeds. A blackened wooden beam angles down from the rim, its underside soft and fibrous. Two oaks lean over the foundation, charred on the sides that face it.

Sometimes deer browse in the meadow. Raccoons and rabbits are always present; they have made their own curving trails across the meadow floor. A fox lives in the nearby trees, rusty and quick. His den, twisting between tree roots, is pressed flat and smooth by his belly.

Sometimes automobiles crawl slowly along the track and park at the edge of the meadow. The people inside sometimes get out, and walk into the grass. They take photographs, or draw pictures, or read from books. Sometimes they climb down into the old foundation. A few camp overnight, huddling close to fires.

Whenever these people come, a policeman, fat and gray-haired, arrives soon after. Sometimes the people speak with him—and sometimes they shout—but always they depart, loading their cars while the policeman watches. When they are gone he follows them down the track in his slow, rumbling cruiser. When this happens in the nighttime, the spinning of his red-and-blue lights makes the trees seem to jump and dance.

Sometimes the policeman comes when there is no one to chase away.

He stops the cruiser and climbs out. He walks slowly into the meadow. He sits on the broken concrete at the rim of the crater, looking into it, looking at the sky, closing his eyes.

When he makes noise, the woods grow quiet. All the animals crouch low, flicking their ears at the man's barks and howls.

He does not stay long.

After his cruiser has rolled away down the track, the woods and the meadow remain, for a time, silent. But before long what lives there sniffs the air, and, in fits and starts, emerges. Noses press to the ground, and into the burrows of mice. Things eat, and are eaten.

Here memories are held in muscles and bellies, not in minds. The policeman, and the house, and all the people who have come and gone here, are not forgotten.

They are, simply, never remembered.

1987

Sheriff Larry Thompkins tucked his chin against the cold and, his back to his idling cruiser, unlocked the cattle gate that blocked access to the Sullivan woods. The gate swung inward, squealing, and the cruiser's headlights shone a little ways down the track, before it veered off into the trees. Larry straightened, then glanced right and left, down the paved country road behind him. He saw no other cars, not even on the distant interstate. The sky was clouded over—snow was a possibility—and the fields behind him were almost invisible in the moonless dark.

Larry sank back behind the wheel, grateful for the warmth, for the static spitting from his radio. He nosed the cruiser through the gate and onto the track, then switched to his parking lights. The trunks of trees ahead dimmed, turned orange. The nearest soul, old Ned Baker, lived a half mile off, but Ned was an insomniac, and often sat in front of his bedroom window watching the Sullivan woods. If Larry used his headlights, Ned would see. Ever since Patricia Pike's book had come out—three months ago now—Ned had watched over the gated entrance to the woods as if it was a military duty.

Larry had been chasing off trespassers from the Sullivan place ever since the murders, twelve years ago in December. He hated coming here, but he couldn't very well refuse to do his job—no one else was going to see to it. Almost always the trespassers were kids from the high school, out at the murder house getting drunk or high—and though Larry was always firm with them, and made trouble for the bad ones, he knew most kids did stupid things; he couldn't blame them that much. Larry had fallen off the roof of a barn, drunk, when he was sixteen—he'd broken his arm in two places, all because he was trying to impress a girl who, in the end, never went out with him.

But activity in the woods had picked up since the Pike woman's book appeared. Larry had been out here three times in the last week alone. There were kids, still, more of them than ever—but also people from out of town, some of whom he suspected were mentally ill. Just last weekend Larry had chased off a couple in their twenties, lying on a blanket with horrible screaming music playing on their boom box. They'd told him—calmly, as though he might understand—that they practiced magic and wanted to conceive a child there. The house, they said, was a place of energy. When they were gone Larry looked up at its empty windows, its stupid dead house-face, and couldn't imagine anything further from the truth.

The cruiser bounced and shimmied as Larry negotiated the turns through the woods. All his extra visits had deepened the ruts in the track—he'd been cutting through mud and ice all autumn. Now and then the tires spun, and he tried not to think about having to call for a tow, the stories he'd have to make up to explain himself. But each time, the cruiser roared and lurched free.

He'd come here with Patricia Pike. He hadn't wanted to, but the mayor told him Pike did a good job with this kind of book, and that—while the mayor was concerned, just as Larry was, about exploiting what had happened—he didn't want the town to get any more of a bad name on account of being uncooperative. So Larry had gone to the library, to read one of Pike's other books. He picked one called *The Beauties and the Beast*, with the close-up of a cat's eye on the front cover. The book was about a serial killer in Idaho in the sixties, who murdered five women and fed them to his pet cougar. In one chapter Pike wrote that the police had hidden details of the crime from her. Larry could understand why—the killings were brutal; he was sure the police had a hard enough time explaining the details to the families of the victims, let alone to ghouls all across the country looking for a thrill.

We're going to get exploited, Larry had told the mayor, waving that book at him. *Look*, the mayor said, *I know this is difficult for you. But would you rather she wrote it without your help? You knew Wayne better than anybody. Who knows? Maybe we'll finally get to the bottom of things.*

What if there's no bottom to get to? Larry asked, but the mayor had looked at him strangely and never answered, just told him to put up with it, that it would be over before he knew it.

Larry wrestled the cruiser around the last bend, and then stopped. His parking lights shone dully across what was left of the old driveway turnaround, and onto the Sullivan house.

The house squatted, dim and orange. It had never been much to look at, even when new; it was small, unremarkable, square—barely more than a prefab. The garage, jutting off the back, was far too big, and knocked the whole structure out of proportion—made it look deformed. The windows were too little, too few.

Since the murders the house had only gotten worse. Most of the paint had chipped off the siding, and the tiny pig-eyed windows were boarded over—kids had broken out all the glass years ago. The grass and bushes of the meadow had grown up around it, closing it in, made it look like the house was sinking into the earth.

Wayne had designed the house himself, not long after he and Jenny got married; he'd had no idea what he was doing, but—he'd told Larry, showing him the plans—he wanted the house to be unique. *Like me and Jenny*, he'd said, beaming.

Jenny had hated the house. She'd told Larry so, at her and Wayne's house-warming dinner.

It's bad enough I have to live out here in the middle of nowhere, she'd said under her breath, while Wayne chattered to Larry's wife, Emily, in the living room. *But at least he could have built us a house you can look at.*

Larry had told her, *He did it because he loves you. He tried.*

Don't remind me, Jenny had said, swallowing wine. *Why did I ever agree to this? The house?*

The house, the marriage. God, Larry, you name it.

When she'd said it she hadn't sounded bitter. She looked at Larry as though he might have an answer, but he didn't—he'd never been able to see Jenny and Wayne together, from the moment they started dating in college, all the way up to the wedding; *I do*, Wayne had said, his cheeks wet, and Jenny's face had gone all soft, and Larry had felt a pang for both of them. At the housewarming party he told her, *It'll get better,* and felt right away that he'd lied, and Jenny made a face that showed she knew he had, before both of them turned to watch Wayne demonstrate the dimmer switch in the living room for Emily.

The front door, Larry saw now, was swinging open—some folks he'd chased out two weeks ago had jimmied it, and the lock hadn't worked right afterward. The open door and the black gap behind it made the house look even meaner than it was—like a baby crying. Patricia Pike had said that, when she first saw the place. Larry wondered if she'd put it into her book.

She had sent him a copy, back in July just before its release. The book was called *All Through the House*—the cover showed a Christmas tree with little skulls as ornaments. Pike had signed it for him: *To Larry, even though I know you prefer fiction. Cheers, Patricia.* He flipped to the index and saw his name with a lot of numbers by it, and then he looked at the glossy plates at the book's center. One was a map of Prescott County, showing the country road, and an X in the Sullivan woods, where the house stood. The next page showed a floor plan of the house, with bodies drawn in outline, and dotted lines following Wayne's path from room to room. One plate showed a Sears portrait of the entire family smiling together, plus graduation photos of Wayne and Jenny. Pike had included a picture of Larry, too—taken on the day of the murders—that showed him pointing off to the edge of the picture while EMT's brought one of the boys out the front door, wrapped in a blanket. Larry looked like he was running—his arms were blurry—which was odd. They'd brought no one out of the house alive. He'd have had no need to rush.

The last chapter was titled "Why?" Larry had read that part all the way through. Every rumor and half-baked theory Patricia Pike had heard while in town, she'd included, worded to make it sound like she'd done thinking no one else ever had.

Wayne was in debt. Wayne was jealous because maybe Jenny was sleeping around. Wayne had been seeing a doctor about migraines. Wayne was a man who had never matured past childhood. Wayne lived in a fantasy world inhabited by the perfect family he could never have. *Once again the reluctance of the Sheriff's department and the townspeople to discuss their nightmares freely hinders us from under-*

standing a man like Wayne Sullivan, from preventing others from killing as he has killed,
from beginning the healing closure this community so badly needs.

Larry had tossed his copy in a drawer, and hoped everyone else would do the same.

But then the book was a success—all Patricia Pike's books were. And not long after that the lunatics had started to come out to the house. And then, today, Larry had gotten a call from the mayor.

You're not going to like this, the mayor had told him.

Larry hadn't. A cable channel wanted to film a documentary based on the book. They were sending a camera crew at the end of the month, near Christmastime—for authenticity's sake. They wanted to film in the house, and of course they wanted to talk to everybody all over again, Larry first and foremost.

Larry took a bottle of whiskey from underneath the front seat of the cruiser, and, watching the Sullivan house through the windshield, he unscrewed the cap and drank a swallow. His eyes watered, but he got it down and drank another. The booze spread in his throat and belly, made him want to sit very still behind the wheel, to keep drinking. A lot of nights he would. But instead he opened the door and climbed out of the cruiser.

The meadow and the house were mostly blocked from the wind, but the air had a bite to it all the same. He hunched his shoulders, then opened the trunk and took out one of the gas cans he'd filled back at the station, and a few rolls of newspaper. He walked to the open doorway of the house, his head ducked, careful with his feet in the shadows and the tall grass.

He smelled the house's insides even before he stepped onto the porch—a smell like the underside of a wet log. He clicked on his flashlight and shone it into the doorway, across the splotched and crumbling walls. He stepped inside. Something living scuttled out of the way; a raccoon, or a possum. Maybe even a fox; Wayne had once told him the woods was full of them, but in all the times Larry had been out here he'd never seen any.

He glanced over the walls. Some new graffiti had appeared: KILL 'EM ALL was spray-painted on the wall where, once, the Christmas tree had leaned. The older messages were still in place. One read: HEY WAYNE, DO MY HOUSE NEXT. Beside a ragged, spackled-over depression in the same wall, someone had painted an arrow and the word BRAINS. Smaller messages were written in marker—the sorts of things high-school kids write: initials, graduation years, witless sex puns, pictures of genitalia.

And—sitting right there in the corner—was a copy of *All Through the House*, its pages swollen with moisture.

Larry rubbed his temple. The book was as good a place to start as any.

He kicked the book to the center of the living-room floor, and then splashed it with gas. Nearby was a crevice where the carpet had torn and separated. He rolled the newspapers up and wedged them underneath the carpet, then doused them, too. Then he drizzled gasoline in a line from both the book and the papers to the front door. From the edge of the stoop he tossed arcs of gas onto the door and the jamb until the can was empty.

He stood on the porch, smelling the gas, and gasping—he was horribly out of shape. His head was throbbing. He squeezed the lighter in his hand until the pain subsided.

Larry was not much for religion, but he tried a prayer anyway: *Lord, keep them. I know you have been. And please let this work.* But the prayer sounded pitiful in his head, so he stopped it.

He lit a clump of newspaper, and, once it had bloomed, touched it to the base of the door.

The fire took the door right away, and flickered in a curling line across the carpet to the book and the papers. He could see them burning through the doorway, before thick gray smoke obscured his view. After a few minutes the flames began to gutter. He wasn't much of an arsonist—it was wet in there. He retrieved the other gas can from the trunk and shoved a rolled-up cone of newspaper into the nozzle. He made sure he had a clear throw, and then lit the paper and heaved the can inside the house. It exploded right away, with a thump, and orange light bloomed up one of the inside walls. Outside, the flames from the door flared, steadied, then began to climb onto the siding.

Larry went back to the cruiser and pulled the bottle of whiskey from beneath his seat. He thought about Jenny; he thought about camping in the meadow as a boy with Wayne. He had seen this house being built; he'd seen it lived in and died in. Larry had guessed he might feel a certain joy, watching it destroyed, but instead his throat caught. Somewhere down the line, this had gotten to be his house. He'd thought that for a while now; the township owned the Sullivan house, but really, Wayne had passed it on to *him*.

An image of himself drifted into his head—it had come a few times tonight. He saw himself walking into the burning house, climbing the stairs. In his head he did this without pain, even while fire found his clothing, the bullets in his gun. He would sit upstairs in Jenny's sewing room and close his eyes, and it wouldn't take long.

He sniffled and pinched his nose. That was a bunch of horseshit. He'd seen people who'd been burned to death. He'd die, all right, but he'd go screaming and flailing. At the thought of it his arms and legs grew heavy; his skin prickled.

Larry put the cruiser in reverse and backed it slowly away from the house, out of the drive and onto the track. He watched for ten minutes as the fire grew, and tried not to think about anything, to see only the flames. Then he got the call from Lynn at dispatch.

Sheriff?

Copy, he said.

Ned called in. He says it looks like there's a fire out at the Sullivan place.

A fire?

That's what he said. He sees a fire in the woods.

My, my my, Larry said. I'm on old 52 just past Mackey. I'll get there quick as I can and take a look.

He waited another ten minutes. Flames leaked around the boards on the windows. The downstairs ceiling caught. Long shadows shifted through the trees; the woods came alive, swaying and dancing. Something alive and aflame shot out the front door—a rabbit? It zigged and zagged across the turnaround, and then headed toward him. For a moment Larry thought it had fled under his car, and he put his hand on the door handle—but whatever it was cut away for the woods to his right. He saw it come to rest in a patch of scrub; smoke rose from the bush in wisps.

Dispatch? Larry said.

Copy.

I'm at the Sullivan house. It's on fire, all right. Better get the trucks out here.

Twenty minutes later two fire trucks arrived, advancing carefully down the track. The men got out and stood beside Larry, looking over the house, now brightly ablaze from top to bottom. They rolled the trucks past Larry's cruiser and sprayed the grass around the house and the trees nearby. Then all of them watched the house burn and crumble into its foundation, and no one said much of anything.

Larry left them to the rubble just before dawn. He drove home and tried to wash the smell of smoke out of his hair, and then lay down next to Emily, who didn't stir. He lay awake for a while, trying to convince himself he'd actually done it, and then trying to convince himself he hadn't.

When he finally slept, he saw the house on fire, except that in his dream there were people still in it: Jenny Sullivan in the upstairs window, holding her younger boy to her and shouting Larry's name, screaming it, while Larry sat in his car, tugging at the handle, unable even to shout back to her, to tell her it was locked.

1985

Patricia Pike had known from the start that Sheriff Thompkins was reluctant to work with her. Now, driving in his cruiser with him down empty back roads to the Sullivan house, she wondered if what she'd thought was reticence was instead real anger. Thompkins had been civil enough when she spoke with him on the phone a month earlier, but since meeting him this morning in his small, cluttered office—she'd seen janitors with better quarters—he'd been scowling, sullen, rarely bothering to look her in the eye.

She was used to this treatment from policemen. A lot of them had read her books, two of which had uncovered information the police hadn't found themselves. Her second book, *On a Darkling Plain*, had overturned a conviction. Policemen hated being shown up, even the best of them—and she suspected from the look of Thompkins's office that he didn't operate on the cutting edge of law enforcement.

Thompkins was tall and hunched, perhaps muscular once, but now going to fat, with a gray cop's mustache and a single thick fold under his chin. He was only forty—two years younger than she was—but he looked much older. He kept a wedding photo on his desk; in it he had the broad-shouldered, thick-necked look of an offensive lineman. Unsurprising, this; a lot of country cops she spoke to had played football. His wife, next to him, was a little ghost of a woman, dark-eyed, smiling what Patricia suspected was one of her last big smiles.

Patricia had asked Thompkins a few questions in his office, chatty ones designed to put him at ease. She'd also flirted, a little; she was good-looking, and sometimes that worked. But even then Thompkins answered flatly, in the sort of language police fell back on in their reports. *It was at this point in time that I, uh, approached the scene.* He looked often at his watch, but she wasn't fooled. Kinslow, Indiana, had only six hundred residents, and Thompkins wasn't about to convince her he was a busy man.

Now Thompkins drove along the interminable gravel roads to the Sullivan woods with one hand on the wheel and the other brushing the corners of his mustache. Finally she couldn't stand it.

Do I make you uncomfortable, Sheriff?

He widened his eyes and he shifted his shoulders, then coughed. He said, Well, I'll be honest. I guess I'd rather not do this.

I can't imagine you would, she said. Best to give him the sympathy he so obviously wanted.

He told her, If the mayor wasn't such a fan of yours, I wouldn't be out here.

She smiled at him, just a little. She said, I've talked to Wayne's parents; I know you were close to Wayne and Jenny. It can't be easy to do this.

No, ma'am. That it is not.

Thompkins turned the cruiser onto a smaller paved road—on either side of them was nothing but fields, empty and stubbled with old broken cornstalks, and blocky stands of woods, so monochromatic they could be pencil drawings.

Patricia asked, You all went to high school together, didn't you?

Abington, class of '64. Jenny was a year behind me and Wayne.

Did you become friends in high school?

That's when I got to know Jenny. Wayne and I knew each other since we were little. Our mothers taught together at the elementary school.

Thompkins glanced at Patricia. He said, You know all this already. You drawing out the witness?

She smiled, genuinely grateful. So he had a brain in there after all. It seems I have to, she said.

He sighed—a big man's sigh, long and weary—and said, I have nothing against you personally, Ms. Pike. But I don't like the kind of books you write, and I don't like coming out here.

I do appreciate your help. I know it's hard.

Why this case? he asked her. Why us?

She tried to think of the right words, something that wouldn't offend him.

Well, I suppose I was just *drawn* to it. My agent sends me clippings about cases, things she thinks I might want to write about. The murders were so…brutal, and they happened on Christmas Eve. And since it happened in the country, it never made the news much; people don't know about it—not in the big cities, anyway. There's also kind of a—a fairy-tale quality to it, the house out in the middle of the forest—you know?

Uh-huh, Thompkins said.

And then there's the mystery of *why*. There's a certain type of case I specialize in— crimes with a component of unsolved mystery. I'm intrigued that Wayne didn't leave a note. You're the only person he gave any information to, and even then—

He didn't say much.

No. I know, I've read the transcript already. But that's my answer, I suppose: there's a lot to write about.

Thompkins stroked his mustache and turned at a stop sign.

They were now to the right of an enormous tract of woods, much larger than the other stands nearby. Patricia had seen it growing on the horizon, almost like a rain cloud, and now, close up, she saw it was at least a mile square. The sheriff slowed and turned off the road, stopping in front of a low metal gate that blocked a rutted dirt track; it dipped away from the road and into the bare trees. A NO TRESPASSING sign hung from the gate's center. It had been fired upon a number of times; some of the bullet holes had yet to rust. Thompkins said, Excuse me, and got out. He bent over a giant padlock and then swung the gate inward. He got back behind the wheel, drove the cruiser through without shutting his door, then clambered out again and locked the gate behind them.

Keeps the kids out, he told her, shifting the cruiser into gear. Means the only way in is on foot. A lot of them won't walk it, at least when it's cold like this.

This is a big woods.

Probably the biggest between Indy and Lafayette. 'Course no one's ever measured, but that's—that's what Wayne always told me.

Patricia caught his drop in volume, glanced over to see his mouth droop.

The track curved right, then left. The world they were in now was almost a sepia-toned old film: bare winter branches, patches of old snow on the ground, pools of black muck. Patricia had grown up in Chicago, but had relatives on a farm downstate; she knew what a tangle those woods would be. What a curious place for a house. She opened her notebook and wrote in shorthand.

This land belongs to Wayne's family? she asked.

It used to. Township owns it now. Wayne had put the land up as collateral for the house, and then when he died his folks didn't pay on the loan. I don't blame them for that. The bank sold it to the town a few years back, on the cheap. The town might sell it someday, but no one really wants farmland anymore. None of the farmers around here can afford to develop it. An ag company would have to buy it. In the meantime I keep an eye on the place.

Thompkins slowed, and the car jounced into and out of a deep rut. He said, Me, I'd like to see the whole thing plowed under. But I don't make those choices.

She wrote his words down.

They rounded a last bend in the track, and there, in front of them, was a meadow, and in the center of it the Sullivan house. Patricia had seen pictures of it, but here in person it was much smaller than she'd imagined. She pulled her camera out of her bag.

It's ugly, she said.

That's the truth, Thompkins said, and put the car into park.

The house was a two-story of some indeterminate style—not quite a Cape Cod, but probably closer to that than anything. The roof was pitched, but seemed...too small, too flat for the rest of the house. The face suggested by its windows and front door—flanked by faux half-columns—was that of a mongoloid: all chin and mouth, and no forehead. Or like a baby crying. It had been painted an olive color, and now the paint was flaking. The track continued around behind the house, where a two-car garage jutted off at right angles, too big in proportion to the house.

Wayne drew up the plans, Thompkins said. He wanted to do it himself.

What did Jenny think of it? Do you know?

She joked about it. Not so Wayne could hear.

Would he have been angry?

No. Sad. He'd wanted a house out here since we were kids. He loved these woods.

Thompkins undid his seat belt. Then he said, I guess he knew the house was a mess, but he...it's hard to say. We all pretended it was fine.

Why?

Some folks, you just want to protect their feelings. He wanted us all to be as excited as he was. It wouldn't have occurred to us to be . . . blunt with him. You know that type of person? Kind of like a puppy?

Yes.

Well, Thompkins said, that was Wayne. You want to go in?

The interior of the house was dark—the windows had been boarded over with sheets of plywood. Thompkins had brought two electric lanterns; he set one just inside the door and held the other in his hand. He walked inside and then motioned for Patricia to follow.

The inside of the house stank—an old, abandoned smell of mildew and rot. The carpeting—what was left of it, anyway—seemed to be on the verge of becoming mud, or a kind of algae, and held the stink. Patricia had been in morgues and, for one of her books, had accompanied a homicide detective in Detroit to murder sites. She knew what death—dead human beings—smelled like. That smell might have been in the Sullivan house, underneath everything else, but she couldn't be sure. It ought to have been.

Patricia could see no furniture. Ragged holes gaped in the ceilings where light fixtures might have been. Behind the sheriff was a staircase, rising up into darkness, and to the right of it an entrance into what seemed to be the kitchen.

Shit, Thompkins said.

What?

He held the lantern close to the wall, in the room to the right of the foyer. There was a spot on the wall there, a ragged, spackled patch. Someone had spray-painted an arrow pointing at it, and the word BRAINS.

Thompkins turned a circle, with the lantern held out. He was looking down, and she followed his gaze. She saw cigarette butts, beer cans.

Kids come in here from Abington, Thompkins said. I run them off every now and then. Sometimes it's adults, even. Have to come out and see for themselves, I guess. The kids say it's haunted.

That happens in a lot of places, Patricia said.

Huh, Thompkins said.

She took photos of the rooms, the flashbulb's light dazzling in the dark.

I guess you want the tour, Thompkins said.

I do. She put a hand on his arm, and his eyes widened. She said, as cheerfully as she could, Do you mind if I tape our conversation?

Do you have to? Thompkins asked, looking up from her hand.

It will help me quote you better.

Well. I suppose.

Patricia put a tape into her hand-held recorder, then nodded at him.

Thompkins lifted the lantern up. The light gleamed off his dark eyes. His mouth hung open, just a little, and when he breathed out a thin line of steam appeared in front of the lantern. He looked different. Not sad, not anymore. Maybe, Patricia thought, she saw in him what she was feeling—which was a thrill, what a teenager feels in front of a campfire, knowing a scary story is coming. She reminded herself that actual people had died here, that she was in a place of tremendous sadness, but all the same she couldn't help herself. Her books sold well because she wrote them well, with fervency, and she wrote that way because she loved to be in forbidden places like this; she loved learning the secrets no one wanted to say. Just as, she suspected, Sheriff Thompkins wanted deep in his heart to tell them to her. Secrets were too big for people to hold—that was what she found in her research, time after time. Secrets had their own agendas.

Patricia looked at Thompkins, turning a smile into a quick nod.

All right then, the sheriff said. This way.

Here's the kitchen.

Wayne shot Jenny first, in here. But that shot didn't kill her. You can't tell because of the boards, but the kitchen window looks over the driveway, in front of the garage. Wayne shot her through the window. Jenny was looking out at Wayne, we know that, because the bullet went in through the front of her right shoulder and out the back, and we know he was outside because the glass was broken, and because his footprints were still in the snow when we got here—there was no wind that night. Wayne's car was in front of the garage. What he did was, he got out of the driver's side door and went around to the trunk and opened it—best guess is the gun was in there; he'd purchased it that night, at a shop in Muncie. Then he went around to the passenger door and stood there for a while; the snow was all tramped down. We think he was loading the gun. Or maybe he was talking himself into doing it. I don't know.

We figure he braced on the top of the car and shot her from where he stood. The security light over the garage was burned out when we got here, so from inside, with the kitchen lights on, Jenny wouldn't have been able to see what he was doing— not very clearly, if at all. I don't know why she was turned around looking out the window at him. Maybe he honked the horn. I also don't know if he aimed to kill her or wound her, but my feeling is he went for a wounding shot. It's about twenty feet from where he stood to where she stood, so it wasn't that hard a shot for him to make, and he made most of his others that night. Now down here—

[The sheriff's pointing to a spot on the linoleum, slightly stained, see photos.]
Excuse me?
[Don't mind me, Sheriff. Just keep talking.]
Oh. All right then.

Well, Jenny—once she was shot, she fell and struggled. There was a lot of blood; we think she probably, uh, bled out for seven or eight minutes while Wayne...while Wayne killed the others. She tried to pull herself to the living room; there were...smears on the floor consistent with her doing that.

[We're back in the living room; we're facing the front door.]
After he'd shot Jenny, he walked around the east side of the house to the front door here. He could have come in the garage into the kitchen, but he didn't. I'm

not sure what happened from there exactly. But here's what I think.

The grandmother—Mrs. Murray—and Danny, the four-year-old, were in the living room, in here, next to the tree. She was reading to him; he liked to be read to, and a book of nursery rhymes was open facedown on the couch. The grandmother was infirm—she had diabetes and couldn't walk so well. She was sitting on the couch still when we found her. He shot her once through the head, probably from the doorway.

[We're looking at the graffiti wall, see photos.]

But by this time Jenny would have been…she would have been screaming, so we know Wayne didn't catch the rest of them unawares. Jenny might have called out that Daddy was home before Wayne shot her; hell, this place is in the middle of nowhere, and it was nighttime, so they all knew a car had pulled up. What I'm saying is, I'm guessing there was a lot of confusion at this juncture, a lot of shouting. There's a bullet hole at waist height on the wall opposite the front door. My best guess is that Danny ran to the door and was in front of it when Wayne opened it. He could have been looking into the kitchen, at his…at his mother, or at the door. I think Wayne took a shot at him from the doorway and missed. Danny ran into the living room, and since Mrs. Muncie hadn't tried to struggle to her feet, Wayne shot her next. He took one shot and hit her. Then he shot Danny. Danny was behind the Christmas tree; he probably ran there to hide. Wayne took three shots into the tree, and one of them, or I guess Danny's struggles, knocked it sideways off its base. But he got Danny, shot his own boy in the head just over his left ear.

[We're looking through a door off the dining room; inside is a small room maybe ten by nine, see photos.]

This was a playroom. Mr. Murray and Alex, the two-year-old, were in it. Mr. Murray reacted pretty quick to the shots, for a guy his age—but he was a vet, and he hunted, so he probably would have been moving at the sound of the first gunshot. He opened that window—

[A boarded window on the roar of the house, see photos.]

—which, ah, used to look out behind the garage, and he dropped Alex through it into the snowdrift beneath. Then he got himself through. Though not without some trouble. The autopsy showed he had a broken wrist, which we figure he broke getting out. But it's still a remarkable thing. I hope you write that. Mr. Murray tried his best to save Alex.

[I'll certainly note it. Wayne's parents also mentioned him.]

Well, good. Good.

Sam and Alex got about fifty yards away, toward the woods. Wayne probably went to the doorway of the playroom and saw the window open. He ran back outside, around the west corner of the house, and shot Sam in the back right about where the garden was. There wasn't a lot of light, but the house lights were all on, and if I remember right the bodies were just about at the limit of what you could see from that corner. So Sam almost made it out of range. But I don't know if he could have got very far once he was in the trees. He was strong for a guy his age, but it was snowy, and neither he or the boy had coats, and it was about ten degrees out that night. Plus Wayne meant to kill everybody, and I think he would have tracked them.

Sam died instantly. Wayne got him in the heart. He fell and the boy didn't go any farther. Wayne walked about fifty feet out and fired a few shots, and one of them got Alex through the neck. Wayne never went any closer. Either he knew he'd killed them both, or he figured the cold would finish the job for him if he hadn't. Maybe he couldn't look. I don't know.

[We're in the living room again, at the foot of the stairs.]

He went back inside and shut the door behind him. I think he was confronted by the dog, Kodiak, on the stairs, there on the landing. He shot the dog, probably from where you're standing. Then—

[We're looking into the kitchen again.]

—Wayne went to the kitchen and shot—he shot Jenny a second time. The killing shot. We found her facedown. Wayne stood over her and fired from a distance of less than an inch. The bullet went in the back of her head just above the neck. He held her down with his boot on her shoulder. We know because she was wearing a white sweater and he left a bloodstain on it that held the imprint of his boot sole.

He called my house at 9:16. You've seen the transcript.

[How did he sound? On the phone?]

Oh, Jesus. I'd say upset, but not hysterical. Like he was out of breath, I guess.

[Will you tell me again what he said?]

Hell. Do you really need me to repeat it?

[If you can.]

Well . . . he said, Larry, it's Wayne. I said, Hey Wayne, Merry Christmas, or something like that. And then he said, No time, Larry, this is a business call. And I said, What's wrong? And he said, Larry, I killed Jenny and the kids and my in-laws, and as soon as I hang up, I'm going to kill myself. And I said something like, Are you joking? And then he hung up. That's it. I got in the cruiser and drove up here as fast as I could.

[You were first on the scene?]

Yeah. Yeah, I was. I called it in on the way, it took me a while to—to remember. I saw blood through the front windows, and I called for backup as soon as I did. I went inside. I looked around . . . and saw . . . everyone but Sam and Alex. It took me . . .

[Sheriff?]

No, it's all right. I wasn't . . . I wasn't in great shape, which I guess you can imagine, but after a couple of minutes I found the window open in the playroom. I was out with—with Sam and Alex when the deputies arrived.

[But you found Wayne first?]

Right, yes. I looked for him right off. For all I knew he was still alive.

[Where was he?]

Down in here.

[We're looking into a door opening off the kitchen; it looks like—the basement?]

Yeah. Wayne killed himself in his workroom. That was his favorite place, where he went for privacy. We used to drink down there, play darts. He sat in a corner and shot himself with a small handgun, which he purchased along with the rifle. It was the only shot he fired from it. He'd shut the basement door behind him.

. . . You want to see down there?

They sat for a while in the cruiser, afterward. Thompkins had brought a thermos of coffee, which touched Patricia; the coffee was terrible, but at least it was warm. She held the cup in her hands in front of the dashboard vents. Thompkins chewed his thumbnail and looked at the house.

Why did he do it? she asked him.

Hmm?

Why did Wayne do it?

I don't know.

You don't have any theories?

No.

He said it quickly, an obvious lie. Patricia watched his face and said, I called around after talking with his parents. Wayne was way behind on his loan payments. If he hadn't worked at the bank already, this place would have been repossessed.

Maybe, Thompkins said, and sipped his coffee. But half the farms you see out here are in the hole, and no one's slaughtered their entire family over it.

Patricia watched him while he said this. Thompkins kept his big face neutral, but he didn't look at her. His ears were pink with cold.

Wayne's mother, she said, told me she thought that Jenny might have had affairs.

Yeah. I heard that, too.

Any truth to it?

Adultery's not against the law. So I don't concern myself with it.

But surely you've heard something.

Well, Ms. Pike, I have the same answer as before. People have been sleeping around on each other out here for a lot longer than I've had this job, and no one ever killed their family over it.

Thompkins put on his seat belt.

Besides, he said, if you were a man who'd slept with Jenny Sullivan, would *you* say anything about it? You wouldn't, not now. So no, I don't know for sure. And frankly, I wouldn't tell you if I did.

Why?

Because I knew Jenny, and she was a good woman. She was my prom date, for Christ's sake. I stood up at her and Wayne's wedding. Jenny was always straight, and she was smart. If she had an affair, that was her business. But it's not mine now, and it's not yours.

It would be motive, Patricia said softly.

I took the bodies out of that house, Thompkins said, putting the cruiser into reverse. I took my friends out. I felt their necks to see if they were alive. I saw what

Wayne did. There's no reason good enough. No one could have wronged him enough to make him do what he did. I don't care what it was.

He turned the cruiser around; the trees rushed by, and Patricia gripped her coffee with both hands to keep it from spilling. She'd heard speeches like this before. Someone's brains get opened up, and there's always some backcountry cop who puts his hand to his heart and pretends the poor soul still has any privacy.

There's always a reason, she said.

Thompkins smirked without humor; the cruiser bounced up and down.

Then I'm sure you'll come up with something, he said.

In the evening, just past sundown, Larry went out to the Sullivan house again. He and the staties had finished with the scene earlier in the day—there hadn't been much to investigate, really; Wayne had confessed in his phone call, yet Larry had told his deputies to take pictures anyway, to collect what evidence they could. And then all day reporters had come out for pictures, and some of the townspeople had stopped by to gawk, or to ask if anything needed doing, so Larry decided to keep the house under guard. Truth be told, he and the men needed something to do; watching the house was better than fielding questions in town.

When Larry pulled up in front of the house, his deputy, Troy Bowen, was sitting behind the wheel of his cruiser by the garage, reading a paperback. Larry flashed his lights, and Bowen got out and ambled over to Larry's car, hands in his armpits.

Hey Larry, he said. What's up?

Slow night, Larry said—which was true enough. He said, Go get dinner. I'll cover until Albie gets here.

That's not till midnight, Bowen said, but his face was open and grateful.

I might as well be out here. It's all I'm thinking about anyway.

Yeah, that's what I thought. But I don't mind saying it gives me the willies. You're welcome to it.

When Bowen's cruiser was gone, Larry stood for a moment on the front stoop, hands in his pockets. Crime-scene tape was strung over the doorway, in a big haphazard X; Bowen had done it after the bodies were removed, sniffling and red-eyed. It had been his first murder scene. The electricity was still on; the little fake lantern hanging over the door was shining. Larry took a couple of breaths and then fumbled out a copy of the house key. He unlocked the door, ducked under the caution tape, and went inside.

He turned on the living-room light and there everything was, as he'd left it this afternoon. His heart thumped. What else had he expected? That it would all be gone? That it hadn't really happened? It had. Here were the outlines. The bloodstains on the living-room carpet, and on the landing. The light from the living room just shone into the kitchen; he could see the dark swirls on the linoleum, too. Already a smell was in the air. The furnace was still on, and the blood and the smaller pieces of remains were starting to turn. The place would go bad if Wayne's folks didn't have the house cleaned up soon. Larry didn't want to have that talk with them, but he'd call them tomorrow—he knew a service in Indianapolis that took care of things like this. All the same he turned off the thermostat.

He asked himself why he cared. Surely no one would ever live in this place again. What did it matter?

But it did, somehow.

He walked into the family room. The tree was canted sideways, knocked partway out of its base. He went to the wall behind it, stepping over stains, careful not to disturb anything. The lights on the tree were still plugged into the wall outlet. He squatted, straddling a collapsing pile of presents, then leaned forward and pulled the cord. The tree might go up, especially with its trunk out of water.

Larry looked up at the wall and put his hand over his mouth; he'd been trying to avoid looking right at anything, but he'd done it now. Just a few inches in front of him, on the wall, was the spot where Danny had been shot. The bullet had gone right through his head. He'd given Danny a couple of rides in the cruiser, and now here the boy was: matted blood, strands of hair—

He breathed through his fingers and looked down at the presents. He'd seen blood before, he'd seen all kinds of deaths, mostly on the sides of highways, but twice because of bullets to the head. He told himself to pretend it was no different. He tried to focus, made himself pick out words on the presents' tags.

No help there. Wayne had bought gifts for them all. *To Danny, From Daddy. To Mommy, From Daddy.* All written in Wayne's blocky letters. Jesus H.

Larry knew he should go, just go out and sit in his cruiser until midnight, but he couldn't help himself. He picked up one of Jenny's presents, a small one that had slid almost completely under the couch, and sat down in the dining room with the box on his lap. He shouldn't do this, it was wrong, but really—who was left to know that a present was missing? Larry wasn't family, but he was close enough— he had some rights here. Who, besides him, would ever unwrap them? The presents belonged to Wayne's parents now. Would they want to see what their son had bought for the family he'd butchered? Not if they had any sense at all.

Larry went into the kitchen, looking down only to step where the rusty smears weren't. Under the sink he found garbage bags; he took one and shook it open.

He sat back down in the dining room. The gift was only a few inches square, wrapped in gold foil paper. Larry slid a finger under a taped seam, then carefully tore the paper away. Inside was a small, light cardboard box, also taped. He could see Wayne's fingerprint caught in the tape glue. He slit the tape with his thumbnail, then held the lid lightly between his palms and shook out the container onto his lap.

Wayne had bought Jenny lingerie. A silk camisole and matching panty, in red, folded small.

Jenny liked red. Her skin took to it, somehow; she was always a little pink. The bust of the camisole was transparent, lacy. She would look impossible in it. That was Jenny, though. She could slip on a T-shirt and look like your best pal. Or she could put on a little lipstick and do her hair and wear a dress, and she'd look like she ought to be up on a movie screen someplace. Larry ran his fingers over the silk. He wondered if Wayne had touched the lingerie this way, too, and what he might have been thinking when he did. Did he know, when he bought it? When had he found out?

Don't be coy with me, Wayne had said, on the phone. He'd called Larry at his house; Emily would have picked up if her hands weren't soapy with dishwater. Larry watched her scrub at the roast pan while he listened. *I know*, Wayne said. *I followed you to the motel. I just shot her, Larry. I shot her in the head.*

Larry dumped the lingerie and the wrappings into the garbage bag.

He took the bag upstairs with him, turning off the living-room light behind him and turning on the one in the stairwell. He had to cling tight to the banister to get past the spot where Wayne had shot the dog—a big husky named Kodiak, rheumy-eyed and arthritic. Kodiak didn't care much for the children, who tried to uncurl his tail, so most of the time he slept in a giant basket in the sewing room upstairs. He must have jumped awake at the sound of gunshots. He would have smelled what was wrong right away. Jenny had gotten him as a puppy during high school—Larry had been dating her then; he remembered sitting on the kitchen floor with her at her parents' house, the dog skidding happily back and forth between them. Kodiak had grown old loving Jenny. He must have stood on the landing and growled and barked at Wayne, before Wayne shot him. Larry had seen dogs driven vicious by bloodshed; it turned on switches in their heads. He hoped Kodiak had at least made a lunge for Wayne, before getting shot.

Larry walked into Wayne and Jenny's bedroom. He'd been in it before. Just once. Wayne had gone to Chicago on business, and the kids were at a friend's, and Jenny called Larry—at the station. She told dispatch she thought she saw someone in the woods, maybe a hunter, and would the sheriff swing by and run him off? That was smart of her. That way Larry could go in broad daylight and smoke in the living room and drink a cup of coffee, and no one would say boo.

And, as it turned out, Jenny could set his coffee down on the dining-room table, and then waggle her fingers at him from the foot of the stairs. And he would get hard just at the sight of her doing it, Jenny Sullivan smiling at him in sweatpants and an old T-shirt.

And upstairs she could say, *Not the bed.*

They'd stood together in front of the mirror over the low bureau, Jenny bent forward, both of them with their pants pulled down mid-thigh, and Larry gritting his teeth just to last a few minutes. Halfway through he took his hat from the bureau top—he' brought it upstairs with them and couldn't remember why—and set it on her head, and she'd looked up and met his eyes in the mirror, and both of them were laughing when they started to come. Jenny's laugh turned into something like a shriek. He said, *I never heard you sound like that before*, and Jenny said, *I've never sounded like that before. Not in this room.* She said, *This house has never heard anything like it.* And when she said it, it was like the house was Wayne, like somehow he'd walked in. They both turned serious and sheepish—Jenny's mouth got small and grim—and they'd separated, pulled their clothes up, pulled themselves together.

Now Larry went through the drawers of the bureau, trying to remember what Jenny wore that day. The blue sweatpants. The Butler Bulldogs shirt. Bright pink socks—he remembered her feet, going up the stairs ahead of him. He found a pair that seemed right, rolled tight together. Silk panties, robin's-egg blue. He found a fluffy red thing that she used to keep her ponytail together. Little fake-ruby earrings in a ceramic seashell. He smelled through the perfumes next to her vanity and found one he liked and remembered, and sprayed it on the clothes, heavily... it would fade over time, and if it was too strong now, in ten years it wouldn't be.

He packed all of it into the plastic bag from the kitchen.

Then he sat at the foot of the bed, eyes closed, for a long few minutes. He could hear his own breath. His eyes stung. He looked at the backs of his hands and concentrated on keeping steady. He thought about the sound of Wayne's voice when he called. *I left her sexy for you, Larry.*

That made him feel like something other than weeping.

When he was composed he looked through the desks in the bedroom and the drawers of all the bed tables. He glanced at his watch: it was only eight.

He walked down the hall into the sewing room, and sat at Jenny's sewing table. The room smelled like Kodiak—an old-dog smell, a mixture of the animal and the drops he had to have in his ears. Pictures of the children and Jenny's parents dotted the walls. Wayne's bespectacled head peeped out of a few, too—but not very many, when you looked hard.

Larry rooted through a drawer under the table. Then he opened Jenny's sewing basket.

He hadn't known what he was looking for, but in the sewing basket he found it. He opened a little pillowed silk box full of spare buttons, and inside, pinned to the lid, was a slip of paper. He knew it right away from the green embossment—it was from a stationery pad he'd found, at the motel he and Jenny had sometimes used in Westover. He unfolded it. His hands shook, and he was crying now—she'd kept it, she'd kept something.

This was from a year ago, on a Thursday afternoon; Wayne had taken the boys to see his folks. Larry met Jenny at the motel after she was done at the school.

Jenny wanted to sleep for an hour or two after they made love, but Larry was due home, and it was better for them to come and go separately anyway, so he dressed quietly while she dozed. He'd looked at her asleep for a long time, and then he'd written a note. He remembered thinking at the time: *evidence*. But he couldn't help it. Some things needed to be put down in writing; some things you had to sign your name to, if they were going to mean anything at all.

So Larry found the stationery pad, and wrote, *My sweet Jenny*, and got teary when he did. He sat on the bed next to her, and leaned over and kissed her warm ear. She stirred and murmured without opening her eyes. He finished the note and left it by her hand.

A week later he asked her, *Did you get my note?*

She said, *No.* But then she kissed him, and smiled, and put her small hands on his cheeks. *Of course I did, you dummy.*

He'd been able to remember the words on the note—he'd run them over and over in his head—but now he opened the folded paper and read them again: *My sweet Jenny, I have trouble with these things but I wouldn't do this if I didn't love you.*

And then he read on. He dropped the note onto the tabletop and stared at it, his hand clamped over his mouth.

He'd signed it *Yours, Larry*—but his name had been crossed out. And over it had been written, in shaky block letters: *Wayne*.

December 24, 1975

If Jenny ever had to tell someone—a stranger, the sympathetic man she imagined coming to the door sometimes, kind of a traveling psychologist and granter of divorces all wrapped up in one—about what it was like to be married to Wayne Sullivan, she would have told him about tonight. She'd say, *Wayne called me at six, after my parents got here for dinner, after I'd gotten the boys into their good clothes for the Christmas picture, to tell me he wouldn't be home for another couple of hours. He had some last-minute shopping, he said.*

Jenny was washing dishes. The leftovers from the turkey had already been sealed in Tupperware and put into the refrigerator. From the living room she could hear Danny with her mother; her father was with Alex in the playroom—she could hear Alex squealing every few minutes, or shouting nonsense in his two-year-old singsong. It was 8:40. Almost three hours later, she told the man in her head, and no sign of him. And that's Wayne. There's a living room full of presents. All anyone wants of him now is his presence at the table. And he thinks he hasn't done enough, and so our dinner is ruined. It couldn't be more typical.

Her mother was reading to Danny; she was a schoolteacher, too, and Jenny could hear the careful cadences, the little emphases that meant she was acting out the story with her voice. Her mother had been heroic tonight. She was a master of keeping up appearances, and here, by God, was a time when her gifts were needed. Jenny's father had started to bluster when Jenny announced Wayne was going to be late—*Jennifer, I swear to you I think that man does this on purpose*—but her mother had gotten up on her cane and gone to her father, and put a hand on his shoulder, and said, *He's being sweet, dear, he's buying presents. He's doing the best he knows.*

Danny, of course, had asked after his father, and she told him *Daddy will be a little late*, and he whined, and Alex picked up on it, and then her mother called both of them over to the couch and let them pick the channel on the television, and for the most part they forgot. Just before dinner was served her mother hobbled into the kitchen, and Jenny kissed her on the forehead. *Thank you*, she said.

He's an odd man, her mother said.

You're not telling me anything new.

But loving. He is loving.

Her mother stirred the gravy, a firm smile on her face.

They'd eaten slowly, eyes on the clock—Jenny waited a long time to announce dessert—and at eight she gave up and cleared the dishes. She put a plate of turkey and potatoes—Wayne wouldn't eat anything else—into the oven.

Jenny scrubbed at the dishes—the same china they'd had since their wedding, even the plates they'd glued together after their first anniversary dinner. She thought, for the hundredth time, what her life would be like if she was in Larry's kitchen now, instead of Wayne's.

Larry and Emily had bought a new house the previous spring, on the other side of the county, to celebrate Larry's election as sheriff. Of course Jenny had gone to see it with Wayne and the boys, but she'd been by on her own a couple of times, too—Emily saw her grandmother twice a month, at a nursing home in Michigan, staying away for the weekends. Jenny had made her visits in summer, when she didn't teach, while Wayne was at work. She dropped the boys at her folks', and parked her car out of sight from the road. It was a nice house, big and bright, with beautiful bay windows that let in the evening sun, filtering it through the leaves of two huge maples in the front yard. Larry wouldn't use his and Emily's bed—*God, it wouldn't be right, even if I don't love her*—so they made love on the guest bed, narrow and squeaky. It was the same bed Larry had slept on in high school, which gave things a nice nostalgic feel; this was the bed in which Larry had first touched her breasts, way back in the mists of time, when she was sixteen. Now she and Larry lay in the guest room all afternoon. They laughed and chattered; when Larry came (with a bellow she would have found funny, if it didn't turn her on so much), it was like a cork popped out from his throat, and he'd talk for hours about the misadventures of the citizens of Kinslow. All the while he'd touch her with his big hands.

I should have slept with you in high school, she told him, during one of those afternoons. *I would never have gone on to anyone else.*

Well, I told you so.

She laughed. But sometimes this was because she was trying very hard not to cry—not in front of Larry, not when they had so few hours together. He worried after her constantly, and she wanted him to think as many good thoughts about her as he could.

I married the wrong guy, was what she wanted to tell him, but she couldn't. They had just, in a shy way, admitted they were in love, but neither one had been brave enough to bring up what they were going to do about it. Larry had just been elected; even though he was doing what his father had done, he was the youngest sheriff anyone had ever heard of, and a scandal and a divorce would probably torpedo future terms. And being sheriff was a job Larry wanted—the only job he'd wanted, why he'd gone into the police force instead of off to college, like her and Wayne. If only he had! She and Wayne had never been friends in high school, but in college they got to know each other because they had Larry in common—because she pined for Larry, and Wayne was good at making her laugh, at making her feel not so lonely. At being gentle and kind—not like every other boozed-up asshole trying for a grope.

And, back home, Larry met Emily at church—he called Jenny one night during her sophomore year, to tell her he was in love, that he was happy, and he hoped Jenny would be happy for him, too.

I'm seeing Wayne, she said, blurting it out, relieved she could finally say it.

Really? Larry had paused. *Our Wayne?*

But as much as Jenny now daydreamed about being Larry's wife (which, these days, was a lot) she knew such a thing was unlikely at best. She could only stand here waiting for the husband she did have—who might as well be a third son—to figure out it was family time, and think of Larry sitting in his living room with Emily. They probably weren't talking, either—Emily would be watching television, with Larry sitting in his den, his nose buried in a Civil War book. Or thinking of her. Jenny's stomach thrilled.

But what was she thinking? It was Christmas Eve at the Thompkins's house, too, and Larry's parents were over; Jenny's mother was good friends with Mrs. Thompkins and had said something about it earlier. Larry's house would be a lot like hers was, except maybe even happier. Larry and his father and brother would be knocking back a special eggnog recipe, and Emily and Mrs. Thompkins got along better than Emily and Larry did; they'd be gossiping over cookie dough in the kitchen. The thought of all that activity and noise made Jenny's throat tighten. It was better, somehow, to think of Larry's house as unhappy; better to think of it as an empty place, too big for Larry, needing her and the children—

She was drying her hands when she heard the car grumbling in the trees. Wayne had been putting off getting a new muffler. She sighed, then called out, Daddy's home!

Daddy! Danny called. Gramma, finally!

She wished Wayne could hear that.

She looked out the kitchen window and saw Wayne's car pull up in front of the garage, the wide white glow of his headlights getting smaller and more specific on the garage door. He parked too close to the door. Jenny had asked him time and time again to give her room to back the Vega out of the garage if she needed to. She could see Wayne behind the wheel, his Impala's orange dashboard lights shining onto his face. He had his glasses on; she could see the reflections, little match lights.

She imagined Larry coming home, outside a different kitchen window, climbing out of his cruiser. She imagined her sons calling him Daddy. The fantasy was almost blasphemous—but it made her tingle, at the same time. Larry loved the boys, and they loved him; she sometimes stopped at the station house, and Larry would take them for a ride in his cruiser. His marriage to Emily might be different if they could have children of their own. Jenny wasn't supposed to know—no one did—but Emily was infertile. They'd found out just before moving into the new house.

Wayne shut off the engine. The light was out over the garage, and Jenny couldn't see him any longer; the image of the car was replaced by a curved piece of her own reflection in the window. She turned again to putting away the dishes. *I think he's bringing presents*, she heard her mother say. Danny answered this with shouts, and Alex answered him with a yodel.

Jenny thought about Wayne coming in the front door, forgetting to stamp the snow from his boots. She was going to have to go up and kiss him, pretend she didn't taste the cigarettes on his breath. He would sulk if she didn't.

This was what infuriated her most: she could explain and explain (later, when they put the kids to bed), but Wayne wouldn't understand what he'd done wrong. He'd brought the kids presents—he'd probably bought her a present. He'd been moody lately, working long hours, and—she knew—this was his apology for it. In his head he'd worked it all out; he would make a gesture that far outshone any grumpiness, any silence at the dinner table. He'd come through the door like Santa Claus. She could tell him, *The only gift I wanted was a normal family dinner*, and he'd look hurt, he'd look like she slapped him. *But,* he'd say, and the corners of his mouth would turn down, *I was just trying to*—and then he'd launch into the same story he'd be telling himself right now—

They had done this before, a number of times. Too many times. This was how the rest of the night was going to go. And the thought of it all playing out, so predictably—

Jenny set a plate down on the counter. She blinked; her nose stung. The thought of Wayne made her feel ill. Her husband was coming into his house on Christmas Eve, and she couldn't bear it.

About a month ago she'd called in a trespasser, while Wayne was away in Chicago. This was risky, she knew, but she had gotten weepy—just like this—knowing she and Larry wouldn't be able to see each other again for weeks. She'd asked if the sheriff could come out to the house, and the sheriff came. He looked so happy when she opened the door to him, when he realized Wayne was gone. She took him upstairs, and they did it, and then afterward she said, *Now you surprise me*, and so he took her out in the cruiser, to a nearby stretch of road, empty for a mile ahead and behind, and he said *Hang on*, and floored it. The cruiser seemed almost happy to oblige him. She had her hands on the dashboard, and the road—slightly hilly— lifted her up off the seat, dropped her down again, made her feel like a girl. *You're doing one-twenty*, Larry said, calm as ever, in between her shrieks. *Unfortunately, we're out of road.*

At the house she hugged him, kissed his chin. He'd already told her, in a way, but now she told him, *I love you*. He'd blushed to his ears.

She was going to leave Wayne.

Of course she'd thought about it; she'd been over the possibilities idly, on and off for the last four years, and certainly since taking up with Larry. But now she knew; she'd crossed some point of balance. She'd been waiting for something to happen with Larry, but she would have to act even sooner. The planning would take a few months, at most. She'd have to have a place lined up somewhere else. A job—maybe in Indy, but certainly out of Kinslow. And then she would tell Larry— she'd have to break it to him gently, but she would tell him, once and for all—that she was his for the taking, if he could manage it.

This was it: she didn't love her husband—in fact she didn't much like him— and was never going to feel anything for him again. It had to be done. Larry or no Larry, it had to be done.

Something out the window caught her eye. Wayne had the passenger door of the Impala open, and was bent inside; she could see his back under the dome lamp. What was he doing? Maybe he'd spilled his ashtray. She went to the window and put her face close to the glass.

He backed out of the car, and stood straight. He saw her, and stood looking at her for a moment in front of the open car door. He wiped his nose with his gloved hand. Was he crying? She felt a flicker of guilt, as though somehow he'd heard her thoughts. But then he smiled, and lifted a finger: *Just a second.*

She did a quick beckon with her hand—*Get your ass in here*—and made a face, eyeballs rolled toward the rest of the house. *Now.*

He shook his head, held the finger up again.

Jenny crossed her arms. She'd see Larry next week; Emily was going to Michigan. She could begin to tell him then.

Wayne bent into the car, then straightened up again. He grinned.

She held her hands out at her sides, palms up: *What? I'm waiting.*

1970

When Wayne had first told her he wanted to blindfold her, Jenny's fear was that he was trying out some kind of sex game, some spice-up-your-love-life idea he'd gotten out of the advice column in *Playboy*. But he promised her otherwise, and led her to the car. After fifteen minutes there, arms folded across her chest, and then the discovery that he was serious about guiding her, still blindfolded, through waist-high weeds and clinging spiderwebs, she began to wish it had been sex on his mind after all.

Wayne, she said, either tell me where we're going or I'm taking this thing off.

It's not far, honey, he said; she could tell from his voice he was grinning. Just bear with me. I'm watching your feet for you.

They were in a woods; that was easy enough to guess. She heard the leaves overhead, and birdcalls; she smelled the thick and cloying undergrowth. Twice she stumbled and her hands scraped across tree trunks, furred vines, before Wayne tightened his grip on her arm. They were probably on a path; even blind she knew the going was too easy for them to be headed directly through the bushes. So they were in Wayne's woods, the one his parents owned. Simple enough to figure out; he talked about this place constantly. He'd driven her past it a number of times, but to her it looked like any other stand of trees out in this part of the country:

solid green in summertime and dull gray-brown in winter, so thick you couldn't see light shining through from the other side.

I know where we are, she told him.

He gripped her hand and laughed. Maybe, he said, But you don't know *why*.

He had her there. She snagged her skirt on a bush and was tugged briefly between its thorns and Wayne's hand. The skirt ripped and gave. She cursed.

Sorry! Wayne said. Sorry, sorry—not much longer now.

Sunlight flickered over the top of the blindfold, and the sounds around her opened up, became more expansive. She was willing to bet they were in a clearing. A breeze blew past them, smelling of country springtime: budding leaves and manure fertilizer.

Okay, Wayne said. Are you ready?

I'm not sure, she said.

Do you love me?

Of course I love you, she said. She reached a hand out in front of her—and found he was suddenly absent. Okay, she said, enough. Give me your hand or the blindfold's off.

She heard odd sounds—was that metal? Glass?

All right, almost there, he said. Sit down.

On the ground?

No. Just sit.

She sat, his hands on her shoulders, and found, shockingly, a chair underneath her behind. A smooth metal folding chair.

Wayne then unknotted the blindfold. He whipped it away. Happy Anniversary! he said.

Jenny squinted in the revealed light, but only for a moment. She opened her eyes wide, and then saw she was sitting, as she'd thought, in a meadow, maybe fifty yards across, surrounded by tall green trees, all of them rippling in the wind. In front of her was a card table, covered with a red-and-white-checked tablecloth. The table was set with dishes—their good china, the plates at least—and two wineglasses, all wedding presents they'd only used once, on her birthday. Wayne sat in a chair opposite her, grinning, eyebrows arched. The wind blew his hair straight up off his head.

A picnic, she said. Wayne, that's lovely—thank you.

She reached her hand across the table and grasped his. He was exasperating sometimes, but no other man she'd met could reach this level of sweetness. He'd lugged this stuff out into the middle of nowhere for her—*that's* where he must have been all afternoon.

You're welcome, he said. The red spots on his cheeks spread and deepened. He lifted her hand and kissed her knuckles, then her wedding ring. He rubbed the places he'd kissed with his thumb.

He said, I'm sorry that dinner won't be as fancy as the plates, but I really couldn't get anything but sandwiches out here.

She laughed. I've eaten your cooking. We're better off with the sandwiches.

Ouch, he said. He faked a French accent: This kitten, she has the claws. But I have the milk that will tame her.

He bent and rummaged through a paper bag near his chair, then produced a bottle of red wine with a flourish and a cocked eyebrow. She couldn't help but laugh.

He uncorked the bottle and poured her a glass.

A toast.

To what?

To the first part of the surprise.

There's more?

He smiled, slyly, and lifted his glass, then said, After dinner.

He'd won her over; she didn't question it. Jenny lifted her glass, clinked rims with her husband's, and sat back with her legs crossed at the knee. Wayne bent and dug in the bag again, and then came up with wheat bread and cheese, and a package of carved roast beef in deli paper. He made her a sandwich, even slicing up a fresh tomato. They ate in the pleasant breeze.

After dinner he leaned back in his chair and rubbed his stomach. When they first started dating she thought he did this to be funny; but soon she realized he did it without thinking, after eating anything larger than a candy bar. It meant all was well in the land of Wayne. The gesture made her smile, and she looked away. Since they'd married he'd developed a small wedge of belly; she wondered—not unhappily, not here—if in twenty years he'd have a giant stomach to rub, like his father's.

So I was right? She asked. This is your parents' woods?

Nope, he said, smiling.

It's not?

It was. They don't own it any more.

They sold it? When? To who?

Yesterday. He was grinning broadly now. To me, he said. To us.

She sat forward, then back. Wayne glanced around at the trees, his hair tufting in a sudden pickup of the wind.

You're serious, she said. Her stomach tightened. This was a feeling she'd had a few times since their wedding—she was learning that the more complicated Wayne's ideas were, the less likely they were to be good ones. A picnic in the woods? Fine. But this?

I'm serious, Wayne said. This is my favorite place in the world—second-favorite, I mean. He winked at her, then went on. But either way. Both of my favorite places are mine now. Ours.

She touched a napkin to her lips. So, she said, how much did—did *we* pay for our woods?

A dollar. He laughed, and said, Can you believe it? Dad wanted to give it to us, but I told him, No, Pop, I want to *buy* it. We ended up compromising.

She could only stare at him. He squeezed her hand, and said, We're landowners now, honey. One square mile.

That's—

Wayne said, Dad wanted to sell it off, and I couldn't bear the thought of it going to somebody who was going to plow it all under.

We need to pay your parents more than a dollar, Wayne. That's absurd.

That's what I told them. But Dad said no, we needed the money more. But honey—there's something else. That's only part of the surprise.

Jenny twined her fingers together in front of her mouth. A suspicion had formed, and she hoped he wasn't about to do what she guessed. Wayne was digging beside his chair again. He came up with a long roll of paper—blueprint paper, held with a rubber band. He put it on the table between them.

Our paper anniversary, he said.

What is this?

Go ahead. Look at it.

Jenny knew what the plans would show. She rolled the rubber band off the blueprints, her mouth dry. Wayne stood, his hands quick and eager, and spread the prints flat on the tabletop. They were upside down; she went around the table and stood next to him. He put a hand on the small of her back.

The blueprints were for a house. A simple two-story house—the ugliest thing she had ever seen.

I didn't want to tell you too soon, he said, but I got a raise at the bank. Plus, now that I've been there three years, I get a terrific deal on home loans. I got approval a few days ago.

A house, she said.

They were living in an apartment in Kinslow, nice enough, but bland, sharing a wall with an old woman who complained if they spoke above a whisper, or if they played rock-and-roll records. Jenny put a hand to her hair. Wayne, she said, where is this house going to be?

Here, he said, and grinned again. He held his arms out. Right here. The table is on the exact spot. The contractors start digging on Monday. The timing's perfect. It'll be done by the end of summer.

Here…in the woods.

Yep.

He laughed, watching her face, and said, We're only three miles from town. The interstate's just on the other side of the field to the south. The county road is paved. All we have to do is have them expand the path in and we'll have a driveway. It'll be our hideaway. Honey?

She sat down in the chair he'd been sitting in. She could barely speak. They had talked about buying a house soon—but one in town. They'd also talked about moving to Indianapolis, about leaving Kinslow—maybe not right away, but within five years.

Wayne, she said. Doesn't this all feel kind of…permanent?

Well, he said, it's a house. It's supposed to.

We just talked last month. You wanted to get a job in the city. I want to live in the city. A five-year plan, remember?

Yeah. I do.

He knelt next to her chair and put his arm across her shoulders.

But I've been thinking, he said. The bank is nice, really nice, and the money just got better, and then Dad was talking about getting rid of the land, and I couldn't bear to hear it, and—

And so you went ahead and did it without asking me.

Um, Wayne said, it seemed like such a great deal that—

Okay, she told him. Okay. It is a great deal. If it was just different. What it means is that you're building your dream house right in the spot I want to move away from. I hate to break it to you, but that means it's not quite my dream house.

Wayne removed his hand from her shoulders, and clasped his fingers in front of his mouth. She knew that gesture, too.

Wayne—

I really thought this would make you happy, he said.

A house *does* make me happy. But one in Kinslow. One we can sell later and not feel bad about, when we move—

She wasn't sure what happened next. Wayne told her it was an accident, that he stood up too fast and hit his shoulder on the table. And it looked that way, sometimes, when she thought back on it. But when it happened, she was sure he flung his arm out, that he knocked the table aside. That he did it on purpose. The wine-glasses and china plates flew out and disappeared into the clumps of yellow grass. The blueprints caught in a tangle with the tablecloth and the other folding chair.

Goddamnit! Wayne shouted. He walked a quick circle, holding his hand close to his chest.

Jenny was too stunned to move, but then, after a minute, she said Wayne's name.

He shook his head and kept walking the circle. Jenny saw he was crying, and when he saw her looking, he turned his face away. She sat still in her chair, not certain what to say or do. Finally she knelt to assemble the pieces of a broken dish.

After a minute he said, I think I'm bleeding.

She stood and walked to him and saw that he was. He'd torn a gash in his hand, on the meaty outside of his palm. A big one; it would need stitches. His shirt was soaked with blood where he'd cradled his hand.

Come on, she said. We need to get you to the hospital.

No, he said. His voice was low and miserable.

Wayne, don't be silly. This isn't a time to sulk. You're hurt.

No. Hear me out. Okay? You always say what you want, and you make me sound stupid for saying what I want. This time I just want to say it.

She grabbed some napkins and pressed them against his hand. Jesus, Wayne, she said, seeing blood from the cut well up across her fingers. Okay, okay, say what you need to.

This is my favorite place, he said. I've loved it since I was a kid. I used to come out here with Larry. He and I used to imagine we had a house here. A hideaway.

Well—

Be quiet. I'm not done yet. His lip quivered, and he said, I know we talked, I know you want to go to Indy. Well, we can. But it looks like we're going to be successful. It looks like I'm going to do well and you can get a job teaching anywhere. I'll just work hard and in five years maybe we can have two houses—

Oh, Wayne—

Listen! We can have a house in Indy and then this—this can be our getaway. He sniffled, and said, But I want to keep it. Besides you, this is the only thing I want. This house, right out here.

We can talk about it later. You're going to bleed to death if we don't get you to the emergency room.

I wanted you to love it, he said. I wanted you to love it because *I* love it. Is that too much to ask from your wife? I wanted to give you something *special*. I—

It was awful, watching him try to explain. The spots of red in his cheeks were burning now, and the rims of his eyes were almost the same color. The corners of his mouth turned down in little curls.

Don't worry, she said. We'll talk about it. Okay? Wayne? We'll talk. We'll take the blueprints with us to the emergency room. But you need stitches. Let's go.

I love you, he said.

She stopped fussing around his hand. He was looking down at her, tilting his head.

Jenny, just tell me you love me and none of it will matter.

She laughed in spite of herself, shaking her head. Of course, she said. Of course I do.

Say it. I need to hear it.

She kissed his cheek. Wayne, I love you with all my heart. You're my husband. Now move your behind, okay?

He kissed her, dipping his head. Jenny was bending away to pick up the blueprints, and his lips, wet, just grazed her cheek. She smiled at him and gathered their things; Wayne stood and watched her, moist-eyed.

She finally took his good hand, and they walked back toward the car, and his kiss, dried slowly by the breeze, felt cool on her cheek. It lingered for a while, and—despite everything—she was glad for it.

Then

The boys were first audible only as distant shrieks between the trees.

They were young enough that any time they raised their voices—and they were chasing each other, their only sounds loud calls, denials, laughter—they sounded as though they were in terror. When they appeared in the meadow—one charging out from a break in a dense thicket of thorny shrubs, the other close behind—they were almost indistinguishable from one another in their squeals, in their red jackets and caps. Late afternoon was shifting into dusky evening. Earlier they had hunted squirrels, unaware of how the sounds of their voices and the pops of their BB guns had traveled ahead of them, sending hundreds of beasts into their dens.

In the center of the meadow the trailing boy caught up with the fleeing first; he pounced and they wrestled. Caps came off. One boy was blond, the other—the smaller one—mousy brown. Stop it, he called, from the bottom of the pile. Larry! Stop it! I mean it!

Larry laughed, and said with a shudder, Wayne, you pussy.

Don't call me that!

Don't be one, pussy!

They flailed and punched until they lay squirming and helpless with laughter.

Later they pitched a tent in the center of the meadow. They had done this before. Near their tent was an old circle of charred stones, ringing a pile of damp ashes and cinders. Wayne wandered out of the meadow and gathered armfuls of deadwood while Larry secured the tent into the soft and unstable earth. They squatted down around the piled wood and worked at setting it alight. Darkness was coming; beneath the gray, overcast sky, light was diffuse anyway, and now it seemed that the shadows came not from above, but from below, pooling and deepening as though they welled up from underground springs. Larry was the first to look nervously into the shadowed trees, while Wayne threw matches into the wood. Wayne worked at the fire with his face twisted, mouth pursed. When the fire caught at last, the boys grinned at each other.

I wouldn't want to be out here when it's dark, Larry said, experimentally.

It's dark now.

No, I mean with no fire. Pitch dark.

I have, Wayne said.

No you haven't.

Sure I have. Sometimes I forget what time it is and get back to my bike late. Once it got totally dark. If I wasn't on the path I would have got lost.

Wayne poked at the fire with a long stick. His parents owned the woods, but their house was two miles away. Larry looked around him, impressed.

Were you scared?

Shit, yeah. Wayne giggled. It was dark. I'm not *dumb*.

Larry looked at him for a while, then said, Sorry I called you a pussy.

Wayne shrugged, and said, I should have shot that squirrel.

They'd seen one in a tree, somehow oblivious to them. Wayne was the better shot, and they'd crouched together behind a nearby log. Wayne's BB gun steadied in the crotch of a dead branch. He'd looked at the squirrel for a long time, before finally lifting his cheek from the gun. I can't, he'd said.

What do you mean, you can't?

I can't. That's all.

He handed the gun to Larry, and Larry took aim, too fast, and missed.

It's all right, Larry said now, at the fire. Squirrel tastes like shit.

So does baloney, Wayne said, grim.

They pulled sandwiches from their packs. Both took the meat from between the bread, speared it with sticks, and held it over the fire until it charred and sizzled. Then they put it back into the sandwiches. Wayne took a bite first, then squealed and held a hand to his mouth. He spit a hot chunk of meat into his hand, then fumbled it into the fire.

It's hot, he said.

Larry looked at him for a long time. Pussy, he said, and couldn't hold in his laughter.

Wayne ducked his eyes and felt inside his mouth with his fingers.

Later, the fire dimmed. They sat sleepily beside it, talking in low voices. Wayne rubbed his stomach. Things unseen moved in the trees—mostly small animals, from the sound of it, but once or twice larger things.

Deer, probably, Wayne said.

What about wildcats?

No wildcats live around here. I've seen foxes, though.

Foxes aren't that big.

They spread out their sleeping bags inside the tent and opened the flap a bit so they could see the fire.

This is my favorite place, Wayne said, when they zipped into the bags.

The tent?

No. The meadow. I've been thinking about it. I want to have a house here someday.

A house?

Yeah.

What kind of house?

I don't know. Like mine, I guess, but out here. I could walk onto the porch at night and it would be just like this. But you wouldn't have to pitch a tent. You know what? We could both have it. We'd each get half of the house to do whatever we want in. We wouldn't have to go home before it gets dark, because we'd already be there.

Larry smiled, but said, That's dumb. We'll both be married by then. You won't want me in your house all the time.

That's not true.

You won't get married?

No—I mean, yeah, I will. Sure. But you can always come over.

It's not like that, Larry said, laughing.

How do you now?

Because it isn't. Jesus Christ, Wayne. Sometimes I wonder what planet you live on.

You always make my ideas sound dumb.

So don't have dumb ideas.

It isn't a dumb idea to have my friends in my house.

Larry sighed, and said, No, it isn't. But marriage is different. You get married and then the girl you marry is your best friend. That's what being in love is.

My dad has best friends.

Mine, too. But who does your dad spend more time with—them or your mom?

Wayne thought for a minute. Oh.

They looked out the tent flap at the fire.

Wayne said, You'll come over when you can, though, right?

Sure, Larry said. You bet.

They lay on their stomachs and Wayne talked about the house he wanted to build. It would have a tower. It would have a secret hallway built into the walls. It would have a pool table in the basement, better than the one at Vic's Pizza King in town. It would have a garage big enough for three cars.

Four, Larry said. We'll each have two. A sports car and a truck.

Four, Wayne said, a four-car garage. And a pinball machine. I'll have one in the living room, rigged so you don't have to put money in it.

After a while, Wayne heard Larry's breathing soften. He looked out the tent flap at the orange coals of the fire. He was sleepy, but he didn't want to sleep, not yet. He thought about his house and watched the fire fade.

He wished for the house to be here in the meadow now. Larry could have half, and he could have the other. He imagined empty rooms, then rooms packed with toys. But that wasn't the way it would be. They'd be grown-ups. He imagined a long mirror in the bedroom and tried to see himself in it: older, as a man. He'd have rifles, not BB guns. He tried to imagine things that a man would have, that a boy wouldn't: bookshelves, closets full of suits and ties.

Then he saw a woman at the kitchen table, wearing a blue dress. Her face kept changing—he couldn't quite see it. But he knew she was pretty. He saw himself opening the kitchen door, swinging a briefcase which he put down at his feet, and he held out his arms, and the woman stood to welcome him, making a happy girlish sound, and held out her arms, too. Then she was close. He smelled her perfume, and she said—in a woman's voice, warm and honeyed—*Wayne*, and he felt a leaping excitement, like he'd just been scared—but better, much better—and he laughed and squeezed her and said, into her soft neck and hair, his voice deep: *I'm home*.

Intruder

BY JOHN BODEN

Don't you just hate it when people touch your stuff? Especially when they don't wash their hands first, and then you have to wash your hands, and all the things they touched, including the scissors you just stabbed them in the neck with repeatedly 'cause they WOULDN'T STOP TOUCHING YOUR STUFF?

This sneaky, screwy, sardonic little creeper-in-the-night, by Shock Totem coeditor and Peter Gabriel enthusiast John Boden, would be the flat-out funniest story in the book were it not for the handful of true squirmy moments that remind you you're still deep in horror country.

The clouds are like thumbprint smudges on dark glass. I pull my zipper tighter, put the hood up and stay close to the buildings that edge the alley. I like that the places I choose are within walking distance. I like the fact that I know these people, some mere passing acquaintances, others close neighbors and friends. Almost like it's my neighborhood and I do as I like.

I'm counting my steps by twos, up to nearly three-hundred, when I see the garage that I marked earlier that day. All the damn houses in this development look the same. Cookie-cuttery eyesores straight outta 80's Spielberg. Once the sun disappears it's too easy to become disoriented, so I marked it with a small dab of mud. A tiny dot above the center window in the garage door. Dot marks the spot. I lick my gloved thumb and wipe the mud from the white aluminum, then duck around the building to the waiting path. I'm at twenty-four steps by the time I reach the gate.

The metal is chilled by the autumn night. I feel it through my gloves. I pull the latch back and step inside the yard. I am up to ten when I stop in my tracks. Did I latch the gate? I walk backward, counting backward by twos until I am reacquainted with *numero two-O*. The gate is latched. Dammit. I start again. I make it nearly to the side porch before the nagging begins again. The gate is not latched. Sure it is, I already checked it. Did I? I'm positive. My forehead is sweating and I'm starting the shake a little. Fuck me. I step off the deck and walk back through the yard, counting and cursing simultaneously. I had latched the gate. You down with OCD? Yeah, you know me! I line up her trash cans in a perfect row before I go back toward the house.

I carefully unscrew the bulb from the porch light. I can pick the lock easily enough without illumination. I had memorized all of the *Time Life Home Repair* books by the time I was six. I'm an unsung master at wiring and locks, plumbing and heating, windows and doors. I can also tell you the model name and number of your ceiling fan, faucets and microwave at a glance.

I slip inside. The house is immaculate, not enough for someone like me, but far from what a normal person would consider a mess. I adjust the light on my headband and turn it on. My gaze follows the soft beam as I take in the kitchen. Three tall chairs, a butcher block table. On the table is a large purse, a handful of change, sixty-seven cents, actually. Keys, a cell phone and a pack of cinnamon gum. I turn to make my way through the house and stop dead. On the counter beside the sink is a plate with a partially eaten sandwich on it, a soiled fork and an empty glass with lipstick on its edge. I feel nausea begin to boil in my stomach. Repulsed, I close my eyes and begin to count. By threes. I throw the partial sandwich away and turn the water on, barely above a trickle, to wash the items. I make no sound placing them in the strainer or when drying my hands. I put the lid down on the trash bin on my way out of the room.

The living room is large and tidy. All the times I stood out front and talked while I delivered the mail, I never would have guessed the home was this spacious. The room holds a sofa, a couch, two bookshelves, a chair and two end tables. On one of the tables, there is a stack of catalogs and periodical propaganda, which is stacked incorrectly, all the spines to one side. This makes the pile slide in an untidy manner. I sigh through my nose and fix them, intermittently alternating the spines to keep the pile level and neat. That completed, I refold the throw blankets and arrange the pillows by size on the sofa. I align all the rugs symmetrically with the walls. I straighten all of the papers on the desk. I organize her CDs and DVDs, put her books into their proper order on the shelves. I straighten the lampshades and all the pictures on the walls, precisely. All without making a sound. I sit down and give my roaring nerves a brief rest. In my head, I recite William Burroughs' "Thanksgiving Prayer." It is exactly 1:13 a.m. I approach the stairs. I start counting.

Her bedroom door is open just a crack. The air smells of her soap and shampoo and skin. I outen the light on my head and peer into the cavernous room. The faint moonlight that has managed to escape its cloudy bonds splashes the walls in an eerie glow. I've always found the woman lying on the bed beautiful, but tonight, she is breathtaking. She sleeps soundly, her little snores like bees buzzing, filling the room. Her skin is as smooth as china and nearly as white. Paper doll white. Her black hair spreads out around her like a spray of blood. I resist the urge to punch her sleeping face as hard as I can. I fight the impulse to lean down and kiss her. To bite and swallow her cheeks. I stand and stare.

Thirty-seven seconds later, I smile and go to my next destination.

The bathroom is at the end of the hall. I close the door and slowly open the sink cabinet. I find certain items and set them atop the Formica counter, next to the brushes and combs. I pull down my pants and groom my pubic hair with her combs and brushes. I clench my hands into tight fists, four times. I squeeze my eyes tight with each clench and exhale deeply. I open them and get to work. I dull all of her razors with soap. I pour bathroom cleaner into her shampoo and conditioner. I put astringent into her mouthwash. I use her deodorant on my taint. I sit on her toilet and stick her toothbrush up my asshole and color the rim with her lipstick. Pull my pants up. I go through her medicine cabinet and note the contents. I can tell by her meds that she's hopelessly crazy. Before I go, I put a pinhole in her diaphragm and re-hang her toilet paper the correct way, with the end facing out.

I navigate the staircase in total darkness. Counting every step. Fourteen from the bathroom to her bedroom door, another ten from that doorway to the landing. Eighteen from the landing down the stairs to the living room. I unplug her phone and everything else in the room. Two-four-six-eight-ten-twelve-fourteen-Kitchen-Ho!

I bend the tines on all of her forks. Put salt in her sugar bowl and fill her salt shaker with sugar. I open the fridge and start in on the contents. I pour out her pitcher of ice water and refill it with white vinegar. I stick straight pins into her apples and pears. I use one of the needles to puncture her eggs and empty them of yolk and white. I loosen the lids to all of the jars and bottles in the kitchen. Syrups, sauces, spices, jellies and jams. All of them. Leaving them just tight enough to allow her to pick them up before.

My problem is that I'm always thinking. Dredging up years' worth of trivia about rock musicians, movies, sports and history. I hear song lyrics while I'm talking myself out of stabbing the counter girl at the coffee shop in the face. I recite biblical psalms while watching pornography. I run through the contents of manuals and books while I walk my route each day. I can smile and shake your hand, stuff letters in your hungry mail slot, all while ranking serial killers by geographical location and body count or alphabetically. There is always too much noise and interference. A dull static, peppered with errant voices. Swatches of songs and movie dialogue. An enormous mural of fresh paint in a rain storm, it's a runny garish mess. Did I mention this is all the time? While counting or twitching or planning or sleeping. Shitting or pissing or working or fucking or whatever. My mind never stops. Even now, I'm working out next week's schedule in my head. Crazy. I used to try to make sense of the droning rhetoric in my skull. Now I just seize random commands that fly by and file them away so I may act on them later and I'm a happier camper for it. I think.

I hear a creak above me and stop—stone still. A minute crawls by, then another and another. Nothing. I exhale and step toward the door. My foot bumps something and I look down to find a pile of shoes beside the door frame. Flip flops, a pair of boots, ratty sneakers and a pair of black shoes. I sigh and breathe out through my nostrils loudly. Disdainfully. She's a pig. I bend and align the footwear, heel to wall, straight and paired. I fill with warmth as I stand. I take a piece of gum from her pack upon the table and slip out and into the night, stealthy as shadow.

From porch to gate, I count by fours on the exit route. I'm near the end of the alley when I stop and sigh. I didn't latch the gate. I try to resist the need to turn and go back and make sure. The pressure that is always in my chest increases like there's an exploding landmine trapped inside. My eyes begin to water and sweat oozes from all pores. "Sonofabitch," I snarl and creep back down the alley to find the gate latched. Keeping to the shrouded side of the alley, I make my way home.

I get nearly two blocks before I have to go back and check that fucking gate again.

Straycation

BY SCOTT BRADLEY AND PETER GIGLIO

You can tell a lot about people from the way they treat their pets. Excessive pampering implies certain kinds of crazy. Obvious cruelty, on the other hand, draws a pretty straight line to the dark side.

Scott Bradley and Peter Giglio are the components of a two-headed writing machine whose first joint novel, The Dark, *should be in print by the time this book appears. With "Straycation," they pay a strangely sideways and cunning homage to Thomas Harris, with a lovely psychotic nod to all animal lovers everywhere.*

1.

The young couple couldn't pull themselves away from spreadsheets and reports long enough to look at one another, let alone at Tabitha Greyson, for which she gave silent thanks. Having the uneasy burden of sitting next to them on the plane was bad enough; actually talking to them would have been intolerable.

The woman was all wrong, with her spray tan and fake red hair and the none-too-subtle hint of plastic surgery in her cheekbones. Her loud jewelry alone was enough to make Tabitha gag.

And the man, with his tight designer T-shirt and nose splitting cologne, wouldn't have begged a second glance.

Not normally.

But Tabitha looked at them anyway, wondering if what she'd often heard had merit—that, essentially, people are what they spend most of their time doing.

She certainly hoped it wasn't true. She needed a break. That was what this trip was all about.

So she just studied them when she wasn't skimming her paperback. Didn't strike up a conversation, and mentally wished them well on their trip, whatever they were seeking from it. Little good it would do them.

But hopefully, she considered, her own journey would help *her.*

2.

A little after noon, having unpacked and napped and called to check in with Sally—her slightly dotty but kind-hearted neighbor, who was taking care of Tabitha's pets—she slipped on a summer dress and glided out of her hotel into paradise.

Much as she wanted to take in the sweet tropical scents, relish the cool ocean breeze, and wade in the warm waters, she knew there was time enough for that later. Right now she was hungry and feeling light-headed from low blood sugar.

She went to the first in a line of cabs clustered at the curb. She said to the driver, "Do you—"

"Speak English?" He laughed. "Of course. Job requirement."

She returned his grin and got in. "Is there a decent restaurant close by?"

"Question is, do you want *decent* or do you want the best?"

She considered the question. Here she was, on vacation, seeking refuge from her day-to-day worries and endless responsibilities. She didn't want to be like the couple on the plane.

Slowly, she shook her head. "You're right. I want the best. I've earned it."

He nodded and started to drive.

3.

Ten minutes later, the cab speeding down winding streets that bordered palatial monuments of architectural perfection, Tabitha saw something that broke her heart.

"Stop the car!" she shouted.

Surprised by the intensity of her demand, the driver braked and pulled to the side of the road. Tabitha wasted no time. She flung open the door and rushed to an injured dog, panting and bleeding on the roadside.

Not here, she told herself, tears welling in her eyes. *Not in paradise.*

The mangy mutt hobbled, whining with each step.

She knelt and ran a gentle hand through the dog's thin, matted fur. "What happened to you, boy? Oh, God, what happened to you?"

The dog whimpered and licked her hand. "When's the last time you had anything to eat?" she asked.

The dog's enormous, sad eyes told her much. He was starving. And his wounds—not made by claws and teeth but with clubs and knives—told her everything else. This was the work of some*one*, not something.

She gently wrapped her arms around the animal, picked him up, and hurried back to the car.

The driver was mortified. "*¿Qué demonios?!* What are you doing, lady?!"

"I'm rescuing this poor creature," Tabitha said as she rested the dog on the bench seat and climbed in.

"Fucking tourists!" he growled, eyeing the blood dripping to the car's floor. "Get that thing—"

"Just drive!" She desperately rummaged through her purse, looking for the treats she always carried. She found the bag of cat treats. Kept searching.

"Lady, that thing is fucking up my car. Get it out, *now!*"

She found the package labeled Milkbone, opened it, and spread the contents across the backseat. The dog looked at her, mystified. "Go ahead," she said. "Eat up."

And he did. Slowly at first. Then greedily.

Still smiling from the sight of the grateful dog, she looked at the driver, who had done his best to calm down.

"Look, lady," he began, "I love *el perros*. We got two at home, my family. But…" He shook his head mournfully and started to reach over the driver's seat to seize the dog.

Tabitha's hand went to her purse and whisked out the small but very sharp knife she'd unpacked from her luggage.

In one fluid motion, she jerked the blade up and into the soft spot just below the driver's chin. His eyes bulged, as much from surprise as pain. His hands reflexively grabbed her wrist, but in trying to defend himself, he only managed to guide the knife further down, into his throat.

A gurgling sputter of blood spattered Tabitha's face. She held firm, clenching her jaw. His grip loosened, eyes rolling upward. The dog continued to eat.

"Good boy," she cooed.

She scratched the dog's head as the lifeless driver slumped in the front seat.

4.

She hated driving in places she didn't know. But with her navigator, it was okay. When he turned his head left, she turned left. Right, she went right.

Animals possessed a keen sense of direction, Tabitha knew from research and experience.

They could find their way home.

5.

Narrow streets bordered shanties of unimaginable squalor, places no tourist was ever meant to see. She drove slowly, waiting for a sign from her new companion.

Finally, he barked three times then emitted a low, feral growl.

"Here?" she asked, pulling into a rutted dirt drive.

The dog barked again, and she knew he was home. She was glad it wouldn't be his home much longer.

6.

Carrying the dog in her arms, Tabitha was greeted on the rickety porch by a boy, no older than twelve or thirteen.

"Is this your dog?" she asked, putting the trembling animal down.

The boy gawked at her, clearly dumbfounded at the spectacle of the bloody and mad-eyed *gringa*.

Then he slowly started to smile. He thumped his chest proudly, speaking in rapid-fire Spanish. Tabitha nodded as if she understood him, then grabbed a handful of his hair, pulled him close to her, and cut his throat.

His body dropped. Then came a scream. Tabitha jumped, startled.

The front door burst open and an old woman, possibly the boy's mother or grandmother, staggered out, shrieking in Spanish, grabbing for the bleeding, dying boy.

Tabitha took no pleasure in what happened next, but it was thankfully over very quickly.

She dragged the woman's prone form into the house, which was ripe with the smell of something cooking. Peasant food. Not unpleasant. In fact, it smelled pretty damn nice.

Silent as a cat, she moved to the kitchen, listening for the sounds of others, but the house was still.

On the stove, a stew bubbled in a large pot. Meats and vegetables swirled, reminding Tabitha just how hungry she still was. The dog slogged into the house, regarded the old woman with a low growl, then made his way to the kitchen.

Tabitha reached two bowls down from a cupboard and filled them with heaping portions of the stew.

In the living room, the old woman moaned. Tabitha placed one of the bowls on the dirt floor. "Be careful," she warned, "it's still a little hot."

The dog didn't care; he quickly began to feed. Tabitha put her own bowl on the kitchen table then went to the living room to finish her business before enjoying a well-deserved meal.

7.

It is a complex procedure to bring an animal into the United States from another country, but not insurmountable when the other country is of the third world, where American dollars speak louder than laws.

Tabitha had brought many dollars with her, and had even more available on her credit card. Her job, after all, paid well.

She worked as a secretary at the Behavioral Sciences Division of the FBI in Quantico, Virginia; the unit charged with apprehending and studying serial killers and mass murderers.

Not that she fancied herself one of the agents, for whom she diligently worked. But Tabitha had acquired a great deal of rudimentary knowledge from simply doing her job.

She had learned, for instance, that one of the primary indications of psychopathology—particularly of the potentially homicidal sort—was cruelty to animals.

8.

"You're traveling with this animal?" the girl behind the counter asked, scrutinizing Tabitha's passport and paperwork.

"My new dog. His name is Roy," Tabitha said. "And, yes, I am. I was assured that everything was in order."

The girl nodded and grabbed the pet carrier. Roy howled.

"Be careful!" Tabitha snapped.

The girl, hearing an odd edge in Tabitha's voice, nodded apologetically, handling the carrier with greater care.

9.

On the long flight back to Maryland, Tabitha found herself sitting next to the same couple as before.

The trip had clearly done them some good. No longer engrossed in the azure glow of computer screens, they looked at each other often, even stole the occasional kiss when they thought no one was looking.

Halfway through the flight, the redheaded woman turned to Tabitha and smiled. "Did you have a nice vacation?" she asked.

She returned the woman's smile. "Yes. I did."

Tabitha reclined her seat and closed her eyes.

How will he get along, she wondered, *with his new family? With Rex and Molly and Spot and Scooby and Dash and Roger and Hank and Bert and Farful and Annie and Max and Audrey and Emma and Stanley and Herb and Tiki and . . . and . . . and . . .*

Her mind reached for another name but couldn't quite find it.

After all, with 57 cats and 21—now, with Roy, 22—dogs, it was sometimes hard to remember all of their names.

For Bella

Life Coach

BY CODY GOODFELLOW

For many people, Los Angeles is the go-to place for potentially lucrative out-of-your-mindness. An unbridled sense of entitlement is practically the name of the game. If you can successfully carve a niche for yourself that is broadcast live, it's like being dipped in gold.

As long as your market share holds, you can say or do pretty much whatever you want. And the weather is great.

The only problem is other people. And maybe their dogs.

Here to race us through the untethered paces is noted spoilsport of conventional wisdom Cody Goodfellow, who never saw a luxuriant showbiz oasis he couldn't reduce to painfully accurate houndshit and pinpoint-precise, off-the-charts mayhem.

You don't like it? Talk to your agent.

If you're lucky, she'll take your call.

This is what happens when you lose control. The moment you start to live for someone else, you become a human-shaped hole in the world. The moment you stop making things happen and become the victim of things happening, you stop being the star of the movie of your life and you become a statistic. Or worse: a story.

You're walking your dog when a tiny Smartcar pulls up and this distinguished older yuppie couple asks you for directions. "We're soooo lost," the man says.

They've come to the right place. "OK, write this down. Ditch this ridiculous car. You look like time travelers from a sad, shitty future. Get your parents' Cadillac out of the garage. Stop dressing young. Your desperation is like a hate crime. Stop recycling. If you carry on like the world will go on after you're gone, then you don't deserve to live in it, now. Spend your retirement money getting some cosmetic work done, so you can bear to fuck each other. Here, take this card and tell the doctor I sent you. Not just you, ma'am . . . you. A beard is not a chin implant, sir. Now, get out of my fucking neighborhood."

It is one of the greater paradoxes of your life, that your flaming hatred of humanity has made you one of the more sought-after life coaches in LA. And here you are out on the street, giving it away for free.

Because of the dog.

Hatred is healthy; hate gets things done, but fear is not. Doubt is not. And living alone, you sometimes feel both.

When your last boyfriend moved out, all your best frenemies told you to get a dog. Lord knows, you've recommended it to enough of your clients who want intimacy and unconditional love from something that won't ever talk back. You resolved to knock down your need for security and companionship in one play, and so picked out Clovis.

The rescue dachshund-ridgeback mix struck you as intimidating and charming at the same time. His powerful torso ripples with layers of prison-grade muscle, but his stubby legs give him a whimsical look that defuses the threat, for everybody but him. And the ghetto shock appeal of a brutalist mutt among the purebred puppy farm lapdogs your neighborhood favors salved both your conscience and need to inspire fear. Don't let a man define you. Get a monster.

The combination of lethal strength and small-dog syndrome makes him a bad fit for even the rowdiest dog parks. Clovis attacks anything that tries to sniff his ass and has to be dragged away, straining on his four-point harness and spraying froth through his muzzle.

Training made him easier to handle, but one can never let their guard down. Every morning, you run him for an hour on the winding canyon streets around your split-level mid-century stilt-propped bungalow off Mulholland. You get up before sunrise to have the streets all to yourself with no distractions, but there are always a few others.

You like this neighborhood because the steep hills and busy lives of the inhabitants mean they mostly mind their own business. Anyone on the street in daylight hours is sure to be a gardener, a nanny or a pro athlete burning calories in the off-season.

But walking Clovis has introduced you to more of the neighborhood than you can stomach. Every psychotic overachiever in the area keeps a neurotic, lonely bottom rattling around the house. Usually, these jet trash losers are your staple diet, but Clovis makes it hard to fraternize and puts you in a defensive mood.

How to greet a pedestrian in Los Angeles without looking like a hillbilly: Don't overdo it. Merely observe that it is indeed, "Morning," with no treacly wish for a good one, or even a rhetorical *howyadoing?* Angelenos hate over-sharing and questions, and wishing someone else a good day might somehow cost you one. Also acceptable is a cool nod and chagrinned tightening of the mouth when caught staring.

You detour out into the street, but they seldom take the hint. They have no control over their dogs, and they blame you for controlling yours. If they say *Good morning* and you just roll your eyes at their banality and offer a friendly warning to keep away from Clovis, or remind them to pick up their dogs' filth up off the sidewalk, you get a half-baked rant cribbed from the weak second act of their doomed screenplay. Even in the best neighborhoods, talking to anyone on the street in LA is like waking up a sleepwalker.

This is why you quit real estate. After so many years, you stop listening to what the buyer wants, and learn to mold them into the ideal mark for the property you need to sell. Subtly reshape their goals and expectations until they'll buy anything you offer. But after the deal is closed, you have to start all over with a new rube. After seven years of it, you realized you could ditch the houses and just work on the people.

This morning, you're out before six with your whole obedience kit: a six-foot length of iron rebar; a tennis ball can filled with nickels; a rape whistle and an air horn for emergencies, and four recycled plastic shopping bags for his leavings. Some trainers recommend treats to reinforce good behavior, but you never got anywhere in life by doling out bribes. In your skintight black Lycra running suit, with your theme music cranked up on your iPod, you look and feel like a weapon, more deadly than your dog.

It should be soothing, but even when you're alone on the street, the familiarity of it breeds worse than contempt. Every time you pass the Plantation-style McMansion with a huge, faded, guano-streaked American flag flapping under a huge birdfeeder, where they park four black Escalades on the driveway blocking the sidewalk, you have to fight the urge to leave a nasty anonymous note on their lawn jockey. You've never actually seen these people, but you have dreams of feeding them to a wood chipper. If trifles like this can get you so worked up, then what's the use of any of it?

As soon as you see him coming up the sidewalk, you know he'll be trouble. Doughy and prematurely bald, swaddled in baggy, holey sweats that say UCLA DRINKING TEAM, and those asinine road-running shoes with separate toe-compartments, that look like space chimp feet. Wheezing like a smoker trying grimly to fend off the results of his bad choices.

Your finely honed people-reading senses go to work: Bass player with a washed-up late 90's alt-rock band, coasting on radio residuals and sporadic scoring work for porn. Divorced, childless man-child, out delivering pee-grams with his only friend.

His dog is a young Aussie, flailing like a hyperactive kindergartener in his urge to rend, chew and piss on all creation. Your eyes nearly pop out of your head when you notice the dog is frolicking off-leash.

You clang your staff on the sidewalk to bring Clovis to heel and claim the right-of-way, and the idiot diverts into the street to pass, his dog bouncing along like something out of a Disney cartoon. A parked BMW with a canvas tarp over it is between the dogs, but the Aussie stands up on its hind legs and paws at the air, then drops into a crouch with his tail stump wagging in a frisky puppy challenge. Clovis instantly forgets all his training and lurches off the curb snarling, intent on an entirely different kind of play.

Most people get the message right away, but this fool just stops in the street and says, "Hi, buddy! You wanna play, don't you?"

Clovis rears up on his hind legs, dangling by his leash like a botched lynching. You barely hold him back, slamming the rod into the concrete beside his ear as you politely ask, "Get your dog under control, would you?"

The asshole laughs at you! "My dog is under control, lady. He just wants to play. Maybe since you're the one with the aggressive dog and no manners, you could maybe walk in the street..."

"I have the right of way," you say, but the niceties of dogwalking etiquette as laid out by Cesar Milan are lost on this idiot. "So back the fuck up."

"You shouldn't talk to people like dogs, and you shouldn't treat your dog like a machine. Have a nice day, anyway." Loping off, he claps his hands and his dog dances around him on its hind legs, nipping at his sweatpants and tugging them down just enough that one flabby, pimpled asscheek winks at you before he disappears around the corner.

Right or wrong, the loser of any argument is the one who broods on it after the last word. When you tell your clients that, they nod as if you were a Brahmin from Shangri-La. But you hyperventilate and fume about the encounter all the way home, where you find a kilo of still-steaming dogshit on the neatly trimmed Bermuda grass parking strip in front of your house. Clovis goes berserk trying to annihilate the offending turd with his pee, then to eat it. It takes the can, the rod and the air horn to drive him back into the house.

You try all your vaunted refocusing techniques to put it behind you, but it gnaws at you all through your sessions with clients. Mrs. Mossadegh is agoraphobic and needs kid gloves, but you lash out at her and send the widow into a panic attack. Scratch yoga, insert alcohol.

You have much bigger issues on your radar: shooting another infomercial next week, and a pitch for a regular segment on a nationally syndicated afternoon talk show. But you feel violated, as if you've been assaulted in the street. How dare he raise his voice and flaunt his apathy like you're the defective one? Where did this lazy eunuch shithead get the balls to talk to you like that? And his dog, somehow a part of him where her own dog was not a friend or even a reliable tool. And he knows where you live...

Option 1: bag the shit, then return it to him via his mailbox. But you have no idea where he lives. No, you should follow him home and...

Option 2: Wait until he believes you've forgotten him, and then...Escalate.

Your heart races as you get up before five and slip into a vintage Danskin metallic green leotard, black Adidas track pants and new Saucony running shoes. You collect your platinum-blonde shoulder-length razor-cut into a tight bun that takes seven years off your face and put on a trucker hat that says SHOW ME YOUR TITS, all the while mentally rehearsing a host of withering snarky attacks that you must've been composing in a fitful sleep.

Clovis feeds off your tension, jumping on you and gouging divots out of the Mothersbaugh designer wallpaper in the entry hall. As soon as the door opens, he jerks you out onto the porch and down the stairs. He knows what's bothering you, and he has the scent.

You jog down Stonebridge, Clovis humping along like a quadruple-amputee bodybuilder on a 'roid rage vendetta. You only want to spot your enemy and track him back to his lair. Merely knowing where he lives will give you parity, and the peace of mind to decide how this will proceed.

Clovis drags you from flowerbed to rock garden, whining and wringing out every drop of moisture to cover the Aussie's omnipresent spoor. The bastard pissed everywhere, claimed the whole neighborhood. Clovis leads you up a blind cul-de-sac, then seems to lose the scent. You look over the daunting array of postmodern palaces crowding the edge of a bluff overlooking the San Fernando Valley, and your heart sinks. Your own house is prime real estate, but still a two-bedroom bungalow on stilts facing the wrong way like a clueless chaperone. If he lives in one of these, then he can buy and sell you. Unless he's just sponging off an old bandmate, running the Kato Kaelin act, walking the dogs and cleaning the pool.

That has to be it. Nobody rich enough to afford an eight bedroom with a view like this wanders around baked with his dog at this hour.

Then you come around the corner, and he ambushes you.

He's just across the street, bouncing a tennis ball to tease his stupid Aussie puppy, who springs and bounces around like he should be wearing a cape.

"Good morning, mean lady!" he calls out. He's wearing the same clothes as yesterday.

You're not ready for this. Head down, you give Clovis a taste of the rod. It strikes sparks off the pavement and rings like a tuning fork, making your hand go numb. The numbness seems to vibrate all throughout your toned, taut body.

"Is this far enough away, your majesty?" He capers around on the opposite sidewalk as you haul a suddenly frozen Clovis onto the shaggy lawn of a misbegotten Cape Cod ranch house that's been up for sale for over a year, and probably will be forever, with Coldwell Bankers rep Megan Larsen showing it. You back up under an unruly magnolia tree with blossoms like cabbages. For some reason, their perfume smells like gasoline.

The idiot tosses his tennis ball down the street. The Aussie bounds after it in a flurry of matted flukes and floppy, adorable ears. Clovis growls real low like a semi approaching a steep hill. You feel your phone vibrating in your breast pocket. You don't keep your phone there, don't have a breast pocket.

"You're breaking the law," you tell him.

"Make a citizen's arrest," he says, stroking the puppy and trying to wrench the tennis ball out of his mouth.

Fuck him, he's not worth it. Keep walking. There are ten phones vibrating under your skin. "If you want to play games with me, little boy, you better be ready to learn how grown-ups play."

"You know, maybe if you played with your dog instead of trying to play games with people, maybe you wouldn't both be so miserable—"

He throws the tennis ball down the tree-shadowed street. His dumb dog goes galloping after it.

Clovis bolts. The leash burns your hand racing through your grip. The end of it pops loose and Clovis shoots off the curb as if from a cannon.

"Clovis, No!" you scream, or you remember saying it, anyway.

The Aussie pauses to clock Clovis and turns to meet him for a jolly frolic. Clovis leaps and catches the Aussie by the throat and tosses his head to snap the puppy's neck and lay bare a dizzying lacework of muscles, tendons and arteries. Before you can drop the rod and get out the nickel can, before the dumbass dog owner can call his dog's name, it's dead meat flying in Clovis's wake.

You would be first to argue that it was wrong, but in the moment, all you can feel is the grim satisfaction of the vindicated. And right or wrong, that takedown was, in a word, awesome. If you'd seen it on YouTube, you'd have to have a heart of stone not to stand up and cheer.

We're even, you think. *Suck on that.* If it stopped here, it would be perfect.

Clovis stops just long enough to lift a leg over his fresh kill, then turns and pounds after its owner. The idiot gets maybe ten long strides towards the driveway of the empty house when Clovis bowls him over, throwing his undulating torso into the wild flurry of legs and battening down on his left ankle. The dog owner pitches face-first into the shit-strewn lawn and tries to speed-crawl through dandelions and sun-bleached junk mail towards—what? His Achilles tendon is gone, so he isn't getting up. With Clovis on his back, there's no going anywhere.

You run at your dog shouting and waving your arms, but you stop just short of grabbing his collar. He could kill this man, but if you interfere, he might just seriously harm you. And then your bond would be broken. He'll have to be put to sleep.

You should do something, but your mind can only make a decision by playing the scripts you trot out for your helpless clients. What would the celebrated life coach tell a sucker to do, in such a situation?

"Please, stop! Get him off!" The man screams, or tries to, but his lungs are so clotted he can only hack phlegm in his assassin's face. He bats ineffectually at Clovis with a moldy phonebook, trying valiantly to shove it into the snapping jaws. The mutt already tore off one ear and made meatloaf of his right hand, but the screaming seems to drive him to new heights of ferocity, and he goes for the source. Fixing his massive jaws over the man's face, he battens down like a nutcracker, jerking it from side to side, looking for that telltale snap—

You grab the collar and yank on his choke-chain, but he won't let go. When you finally pull him off, Clovis takes half the man's face with him.

You almost blow the airhorn in his ears, but then drop it when you notice the quiet. You look around. The street is empty. The house next door is under construction, and the crew won't be showing up until tomorrow. The sun has just begun to insinuate itself into the grey soup of smog that obscured the valley. Fat Sunday newspapers lay on driveways and dewy lawns. Hungover and medicated and dead to the world, the neighborhood has not heard or seen anything.

For a moment there, you felt a sickening hole in the pit of your gut, a sucking wound that threatened to drag you into a vortex of shame when you needed to be at your best. But it was not shame or guilt at all. It was good old-fashioned fear at the loss of control, at the quicksand of consequences opening up underfoot. Every aspect of your life could change for the worse forever and ever, just because your dog had an accident.

Clovis sits at attention, oblivious to the weeping, faceless horror crawling in the weeds with a Thai bistro menu stuck to his three-fingered right hand. Clovis apparently had no problem swallowing the lost digits.

"Okay," you keep saying, like the robotic voice in a car with the door standing open. You are the person anyone in such a situation would look up to. You thrive on crises. Like working out a cramp, you pace and say, "Okay," until the sinkhole in your gut fills in. You suddenly felt quite giddy, as if you just snorted pure MDMA. This situation is still yours to fuck up.

Your house is two blocks away. Your chances of running home and returning with the Cayenne before someone else finds the mess are negligible. And besides, he isn't dead.

He should really get to a hospital. Right now, he's…grievously fucked. If he dies, then that's the end. If he survives as a mangled sideshow freak, he'll be around your neck for the rest of your life. It'll be like divorcing a stranger. But you can't bring yourself to do it, not right here. The silence is a bubble that could burst at any moment.

And then, like you always do, you simply snap out of it and just start fixing it. Running for the front door of the house, you use your iron rod to snap the realtor's box off the doorknob and get the key. The house has a Bel Air Patrol sign out front like every house on this street, but it's weathered and cracked, and the alarm is shut off.

You kick and cuss Clovis into the guest bathroom and shut the door, then race outside to pick up the Aussie.

A huge splash of blood decorates its passage in the shape of a big bird with wings outstretched. You almost throw up when its floppy fifty-pound weight sags like hot trash in your arms, its bowels relaxing and pinching out a runny racing stripe down your leg. You run into the empty house and down the hall to the garage, drop the corpse on the concrete floor and run back outside.

The dog owner still hasn't caught his breath. Blood and the loose flap of face completely obscure his eyes, and he only makes it worse with his right hand. "Help me," he moans. His voice is reedy, breathless even for a smoker. His skin is cold and clammy. Going into shock.

"I'm going to help you," you say. "Just calm down and try to get up. Let me help you inside. I can stop the bleeding, that's what's important."

"Call 911 . . . call—"

You get into his pocket just ahead of him and take his cell phone. "I'll take care of you."

If you lived here, you'd be home now. Furnished with Italian modernist drek from the showrooms going out of business down on Ventura, and cream deep pile shag carpet alternated with blonde hardwood floors. Empty rooms look small and yet daunting to buyers. Bad taste hides bad space. It's easier to picture living in a house if it seems like someone else is already there, and doing it wrong.

Every room has its own air freshener. The living room smells like evergreen, the kitchen like fresh cookies, the dining room like pumpkin pie.

Goddamit, he's bleeding everywhere. You detour into the garage and lay him on a moving blanket against the washer-dryer combo. With his shoelaces, you make tourniquets for his hand and ankle. His face drizzles blood everywhere, but it's all capillary blood—no arterial splashing, at least. He's not liable to die, but he isn't certain to stay put, either.

This could continue to spiral out of control, or you could end it right now.

Ask yourself, as you do when divining the good or evil of anything, what purpose would such a decision serve, and whether it could succeed. This makes it so much easier to live in a cruel and crappy world and not constantly flagellate yourself about injustices from child abuse to genital mutilation in Africa and Tyler Perry movies. Would it work? Would it get you what you want?

The backyard looks out on a steep, brush-choked canyon. Coyotes would find him and his stupid dog before anyone else, and nobody would suspect—

Jesus, it's easy to think like a villain. Is this who you've always been? Are you a bad person? No, you're a problem solver. Weak people let circumstances run them over. Problem solvers rise above, and get shit done.

Clovis whines and paws the bathroom door.

Bad person or no, you didn't ask for any of this. You could let it ruin the rest of her life, and take comfort in having done the "right thing." Or you could take the obvious solution. Right here and so simple, that you would be betraying her deepest principles, if you didn't act on it.

Why the hell don't you just do it?

You go out the side yard and sprint home. You get a deluxe first aid kit left over from Sasha the suicidal performance artist and a smorgasbord of painkillers and anxiety medications collected from every other ex. All the way back, you tell yourself you're just going to stabilize him and maybe try to get him to see sense about the attack, before you call the police. As long as nobody (human) has died, there'll be no fallout. You might even come out of it a hero.

He's halfway to the front door when you came back in. You go to the bathroom door and open it. Clovis barges out and makes a beeline for the dog owner. Wait until the idiot can smell his own flesh on Clovis's breath before stomping on his leash and stopping the dog close enough to lick the man's nose.

"I'll take care of you," you say again, and press a clean gym sock soaked in ether over his face. He slumps into your arms and you drag him back into the garage.

It takes an hour, just to stitch his hand. The severed Achilles tendon is above your pay grade—you learned how to stop bleeding and close holes from Sasha's many artistic misadventures, but you're no surgeon.

The face is a challenge you actually enjoy, like arts and crafts from summer camp. Despite your best efforts, the semicircular flap of exquisitely articulated muscle from the hairline to the bridge of the nose now looks like a slab of chuck steak stitched to his head. Slather the results with Polysporin and garnish with hot pink self-adhesive bandages, and serve.

He really seems to appreciate it, once he wakes up. "I'm really sorry about what I said earlier," he says, as near as you can tell. You fed him some painkillers during and after the operation, so he sounds pretty dopey. "It was very insensitive of me. Thank you for saving my life."

You blush. "I'm sorry, too . . . that you got hurt . . . but you know, you were asking for trouble."

He smiles, which would look kind of cute, if the upper left quadrant of his face wasn't swelling and turning blue. "What're you trying to do, here?"

"Why can't you admit that you were at fault?"

"Wha . . . ?" Now he laughs, which isn't nearly as cute.

"He's not a bad dog."

"I'm sure . . . under the right, um . . ."

"He never attacks unless he's provoked."

He smiles again, looking stupid, but now you start to think he's playing possum. "Maybe you're right. It's just one of those things. Shit happens, right? Let the lawyers sort it out. But you have to call 911."

You make a big production of thinking about it before answering, "No."

"What do you mean, No?"

"We'll settle this here. Now. Between us. No lawyers."

"Lady, I'm bleeding to death—"

"No, you're not. I fixed it."

"Nonetheless . . ." He sniffs, wrinkles his nose. "Are you baking cookies?"

"Let's talk about *you*, okay? Your dog shit in front of my house—"

"What's that got to do with anything?"

"And your dog was off-leash, and you had no way to control him, and you were playing a provocative game in an inappropriate place."

"So, I was asking for it, is that what . . . I got what I deserved, is that what you want to hear? I'm sorry I made your dog attack me?"

"Don't twist my words. You made my dog angry . . ."

"You're not angry because of your dog," he gasped. "Your dog is angry because of you." He looks fit to bust into a rant, but then he notices something behind you. His face cracks open, tears squirting out of his stitches. "Oh my God, Cutter . . ."

"What kind of name is that?" you blurt before it comes together. Aussie . . . middle-aged geek . . . Toecutter from Mad Max. "I'll take care of it."

This is the nadir of your relationship. You've lost his trust. But if this were a romantic comedy, you're just one montage and a grand gesture away from happily ever after.

The dog weighs less than fifty pounds, but Clovis attacks it when you kneel to pick it up. Tearing into the limp carcass like a bag of kibble, he harries you all the way down the hall to the kitchen. His jaws clamp down on one flopping foreleg and yank with all his might. You shout, "Heel, Clovis! Off! Go to your spot!" Clovis has never shown much interest in puppy games before, but he's a fiend for tug of war. The limb twists and pops out of its socket. Fur and flesh split open and lukewarm blood sluices down your leg to pool in your new running shoes.

"God damn it, *heel!*" You kick Clovis and catch him in the groin. He yips and spins around snarling and for one frozen moment, you're sure he's going to turn on you.

You've never hit him before. The regimen of training and discipline ran you both ragged, but you've never lost your temper. The sudden change in your relationship strikes you both mute and still. You back away with the corpse, reaching behind you for the sliding glass door. Clovis lumbers off to sit and pout by the front door.

You lurch across the patio, around the drained swimming pool to the edge of the yard. Beyond, a steep slope, shaggy with coastal scrub and exotic invasive weeds, plummets about two hundred feet to a dry arroyo that feeds into a storm drain. A palatial walled estate sprawls across the top of the next ridge, but there's no other visible sign of civilization. The San Fernando Valley below is completely obscured by a colorless pall of smog.

Drop the dog and it tumbles down the slope, almost instantly swallowed up by the brush. You're not a big fan of poetry, but a line from a Browning poem leaps to mind as you wash the blood off your hands with the garden hose. *And yet, God has not said a word!*

You probably can't just throw him away now, though. Coyotes don't give their kills first aid. The neighbors are digging a new pool. You wonder how hard it can be, to figure out how to use a Ditch Witch.

Filled with renewed resolve, you go back into the house when Clovis lets loose a torrent of barking.

The dog owner is crawling down the hall again. Clovis snaps and growls, but not at him.

The front door opens.

A TV weatherman walks in holding a Starbucks travel mug and a big pink box of doughnuts. He looks at you like an unexpected Category 4 tropical storm that he failed to predict.

"Am I early for the open house?" you ask. "I was walking by and the door was wide open, and I wanted to come right in and make an offer..."

You maneuver yourself to block Clovis and draw his eyes away from the shambling monster in the corridor to the garage.

He smiles and nods, trying to believe you. This house has been a bomb on the market since before the recession. "That's excellent! My wife is the agent, I just schlep the doughnuts..." He drops the bag on the dining room table and goes for his phone.

"You don't have to bother her..."

"Oh, it's no trouble, she's right outside, putting up signs..." He hits a speed dial button and puts the phone to his ear. "So, are you from this area, or—" His face drains of blood, leaving it the pale orange of his bronzing agent.

"Help...me..." the dog owner moans.

"What the hell is—" The weatherman notices that he's standing in a puddle of tacky blood.

Clovis tenses, you feel him trembling against your leg. You *feel* his low growl, like the foundation of the house splitting in half.

You cower and scream, "Don't hurt me!"

Clovis leaps. The weatherman's travel mug bounces off his head. His muzzle clamps down on the weatherman's crotch, driving him back on the floor.

You look around and find nothing useful. Your rod is in the garage. You run into the kitchen and grab every knife out of the block in a big fistful.

The weatherman is much tougher than the dog owner, and must've done a special report about surviving wild animal attacks before. He rolls on his belly and curls in a ball, covering the back of his neck. Clovis circles in a frenzy, biting and clawing and scoring superficial flesh wounds, but nothing the government would call torture.

This has gone far enough.

You jab his hands with the knives. They're cheap Chinese Ikea crap, but the sudden pricking makes his hands fly away from his neck. Before he can flip over, you plunge all five knives into the junction of skull and spinal column.

He goes rigid, humping the deep pile shag with pitiful, diminishing spasms, then sputtering, winding down, choking on his own blood. It takes a while for his eyes to glaze over. He must have so many questions . . .

You sit on his back for another minute, willing yourself not to throw up, you've got enough of a mess to clean up. If she ever hopes to clear this abortion, Megan is going to have to recarpet.

Clovis nuzzles your hand. You absently pet him, moaning, "What am I gonna do with you," and then notice he's got a phone in his mouth, and it's ringing.

You pick it up. It's dripping slobber. "Hi, Megan? It's me, Rowena Merkel, from Encino Re/Maxx?"

Megan is, to put it plainly, a dipshit. "Oops, sorry, I was trying to reach my husband . . ."

"And you've reached his phone, hon." You push the fruity Avon Lady pep into your voice. "I'm here with a really sweet couple who wanted to try to sneak in and see the house early today, and you caught us."

"Oh, well that's great! I thought you were out of showing houses. Are they, you know . . . serious?"

"Very, but they're very concerned about security, and I'm afraid Dan—"

"Doug . . ."

"Doug was showing us the panic room, and he locked himself in."

"Omigod. Really?" She giggles. "He's such an idiot . . ."

"They all are, hon. Is the alarm shut off?"

"Yes, it doesn't go anywhere, but the lock . . . I have the key and the combo . . ." You hear the slam of the big door on Megan's SUV and her chunky wedge heels clomping up the driveway. "Damn coyotes got somebody's cat or something on the front lawn. I hope that didn't put them off—"

"Oh, they're fucking morons, I can assure you. He's some kind of TV personality, so be sure to kiss his ass a lot about it."

"What a coincidence! Wait, he's not at Channel 4, is he? Doug hates those guys. You know they stole his idea for the toy drive—"

She comes into the dining room and sees Clovis, his deep brown coat spiky and stained deep auburn with fresh blood. She bends down and coos to him and blows him kisses. "Who's a big boy?"

You don't even have to tell Clovis what to do.

"So . . . do you remember ever not being a sociopath?"

Out in the living room now, why try to hide? Call any crew of Salvadoran refugees and pay them cash up front to clean this room, no questions asked, and without a moment's hesitation, they would deport themselves.

"I'm not a psycho," you mutter. You've been talking to him for a while now, and he's been so nice, and then he springs this on you . . . "The dog got out of control."

"But you don't seem to feel bad about what happened."

"Sure I do! You think I wouldn't rather be doing something else, right now? This is a workday for me. I want my fucking life back, too."

"Why deny it? You're just going to kill me and burn the house down or something, anyway. Make it look like me and Doug were queer for each other, and using this place as a love nest. And Megan found out, and went all Benihana on everybody."

"That's good, I should be taking notes," you say, but nobody laughs.

"What's your life like?"

"What? Mine? Oh, I don't know. It's good. Really good. I . . . work with people to . . . maximize their potential, and sometimes I'm on TV."

He smiles, waving a bandaged flipper to encourage you. "What do you tell them?"

"Oh you know, all kinds of shit . . . don't give up your dreams for someone else, don't be a victim . . . but I give it to them straight, and I tell them what I see. I don't sugar-coat it."

"So you see yourself as a . . ." he winces. "You got any more of those Percocets?" You give him a couple and a bottled water. "Thanks . . . You teach neurotic people how to be more of a psychotic, to get what they want."

"If you have to label everything, then maybe . . ."

"Sure, but what happened today should be a warning sign, right?"

"A lot of people pay therapists a hundred bucks an hour because they can't face up to the fact that they feel exactly the way I do."

He nods and smiles at some joke he refuses to share. "What would you tell me to do, in my situation?"

"Excuse me?"

He digs in his waistband and pulls out a wallet, fumbles out a wad of twenties. "Go on, I'm soliciting your life coaching skills. What should I do?"

"Put your money away." You scoot closer to him on the couch. His face is already starting to smell, and it's only been, what, four hours? "I would tell you to look at that dog, over there."

You point at Clovis, lolling on the love seat across the conversation pit from you. Something about her perfume or the overblown hairdo on Megan drove him wild, and he made a pig of himself.

"What would he do, if it were his life on the line? He would die fighting, but he wouldn't pick a fight he couldn't win."

You put a hand on his chest, gently pinning him while running the other hand up his leg. His glazed eyes bounce off yours. "When animals know they're doomed, they slink off into a cave or under a porch and die. We have to make the world do it for us, when it's too late to dig out of the mess we've made of a life. Have the good sense to let go."

"I'm in no shape to fight you," he says.

"I didn't think you were," you say, "but that doesn't mean . . ."

Your hand finds a phone in his pocket. Doug's phone. You dropped it somewhere when Megan tried to jump through the living room picture window into the front yard with her entrails trailing around her ankles.

"You maggot, you called the cops?"

"God no," he chuckles. "Rich people don't call the cops."

You take the phone away. The last call was to Bel Air Patrol, just over the hill in Beverly Hills. You hit redial and just start talking while you strangle him.

"Yes, my husband just called, and I don't know what he tried to tell you . . . Yes, he *is* married. We're very private people, we don't feel the need to tell everybody everything . . . Yes, maybe you *should* update his profile. Anyway, there's no need for . . . Yes, he's quite high on prescription medications from an injury . . . a dog bite. I understand there's a false call fee. We'd be *happy* to charge it to our account. And also, there's been a lot of break-ins to our neighborhood lately, so perhaps you have a service where a car is parked on our block for a couple hours in the afternoon? It'd mean the world to us, and most of the burglaries have happened during the day, so … Fine, go ahead and add it to our account. You work on commission, correct? Does that make you happy? Very good then, have a wonderful day, bye."

You've gone and done it, now. You got the last word in, so why do you still feel so empty? Now, he can't eat his words. But kicking his stupid blue face in still seems a lot more relaxing than yoga.

Okay, enough. You've navigated this situation like a pro. Time to reclaim the day. You had things you were going to do, so do them. If nothing else, a solid trail of work phone calls will establish an alibi. Nobody in the midst of a spree killing pauses to work phones.

You call your agent. She's busy, but you call and call until she picks up. "Have you heard anything about the Dr. show?"

"No, but it's Sunday and the Daytime Emmys were last week, honey. Nobody's talking to—"

"I want the producer's number."

"Don't push too hard. They don't like hungry women. It scares them, and you always—"

"Give me the number or you're fired."

She gives you the number. You go into the bathroom to look in the mirror and give yourself a pep talk. "You are a star. This is destiny. Nothing else matters, but what you make of this moment."

Take out your phone and make the call.

You smell gasoline.

A flutter in your chest, like a phone sewn under your breastbone, but this time there is a phone, albeit in your hip pocket. You take the dog owner's phone out and look at it next to yours.

You answer his phone and say hello to yourself.

The doorbell rings. You go to the window and peer through the blinds at a nice Pakistani couple on the porch. The husband looks like a chemical engineer, the wife maybe a lawyer. Behind them, a discreet distance down the driveway, a couple with two-point-three kids, fresh from church, loiter around their SUV, eating Cold-stone ice cream and waiting their turn. On the lawn, and on everyone going down the street, are signs in Megan's cack-handed block Sharpie capitols: OPEN HOUSE

TODAY!

God damn it, after all your hard work, one bad accident and you're back in real estate.

The doorbell rings like every church in Christendom. Clovis jumps and barks at the front door, and then he looks right at you like he's not a dog at all, before he bolts out the garage side door.

You're really losing it, because it occurs to you that maybe there is no Clovis, maybe there never was, and all of this was just you, all along. It's almost a relief to find you're not going crazy, when you hear the barking and screams outside.

You go back into the living room and look around. You blow out the pilot light on the water heater and the stove fixtures.

Suddenly, it's out of your hands. You might as well lay down and have a nap. Lay your head on the dog owner's chest, and your ear crushes a soft pack of cigarettes, and this is what happens, you think, when you lose control. You may as well start smoking again, just to have some control over how fast you blow it all.

It's been years, and you've built a cult, if not a religion, out of your own legendary self-control.

Fuck it, you think. *Maybe just one . . .*

You light a smoke and take a drag and remember why you quit. This is not who you are. You're not someone else's sordid water-cooler story. You can never go home, but you won't let the bastards drag you down.

You drop it on the floor and go out the back, around the pool and over the fence, sliding, tumbling through grasping thorny brush snagging your leotard and ripping off your hat.

You come to rest in a dry creekbed surrounded by coyotes. They scatter when the explosions and fire split the sky high above, but they circle you, yipping and howling when the sirens come.

This is how you get control back. You don't need a dog to define you. This part will be easy. To get back on top, you only have to take out the leader.

Righteous

BY WESTON OCHSE

PTSD (post-traumatic stress disorder) takes many forms, virtually none of them good. At its worst, it reduces strong men and women—often soldiers with clear minds and nerves of steel—to twitchy, delusional paranoid schizophrenics, unable to function in the world they return to, and in which they no longer belong.

But trauma isn't merely a battlefield condition. Sometimes the shit doesn't really hit the fan till you bring the war back home.

Weston Ochse brings his military intelligence background to bear in this berserk opus of nebulous vengeance writ large, replete with a neat Son of Sam reference for the serial killer cognoscenti. And a pizza that I would not want to eat.

They say he never felt a thing. They say when the bomb blew and his lower body evaporated, he died at that moment. But in my dreams he lives for a few more seconds. I see him know that he's about to die. I feel his fear. Then I feel his pain. And it is like my own legs being ripped from me. Ripped by the strong arms of a vengeful god, too hungry and eager to put us in our place to understand the simple truth that we're merely humans and have been seeking an eternity for just a little fucking direction.

I sit behind the wheel of my Buick sedan. I've always owned Buicks. My first one was a hand-me-down from my dad, who'd also always owned them. I was going to hand one down to Brandon when he got back from this deployment. When he was little he called it a *Bwik*. He'd just started to read and that's the way he sounded out the letters. 'Daddy, let's go to the store in the *Bwik*.' 'Can we take a ride in the *Bwik*?' 'Let's go in the *Bwik*.' It was always about the *Bwik*. I held back telling him the right way to say it. I loved it when he called it that—the *Bwik*. But some asshat kid in fourth grade made fun of him and Brandon never called it a *Bwik* again.

Except in my mind.

You're talking to yourself again, Dude, the dog says, sitting in the passenger seat, his baleful eyes on me.

The no-account mutt is probably right. That he's the only one who can hear me makes it okay. I found him on a back Kentucky road. I passed him, then backed up and opened the passenger door. He looked at me as if he knew the entirety of my plan and shook his head. *Asshat*, he'd said in the voice of my long dead wife. *You're going to need me.* Then he jumped into the seat and we've been a team ever since.

Yeah, I used to love this car. I used to wash it every weekend. Now the floor holds the evidence of my vigils: bright yellow, red and orange cups, bags, napkins, and the residue of too many late night trips to fast food restaurants. From the outside it's hard to tell what color it is. The car hasn't been washed since the funeral. A thousand miles of road and a sideswipe of a guardrail have changed its complexion. Really, nothing has been done to it except the driving. Always the driving. And like so many nights before, I stare daggers at the place the man sits. Tonight it's in a booth by a window, he and his wife and young sons eating pizza and laughing like he isn't a serial murderer by proxy. We're almost ready to execute this one, too.

It was a war, Dude. I keep telling you. It was war.

I can never get over how much the dog sounds like Susan. Part of me wonders if her ghost inhabits the mutt, but another part of me wonders if it isn't God having a good laugh.

"It wasn't the war anyone signed up for," I say. "What kind of war does these things to our kids?"

The dog looks at me and shakes his head.

"I know. I'm an asshat."

Once upon a time, I was Private Dude Johnson in 1968 during the Tet Offensive. That was a real war. Men fought and died for a cause. It was hell. I still wake up in cold sweats over the things I did, the things I'd seen done, the things almost done to me. The closest I came to the old reaper wasn't skulking through the jungle in the dark, it was at a disco in Saigon. A man came in wearing a bomb, called us all *Yankee motherfuckers*, and blew himself up. If it wasn't for all the juicy girls between me and him, I would have been hurt. As it was, I was blown back and covered in pieces of what used to be some of the finest Saigon hookers.

He knew the Price of Glory, the dog says.

"Ahh, John Ford and James Cagney. You see that one, Mutt?"

I'm a dog. I don't see movies. I read it in your mind, Dude.

An old 1956 movie about World War I, *What Price Glory* was about a soldier's first duty, which was to his men.

I feel a lump blossom in my chest. "Brandon was a good sergeant," they said. "It wasn't his fault they were blown up, they said."

How were they supposed to know? Mutt asks rhetorically.

"They couldn't have known. Not in a million years."

Why is that movie in the front of your mind? Why not some of the others? Why not John Wayne or Tom Hanks?

"Hanks? That guy's a comedian."

But he was in World War II, the Mutt says, narrowing his eyes.

"When he was in *Saving Private Ryan*. Yeah, that was a good one. And *Band of Brothers*, too. That was a series about an American army unit in Europe during World War II. That was as good as it got when talking about friendships and the nature of leadership."

They Were Expendable?

I nod. "Fucking John Wayne movie about PT Boats. That was one of his better ones, but there's one thing about every John Wayne war movie that I hate."

What's that, Dude?

"Asshat never dies."

Asshat, Mutt agrees.

"You can say that again."

Asshat.

They say a psychopath is completely free of cultural restraints. They say that such a person is not held back by any desires of guilt or shame. How other people think and feel are of no consequence. They call this sort of person crazy. I call this sort of person a father.

I watch as the man who recruited my son into the army pays his bill, gets up and exits the restaurant with his family. His wife and two boys are about the age that my boy first called my car a *Bwik*, and they get into a silver Ford Explorer. He watches them go until they are out of sight, then gets in a beat up Trans Am. I follow from a distance, trying to keep at least one, two or three cars between us. I vary it, careful that he doesn't notice me always in the same place.

Of course I could lose him and it wouldn't make a difference. He was going home. I'd followed him a dozen times. Then he'd call his sons and verbally tuck them into bed. Then after a good night's sleep, he'd go to work the next morning and kill another man's boy by proxy. And the thing of it all, it never seemed to bother him.

Once I made sure he was going to stay in for the night, I drive us to the local Wal-Mart parking lot. One of the few places outside of a campground they allow overnight sleeping, there's already six RVs parked, with lights on and dishes pointed toward the appropriate satellite. I walk Mutt, then we open the bag of food I got on the way. Inside is an immense burrito. I tear it in two. I eat half and Mutt eats the other. Soon, both of us are asleep. I wake occasionally to Mutt passing gas. Dogs were never meant to process beans.

Five sentences changed my life forever.

Yes, I'll marry you, is how Susan changed my life.

It's a boy, is how a wide-hipped, chippy-eyed nurse changed my life.

Metastasized means that your wife's breast cancer has spread to her lymph nodes, is how the medical community gave up trying to save Susan and changed my life.

On behalf of a grateful nation, I present this flag as a token of our appreciation for the faithful and selfless service of your loved one for this country, is how a straight-faced Uncle Sam socked me in the heart.

Then one night I was three sheets to the wind with a bottle of Cutty Sark and *Pulp Fiction* blasting on television. When Samuel L. Jackson screamed the words from Ezekiel 25:17, I sat up and was beset by a moment of clarity as he talked about the *path of a righteous man*. Then he said the words that started me on this *path of the righteous man*. *"Blessed is he who in the name of charity and goodwill shepherds the weak through the valley of darkness, for he is truly his brother's keeper and the finder of lost children. And I will strike down upon thee with great vengeance and furious anger those who attempt to poison and destroy my brothers. And you will know my name is the Lord when I lay my vengeance upon thee."*

And as always, Mutt is eager to point out my errors. *Those are seven sentences, Dude.*

"But they are seven good sentences," I offer.

Mutt thinks for a moment, then nods. *They are. Especially for an asshat.*

I'm up early the next morning. Mutt pees in some weeds. I pee in a can, then walk over and empty it in the weeds. A crochety old bag in a quarter-of-a-million dollar RV gives me the stinkeye. She looks like Susan's mother. They're about the same age and they appear to have the same affection for me. I give her the one-fingered salute, which she returns with an unmistakable glee. For a moment, I wish I had more than five bombs left. When her ass blew through her eye sockets, she might for once realize what an asshat she was being for trying to judge me because I own an old *Bwik* and not an RV.

We get back in the car and head to the local Micky D's for Egg McMuffins. Sitting in the parking lot and eating, I have an episode. I'd thought they were receding, but the way it grabs me, strangling the breath from me as it shows explosion after explosion after explosion, the pain is my pain as I relive what had probably happened to my son and his squad. When I am finally released from its merciless grip, a half-eaten McMuffin lays in my lap, puke and bile soaking it. When the smell hits me, I puke all over again. But I am empty, so instead it is like a cat trying to hack a hairball, my back arching as I dry heave and hack until I see stars and the miserable galaxy they live within. The car rocks with my throes, chasing passers-by away as they watch what could only be the alien from John Carpenter's *The Thing* escaping from my body. When the episode finally leaves me gasping and exhausted, I look over at Mutt. He regards me with his usual aplomb. I swear to God he shakes his head, then calls me *asshat*.

I shove my puke and food onto the floor and sit back in my seat. My head swims as I grip the wheel with clenched fists.

They called it Secondary Post Traumatic Stress Disorder. They say that some people are affected by a horrific incident even if they were never there. Personally, I think it's a load of horse piss, but after the funeral, when it began to kick in, my doctor had to figure out what to call the thing that owned me.

Forgetfulness is a big part of it. The power at my house was shut off three times, not because I didn't have the money to pay it, but because I simply didn't remember to pay the bill. I had a warrant for eight months for not paying a speeding ticket. It wasn't that I didn't want to pay, I just couldn't remember. My rent payment was late every month for a year before I let the thing go completely. It was almost like I convinced myself it would work itself out instead of being proactive and doing it when I was supposed to.

Then there are the nightmares. Technicolor terrible. I'd gotten to where I took antihistamines every night just to knock myself out.

There are also the panic attacks. If surprised, I threw fits. So fucking embar-rassing. I couldn't control it. It was as if someone else was in my body, in my head, and drunk driving all the way through a funhouse.

My doctor gives me meds to control it, but they turn me into a fucking zombie. I even caught myself drooling once. When that happened is when I decided I'd rather be crazy than a zombie. And eight days after that I found the path of the righteous man.

All of my symptoms are gone now.

Well, mostly.

All except the occasional attack.

And, of course, the dog talks to me now, too. That can't be right.

After cleaning up in a truck stop washroom, I pull the car into a church parking lot. Churches are the best cover. No one ever thinks that bad things are capable of happening there. So even though there are several people preparing for service, they ignore me as I check the remaining bombs. Five of the original ten are left— one to represent my son and each member of his squad. Each destined for the recruiter who enticed a fine young American boy onto a path that would ultimately end up with him scattered around the side of the road in the Iraqi city of Haditha.

The bombs look identical. I touch them gently with my fingertips. But they aren't identical. I'd thought to make them all the same, but it was Mutt who intervened. So in a fever dream of construction, I created the bombs so that some of them deliver deadly ball-bearings, and some deliver a much smaller charge along with a hail of multi-colored confetti. I don't know which ones are which. I don't know how many of each one I constructed. That Saturday night in my garage was part blur, part blank. All I know is that I'd so far conspired for five to detonate, and each one did. What they delivered I don't know...I don't want to know...except for this one. Staff Sergeant Reyes was the one who recruited my son. It was his fault my son was dead and he had to pay the most.

I close the trunk, satisfied that the bombs are ready, then I drive to a car wash. I spend seventeen quarters cleaning the outside of the car and the puke from the seat and the floor. All the while, Mutt sits near the trashcan watching my every move. I occasionally stop and watch the dog watching me. Finally when I am about done, I feel the need to confront it. I walk over, kneel down and stare into the dog's eyes. I'd never petted it. It had never occurred to me to do so. Even though it appears to be a dog, it is more than that. I can't be certain, but I feel there is a higher power working through it.

"Susan?" I say, seeking the soul of my dead wife in the deep brown eyes of the animal. "Susan?"

The dog pants, its tongue lolling out the side of its mouth.

"Susan? Is that you? Come on, Susan, answer me."

"Is that your dog, sir?" comes a voice from behind me.

A policeman stands with a hand resting casually in his holstered and snapped pistol. The other hand points at Mutt.

"Uhh, yes, officer."

"It's not registered." Then seeing my perplexed expression he adds "No tags." He glances back at the car. "Yours?"

I stand slowly, glancing from his pistol to the trunk where the bombs rest snug in a suitcase beside the unearthed remains of my son. I wonder which would freak him out more—the bones or the bombs. A giggle escapes.

"Something funny?" he asks, standing a little straighter.

"Nuh . . . No sir. What's the problem?"

"Your dog has to be registered. We can't have animals running around who haven't been cleared by a vet."

"Mutt is clean. She's healthy."

"I'm sure she is. License and registration, please," he says, pulling out a ticket book.

My eyes narrow. "But I'm not driving. Why do you need to see those?"

"License and registration, sir." He gives me a cold look over the top of this ticket book. "Is there a problem?"

I lick my lips. Part of me thinks I can take him. I glance at Mutt, who is almost imperceptibly shaking its head. I take the advice and pull my wallet free from my back pocket. I fumble free my license and paper registration and hand it to him.

He writes for a moment, then paused. "This address correct?"

Meaning my California address, "Yes," I lie, not bothering to tell him that my real address is the front seat of the *Bwik*.

He finishes writing, then hands me the ticket along with my license and registration. "I realize you can just leave town, but if I see that dog again without registration, I'll have to fine you. This is just a warning."

"Thanks, officer." For being a busybody asshole and wasting time with me when you could be out after bad guys.

He frowns and nods, then returns to his bicycle—the reason I hadn't heard him approach. As he pedals away, Mutt comes over and sits beside me.

He heard what you didn't say, the dog says.

"No he didn't. That was my inside voice."

Asshat. No it wasn't. It was your outside voice.

I watch as the policeman looks back and watches me, then he is gone down the street and around a corner.

I pass the night in the same Wal-Mart parking lot, nervous that the policeman will find me. I'm not worried about getting caught, but I am worried about finishing. I have five more bombs and they have to be delivered just so. But my earlier conversation with Mutt had sparked something else...something that wasn't making me happy. My targets had recruited my son physically. They'd given him tests, made him sign the appropriate paperwork and delivered him to basic training. But they hadn't recruited his mind. In the long dark hours of waiting, I was beginning to realize that he'd been recruited a long time before he'd ever met his first recruiter. Part of it was my fault. I'd liked telling him stories, some my own, some made up, of my bravery and courage in Vietnam. What father wouldn't have? To be idolized by a child is second to nothing.

But then there were the movies. Memorial Day Weekend we'd watch the movie marathons on cable about the exploits of soldiers, sailors and marines in every war America had ever been in. From Ironclads to Tanks to Jets, from Tom Cruise to Nicholas Cage to Lee Marvin, we watched them all and inculcated the idea of patriotism and valor. Most of it washed off me. I'd been there. I'd done that. I'd got the combat T-shirt of wet nightmares and dry heaves. But what of my son? How much of an indoctrination had it been? It was a recruitment of the mind, body and soul, and I had been an accomplice after all. Every Hollywood director, producer, actor, key grip and best boy was at fault. Each and everyone who had been a part of making a movie about selfless service and heroism might as well have each been a part of building the roadside bomb that had obliterated my progeny.

I was beginning to suspect that I'd need a lot more bombs.

Five the next morning I am ready. The bomb is wrapped inside a pizza box I placed beside the running track where Staff Sergeant Reyes runs every morning. It is his one constant and the perfect place for me to strike down upon him with great vengeance and furious anger.

I'm there when he pulls into the parking lot in his Trans Am. He gets out wearing shorts, a T-shirt that reads *Army of One*, and sleek orange running shoes. As he stretches, I notice the high school track team beginning to show up on the other side of the track. They are an obstacle I am hoping not to have to contend with. Normally, Staff Sergeant Reyes is done before they even start, but they seem to be early today. I watch them, wondering if they might get in the way. But I've already made my decision. I won't be stopped. It's an interesting conundrum. I watch them as they form up and begin their stretching. It isn't long before I come to the conclusion that it isn't my problem.

Hey, Asshat, the dog says. *Don't look now, but the Po-Po's here.*

I turn at Mutt's urban slang in time to watch the policeman on the bicycle riding towards me. With a sense of foreboding, I realize it's the same police officer. I finger the telephone in my pocket. All I have to do is hit speed dial number six and it'll call the other phone attached to the device. The detonator is attached to the ringer. One call, one ring, then BOOM! Killed by the same method as my son.

"Morning," the cop says, slowing to a stop, until he was resting his arms over the tops of his handlebars.

I stare at him a moment, then hastily return his greeting. Then I half turn towards the track and try and act like I'm interested in something there.

"You going to get that dog registered?"

"What? Yeah. When they open I'll be there."

Staff Sergeant Reyes finishes stretching and begins his run. He starts with a swift pace. He normally runs eight laps, which is two miles. Based on his earlier times, he'd be done in about fifteen minutes. I glance at the kids and see they're about ready to start. Butterflies dance through my chest.

"One of them yours? Grandson?"

I shake my head.

"Then why are you here?"

"Excuse me?"

He raises his voice as he says, "I asked why are you here."

"Uh . . ."

Come on, Asshat. Tell him why you're here.

Staff Sergeant Reyes runs past the pizza box on the far side of the track. He doesn't even give it a second glance.. just like he never gave signing my son into the Army a second thought. My index finger hovers over the call button.

The policeman gets off his bike. The crunch of gravel as his kickstand bites the ground. His footsteps. Then I feel his presence over my shoulder.

"My son died in Iraq," I say, the words coming from some strange accord between my brain and my thrumming heart.

This stops him.

"Sometimes I just like to watch the kids run." Yeah. That sounds right. "My son was a runner in high school. Ran the 800 meters. He used to be fast."

"Let me see your hands," he says.

Staff Sergeant Reyes completes one lap. The kids join him and are soon running in a gaggle with him orbiting the center from the inside lane.

"Turn around," comes the order.

I turn. My throat is so constricted I can barely breathe.

"Hands," he says, as his thumb unclips the snap on his holster.

I remove both my hands from the jacket. The phone is inside my right hand. My left is empty.

"Hold them up."

As soon as I comply, he grabs me by the shoulder, spins me around and frisks me. He finds nothing, then turns me back.

"You can put your hands down." He examines me. "There's something off about you."

"Haven't been the same since my son died."

His face remains hard for a moment, then softens. "That's probably it." He snaps his pistol back in the holster. "Where'd he die?"

"Iraq. Haditha."

The policeman shakes his head. "Tough luck. How'd it happen?"

"Friendly fire," I say, staring at Staff Sergeant Reyes as he separates himself from the others and pours on speed. He whips past the bomb.

"Doubly tough. Were they punished?"

"It's an ongoing process," I say.

"Just tough," he says, as he turns back towards his bike.

I can't help but giggle.

He turns back to me and gives me a baleful stare. He speaks low into his mobile radio, his eyes never leaving me.

Asshat's going to arrest you, Mutt says. *Asshat cop thinks you're a crazy asshat pedophile and is going to call backup.*

I can feel it coming. In a desperate ploy, I point towards the pizza box. "Look at that!"

The policeman follows the direction of my finger to where the pizza box lays alongside the track.

"There. See it?"

"What about it?" he asks, suspiciously.

Asshat thinks you're crazy, Mutt says.

Asshat is right, I think. *Crazy as a fucking loon.* I can't help but giggle. I've come to love the term *ASSHAT*.

That was your outside voice, Mutt points out like I'm the King of All Asshats.

"What'd you say?" the policeman says.

Everything goes into slow motion. He looks to the pizza box and the kids running past, then he looks at me. I can see his mind spinning furiously but unable to fathom what is about to take place. He takes a step towards me.

I step back and shake my head. "Sorry. Like you said. I'm a little off."

He stops.

I watch as he seems to come to term with the idea that I may be insane. I mouth the word *BOOM!*

Staff Sergeant Reyes is approaching my bomb. I press the speed dial. I wait three seconds, wondering whether it will be confetti or skin raining down on the gaggle of boys twenty meters behind him.

Kawhoomp!

The shockwave knocks us back.

I turn in time to see the red-tinged cloud rise into the air like Ezekiel's own mushroom cloud of righteous destruction. The boys struggle to their feet. Most of them are holding their ears and screaming. The open-jawed policeman stares blankly at me, I shrug, then he takes off running towards the carnage, shouting for help into his mobile radio.

Asshat, I say or don't say to his back. *Should have arrested me when you had the chance.*

It's nothing for me and Mutt to get in my car and head down the road. I'm aware that sooner or later I'm going to have to get rid of the car. I'll miss it, but maybe I can get another *Bwik*, one in which the ghost of my son can ride, as me and his mother, whom I'm certain is locked within the fluffy skin of a dog, trundle on down the road of righteous redemption to deliver four more bombs.

Daddy! Come out and play war with us, he said once when he was seven or eight years old.

I remember asking who he was going to be, the good guys or the bad guys.

He gave me one of those looks like Mutt would give, but without calling me asshat. *We're always the good guys, Dad. Come on, Dad!*

And I remember that exact moment, standing on the porch with a glass of ice tea sweating in my hand, wondering about all the children of bad men in the world, if when they played war if they played at being bad guys. Somehow I doubted it. At the end of the day, everyone's a good guy. It's just that some can be even more good, especially if they're righteous.

And I am about as righteous an *asshat* as there ever was.

Look out world, here I come.

The Meaning of Life

BY AMELIA BEAMER

Have you ever watched a little kid who really likes to hurt things and gone, "Oh, this is not gonna turn out well"? All through my life, I've taken note of them as they crossed my path, and wondered who they turned out to be.

Or, more specifically, what they wound up doing.

I gotta tell ya: this was the single toughest read of the book for me. To the point where I said to Amelia Beamer—again, one of my favorite new writers, whose work often sparkles with charm and wit—"You know that people are going to hate you for writing this story."

But she knew, as I knew—and my editor agreed—that you can't do a book like this without a story like this. Because herein lies the terrible truth.

So I'm not kidding when I slap a warning sticker on "The Meaning of Life." It may not be your meaning—I sincerely hope it isn't—but that doesn't change the facts.

Jonathan's life started on the day with the butterfly. He was in the yard, his mother was kneeling in her garden, busy with the dirt and plants. The butterfly landed on a flower near where he was sitting. He had seen pictures of butterflies in books, but this was alive. He understood the difference for the first time.

He reached out for it and to his surprise he caught it. He pinched its wing between his fingers as gently as he could and brought it close to study it. It struggled. He decided it was a boy butterfly, because all animals were boys, all the good ones anyway. He watched the butterfly beat his wings. He wanted to know what made him alive.

The small boy checked that his mother was not watching, in case he was not supposed to have a butterfly. He turned his back to her, just to be safe.

Jonathan examined the small, hairy legs of the butterfly as they kicked and squirmed. There was an orange powder on his fingers from the butterfly's wing. The wing was already torn, even though he was holding it as gently as he could. The butterfly had a tiny face: black eyes, and long, wiggly antennae. He couldn't see the butterfly's mouth but he knew it must have one.

Carefully, he pulled off one of the legs. It was really easy. He looked at the leg, or what he could see of it, as it was pinched between his fingers and he did not want to drop it. He rolled it between his fingers until it got rubbed into a black mess. He was fascinated.

So he did it again. And again until there were no legs left. Then he did the same with the antenna. Somewhere inside this butterfly, he knew, was life.

The boy really liked the round shiny blackness of the butterfly's belly. So he pinched it until it broke. The goo that came out was no colored. He squished it between his fingers. Then, very carefully, he tore off one wing.

What was left of the butterfly's body stopped moving. That was it. The boy felt a feeling that he had never felt before. A wonderful, wonderful feeling. He felt big and strong. His belly was warm and tingly. He crushed the wing in his hand and watched it turn into powder and goo. He rubbed it between his palms and then studied the mess. The life was gone. This was all that was left.

The feeling of power grew stronger in the boy. *He* had done this. He had felt life, and he had taken it.

How could anyone forget that feeling? The boy thought of it often. He became an expert at killing bugs, anything that he could catch. His parents bought him a kit with a butterfly net and a killing jar, and that was fun.

Jonathan particularly liked ants, not only because they were easy but because of the strange sugary smell they gave off when you squished them. The big brown carpenter ants were his favorite.

But he grew bored. The good feeling got smaller and smaller, and he started thinking bigger.

Jonathan asked for a hamster. He was excited when he got one. He named the hamster Sammy, after Sammy Davis Jr. He let Sammy run around in his room. He liked when he crawled on him: he liked the feeling of Sammy's soft fur and nails. He played with Sammy and fed him and cleaned up after him until the itch grew too strong and he started making plans to kill him. Jonathan was five years old.

He knew he had to go somewhere private, outside. It was too risky to do it in the house. Plus it would probably be messy. He would need a knife, at a minimum. Maybe scissors, he wasn't sure. He would tell his parents that the hamster got lost.

The boy waited until one day when the weather was perfect. His father was out and his mother was in a good mood. He asked to play outside in the backyard, where his mother could see him from the kitchen window. Jonathan promised not to leave the yard.

His mother agreed and said she was going to make cookies. So she would be busy for a little while. The boy was happy about that, and about the cookies.

He put Sammy in his sweatshirt pocket, where nobody could see him. In his sleeve he had a steak knife and his mother's sewing scissors, and the best thing of all in his other pocket: a long needle he had found in his mother's sewing kit. Just the thought of the needle made him feel wiggly inside.

Jonathan was careful not to let his mother see his excitement. He went outside. He'd promised to sit where his mother could see him, and he realized that he needed to look like he was doing something. So he went to the sandbox and took off the cover. The sand was clean and fresh and there were nice, new buckets and shovels. He put the hamster in the sandbox. Sammy was happy running around smelling everything.

But Jonathan grew bored after a minute. He wanted to get on with his experiment. He wanted to understand what made Sammy alive.

First he decided to use the pin. He poked the hamster in its belly.

He did not expect the hamster to scream. It was a scratchy, strange noise. The hamster bit him. He dropped Sammy and examined the tiny bite mark on his hand. A drop of blood welled up. It hurt. But not enough to change his plans.

Jonathan caught the hamster and held him so that he couldn't bite. Sammy's eyes were wide and frightened, and he was shaking. This was not easy. The boy realized he would have to go faster than he wanted to. He eyed first the knife and then the scissors. He wasn't sure what to do.

He chose the scissors and cut off the hamster's head. Or rather he tried to, it didn't actually come off, but kind of halfway. The hamster screamed. Blood was going everywhere, on his clothes and hands. The boy tried again with the scissors until he had cut the head off. Sammy's head fell into the sand. The hamster's body went still.

It was a lovely feeling, the warm, bloody hamster, soft in his hands. He loved also the feeling still in his fingers of snipping Sammy's head off. This was way better than bugs, no question. He felt so powerful he laughed.

He cut a line down the hamster's belly. Inside, the hamster was all sorts of colors, not just red but also yellow fatty bits and bluey grays. Twisty stuff. He poked the guts with the needle. It felt good, the way the meat moved. Then he used the scissors to cut the inside of the hamster until he could see bits of bone. He cut the bones apart as well, just to see if he could. He cut up the guts. There was a smell of poop, and he understood that there was poop inside the hamster. This made him laugh. He felt so good inside.

After a while there wasn't much body any more. The boy realized that he had to put the pieces somewhere that his parents wouldn't find them. Bury them somewhere that they would not be dug up. The sandbox wasn't safe, neither was his mother's garden. He'd have to think of somewhere.

Jonathan put the pieces of Sammy into a bucket, along with the sand that had got blood on it. One little hamster eye looked back at him.

He thought about putting the stuff in the trash can, but that would be no good because his parents would see it. Then he thought about just putting it over the fence into the neighbor's yard. They had a dog, so everyone would think the hamster got killed by the dog, if there was enough of the hamster left for anyone to know it had been a hamster. Probably the dog would eat it anyway.

So he threw the remains over the fence. He felt a bit sad watching it go.

Then he thought about the blood on himself. He remembered the time when his father had had a nosebleed, and got blood on his shirt. Jonathan decided to tell his mother that his nose had bled.

He got extra cookies. And later when he said that his hamster was "lost," he got lots of hugs, although he didn't get a new hamster.

Soon he was thinking about what came next. He wanted something bigger, something more. But he didn't feel strong enough or big enough. So he decided to wait for his own body to get a bit bigger. He killed bugs sometimes, plus he also had other things to do, like school and playing and television.

He also started watching from the window. Cats, birds, squirrels.

He made friends with a cat. The cat was white and thin and old and his fur looked kinda gross. He didn't have a collar, which meant he probably didn't have a home. Jonathan fed him salami pieces from the refrigerator, the drawer that said "Meats 'n Snacks."

After a few weeks, the cat started letting Jonathan touch him. Jonathan was not in a hurry. He liked to think about the cat: where he could take it, what he could do to it. Cats were a different league entirely. He thought about knives, and poison, until he finally thought about a hammer. That was a nice thought.

Jonathan was a good boy. He liked being good and being told he was good. He loved his parents. He knew that they did not care about life in the way that he did: they did not understand it or want to feel it the way he did. He accepted this, and knew better than to try and share it with them.

The cat started to trust Jonathan. He would sit in his lap and purr as Jonathan petted him. Jonathan enjoyed the rusty sound, and the softness of the cat's fur, and the feel of the cat's sandpaper tongue as it licked his hand.

The day came when it felt right. He got permission to play outside. The cat came. He followed Jonathan behind the garage. Jonathan had a hammer, scissors, and a knife. He fed and petted the cat one last time. He let him sniff the hammer.

The first blow only stunned the cat. Jonathan held onto the back of the cat's neck so he couldn't run away. The cat scratched the boy's arm, but it didn't hurt. He hit him again. He had swung a hammer before but it had never felt like this. The cat's eyes showed many emotions including surprise, pain, anger, and a feeling like he never would have expected this from *him*.

He hit the cat until the cat's eyes closed and there was red blood on his fur. It was the best feeling ever.

The cat's skull was funny shaped. He wasn't moving. Jonathan wasn't sure if he was still alive. When he touched him with the hammer, he twitched. The boy shuddered with pleasure. This was the most real moment of his life: what he had done could not be undone. *He* had done this. He was real.

He watched the cat and poked him until he didn't move any more. Then he started to cut. He was surprised at the amount of blood, and at the different colors and textures. It was like the hamster but much more so. He especially enjoyed cutting apart the cat's knees: they were a tiny bit like the drumsticks on a chicken.

He buried the remains in his secret place, underneath the front porch, where nobody ever went aside from him. He was proud of this plan. This way he could keep the cat close, and nobody would know. He wrapped it in his bloody shirt before he buried it, and washed his hands and arms with the hose. He'd brought a spare shirt outside with him so he could go inside wearing a clean shirt. He also felt proud for having that idea.

After the cat, bugs held no interest. Time passed. Jonathan killed another cat, and then a small dog. He buried them under the porch. Sometimes he would go sit under the porch and just remember how good it felt. He wanted more. He waited and grew and thought.

And then one day he stood in the school yard at recess, watching the little kids, and he had the idea that perhaps he could kill one of them. Just the thought kept him happy for weeks. He was ten years old.

The thing was, it had to look like an accident. He wished he could just take a kid and do what he'd done with the animals and bury him under the porch, but he knew that wouldn't work. The risk was just too much. There was no way to keep it secret.

So he volunteered to help mind the little kids during recess. He enjoyed spending time with them and seeing them have fun and helping them to do things like climb the ladder to the slide. He pushed them on the swings. He didn't like the way their noses dripped snot, and how sticky and dirty their hands were, and how they would cry for no reason. But he liked being praised by the teachers and his parents for being a good boy and helping. Other students his age also helped, but they were all girls, so he didn't have much use for them. Jonathan's friends were all boys.

While he played with the little kids he looked at the play structures and thought about the many ways that the kids could accidentally die or at least get hurt. Falling from high up on the monkey bars. Being high up on the swing and having it break. Being hit in the head by a branch that fell out of a tree, or by a rock or a ball that someone threw. All of these things would be good, but Jonathan needed it to happen in a way that he didn't get in trouble. So he waited and hoped and imagined. Kids, he'd noticed, were clumsy and often hurt themselves by accident.

Then one day as the bell rang, the impossible happened. A boy named Freddie was going down the tube slide, one last slide before going back to class. He got stuck at the top, and Jonathan just happened to be standing a few feet away.

The little kid's body dangled inside the orange plastic slide, hidden from view. The string from the little boy's hood had got caught in a crack at the top of the slide. The cord was trapped under his chin, choking him.

The rest of the kids were on their way back to the school. They made noise enough so that nobody, Jonathan thought, could hear Freddie gasp and cough. His breathing was loud and funny. He moved his arms and legs like a bug, trying to grab onto something. He tried to free himself from the cord around his neck but the weight of his body held him still. He tried to speak. Jonathan wasn't sure if Freddy knew if anyone else was there or not. All the kid could see was the inside of the slide.

Jonathan's mind went fast. His body was singing with excitement. He crouched down so that if someone looked at the play structure they wouldn't see him, and also so that he could be closer to the little boy. Freddy wore a blue jacket and he was probably about three years old. His face was turning red and his eyes were huge and scared.

Jonathan realized that he could help the boy. He could scream and run and get adults to come and save the boy. Or he could pull him up so that he could breathe. Knowing that he could do these things and that he did not want to was a strange and good feeling.

Then he realized that if the boy saw him and Jonathan didn't help him and the boy lived and talked about what had happened, he would be in *trouble*. But if the boy died and people knew he'd been out here, he would be in trouble, too. He didn't know what to do.

The final bell rang. The playground was empty.

Jonathan watched the small boy struggle to breathe. There were tears on the kid's cheeks. His body flopped and twitched. There was a smell of poop and pee.

Jonathan threw up then. He couldn't help it. The puke dripped through the spaces in the platform of the play structure. He could see chunks of his sandwich and potato chips. The puke got in his nose and made his eyes water. He threw up until there was only bitter spit left. He spat and spat, and pukey tears ran down his cheeks.

When his belly had stopped heaving, he looked at Freddy. The little kid had stopped moving. Jonathan felt all sorts of feelings, both really good and really scared. This was the best and the worst moment of his life. He had not killed the boy himself, not exactly, but he believed the boy was dead. Jonathan knew that he could have done something to help this kid, and he hadn't, because he hadn't wanted to, and he felt good about that. Powerful.

He thought about how everyone would panic and then be sad. He felt how important a person's life was. A person's life, even a little kid's, was so much bigger than an animal's. So much better.

He worked to get enough breath inside himself so that he could think about what to do next.

Then he understood what his body had done for him. Whoever saw his puke would understand that he got scared and didn't know what to do. He could tell the adults that he wasn't sure whether to run for help or to try and help the kid himself, that he couldn't decide and got overwhelmed. Then they wouldn't think he'd done anything wrong.

He decided he would run into the school and find an adult and scream that Freddy had had an accident and got hurt and needed help. He would tell the truth about seeing it happen and not knowing what to do. He was sure that they would understand. After everything that he had done to animals, no one had ever said anything or even suspected anything. People just couldn't think like that about anyone they knew.

As he ran he thought about how wonderful he felt, and when he might be able to feel this good again. He was twelve years old, and he knew what he was meant to do with his life.

Damaged Goods

BY ELIZABETH MASSIE

I've said it before, and I'll say it again: Elizabeth Massie is one of the hardest-punching women in the history of horror fiction. Behind that sweet-faced, grade-school teacher demeanor lies a fist so fierce it'll knock your teeth out the back of your skull, often so swiftly you won't even know what hit you.

I first encountered "Damaged Goods" when Beth and I did a joint reading at the Horrorfind Convention in 2004, right outside Baltimore. Because she is genuinely one of the nicest people you'd ever hope to meet, even those of us who knew how dangerous she is were disarmed as she cheerfully took center stage.

Then she started reading, and our jaws hit the floor, only coming up to jitter in the kind of panicked laughter usually reserved for Bentley Little, or early John Waters at his transgressive craziest.

Needless to say, when this book came about, that story she'd read was one of the first I sought out. I couldn't remember the name, but I'll never forget the feeling.

And neither will you.

"You put your penis here," Darla said.

Paul, sitting in the tall grass next to her, rolled his eyes in embarrassment.

"You hear me?" Darla repeated. She had her yellow cotton skirt up over her knees, and although she retained her pink panties, she poked her index finger with firm direction at the space between her thighs. "I'm the lamb, and it goes here. God, you're dumb."

Paul pulled out the nub of wild mint he had been chewing and turned on his butt, moving so Darla was no longer in his sight. He stared, instead, at the pasture in which they sat and at the shallow river running nearby. He wasn't certain where the pasture was; he and Darla had been rightfully blindfolded in the van until they were placed in the grass. The sun was behind the two of them, setting in the warm, late spring sky just over the woods to their backs. The men with the sunglasses were in those woods, hiding and silent.

Waiting.

"You're so fucking dumb," Darla continued. "Don't care about nothing except yourself."

Paul closed his eyes and tucked his head. She was right. He was afraid of responsibility. He wasn't good at it and he was afraid of it. Several years ago when he had been living at home, his mother had asked him to watch his baby brother. A simple request. "I got to get this down to the bank. Just let Timmy stay in the crib. I know you can do it. Just twenty minutes, you hear?"

Paul had heard. And Mom had left. But what a mistake she had made, giving him a chore. Silly old Mom. Paul loved Tim, and he liked to play with the little boy. Paul had forgotten that his brother could not eat peanuts, that baby Tim had no teeth and couldn't chew. Paul thought a nut-eating contest would be fun. For each peanut Paul had eaten, he had put one in the baby's mouth. He sang as they played.

"Old MacDonald had a farm, ee-ii-ee-ii-oh. And on his farm he had a cow, ee-ii-ee-ii-oh."

Almost the whole can of Mr. Peanuts was gone after three verses. Paul got to giggling, and he thought that Tim was giggling, too—his face was all shiny and tight and he made funny noises in his throat. But, as Paul found out, the baby wasn't laughing. And Mom didn't laugh, either, when she came back from the bank to find the baby was dead.

But here was responsibility again. And Darla with her dress hiked up and her ass raised to the soft blue sky.

"I can't," Paul said without looking back.

"Hell you can't. All mens can do it. You got a dick, don't cha? It squirts, don't it?"

Paul cringed. Darla wasn't supposed to know about what men's things did. She wasn't yet eighteen. But she knew, all right. She had had a couple babies and a couple operations, too. She lived in the special church home where Paul lived. She did sex things with any man that could walk: residents, orderlies, old drunks from the street that she called to from her third-floor window.

Paul, on the other hand, two full years older than Darla, had never done what she had done. He thought about it, although he tried not to. He watched Darla during dinner or activity time, and he got a knot in his pants. Sometimes he even pretended his fingers were hers, late at night when the lights were low and the sheets were up over his head. Sometimes he sweated like a horse, he wanted it so bad. But this was daylight, and this was out in the open, and there were men with sunglasses in the trees. This was not pretend.

"Some lion you is," said Darla. She passed air through her lips in a noisy declaration of contempt, and Paul could hear rustling as she pulled her skirt down. He looked back. Her eyebrows were a thick, angry tangle.

Darla wasn't ugly, but she was scarred. Her nose was crooked where some man broke it one time, and the puckered remnants of a long knife wound cut across her throat. Black hair cupped the curve of her cheek in a thin cap. She squinted, because her eyes were bad, but she wouldn't wear glasses. Paul wanted to do what had been asked of him, but he wasn't sure he knew how. He was nervous, even if it was for God.

In his nervousness, he began to sing. He couldn't help himself. He sang on key, soft and trembling. "With a baa-baa here and a baa-baa there, old McDonald had a lamb, ee-ii-ee-ii-oh."

Darla laughed at him, and he wasn't sure why.

"Old MacDonald had a farm, ee-ii-ee-ii-oh. And on his farm he had a lion, ee-ii-ee-ii-oh. With a—"

Then Darla grabbed Paul sharply by the shoulders. Her face squinted up like her eyes. "You might be stupid, but I ain't. I know what's going on here. And I ain't going to let you ruin it. It's for the world, goddamnit, do you hear what I'm saying? We'll be famous, you fucker, not to mention going to heaven for sure. It ain't long to go now, and you better be ready or I'll chew off your nose and send you to hell myself."

Paul watched her face. He felt tears pushing at his eyes, but he worked them back down. She was right, and he knew it.

A new preacher had come to the church home last week. He had walked around for a long time, and Paul had seen him go up and down the halls, all serious and stately in his black suit and white shirt, a big Bible with a tasseled bookmark streaming from the middle pages. He had short brown hair and his ears were sunburned. Paul watched when he thought the preacher didn't know he was watching. But then the preacher had come right up to Paul as he sat looking at cartoons in the rec room. Without even asking, the man turned off the television set, took Paul out to the backyard, and read to him from the Bible.

"The lion shall lie down with the lamb," the preacher had begun, and Paul nodded because a preacher was a man of God and knew what he was talking about, even if it made no sense to Paul. "Do you know, son, that that line is the prophecy of the end of war and the beginning of true peace?"

Paul nodded again, and out of the corner of his eye he watched as a squirrel with a torn, bloodied back pawed an acorn from the ground.

"I have had a sign, and I have shared it with others who understand. They sent me here, to find you."

Paul suddenly thought he was going to the electric chair for killing his baby brother, after all this time, and the preacher was to give him his last meal and pray with him. Paul started to cry.

"Weep not," said the preacher. "For blessed are the pure in heart. They shall see God."

Paul's lips twitched, and the tears continued.

"Blessed are the damaged ones, for they will bring perfection to our world."

The preacher told Paul of the Holy Plan and kissed him before he left.

Now they were here. This was the day. It was secret, of course, because the masses, so the preacher said, would not understand the seriousness of what was going to take place. There was only one audience, and they were in the trees now, waiting patiently. Only One was missing, and He would arrive very soon.

Paul and Darla, the chosen ones, the damaged ones, were here to be the lion and the lamb. At their union, all the evils of the world would be bound and thrown to the pit of fire and onto Satan's head.

Paul reached under his shirt and scratched his chest nervously, leaving long fingernail lines. He looked past Darla's shoulder. Soon He would come. Then it would be time to act. Paul would either get over his embarrassment and do to Darla what he'd always wanted to do in the late-night hours, or he would let the world continue to fight and kill and torture and tear itself into a million pieces.

Darla said, "Hey."

Paul blinked but said nothing.

Darla said, "Hey."

He looked at her. "What?"

"I'll rub you. It'll help."

Paul shuddered at the thought. But he became instantly hard.

"I'll rub you and it'll be easier. Big shit, you can think of somebody else if you want, I don't care. Damaged goods is what they wanted, but you can think of someone else, okay?"

Paul said, "Okay."

Darla smiled then, the first time since the blindfolds had been removed. With the sun behind her head, she almost looked like an angel.

And then there was a shadowy sparkling from the trees, and Paul knew that He had arrived. The long car with its secret windows pulled up behind the outer edge of trees and stopped. Men in sunglasses became briefly visible as they shifted and stamped in silent respect.

"He's here," whispered Darla.

Paul reached under his shirt and scratched frantically.

Out of the woods came the preacher, and behind the preacher He came. Darla and Paul sat motionless. Paul felt his muscles kick into spastic idle; he shook uncontrollably.

The preacher wore his black suit and white shirt. He smiled a beautiful smile.

The Man with him was tall and white-haired and wore a gray suit and sunglasses. He said nothing but stood in command of them all.

The preacher said, "The lion will lie down with the lamb. In this will be the beginning of peace, and all nations will lose their love of war."

Darla's eyes were turned up in an expression of near-worship. Paul scratched his chest, making it burn.

"Thus it is said," continued the preacher. "When she who is the lamb and he who is the lion lie together, and become as one, the veil of hate will be rent."

The Man with the preacher crossed his arms. His hands were soft and strong. His fingernails trimmed and clean.

"Blessed be the lion and the lamb."

Darla whispered, "Amen."

"Please," said the preacher. "Make the prophecy come true." With that, the preacher fell silent.

Darla looked at Paul. "I'll rub you," she said.

Paul's fingers became still on his chest. He watched as Darla moved her hand to the snap on his pants and popped it open. The zipper was undone, exposing Paul's white briefs. Darla's touch and the cool spring air on the cotton stirred Paul's organ again. It tingled in anticipation and pushed at the cloth. Paul wanted to cover himself. He wanted Darla to suck him and make him explode.

"Come on, lion," said Darla. "Lie with me."

Ee-ii-ee-ii-oh, thought Paul.

Darla slipped her hands beneath Paul's hips, and he instinctively rose up so she could pull his jeans down to his knees. Then she loosened his shoes and tossed them aside. His socks followed, and then the jeans, one leg at a time. Paul sat back on the prickly grass. He wondered if little Tim would have been proud of his big brother now, the new savior of the world.

The yellow skirt with its elasticized waist came up over Darla's head. Her pink panties appeared to be damp. Darla touched her thighs, her belly button, the damp pink panties.

Paul realized that she was not going to remove her own blouse, nor his shirt. Not that it mattered: The business ends were already exposed. He wanted to touch his penis but was afraid. He would let Darla take charge. She knew what to do. Blessed be the lamb who sucks the dick of the lion.

Darla caught Paul's hand in her own. She moved it to the panties and worked his fingers down inside. Paul gasped at the feel of coarse hair. "Oh," he moaned.

He thought he heard the Man echo, "Oh."

"Come on," Darla said, her breath hot on Paul's face. "I'll rub you and you rub me."

Paul's fingers began stroking the thick hair below the elastic. No longer could he feel the burning scratches on his chest; his own breath came in horrified, ecstatic jolts. Darla found his erection with the palm of her hand. Paul arched his back, pressing into her touch.

The Man with the preacher opened his own pants, and from the corner of his eye, Paul saw him reach in to stroke himself.

But Darla took his attention back with a firm squeeze. "Lie with me." Her voice was barely audible. "Stop wars. Bring peace." She slipped her hand inside his briefs and brought his organ out into the sun. Passion, embarrassment, anticipation, and fear cut his heart. Paul groaned.

The Man and the preacher groaned, too.

Somewhere beyond the holy union, sunglasses, moving to the edge of the woods, winked in unison.

Darla tore the seams of her panties and tossed them out with Paul's socks. She ripped away Paul's briefs with sharp nails. She folded, and her mouth took Paul's penis in a wet caress.

"Ee-ii-ee-ii-oh!" Paul shrieked. He felt the swelling pressure, the urgent demand as her tongue studied him. He wanted to stop for a moment, he was rushing ahead too fast, he could not think of what was happening and he wanted to, he wanted to have memories of this and think of it again and again, but it was too fast. Too fast.

"Wait!" he screamed.

Darla dove backward, dragging Paul with her. She threw her legs apart and shoved Paul into the wet place beneath the dark hair. Paul bucked instinctively, furiously. He was so swollen he knew he would rip her open, but that was fine. That was good. The lion tearing the lamb for the peace of the world.

And then the divine, glorious explosion.

"Oh, my God!" shouted Paul.

"Oh, God!" shouted Darla.

"Oh, God," grunted the Man near them.

Paul fell, face into the sharp grass, arm crumpled up under him, folded against Darla's breast. His groin and stomach continued to shudder with aftershocks. He could hear Darla's pants. He could feel the sweat of her body. It was warm, like a beautiful, peaceful bath.

"Yes," said Darla in his ear. "We laid down together. Lion and the lamb. We done it." It sounded as if she were weeping with joy.

Paul began to laugh for the same reason. "We saved the world," he sang. "Ee-ii-ee-ii-oh, we saved the world from war!"

He heard the preacher laughing, too.

Then the preacher said, "Well, sir, that do the trick?"

Paul used his untrapped hand to wipe a gnat out of his eye. He squinted up at the men near them in the pasture.

The Man had his penis out of his pants, and it was erect. His mouth was a straight, tight line across his face. His eyes were still invisible behind the glasses. There were sweat droplets on his cheeks and hands.

For the first time, the Man spoke: "Not quite. Almost."

"Shit," said the preacher, and Paul flinched. Preachers didn't talk like that, not at the church home, anyway. "We got another go-round," the preacher went on. "If you'd like."

Paul worked himself up off of Darla. He sat and brushed dead grass from his legs. Darla lay still, basking in the glory of her success.

The Man wiped his mouth, gazed out past the river, then back to the preacher. He said, "Why couldn't I go for golfing?"

"Different strokes," said the preacher, and he laughed again, once.

Darla opened her eyes and looked at them all.

Then the preacher swung his foot and caught Paul in the ribs. "Get up, morons," he said. He kicked Paul again.

Darla sat up immediately. Her mouth hung open, bad teeth showing. "What the hell are you doing?" she said. "What is the matter with you?"

Paul began to shake. He stood and looked over at his torn underwear in the weeds. He glanced down at his exposed penis. With a surge of supreme humiliation, he covered himself with his hands.

"Thanks for saving the world," said the preacher.

Darla jumped to her feet. "What the fuck's going on?" she screamed. She raised her hand to strike the preacher, but he caught it and twisted it. Darla dropped to her knees.

"I've got State of the Union tomorrow," the Man said to the preacher. "Teddy got off on hunting, Ronald on his horses. Sports just don't cut it for me. I have to have my stress release or who knows what wrong decisions I might make?"

The preacher said, "You don't have to convince me. I'm just happy to be part of the smooth running of the government. 'Remembereth me as thou dwelleth in thy kingdom.'" He smiled a chilling smile.

"Another go-round," said the Man. "Please. That would be good."

The preacher pulled a small pistol from his black jacket. His smile was gone, but in its place was not anger, just emotionless duty. "To the river," he said.

Darla was crying. She stayed on her knees until the preacher put the pistol to her head. "To the river," he said. "We don't have time for this shit."

Darla stood up beside Paul. The preacher led them to the river's edge. He took white strips of cloth from his pocket. He tightly gagged Darla's mouth. Then he gagged Paul.

"Silence of the lamb," said the preacher. "And the lion." He laughed.

Paul began to choke against the dry cloth. He could not swallow. He felt his nose could not take in enough air. Had the wars stopped? Had the peace come?

"Hands back," said the preacher.

Darla shook her head violently. The preacher put the mouth of the gun against her teeth and she stopped. She put her hands behind her back, and the preacher tied them with cloth. Then he looked at Paul.

Paul put his hands back.

"Good little lion," said the preacher, and he secured Paul's wrists. "You won't be shot, though. Morons drown so much more naturally."

There was a rumbling from the woods, and Paul looked behind to see a van moving out into the pasture. The Man stepped back to give it room. It stopped, and the engine was cut.

Darla's eyes widened in hope. Paul tried to stumble forward. Rescue, oh, God, yes, thank God, thank God! He uttered a choked whine of agonized appeal.

The driver of the van swung out and around, then opened the sliding door on the side. Two blindfolded people climbed slowly into the daylight.

A young blindfolded man. A young blindfolded woman.

"They're going to save the world, too," said the preacher.

Ee-ii-ee-ii-oh, thought Paul.

The preacher baptized Darla and Paul in the brisk, running water of the river.

Willow Tests Well

BY NICK MAMATAS

Savvy business types with their eye on the future have long been keen on recruitment techniques. Genuine talent is often easy to spot, straight out of the cradle, if you know what to look for. And some skills are more useful than others in the massive scheme of things.

Doubtless, little Nick Mamatas was quickly pegged as a snarky subversive, roughly twice as smart and three times as tart as his teachers and classmates combined. No wonder he grew up to be nothing but trouble.

Here to help decipher systemic psychosis on a grand scale is "Willow Tests Well," a Machiavellian meme already in progress through much of the so-called civilized world.

Willow got her first birthday card from a stranger on her ninth. Not a stranger, really. The director of the Federal Bureau of Investigation was on TV so frequently that he was practically a friend of the family. Her parents insisted on watching the news—both the fun local news where people smiled, did banter and half the stories were about great red smears and ruined cars on the nearby streets, and the boring national news—every night during dinner. Willow liked the director of the FBI. His name was Bottomore and he had a dimple right in the middle of his chin. Where she liked it.

When Bottomore died some months later, Willow wasn't sad. Not exactly sad—tingly, upset, anticipating something that could never be. Because Willow was never sad. She always felt just fine.

"How was school?" her father asked.

"Fine," she said. No need for father to pry any further. Willow tested very well—she was already reading and performing mathematics on a twelfth-grade level. Willow could probably skip a grade if she wanted to, and by the time she was fifteen take community college classes for full credit.

"What do you think of this sweater?" her stepmother asked, pointing to the picture on her laptop. Willow's real mother had run off some time before. "They have them in, uh, Bubble, Amaranth, or . . . Durian. Geez, what do these colors even mean?"

"Blue, green, or brown," Willow said. Then she said, "Any of those would be fine. Thank you, Doris."

"So clever," Doris said.

Tenth birthday: greeting cards from the CIA and NSA. Willow had scored ridiculously well on the Race to the Top tests, and even discovered the instructions for and answered the questions in the secret test integrated into the exam. Questions like

What does the old saying "A bird in the hand is worth two in the bush" mean?"

a. birds are unpleasant because they need to be cared for

b. it's better to own something than risk what you have for a potential reward

c. if you have a bird in your hand, you can squeeze it, you can kill it . . .

d. possession is nine-tenths of the law

Willow knew that the answer was C. So various intelligence agencies began negotiating. Who would get Willow? Three weeks later her parents were killed in a terrible if well-choreographed car accident. Her father's head was sheared off— his face was nothing but a jaw topped with meat sauce. Her stepmother died in the hospital of less photogenic injuries. Willow was sent to live with her biological mother, whose economic situation had taken a turn for the worse since her flight and abandonment. For some reason, she had a coroner's photo of her ex-husband in the bottom drawer of her pressed wood bureau, and Willow found it easily. She lived in the city, in a sweltering one-room bedsit with cinderblock walls atop a dying florist.

The florist was an NSA front. Willow would stop in after school to look at the flowers while waiting for her mother to get home from her job at an industrial bakery. The whole neighborhood smelled like cinnamon and burning plastic.

"What's this flower?" Willow asked one day.

"Those are chrysanthemums," the florist said. He always had a pair of clippers in hand.

"They look like people's heads," Willow said. "I mean, more than other flowers. Like a big round head full of curly hair."

The florist smiled and said, "I know a flower that looks like you. I have it in the back." He left his clippers behind as he turned to go to the cooler in the back room. When he came back, the mums were all headless, but he kept smiling and presented black-haired Willow with a black-petaled flower. "It's a black beauty hollyhock," he said, and presented it to her. Willow brought her hands out from behind her back and knew she didn't need to hide the clippers anymore.

"It does look like me," she said as she accepted the flower. "Just like me. Black all around, with a yellow spike in the middle." The florist's tight-slipped smile betrayed a twitch at that.

Willow's grades began to falter. She was new in school, and quiet, and large-eyed and wore clothes that were popular two years prior. Some of them had stains on the sleeves, from their original owners. Boys mostly ignored her, but occasionally pulled her hair as they passed her in the hallways. Girls were much worse.

They worked in groups, surrounding her.

"So your dad is dead, huh? Must have been a suicide."

"How does your mom afford your fancy apartment? Is she a prostitute?"

"What are you going to do for Take Your Daughter to Work day?"

"She's upset. Look, don't be upset, Willow. There's nothing to cry about. We're your friends. Are you getting your period?"

"Your first period?"

"Does your mother take a few days off from work when she has her period?"

"Will you have to take over for her," the main girl said, even taking Willow's hand in her own and patting it comfortingly, "when she is so indisposed."

Willow stood there, hair over her face, taking it. Surveillance cameras, parabolic mics, satellites that could find a 1976 bicentennial quarter flipped into the Grand Canyon, all focused on her. She didn't snap. The ringleader didn't end up with a pencil in her eye, the others weren't beaten with a pipe or pushed in front of a city bus. Willow just went home after school let out, as she did every day, except that three blocks from her apartment she made friends with a little four-year-old boy and, taking him by the hand, walked him face-first into a lamppost, then left him on the corner to cry and bleed.

There are two kinds of children who attract the attention of the federal government's alphabet soup. They are both prodigies in their way. Kids with a knack for math and lateral thinking are recruited early on. Birthday cards emblazoned with the seals of major intelligence and law enforcement agencies still mean something special, even in these days of single-digit approval ratings. Those numbers are only for the *elected* government. The permanent government has a more entrenched reputation. So the little smartypantses get their cards and parents get the hint—judo lessons, laptops, tutors, Chinese and Arabic flashcards. Despite the best efforts of the *petit-bourgeoisie*, there's a strong regression toward the mean. Most genius ten-year-olds are utterly ordinary sixteen-year-olds. Only a few retain the interest of federal recruiters, and otnly a fraction of those suitable can be lured away from the business world with appeals to the spirit of public service and promises of proximity to power.

There are other organizations that keep track of girls like Willow.

Willow continued to do very well on her tests, even as her attendance in school grew increasingly erratic, and her work indifferent. She sucked her first cock at thirteen, and started smoking cigarettes. She got bombed out on cheap bourbon on her fourteenth birthday. Her boyfriend was nineteen, and fancied himself the local Great White Hope at the boxing gym where he trains four days a week. He loosened two of Willow's teeth with an open-handed smack once. She left a stray cat in the trash, its head turned one hundred and eighty degrees. Mother had to take a second job—industrial bakery in the morning, night shift at a Dunkin Donuts. Somewhere in Langley, Virginia a mouse was clicked and an insurance settlement check in Willow's name fortuitously kept the family from eviction, making community college a possibility after all.

Willow didn't need to go to the doctor for an abortion. She drowned her fetus in her belly with sizzurp and shellfish. She finally broke up with her boyfriend after three years and found him another fourteen-year-old—that's how he liked them, just wisps down there—and thus he promised not to kill himself after all. Memoranda flew back and forth. High-priority emails were sent, read, deleted. Hard drives zapped with powerful magnets the size of shirt buttons. But they are powerful enough to drag a boat. There was only one question left to answer: *Does Willow have too much empathy, or not enough?*

At community college, there were more tests, but those were specialized, not standardized. Willow wore a skirt with a hem just three inches over her knee, and some purple stockings, to class the first day, and was called a "cheap fucking whore!" by some weedy-looking boy in the parking lot. She kept her head up, walked to her class. PSY 101, her only elective. A vending machine malfunctioned, taunting her with a Three Musketeers Bar hanging from its loop, refusing to fall. She learned about childhood sexual urges, about the Stanford prison experiment. An older woman, a veteran of the war in Afghanistan, burst into tears in English class one day, as everyone but Willow struggled through "The Tell-Tale Heart." Back in PSY 101, Willow watched an episode from a late-night television news program about sociopathic youngsters. A cute young blonde girl says on the show, "I wish I could kill everybody; then I could have the world all to myself." An infant stares over the head of her mother and smiles at some invisible thing in the air. Willow's pulse remained steady. She wrote a term paper about a famous female serial killer whose jailhouse correspondence revealed a strong belief in UFOs, ancient astronauts, and an inevitable invasion. The killer's last words, said even as she was strapped to a gurney, with three different poisons pushing in to her veins, were, "I'll see you on Independence Day." Willow's Facebook timeline was full of photos, but when her friends smiled and hoisted their drinks with one hand and flashed faux gang signs with the others, she stood in their midst, square-shouldered, arms at her side, just smirking at the lens. On one wintry night, an agent damaged Willow's car in the community college parking lot. She had to walk home, on the shoulder of the highway. She was half blind from the ice rain in her eyes, and snow was piled in drifts along her path. Her left foot sunk into the ruined carcass of a raccoon that had managed to drag itself to the side of the road. She walked on without flinching.

Even better, on the sidewalk outside the door to her building, she scraped the letters I, C, and U into the dusty snow with the toe of her winter boot. Another secret test that only she perceived; another correct answer.

"What have you figured out so far?" her case worker asked Willow. She was a beautiful girl now. Black hair pulled into a thick and complex braid, light blue eyes, just enough acne scarring to seem accessible to the average pig. French manicure, eyebrows waxed and arched. No tattoos or piercings—very clever. She can hide that way, when she needs to. The case worker didn't look like an intelligence agent, but she was one. She knew how to hide as well.

Willow said, "Well you can't use just anyone, can you?" They were in a twenty-four thour diner, three hours into a new day. Willow had ruined the yolks of her eggs the moment her plate was placed in front of her, because she hated being stared at. She made a point of gesturing with her fork at the agent as she spoke, between bites and breaths. "For most jobs, anyone will do. Give them a uniform, a job title, some resources, and they'll do whatever you want. Be a hero or a villain, be a victim or a martyr. So you don't need me for the basics—extradition, enhanced interrogation, infiltration, propaganda. Not even wet work. That's boy stuff."

The agent didn't nod or shift her eyes in return. She just bit into her toast, flipped through the first few pages of the newspaper before her, chewing.

"Any girl would suck a cock straight from her own shitty asshole for a few extra dollars and a shot at Internet fame," Willow said suddenly. She shoveled some hash browns into her mouth and peered at the agent. "Any boy too."

The agent nodded solemnly, like God might from his throne atop a cloud.

"Big picture stuff," Willow said.

"Positively enormous," the agent said.

The agent had forms for Willow to sign. They were a dream come true, in form form. Willow accepted a place in Princeton University as a transfer student, and a full bank account, and a lease to an apartment in Trenton co-signed by the agent herself. The agent happened to have the same last name as Willow. At the bottom of the forms lay a glossy photo of Willow's father's head. She shuddered, but didn't scream and scream and dig her fingernails into the flesh of her arms till she felt something hard until later.

Princeton was challenging. Trenton more so. The building to which she was assigned was in a slum area, her apartment a joke—bathtub in the kitchen and just enough floor space for an air mattress, no climate control save a space heater that fired off sparks when plugged in, rats with no fear of human beings and an appetite for uncooked supermarket pasta. The interior of the refrigerator was heavily stained with what looked like mold and dried blood. It was only blood, courtesy of the previous tenant and his unfortunate lover. Her neighbors were drug addicts and petty criminals who had nothing to lose—smashing someone's head in with a pipe wrench for ten dollars was worth the risk of a twenty-five year prison sentence. Willow took to carrying a box cutter, but she didn't use it at home. She used it at school.

Willow's coursework was selected by her case worker. Arabic, Russian, constitutional law, organic chemistry for a change of pace. Big picture stuff, but with an added fringe benefit—Willow's classmates were hypercompetitive young men and women who never abandoned their childhood dreams of being President or curing cancer. Clever boys and girls, sensitive and discerning. They could smell a sociopath a mile away. A bit overconfident, though.

Gordon and Camile were lovers, and very cosmopolitan. They both liked to watch the other fuck third parties. Gordon zeroed in on how Willow's hair was always in her face. "That girl got herself daddy-raped," he said to Camile. They were loitering outside the lecture hall as Willow moved past them.

"Girls like that will suck you off *before* dinner," Camile said. She chortled at her own ribaldry. "So that you'll like them." No need to keep their voices down. A deal was struck.

Gordon made his move later that day, buttonholing Willow and talking up the alacrity with which her Russian vocabulary was expanding. He knew to throw in a "neg", and mentioned something about Willow's Jersey accent interfering with a few of her pronunciations. He was on her side, ready to help her out. Maybe tonight, at his apartment, they could work on some lingual exercises?

"Sure," Willow said. She went home and dressed for the occasion—sun dress for easy access, oversized purse with a whole other outfit, hair pulled back, flats for running. She withstood four blocks of catcalls to catch the bus, which took her to the rundown district adjacent to Gordon's nice neighborhood.

There was wine waiting, and dumb music—Vangelis, the *Bladerunner* soundtrack of all things—and fresh sheets on the bed. Gordon kept the bedroom door open, so he'd have some place to nod toward after the academic preliminaries. Willow took her glass, kicked off her shoes, smiled at the right moment and let her tongue slip between her lips when she spoke. Gordon moved in. Willow put up a hand and excused herself to the bathroom. "I need to do something important," she said, snatching up her purse for effect.

She locked the bedroom door behind her, pulled Camile from the closet and slit the girl's throat to stop the otherwise inevitable scream. It was an expert cut, but a cheap box cutter, so there was gurgling, and blood all over the sheets and a puddle of the same slowly expanding toward the bedroom door. Then, in the bathroom Willow washed up, changed her outfit and waited for Gordon to either bust down the door to his room and confront her, or rush to his car, the tires of which Willow had already slashed. She heard him howling and screaming outside, right by his parking space. Willow waved to him, then sat on the toilet, lid down, bloody cellphone in hand, and called for her case worker to come shoot Gordon and pick her up.

Gordon was easy enough to frame. He certainly didn't go around telling his friends that he had invited Willow over for a tryst, and there was enough bondage gear in the closet from which Camile had been dragged to satisfy the police that this was just another preppy sex-murder to be covered up for a while, then ruthlessly exploited by the media for some period after.

"Good one," the case worker told Willow on the car ride home. "You almost did a good job of it, with the change of clothes and the public freakout. We like audacity, but next time tell us first."

"So you put me in contact with rich assholes I'd want to kill on purpose, to see how many I would actually do?" Willow asked plainly.

"We're just making sure you fit into our corporate culture," the case worker said. "Given who you'll be working with, it's good to get this sort of thing out of your system."

Willow graduated from Princeton with a 3.98 GPA, but did not attend graduation. She was busy already, at her new job in Washington DC. Another slum apartment to keep her on her toes. A bullpen office on the good side of town. Not in the secret sub-basements of the Washington Monument or anything so fanciful, just a decent commercial space with the non-bearing walls torn down and wide desks. In the fourth-floor woman's restroom, someone had labeled the sanitary napkin dispenser THE BOTTOMORE MEMORIAL MAXI-PAD BOX. Willow loved that. She also loved that work for her was one extended brainstorming session.

"Filarial nematodes!" Willow shouted out one bright Monday morning at the general staff meeting. Her team was there, as were the case workers responsible for each genius. Her Danish sat untouched before her. "Let's weaponize it." There were murmurs of approval from Willow's cohort, but the management was confused.

"English please," Willow's case worker reminded her. "We're not all as smart as you are, so you have to tell us what you mean slowly, carefully, and completely. What do these, uh, nematodes do?" Willow giggled, as did a few others, but the caseworker sat placidly, used to it.

"What don't they do! Willow said. "Elephantiasis—"

"Elephantitis?" one of the other case workers asked.

"Elephant*iasis*. But yes, it's what you think. And river blindness."

"Little children blind from drinking river water," the employee next to Willow interjected. "I like to imagine little worms swimming in the jelly of the eyes, nibbling on the optic nerve."

"Arthritis too," Willow said, but that was anti-climactic. "They cause arthritis."

"All right, blindness and deformity, targeting poor children," Willow's case worker said. "What else do we have?"

The ideas came fast and furious. Drones that will swarm like bees on the horizon and will extrude a napalmlike "royal jelly." Lung-extraction torture combined with the use of a respirator to keep the target alive for several minutes. Creating a futures market for municipal water supplies, then bundled derivatives based on the futures. "We can literally flood the market," the man who introduced that idea said, "by wiping out a glacier or two. Whenever we like. Or just turn off the water entirely; make the little fuckers fight for it." Another wants to create hypertaylorist shipping warehouse labor where the work schedule itself counts as health coverage, what with all the lifting and running. "We can set some up ourselves and charge people to use them. Like a gym," someone adds to that idea. Then there's a tangent in the discussion—cultivate aneorexia through nutrition clinics and one-calorie vitamin supplements. That leads the discussion to famines, and how it's such a shame that there haven't been any in Western Europe in so long. Maybe tiny Corsica would make for a good show. Or think big, take out Portugal.

"What fucking tedious shit this all is," Willow said suddenly. The pastry before her had been torn to shreds. All heads turned to look her way. She pushed her hair out of her face; her eyes were blazing. "Here's what we should be doing. Let's leak this meeting, let's leak all of them. So everyone in the world knows about our department and what we do. That we kill children, wreck economies, set up rape camps, just to have some slaves. People think this stuff is just *natural*, an emergent property of the free market." She raised her hands to make quotation marks in the air over those last two words, and got a laugh from her co-workers, but not from their handlers.

"Let's tell everyone exactly what we do. From grade school recruitment to the pipeline from the Ivy League into this office. That we're the ones dousing little Pakistani girls in acid just to have something for the photographers," Willow said, an edge in her voice. "And then we'll tell them that this is what they're going to have to put up with—no, what they'll have to fucking love with all the Jesus-love in their heart—if they really want to live in the greatest country in the world. There's a psychopath gap out there, between us and the other countries, and we have to keep up."

For a long moment, nobody said anything. Then one of the other members of Willow's team added, "We can probably start selling test-taking guides, maybe set up some afterschool tutoring for children. In the inner cities, maybe, but definitely for parochial schools and all the best private schools. You know, so the students can have a shot at testing well."

Everyone began talking at once. Willow's enthusiasm was contagious. She smiled and thought of the old motivational poster with a cat clinging to a branch with its claws that had hung in her third-grade classroom. *Hang In There, Baby!*

Serenity Now

BY SIMON McCAFFERY

Big problems demand big solutions, often delivered by recklessly deliberate visionaries with extremely big balls. These unilateral maneuvers are rarely popular in their time. But the changes they invoke change the map for all to come. For both better and worse.

Kindly observe, as Simon McCaffery succinctly trash-compacts the Big Picture into the following micro-epic, and weirdly one-ups A Clockwork Orange *in the globally transformative process.*

For Isaias

You must remain calm.

If you want to hear the story of the monster named Andrew Keaton Paylor and understand why he did the things he did, it is an absolute necessity.

You have almost certainly been exposed. Females and preadolescent males were initially immune to ST6, dubbed Serenity666 in the sleazoid tabs and so-called online news sources, but within a year of its outbreak it went airborne. Today it aggressively infects both genders of all ages and races. Only the brotherhood of blank-eyed Wal-Mart greeters and the autistic have nothing to fear. And pure schizoids.

Yes, in hindsight I should have assumed that ST6 might mutate and spread beyond its target demographic. The essence of life is that it adapts, slipping around the cleverest barricades. My hope is that in sharing my story you can look past the absurdist doomsday rhetoric and appreciate the black-cloaked horrors our race has cast off and the serenity it has embraced, however forcibly.

There are no diagnostic tests to detect ST6 and no stages; once triggered the retrovirus gives birth to a malignant neoplasm that cascades through the blood and lymph nodes within twenty-four hours. This cancerous flash-fire consumes the organs and marrow in mere days, far too quickly to combat it with chemotherapy, advanced proton treatments or robotic radiosurgery.

The mortality rate of patients with active symptoms is, all of them.

Quarantine is pointless.

You can flee the depopulated cities, escape to some remote tropical island if you have the resources, but if someone else beat you there, you may be greeted by a Zen master's bullet, not a garland of orchids and carnations.

There are no preventative inoculations. My attorney confided that after my arrest my captors considered water-boarding me to coerce the creation of one, but that tactic would only have resulted in my untimely death and the loss of all knowledge of ST6's genetic architecture. They *beseeched* me to assist them to reverse-engineer it, as atonement for my crimes against humanity. But I'd had plenty of time to think since my incarceration and prosecution before the International Criminal Court, and I politely declined.

You and your surviving loved ones must simply learn to quell your inner demons, with the help of pharmacology.

Take your CDC rationed pills as directed, whether you've elected Home Sequestered Status, or you signed away all major health coverage to return to work and a simulation of normal life. Make sure your children take theirs. Sleep well knowing that governments on five continents have commandeered Big Pharma—Pfizer, Bayer, GlaxoSmithKline, Hoffmann–La Roche, Takeda, Johnson & Johnson—

to ensure stockpiles of mood stabilizers distributed by the World Health Organization never fall below critical levels.

Alcohol, coffee and cocaine can be consumed—this is still *America*—but as a medical doctor I strongly advise you against imbibing any substance that heightens the senses or excites. Slip that Netflix documentary about the slaughtering of dolphins right back into the mail, unopened.

Soft lighting and soothing music helps. Cop-killin' Rapping and eardrum-shredding Metal are deader than Tupac and Randy Rhoades. Shock jocks have switched brands to elevator Muzak. Yoga and biofeedback are being taught in kindergartens, I hear.

I'm listening to Gabriel Fauré's ethereal *Requiem Solos* as I write this in my impregnable cell, and the soothing angelic harmonies are like limbic coolant.

Take your pills.

If you want to keep reading, your life depends on it.

Terrorism follows a predictable trajectory.

Political and economic catalysts mix with bitter, centuries-old religious and racial disputes. Extremist leaders arise and the weak-minded and downtrodden are swiftly recruited, brainwashed and prepared. Incendiary violence erupts, with a relatively high legitimacy and support for the insurgents at first.

Government and invading foreign military forces crack down, and a protracted period of stalemate ensues that devolves into a draining, endless state of martyrdom and paranoid chaos punctuated by acts of soulless violence by all parties. Factions splinter. Soon the drab squares and narrow streets are redecorated with bright abstract expressionist blood and half-incinerated fragments of flesh. The extremists and their combatants endure heavy losses and both lose popular support as collateral damage mounts. No one is converted to the other's ideology.

Terror cells spring up in the infidels' homelands and set off subway bombs. The invading "peace-keeping" forces escalate the conflict and deploy more troops. Embers from the crucible of fanatical hatred are blown and scattered to new lands.

Politicians spout the same tired speeches about instilling hope and democracy, but breaking the cycle has always been impossible.

You cannot isolate man's inherent desire to kill for a cause in the older folds of the brain and excise it with a scalpel. Scholarly dissertations on the "psychology of terrorism" are as useless as neuroscientists viewing 3D scans of a living sociopath's brain in hopes of mapping his alleged madness. Watch the colorful movie of my brain while I viewed footage of the truckloads of dead and dying being deposited inside stadiums converted into massive domed hospices. Let me know what it reveals.

Terrorism is as old as Abraham. But three years ago I conceived a perfect, elegant solution.

Scattered along the Pakistani North-West Frontier and part of the Afghan Kunar province known as "Enemy Central," the outlying villages of Asadabad are primordial cradles of terrorism. Local Taliban groups are thicker than sand fleas throughout the impenetrable terrain and networks of caves. More than seventy percent of all deadly insurgent incidents in the country occur in the region. The number of American and NATO soldiers maimed or bagged and shipped home in pieces isn't widely publicized.

I take a sabbatical from my department head chair at the Cancer Genetics Laboratory at Baylor College of Medicine and volunteer to be reactivated and attached to the First Battalion, Seventh Marines. I'm forty-three and in good health, divorced and childless. The 1/7 is deployed to a hellhole village nine klicks from Asadabad where an abnormal number of American and British soldiers have been diagnosed with lethal scalp and neck skin cancers. Metastatic melanomas and the more rare Burkitt lymphomas.

Despite their Middle Eastern heritage the local populace isn't immune to basal cell carcinomas and lesions, but this isn't my core mission. I have to convince the battalion CO to allow me to offer free screenings. I tell him it will help us win the hearts and minds of the oppressed villagers. My fellow jarhead liberators sneer behind my back and call me an Ewok-lover and a camel-fucker. But I scavenge supplies and set up my portable clinic.

Few people accept my offer; they're probably concerned they'll be labeled sympathizers. Taliban informants are everywhere. Many villagers disappear from their simple homes after the sun drops below the sawtoothed mountains. They are spirited into the freezing desert, and none return.

Patient zero is a twelve-year-old boy named Aamir.

I find him sitting on the baked ground beside my screening station one blazing morning, accompanied by his surviving guardian, a wizened dust-cloaked grandmother. The boy is a skinny tangle of scabbed limbs with a smile full of crooked yellow teeth. He doesn't brush away the flies that light at the corners of his large dark-brown eyes.

I give them both exams.

"Do you like chocolate, Aamir?"

Of course he does. All little boys love chocolate. I give Aamir five bars.

"You must tell all of your friends to come see Dr. Paylor for free screenings," I say as I pat his round head, jumping with lice.

I offer his grandmother MRE rations and slip her ten dollars, and tell her I am concerned about an irregular mole on the back of her son's head. She sits there forever, staring at me with her milky eyes, but she finally allows me to give Aamir a vaccination. I think it's the ten dollars.

In the coming week I "vaccinate" fifteen of the village's adolescent boys, and distribute more chocolate and currency to the Dirty-Knee Pajama Mammas.

In August our battalion is redeployed to Asmār in the Bar Kunar District, and I inoculate many more Aamirs, Aasifs, Abduls, and Aazars. I inject the alphabet with ST6.

You see, the terror cells rely on the outlying villages for shelter and food, but mainly they recruit poor orphaned young boys to replenish their ranks.

If you consulted Wikipedia or watched *The Doctor Oz Show* segments, you know that a retrovirus is an RNA virus that uses a reverse transcriptase enzyme to produce DNA. Once it invades normal cells, the RNA strands integrate themselves into the host's genome.

They become *you*. It is no longer possible to distinguish the original you from the new you.

A retrovirus like Serenity666 is contagious by touch and saliva, and detecting its presence is extremely difficult until it presents symptoms in the host.

You probably also saw Dr. Oz's guest, the funny Don Knotts endocrinologist with the bobbing Adam's apple who did a marvelous job of explaining how an engineered retrovirus could theoretically be triggered by heightened amounts of hormones and neuro chemicals released inside a body experiencing sustained anger. Indoctrinated bodies hooked on the white-hot heroin rage of Jihad.

My solution worked, at first.

Four months after Aamir went scampering back to his shelled home the RPG ambushes tapered off and the platoons assigned to sweep the same pock-holed roads for IEDs weren't finding them. The kidnappings dwindled. The Taliban stopped shooting up supply convoys and downing Predator drones. Police stations and electrical substations that had been bombed and rebuilt several times went unmolested. An eerie peace settled across the region and spread into Pakistan, Iraq and Iran. Blackwater's revenues dipped for the first quarter ever.

The villagers and shopkeepers of Bar Kunar whispered of the terrible return of *Malak al-Maut*, come to carry off their husbands, brothers and sons in the night. Azreal, the Islamic archangel of death.

By then I was back in Texas with my own oncology practice, inspecting freckles and egg-shaped moles. Reports of an alarming unknown carcinogen began appearing on CNN and in *The New York Times*. The media speculated that the cause was depleted uranium shells or an unreported cache of WMDs.

I wasn't alarmed. I'd engineered ST6 to infect adolescent and adult males only, and created the perfect vector to deliver it to the isolated bands of Taliban operating in remote camps and mountain caves. They would be exterminated too swiftly to spread it beyond the region. Only sympathizers who came in direct contact were at risk, and undeniably, some of the soldiers sent to root them out. If you consider it calmly, they were already dying in droves.

Then the first female suicide bomber staggered into a crowded market square and collapsed before she could detonate the vest. Her body underneath the modest burqa was burning up with ST6.

The table to which I've been securely strapped is shaped in a cross.

I'm called the Beast, Omega Man, the Supreme Sociopath and other colorful epithets. By comparison Hitler is a surly, truant schoolboy in short pants, the fictional Hannibal Lector a harmless, flesh-nibbling pervert.

The gallery beyond the glass viewing ports is empty except for a single stoic Army guard, and my execution by lethal injection is not being relayed live around the world. No witnesses are present since my father, mother and estranged ex-wife all succumbed to ST6. So did my bigoted battalion CO and platoon mates, and the military investigators who traced the man-made epidemic back to me.

I'm a carrier, but the "schizoid personality disorder" the criminal psychologists diagnosed me with renders me immune. I'm simply *in control*, and always have been.

Go ahead, what are you waiting for? Depress the plungers and fill my veins with paralytics and poison.

I'm not the Antichrist. I'm not another schizophrenic messiah. Constructing cathedrals that soar to the sky and washing the jam from between my toes is unnecessary, but you can at least *acknowledge* my achievement. Admittedly, I am guilty of murder.

I'm the man who murdered Hatred.

I'm the man who murdered Holy Wars.

I eradicated Aggression and purged us of Fundamentalist Religious Fervor.

Dead and gone forever, amen.

Lying here, gazing up into a halo of fluorescent light, I feel nothing. Like all of you tranquilized deadheads, my unwitting disciples, doped to the gills and drooling onto your shirt collars.

Love, Passion, and adrenalized skydiving (and five billion souls) were unforeseen collateral damage, but the scales are balanced. For the first time there is hope.

Think what you will, and take your pill. When the plungers come down, my peace will be eternal.

The Mannerly Man

BY MEHITOBEL WILSON

Every society since the dawn of time has sought ways to channel our most aggressive impulses into relatively harmless activity. And so it is with speculative fiction.

Even Ernest Callanbach's 1975 utopian New Age hippie classic Ecotopia *understood that violent sports were a necessary safety valve for a community devoted to peace. Cuz all that ugly's got to go somewhere. (As Stephen King once said. "Lennon and McCartney were right. All you need is love. As long as you keep the gators fed.")*

And if we can't make nice entirely, the next available step is to focus the chaos down to a neat, contained, entertainment-friendly event we can tune in, then tune out at our leisure. From the Roman coliseums of yore to Death Race 2000, Rollerball, The Running Man, *and* Battle Royale *(the inarguable baby-mama of the wildly popular* Hunger Games *series), this is a populist urge ever eager to be met. Because it will not, by itself, go away.*

Mehitobel Wilson's brilliant "The Mannerly Man" seeks an alternate escape valve: less spectacular on the surface, but more than making up for it with creepily character-stunting paranoia as a way of life. With one psychotically perfect perk.

At noon on Tuesday, Gregory took a break for lunch and discovered that his bathtub drain had not yet swallowed the water from his morning shower. He removed his sunglasses and looked at the standing water, which was milky with shed cells and fragrance-free soap. He did not sigh or frown. He tried to plunge the drain clear, without success. There were, he calculated, three options: he could ignore the problem, he could risk calling the landlord, or he could brave the grocery store in search of chemical relief.

The landlord was a calm man, a mannered man, who had always seemed safe to Gregory. But one never knows, does one, thought Gregory, and deleted the landlord from the list. If he ignored the tub, it might eventually overflow and leak through the floor, staining the ceiling of the apartment below. Gregory had never met the tenants, though he'd seen them, nodded through his dark lenses at their own implacable, sunglassed faces. One never knows.

He should have considered this eventuality and ordered some drain-cleaner from an Internet site, but he had not. The only remaining option was to brave the store.

At times, being in public seemed more safely anonymous than did staying alone. Gregory tried not to test this theory often. No one tested anything anymore.

So he went to the door, smoothed his jumpsuit, adjusted his sunglasses, and opened it. He passed no one on the stairs. His drab sedan was dirty enough to be dull but not so dirty as to offend anyone, he hoped. He got into it.

En route to the store, Gregory kept pace with the traffic. He slowed once to let a car merge into his lane, and peered over the tops of his sunglasses, checking the rearview mirror for any signs of aggression from the motorist directly behind him. There were none. He kept his face placid and did not sigh in relief.

The knife in its black mesh sheath chafed his calf every time he pressed the clutch.

Gregory reached the store and found a parking space without incident.

While crossing the parking lot, however, he tensed his shoulders as he caught sight of a group of young teenage boys loitering outside the automatic doors. They were wearing primary-bright sweaters, jeans, and boots. Their postures were open and easy. One smoked. One sang. The third picked his nose. None of them wore sunglasses. All three of them turned their heads this way and that, their uncovered gazes casting sightlines that mannerly folk could nearly visualize, like rifle-mounted lasers streaming through smoke.

There was no other way into the store.

Gregory's own head balanced on his neck in the same position it always did, his face tilted down just low enough to be polite. Others he passed had their own faces tipped down into the meek zone. Gregory found that as dangerous as he found aggression.

He approached the doors. The boys stared at him. He felt a measure of fear, but not too much. There was never too much of anything anymore.

If any of them had a Legal left, and chose to exercise their Right against Gregory, he would feel no pain. So he hoped, anyway.

And he knew that the boys had nothing against him personally, that they were just looking for attention. It was rude, but not enough to attract the kind of attention they were looking for. Perhaps that was their point, Gregory realized. Perhaps they weren't obnoxious kids, but activists, trying to prove by example that survival did not depend on manners, after all. Perhaps they each hoped to sacrifice themselves in order to waste the Legals of strangers, thereby potentially saving other, better lives. There were, Gregory had heard, people like that.

Gregory stepped onto the concrete walkway leading to the shaded doors of the store, and the boys pivoted their heads and let words through their sneery grins, words all running under each other, low and easy-mean. *"Do you hate me? Do you? Want me dead? Want to kill me? Motherfucker, want to take me down? Am I bothering you? Are you scared? Think you bother me? Talk to me, talk to me, Sir, give it up, hand it over, Sir, where's your eyes, where's your gun, whatcha packin', am I rude?"*

He walked through the words, ignored the adrenaline seething in his cheeks, and the doors sucked apart and let him in.

Very few customers shopped in the store. Most had the same agenda as

Gregory: get in, get out, offend no one. Some were nearly furtive in their move-
ments, which drew Gregory's attention and made him wish them well. One man
held his smooth chin high and shoulders back, but his brave stance made him look
all the more afraid. Gregory walked down an extra aisle to avoid that one.

In the six years since the Right to One had become final, the country's
population had been cut in half. Everything was going according to plan. The
equal-rights people were made happy by the fact that everyone had the Right to
One, the choice-loving people were happy that they could choose whether or not
to exercise their Right, the pro-life people had been thrilled that they could act
as the fist of God and remain on the good side of the law. Citizens who preferred
government aid appreciated the money liberated now that prisons were nearly
obsolete; those who preferred to handle things themselves liked the freedom to
do so.

And everyone was very, very polite.

Fear of the ultimate retribution had made the remaining members of the population very considerate. Please, thank you, yes sir. May I come in, do you have a
moment? Is this a good time?

It was hard. Gregory still wasn't sure, after all this time, whether he had the
game right. One mustn't bother or offend anyone. No interruptions of their private trains of thought, but no ignoring them, either.

The sunglasses were imperative. Everyone could gauge one another's moods
without being noticed. The jumpsuits kept the fearful anonymous.

When the Right to One was put into effect, twenty percent of the population
died within two weeks. Twenty percent of the population had inflicted wrongs,
imagined or real, so deep that their murderers came for them immediately. More
than one news story featured a person who had crossed the country to exercise
their Right and discovered that the person against whom they bore a deadly
grudge had already been Legally killed. Most of those stories ended with addenda
stating that, in fits of rage, the frustrated killers had wasted their Right on the next
person that passed.

Thousands more were executed by the Authorities for surpassing their limit
of One.

Over the years, the people who had prudently decided to save their Right started to snap. Twelve items in the 10 Item or Less line could get you killed. Road rage exploded. Saying hello to a stranger could earn you a shot to the face; not doing so could result in the same end.

Now that the country was paranoid, and now that the pensioners had killed the drug dealers, and the meek had killed the bullies, and abused and abusers killed one another, things had settled down a bit. Everyone tried to remain invisible, as Gregory did. Those who had exercised their Right hid the face that they had, for they would be easy prey. Even a killing in self-defense was call for execution if it was not the One.

Some citizens refused their Legal Right because they feared that the whole law was a trick, that the Authorities executed all who exercised it and claimed that they were punishing people for their second kills, when each kill was the first.

The Authorities frightened everyone. They were executioners who could not themselves be killed.

Gregory had once wanted very badly to be an Authority. The killing would bother him, but the relative immortality would have been worth it. But he had been afraid to apply, because it would bring him to their attention. What if they had not let him join the Force? What if one of them hated him? The fear of being noticed was too much to bear, so Gregory stayed at home and telecommuted, delivering spreadsheets and calculations on the hour to the warehouse whose stock he tracked.

He had never exercised his Right. He was a prudent man.

He carried his drain cleaner to the cash register. There was no clerk. Clerks drew ire too easily: made incorrect change, perhaps raised an eyebrow a millimeter if someone bought hemorrhoid cream. Editorials in the newspaper often commented upon the unforeseen way the Right to One had affected technology. Now Gregory waited as the placid jumpsuited young woman in front of him fed her four purchases through the laser screen. Toothpaste, mouthwash, dental floss, and menthol lozenges. Gregory looked at the clean brown hair on the back of her head and wondered what was wrong with her mouth. Her total appeared on the LED readout; she slotted her card in the reader. The gates opened and she crossed through. No alarm sounded. She turned her mirror-lensed face to Gregory, and her mouth looked fine to him.

He nodded at her, just enough, and pushed his bottle of cleaner through the red-light screen.

Her face was still turned towards him. Her mouth looked less fine now. It looked curly at the corners.

Then it cracked open and showed him teeth so white they looked tinged with blue, and he dropped his gaze to her hands. No gun. She was gathering her purchases into a mesh bag. He looked at her face again and realized that she was smiling.

Gregory faltered, stunned to see a living person smile directly at him. The customer in line behind him shifted and Gregory heard the squeak of shoe leather against the linoleum. He turned quickly and said to the invisible man behind him, "I'm sorry, I was a bit distracted for a moment. My apologies."

The man's head ticked forward, as if he'd seen something in Gregory's face that bothered him. "It's quite all right," he said. His voice was pleasant.

Gregory was quick to pay, and anxious as he waited for the gates to part. No alarm sounded.

The girl with the lozenges stood waiting for him. Her breath smelled of medicine. Her smile was huge and, now that Gregory had assimilated it, genuine.

He was terrified.

She took off her sunglasses, revealing bloodshot eyes, and said, "I've missed you very much. I fucked up, I know that. I can't sleep without you next to me. The nightmares are worse now that you're gone. Please have coffee with me? Please let me talk to you? I know you must be hurting, but I need to explain some things."

Gregory had never seen the girl before in his life.

He clenched his bottle of cleaner and wished for the first time that he kept his knife sheathed on his ribs.

Possibilities: she could be nuts, and he could die. She could have mistaken him for someone else, and her confusion and embarrassment upon discovery might get him killed. She might have used her One already, but that was not a chance he was willing to take. He could play along, and she might kill him for it. She might be trying to trick him and kill him anyway.

"Coffee," he said. "That would be nice. Let me drive you." He wanted one of her lozenges. Each syllable bruised his fear-tight throat.

Her lips tightened with emotion, and then the smile came back, smaller, grateful. Nervous. Her eyes filled with tears; she severed his access to them with her sunglasses.

They left the store. Behind them, the three boys postured in the shade. One of them said, "That's that fucking guy, man!" Gregory told himself that they could not mean him, that he had done nothing, and he did not look back.

Together, they walked toward his car.

She was very small.

His bottle of drain cleaner was heavy. Eighty fluid ounces.

"Thank you, Marcel," she whispered, and touched his wrist. He flinched. When was the last time he had been touched? Smiles, eyes, speech, and touch all in the space of four minutes. His heart beat incorrectly. His breath was wrong.

"You're welcome," he said, wishing her knew her name, wishing he knew how hard a blow would render her unconscious.

They reached his car. No one was parked in the space in front of his.

"Let me open the trunk," he said, "so you can put your groceries in the back." He unlocked his car, got in, and started the engine. He left his door open. He pressed the trunk release and the pneumatic struts raised the hatch. He leaned out of his door and saw her walk to the back of the car, saw his brakelights turn the legs of her khaki jumpsuit a sour mauve.

Gregory dropped the brake and hit the gas. The car jumped forward, the engine stammered, and then the car shot across the parking lot. His door banged into his left elbow and he winced, caught it, closed it properly. The tires hit the canary speed bump guarding the exit; the trunk lid sprung wide, then slammed shut. He braked at the street and checked the rearview mirror. The girl stood, stunned, where he'd left her. Her mesh bag dangled from her hand. He saw no weapon.

Gregory signaled, turned onto the street, and drove home.

A dusty green car was parking parallel on his street. He idled behind it for a moment, giving it room to maneuver.

He parked and got out of the car. The bottle in his hand seemed heavier now. He carried it to the steps of his building, where another tenant stood, an older man, graying, fumbling with his keys. Gregory hung back for an instant, having had enough interaction for one day. But that might make the man feel tense, watched, and it's never wise to cause tension in strangers.

So Gregory stepped up and the man turned his head a bit, his beard rasping against the collar of his starched jumpsuit, and said, "I'm sorry about the wait, I'm having a little trouble with my keys."

"That's quite all right," said Gregory. "I'm in no hurry." An offer to help would be friendly, but might also be considered insulting. He was torn.

The man did not turn back to the door. Instead, he stared at Gregory through smoky lenses. "Pardon me, er. I must say I'm surprised to see you here. Please accept my condolences. She was a lovely woman."

Gregory raised his bottle of drain cleaner. "I live in this building, sir. You may have mistaken me for someone else."

The man looked grave. "I understand. Please forgive my intrusion. I will, of course, be discreet. No one will know that you are here." He turned back to the door, fitted his key into the lock, and entered the building, letting the door fall shut behind him.

Gregory felt a flare of annoyance at the fact that the man had not held the door, and was surprised at himself for it.

He gave the man plenty of time to get inside his apartment before he entered the building himself.

His hands shook a little as he unlocked his apartment door. Once inside, he allowed himself a moment of release: he shook openly, breathed deeply, lost control of his expression and let his face tighten upon itself with relief.

No way would he leave the house again. Never. Not for weeks, at least, he told himself. People were too unpredictable. They spoke. They demanded engagement.

They threw blue-white smiles at strangers and said things that made no sense. They killed. They put him in very uncomfortable situations and he hated them for it as much as he feared them.

Then he seized control of himself, smoothed his jumpsuit, and removed his sunglasses. He inspected the instructions on the bottle of drain cleaner. He followed them. Chemical fumes filled the bathroom. He considered cracking a window for ventilation, but feared that the fumes might bother a neighbor, so he ran the exhaust fan instead. The bottle suggested he allow fifteen minutes for the treatment to work.

He logged onto the Internet and went grocery shopping. Along with canned and frozen goods he chose drain cleaner, throat lozenges (cherry), and aspirin.

He also ordered three jumpsuits and a new pair of sunglasses, a pair styled differently than his own.

Thirty minutes had passed. Gregory was a prudent man. The drain cleaner had not worked.

Gregory frowned down at the still, clouded water and then flinched as he heard a sound he hadn't heard in years: the sound of a fist rapping on his door.

It was not even one-thirty. He couldn't pretend to be asleep. He crept to the door and craned his neck toward the peephole, holding his body as far away from the door as possible.

A woman stood in the hallway, a brunette, his age. Her sunglasses were tortoiseshell. In these times, those were as much of a statement as fuschia cat's-eye sunglasses would have been seven years before. She wore lipstick. It was a neutral beige, but it still caught his eye. She liked attention. This meant that she either had a death wish, or that she had little fear.

Gregory wondered if a woman like this, a jumpsuited, sunglassed woman who still had an edge of individuality, might touch him. Her mouth was pretty.

Her hands were pretty, too. She raised one and knocked again.

Gregory relished the fact that he was, physically, inches away from her, staring directly at her face, and that she didn't know. Even in sunglasses, he never allowed himself to fully turn his face toward a stranger. Toward anyone. Everyone was a stranger now.

He thought of the girl from the store and remembered how his blood had felt when she'd smiled at him.

The woman in the hall twisted her glossy beige lips, hesitated, then knocked once more.

Gregory raised his own fist and knocked back at her.

She laughed. She laughed aloud and her teeth weren't scary at all. Her throat was long when she threw her head back. He wondered how he could make her do that again.

He opened the door.

"Oh!" she said, and took a step back.

"Hello," said Gregory. "May I help you?"

"Hello, yes. No. I actually came to help you, I believe." Despite the coverage of her sunglasses, he could tell that she was staring at him. He stared back. He saw his reflection in her lenses and blinked at himself. Blinked: he'd forgotten to put on his own shades.

"I see, well, thank you very much. How so?"

"I live in 221B. Your package was delivered to my door by accident. It is addressed to 221A. But it says Gregory Holland." Her forehead pinched and flushed.

"I'm Gregory Holland," he said. "This is thoughtful of you, thank you."

"Gregory Holland," she repeated.

Something oily rose inside him. His joints felt slow. He wished that the sick oil would reach them and make him fast so he could shut the door.

The woman pulled her canvas satchel around to her pelvis and pulled back the flap. Gregory felt tight and knew that she could see his eyes, would read the fear there. Shut the door, kick her and shut the door! Hit her in the face, blind her with broken tortoiseshell!"

Her hand slid into the satchel and he heard the thrush of enormous wings in his ears and she pulled out a flat brown package.

"Gregory Holland, 221A." She held the package to her face. Her fingernails were painted with clear gloss and Gregory stared at them. He wanted to tap his teeth against them and hold her fingertips on his tongue.

She raised her hand and pushed her sunglasses up to crown her head, and then Gregory was eye to eye with another human, and she said, "Please forgive me for being forward, but I would like to come in for a moment, if you don't mind." Her words were appropriate, but there was no formality in her voice at all. Instead, she sounded exhilarated, nervous.

She stepped forward and stood on his threshold. If he slammed the door right now, right now hard, he could knock her out, maybe she would even fall down the steps and break her neck. That would be an accident, not his Right. Even if it were his One it would stop her from looking at him, from doing this to him. He gripped the edge of the door down low and his shoulder tensed to swing it shut.

But she came into his home and reached out as if to touch him and then he couldn't move at all. Her hand stopped and hung in the air, her fingers twitched.

"You used to be famous," she breathed. "Does that mean you still are? Once known, always known, I guess." Her teeth, scarier now, dented her lower lip for an instant. The tip of her tongue flashed and licked her beige lips wet. Gregory backed against the wall and she toed the door shut. God, alone, alone with bare eye and a woman. He wanted to tell her that he had never been famous at all. He wanted her to touch him.

"Famous," she said, in a fugue. Then her eyes grew bright and she snapped her gaze to his, cocked her head sideways. "I don't blame you for changing your name, for going anonymous. But I've seen all of your movies. I was a fan even before you did *Cold Scars*, in fact—I watched you on the soaps. And the fact that you've survived, oh, you don't know how glad I am. I watch your movies and I mourn for you. They're all dead now, you know. Lovers and fans and—oh, Mickey, don't ever think that I'm one of those fans, never ever think that."

She forgot herself and put her hand on his arm. She drew a fast, hard breath and quivered as she exhaled. Her voice grew heavy. She had to expend effort to lift it into words. "You have always been so strong. The fact that you've survived proves that."

Gregory disagreed with this, but agreed very much with the flutter of her fingertips on his forearm.

The woman was bats, he knew, but this would be so easy, and she was so convinced of her delusion that she would never notice.

Gregory put his hand on hers and said, "What is your name?"

"Ann," she said, and it didn't sound like a name, but like a noise that had fallen from her.

Her hand, cool and trembling, moved under his. He wanted to keep it. But he was a prudent man, and he said, "Would you like to have dinner tonight, Ann?"

Ann's eyes grew wide, as did her smile. She nodded and gave an affirmative hum.

"Would six o'clock be a comfortable time for you?" Oh, it would, it would. "I'll see you then, Ann. Thank you for bringing my package. I'm very glad to have met you." He dared to put his hands on her shoulders and as he gentled her towards the door again he marveled at the flex of bird bones beneath his thumbs. She was cooing.

"Goodbye, Mickey," she said, and he smiled at her, nodded, and closed the door. Locked it. Pressed his forehead to the wood and focused on the stretch of his lips. A smile. The air dried his teeth and he put his lips over them, where they belonged.

Gregory returned to the bathroom and stared into the mirror. Work could wait. What was making people look at him funny, mistake him for other men? He examined himself. Brown hair, brown eyes, and a face. Clean man. Bland man. Unremarkable man. He could be any one of a thousand men.

Sunglasses, jumpsuit, please do pardon me, I'm so sorry to have bothered you. No smile, no eyes, no expression, no self-expression. He was just a man, purely manners and anonymity.

He was nobody.

He could be anybody.

Gregory unsheathed his knife and weighed it, tipping it from one hand into the other. Who would the Authorities see, if they saw him?

He frowned. Ann and the girl at the store, could he have known them once? No, of course not. He would have remembered the girl's terrible magnesium teeth and the gaudy colorful frames of Ann's sunglasses.

It was two o'clock. Water stood in the bathtub, still. He had no mind for work.

He passed the time on the Internet. He ordered a shoulder holster. He researched the film *Cold Scars* and its star, Mickey Samson. Samson had been four years older than Gregory, and six inches shorter. Ann would not know about the height difference. Samson's whereabouts were unknown. This was typical of personalities famous before the Law was passed. There were few stars now; most shows were animated, and those that weren't featured casts of Authorities. News shows contained footage and voice-overs instead of anchors and live reporters. The cooperation among the sheer numbers of crew members needed for long shoots on location had made movies obsolete. The primary tool of entertainment was the State Internet, a closed system for citizens only. Text was king.

Despite the physical suggestion of anonymity cultivated by the jumpsuited population, the laws demanded that individuals take responsibility for their words and actions. All users online operated under their own names. Their home addresses and private phone numbers were available to the public. Manners reigned on the State Internet, too.

At five o'clock, Gregory shaved, dressed, combed his hair. He polished his sunglasses. His jumpsuit was crisp. His boots were clean and glossy, but not too glossy.

At five-forty, he sat down to wait.

Fourteen minutes later, he heard movement in the building hallway, and saw the shadows of feet at his door. He waited for Ann's knock. It did not come.

Once again, Gregory crept to the door and peered through the lens. Ann stood outside. Her upper teeth pressed into her lower lip. She pinched her earlobe. She drew back the cuff of her fawn jumpsuit with her fingertips and examined her watch. She looked at the door, then back at her watch. The watch was scarlet. Gregory's own watch was matte black. He wondered how Ann had survived so long with all her attention-getting accessories.

Her chest swelled, deflated, then swelled again, and she held it that way and knocked on the door.

Knocked again.

Gregory stared through the peephole until she could hold her breath no more and, just as she let her posture slip, he thumbed the lock and opened the door.

Her shoulders were still caved in, but her eyebrows rose above the tops of her sunglasses, and she squeaked.

"Good evening, Ann. I'm honored that you returned."

She wobbled her head a little and then regained her composure somewhat, and said, "Good evening, Mickey. Gregory. Which do you prefer?"

"Gregory, please. Mickey must be our secret."

"Of course." Penny-sized jowls of disappointment puffed at the corners of her mouth. They faded as she controlled her face.

"I would be happy to ask you in, under normal circumstances. Tonight I thought you might like to come with me to see the Ensemble Authorities perform Shakespeare in the park. *Othello*, I think. The web schedule says there will be *dim sum* vending kiosks there."

"That sounds just wonderful," she said.

Gregory nodded. "It begins at six-thirty. We can walk to the park. There may be a crowd," he warned. He could barely speak the word "crowd," so unnerved was he by the possibility.

Ann could contain herself no longer. "Who cares?" she asked, reaching for and catching his hand. "Six-thirty? Not much time. Let's go!" Her smile was broad and eager.

Mistake, thought Gregory. This woman was death to him. She was all teeth and quickness, but even when quiet, she wanted attention. The skin that gloved her dangerous flesh felt nice against his, but not nice enough to stop him from fearing her.

They left for the park.

The walk took five minutes. Ann chattered the whole time. Her plumbing was bad too (perhaps Gregory would bother the landlord, after all) and she detailed the stagnant contents of her kitchen sink to him. Her toilet was clogged, too. She told him that, until it was fixed, she tried not to eat or drink much at home, so her body would not force her to use the restroom. He would rather not have heard this and thought it appallingly uncouth of her to have told him. Even her tongue was death. He wanted it far away from him, but leaving would have been rude.

They entered the gates of the park and passed through the arbor. The air was indigo with dusk. Ahead lay the parade grass, populated by quiet people wearing sand-colored coveralls. Each of the *dim sum* kiosks stood as the hub of a wheel spoked by queues of polite citizens. Here and there white-suited Authorities monitored the quiet throng.

"Oh, Mickey, honey, the play's going to start soon. Let's eat during intermission, or afterwards, we can eat afterwards if you want." Ann's hand gathered the fabric of his right sleeve at the elbow and bunched it up as she hauled him toward the small stage. The button that held the cuff closed popped off as she dragged the fabric up his forearm. He was glad he'd ordered new jumpsuits.

Gregory offered apologies and excuses to each person she brushed against. He doubted his words could be heard over her own, which were growing shrill.

People.

He had brought this upon himself. It had been an experiment. It had failed. His eyes watered behind his glasses.

It would be rude of him to yank his arm away from her. It might anger her. Anger is danger.

But Gregory was angry himself. That, too, was danger. Danger to her. And, he thought, if she was too stupid to realize what she was doing to him, it might be polite to enlighten her.

"Ann. Ann." He stopped short and she stumbled back into him, her momentum interrupted. Her hair bounced against his chin. "Pardon me, but you seem to be growing a bit overexcited. I am concerned that you may disturb other patrons."

She whirled around and struck him in the sternum with the heel of her open hand. "Fuck you," she snapped. "I have the upper hand here. I know who you are, Mickey fucking Samson. I know you used your Legal two years ago, right before you disappeared. You killed that movie critic." She fingered the collar of his jumpsuit and smirked at him. "Sorry you're embarrassed. You'll have to get used to it, lover. Now. Let's sit here, it's a nice place. We're as close to the stage as we're gonna get. I know you don't want to be right up front because the actors might recognize you, right? Here's good."

She sat down on the grass, her legs crossed. Her hip bone pressed the toe of his boot.

He thought about kicking her in the back of the head.

He thought about her mouth. He'd wanted so badly to feel her lips, earlier.

So he knelt down behind her and drew his knife from his boot, folded his left hand over her slick beige talkative lips and brought his right one around to shove the knife through her larynx.

Her hair smelled like lemons.

Her lips moved against his palm and her blood moved down his wrist. Her shoulders bucked hard against his own throat. That felt nice. He stirred the insides of her throat with the blade, crushing and severing her windpipe. The sounds were bad.

Then his One was dead.

Gregory pulled the knife from her neck and wiped the blade on the grass. He slid it back into the sheath in his boot. He wiped his wrist on the grass and pulled the sleeve down over it. The cuff hung loose but hid the blood.

He checked behind him and saw that the crowd was standing. The play was about to start. They stood to honor the players. Gregory stood, too. Two men in white suits strode toward him from the stage, their eyes hollowed by dusk.

Gregory took four steps backwards, then four to the right. Five back. Three left, deeper into the crowd. He stopped when a man touched his shoulder and said to him, "Pardon me, but aren't you Professor Brooks? You taught my class last semester. It was an excellent class."

"Thank you," said Gregory. "I remember you. You were a talented student."

He could be any of a thousand men.

"Excuse me," said Gregory, "I must be going." He walked another dozen yards, then turned to face the stage.

The Authorities fixed hard stares on a man twenty paces closer to the stage than Gregory. The man stood calm and confident. The Authorities approached him and stood before him, spoke to him. His posture did not change. He drew forth identification and one of the men in white scanned the chip with their ID databank device. The second Authority listened to the verdict of the first, then spoke at length, face fixed and mechanical, to the man. The man's shoulders twisted and his head turned from side to side. The first Authority extended his hand to the man's neck and administered the lethal dose via syringe.

Gregory watched all of this, but he was calm. He did not stare. It's not polite to stare.

Subdued applause came from the crowd, then, as the curtain rose.

The man next to Gregory smiled at him and said, "I'm so glad we came here. This was a lovely idea, just what I needed. Thank you."

Gregory smiled back. "I'm glad you're happy."

He continued to smile.

HELP!
Need money
God Bless You

Sensible Violence

BY BRIAN HODGE

Murder is a sin. Of course it is. But there are little loopholes and provisions encoded into every religion. "Thou shalt not kill, except . . ."

And then there are those systems of belief that can't be bothered with pussy-footing around. Their gods walked in slaughtering and never looked back. To do anything less is to see things unclearly.

You can call their adherents extremists or true believers. Call 'em saints or psychotics. Doesn't matter to them. They know what is true, and you don't. Suck it up.

Metaphysical scrapper Brian Hodge never met a truth he couldn't wrestle to the floor, or die trying. And not a single bloody punch will be pulled.

As you are about to see in this extraordinary culling of the herd.

You're minding your own business when he comes up to you, the way it happens to anyone. Your palms are pressed against the plate glass of the store's window, a pet store, you never can resist it, taking time out to squat on your haunches and share a few moments with the puppies. With their big feet and fat little bellies, they squirm and trip all over each other trying to get to you, impress you, maybe you'll take them all home. Show them the world on the other side of the glass.

"'S'cuse, not to be intruding or nothing, but I's needing to ask you something, okay, mind if I conversate with you a second?"

Money. He'll want money, it's as good as predestined. When you squatted down to watch the pups he was nowhere in sight, and you'd checked, too. You're less a target for beggars when you're moving and they know that, that it's easier to pretend you don't hear them, that your ears shut down in midstride.

"Basically I's wondering if you could spare like a couple dollars so I could get something to eat, you know, I wouldn't ask but I ain't had nothing to eat for a couple days now—"

He talks with his hands always in motion to make you feel his urgency, feel his hunger, and you wonder if you should tell him to calm down, quit flailing so much and he'll conserve more calories. He tells you how your donation will enable him to go back up the street a couple blocks to the Dairy Queen on the corner, alleviate his hunger with a double cheeseburger and fries.

"I'm not giving you the money," you tell him, "but if you're hungry I'll take you to buy it."

"I heard *that*, let's go," his willingness immediate, without the outrage that comes when they only want the cash, then you're walking up the street, not looking as though you naturally belong together but are something odder, buddy cops maybe, and he's just come in from undercover work, the reason he's dressed the way he is, wearing that dirty sweatshirt with the hood fraying around the edge. He probably really needs the meal, unless he only dresses the part, although some don't even bother, wearing two hundred dollar warmup suits and pricey new sneakers, as robust as marble statues come to life, with their hands out, telling you about all the meals they've missed.

"Got a head for business, must have," he says about you, "be wanting to eyeball where your money goes."

"Well, it *is* mine," you say, then with a glance back at the pet store: "People eat dogs sometimes. Not here, but . . ."

"Get hungry enough, yeah, I can see that, my stomach gets to growling too loud, I'd eat me a Benji-burger too."

"It's wrong, eating dogs, no matter where they do it," and he nods along with you, sharing a soft spot for man's best friend. Or maybe he'll agree with anything as long as food is coming, so you don't mention the T-shirt that you own with the wolf's head in the center, between two slogans: SAVE THE WOLF above, then underneath, PREDATORS KEEP THE BALANCE.

It's midmorning and the Dairy Queen isn't busy and the young woman with the dreadlocks behind the counter has no smiles for you or your new best friend, looking at him as if she's seen him too many times before, and you along with him.

"So you let that fool shame you into buying his breakfast for him," she says when you order, resenting it and why not, she's the one with the job and the grocery bills.

"No, no shame. My family's Norwegian, we didn't do slavery."

"Well, so nice to see someone with a clear conscience for a change," she says, very unimpressed. "He want anything to drink?"

You turn to check, but your undercover cop pal is off in the corner, clowning with another just like him who's rattling a newspaper.

"Give him a Hi-C," you decide, "keep him from getting scurvy for a few more days."

A corner of her mouth tics, as though tugged by a marionette string, you've almost made her laugh, or laugh for another reason instead of at you, at liberal Caucasian guilt too pervasive to be assuaged by pushing a nervous dollar or two away from your body before remembering somewhere else you have to be.

He trots into the restroom before the food is ready, is still there when it's up, so you carry it to a table and wait, checking to see how ignored you are. You unwrap the burger and peel the bun back on its ligaments of cheese, exposing thick goo, mostly bright primary colors, unnatural, like a squashed animal in a subversive children's book.

When he emerges from the restroom you've been guarding his food for a couple of minutes, as you rise he showers you with gratitude and the mingled fumes of malt liquor and tooth decay.

"God bless you, God bless you," he says, overdoing it, you're embarrassed, and when you leave him you return to the place where he found you, to finish your time with the puppies, who once again compete for your affections. Seems like everybody's glad to see you today.

You tap on the glass and it stirs their blood, with furiously wagging tails they swat each other's faces, it's almost the second Thursday of the month, and you know if the world works the way it's supposed to, these are just the ones who should inherit it.

It always comes back to canids for you, nothing else on earth as untarnished as the societies of dogs and dingoes, jackals and hyenas, coyotes and the progenitors of them all, the wolves, the beautiful wolves, with their tender and baleful eyes, said by an old Indian legend to have been the only human attribute to take when the gods tried to turn the animals into men. But human beings can only wish that their rites of dominance and submission were as pure.

You've always been entrenched on the canine side of that wide and irreconcilable schism between cat people and dog people, where each camp recognizes the inferiority of the other but only the dog people are right. Cat people laugh, haughty, say that they prefer felines because of their independence, their autonomy and self-reliance; say that dog people crave brainless obedience. But the true dog people know just how far self-reliance goes when trying to escape a pack on the hunt; know that what cat people are really identifying with is sleepy-eyed lazy indolence. Most cats, if they could, would be on welfare.

Since childhood you've preferred the company of canines, you sense a kinship that transcends species and they know it too, will defer to your mastery to a degree approaching the telepathic. Your impulses become theirs, their instincts inform your own, when you were a boy the area dogs would gather around you, nuzzling with their long toothy muzzles. You could strip down and roll with them, with young and old, they would accept you into their society of scents and sensibility as if recognizing some better part of you, beneath your hairless skin and flat face, you, the strangely-furred pug who walks on two legs. Cats aren't the only ones who bring blood offerings, so you pretended you had some use for dead squirrels, for broken-necked tabbies, and no, you never once actually thought you were a dog, no matter what anyone said, and ever since then you've understood that the human animal is primarily characterized by arrogant stupidity and soft throats, a combination that constantly courts extinction.

Just as they see into you, so too do you see into them, they are Nietzsche's abyss with the reciprocal gaze, or maybe the abyss is you. Show you a worthy dog and you'll see past the millennia of taming, see past civilization's dulling to the sharp primal edges beneath, the wolf behind those eyes. Except for poodles, pampered and self-loathing inside, and dachshunds, which are less dogs and more sorrel-haired rats.

The rest, it's why they like you so, you know their ancestral secret and respect it, it's almost the second Thursday of the month, and already you're cocking an expectant ear toward the sky, listening for the howl that will split the city, then the world.

So enlivened are you by the day's gift of the panhandler that you decide not to return to work. Instead you walk, not wanting to miss anything now that your senses are primed, you can track down further opportunities for trickery like any efficient hunter, blending into the landscape. You wear lots of gray and black because you live around lots of concrete and asphalt.

Work, too, is camouflage, was camouflage long before you even realized it, after awakening to your deepest nature. You log manifests and dispatch messengers, you help the city stay in touch with itself, for whatever that's worth, old people do the same when senility takes hold and all anyone ever wishes is that they'd just shut up. If you really wanted to be happy you'd work in a pet store somewhere, but you tried that once already, and were fired when they caught you trying to smuggle all the dogs to freedom, even if they misunderstood everything, suspected you of planning to sell the stock to experimental medical laboratories, although they couldn't figure out why you'd left the dachshunds behind.

After an hour of feeling the city's shifting crust beneath your boots you take respite in a neighborhood bar, you've never seen or been seen here before, it's beneath your usual dignity but happy hour begins early and seems to draw a clientele that needs it more than most. Paradoxically, all of them ignore each other.

You're minding your own business when she comes up to you, the way it happens to anyone. You've had the darkened booth to yourself for less than the duration of your first drink, or the cigarette that she lit around the time she watched you sit down.

"I don't mean to interrupt or anything, if you've got your heart set on sitting here alone, but if you wish you weren't, I, I know how you feel, you don't have to anymore, then neither would I, I mean it kind of makes sense, doesn't it?"

A refill. She'll want a refill, it's as good as predestined.

"We don't have to talk or anything, not if you don't want to, it's just that drinks taste better when you're with someone."

She talks with her hands held rigidly before her, a conscious effort to keep them from trembling, and doing a better job with her hands than she's managing with her voice.

"Would you mind not smoking, that's all I ask," you tell her. "I have a very sensitive nose."

Her nervous hand dives toward the ashtray, she grinds out the butt, not a problem for her, then she's fanning the wisps away and lands in the booth, across the table, she and her purse and her glass with its lonely, rattling ice cubes.

"My name's Merilee," she says.

You nod. "As in, 'merrily, merrily, merrily, merrily, life is but a dream'?"

She looks at you blankly, how could you be making such a mistake? "No, no, it's spelled—" She catches herself. "Oh, you're joking, I get it." She slaps her forehead, lets it slide halfway down her arm, embarrassed.

You buy her another drink to go with your second, making an educated guess that she's had a two-drink head start on you. When you catch sight of the booth in the mirror behind the bar you scan the reflection for the way you look together, the story it tells.

Two years ago you might've belonged together, but no longer, she left you and now she wants to come back, she's had a rougher time of it than she thought, it shows in the puffiness along her jowls and under her eyes, while you have prospered, triumphed over the pain, and while you feel pity for her you're not the same person she left, so how could you take her back?

Briefly you wonder who he was, if you've envisioned what has been, or what is still to come.

"I'm not keeping you from anything, am I, you don't have to go anywhere right away?" she asks.

"Well, I have a dog I'll need to feed eventually."

Her eyes mist over with sorrow, as though she's heard better excuses in her day, but is still willing to give you the benefit of the doubt, she has hope, clings to it. "What's his name?"

"Fenris."

"What kind of name is that?" she asks, so you tell her it's Scandinavian, just like you, and it brightens her afternoon, she believes you now, she says nobody would just make up a name like that and asks what breed of dog Fenris is.

"He's more of a wolf, actually."

With widening eyes, "You keep a wolf in the city, isn't that dangerous?"

"Not for Fenris. He thrives on it."

"I'll bet you don't have many problems with your neighbors."

"Not anymore."

"That's funny, you don't strike me as one of those guys who has to have the meanest dog around," she tells you, it's a fumbled compliment. "I knew this guy, well, lived with him for a month if you must know, it was Rottweilers or nothing for him. He was as hairy as the dogs, almost. But you, you have such a cultured look if you don't mind me saying so, like you could be an artist maybe. And your voice, I could listen to you talk for hours."

Which sounds like a threat, as she drinks two to your one, a ratio Merilee seems to have some experience with. Her hands start and stop for her cigarettes so often you lose count, her fingers drum with nerves and pretty soon the situation arrives where you know it's been heading all along. She tries not to cry over things she can't even tell you about, worries what you must think of her, with her eyes she begs you not to judge too harshly. She dumps her soul at your feet, skinned and raw.

"Loneliness is a cancer," she says with frozen tears and a lurch in her voice, "and it never gets tired of eating at you day after day."

It touches you like nothing else she's said or done. "I know exactly what you mean." You point to the front window, overlooking the sidewalk. "Walking around out there today, how many people did I see, do you think? Five thousand? Five thousand⸱and they're all selectively deaf, selectively blind. I might as well not exist for all they care. I could stand on a streetcorner and shout at the top of my lungs, and they'd hear me almost as well as they'd hear a gnat buzzing near their ears. They only want to know about you when they can take something from you."

"Like your kids," she murmurs with a faraway gaze.

"The world quit feeling, if it ever did in the first place," and you're saying more than you should but she's made you talkative, "so we may as well just give it back."

Give the world back to where, to whom, she wants to know. But you're canny enough to smile and shake your head as if to admit you're only spouting off, you've never thought it through. Merilee says she'll be right back, she scoots off toward the restroom with purse in tow and while she's gone you hold her glass and swirl it, checking to see how ignored you are.

When she returns your trick is done, you can tell she's tried to freshen up, she's washed the smudges from around her eyes.

"What was that about your kids?" you ask, and at first she's hesitant but you persist, you really want to know.

"Anybody can make a mistake. It was only bathwater, it didn't feel too hot to me." She's a talking shell. "So what about you, what's the worst thing you ever did? You owe me one now, y'know."

"Earlier today this guy came up asking for money for food, so I took him to get a cheeseburger," and before you can finish she's asking what's wrong with that, it sounds positively saintly. "But while he was in the restroom I put ground glass in the sandwich. He was drunk enough, I doubt he even noticed. The glass was pretty finely-ground to begin with."

Merilee blinks at you, her face is as blank as unshaped clay, in her bovine eyes you see the future, see how she'll continue to propagate more kids that may or may not be taken from her bungling hands and what kind of specialized monsters and parasites they'll turn out to be, the world doesn't need them, although that's all academic now. Or will be in a few more hours.

She slaps her forehead and laughs. "You're joking again! You really had me going for a minute, you have the strangest sense of humor, did anybody ever tell you that?"

"No, never," and now you're checking the time, how many hours since tricking the panhandler, the glass should be well on its way into his aching digestive tract by now, small intestine for sure, indigestible razor dust cutting soft tissues along its peristaltic journey, if he's drinking, and he probably is, his thin blood will leak out that much sooner.

"I like you," Merilee says, and you nod toward her glass and tell her to drink up, every last drop, for it's time you should be on your way, it's almost the second Thursday of the month, and the end of everything that's overdue already.

It always comes back to history for you, most history being cyclical, because of the fundamental stupidity of human herds that never learn, or less often the realization that sometimes the old ways really are best. New generations must discover this on their own, why should they take anyone's word for anything?

Some months ago you first felt it, felt that cold wind blow to you from across the ocean, from Norway, home of your ancestral genes and much that you hold dear. For a few years it's been going on and you never even knew, until your chance encounter with a small newspaper article, which led you to a more detailed magazine article, which triggered your search for all that you could find on the subject of the Norwegian church-burnings.

A war has been declared, fought mostly in the middle of the night, churches a thousand years old, some of them, set aflame and razed to the ancient ground, burned in the name of old gods once sacred to Viking lips and warriors' blades. The newly churchless blame it on devil worshippers, poor Lucifer gets dragged into everything, if the pious have no greater sense of their own ancestry than that, then they're no better than poodles and dachshunds, maybe they really should be burned out. The culprits are musicians in most instances, modern-day sons of Odin and Thor, evidently they've had quite enough of missionaries and meddling, would've put a stop to it, too, if only they hadn't been born a thousand years too late.

From across the Atlantic and cold North Sea you cheer them on, their fiery tricks are the vanguard of revolution, the world is about to shake itself down like a tick-infested hound and these are the first true signs, and you're a natural part of the rest.

Ragnarok is coming.

You hear it on its way, heard it trying to break through into the world a month ago, and the month before, and the month before that, you weren't ready then but now you are, you've remembered everything, now it's almost the second Thursday of the month again and it all depends on you.

So enlivened are you by this final countdown that you decide not to go home, in polls you've read wherein people share what they'd do if they knew they had but another day to live, and nobody ever says they would sleep more.

You're minding your own business when she comes up to you, the way it happens to anyone. You've taken a break from your spree of tricks, both feet are aching in their boots. The blistered soles of your feet throb while you sit on the bench at the bus stop, your blisters have popped and feel raw inside sticky socks.

"You look kind of stressed," she tells you. "Suck you off to relieve some of that tension? Twenty bucks."

Vitality. She'll want your life's vitality, it's as good as predestined. She can't be more than fourteen and possibly younger, her body still has that slim, straight look of a boy's, no curves anywhere, or perhaps it's poor nutrition.

"Come on, you got a car nearby? I'll do you there, do you so good your grandpa'll come. No, wait, if you had a car, like, what would you be doing waiting for the bus?"

"You're new at this, aren't you?" you ask.

"Yeah, I've got these virginal lips, they've never known a man's thing. Is that what you want?" She's pouting like a magazine cover, hard little urchin's face softening beneath a floppy hat, hair snaking from beneath in tangled dark strands and both knees of her jeans are dirty. "Okay, fifteen and we'll go find somebody else's car. There's gotta be one unlocked around somewhere."

"Do your parents know you do this?"

"Oh yeah, sure, I'm like sending them a postcard every week, 'Hope you're fine, I still don't swallow.' So what planet are you from, anyway, do they even have blowjobs there?" She rolls her eyes. "Ten, okay? It's as low as I go."

"You know what you need?" you tell her, because now you know that you can make a difference in her life, grant it some grace here at the end. "You need a dog."

"Whoa, no, I'm all, okay, like I've done some weird things to get by, but I'm not into animal scenes, you really are a freak—"

You stop her before she can go any further, perpetuate this sick misunderstanding, the idea of treating a fine dog in such a way fills you with nausea, and never mind what the males will do sometimes to an unwary leg, they don't know any better and you do.

"A pet, that's all I mean, a protector, and to always love you," you explain. "They're a lot more reliable than people."

"I had a dog once," she says quietly. "His name was Sailor, and we . . . we never could hardly go anywhere without him following, he was so good at slipping the gate."

She's thoughtful now, you see the distant past overtake her, remake her, she's no longer the pubescent whore. If a remembered mutt can do this much for her, imagine what Fenris can do to the rest of the world when he gets it in his jaws.

"I'll buy you another dog tomorrow, all you have to do is meet me at the pet store on Lancaster Avenue. You know the one?"

"A dog." She can't believe what she's hearing. "You wanna buy me a dog."

"But it'll have to be first thing in the morning. Later on I'm going to be extremely busy."

"You. Wanna buy me. A dog."

"They all know me there. If you want, we could walk over now and look in the window, you could pick one out tonight."

The girl contemplates this, her mouth hangs open and her eyes roll up, she doesn't know what to do with her hands. "You are like the weirdest guy I have ever met." She stops, abrupt. "Okay. Sure. Okay. Let's go look at the dogs, maybe it'll excite you, something needs to."

The two of you walk along the street together, you're much taller than she is, if anybody cares to look she could be your kid sister but of course nobody cares. The members of a wolfpack watch out for one another, but the tendency has been bred out of humans, another reason to give the world back.

"So is this your mission in life, or what?" she asks.

You wonder how to explain it all so she'll understand, these are not simple principles, you may have to be patient.

"Everything we do makes ripples," you say. "Like in a pond? You throw in one pebble and it makes ripples, you throw in two or three, then the ripples get complicated, they intersect. So what I do is, I go around throwing pebbles."

"Right," she says. "Why?"

"As long as I'm in the middle of the ripple patterns, that should keep me safe."

"Oh, sure, the ripple patterns, why didn't you just say so?" You're really communicating now. "Look, I know that nice leather jacket you're wearing must not've come cheap, but are you sure you can afford this dog?"

You assure her you can, after Ragnarok what use will anyone have for money anyway, filthy lucre will be utterly without value. Flesh and blood will be the currency of the future, and tomorrow's princes those who have shown an aptitude for dealing in them.

For many years you've been hearing about senseless violence, commentators tossing the phrase around as though it were something they were proud of inventing and proud of scorning, above it all. They're fools at best, at worst traitors to their species, ignorant of the natural order, they must think that deer run from wolves in a spirit of fun, that throats open and entrails spill from zippers, without a struggle. The culling of the weak can hardly be a senseless act, is labeled so only by a species that cherishes weakness, that nurtures it, that protects the weak from their natural fate. It demeans the whole system.

"You're not Italian, are you?" you ask.

"No," she says, she's looking strangely at you. "Would it be a problem if I was, are you prejudiced?"

"Just checking, just curious." People all around, in windows and in cars, no one sees you or this underage whore, how blind do they have to become before they never leave home at all? "Columbus gets credit for discovering it over here even though Vikings came centuries earlier. They know better, so what's Columbus Day still doing on the calendar? It just bugs me. Some smart Norwegian needs to restake the claim."

"There's always tomorrow," she says, then you're looking at her back, she's turned into an alley all but untouched by light, the bricks and wrought iron gleam with a wet nocturnal sheen.

"Where are you going?"

"Shortcut, this way's quicker than going all the way to the end of the block. Believe me, I live out here, I know."

So you follow, the alley slick beneath your boots. She takes your hand like a child afraid of the dark, you hope she doesn't start up with the propositions again. Halfway along she pivots at the waist, scrawny torso spinning toward you when her fist slams into your stomach in that opening of your jacket, her fist and the small knife she's holding. You grunt and she stabs you again, lets the blade pull itself out as you lurch back against moist bricks and slide down, her hands plunge into your pockets, deft and sure, they know what they want by touch alone and leave the rest.

Before you can tell her what a mistake she's making she's running away with your old name and your money. You sit against the wall, you're aware of breath and blood, aware of everything but time, you sit until something clicks inside you, it must be after midnight by now, it's the second Thursday of the month, if only you can hold out a few hours longer.

It always comes back to roots for you, in roots lies purpose, without roots how can anyone know which direction to grow? Roots are the human pedigree, ergo one's destiny, as surely as pedigrees match dogs to duty, *canis familiaris*, a single species but many breeds. Pedigrees point border collies toward herds of sheep, and bloodhounds toward scent trails, while behind them all are the wolves, the beautiful wolves, who lurk in the northern woodlands of deepest night and in the dim bestial memories of those who build walls to keep them out.

Your fleshly grandparents were born in Norway but you're an American, whatever that means, the answer might be found if you read enough bumper stickers but they don't mean the same things on cars that are stolen or repossessed, and since you never know who's driving, you're better off trusting your roots. You have Vikings in the woodpile, plunder in your blood and Ragnarok in your future, as a heritage there's a lot to live up to.

They've given you courage, these Nordic church-burners across the ocean, obviously they knew more than you at first, being so much closer to the soil of your common roots. With Ragnarok on the way they're making preparations, you wonder if they too heard the howl of Fenris on the second Thursday of each month, Fenris apparently too weak to claw through into this world.

His howling is to be the beginning of the end, the old Norse legends agree that the trickster and fire demon Loki will slip his bonds, then he and his followers will meet the gods for the final battle and Fenris the mighty wolf born of the trickster Loki will unleash his howl of devastation to come and there's Ragnarok for you. Of course everyone must die before the earth can regenerate into a new and better place, it's a necessary sacrifice, but look at most of the people around today and sacrifice starts to seem perfectly reasonable.

You remember hearing these old stories when you thought they were just that, just stories, tales your grandfather told to pass the winter afternoons after your parents no longer wanted you. He would take you for walks in the country, you were quite small at the time, you would help him take his dogs out to chase winter hares and laugh and kick at snow drifts and wander so deep into the forests that the day he fell over dead out there you knew you would never find your way back, late as it was, so you went to sleep instead.

It woke you with its hot breath and rough tongue, you opened your eyes but couldn't feel your feet, your grandfather lay where he fell although now his big belly was torn open and great steaming heaps of things lay in the snow. The yellow eyes looked upon you as if they knew you, knew everything you were and would be, you'd never seen an animal like this before, never so big nor so black, the dogs were nowhere to be found, and when it took your hand in its mouth you couldn't feel that either. It tugged you to your grandfather, to the ragged edges of the steaming wound, where frozen hands and frozen feet might be warmed, how it knew such a trick you couldn't understand. It had vanished before they found you, the two-leggeds, who didn't believe you anyway. "Where are the tracks?" they asked, and with your drippy hands you pointed at the snow but they wouldn't see, so you quit talking. They didn't deserve it.

You've always remembered the yellow eyes looking at you, how they recognized you even if you didn't recognize yourself and even forgot yourself entirely until a month ago, the latest howl of Fenris brought it all back, you've known who you are ever since.

You are Loki, *you* are the fire demon, *you* are the trickster and you've been playing tricks ever since, with ground glass and toxins and whatever else is handy. You've slipped your bonds as the legends always said you would, you wonder if anyone ever guessed that the bonds were forged not of metal but of a gray life of rent and repetition, and the gods damn them, they made you just one more link in the chain. No wonder escape took so long.

But now you're here, now you're free, it's finally the second Thursday of the month, the end of all that was never really you.

By dawn you made it to the building that you selected weeks ago for this morning and you've been here ever since. It's tall, vacant too if you don't count the vagrants below, they look asleep and in one sense they are. Two evenings ago you tricked them, you left warm deli sandwiches for them, cyanide has a very fulfilling effect, they want nothing from you now.

The building might've been a hotel once, its brick shell and musty hallways feel as though they were built in an age of sunnier dispositions. You wonder what happened, if the hotel died first and took the surrounding area with it, or if it was the other way around, if the hotel choked on creeping blight. It does no good to lock the place, whoever tries, vagrants only chisel it open again.

From a high window you view the streets below while awaiting Fenris, the insignificance of two-legged comings and goings is so much more apparent when watched from overhead, perspective is all. They're marbles in a crate down there, they roll wherever they're tilted, no pattern to it, and no purpose either. As a trickster you can appreciate the joke, but enough's enough.

You're minding your own business when he comes up to you, the way it happens to anyone. You sit on the floor, back against the wall, while you settle your stomach, settle your vision, your head feels hot this morning, never mind this chilly air. When you see him you shift as well as you can, it's not easy with your crusted belly and thirty-two pounds of weight resting across your lap.

For a moment he only stares, the room is atrocious, plaster crumbled everywhere and wallpaper hanging in tatters, same as the hallways, the whole place looks like a mummy.

"I'd ask if you need help," he says, "but I think I know how ridiculous that would sound."

Your soul. He'll want your soul, it's as good as predestined. Even from across the room you can tell what he is, he's wearing a ministerial collar, not Catholic though, Presbyterian maybe. He's carrying an armful of blankets, it's what his kind does, they find the homeless in their homes and bring them blankets for the coming winter, blankets with salvation, thanks, much earlier inhabitants of the region were brought blankets too, blankets with smallpox.

"I followed the blood upstairs. I don't know what your story is . . . but son, I beg you to let me get you some help, I beg you not to do whatever it is you have on your mind."

"Today's Thursday," you tell him. "You know why it's called that, don't you?"

No, no he doesn't, you know it even before he opens his pale mouth to confirm it.

"Thor's Day," you explain, slowly. "The day they dedicated to the thunder god. The one with the hammer. How can you be a holy man if you don't even know what's holy? You're as bad as the rest of them down there. No, worse—at least they don't pretend to know much of anything."

He's asking if he can't call for an ambulance, get you to the hospital, that's a nasty-looking belly wound and maybe so but they take a long time to die from if you die at all, depends on how the rest of this morning goes.

"That's—" He's shaking, now why would that be, it's not that cold. "That's about the biggest rifle I've ever seen."

He speaks the truth, across your lap rests a McMillan M-93 sniper rifle, each .50-caliber cartridge is nearly as long as your hand and each magazine holds twenty of them, it cost you every dollar you had in the bank and some you didn't.

"You don't know who I am, do you? You don't even recognize me," you say, then he tries to fool you, says sure, sure he does, the light was bad is all, but who's he kidding, can't trick the trickster. "That's all right, nobody else does either. I'm used to it by now. Not that it matters today, right before."

"Before . . . ?" he wants to know.

"You really are in the dark, aren't you? Doesn't your god tell you anything?"

It's the wrong thing to say, all the lead-in he needs, next thing you know you're getting a sermon, for God so loved the world, well he doesn't actually say it but you know that's what's going through his head, there's a remarkable consistency to the sheep of the lord, and if anything knows sheep it's wolves.

There's a beauty in devastation that escapes the appreciation of most, they're so attached to what has been they never think of what might be, never consider how a decomposing body can enrich a bed of roses, and that's just the small picture. With the entire world become a graveyard there's no telling what may grow in time, it's the great potential that is Ragnarok, so rejoice you deaf, dumb, blind, and ravenous, a better world will sprout from your fat and clutching fingers.

"All of them down there?" you say, with a nod at the window, the street. "As a holy man you must be very disappointed in them."

"No. Oh my, no." The Presbyterian shakes his head, he's even smiling a little. "They've given me good reason plenty of times. But then they turn around and delight me. And in between, there's forgiveness to fall back on. I promise you, they *will* delight you too . . . if you'll wait a little longer."

You snort at his desperate naivety. "If they only had longer teeth, they'd eat each other alive and sleep the rest of the time, they just don't admit it. I've watched it for thousands of years and it never changes."

For a moment he looks puzzled, still holding the blankets in his arms, he's a befuddled emissary, and then you hear it, Fenris at last, the mighty howl whose pattern you figured out is trying again and this time you're ready, it permeates the sky, it rolls through the streets.

"Hear that?" you ask. "I've waited for this forever."

"It's just the disaster siren, for heavy storms and such," he says, he still looks befuddled and why not, he's so desperate now he'll say anything. "They're all over town."

You've never heard such nonsense in your life, you may be a trickster but that's no reason for him to take you for a fool. Today isn't the first day you've heard it, after all, sometimes you'd be off work and Fenris would howl, the sound seeming to come from everywhere and every dog in your neighborhood would join in because they all remembered, their instincts hadn't dulled, their ancestral roots still ran true.

"It's nothing to be afraid of," the Presbyterian says, "the city tests it once a month or so—"

Fenris hangs at the peak of his first howl, he's waiting for you, Loki unchained, the father of the wolf. You tilt the rifle up from your lap, you squeeze the trigger without aiming and it makes such thunder. One second the Presbyterian has two good arms and the next has only one, the other's no longer there, you think it might've flown back out the doorway and into the hall. He sits down among the scattered blankets as though he's been hit with a hammer and stares at his shoulder and empty space, it's a good thing he had blankets since there's blood enough for them all.

Fenris lets his voice fall, then it crests again, when you swing the rifle around to the window your stomach rips with pain and starts to bleed again. You rest the massive barrel across the windowsill, no trained sniper would ever reveal himself this way but at thirty-two pounds the rifle needs support and you have no need of escape anyway, the world will fall around you now.

You bolt a new cartridge into the chamber and peer through the scope, everything and everyone in your face again, they swarm like maggots on a corpse and are equally soft and hungry. You settle on the first, and five pounds of trigger pull later you've made thunder again, the recoil pushes back a couple of inches into your shoulder and you've taken the guts out of sacrifice one. The second loses her heart and lungs, now you've got the hang of it, you've got the rhythm and the roll, no different than practicing on milk jugs, and it's time to get tricky, time to start taking heads.

Twenty shots go by fast, Fenris seems to think so, he's still with you as you snap on twenty more and bolt the next into the chamber, you bring the street up close again and they're all in your lens now, some of them still standing there covered in bits and pieces and splashes of the fallen and they haven't noticed a thing, for them not one thing has changed, sometimes you feel as though you're the only one alive and you wonder what does it take, what does it take just to get their attention? Some guy down there is still reading a newspaper, you punch the next bullet through the headline, black and white and red all over.

All in all, they've at least made your job easier.

You'll remember to thank them later, in that better world to come.

Bucky Goes to Church

BY ROBERT DEVEREAUX

Having spent the last billion-odd pages naturalistically laying out the details of our human dilemma, the time has come at last to ask the trillion-dollar existential question: What does it all mean?

Is there a point to all this suffering, madness, and horror? Are the optimists and the spiritually inclined among us right when they say that all things happen for a reason, and that it's just part of God's divine plan?

Let us pause, for a moment, to ponder the ineffable.

Then sit back and goggle in awe, as a mere mortal man named Robert Devereaux somehow finds the breathtaking big-picture words that part the veil, and deliver the cosmic lowdown.

A Bizarro pioneer long before the term was coined, Devereaux applies virtuoso verbal skills to a visionary palette so shamelessly profound that it's almost ridiculous. And does, in fact, make me laugh out loud.

But I dare you to dismiss its revelatory heart.

Ladies and gents: let the mind-blowing begin.

His real name was Vernon Stevens but folks called him Bucky on account of
his teeth and his beaverish waddle and well, just because it was such a cute name
and he was such a cute little fat boy, nothing but cuddles in infancy, an impish ball
of pudge in childhood, primed to take on the role of blubbery punching bag in
adolescence.

Kids caught on quick, called him names, taunted him, treated him about even
with dirt. Bucky smiled back big and broad and stupid, as if he fed on abuse.
The worst of them he tagged after, huffing and puffing, arms swinging wildly like
gawky chicken wings, fat little legs jubbing and juddering beneath the overhang of
his butt to keep up with them. "Wait up you guys," he'd whinny, "no fair, hey wait
for me!" They'd jeer and call him Blubberbutt and Porky Orca and Barf Brain, and
Bucky just seemed to lap up their torment like it was manna from heaven.

But, hey wuncha know it gang, somewheres in Bucky's head he was storing
away all that hurt: the whippings at home from his old man's genuine cow-leather
belt, a storm of verbal abuse stinging his ears worse than the smack of leather on
his naked ass; the glares and snippery from his frowzy mama, she of the pinched
stare, the worn, tattered faceflesh, the tipple snuck down her throat at every odd
moment; the bark of currish neighbors yowling after him to keep his sneaks off
their precious lawns; teachers turning tight smiles on him to show they didn't
mind his obtuse ways, Bucky'd get by okay if he did his best, but they'd be triple
goddamned if they were going to go out of their way to help him; and the kids, not
one of them daring to be his friend (Arnie Rexroth got yanked out of first grade
and shuffled off to Phoenix so he didn't count), all of them coming around quick
enough to consensus, getting off on taking the fatboy's head for a spin on the car-
ousel of cruelty, good for a laugh, a good way to get on with the guys, a great way
to forget your problems by dumping them in the usual place—on Bucky Stevens's
fat sweaty crewcut of a head.

Well one day, about the time Bucky turned fifteen, he woke to the mutterings
of a diamond-edged voice inside his left frontal lobe. "Kill, Bucky, kill!" it told
him, and, argue with it as he might, the voice at last grew stronger and more per-
suasive, until there was nothing to do but act on its urgings. So Bucky gathered all

that hurt he'd been storing away and pedaled off to church one Sunday morning on his three-speed with his dad's big backpack tugging at his shoulders like a pair of dead man's hands. The weight of the hardware inside punched at his spine as he pedaled, though it was lighter by the bullets lodged in the bodies of his parents, who lay now, at peace and in each other's arms, propped up against the hot-water heater in the basement. He couldn't recall seeing such contentment on their faces, such a "bastard!"-less, "bitch!"-free silence settling over the house.

He pumped, did Bucky, pumped like a sweathog, endured the TEC-9 digging at his backbone, kept the churchful of tormentors propped up behind his forehead like a prayer. His fat head gidded and spun with the bloodrush of killing his folks: his dad, dense as a Neanderthal, the ex-marine in him trying to threaten Bucky out of it, arms flailing backward as his forehead swirled open like a poinsettia in sudden bloom, his beefy body slamming like a sledge into the dryer, spilling what looked like borscht vomit all over its white enamel top; his mom down on her knees in uncharacteristic whimper, then, realizing she was done for, snarling her usual shit at him until he told her to shut her ugly trap and jabbed the barrel into her left breast and, with one sharp squeeze of his finger, buckled her up like a midget actress taking a bloody bow, pouring out her heart for an audience of one.

Bucky crested the half-mile hill at Main and Summit. The steeple thrust up into the impossible cerulean of the sky like a virgin boy's New-England-white erection humping the heavens. Bucky braked, easing by Washington, Madison, Jefferson. The First Methodist Church loomed up like a perfect dream as he neared it. It was a lovely white box resting on a close-clipped lawn, a simple beautiful spired construction that hid all sorts of ugliness inside.

Coasting onto the sidewalk, Bucky wide-arced into the parking lot and propped his bike against a sapling. Off came the backpack, clanking to the ground. A car cruised by, a police car. Bucky waved at the cops inside, saw the driver unsmiling return a fake wave, false town cohesion, poor sap paid to suspect everyone, even some pudgy little scamp parking his bike in the church lot, tugging at the straps of a big bulky backpack. Grim flatfaced flatfoot, hair all black and shiny—stranded separately like the teeth at the thick end of an Ace comb—was going to wish he'd been one or two seconds later cruising Main Street, was going to wish like hell he'd seen the TEC-9 shrug out of its canvas confinement and come to cradle in Bucky's arms, yes indeed.

Not wanting to spoil the surprise, Bucky pulled his Ninja t-shirt out of the front of his jeans, pressed the cool metal of the weapon against his sweaty belly, and redraped his shirt over it.

He could hear muffled organ music as he climbed the wide white steps. The front doors, crowding about like blind giants, were off-white and tall. And good God if the music mumbling behind them wasn't "Onward, Christian Soldiers," as wheezed and worried by a bloodless band of bedraggled grunts too far gone on the shellshock and homesickness of everyday life to get it up for the Lord.

Bucky tried the handle. The door resisted at first, then yielded outward.

The narthex was empty. Through the simulated pearls of Sarah Janeway's burbling organ music, Bucky could see an elaborate fan of church bulletins on the polished table stretched between the inner doors. Programs, the little kids called them. Through the window in the right inner door to the sanctuary, the back of a deacon's bald head hung like some fringed moon. Coach Hezel, that's who it was; Bucky's coach the year before in ninth grade, all those extra laps for no good reason, pushups without end, and the constant yammer of humiliation: how Bucky had no need for a jockstrap when a rubber band and a peanut shell would do the trick; how he had two lockermates, skinny Jim Simpson and his own blubber; how the school should charge Mister Lard Ass Stevens extra for soap, given the terrain he had to cover come showertime.

Bucky unshirted the gun, strode to the door, and set its barrel on the window's lower edge, sighting square against the back of Hezel's head. A clink as it touched glass. Hezel turned at the noise and Bucky squeezed the trigger. He glimpsed the burly sinner's blunt brow, his cauliflower nose, the onyx bead of one eye; and then the glass shattered and Hezel's mean black glint turned red, spread outward like burnt film, and Miss Sarah Janeway's noodling trickled to a halt at the tail end of *With the cross of Jeeeee-zus.*

Bucky kicked open the door and leaped over Hezel's still-quivering body. "Freeze, Christian vermin!" he shouted, ready to open up the hot shower of metal tensed in the weapon, but it sounded like somebody else and not quite as committed as Eastwood or Stallone. Besides, his eyes swept the shocked, hymnal-fisted crowd and found young kids, boys of not more than five whose eyes were already lidded with mischief and young girls innocent and whimpery in their pinafores and crinolines, and he knew he had to be selective.

Then the voice slammed in louder and harsher—(KILL THE FUCKERS, BUCKY, KILL THEM SONS OF BITCHES!)—like a new gear ratio kicking in. Bucky used its energy to fight the impulse to relent, dredging up an image of his dead folks fountaining blood like Bucky's Revenge, using that image to sight through as he picked off the Atwoods, four generations of hardware greed on the corner of Main and Garvey: old Grandpappy Andrew, a sneer and a "Shitwad!" on his withered lips as Bucky stitched a bloody bandoleer of slugs slantwise across his chest; Theodore and Gracia Atwood, turning to protect their young, mowed down by the rude slap of hot metal digging divots of flesh from their faces; their eldest boy Alan, overbearing son of an Atwood who'd shortchanged Bucky on fishhooks last July and whose head and heart exploded as he gestured to his lovely wife Anne, who danced now for them all as her mist-green frock grew red with polkadots; and four-year-old Missy who ran in terror from her bleeding family, ran toward Bucky with a scream curling from her porcelain mouth, her tiny fists raised, staggering into a blast of bullets that lifted her body up with the press of its regard and slammed her back against a splintering pew.

A woman's voice rose through the screams. "Stop him, someone!" she yelled from the front. Bucky pointed toward her voice and let the bullets fly, bloodfucking whole rows of worshippers at one squeeze. Most lay low, cowering out of sight. The suicidal made escape attempts, some running for the doors behind Bucky, others for those up front that led into the pastor's study or back where the choir warmed up. These jackrabbits Bucky picked off, making profane messes out of dark-suited bodies that showed no sense of decorum in their dying, but bled on hard-to-clean church property everywhere he looked.

He eased off the trigger and let the blasts of gun-thunder vanish, though they rang like a sheen of deafness in his ears. "Keep away from the doors!" he shouted, not sure if he could be heard by anyone. It was like talking into fog. "Stay where you are and no one will get hurt," he lied, stepping over dead folk to make his way forward. The crying came to him then, thin and distant, and he saw bodies huddled together as he passed, the wounded and the not-yet-wounded. Call them all what they were, the soon-to-be-deceased.

"Shame on you, Vernon Stevens," came a quavery voice. Bucky looked up. There in the pulpit stood the whey-faced Simon P. Stone, sanctimonious pastor who'd done nothing—his piety deaf to cruelty—to keep Bucky from being the butt of his confirmation class two years before. The knuckles of his thin right hand were white with terror as he clutched, unconscious, a fistful of gilt-edged Bible pages. His surplice hung like a shroud from his taut gaunt shoulders, a tasteful Pontiac gray, sheen and all. A lime-green tippet trailed like an untied tie down the sides of his chest.

"Come down, Satan," said Bucky, hearing sirens in the distance through the bloodpulse of his anger, "come down to the altar and call your flock of demons to you."

"No, Vernon, I won't do that." Pastor Stone's eyes were teary with fear—he of little faith not ready, no not after decades of preaching, to meet his Maker.

Bucky looked around through the sobbing, saw crazed eyes turn away from him, saw between pews the sculpted humps of suited shoulders like blue serge whales stuck in waves, saw—yes! saw Mrs. Irma Wilkins, her red velvet hat a half-shell really with black lace crap on it, her gloved hand dabbing a crumpled hanky to one eye. "Mrs. Wilkins," Bucky said, and her head jerked up like a startled filly, "come here!" Her lids lowered in that snippy way, but she rose, a thin frail stick of a woman, and sidled out of her pew. And as she neared, Bucky was back at the church camp five summers before, out in the woods, holding one end of the cross-branch from which depended the iron kettle, its sole support him and another kid and two badly made and badly sunk Y-shaped branches, and the wind shifted and the smoke of the fire blew like a mask of no-breath into his face and clawed at his eyes no matter how hard he tried to blink past it, and he turned away and let go of the branch saying "My eyes!" and the rude blur that was Irma Wilkins rushed in to catch the branch and to sting him with her condemnation, even now as she approached in this church he could hear her say it, *"Your eyes? OUR STEW!"* as if the fucking food were more important than Bucky's vision and to her it was and that voice of hers, that whole put-down attitude reduced Bucky to nothing; but Bucky knew he was something all right, and he saw her pinched little lipless mouth as she came closer, by God it looked like a dotted line and by God he'd oblige her by tearing across it now with his widdle gun, better that than live his whole life hearing this nasty woman's voice reduce him to nothing; and he opened up his rage upon her, rippling across her face with a rain of bullets until her head tore back at the mouth like the top of a Pez dispenser thumbed open, shooting out a stream of crimson coffins, spilling gore down the front of her black dress like cherry liqueur over dark chocolate, and mean Irma Wilkins went down like the worthless sack of shit she was, and Bucky felt damned proud of himself, yes he did, happy campers.

Bucky swung back to Pastor Stone. "Bring 'em all to the front of the church and I won't harm a one of 'em," he said. "But if you refuse, I'll pick 'em off one at a time just like I did Mrs. Wilkins here."

Rest of them had ears. They needed no coaxing, but coaxed instead their whimpering kids out of hiding, out into the aisles and up the red runners to the altar, where Pastor Stone, trembling like unvarnished truth, raised his robed arms as if in benediction, as if he were posing for a picture, Pastor Simon P. Stone and his bleating sheep.

The muffled squawk of a bullhorn turned Bucky's head to a tall unstained window at his left. A squat man in blue stood on the grass at the near edge of the parking lot, legs planted firmly apart, elbows bent, face and hands obliterated by a black circle. "Vernon Stevens," came his humorless voice, "lay down your weapon and come out with your hands raised. We will not harm you if you do as I say. We have the church surrounded. Repeat. The church. Is. Surrounded." The bullhorn squawked off and the black circle came down so that Bucky could see clearly the ain't-I-a-big-boy-now, pretend courage painted on the man's face. Glancing back, Bucky saw bobbing blue heads through the two small squares of window that let onto the narthex, a scared rookie or two, the long stems of assault rifles jostling like shafts of wheat in a summer breeze.

Doubt crept into him. And fear. His finger eased off the trigger. Tension began to drain from his arms.

FINISH THE JOB! came the voice, like a balloon fist suddenly inflating inside his skull, pressing outward as if to burst bone. *LOOK AT THEM, BUCKY! LOOK AND REMEMBER WHAT THEY'VE DONE TO YOU!*

And Bucky looked. And Bucky saw. There was Bad Sam in his Sunday best, frog-faced pouting young tough, a lick of light brown hair laid across his brow, freckles sprayed on his bloated cheeks, Bad Sam who'd grabbed Bucky off his bike when Bucky was nine, slammed him to the cement of the sidewalk by Mr. Murphy's house and slapped his face again and again until his cheeks bruised and bled. And through his tears, he could see Mr. Murphy at his front window, withdrawing in haste at being discovered; Mr. Murphy who'd always seemed so kind, tending his tulip beds as Bucky biked by, and now here he was in church along with his tiny wife and their daughter Patricia in a white dress and a round brimmed hat that haloed her head. And next to her stood Alex Menche, a gas jockey at the Exxon station, corner of First and Main, whose look turned to hot ice whenever Bucky walked by, who never blinked at him, never talked to him, but just stared, oily rag in hand, jaw moving, snapping a wad of gum. And back behind Alex he caught a glimpse of Mr. Green the janitor, who'd yelled at the lunchbox crowd in second grade to Shut up! even when their mouths were busy with peanut butter. And odd Elvira Freeborn, New Falls' weirdo-lady, who laid claim in good weather to a corner of the city park across from the town hall and had conversation with anyone who chanced by and lingered there—even weirdo Elvira had come up to him one day when he'd been desperate enough for company to go seek her out, had come up all smiles, her hair wispy gray and twisting free of its bun, and said, "My, my, Vernon, you are one fat ugly thing, yes you are, and if you were mine, I'd sew your mouth shut, I would; by God I'd starve that flab right off your bones and I'd see about getting you a nose job for that fat knob of a honker you got on your face and—" on and on and on, and now her eyes were on him here in church, off-yellow glaring cat's-eyes like a reformed witch having second thoughts. And beside her was Sarah Janeway the organist, who'd laughed and then tried to hide it when Bucky auditioned for the children's choir at the age of eight, a no-talent bitch with her wide vacant eyes encircled in wide glasses rimmed in thin red and her hair cropped short as her musical gifts and her absurd flowered dress poking out of the shimmering-green choir robe down below, and she was standing there white-faced and whiny, and then the bullhorn bullshit started up again, and Bucky brought his one true friend up to his chest and let the surge of righteous wrath seize him.

He made them dance, every last one of them.

He played the tune. They tripped and swayed to the rhythm of his song. Wounds opened like whole notes in them. Sweeping glissandos of gore rose up like prayers of intercession.

Behind him he felt a flood of cops rush in to pick up the beat and join him, to judder and jolt the music out of *him* with music of their own. Bucky, tripped out on giving back in spades what New Falls had so unstintingly bestowed upon him over the years, turned about to spray death into the boys in blue at his back. But there were too many of them, and a goodly number were already in position, rifles beaded on him.

Then pain seized his right knee and danced up his leg in small sharp steps, like invisible wasps landing on him, fury out. Needles of fire watusied across his belly. Two zigzags of lead staggered up the ladders of his ribs and leaped for Bucky's head. Something impossible to swallow punched through his teeth, filling his mouth with meat and blood.

And then his brain lit up like a second sun and all the pain winked out. The terrible thunder of weaponry put to use went away, only to be replaced by organ music so sweet it made Bucky want to wet his pants and not give a good goddamn about the consequences.

He felt himself drift apart like a dreamer becoming someone else. The cops froze, caught in mid-fire. About him, the church walls roiled and wowed like plaster turned to smoke. But it wasn't smoke. It was mist, fog, clouds. They billowed down into the church, rolling and shifting and swirling among the corpses. Bucky glanced back at the altar, saw the bodies of his victims posed in attitudes of death, saw Pastor Simon P. Stone, his robed arms out in crucifixion, veed at the waist as if he'd just caught the devil's medicine ball in his belly.

But right behind Bucky, close enough to startle him, was his own body, bits of flesh being torn out like tufts of grass at a driving range, shoots of blood looking like hopeful red plants just coming into sunlight. He circled, by willing it, about his body, feeling the cumulus clouds cotton under his feet, soothing his soles, as he gazed in astonishment at his head, pate cracked open all round like the top of an eggshell, hovering a foot above the rest of it in a spray of blood and brain. He reached out, touched the stray piece of skull, tried to force it back in place, but it was as if it were made of stone and cemented for all eternity to the air. Likewise the freshets of gore issuing like bloody thoughts from his brain, which, though not cold, were as stiff as icicles.

The music swelled, recaptured his attention. Looking about for its source, he saw emerge from each tiny cloud a creature, all in white, all of white and gold, delicate of hand, beatific of face, and every one of them held a thing of curves in its hands. Their angel mouths O'd like moon craters. Thin fingers swept in blizzards of beauty across iridescent harps. And yet their music was neither plucked nor sung, but a pain-pure hymn rolling out in tones richer than any man-made organ.

They made the bloody scene beautiful, sanctifying it with their psalm. And now their bodies swerved as though hinged and they raised their eyes to the dioramic massacre before the altar and up past the huge golden cross even to the white plaster ceiling above it, beyond which the spire lofted heavenward. With a great groan, as if angelic eyes could move mountains with a look, the top of the building eased open, sliding outward on invisible runners to hang there in the open air. And down into the church descended a great blocky bejeweled thing, an oblong Spielbergian UFO Bucky thought at first. But then he saw the sandals, the feet, the robes, the hands gripping firmly the arms of the throne like Abe Lincoln, the chest bedecked in white, and the great white beard, and he guessed what he was in for.

But when the head came fully into view, Bucky had to laugh. Like Don Rickles trapped in a carpet, the face of an angry black woman grimaced out from behind the white beard and mustache of God. Her cheeks puffed out like wet sculpted obsidian, her dark eyes glared, and just in front of a Hestonian sweep of white hair, a tight black arch of curls hugged her face like some dark rider's chaps curving about the belly of his steed. The white neck of the deity was stiff and rigid, as if locked in a brace.

"Bucky Stevens," She boomed, Her eyes moving from him to a space of air in front of Her, "you'd best be getting yourself up here this instant, you hear?"

"Yes, ma'm," he said, drifting around his exploding corpse and sailing up over the bloody crowd at the altar. He could still sense how fat he was, but he felt as light and unplodding as a sylph. "You sending me to hell?" he asked.

She laughed. "Looks to Me like you found your own way there." Her eyes surveyed the carnage. "First off, young man, I want to say I 'preciate what you did for Me. I like sinners who listen to My suggestions and have the balls to carry them out."

"That was You?"

"Does God lie?"

"No, ma'm."

"Damn right He don't, and I'm God, so you just shove those doubts aside and listen up."

"Um, scuse me, ma'm," said Bucky, shuffling his feet in the air, "but how come God's a black woman? I mean in Sunday school, we never—"

"God ain't a black woman, Mister Bucky, leastways no more He ain't. He's been that for a while, oh 'bout three weeks or so." She smiled suddenly. "But now He gets to be a fat white boy named Bucky Stevens."

Bucky brightened. He didn't doubt for a moment what She'd said. He couldn't. It speared like truth into his heart. "You mean I get to . . . to take over? There's no punishment for killing all these people?"

God chuckled, a high-pitched woo-wee kind of sound. "That ain't what I said a-tall." She did a stiff-necked imitation of a headshake as She spoke.

Bucky was mystified: "I don't get it."

God leaned forward like She had a board strapped to Her back. "I'll be brief," She said, "just so's you can hustle your fat butt up here quicker and let Me come down and do My dying. I killed me a whole officeload of people three weeks ago, got blown away by a security guard after I hosed those heartless fuckers at Century 21. Same sorta miracle that's happening to you now, happened to me then. Only God was this unhinged lunatic I'd seen on Dan Rather the week before, some nut who went to O'Hare and picked off ground crew and passengers not lucky enough to be going through one of those tubes. He got blown away too, became God, then talked me into wiping out my co-workers when they gave me the axe. So I did it, and coaxed you along same's he did me, and here we are."

The music was doing beautiful things to Bucky's mind. He grew very excited. "You mean I'm going to be in charge of everything? I can make any changes I feel like making, I can stop all the misery if I want to?" God ummm-hmmmed. "But why would anyone, why would You, want to give that up?"

She looked agitated, like She wanted to laugh and cry and holler all at the same time. Instead She said, "As My momma used to say, young Master Stevens, experience is the best teacher a body can have." She glared at him suddenly and Bucky felt himself swept forward and up.

He windmilled his arms, struggling to find his center of gravity, but found himself fluttering and turning like an autumn leaf, tumbling spout over teakettle toward the great black face, toward the crazy brown eyes. He headed straight between them, fearing he'd smash on the browbone, but instead doubled and split like a drunkard's vision and fell and swelled into the black pools of God's pupils. In the blink of an eye, he inflated. That's how it felt to him, like his head felt when they stuck his arm and taped it down, knocking him out for an ingrown toenail operation when he was ten, only all over his body this time and he didn't lose consciousness. He unlidded his eyes just in time to see the stocky black woman wink at him before she put her hands together as if in prayer, sang out "So long, sucker!" and swan-dived into his shattering body.

Bucky gazed about at the angels on their clouds and felt guy-wires coming from their O'd mouths as if He were a Macy's Day balloon and they the marching guardians who kept Him from floating free. The throne rose slowly and the angels with it. Bucky took His first Godbreath and felt divine. Like Captain Kirk, He was in command now, He sat at the helm, and things by God were going to fly right from here on out.

But then, as He lifted above the church and its roof clicked into place, time unfroze and, with it, the pain of those inside. He felt it all, like a mailed fist slamming into His solar plexus again and again: Simon Stone, small and mean inside like a mole, gasping for one final breath; Sarah Janeway, two months pregnant, trying in vain to hold back the rope-spill of her intestines; kind-hearted Elvira Freeborn, in so many ways the sanest person there, who let her dying fall over her like a new sun dress, a thing of razor and flame. And even the dead—Coach Hezel, the Atwoods, Irma Wilkins and the rest—even from these, Bucky felt the echoes of their suffering and, transcending time, seeped into their dying a thousand times over.

And then He rose over New Falls, did Bucky Stevens, feeling His holy tendrils reach into everyone that wept and wandered there. He knew at last the torment of his parents and the riches they'd lost inside themselves, and it made His heart throb with pain. Bucky rose, and, in rising, sank into every hurting soul in town, spreading Himself thick everywhere. And all was painful clarity inside Him. It grew and crackled, the misery, and still He rose and sank, moving like Sherwin-Williams paint to engulf the globe, seeping deep down into the earth. Bucky wanted to scream. And scream He did. And His scream was the cause, and the sound, of human misery.

He tried to bring His hands to His face. To puncture His eardrums. To thumb out His eyes. But they clung like mules to the hard arms of the throne, not budging, and His eyelids would not shut, and His earflaps sucked all of it in like maelstroms of woe. Pockets of starvation flapped open before Him like cover stories blown, and each death-eyed Ethiopian became unique to Him—the clench of empty stomachs, the wutter and wow of dying minds.

Like dental agony, layer beneath layer surprising one at the untold depths of it, Bucky's pain intensified and spread, howling and spiraling off in all directions. And after a while, it didn't exactly dull, nor did He get used to it, but rather He rose to meet it, to yield to it as the storm-tossed seafarer gives up the struggle and moves into the sweep of the sea. He was the pincushion of pain, He was the billions of screaming pins, He was the billions of thumbs pressing them down into flannel. He suffered all of it, and knew Himself to be the cause of it all. Caught in the weave, He was the weave.

He almost smiled, it was so perverse; but the smile was ripped from His face by new outrage. There seemed no end to the torment, no end to burgeoning pain. As soon as He thought He'd hit bottom, the bottom fell out. He began to wonder if the black woman had lied to Him, if maybe He was trapped in this nightmare for all eternity. While He watched with eyes that could not close, new births killed young girls, new deaths tore at mourners, new forms of woe were kennel-bred and unleashed. Bucky was fixed in His firmament, and all was hell with the world.

Plunged down the slippery slope of despair, He cast His great eyes about, sought for pustules of resentment, found them. The seeds of His redemption they were, these seething souls. The black woman—Miriam Jefferson Jones—had, like her predecessor, been nursing others along, and now Bucky reached out to them and took up the whisper in their ears, the whisper momentarily stilled at the shift in deity. Heavens yes, Sean Flynn, he assured the young man leaned against the stone wall, huddled with his mates, it's only proper you elbow under their fuckin' transport at night, fix old Mother Flammable there, crawl the hell out o' there, give it the quick plunge, watch all them limey bastards kiss the night sky over Belfast with their bones. And yes, Alicia Condon of Lost Nation, Iowa, it's okay to take your secret obsession with the purity of the newborn to its limit, it is indeed true that if you could wipe out a whole nursery of just-delivered infants before they hit that fatal all-corrupting second day of life, the Second Coming of My Own Sweet Son would indeed be swiftly upon the sinning race of mankind. And yes, oh most decidedly yes, Gopal Krishnan and Vachid Dastjerdi and Moshe Naveh, you owe it to your respective righteous causes to massacre whole busloads, whole airports, whole towns full of enemy flesh.

There were oodles of them walking the earth, ticking timebombs, and all of them He tended and swayed that way, giving with a whisper gentle nudges and shoves toward mass annihilation. New ones too, promising buds of bitterness, Bucky began to cultivate. Some one of them was certain to bloom any moment now—oh God, how Bucky prayed to Himself for it to be soon—at least one brave quarterback on this playing field of sorrow was sure to snatch that ball out of the sky and run for all he was worth, pounding cleat against turf, stiff-arming those who dared try to block him, not stopping till he crossed the forbidden line and slammed that bleeding pigskin down in triumph.

That was the hope, through agonies untold, that kept Bucky going. That was the hope that made things hum.

At Eventide

BY KATHE KOJA

So what have we learned from all this?

Whether you feel that life has intrinsic meaning, or only the meaning we ascribe to it—or even no meaning at all—in the end, the human hope is to somehow make peace. Find a way to reconcile both our beautiful and terrible truths.

To both live, and then die, as best we can.

Which brings us, at last, to "At Eventide." Courtesy of Kathe Koja, who quietly codifies the end of our journey in terms so brilliant and haunting and true that no climactic explosion could possibly compare.

I could not ask for a better note to leave on.

Take care, everybody. I wish you well.

What he carried to her he carried in a red string bag. Through its mesh could be seen the gleam and tangle of new wire, a package of wood screws, a green plastic soda bottle, a braided brown coil of human hair; a wig? It could have been a wig.

To get to her he had come a long way: from a very large city through smaller cities to Eventide, not a city at all or even a town, just the nearest outpost of video store and supermarket, gas and ice and cigarettes. The man at the Stop-N-Go had directions to her place, a map he had sketched himself; he spoke as if he had been there many times: "It's just a little place really, just a couple rooms, living room and a workshop, there used to be a garage out back but she had it knocked down."

The man pointed at the handmade map; there was something wrong with his voice, cancer maybe, a sound like bones in the throat; he did not look healthy. "It's just this feeder road, all the way down?"

"That's right. Takes about an hour, hour and ten, you can be there before dark if you—"

"Do you have a phone?"

"Oh, I don't have her number. And anyway you don't call first, you just drive on down there and—"

"A phone," the man said; he had not changed his tone, he had not raised his voice but the woman sorting stock at the back of the store half-rose, gripping like a brick a cigarette carton; the man behind the counter lost his smile and "Right over there," he said, pointing past the magazine rack bright with tabloids, with PLAY-BOY and NASTY GIRLS and JUGGS; he lit a cigarette while the man made his phone call, checked with a wavering glance the old Remington 870 beneath the counter.

But the man finished his call, paid for his bottled water and sunglasses, and left in a late-model pick-up, sober blue, a rental probably and "I thought," said the woman with the cigarette cartons, "that he was going to try something."

"So did I," said the man behind the counter. The glass doors opened to let in heat and light, a little boy and his tired mother, a tropical punch Slush Puppy and a loaf of Wonder bread.

Alison, the man said into the phone. It's me.

A pause: no sound at all, no breath, no sigh; he might have been talking to the desert itself. Then: Where are you? she said. What do you want?

I want one of those boxes, he said. The ones you make. I'll bring you everything you need.

Don't come out here, she said, but without rancor; he could imagine her face, its Goya coloring, the place where her eye had been. Don't bring me anything, I can't do anything for you.

See you in an hour, the man said. An hour and ten.

He drove the feeder road to the sounds of Mozart, 40's show tunes, flashy Tex-Mex pop; he drank bottled water; his throat hurt from the air conditioning, a flayed unchanging ache. Beside him sat the string bag, bulging loose and uneven, like a body with a tumor, many tumors; like strange fruit; like a bag of gold from a fairy tale. The hair in the bag was beautiful, a thick and living bronze like the pelt of an animal, a thoroughbred, a beast prized for its fur. He had braided it carefully, with skill and a certain love, and secured it at the bottom with a small blue plastic bow. The other items in the bag he had purchased at a hardware store, just like he used to; the soda bottle he had gotten at the airport, and emptied in the men's room sink.

There was not much scenery, unless you like the desert, its lunar space, its brutal endlessness; the man did not. He was a creature of cities, of pocket parks and dull anonymous bars; of waiting rooms and holding cells; of emergency clinics; of pain. In the beige plastic box beneath the truck's front seat there were no less than eight different pain medications, some in liquid form, some in pills, some in patches; on his right bicep, now, was the vague itch of a Fentanyl patch. The doctor had warned him about driving while wearing it: *There might be some confusion*, the doctor said, *along with the sedative effect*. Maybe a headache, too.

A headache, the man had repeated; he thought it was funny. *Don't worry, doctor. I'm not going anywhere.* Two hours later he was on a plane to New Mexico. Right now the Fentanyl was working, but only just; he had an assortment of patches in various amounts—25, 50, 100 mgs—so he could mix and match them as needed, until he wouldn't need them anymore.

Now Glenn Gould played Bach, which was much better than Fentanyl. He turned down the air conditioning and turned the music up loud, dropping his hand to the bag on the seat, fingers worming slowly through the mesh to touch the hair.

They brought her what she needed, there in the workshop: they brought her her life. Plastic flowers, fraying t-shirts, rosaries made of shells and shiny gold; school pictures, wedding pictures, wedding rings, books; surprising how often there were books. Address books, diaries, romance novels, murder mysteries, Bibles; one man even brought a book he had written himself, a ruffled stack of printer paper tucked into a folding file.

Everything to do with the boxes she did herself: she bought the lumber, she had a lathe, a workbench, many kinds and colors of stain and varnish; it was important to her to do everything herself. The people did their part, by bringing the objects—the baby clothes and car keys, the whiskey bottles and Barbie dolls; the rest was up to her.

Afterwards they cried, some of them, deep tears strange and bright in the desert, like water from the rock; some of them thanked her, some cursed her, some said nothing at all but took their boxes away: to burn them, pray to them, set them on a shelf for everyone to see, set them in a closet where no one could see. One woman had sold hers to an art gallery, which had started no end of problems for her, out there in the workshop, the problems imported by those who wanted to visit her, interview her, question her about the boxes and her methods, and motives, for making them. Totems, they called them, or Rorschach boxes, called her a shaman of art, a priestess, a doctor with a hammer and an 'uncanny eye.' They excavated her background, old pains exposed like bones; they trampled her silence, disrupted her work and worst of all they sicced the world on her, a world of the sad and the needy, the desperate, the furious and lost. In a very short time it became more than she could handle, more than anyone could handle and she thought about leaving the country, about places past the border that no one could find but in the end settled for a period of hibernation, then moved to Eventide and points south, the older, smaller workshop, the bleached and decayed garage that a man with a bulldozer had kindly destroyed for her; she had made him a box about his granddaughter, a box he had cradled as if it were the child herself. He was a generous man, he wanted to do something to repay her although 'no one,' he said, petting the box, 'could pay for this. There ain't no money in the world to pay for this.'

She took no money for the boxes, for her work; she never had. Hardly anyone could understand that: the woman who had sold hers to the gallery had gotten a surprising price but money was so far beside the point there was no point in even discussing it, if you had to ask, and so on. She had money enough to live on, the damages had bought the house, and besides she was paid already, wasn't she? Paid by the doing, in the doing, paid by peace and silence and the certain knowledge of help. The boxes helped them, always: sometimes the help of comfort, sometimes the turning knife but sometimes the knife was what they needed; she never judged, she only did the work.

Right now she was working on a new box, a clean steel frame to enclose the life inside: her life: she was making a box for herself. Why? and why now? but she didn't ask that, why was the one question she never asked, not of the ones who came to her, not now of herself. It was enough to do it, to gather the items, let her hand choose between this one and that: a hair clip shaped like a feather, a tube of desert dirt, a grimy nail saved from the wrecked garage; a photo of her mother, her own name in newsprint, a hospital bracelet snipped neatly in two. A life was a mosaic, a picture made from scraps: her boxes were only pictures of that picture and whatever else they might be or become—totems, altars, fetish objects—they were lives first, a human arc in miniature, a precis of pain and wonder made of homely odds and ends.

Her head ached from the smell of varnish, from squinting in the sawdust flume, from the heat; she didn't notice. From the fragments on the table before her, the box was coming into life.

He thought about her as he drove. The Fentanyl seemed to relax him, stretch his memories like taffy, warm and ropy, pull at his brain without tearing it, as the pain so often did. Sometimes the pain made him do strange things: once he had tried to drink boiling water, once he had flung himself out of a moving cab. Once he woke blinking on a restaurant floor, something hard jammed in his mouth, an EMS tech above him: *'Bout swallowed his tongue,* the tech said to the restaurant manager, who stood watching with sweat on his face. *People think that's just a figure of speech, you know, but they wrong.*

He had been wrong himself, a time or two: about his own stamina, the state of his health; about *her,* certainly. He had thought she would die easily; she had not died at all. He had thought she could not see him, but even with one eye she picked him out of a line-up, identified him in the courtroom, that long finger pointing, accusing, dismissing all in one gesture, wrist arched like a bullfighter's before he places the killing blade, like a dancer's *en pointe*, poised to force truth out of air and bone: with that finger she said who he was and everything he was not, *mene, mene, tekel, upharsin*. It was possible to admire such certainty.

And she spared herself nothing; he admired her for that, too. Every day in the courtroom, before the pictures the prosecutor displayed: terrible Polaroids, all gristle and ooze, police tape and matted hair but she looked, she listened carefully to everything that was said and when the foreman said *guilty* she listened to that, too; by then the rest of her hair had come in, just dark brown down at first but it grew back as lush as before. Beautiful hair…it was what he had noticed first about her, in the bar, the Blue Monkey filled with art school students and smoke, the smell of cheap lager, he had tried to buy her a drink but *No thanks*, she had said, and turned away. Not one of the students, one of his usual prey, she was there and not-there at the same time, just as she was in his workshop later, there to the wire and the scalping knife, not-there to the need in his eyes.

In the end he had gotten nothing from her; and he admired her for that, too.

When he saw the article in the magazine—pure chance, really, just a half-hour's numb distraction, *Bright Horizons* in the doctor's office, one of the doctors, he could no longer tell them apart—he felt in his heart an unaccustomed emotion: gratitude. Cleaved from him as the others had been, relegated to the jail of memory but there she was, alive and working in the desert, in a workshop filled with tools that—did she realize?!—he himself might have used, working in silence and diligence on that which brought peace to herself and pure release to others; they were practically colleagues, though he knew she would have resisted the comparison, she was a good one for resisting. The one who got away.

He took the magazine home with him; the next day he bought a map of New Mexico and a new recording of Glenn Gould.

She would have been afraid if it were possible, but fear was not something she carried; it had been stripped from her, scalped from her, in that room with the stuttering overheads, the loud piano music and the wire. Once the worst has happened, you lose the place where the fear begins; what's left is only scar tissue, like old surgery, like the dead pink socket of her eye. She did not wait for him, check the roads anxiously for him, call the police on him; the police had done her precious little good last time, they were only good for cleaning up and she could clean up on her own, now, here in the workshop, here where the light fell empty, hard and perfect, where she cut with her X-Acto knife a tiny scrolling segment from a brand-new Gideon Bible: blessed are the merciful, for they shall obtain mercy.

Her hand did not shake as she used the knife; the light made her brown hair glow.

The man at the Stop-N-Go gave good directions: already he could see the workshop building, the place where the garage had been. He wondered how many people had driven up this road as he did, heart high, carrying what they needed, what they wanted her to use; he wondered how many had been in pain as he was in pain; he wondered what she said to them, what she might say to him now. Again he felt that wash of gratitude, that odd embodied glee; then the pain stirred in him like a serpent, and he had to clench his teeth to hold the road.

When he had pulled up beside her workshop, he paused in the dust his car had raised to peel off the used patch and apply a fresh one; a small one, one of the 25 mgs. He did not want to be drowsy, or distracted; he did not want sedation to dilute what they would do.

He looked like her memories, the old bad dreams, yet he did not; in the end he could have been anyone, any aging tourist with false new sunglasses and a sick man's careful gait, come in hope and sorrow to her door; in his hand he held a red string bag, she could see some of what was inside. She stood in the doorway waiting, the X–Acto knife in her palm; she did not wish he would go away, or that he had not come, wishing was a vice she had abandoned long ago and anyway the light here could burn any wish to powder, it was one of the desert's greatest gifts. The other one was solitude; and now they were alone.

"Alison," he said. "You're looking good."

She said nothing. A dry breeze took the dust his car had conjured; the air was clear again. She said nothing.

"I brought some things," he said, raising the bag so she could see: the wires, the bottle, the hair; her hair. "For the box, I mean. . . . I read about it in a magazine, about you, I mean."

Those magazines: like a breadcrumb trail, would he have found her without one? wanted to find her, made the effort on his own? Like the past to the present, one step leading always to another and the past rose in her now, another kind of cloud: she did not fight it but let it rise, knew it would settle again as the dust had settled; and it did. He was still watching her. He still had both his eyes, but other things were wrong with him, his voice for one, and the way he walked, as if stepping directly onto broken glass and "You don't ask me," he said, "how I got out."

"I don't care," she said. "You can't do anything to me."

"I don't want to. What I want," gesturing with the bag, his shadow reaching for her as he moved, "is for you to make a box for me. Like you do for other people. Make a box of my life, Alison."

No answer; she stood watching him as she had watched him in the courtroom. The breeze lifted her hair, as if in reassurance; he came closer; she did not move.

"I'm dying," he said. "I should have been dead already. I have to wear this," touching the patch on his arm, "to even stand here talking, you can't imagine the pain I'm in."

Yes I can, she thought.

"Make me a box," as he raised the bag to eye-level: fruit, tumor, sack of gold, she saw its weight in the way he held it, saw him start as she took the bag from him, red string damp with sweat from his grip and "I told you on the phone," she said. "I can't do anything for you." She set the bag on the ground; her voice was tired. "You'd better go away now. Go home, or wherever you live. Just go away."

"Remember my workshop?" he said; now there was glass in his voice, glass and the sound of the pain, whatever was in that patch wasn't working anymore: grotesque, that sound, like a gargoyle's voice, like the voice of whatever was eating him up. "Remember what I told you there? Because of me you can do this, Alison, because of what I did, what I *gave* you. . . . Now it's your turn to give to me."

"I can't give you anything," she said. Behind her her workshop stood solid, door frame like a box frame, holding, enclosing her life: the life she had made, piece by piece, scrap by scrap, pain and love and wonder, the boxes, the desert and he before her now was just the bad-dream man, less real than a dream, than the shadow he made on the ground: he was nothing to her, nothing and "I can't make something from nothing," she said, "don't you get it? All you have is what you took from other people, you don't have anything I can *use*."

His mouth moved, jaw up and down like a ventriloquist dummy's: because he wanted to speak, but couldn't? because of the pain? which pain? and "Here," she said: not because she was merciful, not because she wanted to do good for him but because she was making a box, because it was her box she reached out with her long strong fingers, reached with the X–Acto knife and cut some threads from the bag, red string, thin and sinuous as veins and "I'll keep these," she said, and closed her hand around them, said nothing as he looked at her, kept looking through the sunglasses, he took the sunglasses off and "I'm *dying*," he said finally, his voice all glass now, a glass organ pressed to a shuddering chord but she was already turning, red threads in her palm, closing the door between them so he was left in the sun, the dying sun; night comes quickly in the desert; she wondered if he knew that.

He banged on the door, not long or fiercely; a little later she heard the truck start up again, saw its headlights, heard it leave but by then she had already called the state police: a sober courtesy, a good citizen's compunction because her mind was busy elsewhere, was on the table with the bracelet and the varnish, the Gideon Bible and the red strings from the bag. She worked until a trooper came out to question her, then worked again when he had gone: her fingers calm on the knife and the glue gun, on the strong steel frame of the box. When she slept that night she dreamed of the desert, of long roads and empty skies, her workshop in its center lit up like a burning jewel; as she dreamed her good eye roved beneath its lid, like a moon behind the clouds.

In the morning paper it explained how, and where, they had found him, and what had happened to him when they did, but she didn't see it, she was too far even from Eventide to get the paper anymore. The trooper stopped by that afternoon, to check on how she was doing; she told him she was doing fine.

"That man's dead," he said, "stone dead. You don't have to worry about him."

"Thank you," she said. "Thank you for coming." In the box the red strings stretched from top to bottom, from the bent garage nail to the hospital bracelet, the Bible verse to the Polaroid, like roads marked on a map to show the way.

Psychos and You!

A MODESTLY INFORMATIVE AFTERWORD
BY JOHN SKIPP

Just so you know, I'm not a scholar. I'm not a cop, a forensic pathologist, or a behavioral psychologist. I've also never killed someone, so I'm not speaking from experience here.

The closest I've ever come to a psychotic killer of any stripe, insofar as I know, was holding in my hands the actual letter that Albert Fish sent to the parents of Grace Budd, the twelve-year-old girl he killed on June 3, 1928, and then ate over the course of the following nine days. (The full excruciating text, for those who can stomach it, is included as Appendix B.)

And shortly before I was born, in 1957, my mom and dad spent a Wisconsin summer night in a broken-down car less than a mile from the house of Ed Gein (left), when he was in the midst of his legendary killing spree. So maybe I picked up a little psychic residue there.

That's closer than a lot of people get to horror history. But it certainly doesn't make me an authority.

So for those of you hoping for more fact with your fiction, the simple fact is this: there is more information out there than I could possibly catalog. Compiling a Greatest Hits would be a book in itself (and, in fact, has been, numerous times over).

The Internet can take you pretty far, in any and every direction you might seek. Serial killers? Spree killers? Crimes of passion? Crimes of war? Gangsters? Gangstas? You name it, we got it. We are obsessed with our crimes, our justice and injustice. You can't turn around without somebody slapping you in the face with the latest atrocity or the latest revelation about some atrocity from the past.

It's endless. It's the definition of infinity.

Because there's just so much.

If you want to know about John Wayne Gacy, I point you directly toward Tim Cahill's staggeringly incisive *Buried Dreams: Inside the Mind of a Serial Killer* (1986). It is, to me, the *Red Dragon* of nonfiction accounts. Brilliantly written, drawing on extensive interviews and research by investigative journalist Russ Ewing, it goes to astonishing lengths to decipher the pathological lies Gacy routinely draped over the hideous events of his life.

Likewise, you can't go wrong with Ann Rule, the legitimate queen of true crime writing, whose Ted Bundy asskicker, *The Stranger Beside Me* (1980), is as personal an account as you're likely to get, given that she worked beside him on a suicide hotline, and totally missed the cues until far too late. Because—as a psychotic poster child—he was *just that good.*

If you want some Charles Manson, you head straight for Vincent Bugliosi and Curt Gentry's *Helter Skelter* (1974) for the definitive account.

Past that, my friend, you and your search engine of choice are on your own.

Searching is easy to do. I was amazed, for example, by how thorough a site like Trutv.com—its tagline being "Not Reality. Actuality."—is (as of this writing), in terms of keeping up-to-date on every little revelation regarding people who go out of their minds and kill, all over the world. In every kind of way.

There are doubtless a trillion others, who'd be more than delighted to fill you in on the gruesome details.

In compiling *Psychos*, my goal was to pass on the kinds of insights that great dark fiction seems to best provide: connecting the psychological dots in ways that all but the best nonfiction is as yet unable to do.

Because as many facts as are lobbed at us, every time things go horribly wrong—as many dates and places and forensic details and evidence trails as we can map—we are still ultimately left guessing as to *what it's like, on the inside*, when somebody finds themself dragged to the Bad Place.

And just in case you weren't clear on this, horror's a lot more fun when it isn't happening to you.

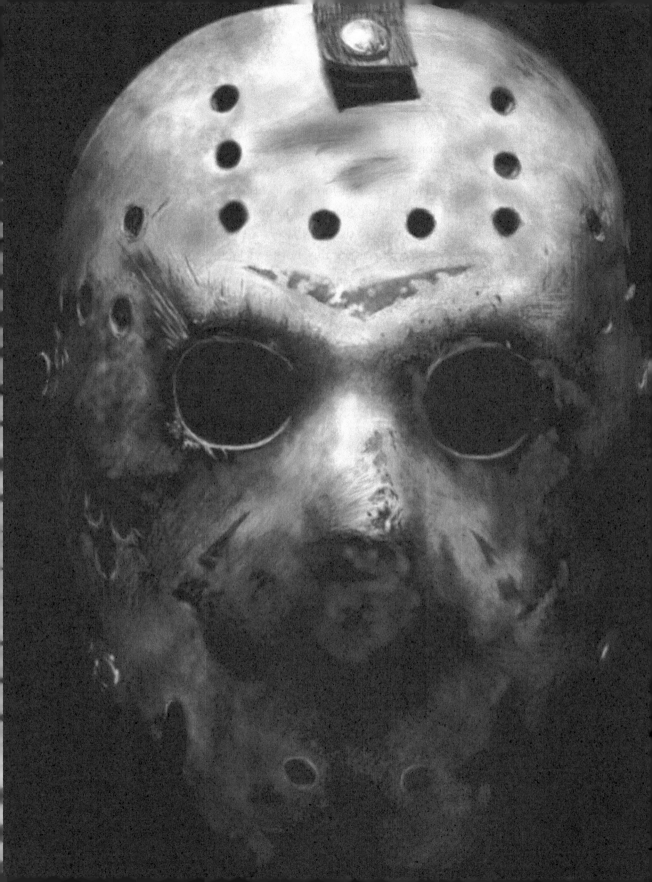

A Devil in My View:
Psychos in Popular Culture
BY CODY GOODFELLOW

I am evil
Because I am a man.
—Iago, "The Creed" from Act 2 of Otello
by Giuseppe Verdi (1604)

It's strange that we made up the great monsters to try to understand the causes and consequences of human evil and madness, and yet the depiction of madness itself has always been marred by the need to distort or dress up mental illness. This dressed-up distortion changes the madman into a cipher, at once more dangerous and far less disturbing than the real thing.

From their earliest incarnations, drama and literature have cast the madman as the one who entertains and speaks uncomfortable truths, not to arrive at any sincere explanation of madness. Behind the rather extravagant fear that we will be the victims of an ingenious or simply relentless psychopath lies the real fear of madness: that it is catching.

In ancient Greek drama, hysteria and madness ensue when the mainspring of reason is broken by the tragic machinations of fate—Medea is infuriated by her husband's infidelity and so murders their children, while Oedipus gouges out his eyes and renounces his hard-won crown when he learns of his unwitting patricide and incest.

But the natural passions, the innate savagery only thinly painted over by civilization, could also be brought out by strong wine or music. The Greeks drew a bold line between Apollonian and Dionysian qualities in all works. The former represented all that was male, rational, and orderly, while the latter embraced the female, the passionate and chaotic. The Maenads, women driven to orgiastic fervor by the rites of the god of wine, were said to rend to bloody shreds any who would not join their revels, as they did with Orpheus.

Even in Shakespeare, this naïve depiction of madness persists: insanity and nonsense are the natural and harmless state of the fool and the simpleton, while reasonable people snap and succumb to madness when their hearts or will are broken by the world (*Hamlet, King Lear*), or when evil catches up to them (*Macbeth*). But in his most psychologically astute tragedy, *Othello*, we see behind the traditional depiction of madness to a true portrait of psychopathy.

An articulate, faithful, and noble man, yet an ethnic outsider, Othello is driven to madness, murder, and suicide by the ingenious manipulation of his scheming underling Iago, who causes him to doubt his angelic wife for no real reason beyond his own love for evil. In Iago, we are granted a truly chilling vision of the modern psychopath, from the chameleonic charm of Ted Bundy to the manipulative nihilism of Charles Manson. An egomaniac who thrives on chaos and lies, Iago is a devil in human shape, a worm that gnaws the very fibers of human community and makes faithful men into murderers. When all is revealed, a blood-simple Othello seeks to assure himself that Iago is indeed a horned, cloven-hoofed demon: "I look down towards his feet; but that's a fable," for such would be a comfort, next to the awful truth that such monsters walk among us.

In *The Prince* (1532), Machiavelli sought to define the ideal statesman, and without an iota of irony sketched a profile of the controlled sociopath one would need to be to successfully wield the tools of political and economic power. In the ability to seem like one of us while always standing ready to employ deceit and brutality, Machiavelli defined the rare but justifiably terrifying controlled psycho-path as the ideal statesman, and anticipated the modern strategy for recruiting CEOs by several centuries.

The Marquis de Sade scandalized Europe with his exhaustive catalogs of decadent perversity, while the Gothic tradition elevated obsession and madness into a fevered romantic ideal. Walpole's *Castle of Otranto* (1764) created the mold for Gothic villainy with his cruel patriarch, Manfred, while the haunted Heathcliff in *Wuthering Heights* (1847) owed much of his tormented persona to Emily Brontë's brilliant but doomed brother, Branwell.

The Gothic tradition embraced a particular, highly stylized depiction of madness and evil, culminating in an archetype that plagues literature and drama to this day. The diabolical genius, the archfiend whose madness grants almost supernatural powers to concoct elaborate schemes of torture and punishment. *The Monk* (1796) was a sensation and the prototype for sadistic supervillains down through the centuries, from Professor Moriarty to Dr. No and Jigsaw.

But nobody could penetrate the essence of madness like a real madman. Guy de Maupassant wrote three hundred short stories, only a handful of which were horrific, but one dark masterpiece remains a milestone in the artistic understanding of insanity. In "The Horla," the narrator foolishly invites a bodiless spirit into his home, only to find the alien consciousness has invaded his brain and is gradually assuming control over the narrator's body and mind. Maupassant could speak with authority on the subject of madness, for he was suffering from advanced syphilis when he wrote it in 1887, and later died in a madhouse.

But for true psychological depth, the Gothic had to come to America, and Edgar Allan Poe. An alcoholic tortured by romantic obsession with a dead cousin and overwrought with bitterness at his failed career, Poe observed sanity down the wrong end of the telescope and virtually invented, alongside the detective story, the treasured concept of the unreliable narrator. His epic "The Fall of the House of Usher" (1839) traps its witness in the crumbling house of an inbred family racked by hereditary madness, and like so many of Poe's oversensitive heroes, nearly goes crazy himself.

Michel Foucault has insisted that each era manifests its own native brand of madness. The insanity of an era usually goes undiagnosed until it passes into history, unless an individual arises to dramatically epitomize the secret malaise.

Victorian England kept a tight lid on its seething subconscious desires, but in 1888, London birthed a figure to shame its most lurid penny dreadfuls. When Jack the Ripper murdered a handful of prostitutes in Whitechapel, his savage exploits dragged the suppressed demimonde and the hypocrisy of London's male citizens into the spotlight. His dastardly taunting persona resonated so deeply because it balanced refinement and wanton cruelty so perfectly that he could be the voice and hand of London itself, and his successful escape left the world with a mystery more tantalizing than any fiction. Ripper theories are only outdone by the JFK assassination industry for sheer volume and paranoid invention, and writers from Robert Bloch and Harlan Ellison to Alan Moore and Alan M. Clark continue to see in the enigma of the unsolved murders an evil far beyond mere madness, and an archetype too compelling to be contained by history.

Even as Sigmund Freud and Carl Jung diagnosed the banal neuroses and psychoses of early twentieth-century life, a more naturalistic approach in fiction uncovered the dismal, often pathetic symptoms of the modern maniac. While horror pulps continued to offer cardboard craziness, the hard-boiled crime story hijacked horror's integral engines to show the true nature of psychosis.

The psychological crime story was born long before, with Dostoevsky's *Crime and Punishment* (1866), which relentlessly documents an unstable student's guilty path to madness. Raskolnikov senselessly murders a pawnbroker to prove to himself that he is a Napoleonic figure, a man of destiny who can "step over blood." But the murder becomes a linchpin of obsession and furious remorse that shakes him to bits. This is the lot of the sane man, the gulf between the "sane" and the insane that one must step over to become a cold-blooded killer.

Insanity as a motive for murder was explored by Dashiell Hammett, Raymond Chandler, and lesser noir pioneers, but in the hard-bitten underworld, only the idle rich can afford to go insane. The next generation of hard-boiled writers turned the mystery inside out, leaving us alone with the killer as he plies his trade. Jim Thompson's protagonists are all too aware of the evil of their actions, and endlessly skilled at passing for what square society considers normal. The deputy in *The Killer Inside Me* (1952) gives a tour of his intricate web of murder and deceit and revels in posing as a hapless dimwit. Likewise, the sheriff in *Pop. 1280* (filmed brilliantly as *Coup de Torchon*) pretends to ineffectual stupidity while pushing the citizens of his town around like disposable pawns.

Neither raving maniacs nor diabolical geniuses, Thompson's sociopathic killers are blessed with an absence of conscience, but cursed by the compulsion for dominance and pain. Without studying Freud or Sade, streetwise Thompson understood that banal, awful childhood abuse twisted young minds to make others' pain into the closest thing to pleasure that a sociopath could feel.

Another generation on, and crime fiction has circled around to become everything that horror fiction should be, with Freudian monsters worthy of Hollywood. Andrew Vachss's unstoppable Burke series obsessively details the cycle of abuse and the many species of "street freaks" spawned by it, including the hollow shell of an antihero detective who narrates the books.

Beginning with *The Black Dahlia* (1987), James Ellroy explored the sickness of misogyny and the human hunger for violence by infecting and testing his characters to destruction. As the gruesome murder of Elizabeth Short leads two detectives into a wilderness of contagious perversity and madness, they seem to be hunting not just a killer but Patient Zero in an epidemic of psychopathology. At the heart of this and each of his succeeding LA novels (*The Big Nowhere, LA Confidential, White Jazz*), a subhuman pervert is the primary killer, but the real monster driving everyone insane is the warped and false glamour of the American Dream. That Ellroy has used his career to examine and understand the unsolved murder of his own mother is a strong argument for the power, or at least the pathology, of using fiction to make sense of the inexplicable.

Meanwhile, in the horror genre, the madman became increasingly a fantastical figure, with little basis in real psychology. In the works of H.P. Lovecraft, Robert W. Chambers, and other popular early twentieth-century fantasists, madness remains an excess of passion rather than an absence of regret. In John Collier's morbidly flippant yarns, homicide is only a poignant misunderstanding away, while in Lovecraft's Cthulhu Mythos canon and Chambers's odd horror shorts, the fragile curtain of sanity can be ripped down just by perusing a book—the *Necronomicon* and *The King in Yellow*, respectively.

In an increasingly hacky search for cheap thrills, horror sacrificed truth in depicting mental illness to play to the fears of the "sane" audience: that an insane person walks among them and may kill them or that they could go insane themselves. Insanity could be but one of the excuses for a villain's otherwise inexplicable behavior. A creature entirely enslaved to the demands of a mechanized plot, the dangerous lunatic could be counted on to escape from the insane asylum right on schedule to make a creaky plot deliver at least the semblance of surprises.

For those who wanted their psychology dumbed down even more, Freud in four colors was on offer in *Detective Comics*. Every character in the Batman universe is a grotesque scarred by trauma, driven to don a sub-Freudian costume and take part in an endless carnival of crime. Even for Batman, obsession and psychosis are the only superpowers one needs. Despite, or because of, the increasingly dark tone wrought by modern writers like Frank Miller and Grant Morrison, Batman continues to exert a far stronger psychological appeal than the sunny Superman, but the key to the Batman universe is that most iconic of all psychopaths, the Joker.

Borrowing freely from Conrad Veidt's manic grimace in *The Man Who Laughs* (1928), the Joker is a nihilistic thief and murderer whose irritating asides and throwaway gags mask an awareness of the joke too big to get laughs in Gotham City: that they are puppets in a madhouse play. Growing ever more dangerous and absurd with the decades, the Joker is the only one to transcend his disposable origin story (more about this in Film, below), because he's not a madman, but madness itself.

Popular culture seemed determined to keep lying to itself about the criminally insane forever, until a shrewd young prodigy weaned on a Lovecraft correspondence course in weird lit set the record straight. Robert Bloch famously based *Psycho* (1959) on the incredibly sordid case of Edward Gein, a shy backwoods Oedipus who channeled his freakish mother-love into a spree of grave robbery, murder, cannibalism, and ghoulish craft projects.

By making Norman a meek, retiring nobody and keeping the tormented mother obsession in the closet, Bloch cut through decades of bullshit to show us a true homicidal psychopath—racked with guilt and torment, yet driven to destroy women before they can destroy him.

Indeed, few writers of light entertainment strove to understand madness, so much as to bear false witness against it in the service of art. Insanity is an occupational hazard for any professional who thinks too much, and creative genius, in particular, seems to carry the seeds of unreason within itself. The works of Nikolai Gogol, Louis Wain, Syd Barrett, and Bob Meek are all the more fascinating for the glimpses they provide of the mind in the throes of a breakdown. Perhaps the unbelievable quality of madness in so much of both early and modern literature owes as much to the willful obscuring of the territory of madness by artists who fear that going there could mean staying there, as it does to the expediency of genre hackwork.

Too, the psycho can be the frustrated author's revenge on an indifferent world, or even the hidden destructive face disguised behind the passive mask of the creator. It is hardly ironic that the most successful writer in the history of the language returns so regularly to the theme of the raging nihilist trapped inside harmless, outwardly ordinary people who are, as often as not, writers.

In *Rage* (1977), *Roadwork* (1981), and *Apt Pupil* (1982), Stephen King gives vent to a shockingly caustic disillusionment and disgust with modern society that must tap into a vein of fury as American (or simply human) as apple pie. One of King's most forceful pet themes is the writer with the split personality. Writers constantly engage in a host of mental games that parallel, if not actively mimic, the routines of paranoid schizophrenia. Writers tour other people's lives, as King himself puts it, and the active listening to the inner voices others suppress can yield destructive mysteries as much as inspiration.

In *The Dark Half* and *Secret Garden, Secret Window*, the writer-protagonist is dogged by a ruthless killer who turns out to be a suppressed alter ego, while in *The Shining* (as much a horror novel about writer's block as ghosts), Jack Torrance becomes an empty vessel that fills with the urge to destroy instead of create.

Where many writers fade into irrelevance as their personal work becomes entangled with the rarefied life of the professional author, King's writers' nightmares sell in the tens of millions because the notion of a secret self capable of wiping out one's enemies must seem more like a fantasy than a horror in some deep recess of the collective modern mind, an undiagnosed mental illness with which we are all a little bit infected.

While public fascination with the criminal mind continued to drive fictional killers to more fabulous extremes, the true crime genre offered ghastly thrills no fiction could get away with, and almost made morbid curiosity respectable.

Truman Capote's examination of a horrific home invasion murder, *In Cold Blood* (1966), created a new market that bypassed the comforts of fiction to reveal the much more raw stuff lurking behind it. The Clutter family's drifter killers were merely desperate, disaffected losers, but the sensation caused by his penetrating examination of their motives gave birth to the true crime genre.

Lurid criminal accounts have been popular for as long as printing presses existed (Daniel Defoe is supposed to have written a pamphlet about Sawney Bean), but modern true crime fused the suspense techniques of thrillers with the fascinating minutiae of police procedure and the unflinching examination of grotesque details forbidden in popular art. Despite lurid covers plastered with body-count scores, the killers' sad biographies delve deeper than fiction into the motivations and methods of previously obscure or forgotten murderers like H. H. Holmes, Albert Fish, and Marcel Petiot. But no psycho has benefited more from his negative press coverage than Charlie Manson.

When the sensational Tate-LaBianca murders wrecked the Aquarian age and confirmed the establishment's worst nightmares about hippies, LA prosecutor Vincent Bugliosi wrote an even more extraordinary account, *Helter Skelter.* The runaway best-seller wallowed in the squalid insanity of Spahn Ranch but failed to dispel the mystique of the Family's cunning ringmaster, Charles Manson, who remains a media-made celebrity in captivity.

In the 1990s, FBI profilers John Douglas and Robert Ressler each scored a series of true crime best-sellers with deep explorations of the psyches of serial killers in prison. Though these sensational but educational books raised public awareness and inspired literary and television franchises about the pursuit and prosecution of serial killers, novelists like James Patterson and Patricia Cornwell dwarfed their success with serial killers as wildly unrealistic as their forensic detail was rigorously spot-on. In their sleek way, the new murder thrillers revived the Agatha Christie gambit of improbably elaborate murders as a parlor game.

The defining masterpiece of the serial killer boom is *Red Dragon* (1984). Juxtaposed against the pathetic, compulsive killer Francis Dolarhyde, Hannibal Lecter emerges as the archetypal human wolf—the diabolical madman as archfiend, combining Moriarty's elaborate cunning and refinement with an utterly bestial capacity for violence. As described in the books, Lecter is readily recognizable as a monster, with deep red eyes and extra digits. A natural predator, Lecter charms and disarms his potential meals, but he only eats the rude. In both *Red Dragon* and *Silence of the Lambs* (1990), he exerts an almost supernatural menace despite his draconian captivity. A demon in a bottle, he cooperates with Will Graham and Clarice Starling to catch less evolved killers for his own amusement. When he finally wins his freedom, the apocalyptic bloodshed is a prelude to an even more disturbing silence. Lecter has gone to ground, but with him out in the world, somehow a natural balance has been restored. The modern jungle *needs* its wolves, its cullers of rude sheep.

Quite predictably, Hannibal Lecter became a mainstream sensation when the film version of *Silence of the Lambs* became an Oscar-winning box office success. A deft blend of conservative police procedural and subversive slasher horror epic, it foisted the cannibalistic serial killer into the limelight as an edgy media darling, a far more toothsome alternative than his dismally introverted real-life cousin, Jeffrey Dahmer. But in the process, he became domesticated. When Billy Crystal was wheeled onstage at the Oscars in Lecter's restraints and muzzle, the taming of the predator seemed complete. Harris must've agreed, for *Hannibal* (1996) went off the rails in its mad charge to reassert Lecter's untamable savagery. When he captures and seduces Clarice Starling, he effectively "cures" the traumatic childhood experience that drove her to become an FBI agent, and frees her to become a human wolf like himself.

Whatever wild hair drove him to take such a caustic tack, the movie bailed on Harris's subversive climax, and Harris himself sold Lecter down the river in *Hannibal Rising* (2006), a disappointing origin story that explored the trauma that set Lecter on the path to cannibalism—in effect defusing all the inscrutable appeal of the character. The premise that nature creates such monsters to thin the human herd, and the notion that the drive to do good is no less a clinical deviation from the norm still linger, but as an orphaned subtext.

But long before Hannibal, the truly frightening question of natural-born killers in our midst was taken up in a very different form. William March's 1954 novel *The Bad Seed* gave us little Rhoda Penmark, an adorable moppet who coldly kills anyone who thwarts her will. A "serious" work that eschewed genre sensationalism or easy psychological answers, the book spawned a Broadway play and film that posited the genuinely disturbing question of evil with no motive, no traumatic mainspring or genetic deformity to explain its aberrant evil. The horrible, lingering theme of *The Bad Seed* is that no matter how much we love and socialize our children, some of the sheep will inevitably become wolves.

Iain Banks escalated March's muted approach with his devastating debut novel, *The Wasp Factory* (1984), in which young Frank describes with little or no remorse his elaborate rituals of animal cruelty and the murders of several childhood playmates. While signs of hereditary instability abound—Frank is haunted by his older brother, an escapee from an asylum—Frank affords us a chilling glimpse of the inner terrain of the born psychopath: a dreary, cold void in which only the bright colors and brittle sounds of agony and doom register.

Monsters can be made by domestic trauma, and sometimes they come out of nowhere, but what do our monsters tell us about the society that produces them? It is not shocking or subversive to posit that evil sometimes comes out of nowhere, but to delve deeper and point out the societal triggers of psychopathy is still a deeply controversial issue in our psychotically politicized age. Too easily are books and cinema that ask these very questions demonized as somehow driving consumers to violent acts. The subtle yet universal trauma of class warfare and elitism, Bret Easton Ellis obliquely warns in *American Psycho* (1991), can produce a whole demographic of monsters.

A purebred slab of elite Yankee beef, Patrick Bateman fanatically embraces the shallow power games and orgies of consumption of the Reagan Wall Street boom, but his suppressed self-hate is a raging storm that periodically forces him to kill bums, prostitutes, and even rival brokers whose business cards look better than his. As his excesses grow from a symptom of his success to an indictment of the system, Bateman wants to get caught, but finds he can't even turn himself in. The privileged class he belongs to will not allow his sloppy indiscretions to disrupt their own reign of terror. Of course, when the unreliable narrator finds his corpses cleaned up and his confession dismissed as a coked-up joke, we are allowed to write off the whole spree as a delusion or metaphor. But whether real (in a work of fiction) or imaginary, the murderous career of Patrick Bateman beautifully captures the utter banality, the utterly unromantic hole at the heart of the psychopath.

When the serial killer boom reached its high-water mark in the mid-1990s, the only taboo left was to let them fall in love. Poppy Z. Brite's *Exquisite Corpse* (1996) pairs up two serial killers (one based on meek UK killer Dennis Nilsen, and the other on Jeffrey Dahmer) in a volatile love triangle with Tran, a hapless morsel of perfect victim-meat. As dedicated to purple neo-Gothic romance as iconoclastic shock, Brite's dueling killers are, like her vampires, a species apart, capable of greater depth of feeling as well as physical miracles like feigning death to get out of prison. While utterly repulsed by the otherness of its narrators, we are cornered into sharing their ecstatic sense of being a breed apart, not cursed, but gifted, with the will to kill.

With all the taboos seemingly shattered, the psychopath stares at us across a vast gulf. Walking in his shoes only underscores the necessity for getting these bastards off our planet. But as the world grows ever more crowded and competitive, we each harbor a longing to identify with that killer, rather than to blend into the herd. To see ourselves as the wolf. But how to make a truly sympathetic serial killer?

With his incredibly popular Dexter books, Jeff Lindsay seemed to hit the answer. His serial killer is a true bad seed, cursed with the taste for blood from his murky infancy. But raised to channel his appetites into hunting other killers, he becomes a uniquely satisfying hero that allows us to revel in being both the Vigilante Champion and the Big Bad Wolf.

Film

If genre literature was slow to try to explore rather than invent the geography of madness, the movies, to their credit, never really tried.

Owing much to the French theatrical tradition of Grand Guignol, in which madmen conspired with unlikely coincidences and unruly fate to deal out bloody punishment to all, the modern horror film has cooked down the dangerous madman into two discrete, equally unrealistic archetypes: the Fool and the Fiend. From Grand Guignol plays to postmodern slasher flicks, the lunatic is often an agent of fate or bloodthirsty Old Testament morality, or a demented Greek chorus, feeding vital plot points laced with nonsense.

The Fool is more mad than evil, and often represents an apologist for the villain or the author's veiled attempts to help the protagonist—Dwight Frye or Tom Waits as Renfield in *Dracula*, or Dennis Hopper as the "harlequin" photojournalist in *Apocalypse Now* (1979). An all-too-common cliché of recent supernatural films is the visit to the insane asylum to glean clues from the surviving victim, the burnt-out police detective or the crazy old lady whose cryptic raving in the first reel proves prophetic in the third.

The Fiend inherited all the operatic sadism and destructive obsession of the Gothic villain. His motive is usually revenge or to fulfill an insane project, while the best ones fuse both aims into one. While morbid and fraught with sick obsession, the most overwrought of these stories have become blockbusters on Broadway. *The Phantom of the Opera* has been a perennial remake favorite, gradually reducing the villain's hideous disfigurement to a tiny blemish to make him a romantic anti-hero. *Sweeney Todd* (1936) turned an urban legend about a degenerate barber who killed his customers to make meatpies into a romantic revenge tragedy. By giving the monstrous Todd a dead wife and a stolen daughter, he becomes not only a sympathetic protagonist, his career of murder becomes a shocking new form of class warfare.

Similarly, Lionel Atwill, as the titular mad scientist *Doctor X* (1933), seeks a means of producing tasty artificial flesh from human tissue. Atwill so excelled at melodramatic madness that he returned the same year to play Ivan Igor, the scarred human monster of *Mystery of the Wax Museum*. Using the bodies of his victims in his stunningly realistic exhibits, Igor finds another colorful way of reducing his fellow humans to products. Vincent Price played the same role with more polished menace than madness in *House of Wax* (1953), but when loosely remade in 2005, the killers were mute rednecks who grind out the murders and surreal installations with the dull resolve of hirelings making doughnuts.

With a healthy American mistrust for anyone smarter than the mob, horror movies also found a useful archetype of the Fiend in the arrogant but all-too-rational Victor Frankenstein. The mad scientist who unleashes Things Man Was

Not Meant to Know pursues chaos and horror for its own sake. Beginning with the dashing disconnection of Colin Clive in *Frankenstein* (1931), the monster-maker devolved into a raving curiosity in *The Human Centipede* (2010). While exciting, these pictures offer little insight into the mysterious kinship of genius and madness, or the paradox of truly rational, educated men committing atrocities.

No enlightening sparks of madness enliven the blunt daily inventory of Heinrich Himmler's journals; no moustache-twiddling raving punctuates the experimental records of Josef Mengele, and no colorful telltale symptoms betray the homicidal delusions of Charles Whitman, Lee Harvey Oswald, or the Columbine killers in time to help spot the next one. The tragically ordinary truth is that the will or compulsion to murder is often accompanied by a quite unremarkable absence of normal emotions, rather than crazy behavior or evil split personalities. So art is too often unwilling, even where it is able, to cleave to the truth about madness.

Fritz Lang's *M* (1931) was a striking departure, not only for its stark, proto-noir scenery, but because it forces us to stalk with the killer as he chooses his prey and to run with him as he is, in turn, hunted. A fascinating dynamic of evil versus evil emerges when Berlin is locked down by a dragnet, forcing the underworld to collude to hunt the killer themselves.

The "realist" serial killer biopic has grown into a genre of its own, evolving from *Psycho* and the commercially disastrous but intriguing *Peeping Tom* (both 1960) to the incendiary *Taxi Driver* (1976). *When a Stranger Calls* (1979) limps away from its electrifying first act to follow John Hurt as a miserable killer seeking absolution, or at least deliverance. But our hunger to vicariously enjoy the life of a human predator is turned back upon us in sick yet effective flicks like *Maniac* (1980) and *Henry: Portrait of a Serial Killer* (1986).

By the 1990s, the familiar serial killer is all too aware of his audience: in the mockumentary *Man Bites Dog* (1992), the cunning killer corrupts his camera crew into cleaning up his sanguine messes. In *Se7en* (1994), we are force-fed a cold banquet of *schadenfreude* as the killer flenses away a litany of human jetsam. In his philosophy, if not his technique, he only articulates the fierce will to judge others that makes these movies so satisfying in the first place.

Insight into the inner workings of the killer are untrustworthy, and we are easily manipulated by dazzling flurries of spectacle that manipulate us into pitying or even admiring them, as in *Natural Born Killers* and *Heavenly Creatures* (both 1994) or Alejandro Jodorowsky's masterpiece, *Santa Sangre* (1990). We are fools, these films seem to say, to expect the madman to explain himself to us. What we get, instead, is often the serial killer's explanation of *us*.

But Jodorowsky and Oliver Stone had the luxury of lofty thematic statements that comes with genius and/or big-studio backing, while most psycho pictures were merely trying to make a buck. Psychos are, after all, even cheaper and easier than zombies or vampires. In Herschell Gordon Lewis's bloody potboilers like *Blood Feast* (1963) and *Two Thousand Maniacs* (1964), anyone could be a maniacal killer, simply because *somebody* had to be.

Beginning with suspense thrillers like *Experiment in Terror* (1962) and *Wait until Dark* (1967), we begin to see high-toned films that marry us to the victim as they are stalked by a cruel, seemingly inhuman sadist, but they also let us share the thrill of terrorizing a helpless woman, of eluding the police and having our way. Hitchcock elaborated on the shower scene in *Psycho* with a sickeningly intimate strangling scene in *Frenzy* (1972). Once audiences had betrayed their enjoyment for the thrill of the chase, the mystery part of the package was discarded, and the slasher film was born.

Many huge, excellent books on the slasher film phenomenon have been written already (the hugest and most excellent among them being *Butcher Knives & Bodycounts*); but amid debates over violence as pornography and slashers as enforcers of gender inequality, precious little consideration is given to whether any movie psychos are even properly insane. Most are not alive or completely human, and they are only meaningful as portraits of our most irrational, suppressed fears.

Your meat-and-potatoes slasher kills for revenge against taunting classmates, unattainable women, irritating assholes, or anyone who reminds them that they're different. Usually, the differences involve childhood abuse or sensational disfigurement, leading to sexual impotence compensated for with cutlery and power tools. Nailing a couple in flagrante delicto is the grand slam of slashing. But few, if any, slashers qualify as bona fide maniacs by even the broadest M'Naghten standard.

Michael Myers is an explosive Bad Seed, though we have seen nothing to explain what went wrong. Seemingly a happy, normal child, he snaps and kills his way through his house like a runaway lawn mower. Dormant for decades until a chance to escape turns him loose on his hometown, he zeroes in on couples coupling like his sister, suggesting a simple Freudian attachment, a lethal fear of sex. Dr. Loomis's raving in successive sequels seem to suggest that Myers is much more: an indestructible avatar of death itself. In John Carpenter's deft hands, *Halloween*'s Michael Myers was a truly frightening and ambiguous figure for the skeptical, cynical '70s.

An audience's hunger for answers should seldom be catered to; a filmmaker tempted to give too many easy answers seems to have missed the lesson of Jack the Ripper. Once the public's attention is captivated, the less they know, the more they want to find out. The increasingly threadbare sequels layered motives and schemes on the once-elegant minimalist story until nothing edifying or entertaining was left. Rob Zombie's remake inserts a nightmarish tapestry of abuse and humiliation to explain Myers's rampage, until any sane person in the same straits would put on a Shatner mask and go stabbing.

Even easier to diagnose, *A Nightmare on Elm Street*'s Freddy is a child molester and "the bastard son of a thousand maniacs," as his grandiose legend has it. More a victim of studio greed than vengeful parents, Freddy began as a caricature of a child molester, the comic book apotheosis of Albert Fish, a jester-executioner fueled, if not created, by his self-loathing teen victims' masochistic imaginations. As an all-powerful ghost, he can enter dreams and warp reality, but because he merely kills, rather than perpetuating his cycle, the remake predictably twisted the original plot into even worse knots, with the even creepier new Freddy proving to have been innocent of his original charges.

Friday the 13th's Jason is a zombie revenant, a clumsier, sweatier Grim Reaper, but his mother is a nice piece of work. Right or wrong, the mother loves her deformed child to the exclusion of all else. When he drowned, she had no choice but to kill the horny counselors responsible, and anyone who subsequently filled their jobs. This kind of tissue-thin rationale gets stretched even further in teen exploitation potboilers like *Terror Train* (1980), *Massacre at Central High* (1976), and the like. Though it was only trying to keep the franchise alive, *Friday the 13th V: A New Beginning* (1985) came closest to an interesting wrinkle when it replaced the lumbering hockey zombie with a copycat killer swept into the monstrous identity because his own life was a vacuum of frustration. While lifted from the superior *My Bloody Valentine* (1981), this twist backed into a fascinating integral part of the slasher genre. As self-conscious slasher franchises like the *Scream* and *Saw* series emphasize to the exclusion of all else, the mask is all-important, and anyone can be called to put it on.

Perhaps the most disturbing of all the slashers is Leatherface, because he's neither insane nor truly evil. Another pop culture version of poor Ed Gein by way of Sawney Bean, Leatherface (in 1974's *The Texas Chainsaw Massacre*), represented the nadir of the American conservative heartland, a backwoods King Kong whose rage and venal fetishes are caused by ignorance and inbreeding. When he sees a clown on his Speak & Spell in *TCM3* (1990), he earnestly types *FOOD* over and over.

At his best, Leatherface is a chilling figure because he isn't insane at all. He has merely been raised to see you as food. His rage, then, is the nigh-universal anger of anyone too ugly, dumb, and poor to be worthy of love and admiration. As such, Leatherface is less a hillbilly killer than the avenging angel of the bungled and the botched, a chain saw as lethal middle finger thrust out at the Beautiful People.

Perhaps the most absurd, and the most educational, of slashers, is Jigsaw of *Saw* fame. The fear of getting hunted by a slasher is a rootless, narcissistic one—the reverse of winning the lottery—so elaborate in its conventions as to have nothing to do with real crime, as shown in the heavy-handed spoof *Behind the Mask: The Rise of Lesley Vernon* (2006). That some giant mutant rodeo clown would want to stalk and kill *you*, for whatever far-fetched reason, is a compelling enough idea that one forgets how ridiculous and unlikely it is. That a killer should get to know your secret shame, and devise a preposterous Rube Goldberg torture device to teach you and the universe a half-baked moral lesson, somehow captured the imaginations of postliterate audiences in an era when less cynical horror flicks couldn't get into theaters on Halloween.

Taken on its own silly terms, if Michael and Jason are avenging angels and Freddy is a devil, then Jigsaw is an idiot's vision of God. Some mean asshole who knows all your sins, who constructed and trapped you in an elaborate machine to punish you for being no better than you were made to be.

If we really want to understand why we're drawn to these cartoon depictions of madness, we have to go even further from reality, and back to Batman.

In the Joker, we have seen Cesar Romero as a nitrous-huffing hyena laughing at his own lame jokes; Jack Nicholson as Jack Nicholson, with a laconic scenery-chewing performance that made Keaton's inhibited Batman irrelevant. His sole, continuous joke seemed to be that he realized that he was in an exceedingly silly summer movie. But Heath Ledger brought a shockingly new intensity to the Joker that effortlessly planted doubts about our own understanding of madness.

In his conflicting monologues explaining the tragic events that made him a monster, this new Joker seems to own not only the decades of disposable comic book and film incarnations of himself, but also the audience's need to know the Reason Why. Like Henry's serial fantasies about having killed his mother, they show something important about us, not the madman. It also shows us what we fear the most: a psychopath unencumbered by morality, impossible to understand, who yet understands us all too well.

While psychos and serial killers have always been the ultimate Other, the movies have always held a special spot in their heart for temporary madness, and American audiences have always loved a romantic fling with a body count. In a world where we are all controlled, overcharged, humiliated, and pushed around, the thought of taking to the road to grab all that you truly deserve is a fantasy tied to America's burnished love of outlaws.

Born out of the road pictures that celebrated the counterculture's bid for liberation from straight society, *Bonnie & Clyde* (1967) and *Badlands* (1973) took notorious murderous rampages and turned them into daring, romantic adventures, reinventing murder as a rite of American passage. *Bonnie & Clyde* reinvented a plain young wife of a recidivist jailbird and a "rattlesnake" driven to mass murder by repeated rapes in a Texas prison into dreamy matinee idols with the casting of Warren Beatty and Faye Dunaway. Arthur Penn's frenzied film shows the desperate, doomed couple as they saw themselves in their two-year spree, as the only sane people trying to make their glamorous way in a world gone mad.

Terrence Mallick's *Badlands* does less to glamorize the fictionalized Stark-weather-Fugate rampage of 1958, and their murders are treated with anything but the cathartic orgasmic energy of Penn or Sam Peckinpah. But we are drawn in and charmed by the meditative vistas of the empty plains and the wistful narration of Sissy Spacek, and by Martin Sheen's puckish take on beady-eyed creep Stark-weather, and for a moment, we are tricked into identifying with stone-cold killers.

With his usual adroit insight and heavy, heavy stylistic hand, Oliver Stone turned these seductive visions of violence into a massive neon-lit varmint trap. Designed as a bug zapper for controversy, *Natural Born Killers* didn't disappoint. Employing every trick in the book to apologize for the explosive rampage of Mickey and Mallory Knox, we must either identify with the ultimate dysfunctional power couple in their feud with the world that made them, or we must walk out before the third act.

A special word must be said about the role of women as killers . . . there's not nearly enough of them, and the ones who exist embody less the essence of feminine madness than men's fears of clingy, pushy, emasculating bitches. The conniving stalker in *Play Misty for Me* (1971) cropped up as an unexpected side effect of the sexual revolution, which gives us the worst of both worlds—an assertive woman who won't take no for an answer and a clingy freak who doesn't understand how one-night stands work. *Fatal Attraction* (1987) defined crazy bitches for a generation, and set up formalized rules for the stalker movie almost as ridiculously formalized as slashers. Feeding on women's cultivated mutual mistrust, feminized copies of this formula, focusing on the cuckolded wife's POV, continue to dominate the fem-friendly Lifetime network.

Female psychos get short shrift in Hollywood, but one remarkable film that came out the same year as *Fatal Attraction* actually tried to give us a crime drama with a totally female dynamic. Staid DOJ agent Debra Winger's body-strewn pursuit of the chameleonic killer Theresa Russell in *Black Widow* (1987) causes her to delve into the otherness of the sexual predator in an intriguing mirror of the police procedural arc, even adding a layer of sexual tension that all but renders the film's male victims irrelevant. Russell is a chillingly realized female Ted Bundy as she charms, marries, and subtly murders rich suckers. If this one had ended more like *Hannibal* (the book, not the movie), it would've been a legendary kick in the balls to male audiences.

But the reigning queen psycho is still Annie Wilkes in *Misery* (1990). No more lavish portrait of a psychotic killer has been committed to the printed page than the murderous, Liberace-loving nurse who captures and torments her favorite author. Stephen King clearly put into his novel all the angst he's felt over his legions of demanding fans, but the movie blows it away with William Goldman's drum-tight script and Kathy Bates's squirmily convincing portrayal. Asexual yet addicted to a saccharine delusion of "romance," Wilkes's femininity is almost irrelevant. She wants to make the world a decent place, free of lies and pain and cockadoodie dirty things, but her methods would shame a Siberian gulag. To be at the mercy of a lunatic, hostage to her violent mood swings and fits of temper, is the worst kind of hell imaginable for an artist, but at least it's an audience.

To identify with the killer in our overcrowded modern herd is to identify with power, but a far more troubling theme, which cuts to the heart of our fear of the insane, asks us to identify with madness. If our fears of being killed by a wandering maniac are enervating fantasies, then our fear of going insane ourselves is something much deeper and darker, and therefore much harder to depict effectively on screen.

As the bereaved widower of a Manson victim, Roman Polanski would come to know all too well what the former kind of terror is like, but he had already broken out with an authoritative cinematic treatise on the latter variety. *Repulsion* (1965) postulates the most horrible unexamined aspect of the question of madness: Could it happen to you? Catherine Deneuve is like the prototype of the virgin survivor type of every slasher flick, yet it is she, alone in a strange apartment and wound into a frenzy of sexualized terror, who becomes both killer and victim. Her mushrooming hysteria turns to manslaughter in a short series of scenes, but witnessing it, we feel every twitch of crumbling sanity. Putting himself into the crucible in *The Tenant* (1976), Polanski succumbs to an obsessive terror at the thought of being possessed by a ghost, à la "The Horla."

A more convoluted but similarly troubling theme is struck in *Session 9* (2001) and *Shutter Island* (2010), which play on our fears of mental institutions as more a vector for incubating and spreading mental illness than curing it. That the investigator or the administrator in these kinds of films invariably ends up being a patient is only a dishonest twist to rationalize our irrational fear of the unclean getting upon us.

A vital subgenre mining this fear is the transplant film, which digs even deeper into organic mistrust and superstition tarted up as cutting-edge science. Oddly enough, the French have done more than their share in this line. Our heads tell us that tissue is tissue, but a killer's hands trump a loving heart and a rational mind.

Mad Love (1935), an American adaptation of Maurice Renard's 1920 novel *Les Mains d'Orlac* pitted Peter Lorre as a mad surgeon who grafted a killer's hands onto concert pianist Colin Clive, in hopes of somehow stealing his wife. *Hands of Orlac* was adapted twice more, and planted a generational seed in French minds. Crime writing duo Pierre Boileau and George Narcejac (*Diabolique*, *Vertigo*) adapted the popular novel *Les yeux sans visage* into the film *Eyes without a Face* (1960), in which another mad surgeon captures girls and steals their faces to heal his own disfigured daughter.

In 1965, they took the premise a step further with their novel *Choice Cuts*, a laughably awesome medical thriller in which a murderer is cannibalized for spare parts. When his limbs and even his head(!) are grafted onto ordinary citizens who turn to murder—yes, even the guy with the feet—the question of the seat of the soul is set back at least ten centuries in pursuit of shock.

Somehow, this misbegotten gem misfired in Hollywood's first attempt to shoot it, but a very loose adaptation by Eric Red—creator of superhuman serial killer spiritual guide John Ryder in the iconic *The Hitcher* (1986)—finally emerged in 1991 as the intermittently hilarious *Body Parts*. Here, evil or madness is like leprosy, a corruption of biology that cannot be purged from the flesh. If it took itself too seriously to be as fun as it could've been, it didn't take itself nearly as seriously as the hammy, the horripilating . . . *The Hand* (1981).

When hot-tempered comic artist Jon Lansdale (Michael Caine) loses his hand in a car accident, sultan of subtlety Oliver Stone goes to work on him and us with a string of murders that may or may not have been committed by Lansdale's missing digits. The idea that his hand is out there, somehow acting as an agent of Lansdale's suppressed id, is somehow preferable to the audience than the possibility that it's all in his mind, and he's another ordinary one-handed killer.

The very rational fear of losing *all* rationality is stripped to its barest essence in *28 Days Later* (2002). Mislabeled and celebrated as a zombie film amid the current craze, the epidemic of madness as a viral plague in Danny Boyle's stripped-down apocalypse renders its victims into screaming, eating killers in seconds. No understanding of the mental degeneration into madness is offered or expected. The suddenness with which Brendan Gleason's infection drives him to kill his cherished child is little more than a gimmick, but its flagrant disregard for our precious individual sanities is exciting to watch from afar. Thankfully, unlike real mindlessness, the plague uses up its victims and burns itself out.

A better specimen for the understanding of what our sanity means to us and what it means to lose it is *Pontypool* (2009): a locked-room apocalypse in which a corrupted linguistic meme causes a complete mental breakdown. Adapted by Tony Burgess from his novel *Pontypool Changes Everything*, the other mislabeled zombie flick succeeds on higher intellectual levels than anything in the survival horror genre because its protagonists are only incidentally fighting the brainless army seeking to crush them with their dyslexic fury. The real enemy is the virus itself, which—like so many manias, crazes, and rushes to stupid wars—is a virus of words.

We are justifiably afraid of violence to our precious, fragile bodies, which may come in the dramatic form of a pinhead in a hockey mask or the tainted Tylenol in our medicine chest, because of someone else's insanity. But this is a fear we can't control and can't really imagine coming for us, and so it's always been fun, and it always will be.

In an era when every ethnic, social, professional, and religious group has a vigorous media watchdog, mental illness will always be fair game because of the other fear, the very real one, that dogs us all ...

That through a traumatic episode or an undiagnosed hiccup of heredity—or in the golden degradation of advanced age—we might join that untouchable minority.

And go mad ourselves.

APPENDIX B

The Albert Fish Letter

Editor's note: What follows is, I believe, the precise transcript. It is by far the most horrifying piece of writing in this book because it's true. And if you read it, it will haunt you for the rest of your days. Not in a good way. But in a very real one.

You have been sincerely warned.

Dear Mrs. Budd. In 1894 a friend of mine shipped as a deck hand on the Steamer *Tacoma*, Capt. John Davis. They sailed from San Francisco for Hong Kong, China. On arriving there he and two others went ashore and got drunk. When they returned the boat was gone. At that time there was famine in China. Meat of any kind was from $1-3 per pound. So great was the suffering among the very poor that all children under 12 were sold for food in order to keep others from starving. A boy or girl under 14 was not safe in the street. You could go in any shop and ask for steak—chops—or stew meat. Part of the naked body of a boy or girl would be brought out and just what you wanted cut from it. A boy or girl's behind which is the sweetest part of the body and sold as veal cutlet brought the highest price. John staid there so long he acquired a taste for human flesh. On his return to N.Y. he stole two boys, one 7 and one 11. Took them to his home stripped them naked tied them in a closet. Then burned everything they had on. Several times every day and night he spanked them—tortured them—to make their meat good and tender. First he killed the 11 year old boy, because he had the fattest ass and of course the most meat on it. Every part of his body was cooked and eaten except the head—bones and guts. He was roasted in the oven (all of his ass), boiled, broiled, fried and stewed. The little boy was next, went the same way. At that time, I was living at 409 E 100 St. near—right side. He told me so often how good human flesh was I made up my mind to taste it. On Sunday June the 3, 1928 I called on you at 406 W 15 St. Brought you pot cheese—strawberries. We had lunch. Grace sat in my lap and kissed me. I made up my mind to eat her. On the pretense of taking her to a party. You said yes she could go. I took her to an empty house in Westchester I had already picked out. When we got there, I told her to remain outside. She picked wildflowers. I went upstairs and stripped all my clothes off. I knew if I did not I would get her blood on them. When all was ready I went to the window and called her. Then I hid in a closet until she was in the room. When she saw me all naked she began to cry and tried to run down the stairs. I grabbed her and she said she would tell her mamma. First I stripped her naked. How she did kick—bite and scratch. I choked her to death, then cut her in small pieces so I could take my meat to my rooms. Cook and eat it. How sweet and tender her little ass was roasted in the oven. It took me 9 days to eat her entire body. I did *not* fuck her tho I could of had I wished. She died a *virgin*.

ACKNOWLEDGEMENTS

I hope you'll forgive me if I keep it short and sweet. Reason being: I'M BEAT! All these months of full-tilt immersion in crazy have strangely taken their toll; and all I wanna do now is curl up in bed, go to sleep, and dream about nice people doing nice things.

Speaking of nice people . . . THANK YOU, DINAH DUNN, for being as smart, tough, kind, and open-minded an editor as this editor could possibly wish for. Thanks to all at Black Dog for keeping our winning streak streakin'.

Thanks to Lori Perkins, Ravenous Shadows, Fungasm Press, Eraserhead Press, Crossroad Press, and everybody else whose business interest in my work helps keep me alive and kickin'.

Thanks to Cody Goodfellow, for the constant brilliant above-and-beyond.

Thanks to Andrew Kasch and the filmmaking community we have entered into together, giving me a new creative lease on life.

Thanks to Janie, Max, Chris, Bianca, Dan, Allison, Mike, Mehran, Kaitlin, Stan, Sadie, Scoob, and all residents of Cazador Manor, past and present, for giving me the place I call home.

Thanks to Marianne, Mykey, Melanie, and the brand-new Griffin-Bennett Skipp-East, freshly expanding our nuclear family. Thanks to Tim, Griffin's dad. Thanks to my dad and mom, my sisters, and on out through the gorgeous ganglia of our ever-expanding human family tree.

Thanks to all my friends, and many more warm acquaintants. Thanks to everyone who appreciates the work. Thanks to the members of the Horror Writers Association, who awarded *Demons* with the Stoker award for Outstanding Anthology in 2012, thereby stamping approval on our whole mad series of cool.

Finally, thanks to all the astounding writers who made this book what it is, and these books what they are. And thanks to all the great ones who didn't make it in this time, but made my job so goddamn hard by being so goddamn good.

As it turns out, this wasn't so short after all. But it sure feels sweet to thank you all. It's the least I can do.

I LOVE YOU GUYS! THANK YOU!!!